THE FLAME

BETROTHAL AND PROPHECY

S R JAMES

THE FLAME OF ARVEN I

BETROTHAL & PROPHECY

S R James

COPYRIGHT

DEDICATION

To my wonderful family who have put up with my abstractions for so long, getting these stories into the world and to those of you who have been so kind, enjoying what I've written, I can only hope you enjoy this too.
This is especially for Helen, best friend and sister-in-law who has been with this from its conception and all the way through to the end; for Steve, who has always provided the best support and battle assistance, and Anne, for her expert critique and support.
To everyone else – you know who you are! Mum, Archie, Harvey, Roisin, Rebecca, Mary, Grant & Michelle especially – I could not have done this without you!
And our most special Grandson James, hoping that you enjoy this when you're older.

MOONS OF THE IULLYN YEAR

Ertam – 1 Spring Equinox - Selith
Rhellay – 2
Atlaire – 3
Shilare – 4 Summer Solstice - Selith
Kharsare – 5
Jawell – 6
Vhisson – 7 Autumn Equinox - Selith
Thurton – 8
Umttarn – 9
Instur – 10 Winter Solstice - Selith
Penttar – 11
Staipe – 12

MAP OF WEST IULLYN

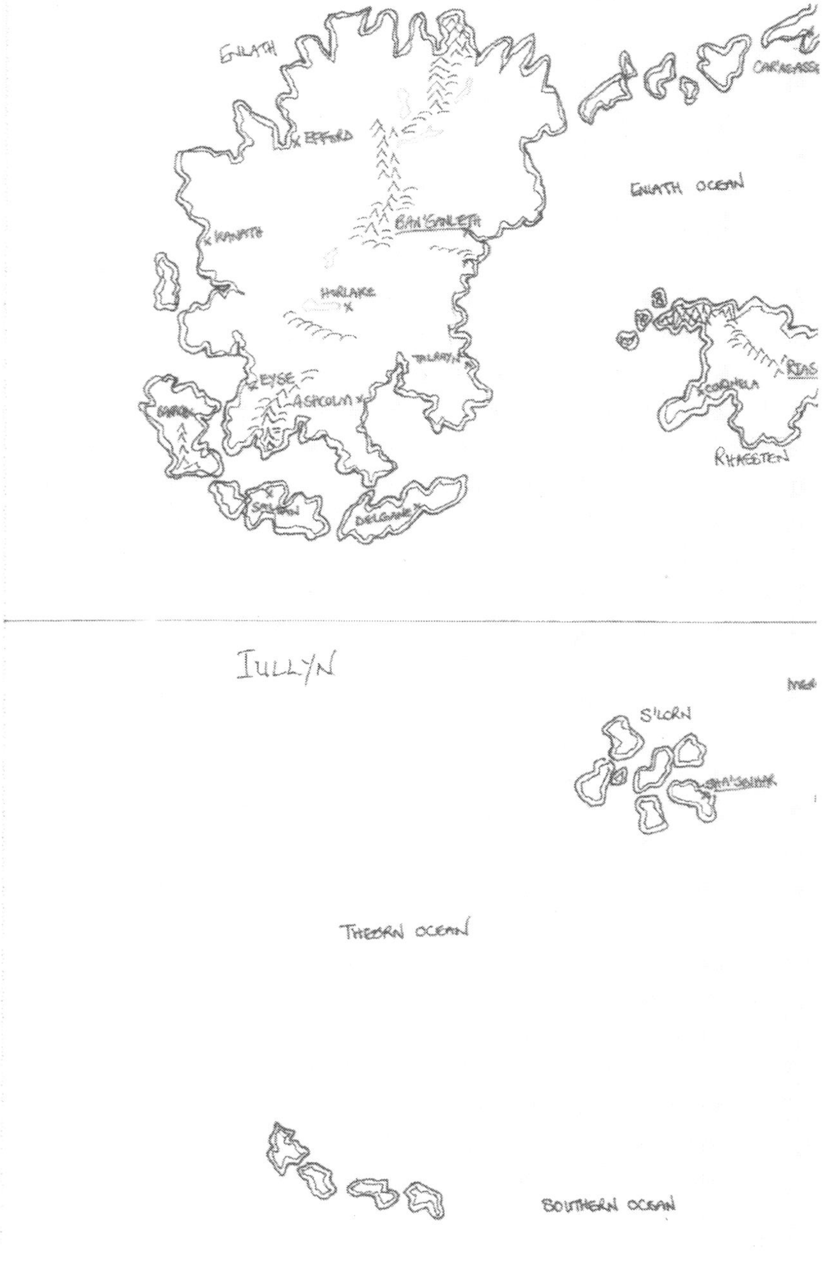

MAP OF EAST IULLYN

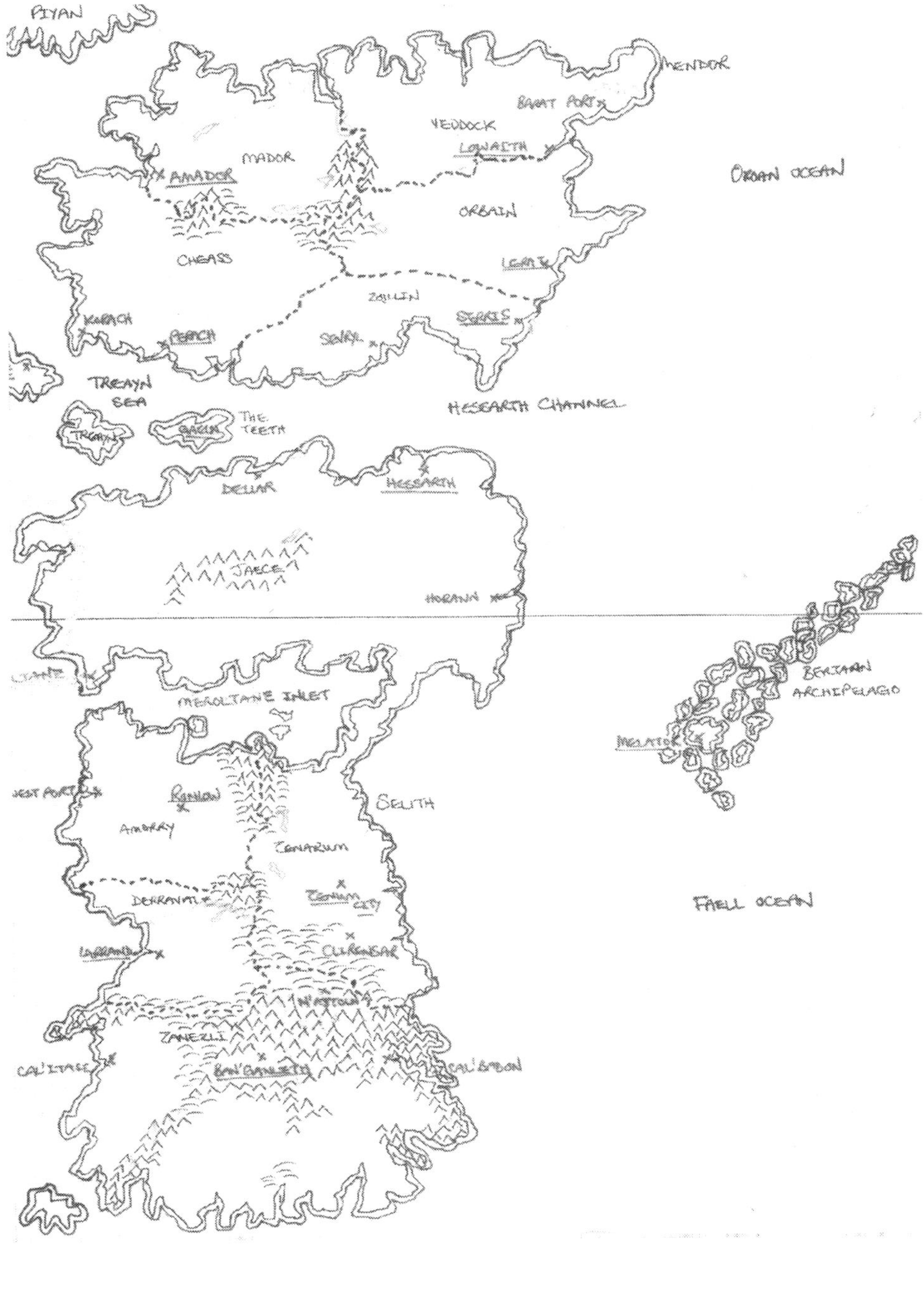

MAP OF SELITH

CHAPTER 1

Lady Ethrayne of Clirensar joined her family for a private breakfast with the king and his only son, early that morning, liveried servants serving them with drinks and a vast range of freshly prepared viands, from fruit, porridge to ham, eggs and grilled kidneys, there in the private dining room of the royal family; she was eating slowly, listening to the others talking rather than joining in. It was peculiar, she thought, to feel so uncertain. This day was the eve of the occasion when her life would change irrevocably. Tomorrow, before noon, she would be officially betrothed to Prince Jerryn. It was a strange concept, one she could not properly imagine as fact – being wed to him.

Discussion between the members of this exalted group was light; Lady Lyria, her best friend and prospective sister-in-law was as quiet as she was, but Lyria always behaved faultlessly in all situations; whilst Prince Jerryn and her older brother, Pualyn, sat with their heads close and talking quietly in each-other's ear, glancing quickly around at their companions, grinning broadly, before they turned their attention back to their plates, eating heartily.

The looming event of the next day, at least, certainly did not seem to be dulling the prince's appetite, she realised, with mingled exasperation and amusement. But he never did seem to allow every day or even extraordinary matters to affect his enjoyment of a good meal.

Ethrayne, daughter of the Duke and Duchess of Clirensar, was sixteen years old, a little more than average height, about five foot five; she was beautiful, with bright blue eyes and luminous pale skin, whilst her longer than waist-length hair was the colour of light-brown honey. She also had an amiable manner that quite effectively disguised both a strong, determined personality and a quick mind: she had received an excellent education due to her position; and thanks to her father's stud south of their home city, she was also fearless, quite physically strong despite her slender frame and able to ride any horse in his extensive stables.

She, her mother and Lyria were dressed very stylishly; at first glance, their gowns were plain, but on closer inspection the fabrics were rich with embroidery and other details. The men were informally dressed in fine linen shirts, their doublets unfastened, soft boots on their feet. This was, afterall, only the eve of momentous events, the chief of which the young woman was trying to forget, for now at least, although the rest of their families were not: her parents and King Marrand had been discussing it jovially since they sat down together. She wondered just how she was going to fill this day, her nerves already stretched tight.

Jerryn was a couple of moons older than she; just over six feet tall, with dark chestnut hair that tended to wave, hazel eyes and regular, pleasing features. Like most noblemen of his age, his body was well-muscled from years of weapons-training, hunting and summer tournaments; his father's kingdom had not been to war for hundreds of years, yet it was not deemed sensible to abandon the traditions of many centuries, although Tenarum was on excellent terms with her neighbours across the Selithian continent and beyond.

Yes, Jerryn was handsome, but he was also nice, very clever and they had spent a great deal of time together since early childhood, best friends for a great deal of it . . . Of course, their interactions had changed somewhat over the past few years, as they had grown up . . . And he was pleasant enough company; he could spin a good story; he was kind; sometimes he could even make her laugh . . . But, a husband?

Ethrayne's older brother, Pualyn, now twenty-one, was slightly taller than the prince, also strong and good looking – a younger version of their father with mid-brown hair and soberer than his friend, whom he would always serve as their father the duke served the king.

His semi-official betrothed was Lyria, who was two years older than Ethrayne; she was a few inches shorter, five-foot-three, with lovely blonde curls, a rosebud mouth and pale blue-green eyes shining in her pretty face; in fact, she was the Duchess's lady's maid yet, since she was walking out with Ethrayne's older brother, she was far more a member of their family than a servant and, consequently, she had been the younger girl's constant companion for at least two years.

"What are you two young men planning?" Duchess Riyala asked levelly, glancing from Pualyn to Jerryn over her porridge bowl. "I know you are up to something."

"Us, Madam?" Prince Jerryn asked in a mock outraged tone. "What on Iullyn makes you say that?"

"Because we know you so very well, your Highness." She replied dryly, smiling. "Come on, spit it out."

"But of course, your Grace." Jerryn answered with a flourish of his right hand and an inclination of his head. "My esteemed nearly brother-in-law has tentatively suggested that we ride out up into the hills to clear our heads before the extravagance of tomorrow. It's turning into a lovely day, so far at least." He flashed them his winning smile, his eyes shining and Pualyn guffawed. "Of course, it might well rain later, but the sun is shining, and we've spent so much time organising for tomorrow that we really deserve a day out, don't we?"

Duchess Riyala and King Marrand exchanged glances and groaned in unison, shaking their heads, whilst Ethrayne, Lyria and Duke Sarant all laughed.

"You just want to try out Vachane, Jerryn, but you've certainly thought of an inventive and probably popular way to escape the palace, although you and Pualyn were meant to attend the Council with us." King Marrand stated, leaning forwards across the table. "And don't you dare to deny it, young man."

He added with a fake glare.

"Deny it? I'd never do that, Father." Jerryn countered with a broad grin, straightening. "If you approve, Sire, we'll rouse the other young people in the palace, have some food boxed up for luncheon and I can finally ride Vachane."

"Jerryn, you are quite outrageous, do you know that?" Ethrayne declared as his eyes widened in that boyish, enthusiastic way he still had when he had need of it. "Oh, please your Majesty, Mother, Father, may we go?" She asked eagerly, appealing to all the adults. A ride, a picnic, would certainly fill the day nicely and reduce all her fears.

Their parents exchanged long looks and maintained a unified silence until the king sighed slightly, glanced from one young adult to another and finally smiled. "Go along with you then but ensure that you are back well before dinner."

"We will, Father, I promise." Jerryn assured him quickly, grinning as he rose to his feet and bowed. "Your Graces, your Majesty. Thank you, Father; come on, you three -."

*

It took time, of course, to gather together those were eager for the exercise, mostly young people like themselves, but not entirely. There was a certain amount of bustle amongst the various servants of those interested, fetching and carrying; yet, surprisingly quickly, they congregated in the main courtyard. The ladies had changed into the latest in fashionable riding habits in jewel bright shades; the men were similarly striking in colourful outfits and would probably be a lot more comfortable.

Ethrayne had changed into an elegant, understated riding outfit in garnet velvet and crisp white silk, a matching velvet cap sat jauntily on her head; Lyria was striking in pink, whilst Pualyn, Jerryn and the other men wore the smart leather leggings and matching jerkins most suited for riding. The prince was busily organising the group, the very centre of attention, his new weapons resting easily at his hips, the metalwork shining in the sunlight fighting against a bank of clouds gusting across the sky. He was not the only one armed; Pualyn and the other men were similarly weighed down with swords, as was customary.

About twenty-five nobles set out, followed by twenty guards and four male servants in charge of the horses bearing luncheon in large baskets strapped to their backs. The clatter of their horses' hooves preceded them down the winding way from the palace, and the main street of the city cleared of pedestrians as they saw the prince's company advancing, people stopping at the edge to wave and cheer. Even more people awaited them in Cathedral Square, alerted by the cheering from further up the hill.

Ethrayne, riding beside Jerryn at the head of the group, heard both blessings and congratulations shouted to them; clearly, the official announcement of their imminent betrothal had been widely discussed by the populace since the previous morning. She smiled, waved and occasionally called back thanks to left and right, gazing down at the faces of those hard-working folk who had paused in their own busy lives to wish her and Jerryn well; men, women, children of every spectrum of life in the kingdom passed before her eyes. Some nobles despised the ordinary folk, she knew that, but her parents had taught her and Pualyn that everything in their own exalted world was underpinned on two vital foundations: the rural economy, that provided the food on everyone's table and the villages, towns and cities, the base of the intricate network of trade and commerce that spread right across the continent and far beyond. Without that dual base, the kingdom was nothing.

Then, as they rode past the junction of Brewers Street, abruptly and horribly sharply, a feeling of actual hatred hit her, almost like a hard slap across the face. Ethrayne's hands tightened on the reins and she straightened in the saddle, as the feeling strengthened. But what was it? How could hatred hurt like that?

"Are you all right, Ethrayne?" Jerryn asked jovially, seeing her sudden change of expression, then he grimaced. "Ow! What *is* that?"

"You can feel it too?" The girl asked, slightly reassured by that fact. "You can feel it, that hatred, Jerryn?"

"Dear Arven, yes, intense hatred." He exclaimed, frowning. "I can sense fury, too. But how can we feel *feelings*?"

"Hurry up, Jerryn!" Earl Orthen called from behind Pualyn, for they had both allowed their mounts to slow as they considered the strange feeling that had come over them.

"Yes, sorry everyone." The prince answered, turning slightly to grin and wave back at the others in apology as, almost at the same moment, he and Ethrayne both felt a lessening of the unfriendly emotion which beat at them. In a breath, it was gone as if it had never been, as they continued at a trot down the hill towards the massive gates in the western wall of the city. "Now that was strange." He commented to her, frowning.

"It just seemed to stop, like a candle snuffed." Ethrayne agreed. "It's very peculiar."

Leaving the city, passing the bustle of those waiting to enter the gates with their animals, produce or business, the others laughed and talked together merrily, the group spreading out a little on the open highway; but the newly betrothed couple rode ahead in quiet thought. Ethrayne found herself wondering what had happened, doubting uneasily that it had been their imaginations. Then, after a few hundred yards, the conversations surrounding them impinged on their thoughts and Ethrayne and Jerryn began to join in, abandoning the puzzle, riding towards the wooded hills over a league away to the west, past crown-owned farmland and small, neat estates.

It was not until they stopped for luncheon in the shade of a stand of blossom-covered rowan trees, sometime in the early afternoon, that the young couple could begin to discuss that odd event, as the group arranged themselves around, the servants setting out the bread, cheeses, meats and so forth, pouring ale and wine with generous hands. It was sunny, yes, but the wind was chill from the south.

"Did you feel the beat of that emotion?" Ethrayne asked, with a shudder, as Jerryn spread his cloak over a fallen log, and politely helped her to sit, a short distance from the chattering group. "Thank you. I've never faced antagonism like it -."

"Nor in such a strange manner, Ethrayne!" Jerryn interjected, smiling as Lady Lyria brought them a platter of food, followed by young Deerne, son of Lord Chamberlain Ferman, who bore pale wine in fine silver goblets. "Thank you, both." Then he sighed, as their privacy was restored. "I don't think anyone else felt it, though, else they would surely be talking about it."

"But who could hate us so vehemently, Jerryn? We are prominent I suppose, you especially as Marrand's son and heir -." He snorted disgustedly at her remark. "Yet we have no real influence over the kingdom and we won't for years, even though you are a member of the Council." Ethrayne shrugged and took a bite of thinly sliced beef on bread.

"Somehow . . . somehow it felt personal, I think; but why? And how could a blast of unfriendly hatred make me think that, anyway?" Jerryn mused, sipping at his wine. "Oh, I don't -."

"Come on, you two!" Lady Bettana called rather shrilly. "There'll be plenty of time for *that* when you are safely wed, or at least after tomorrow! We're trying to organise the midsummer pageant over here, please help."

Rather reluctantly, smiling ruefully at the laughter and comments, they took their plate and goblets across the grass to where the rest of the group were sat or sprawled with easy nonchalance, unconcerned with anything more pressing than a day spent away from court; even Pualyn and Lyria, Ethrayne noted, who were sat close and hand in hand, talking quietly together as if a bubble separated them from the others, despite the interruption of the wider conversations around them.

Looking back across the space to where the guards were stood, Ethrayne caught the smirk of one of the men, Tymain, who had been assigned to Jerryn's protection a few months previously. The young man was a few years older than they, and he viewed the prince, as far as she could tell, with contempt, although she was not at all sure why; men were strange. Privately, she wondered whether it was simply because Jerryn was Marrand's son, nearly betrothed, powerful, rich, yet still officially a youth. The soldier was broader of build, probably adept with his weapons and quite ruggedly good looking besides, yet only ordinary; but Ethrayne knew that whatever anyone in the palace thought of the prince or herself, Tymain included, it certainly did not come close to that mental smack of hatred that had affected them both earlier.

Luncheon over, the servants and guards hurriedly ate as the nobles rested again, before the remnants of the food, drink and equipment were efficiently lashed back into the baskets on the pack horses and they rode on, loud and bright as a group, Ethrayne and Jerryn again leading the way, continuing their roughly circular route between the village, the well-farmed slopes that edged the valley and the greening heights of the hill country which loomed above it to the west of Tenum City; they were wending their way between the many crisscrossing lanes that led, meanderingly, back to the broad valley they could see below through the trees, the wide river at its heart curving around the vast walled city looming grey, black and brown in the distance. The lane they followed had broad stripes of grass on either side, separating it from the fields beyond.

Many people were working in the fields, weeding, casting seed or ploughing, but none were so intent on their tasks that they did not lift their heads to stare at the riders. Some, closer to the lane, called blessings, recognising the soldiers wearing the green, blue and gold of the royal family, if not the prince; others pulled their hats from their heads and essayed clumsy bows. Jerryn did his best to respond, halloing greetings across the furrows and waving cheerfully back at them. "Arven's blessings on you and yours, good people."

"You are very good at this, Jerryn." Ethrayne remarked quietly with a smile, as they passed an ancient, moss-covered boundary wall. "Father always says that it is these informal meetings that can be the most trouble."

The prince pondered this seriously. "Yes, but I think I prefer it to the official speechmaking our fathers' will perform tomorrow. Somehow that feels too impersonal, when it's written in front of you, my Lady."

"But you are not really a person, Jerryn, you are the heir of their king and probably their landowner too." The girl pointed out.

"And what does that make you, Ethie my dear?" He teased her. "We'll be husband and wife before the end of the year."

"Oh, you!" She retorted with a toss of her head, the flash of a smile. "I'll race you, Jerryn, see just how fast Vachane is against Oxalla?" Before he could answer, she urged her mare on with a billowing of skirts and set off quickly, turning the mare onto the smooth grass, leaving the hard lane to the right; her dark blue cloak was spread behind her like a standard as her mount sped to a canter. Swearing audibly, Jerryn followed a moment later, outstripping the others quickly.

"Ethrayne, that's hardly fair, slow down." He called, laughing. "This is embarrassing."

She heard him, dimly and glanced back quickly, grinning, his by far the clearest voice amongst the group as the rest milled together, far to the rear. Vachane had certainly surpassed them, but she had ridden Oxalla for two years now and she knew that the mare was swift and stong, as important a part of her father's stud as Vachane. She raced on, relishing the cool wind in her face, buffeting at her hat, her cloak, across the smooth grass that bordered the fields, laughing aloud in delight simply because no-one could hear her.

"Ethrayne, wait!" That was Jerryn and Pualyn together, their voices distant, and she raised her left hand in a wave of acknowledgement, as Oxalla galloped onward.

Off to her left, beyond a stand of elms and oaks, at most a hundred yards distant, was a collection of buildings, most likely a farm for she could hear fowl calling; to the right, a series of fields made their irregular way along the slope, sprouting grain and other seedlings just visible and bright above the dark soil. Still some way ahead was a sunken lane meeting the one they followed, an earth-coloured rope advancing down from the farm and across her route to the right; bordering that, on the far side of the lane, was a double line of ancient orchard trees, the gnarled branches a riot of pale pink and white blossom and new-green leaves.

Slowing Oxalla, Ethrayne approached the crossroads at a more manageable rate, noting tumbled moss- and nettle-covered remains of walls amid the fruit trees; clearly, at some time in the past, there had been a building there, but not for a century at least. She reined in some distance from the lane, turning in the saddle to gaze back along her route, but something else caught her eye as she moved; a figure stepped out through the mistletoe- and lichen-spotted tree trunks, striding through the rough undergrowth, stepping over the ruined walls.

At first, Ethrayne thought that one of the locals had become far bolder than was usual, but she instantly discarded that supposition, for the man approaching her wore black leather and jingled as he moved. This was certainly no farm hand. He wore a long, luxurious dark grey cloak, but a gust of wind caught it and as it opened, his weapons were prominent: a long sword at his left hip, a shorter blade on his right; there was a glint of mail and his high boots gleamed, beaded with dew from the long grass. He was tall, taller than average, she assessed, even taking her own position in the saddle into account; his hair was blond and short, shining pale in the sunlight which escaped the clouds; his face might have been handsome, but the expression there and in his light blue but burning eyes were dark, forbidding and the girl was suddenly certain that she had found the source of the intense hatred which had assailed her and Jerryn earlier – for that emotion, along with clear contempt, seemed to radiate from him.

"We meet at last, Lady, even if only briefly." The man said in a mild, slightly accented voice, bowing politely; but both the gesture and the look in his eyes made it clear that there was no subservience there.

"Who, who are you?" Ethrayne forced the question out despite the fear that had taken hold of her so abruptly. He was perilous, she knew that. She kept her grip on the reins tight, every part of her tense and alert, letting Oxalla sidle away a step or two further away from the stranger, nudged her with her heels to retreat further. Somewhere behind, she could hear the voices of her companions, closing all the time, thank Arven! Why was it taking them so long to arrive? She did not dare to look away from the stranger, tense and watchful in case he moved closer. "What do you want with me? How dare you -?"

"Please, contain your unease. I am commanded to convey the congratulations of my master to yourself and yonder prince on your impending betrothal, Lady." He stated, with a second bow, irony thick in his tone. "But I must warn you that future events may serve to delay your wedding." He smiled and gestured broadly, his dark eyes glittering with malice as the smile became a sneer. "Until we meet again, Lady. Matters would only end in bloodshed on their part, should I have to deal with your silly young friends. Farewell."

Ethrayne could only stare, alarmed and amazed in equal measure, exceedingly glad that the stranger was striding away, disappearing quickly back through the ancient fruit trees; she shuddered in sudden reaction as the chokingly overwhelming touch of his hatred faded, feeling as much as hearing the oh-so-welcome drum of hoof-beats closing on her from behind.

"Ethrayne!" Jerryn shouted urgently. "Are you all right?"

Turning, she saw that he led the group, with Pualyn and Private Tymain hard on his heels; he had his sword in his hand, the pristine steel shining brightly in the sunlight. Her brother and the other lords were also armed and ready, whilst Lieutenant Connah was barking commands to the soldiers, some spreading out along the lane to left and right, more advancing through the edge of the orchard and out of sight. Everyone looked grim and frightened and the ladies rode separately to the rear, out of the way with the servants, their faces pale, their manner unsure.

"Oh, Jerryn!" She said, shivering all over, relief making her ridiculously weak and cold. "Dear Arven! I -."

"Did he threaten you? Touch you? Who was he?" The prince asked, his words tumbling over themselves as he sheathed his sword and jumped down out of the saddle, holding out his hands to help her dismount and he quickly embraced her when she was stood before him. "I felt that hatred again, it was really strong! Was -."

"Yes, I think it came from him." Ethrayne confirmed, feeling so much safer in his arms that it was almost indecent. Oh, how she wished that she had faced the strange man with Jerryn at her side. "I rode across to here." She pointed. "The man just walked out of those trees from nowhere and he strode back through them, to the left of the twisted apple tree there, before you rode up. He could be well away by now -."

"Tymain, Pualyn, go on through the orchard, but carefully. See what prints or evidence is there, but don't follow him if you see him, though I doubt he's anywhere nearby." Jerryn commanded at once, stepping back from Ethrayne, taking her gloved left hand in his right as they watched both men, their weapons back in their hands, head across the lane, into the overgrown orchard and out of sight, the babble of the rest of the group behind them not even registering.

"Oh, Ethrayne, when I felt that strong hatred again, I somehow knew that something was amiss." He squeezed her hand, leaning close. "It was even as if our horses slowed, but that's probably my imagination playing tricks. It seemed to take ages to catch you up, however. Who was he? What did he want?"

"He wasn't Tenarean. I don't believe so, anyway. He was very tall, blonde, fully armed, he wore mail. And he was chilling; maybe handsome, if that means anything. He spoke with a slight accent – quite musical, really, though he was arrogantly mocking, Jerryn. He knew who I was, congratulated us on our betrothal." Ethrayne paused, smiled thinly and took a deep breath before relating exactly what the man had said, her tone urgent and quiet, determined to keep the details private as the rest of the group chatted and moved about them. "I just was so alarmed, for he seemed dangerous, although he didn't try to move closer or even lay a hand on his weapons."

"Dear Arven, Ethrayne! He might have attacked you, or even taken you away!" He breathed, as if the realisation had just come to him.

"Please excuse me, your Highness." The soldier, Tymain, called, pitching his voice over those of the others and all the conversations died in a moment as everyone turned to stare at him and Lord Pualyn as they came back across the lane, both slightly dishevelled, stained with lichen and mould, still holding their weapons in their hands.

"Tymain, Pualyn, what have you found?" Jerryn asked with a calm confidence that surprised not a few of the group.

The young soldier seemed startled by that, by Jerryn's focus on him; perhaps also by the way that Lord Pualyn, older than he and outranking everyone there but the prince, waved at him to speak; the lowly soldier. Ethrayne realised that he was trying to hide his surprise as he sheathed his sword, coughed nervously and glanced from the prince to herself, bowing slightly, his face solemn.

"Your Highness, my Lady." He said, bowing politely. "It seems that the stranger, whoever he was, was alone and had been waiting there in the cover of the trees for some time: there were numerous footprints in the long grass and hoof-prints from one large horse in the scrubland beyond. He had discarded some foodstuffs: bread crusts, an apple core and so on. He approached from the direction of Tenum City, but he rode off into the west, as far as Lord Pualyn and I could discern and there was no sign of him: the hoofprints vanished when he rode onto the lane which lies beyond the orchard, heading west into the valley beyond. There was no sign of him, however." He paused and sighed. "I am sorry that I can tell you no more of substance."

Lieutenant Connah nodded his agreement, also having returned from his perusal of the area. "It's almost as if he's vanished, your Highness. I can only apologise that there are no more guards here, but we dare not divide our number to pursue the man, for that would leave you and your lady with insufficient protection." And, bowing more deeply, the officer frowned, almost as if it was their fault.

"Yet we know nothing about the man." Ethrayne noted, startling all of them. "It was a strange encounter, yes; even threatening; but not *really* dangerous." She said the words, but she did not believe them: she knew that she would have been less than a moment from some terrible fate, if the stranger had decided it! The truth of that made her angry, she found, at her helplessness.

"Humph!" Jerryn snorted. "You don't pale easily, Ethie, but you were as white as a sheet when we finally reached you. You must not set off by yourself again, dearest; what if he had carried you away?"

"His Highness is correct, my Lady." Tymain agreed unexpectedly, even as Lord Pualyn and Lieutenant Connah opened their mouths to speak and Ethrayne herself took a breath to argue. "As the daughter of the Duke and Duchess of Clirensar and, more importantly, betrothed to Prince Jerryn, you must -." He faltered there, fishing for a word and failing. "Please excuse me, I, I . . . I rudely spoke as if you were-were my young sister, my Lady." He said then, lamely, blushing bright red, quickly kneeling in the long grass.

"Private!" Connah growled warningly, but subsided, still glaring, as the prince spoke.

"No, you are right, Private. Get back on your feet. It's not important, Lieutenant. You really must behave like a princess now, I suppose, Ethrayne." Jerryn supplied in a gentle tone and grinned quickly at Connah, Tymain and Pualyn, before raising one eyebrow to his betrothed as Ethrayne glared at him. "How old is your sister, Private?"

"Erm . . . Genallie is nearly fifteen, your Highness." The young soldier answered. "Please forgive me -."

"It is not a problem, Private Tymain. Now, we really ought to get on our way back to the city, ladies and gentlemen; and we should speak to my father immediately when we return." The prince said smoothly. "Come on."

"Most decidedly, your Highness." Pualyn interjected then, giving his younger sister a quelling glance. "Let us return to safety at once."

Mounting again, with Jerryn's polite assistance, arranging her seat and skirts in the side saddle, Ethrayne sighed deeply to herself, catching Lyria's eye; she had kept back during the wait and she thought her friend looked decidedly tense. Lyria nodded slightly at her compliance, as if approving, but Ethrayne was a little despondent as well as strangely frustrated. It seemed that those peculiar golden chains of marriage and propriety had looped and locked tight around her even sooner than she had ever imagined – even before her betrothal! Still, she admitted to herself, she was very glad to be flanked by Jerryn, her brother, the other nobles and the soldiers all close behind, well-armed. She was safe and, thank Arven, that man had not actually endangered her . . . But another part of her hated the fact of her vulnerability if he had!

*

It was heading towards late afternoon by the time the very alert group re-entered Tenum City and ascended back up to the palace complex, causing a bit of a stir as Lieutenant Connah and his soldiers now rode ahead of the rest, clearing the streets in a most peremptory manner. Ethrayne despised herself for breathing a little easier, but defiantly acknowledged that she was relieved.

"Captain Berdon." Prince Jerryn accosted the officer as the inner gates of the central courtyard closed behind them. "Where are his Majesty and the Duke and Duchess of Clirensar at present?"

"I belive that they are in the royal apartment, your Highness." The middle-aged man replied with a bow. "A meeting was arranged with his Grace the Archpriest."

"Thank you; we really should see them immediately, if you can send someone?" Jerryn ordered.

"Your Highness." The captain beckoned to one of the nearby guards, and the young man strode on up the steps and into the palace, as Jerryn, Ethrayne and the rest of the group dismounted, surrendering their mounts to the throng of stablemen who had hurried to assist.

"Pualyn, Tymain, if you could accompany us." Jerryn did not make it a request but an order yet the young soldier smiled, which surprised Ethrayne.

"Of course, your Highness, but do you really need my presence? Lord Pualyn is far more experienced -." He questioned, even as Connah nodded his approval.

"Thanks, I think." Pualyn interjected dryly.

"You're the professional, however, Private Tymain." Jerryn answered with a grimace and turned to the others. "I'm sorry, everyone, you all might as well go on and get ready for dinner, thank you. Lady Lyria, please, join us."

"Oh, for Arven's sake!" Ethrayne glanced around at the milling group causing so much mayhem and felt her roiling emotions flare into irritation. "Come on -." She strode away from them, her boots ringing as she ran up the sweeping steps and aware that Jerryn, Lyria, Pualyn and Tymain were all hurrying in her wake; she paused only to surrender her cloak and hat to one of the servants loitering in the entrance hall.

They caught up with her as she ascended the ornate staircase to the main private apartments, some distance past the public halls and offices and the guards on duty all saluted Jerryn and herself as the group passed; the corridor at the top which led to the king's suite was long and wide, lined with more guards, huge tapestries and the occasional new innovation: a few large, solemn portraits that were painted in amazingly bright shades. As the five of them approached the heavy, iron-bound oak doors at the far end, one of the soldiers at attention there bowed low and stepped forward to open them with a flourish, then stepped back.

Jerryn took the lead as they walked into an oak-panelled foyer, facing a second pair of doors, where two more liveried soldiers stood and again the man on the left bowed, opened the doors, and bowed again as he stood in the doorway. "His Highness, Prince Jerryn, your Majesty, with Lord Pualyn, Ladies Ethrayne and Lyria and Private Tymain." He announced, and stepped back out, pulling the doors closed quietly behind them once they had passed him.

King Marrand and his guests were sat on comfortable blue or green upholstered chairs and settees around a merrily blazing fire in the hearth some thirty feet from the outer doors, a hearth that could have easily roasted half an ox; the king's private sitting room was pleasantly furnished but rather understated, the walls palely panelled, the curtains and carpet of striped blue and green silk. It was familiar to all of them, except for the wide-eyed young soldier who had clearly never been here before.

"Is something wrong, Jerryn?" The king asked, rising to his feet as he looked from face to face.

"Father. Your Graces, I apologise for intruding so rudely, but something strange happened earlier; we thought it best to tell you at once . . . Ethrayne -."

"Please, do sit down. You look tense." Marrand noted as everyone bowed and curtsied, whilst the soldier saluted crisply.

"My dear, are you all right?" Duke Sarant also rose and approached them, taking his daughter's hand for a moment. "I don't think I've ever seen you at such a loss for words." He asked with a mischievous wink as everyone but Private Tymain took seats, the young soldier stood stiffly to attention there by the door.

"Father, please!" Ethrayne protested mildly, took a deep breath and related her encounter with the stranger, describing his appearance as well as she could, recounting his conversation, or rather discourse, for she had hardly said a word, exactly. She did not, however, mention the sharp, clear feeling of hatred that had struck right into her mind. As Jerryn reported what he had seen, Ethrayne noted that he also kept that personal mental assault private; and he quickly passed the duty of explanation to the young soldier, Tymain and then to Pualyn.

"My word!" Marrand remarked, gazing from one serious young face to another, then focussing back on Tymain. "Is that all, Private?" He asked gravely. "Has every detail been reported?"

Tymain took a breath. "Y-yes, your Majesty, I do not believe that anything has been forgotten. I only wish that we had been closer to Lady Ethrayne; it was strange that her horse got so far ahead, given the equally fine mounts of his Highness and Lord Pualyn." And he bowed shakily.

"Thank you for your input, Private Tymain." Jerryn said earnestly. "I expect you want to go and rest."

"Thank you, all of you." Ethrayne added with a lopsided smile. "I'm sorry that I've ruined everyone's afternoon."

"Ethrayne, my dear, this is hardly your fault." King Marrand pointed out. "Now, Private, find Lieutenant Connah, then report to Commander Vedeigne: I want a concise assessment of everything that happened; and I add my heartfelt thanks to his Highness's and Lady Ethrayne's."

"I am honoured, your Majesty, your Highness, your Graces, my Lord, Ladies." The young soldier bowed again, saluted, and quickly left the room.

“My word, what an awful shock.” Archpriest Lurco, who had been sat quietly during the discussion, leaned forward in his chair. “Hopefully this is not involved with our earlier conversation, Sire. Naturally you wish to discuss this singular event and I am only going to get in the way, your Majesty, my dear Duke and Duchess; this meeting can be easily rearranged on a less busy occasion, so I will take my leave of you at once. I extend my congratulations to you both on your forthcoming betrothal, your Highness, Lady Ethrayne; and you also, my Lord Pualyn, Lady Lyria. I will commend all of you to Arven.” Lurco was a hale man in his sixties, with a gently lined face around his brown eyes; he wore a richly embroidered open-fronted white robe over a rather plain white shirt and leggings, denoting his position as the head of the church in Tenarum; he got easily to his feet, smiling genuinely, as they all stood as well, everyone bowing or curtsying, but for the king.

“Thank you so much for your understanding, Lurco, and I can only humbly apologise. We will swiftly be in touch to re-arrange our meeting for a later date.” Marrand said gratefully, his hand on the man’s shoulder as he accompanied the Archpriest to the doors. “Your support means a great deal to us.”

“There is no need for any apology, the wellbeing of your families is paramount. Bless you all! I am honoured, Marrand, good afternoon.” He bowed, and left with a wave and a broader smile, nodding pleasantly at a servant who passed him, bearing more glasses, a carafe of wine and other refreshments.

“Are you feeling all right, Ethrayne, my dear?” Duke Sarant asked earnestly.

“Yes, I am, Father, yet it was such a strange meeting, for how could he have known that we would ride that way, when all is said and done?” The girl frowned, thinking her way again through the events of the afternoon. “He seemed so confident, even though he was alone as Jerryn, Pualyn and the soldiers approached at speed, and they were all armed. But who he was, what he wanted, I don’t know at all.”

“Oh, Ethrayne!” Her mother cried, taking her hand. “How unwise you were, to ride ahead of the others!”

“Jerryn and I were racing, Mother.” Ethrayne pointed out mildly. “I had no idea Oxalla had got so far ahead of the rest. She is fast, yes, but Jerryn should have been much closer than he was: Vachane usually outstrips Oxalla within a hundred yards.”

“Why should she not ride out, Riyala?” King Marrand queried then, to her surprise. “How often have our children escaped supervision from their guards and servants, hey?” He shook his head and took a sip of wine. “They were all out hawking six days ago, remember? We had young nobles dotted all over the countryside; and what about last summer, in Clirensar: our children were down by the Sare, fishing pretty much alone, for a few days; and they have often ridden from the city to your South Vale Farm to help with the animals and not every outing was robustly supervised, was it?"

His assertion made Ethrayne feel slightly better, but also more like a child than ever which, overall, did not really help. Annoyance warred with a lingering unease at the constraints she could see looming over them, the freedoms vanishing.

"Ethrayne, my dear, and the rest of you as well, I am afraid that you will have to stop leaving the palace without your guards or visiting the markets with only servants. Oh, we are all so relieved that you are safe!" Her father said, his tone light, but the look in his eyes, on his face, was troubled.

"Yes Father, so am I." She acknowledged quietly and Lyria, Jerryn and Pualyn echoed their agreement to the new, expected, restriction.

"Oh, what an afternoon!" Duchess Riyala said, shaking her head. "This is quite unsettling. You had all better go and get ready for dinner, go on now."

"Yes, Mother." Ethrayne replied meekly for all of them. "I am sorry to have caused you all so much concern so suddenly, your Majesty, Father, Mother." She got slowly to her feet and Lyria, Jerryn and Pualyn followed suit, bowing and curtsying, then quitting the sitting room, leaving their elders talking, heading back along the huge corridor to the stairs that led up to more apartments.

"Well, that could have gone worse." Jerryn remarked heavily. "Dear Arven, Ethie, when I saw that man, my heart thudded with fear."

"As did mine, I assure you, but he just walked straight out of that orchard, out of nowhere." Ethrayne restated. "If I had thought -."

"But our father was right, Ethrayne. You – we all – will have to take especial care." Pualyn replied gravely. "You are practically betrothed to Jerryn, our princess in effect . . . Yet Tenarum has no political enemies; we have no real personal enemies, I am sure, or we would know about them. There has been peace for centuries – who would threaten us? Why should any one of us think that a simple race would compromise our safety? We are hardly reckless, any of us . . . But I wonder who he was?"

Jerryn only shrugged as they walked on.

"We could talk in circles forever, I'm sure." Ethrayne said with a sigh as she and Lyria headed to the left at the top of the stairs. "We'll see you at dinner, your Highness, my Lord; and thank you."

"Ladies." Jerryn bowed floridly, Pualyn grinned and bowed to Lyria and the men went on alone, talking quietly.

Their maids separated the young ladies as they entered the suite and Ethrayne quickly had her snood removed, her dusty riding outfit unlaced by Fionn and Sallie, who chatted away cheerfully as normal as they dealt with Lyria and herself, even though she was so uncharacteristically quiet. She washed, then her long hair was brushed ruthlessly and rearranged with many pins, as she continued to try not to think too deeply on what had happened and, perhaps more pertinently, what might have happened.

Just the thought of abduction or attack, however unlikely, turned her icy cold for a moment and she shivered. But what did it mean? She wondered.

Ethrayne chose a deceptively understated gown of silvery-green velvet, donning a plain silver circlet and earrings which she had loved for years. And, considering what had occurred, she had decided that she certainly did not want to stand out; she wanted to prove to her parents and the king that she wasn't a foolish girl.

Lyria came through from the dressing room as she slipped her feet into delicate shoes by her bed, the blonde girl wearing creamy-yellow satin and a gold chain and bracelets that had been a gift from Pualyn.

"Are you all right, Ethie?" The older girl asked earnestly. "You're very quiet and I know that you were frightened, although you controlled it well. I would have been terrified, I know that – but what a strange meeting. And I really can't see that you did anything amiss, other than completely outstrip all of us – Oxalla seemed to fly and it was as if we were all stuck in mud behind you."

"Yes, I'm fine, Lyria, really I am." Ethrayne reassured her, opening the outer door and realised that she was ridiculously pleased to see the two guards in the corridor come to attention and then fall in behind them to escort them. Abruptly, from nowhere, she wished she had the training, the assurance, of Jerryn, Pualyn and the soldiers, with their long familiarity with the weapons at their hips.

*

Ethrayne had not considered it, but of course the news of her irregular adventure during the afternoon seemed to have reached the ears of everyone in the palace by the time that she and Lyria entered the dining hall. Those who were her acquaintances talked loudly, pointing her out to their companions quite unnecessarily; whilst certain others, whom she might have considered friends, stared openly, but were talking behind their hands. This evening was bound to be rather tedious, she realised, taking her seat between her parents; Lyria had been placed between Duke Sarant and Pualyn, whilst Jerryn was sat between the Duchess and King Marrand. He caught her eye and grimaced, rolling his eyes at the apparently universal topic of conversation.

Wine and ale were poured for the king and his principal guests, the silver jugs set down before the many platters on the top table were broached, as the lower tables were served. The conversations began to fade a little, but some, especially the older members of the court, continued to shake their heads and voice their disapproval, or so Ethrayne believed.

"Don't worry about them, Ethrayne." Her father advised, speaking quietly in her ear, nodding his head in the direction of the Lord and Lady of Calshore, who were regarding her almost as if her hair had turned green, she thought. "A modern-minded miss you might be, with no thought for the proprieties or traditions of your rank and position, but you are safe and that is what we are grateful for." He smiled and patted her hand. "How often have even proper, high-born young ladies rebelled to ride or walk out alone into the city? Times without mention, I suspect, and no one else would expect to be accosted by a stranger, any more than you did." He sighed. "Thank Arven you are safe!" He added fervently.

"So, it is my fault, even though it was only a race? I didn't expect to outstrip Vachane so comprehensively, Father! He's bigger than my mare and I still don't know how Jerryn didn't catch up with me, he's a superlative rider." Ethrayne replied in an aggrieved tone, knowing that she was behaving childishly, but feeling a mixture of anger, frustration and helplessness that was quite unsettling. "Dear Arven, Father, sometimes I wish I had been a boy!" Yet it wasn't that she was constrained by propriety so much that rankled, just her inability to protect herself, she realised again.

Her mother laughed aloud at that. "Oh, Ethrayne, sometimes I think that every young woman says that at some point. Honestly, though, I think that in the long run you will be glad to be just as you are, female, even if growing up has rather narrowed your horizons a little. Balancing that, of course, you will soon be our princess and one day, you will be our queen and the most powerful woman in Tenarum. The sense of not riding off alone now that you are grown up is a constraint on your sex generally, not on you personally, my darling."

Ethrayne wanted to snort and proclaim the whole business completely unfair but kept quiet; such behaviour would likely only label her as being more childish than ever and a fool, in the eyes of her elders.

But who had he been, that stranger, and who was his 'master'? She mused, for the third time at least, picking at her food with little appetite. How had he known where they would be riding, when their route had been chosen at random? There were many green lanes winding and crisscrossing through the countryside around the capital between the farms: they could have chosen any of them, one of numerous routes. And why and exactly how had she and Jerryn been able to feel that silent animosity, the hatred that had emanated from him like the heat of a fire? He had been so confident, so arrogant – so dangerous.

Eventually, however, as the meal came to an end she decided to stop trying to make sense of the questions: she was getting a headache, whilst getting nowhere at all; she had volunteered not a single answer to her questions all evening. She could only hope that the mystery would perhaps become clearer in time. So, deliberately, she locked the event, the fear and her confusion away in her mind, as described by her long-term tutor, the middle-aged deacon assigned by her family priest, for consideration later.

Coming out of her introspection, Ethrayne became aware of the conversations flowing about her, most of which hardly seemed to have progressed at all during the sumptuous meal, from what she heard.

"Are you feeling all right, Ethrayne?" Jerryn asked then. "You've been very quiet this evening. I'm sorry -."

"Heavens, please don't apologise, Jerryn. It's just that I've been trying and failing to make any sense of it all. I'm perfectly fine, honestly." And she essayed a smile which failed to reach her eyes. "At least I will be able to continue to perfect my embroidery, won't I?"

King Marrand, beyond his son, heard both her words and the bitterness in her voice and chuckled aloud, startling many others on the top table, and the servant who nearly spilled the wine as it was poured into his goblet.

"I think that we can do better than that, my dear Ethrayne." He said, smiling, waving the servant away. "I am sure that you know Lady Celia, who has recently joined my Council?"

"Yes, your Majesty, I do."

"I thought so. Well, I know that you have been a diligent pupil with commendable conscientiousness and intelligence, for the reports I have received from Deacon Pettar have all been excellent. I believe it is time for you to start to learn what our Council's purpose is within the kingdom, before you join us formally upon your wedding." Marrand grimaced slightly, then smiled at her rather stunned expression. "I freely admit that, generally, it's rather tedious and your father, Jerryn and your brother will agree with me, I'm sure, but our work is vital. What do you think, hey? Do you want to sit in with us, the day after tomorrow?"

"I, well, your Majesty, I am honoured that you think so highly of me, Sire, and I . . . I am doubly honoured to accept." Ethrayne replied earnestly, rising to her feet to curtsy very formally. She was stunned, overwhelmed; so much had happened in such a short time that she knew that it was going to take ages to get it all straight in her mind.

* * *

CHAPTER 2

Ethrayne gazed out of the window of her bedroom at the lightening sky. The sky was turning a lovely shade of pale blue now that the stars were fading, and the clouds above were lightly stained in shades of gold. She had been awake for quite some time, lying in her bed, thinking; but now that it was nearly dawn, she had had enough of pretending to sleep, pulling on a robe, then she slipped past the full-length closed curtains over the east-facing window, hoping not to disturb Lyria, who was still asleep in her own bed on the other side of the room. Quietly, privately, she realised that she was worried. This fact even dominated her concerns at that stranger's appearance and arrogant words the previous afternoon.

It was not that she did *not* want to marry Jerryn. She had known him all her life; indeed, since the death of Jerryn's mother, Queen Tanallyse, in childbirth twelve years previously, the friendship of king, duke and duchess had only strengthened and that of their children likewise – he had called her parents aunt and uncle; she called his father uncle as well, when they were in private . . . they were already almost as close as family, Ethrayne acknowledged.

This occasion had long been in her awareness and yet it had been somehow unreal: the Ethrayne who would wed the prince was not *her*, inside her own head, but another person entirely, since she had first learned of this intention at the age of twelve or so; and that adolescent thought was clearly utterly ridiculous. It was alarming, that the long-term plan of her parents and King Marrand was coming to fruition . . . That, all too soon, quite apart from the previous day's events, her life would no longer be in her control; that politics and practicality would take precedence . . . Ruefully, she acknowledged that, honestly, her life never had been at her command, which proved only that she was a fool!

She considered the prince seriously, with as much dispassion as she could manage. Ethrayne certainly was not sure if she was ready to commit to this; promising to become Jerryn's wife and princess of Tenarum, one day queen . . . But, truth to tell, she knew that it was far too late to change anything. Their betrothal was happening, today.

"Oh, damn it!" She muttered quietly, leaning her forehead against the cool glass of the diamond paned window, wondering whether she could run away right now, before anyone else was awake . . . although that blonde stranger might be somewhere around, she realised, with his strange hatred – *watching her.*

Then, behind her, she heard Lyria yawn and stir.

"I thought you'd be awake early." Lyria said a short while later, pulling the curtains open. "Good morning, my Lady."

"Hello." Ethrayne sounded a little disgruntled, she knew, but she smiled at the older girl and felt her odd mood recede slightly. "I hope I didn't wake you. And how did you guess?" She asked with a chuckle.

"Because I know I'll feel the same when it's my turn, Ethrayne." Lyria shrugged elegantly. "Come on, Mistress reluctant, let's start getting you ready, shall we?"

"I'll feel like one of father's horses being put through its paces to a buyer." Ethrayne said with a toss of her head.

"Hardly, Ethrayne: that gown has taken us all a great deal of effort. No one is going to want to see how well you can jump or gallop, not dressed so well. Your beauty will shine out today and silence even those decrying your forward behaviour yesterday." Lyria said, now laughing at her. "I'll get Fionn and Sallie, yet I imagine they are already starting your bath. Then, you can have breakfast."

"Very well, my Lady Lyria." Ethrayne agreed. "But I really don't think I can eat."

*

The throng of immaculately dressed courtiers and hangers-on seemed to ebb and flow before the dais where Lady Ethrayne, Prince Jerryn and their elders stood in their finery, raised higher than everyone else and so, of course, the absolute centre of attention. Their location was the old Tapestried Hall, with its tall, narrow, ancient mullioned windows holding rare stained glass of equal antiquity; and the far newer, brightly configured tapestries that covered nearly all the whitewashed stone walls between. Bright sunshine was, now and again, reflecting off other walls in the vicinity, shining through the windows and dotting the tapestries and walls with more vibrant hues.

Even brighter were the fine clothes of the guests, who swirled around them, looking strangely truncated, Ethrayne thought, as if their legs had been removed at the knees. Visible to her eyes was practically every colour imaginable, in the latest fashions of the season; yet, looking out over them as she and her companions received the best wishes of the throng, the young woman rather smugly considered that she and her family, in addition to and the king and his son, were dressed far more exquisitely. They were also, quite deliberately, coordinated in colour and far more visible due to their positions on the dais.

The surrounding noise of the many conversations was becoming baffling; the numerous scents and pomanders that drifted on the air were equally an assault on the nose, some pleasant, others less so; yet Ethrayne, feeling suddenly and ridiculously vulnerable and far too exposed, held back a sigh and maintained her smile.

Ethrayne wore a beautiful gown of bluebell blue satin and it was deceptively and purposefully simple, demure rather than revealing, edged with lace and a great deal of delicate embroidery. This was augmented by glittering jewellery: a tiara, earrings, necklace and ring in sapphires, emeralds and diamonds set in gold, exquisite and noticeable: jewellery worthy of a queen, ensuring that she stood out even against her mother's beautiful pearls.

Now speaking quietly with her older brother, Prince Jerryn wore mid blue brocade, also embroidered, over a fine silk shirt, his crown of gold and studded with emeralds and sapphires, whilst Pualyn, her brother, was staid but handsome in a dark green of a similar material and cut; both looked a little uncomfortable in the heavy, slightly tight doublets and hose. The king wore a slightly darker shade of blue than his son, his dark, slightly greying hair offset by his heavy crown, whilst Ethrayne's mother, Duchess Riyala, was imposing in jade green silk, of an exquisite, shimmering quality that was clearly imported and her father, Duke Sarant, complemented his wife and King Marrand in midnight blue velvet offset with silver. Lady Lyria wore a beautiful gown in a similar shade of light blue to the sky that morning and she was below the dais since she was not yet officially betrothed to Pualyn; she was stood beside another young woman, striking in deep pink.

Ethrayne caught her friend's eye and smiled quickly, rolling her eyes slightly and Lyria smiled back, then blushed a deep rose as she caught Pualyn's gaze without meaning to. The other young woman laughed and murmured something in Lyria's ear, nodding politely to Ethrayne, then winking slightly. Ethrayne nodded to her as well in amusement: trust Lady Celia to take Lyria under her wing.

"My Lords, Ladies and gentlemen, I am absolutely delighted to present Ethrayne Hallainne Tanallyse, Lady of Clirensar, daughter of Duke Sarant and Duchess Riyala, and now the betrothed of Prince Jerryn Marrath Sarant, my son and heir to the throne of Tenarum." King Marrand declared with a wide grin and a flourish of his arms, followed by a well-rehearsed fanfare from liveried musicians playing silver trumpets, stood along the far wall. At that signal, the prince bowed to his betrothed and kissed her hand and Ethrayne curtsied to him in return. Marrand laughed aloud at that display whilst some of the crowd cheered and applauded. "This is the next step towards a most wonderful conclusion which their Graces and I have been working towards for years. I can only express my sincere apologies for not yet being able to announce a date for Ethrayne and Jerryn's wedding, but the year is just beginning, and I am very sure that this young couple will let me know their wishes soon enough."

There was a wave of polite amusement around the hall and the duke and duchess exchanged smiles with the king as Ethrayne curtsied very politely to the hall at large, a movement that was precise in every detail, yet not at all submissive, by the almost defiant gaze that she swept from face to face below as the crowd bowed or curtsied back.

"Hold to your courage, my dear Ethrayne, this pageantry will be over soon enough, and our guests will soon be concentrating on the feast awaiting us." King Marrand quietly assured the girl with a warm smile, squeezing her hand for a moment. "The servants have been working on the occasion for a moon at least; it would be rude in the extreme to abandon this event before time."

For a moment a natural smile crinkled her nose and made her blue eyes sparkle – for Uncle Marrand obviously knew her too well; Ethrayne chuckled. "This would not be too arduous to endure, your Majesty, if I did not know full well that many of these good people wished so plainly that you had chosen their daughter, sister or niece to wed Jerryn and not I." She glanced at Prince Jerryn on her left, then back at his father. "I am, of course, greatly honoured, your Majesty, but I do remember that little boy sitting high in the apple tree with me all those years ago, pelting Pualyn with fruit." She broke off as both the prince and her brother snorted with evident amusement. "Dereck the gardener was not best pleased with us."

"No, he wasn't, was he? The three of you have surely led us a few merry dances over the years, dear Ethrayne, so who would be better suited to keep his Highness here in line than you, his partner in mischief?" Marrand enquired with a wink that included all of them.

"Father!" Jerryn protested with false outrage.

"Those damned apples hurt." Pualyn remarked then, grimacing slightly. "I had bruises for ages; I think I thrashed you conclusively a few days later, however, your Highness."

The prince grinned. "I know you did, but we had a good aim, didn't we? And Dereck chased us all from the garden conclusively, bellowing threats. I hope he's having a good retirement, there in Clirensar, not worrying about the duke's gardens."

There came a second musical blast from the musicians, announcing that the guests of honour should lead the procession through to the oak-panelled hall next door. Prince Jerryn bowed low again and escorted his beautiful, jewel-bedecked lady into the banqueting hall, where the north-facing wide windows in one long wall looked out over a courtyard garden where bright spring flowers were set between ancient paving and lichen-covered walls. Light, floral scents wafted in through a few open panes, soon competing with the huge platters of intricately dressed dishes quickly set out for their delight, the first of many courses in the well-appointed feast prepared.

Course followed course and wine and ale flowed freely for a time, the volume of noise increasing apace, until musicians with different instruments began playing more loudly in the gallery above and Jerryn and Ethrayne, laughing, got up and began the dancing alone, mirroring their future marriage. Even those who were jealous of the young lady's good fortune had to admit that they made a fine couple as they moved through the intricate steps of one of the most popular dances of the year. As the music ended with a flourish from the musicians and a graceful bow and curtsey from the couple, everyone joined in with enthusiastic applause before other couples joined them on the floor when the musicians began a hugely popular country tune. Ethrayne moved quickly across to the left side of the high table, pulling Lyria up from her seat, pleased that her brother stood as well.

"Come on, please do dance with us." She urged, feeling calmer than before. A banquet and dancing were always to be enjoyed, after all, now that she was not singled out for so much attention as she and Jerryn had been earlier, or that she had experienced the previous day.

"Oh, all right, Ethrayne, if you insist." Lyria was laughing, but her suitor already had her hand in his.

A stomping, whirling dance of great antiquity was begun, one familiar throughout the realm and danced at all occasions and locations from royal palace to village greens. It was perhaps not the best for such formal, tight clothing, but such details did not matter. The hall's centre was full of moving shades of colour.

"They make a good couple, Sarant." Marrand remarked to his old friend, the Duke of Clirensar. "Ethrayne will be a very good queen for Tenarum and for Jerryn -." He laughed. "Well, if the business of the next few moons doesn't scare her away from the palace entirely. This union will serve to strengthen the kingdom as none other could. Thank you, your Graces."

"The honour is ours, Marrand." Duchess Riyala answered with a smile, patting his hand. Her hair was a little darker than her daughter's, now lightly marked with grey but it was clear where Ethrayne had got her beauty and blue eyes. "And she certainly knows all the dangers of court, from cellar to tower, if I remember. Do you recall, when they were small and practically everyone in the palace complex was searching for the three of them? They had evaded all the guards and servants, left the palace, walked through the city alone and were fishing down in the river beyond the wharves?" She chuckled, shaking her head at the memory.

"Dear Arven, their clothes were completely ruined; they were, what? Only six or so? Pualyn might have been ten. And now look at them." Marrand grinned, gesturing proudly to where the young people danced: Jerryn and Ethrayne, Pualyn and Lyria. "Our children are all grown up! Where have the years gone?"

"Tanallyse would be so proud of you, your Majesty." Sarant said with a gentle smile. "Jerryn is a fine young man, a worthy heir."

"As is your son, old friend." The king added as Pualyn and Lyria pranced past the front of the high table, leading their group in the dance. "They look happy together. I imagine that more congratulations and festivities will be soon in order." And he waved one hand slightly to the tune, still grinning at Pualyn and Lyria, who were looking very content.

"The announcement will be imminent, Marrand." Sarant admitted. "Pualyn has already asked for permission from Lyria's father; you remember Lord Terfylls and Lady Allara from Callorton, don't you? Her third brother runs our stud, the fourth is in the army."

"Yes, of course and she's the only daughter, isn't she?" Marrand nodded. He knew the girl's parents, for he enjoyed the quiet periods he occasionally spent relatively anonymously in the south of his realm, where he and Sarant were almost merely local landowners, away from the complications and convolutions of court. "They're a very good family."

"She is a lovely young woman, a great help to both Ethrayne and I; we will be immensely lucky to gain her as daughter. Lyria will become an excellent duchess, in time." Riyala stated easily and at her smug tone, both men laughed, before they turned their attention to appreciating the dancing again.

*

Much later that night, Ethrayne sat before the ornately framed silver mirror in her bedroom, part of her parents' apartment in the vast palace. Wearing a soft velvet robe in pale pink, she was humming a tune as Lyria, in green silk, gently combed out the last of the complex style in which her hair had been confined all day. Their beautiful but heavy and restrictive gowns had already been hung up in the dressing room by their maids, girls from Clirensar, friends as well as servants, who had now retired, giggling together.

Ethrayne picked up the jewelled pins that had held the braids so elegantly and placed them in a small silver box, before reaching up to remove the earrings that sparkled on her lobes, matching the delicate-looking tiara, ring and necklace that lay in the centre of the dressing table, which had been delivered by King Marrand himself before breakfast time to her amazement: a wealth of precious gemstones in the colours of the king's standard. The sapphires and emeralds had been styled to look like forget-me-nots with eyes of gold and surrounded by oak leaves in graduated shades of blue and green, edged with scintillating diamonds throwing the light every-which-way.

"They are lovely, Ethrayne." Lyria said wonderingly. "You looked so beautiful today, even more so than usual, dear."

The younger girl laughed a little. "Dear Arven, if that is beauty, I really don't want to endure it every day Lyria, for my scalp aches awfully: that little tiara weighs nearly as much as a bag of flour and the gown seriously constricts my breathing. Do you think I'll be able to wear my old, loose linen dresses for the next month or two? The ones we wore to conduct the cleaning in the autumn?" Carefully she laid the jewellery in its large ebony case lined with white satin and edged in filigreed gold, locking it away. "But it is very lovely. I expect Jerryn likes his betrothal gifts even more: the weapons father commissioned from Master Queyt are the best in the kingdom by far; and quite a few young men at court were hugely envious of his receipt of Vachane."

Lyria smiled, shaking her head as she continued working Ethrayne's hair into one waist-length braid. "A few? You are too modest of your father's expertise, Ethrayne. Likely every man in the city would give his left arm to own a horse from the stables of Clirensar, and Vachane is the best stallion bred by far. He's the pinnacle of your father's success to date, you know. You should have heard the men talking, yesterday, during our ride back to the city: they were envious of Vachane and Oxalla both. Even my father says so, and you know how he always teases his grace for playing at farming."

"Well, that is true I suppose. Anyway, Salyar and Deanne really run South Vale Farm, Lyria, not father. Men!" Ethrayne snorted a little resentfully. "They prefer weapons and horses to us!" She turned about as Lyria fastened a ribbon securely about the braid, frowning.

"Now that is certainly not true." Lyria countered gently. "You're only tired, for you were the complete centre of attention today, Ethrayne, in every way. The prince might have superb weapons and the beginning of his own stud, but he will also have you –."

"With the accompanying steel and horses!" Ethrayne interjected, feeling uncharacteristically ungrateful. All at once, her disgruntlement from the previous evening and that morning had re-emerged even stronger than it had been.

"Ethrayne, you know that your marriage will strengthen the kingdom greatly: the iron and steel of the south will be allied to the kingdom by blood, the risk of one single heir negated by your wedding. And Clirensar will be connected even closer to the throne, forever." Lyria answered firmly. "Your father's gift to the king is vast, whereas poor Pualyn will have my hand and only a token dowry from father."

"Oh Lyria, I'm sorry. Not only have we completely set back your own wonderful news, I am moaning ungratefully when you're tired as well. Your betrothal should have happened first this spring." Ethrayne said contritely, feeling suddenly spiteful and embarrassed by her burst of bad temper, kissing Lyria quickly.

"Honestly, it doesn't matter, Ethrayne. Pualyn also is a member of the Council, after all: he spoke on the matter of your betrothal and voted against Jerryn's wishes." Lyria shrugged a little and smiled cheerfully. "Everyone deserves a good party after the winter and the king can afford it. The prince's betrothal is far more important than even the heir to the Duchy of Clirensar's."

The plain truth of that caused Ethrayne to laugh, but a knock at the door to their left caused her to decorously halt her amusement as she called entry, before she hugged her friend tightly; fortunately, that burst of bad humour was leaving her as suddenly as it had emerged.

"Are you two girls going to be talking all night long?" Duchess Riyala asked, sweeping into the room in a fine cream dressing gown buttoned to her neck, two long braids hanging over her shoulders; she was followed by her tall husband, imposing in black. "Oh, if only I still had your stamina." And she sighed with apparent weariness.

"Mother!" Ethrayne got up, her own braid swinging and moved to embrace the duchess, kissing her and then her father. "Father! Oh, my! I just . . . I'm sorry, it is very late, isn't it?"

"Ethrayne, my darling." Sarant held her close and kissed her on the brow. "And all grown up now; it seems only moments since you were a baby. Oh my, we are so proud of both you young ladies." He reached out and cupped Lyria's chin as he spoke, including her in the compliment, smiling and Lyria curtsied.

"Thank you, your Grace." She murmured.

“We have only come to wish you good night.” Riyala hugged Ethrayne again when her father released her, then Lyria also, kissing them both. “Gosh, with all this excitement I am exhausted, even if you two aren’t. Sweet dreams, girls.”

“Mother, Father, good night and thank you.” Ethrayne said, curtsying and her parents disappeared back into the corridor beyond, quietly closing the door.

“Your family is lovely, Ethrayne.” Lyria commented with a smile. “And so is the prince. He and King Marrand have been so kind to me. You are clever, and you have nothing to fear here in Tenum City, my dear.”

Ethrayne grinned at that. “Clever doesn’t really count for much, Lyria, not for a girl.” She gestured to her friend to take her place at the mirror and picked up the comb to braid her hair in turn. “And the hordes of people here in the palace make wolves look friendly, I think. I doubt they will like a clever princess.”

“That is not true either and you know it; you’re already far beyond those minor courtiers. And look at Lady Celia: she’s hardly stupid, she inherited Pellerton Court in her own right *and* she has joined the Council. Those scary old men who advise the king must have been terribly shocked at that occurrence, I’m sure.” Lyria stated calmly. “And she was nothing before, was she?”

“Well, that’s true, did Celia tell you that she has asked us both to join her for lunch tomorrow?” Ethrayne said as she combed Lyria’s hair. “I spoke with her briefly, earlier and she’s not as scared at speaking and appearing in public as she was last year, when she first came to court. And look at her: Lady and Mistress of Pellerton Court in her own right, not just that-young-niece-of-Lord-Junnet.” She made a noise of disgust. “Apparently Lord Ellett was horrible, Junnet’s nephew. I only ever saw him at a distance, but, gosh, I’ve heard awful stories: apparently quite a few women of all ranks had trouble with him. He drank, gambled and fought all over the countryside, I think and left debts everywhere. He caused so much trouble that King Marrand lost all patience and disinherited him completely.”

“It serves him right. It’s no way for a member of the Council to behave.” Lyria agreed as her blonde hair was deftly plaited. “We are both very lucky, you know Ethrayne: we know our husbands-to-be, which is quite unusual.” She smiled broadly.

“Yes, that is so.” Ethrayne chuckled. “You have lived with us in the castle for years, helping mother, but we’ve known you and your family for ever, longer than I’ve been alive, certainly. Do you remember how we all kept running across the fields between Callorton and South Vale Farm when we were younger? Pualyn and I, you, and your older brothers as well? We could never keep up with any of them, of course, though we tried.” She laughed at that: the youngest of Lyria’s brothers were all at least four years older than even Pualyn, she thought she recalled. “Jerryn and I have known each other for ever, too, I suppose, even from when we were babies, since mother and the queen were so close, although we fell out completely when we were little. I can't really remember why, but I suppose it was over something silly and childish. Jerryn and Pualyn have been close friends for years and it's clear that my brother adores *you.* I just wish that our betrothal had not squashed your plans, Lyria." She apologised again.

"But it hasn't, and we really don't mind, Ethrayne." Lyria hugged her tight. "I'm going to bed, it's been a very busy day, good night."

"Yes, hasn't it? Sleep tight." Ethrayne agreed, turning to her bed, removing her robe and climbing in, pulling up the covers, stretching out her toes as far as she could reach. Lyria blew out the lamps, got into her own bed and, soon enough, after a little more conversation, silence filled the room.

The young woman lay still, hearing her friend's breathing slowly change as she fell asleep, but although she was tired, Ethrayne still was too wound up to sleep herself . . . Jerryn's apparent nervousness earlier was heartening, she thought, as was King Marrand's clear delight that she would soon be a permanent resident in the palace. The prince's handsome face filled her mind for a while – like his father's but with a squarer jaw. Odd thoughts and images moved in her mind: splashes of colour from the tapestries and people's clothes, faces, some familiar, others unknown and all intent on her and her betrothed; the feel of Jerryn's lips on her hand as he had kissed it formally . . . kissing was another thing that she did not feel at all comfortable considering; another was bed, of course . . . again, that step forward from childhood to adulthood seemed too great to make. She did her best to ignore any thoughts concerning the blonde man, however.

*

In his large, well-appointed suite at the other end of the corridor, Prince Jerryn of Tenarum had dismissed Karne, his valet and his other servants, his ears still ringing from the conversations, the music and noise that had filled the halls earlier. Only Holly, his favourite hound of the lot, was laid before the smouldering fire, sleeping. Now thankfully alone, he slowly unfastened his shirt, stripped off the rest of his clothes, donned the nightshirt laid out neatly on his huge four posted bed, then pulled on a robe; he was weary, but still keyed up after the events of the day, so he poured a small goblet of red wine and sipped at it, before taking up the sheathed weapons that had been set rather incongruously on the sideboard, before a bowl of fruit. The ones he had drawn the previous day, so utterly afraid for Ethrayne's safety.

He had known that Duke Sarant would present him with weapons, of course, since Clirensar held the best reserves of ore yet discovered in the realm and the best smiths besides; but the quality of the sword, long dagger and table knife, the finish of the steel, the hilts and leatherwork was all superb. A small circle of bright gold on the hilt held a single large emerald which was nearly two thirds the size of a hen's-egg as the pommel stone on the sword, whilst quail's-egg sized sapphires and more gold reflected the warm lamplight in odd directions on the two knives, a fortune of gems that balanced the weapons perfectly, if ostentatiously, creating items that would be a good part of a king's ransom. Despite this wealth, however, these weapons were certainly designed for use: Jerryn was not about to test the edges, that was for sure. The weight of the sword was perfect, he recalled, and it was only a pity that the previous day's encounter had threatened them all, in effect.

The sight of the glittering gemstones made Jerryn smile slightly; this gift certainly equalled the price of the jewellery that his father had commissioned for Ethrayne and those items had only served to enhance her phenomenal beauty, a beauty of which she seemed completely oblivious, a fact that always slightly puzzled him. How could she be so unaware of the effect she had on everyone around her? He wondered if Tymain, for instance, was just jealous of his good fortune, betrothed to so pretty a girl. Also, she was at least as clever as he and her brother, whilst she was fortunately far better looking, beautiful, shapely and pleasant to spend time with, even if she often beat him at Stepping Stones; he usually tried to tell himself that this was because he let her win, but he knew that this was a lie: she was damned good at the strategy game.

This marriage, which had been arranged by their parents, was political of course, but he knew that he and Ethrayne were very lucky: they might have grown apart as they had grown older, moving into their very different roles and spheres as man and woman. Some of his other friends as adults were not the people he had known as a child. He had spent a long period of nearly every summer in Clirensar with the duke's family he remembered that, along with long days at South Vale Farm. They had been great times, spending days at a time well away from the intrigues of court and helping with the animals, the harvest, playing with relative freedom. Consequently, he knew Ethrayne well, her vibrant personality and moods and, even more uniquely, their families were close. The duke was his father's most trusted advisor and Pualyn was one of his best friends in the realm. He, Ethrayne and the kingdom also, would hopefully all flourish . . . But marriage? It was a huge leap into the unknown. Jerryn wondered, taking another sip of wine, if his betrothed was as nervous as he.

"Well, it's back to normal again, anyway; well, as normal as it ever gets here." He murmured with a short laugh and turned out the lamps about the room before climbing into bed.

But, lying there, he found himself thinking about that stranger, with his oddly radiating hatred and contemptuous words. Jerryn hoped the explanation would prove straightforward, regarding his purpose and background, when the soldiers found him.

* * *

CHAPTER 3

The Royal Council of Tenarum traditionally gathered in the Painted Hall, a large space in one of the oldest parts of the palace, connected to the throne room by a dim, windowless tunnel of a corridor down which the members processed formally after breakfast the next morning, Ethrayne following at the rear of the line with Jerryn, smiling, at her side.

She was amazed when she walked in to it: this was a hall she had only ever heard of, for it was usually locked, and she was amazed to see that the walls and vaulted ceiling of the hall really were painted; the high walls were a riot of colours and images: of forests, animals, fantastic monsters, hunters, towns, landscapes; contrasting and even clashing themes were right next to each other, whilst the ceiling and the supporting beams were in contrasting red and yellow. It had all been painted by hand and was starting to fade and peel with the slow passage of years. There was a vast stone fireplace at either end of the hall, but heat in winter was also supplied by large cast iron braziers, spaced around the perimeter. The massive oak table in its centre was so highly polished that its surface reflected firelight, lamplight and almost entire faces with nearly the clarity of a mirror.

The king's seat was large and ornate, the only one upholstered in royal blue, whilst the other chairs were plainer, although still padded, covered in dark green leather. Silver lamps and large silver candlesticks holding tall, sweet-smelling beeswax candles, all lit, were regularly spaced along the table and also on the three long sideboards along the long inner wall, on which lay quills; covered silver inkwells; bottles of ink; stacks of parchment; some innovative pages of new wood-pulp, plus a large number of large, green-leather bound books, and neat, ribbon-bound piles and boxes full of scrolls.

To Ethrayne's eyes, the vast hall was garishly decorated, and it smelled very much like the school room had in the castle in Clirensar, a mixture of old wood, parchment and leather. She moved to stand beside her father as King Marrand led the group towards the table and felt overawed by the spectacle and the old-fashioned grandeur of the place. This space was one she had not ever thought she might see, this seat of innovative government, the Royal Council of Tenarum, established two and half centuries before; even their arrival had been of high ceremony: gathering in the throne room after breakfast, to progress behind the king into this hall, where honoured noblemen and now the occasional noblewoman would decide the future of the kingdom.

"Please, sit down, my Lords and Ladies." Marrand said, gesturing as he took his seat at the centre of the table, the chair legs grating loudly on the flagstone floor. For a short time, the sound of the moving of heavy chairs was prominent, before silence returned and the assembled gazed at their ruler.

Not knowing if there was a seating protocol, Ethrayne hung back, until Jerryn and Pualyn guided her towards three chairs arranged at a corner of the left-hand side of the table and she found herself sat next to Lady Celia, the heiress of Pellerton Court, a slight, dark haired young woman in her early twenties, who smiled at all of them.

"My Lady Ethrayne, we *really* must get together with Lady Lyria and chat. We had no time during the ride, did we?" She said almost reproachfully. "I mean, I know you've been rather busy since you arrived, but -." She broke off, laughed aloud and winked. "Don't be alarmed, Ethrayne, you look just how I remember I felt when his majesty asked me to join the Council." She glanced around at the group, now mostly settled. "They won't bite too much, no matter how fierce they seem."

Ethrayne felt her spirits lifting a little for, despite all the rather intimidating expressions of most of the older men surrounding her, King Marrand nodded pleasantly at her as Lord Ferman introduced the first item of the agenda in a dry tone. The sorry state of the highway through the North Keslione Forest, as reported by a caravan of merchants on their return to the capital occupied some time, and the debate was extensive as to whose jurisdiction the region was in; whose workmen would be tasked; how much money would be required, once they had established that the road was in fact the Crown's responsibility and not the remit of any local landowner. It was rather more mundane than Ethrayne had supposed and this realisation was startling, as was the next item, which began a discussion on the lawlessness and lax morals of Clorport.

After a short break for refreshments, the conversation turned to agriculture and commerce. Again, Ethrayne was surprised by the depth of detail gone into, and the levels of knowledge shown generally around the table. It was rather alarming to realise that she would be expected to join in with them in discussions on such diverse matters in a sensible and useful manner after her wedding to Jerryn; might she have to start learning about general farming, economic and legal matters, although her formal schooling had finished in the winter a few moons ago, around her sixteenth birthday?

*

The Council was concluded in the early afternoon, whereupon Lady Celia spirited Ethrayne away to meet Lyria, as promised, and Pualyn and Jerryn found themselves alone as the older men left the hall in a large group.

"You know, Pualyn, I meant to mention it yesterday, but Ethrayne's horse is incredibly fast." Jerryn remarked admiringly. "Events rather quickly took the thought from my head but she's very fleet of foot."

The Lord of Clirensar smiled. "Another of father's successes, and Oxalla's bloodline is separate to Vachane's. You've got the makings of a first-class stud in a few years, Jerryn, if you breed from them." He pushed open one of the side doors that took them into a plain corridor, empty of even the customary guards, which made its way eventually back towards the domestic wings of the palace. "Where do you want to go? Any plans for this afternoon, now the girls have vanished?" And his grin broadened as he gazed at his friend.

"My rooms, I've got some rather nice Rothern Red." Jerryn replied, leading the way and ignoring the pair of guards who were soon trailing along behind them. Upstairs, in the base of the south tower where his apartment was situated, he held the door wide for his friend, shut the outer door firmly and went to the old but finely carved sideboard in the large living room, pouring two goblets of wine.

"Pualyn, do you really think that Ethrayne wants to marry me?" He asked, plunging in directly; he trusted her brother implicitly, and whom else could he ask? "I know we really don't count in the matter, but some of her remarks lately, and . . . oh, I don't know!" He crossed the soft carpet, handing her brother one of the silver goblets and gave him a rather embarrassed smile as he sat down in a comfortable chair opposite.

"Jerryn, you idiot!" Pualyn laughed aloud at his expression. "What girl would not want to become your wife? I ask you! Of course, she wants to wed you. It's just -." He paused. "It's probably that she will lose her freedom and I think it hit home after our ride."

"She'll hardly be a prisoner!" Jerryn interjected in an injured tone.

"Think, Jerryn: you know how it is in Clirensar. Ethie could go down to the kitchens and help the cooks make bread or whatever, and you helped enough times yourself, when you were younger. She, Lyria and Mother got stuck into spring cleaning the castle; they organised the produce laid down through the year, she helped with the work and the endless lists. They could just take a maid and go shopping with no complications. Things like that. And we have South Vale Farm, where we all ran riot."

Jerryn smiled a little. "I remember."

"You have all these extra noble courtiers and imposing servants here running the palace, and although I've been here longer than you have, youngster, it is unnerving sometimes. Your princess won't be able to sneeze without everyone in the city commenting on it." Pualyn continued soothingly. "She'll get used to it; mother has been advising her on the protocols, I know, but she's still finding it a shock, I suppose. It's different for women." He shrugged and made a face. "They carry the babies whilst we do the lesser job of running everything."

Jerryn frowned a little, thinking about it. "Mmm, I'd not really considered that." He allowed. "Just thought that we were all quite lucky, knowing each other all our lives."

"Yes, especially since you fell out so adamantly when you were ten or so; we never did find out what happened, Jerryn. You wouldn't speak for months."

"I broke her necklace and she threw my knife into the river, I think." The prince admitted with a grimace. "It was all utterly stupid, but we were children. Your wise and esteemed mother eventually persuaded me to buy a new necklace for your sister, she gave me a new knife at the Solstice and we were friends again."

"Dear Arven, wasn't it wonderful when everything was so simple?" Pualyn's tone was almost wistful. "I remember, it seems so long ago -."

"You're only about five years older than we, Pualyn." Jerryn pointed out. "You were playing with toy boats and soldiers yourself not too long ago. Are you and Lyria getting married before Ethrayne and I?" That event kept intruding into everything, it seemed.

"Our fathers seem to be talking about the end of autumn for you two and perhaps the Winter Solstice for Lyria and I. These things must be done in a certain way, it seems. No impromptu jumping over broom handles for the likes of us." Pualyn laughed. "Instead, there's more of that interminable pomp and ceremony and the accompanying uncomfortable but very smart clothing."

"Ethrayne would look good in sackcloth, let alone satin." Jerryn grinned. "She is beautiful, as well as clever and very talented."

"She wasn't so clever the day before yesterday, Jerryn."

"Don't be stupid, Pualyn, we were racing, we've all done that sort of thing loads of times, here and at Clirensar. I just can't work out how she got quite so far ahead of us: that was uncanny. I set off ahead of everyone myself on a ride, before you arrived a few days ago, and left my guards way behind." The prince countered easily, his tone rather firm. "She was always in sight and how, by Arven, could anyone predict that man's appearance? I think a lot of people were rude that night, I really do . . . I wish I knew who he was and what he wanted."

"Aye, me too." The other man agreed. "Now, what do you think of Vachane?" And the conversation turned to horses.

*

Next morning, after breakfast, Ethrayne and Jerryn were both in receipt of identical notes from Archpriest Lurco, requesting their attendance at the Cathedral, apparently 'on a matter of liturgy' the next day, likely to discuss the state of their souls, prior to their very public wedding, Ethrayne assumed. Since they were still sat in the private dining room, they sent back a joint reply, then decamped to the family's sitting room with Lyria and Pualyn, for it was raining hard; the king, duke and duchess had other business that day.

"That's it: you can't escape, now the priests are involved." Jerryn joked.

Ethrayne gave him a haughty look that was marred by the smile quirking her lips. "I don't want to; yet I don't think we ever could escape, Jerryn." She answered seriously. "And I like Archpriest Lurco, he's a good man."

"Yes, but he's a bit stuffy." He added.

"Priests usually are. So, Ethrayne, what do you think of the Council?" Her brother asked, setting out Stepping Stones, a popular board game.

"I'm too stupid for the Council of Tenarum, no matter what his Majesty so kindly said!" Ethrayne replied with a groan. "I don't know anything about wheat, or sheep, or trade taxation, Pualyn."

He laughed. "No, you don't, but that is what the group is for: some people know farming; or ironworking; or basic taxation; making wine or whatever, and all those books and scrolls hold centuries worth of information and history for reference. Not even King Marrand could know everything, Ethie."

"Oh, you know, I hadn't thought of that." She admitted, and chuckled, shaking her head. "Are matters usually so ordinary, though?" She glanced from Pualyn to Jerryn, who had taken a seat opposite and had picked up his game pieces. "Can I ask how long you have been a Member of the Council, Jerryn?"

"Since my sixteenth birthday on towards last winter, officially, but I'm generally not very vocal; father wants me fully involved, but I know that most of the lords just think I'm too young yet." He shrugged and frowned. "But I'll be seventeen in Umttarn, we will likely be wed by then and with Pualyn, Lady Celia and you yourself, at least I won't feel like a child." He grinned. "It's interesting. Now, who's going to play which colour?"

After a while, when there were more counters on the table than the board, they took a break for refreshments.

"Jerryn, would you teach me how to fight?" Ethrayne asked quietly, the remark coming completely out of nowhere, but the concept, the thought, had been brewing in her mind since meeting the menacing stranger so suddenly; her utter helplessness rankled.

"*What*?" He stared at her in shock; Pualyn and Lyria also looked amazed and rather astounded.

"I've been thinking, you see: I can use a knife to cut meat and vegetables, but I could not actually defend myself with one, not usefully. I want to learn how to use a sword and a bow and arrows if that's possible?" Ethrayne was heartened that neither young man had just laughed outright at her request and realised that was certainly one of the prince's best points, and her brother's as well; unlike some other men she knew, they listened to women as if they were sensible people.

"Surely not, Ethrayne! You're not serious, are you? You are joking?" Lyria asked, shocked.

"Yes, I am, I am very serious, Lyria." She answered levelly. "I want to learn how to protect myself, after what happened during our ride. Honestly, I do, Jerryn." She met his gaze, almost daring him to protest.

"Well, you know, I didn't think of that." Her betrothed said, his tone surprisingly respectful. "But swords are heavy, you know, the work isn't easy. And it's damned dangerous."

"I'm strong." Ethrayne countered, sitting straighter, thankful that he was at least considering the matter. "I can control any horse I've ever ridden, including Vachane, I'll have you know. And, surely, I'd get stronger anyway? I know it's an on-going process – you never seem to stop the learning."

"Well, yes. But -." Jerryn stopped, clearly thinking hard. Ethrayne was pleased that he and her brother hadn't told her to stop being foolish. "You'd have to do exactly what you're told, there's no alternative. And we'd have to be discreet; Arven only knows what the older members of the court will say to this. But . . . I could teach you, yes, but not alone; Pualyn, would you help me?" He asked.

"Yes, I suppose I could." Pualyn acknowledged doubtfully. "But this is just theoretical, isn't it? You will our princess soon – and whoever heard of women fighting, especially royalty? It's just not done, Ethrayne. That's what we and your guards are for, your protection . . . You don't really want to learn how to hurt people, do you?"

Ethrayne only gazed at him, solemn, for a moment. "I wish to learn how to protect myself, my Lord Pualyn. I certainly know what it entails, Brother."

"Well, how often have any of us actually used our skills, my Lord Pualyn?" The prince asked with a shrug. "None of us who aren't keeping the peace across the kingdom. We just keep very supple, practising, really . . . And we would need -." Jerryn paused and rang the bell. A maid quickly appeared and curtsied low. "Can you please send someone for Private Tymain, Ceyal?" He asked politely.

"Why him?" Ethrayne asked aloud what the small group was wondering. "He doesn't even seem to like you, Jerryn."

"He's a professional." Jerryn said with a shrug. "And he's not too old, so he might not scream in horror like some of the other soldiers. What do you think, Pualyn?"

"I-I think you're both mad!" Her brother snapped. "And what about our fathers? The king will never agree to this, let alone the duke! . . . But, if it makes you feel safer, learning such skills then, all right, you can count me in."

The soldier arrived a while later, as Pualyn was stealing a good number of Lyria's pieces. He came into the sitting room as quietly as possible behind the maid and bowed low.

"You sent for me, your Highness?" He bowed again to each of them as they faced him. "My Lord, my Ladies."

"Yes, thank you for coming." Jerryn paused and took a breath. "Lady Ethrayne has asked us, Lord Pualyn and I, to teach her how to fight; to be able to defend herself, handle weapons and so on. But you're the soldier, do you think it's a good idea, Tymain?"

Tymain's mouth fell open, and he stared at Ethrayne, for a moment, his eyes wide, before shutting his mouth with a snap and turning his attention back to the prince. "I, y-yes, your Highness, I believe that it might well be. But you would have to take care. Combat is serious, Ma'am, for the whole purpose is to kill one's opponent, my Lady. It isn't a game." He said in a rather stunned tone of voice and then took a deep breath, meeting her gaze again. "It certainly isn't a game." He repeated.

"Yes, I am aware of that, Private." She replied levelly, holding his gaze, wondering if she could look at all serious dressed so elegantly in fine silk and jewellery. "I am not viewing this at all as a joke or an amusing diversion, I can assure you all, on my honour. I want to learn how to protect myself."

"Well, my Lady . . . If you really are determined . . . Yet it will be difficult, I'm sure . . . And if his Majesty and my superiors agree to this, then-then yes." The soldier stated, bowing rather jerkily.

"Excellent, thank you." Jerryn grinned. "Right, then we'll sort out the practicalities later and we'll discuss this with our parents next. Just please don't tell anyone yet, Tymain, but you can go. Thank you."

"On my honour, I will keep this private, your Highness. My Lord, my Ladies. Good day." Clearly nonplussed, he bowed again and departed.

"I think you stunned the young man." Lyria noted quietly.

"Well, I don't think it's too shocking, to ask to learn such skills." Ethrayne replied. "But I certainly don't want to be a soldier, Lyria."

"His Majesty and our father might well view the matter differently, Ethie. Don't be surprised if they refuse." Pualyn warned her.

*

The next day dawned grey, but the rain had passed overnight, leaving the streets and rooftops gleaming. Ethrayne rose early and picked a reasonably understated gown of dark green for their later meeting with the Archpriest, for appearances were of vital importance, something she had learned in early childhood. Her maids organised her hair more loosely than she had worn it of late, so that it spilled down her back, held back from her face with silver combs.

"You do look lovely." Her mother declared as she entered the dining room, sounding almost surprised and that made her smile as she thanked her with a kiss, sitting down to porridge and fruit compote.

It was nearly midmorning when she, Fionn and the prince set off through the palace, warmly cloaked, their guards behind them as always, but ostensibly alone. Making their way to the main courtyard, they quickly entered the small coach awaiting them for their journey to the Cathedral, as it was raining again, which meant that riding or walking would not be appropriate for what was a semi-official meeting with the Archpriest. Their guards, however well cloaked, were on horseback, of course, and resigned to the rain.

The Cathedral was set further down the hill and closer to the river than the palace, an imposing edifice of pale limestone that contained not only places of worship, but the accompanying monastery that provided the Archpriest with his staff and clergy.

The carriage entered the walled complex through an arch beside the Penitents' Gate, close to the buttressed bell tower and Ethrayne,Jerryn and her maid emerged by the steps to the closest building, where a pair of respectful, black-robed priests waited, to be swiftly shown through the place to a foyer where Fionn was politely shown to a seat, whilst the pair of them entered the Archpriest's lavish study which was a wealth of tapestries and ancient panelling. The public parts of the Cathedral were reasonably familiar, but she had never ventured into this area before and Ethrayne felt rather uncertain.

Beside her, she saw Jerryn's set expression; perhaps he was unsure as well.

Two men were waiting by the fireplace, only one of them familiar. Archpriest Lurco had startlingly bright brown eyes and rosy cheeks; he was such a man as always seemed to be happy and smiling. Today he wore a plain but well-made shirt and trousers, with the over-robe of his rank and responsibility above, made of white silk, embroidered with gold thread in the elaborate symbol of Arven: a hand cupping a globe, surmounted by stylised flames.

"Your Highness, my Lady." He greeted them with a beaming smile, striding forward from beside the fireplace. "Thank you for consenting to join us this morning. May I present ex-archpriest Bahlien? Bahlien, this is Prince Jerryn and Lady Ethrayne of Clirensar."

The other was very tall, at least a head taller than Jerryn, with a long face dominated by a beak of a nose, sparse, wavy white hair, dark blue eyes and a very upright though thin physique that covered by an open-fronted pearl grey robe with less embroidery than Archpriest Lurco's, over a plain dark green tunic and leggings.

"Good morning, my Lady, your Highness." The ex-archpriest said quietly in a lilting accent and bowed, then stepping forward to clasp their hands in his, smiling. "I am very honoured to meet you."

"The, the honour is ours, your Graces." Ethrayne answered, with a polite curtsy to them both as Jerryn bowed. She was puzzled by the odd tingling which had coursed through the hand that Bahlien had clasped and through her mind; also strange was a feeling, a certainty, that this man was a definite friend.

"Please, do sit down my dears and I will send for refreshments." Archpriest Lurco urged with a gesture and another smile, taking their cloaks and guiding them towards two well-padded chairs near the fireplace. "It is a disappointing day, better spent indoors by the fire. May I again, on behalf of our Church, congratulate you both on your betrothal? Tenarum is blessed."

"Thank you, your Grace, as am I, to have such a most intelligent and beautiful young lady consent to wed me." Jerryn said with a clear sideways glance at Ethrayne to gauge any reaction to his compliment and a quick flash of a grin when her expression did not change, though she was pleased by his words. "And I can only apologise for our rude intrusion when you were talking with our parents."

"Great heavens, your Highness! Naturally such a strange encounter and the possible threat involved to yourself, Lady Ethrayne, takes priority over other matters." Lurco waved away the apology. "I hope that you feel calmer, my Lady?"

"Oh yes, your Grace. Also, Jerryn, my brother Pualyn and his guard have agreed to teach me how to defend myself with weapons." She confirmed with a hint of a mischievous smile, wondering what their reaction to such news would be.

Lurco, predictably perhaps, spluttered a little at that declaration, but Bahlien nodded in evident approval. "Good." He said shortly.

"Good? My dear Bahlien!" Lurco interjected with an air of unease. "Lady Ethrayne will be queen of Tenarum one day; a great many years hence, please Arven! This is a stark departure from the traditional! . . . Quite unprecedented! . . . Really -."

"Yet we live in uncertain times, good Lurco and who knows which skills will prove the most useful, even to a princess?" Bahlien answered in a mild, rather conciliatory tone and Ethrayne noticed that the archpriest shivered slightly.

"We have not yet asked his Majesty's permission, nor Duke Sarant's, sir." Jerryn offered then.

"It would sensible to speak to your fathers, yes. " The ex-archpriest agreed and she and Jerryn exchanged glances at that remark, both opening their mouths to ask what he meant by it, but two servants in white swept into the study with silver trays; the moment passed as drinks and nibbles were laid out on a convenient table by the window and Lurco and his guests were served with fragrant tea and crumbly sweet tarts.

"You mentioned uncertain times, your Grace." Ethrayne turned to Bahlien, sitting across from her in a large armchair, and offered him the plate of tarts that Jerryn had handed to her on its second passing. Something about the old man's manner was very reassuring, she found, just as much as Archpriest Lurco. "Might we know what you mean by that? The kingdom is enjoying excellent relations with her neighbours and as far as I am aware there are no internal troubles that his Majesty's Council have discussed."

"Indeed, you are correct, Lady Ethrayne, to a point." Bahlien replied in a low, grave tone, getting to his feet to set the plate on the table, then moving across to Lurco's imposing oak desk that dominated the room, where he lifted a large book covered in faded crimson leather decorated with gold, with three hefty locks holding it secure. He set it back down again the opposite way up, with a thump that told them that the leather covered wood.

"This is an ancient book that has been stored here securely in Tenarum for nearly three thousand years." He said quietly, unlocking the volume with three small silver keys that jingled lightly on a ring attached to his belt by a chain, carefully lifting the cover. "There is copy kept safe in Lerat, but this is the original Book of Days."

"A Book of Days?" Jerryn repeated, puzzled. "What is that, your Grace?"

Ethrayne was glad that Jerryn had asked that question, for she had never heard of it either.

"This is Lord Arven's book of prophecy, your Highness." Bahlien explained. "It has been my major source of study for quite a few years now, which is why I am here." He stopped abruptly, the look on his face suddenly guarded and uncomfortable.

"Of which kingdom were you the Archpriest, your Grace?" Ethrayne asked then. "Your accent is not familiar to me and your robe is quite unusual, I must say."

"Most astute, my Lady." His guarded look vanished as Bahlien laughed and shook his head. "Yes, my robe is different. Whilst the Selithian Kingdoms generally conform on their symbols of office and clothes, the Razine Protectorates differ slightly. I was Archpriest in Lerat, the capital city of Orbain. Our version of the Church is a little different to yours in a few superficial ways, but we have all been worshipping Arven for many thousands of years now."

Jerryn frowned at that and glanced from Bahlien to Ethrayne and then to Lurco. "Forgive me for being rude, your Grace, but is Bahlien correct?" He asked the older man.

"Oh, indeed he is, your Highness." The Tenarean Archpriest confirmed. "Little is really known about the razine throughout this continent these days, but it is a widely known fact here in the Cathedral, and amongst our fellows in Derravale and Amorry that the people who went on to form the kingdoms of Selith, learned most of Arven's benevolence alongside the men and razine in Mendor. Bahlien has been a regular visitor here over the last few decades. I can promise you that he speaks the truth."

"The razine are reported to be immortal and to be some eight feet tall." Ethrayne said quietly, unsure whether she was reassured or not by his words. She did not think she had ever met a razine before, anywhere. The race seemed mysterious, remote, to the human kingdoms of Selith. "And do you not have magical powers, your Grace?"

The ex-archpriest laughed again at that. "Nay, my Lady, the tales have become garbled over the centuries; although we generally live longer than your people, we are not immortal; our tallest men generally don't even reach seven feet; and we do have some capabilities beyond the usual in *your* eyes, say, but not everyone by any means and it isn't magic."

"But, forgive me, we can *feel* your presence, sir and-and I *know* that you are speaking the truth." Jerryn declared. "May I ask why you are here?"

"My purpose here is prophecy, your Highness. My honoured colleague mentioned the matter to your parents in passing, the other day. This is a prophecy which seems to concern you two young people intimately, although we pray that we are alerting you well in advance of any action, hopefully by some years . . . Please, come over here and I will read the passage to you."

Puzzled, Ethrayne rose to her feet and she and Jerryn moved across the room to stand on either side of him around the back of the desk. Bowing his head to gaze down at the huge tome, Bahlien turned fully two-thirds of the thick, crackling parchment pages, then laid one long forefinger at the top of a sheet where a greatly detailed yet small painting of a fabulous and mythical dragon was wrapped about an oak tree, it's scales a wonder of gold and silver leaf, the leaves of the tree shining like emeralds, a work of art. The book would be a beautiful thing to own, just for the beauty of it. Below this, stylised letters made words that were also more works of art than writing. Bahlien cleared his throat and began:

"'And behold, my loyal servants.
In the time following the promise
Of the Daughter of the Iron Duke,
To the Son of the Eastern Realm ~
Take Heed.
He, The Betrayer.
He, who stole part of Me ~
He, who would Command All,
Ruling the ice of glacier and jungles hot.
He will seek to gain that which has long
Been guarded ~ And,
In the hands of this Marriage lies our Hope.
Guard this Couple well.
In the hands of the Betrayer always lies despair.'"

He declaimed.

"Dear Arven, is that meant to make sense, sir? It's just poetry!" Jerryn objected.

"Poetry!" Lurco exclaimed. "It is indeed most poetic, your Highness, but this volume details prophecy which are the words of our God, and it is far more important in every way than mere poetry. Perhaps our very lives may depend upon these verses here."

"Do you believe that this, this prophecy refers to *us*, your Grace?" Ethrayne asked, stunned, trying to read the archaically spelled script for herself, but succeeding only slowly. "Am I meant to be this 'Daughter of the Iron Duke'? And Jerryn 'The Son of the Eastern Realm'?" She sighed and blushed a little, hating to admit to ignorance. "But what does it mean, please?"

Bahlien reached up and scratched at his scalp. "It relates to you and Prince Jerryn, I am certain, my Lady. I am deeply sorry to confuse you, my dears. Arven, it seems, has great need of you both to wield his Flame against the one known as 'The Betrayer'!"

"But -." Jerryn stopped, tipping his head to one side, clearly thinking hard; he looked amazed, stunned, to Ethrayne's mind. "But the Flame of Arven is lost, it has been lost for centuries, ever since -." He paused again, gulped, then sank down into the closest chair.

"It has been lost ever since 'The Betrayer' betrayed our God and locked Arven in the ice at the top of the world, in Car'Agasse." Ethrayne said very quietly, recalling lessons and church services which had formed the background of her life. "Centuries ago."

Archpriest Lurco chuckled at that moment with an almost unseemly amusement. "Lost? Never, my dears. The Flame of Arven has been kept safe here in Tenum City amid the tightest security we in the church could devise."

The story was the central tenet of the liturgy of the Church of Arven but was never celebrated or turned into the teaching playswhich educated the young and the illiterate around the world. '*The Parable of the Hungry Child*' was regularly shown, for every festival saw it performed without fail; *'The Parable of the Good-Hearted Whore and the Injured Man'* was recounted every Spring Equinox; '*The Creation*' was constantly playing, along with many other interactions between their God and his worshippers. But '*The Betrayer'* was only mentioned at the Winter Solstice there in the south and the priesthood wore only black. No bells rang. No hymns were sung.

"He was a Beloved Disciple." Jerryn stated, clearly recalling his childhood schooling. "He sat at Arven's feet with his fellows, one of the *First Race* . . . So, does that mean that he was razine?" He wondered, frowning deeply.

"Oh yes, he was razine. That 'first race' description is very old-fashioned and not entirely accurate, actually." Bahlien replied heavily. "As it says in the liturgy, he turned from Arven, hiding his changing heart and blackening soul from our God, craving the power and the might that was Arven's alone, although our God was free with his gifts and gave many of his Disciples abilities that even the razine could only dream of."

"The Betrayer persuaded Arven to place his power and strength *outside* of himself, they were discussing the real taste of need and want, apparently; is that right, Bahlien?" Lurco glanced questioningly at Bahlien.

"Were you there, sir?" Ethrayne asked loudly, aghast, seeing the query in that look. "But -!" She paused. Details were not given in church around those southern Winter Solstice services, beyond the basic information of that betrayal, their God's imprisonment since then, unreachable, although many had tried to reach Car'Agasse over the centuries, to fail.

"I was a boy, younger by six years than you are now, my dears. A mere servant in a way, but it was an honour to serve our God, and we were present in Car'Agasse for only three moons before returning to our families. Arven loved having children around: relishing their innocence, their thirst for knowledge, their delight in the world." Bahlien said sadly and sighed. "It was the Summer Solstice in the north of Iullyn. Lord Arven placed his power aside and the Betrayer used his own abilities to confine our God deep in ice there. Then he slew all his fellow disciples in an orgy of bloodlust, even Holy Ayline who had been his own constant companion. I was chased by the Betrayer in a murderous rage, I was terrified: the halls were full of dead bodies and blood, but the Flame of Arven, contained in a crystal casket, seemed to act of its own volition: it called me to it, there in the Iullyn Hall and it and I were instantly transported to Lerat, to the Cathedral. Our appearance caused a huge panic. My family were justifiably horrified, considering all that had occurred, but I pledged my service to our God.

"Some years later, as the Betrayer's gathered forces wreaked havoc throughout Orbain and the other kingdoms in Mendor as well – he was always very eloquent – I became a priest and dedicated myself primarily to protecting the Flame and I have done so now for a very long time, in between serving as Archpriest in Orbain for a few centuries or so. The Betrayer took his loyal followers away after murdering many thousands across Mendor and left to establish his own Empire in Enlath. It was years before we could recover from our losses at their hands."

"Oh, dear Arven!" Jerryn exclaimed, still frowning, then gulped. "The Betrayer is the emperor of the jajozeli-razine. We are meant to *fight* them?"

"You will both certainly lead our forces, your Highness." Bahlien confirmed, bowing his head slightly.

"What, me as well?" Ethrayne said, startled, and caught at a thread of thought, from something that Bahlien had said earlier, something she had never realised before. Her face felt suddenly cold and she shivered. Suddenly, things seemed to be making an uncomfortable sort of sense. "That man, the man who approached me at the lane when you fell behind, Jerryn . . . he said: '*I must warn you that future events may soon serve to delay your wedding.*' Was he one of the Betrayer's servants, your Grace? A-and are they *watching* us? Do they know of this . . . prophecy?"

"We are to Wield the Flame of Arven against the *Betrayer*?" Jerryn shuddered. "We know nothing, your Grace. Nothing!"

"It is true that it will take some time for you to learn of your roles and your strength. Yet you will be surprised how much you will intuit during your training. And, yes, you are equally to lead us, my Lady." Archpriest Lurco said comfortingly, although his tone seemed overly jovial, Ethrayne thought. "Also, Bahlien is certain that the jajozeli-razine must know of the prophecy, although I am sure that the enemy are just watching, biding their time and scaring you."

"Time is passing." Bahlien's face was stern and Ethrayne privately thought that his lack of platitudes was rather telling. She saw that Jerryn's frown became a deep glare at his words. "We have taken up all your morning, your Highness, my Lady. Now, you had better return to the palace and please discuss everything that we have said with your families. I am deeply sorry -."

"You will be speaking to our parents soon, I hope?" Jerryn asked. "I really don't think that they will believe us, your Grace."

At that question, the old razine grinned quickly. "Most certainly we will, your Highness, my Lady. I suggest, Lady Ethrayne, that you do begin your weapons training, just to be on the safe side, my dear."

"Yes, your Grace, I will." She assured him, frowning. The church took a very dim view of violence, it always had. This was a singular suggestion for even an ex-archpriest to make!

"We have a copy of the prophecy for you to take back to the palace, and I know that I don't have to ask you both to only discuss this with your families at this stage. We hope that we have not alarmed you." Archpriest Lurco said with a small sigh. "I think that it may confuse too many people to start discussing such religious matters widely – circumspection will be key, we believe. Thank you so much for coming here this morning." And he bowed low after handing a small scroll to Ethrayne.

"Thank you for confiding in us, your Graces." She said, curtsying deeply, accepting her cloak from Bahlien, who draped it around her shoulders most solicitously.

"We will be guarded, your Graces." Jerryn assured them and bowed politely. "Good morning."

"May Arven grant you peace. Good morning." Ex-archpriest Bahlien said, blessing them, and they were reunited with Fionn at the door and escorted back to the courtyard where their carriage and guards waited.

Ethrayne did not speak at all during their return to the palace: deep in thought, shocked, amazed and simply overwhelmed at what they had been told; she still held the scroll in her hand, swaying slightly with the movement of the coach up the cobbled street to the palace, her gaze lost in nothing as she looked through the leather-clad interior, only glancing once at her betrothed to see that Jerryn was staring blankly out of the window, frowning again. Beside her, Fionn was demure and silent, although the girl did look puzzled at their tense silence.

The coach came to a halt in front of the ornate main entrance and one of the grooms stepped down to open the door closest to the steps.

Fionn coughed, but neither of them moved. "My Lady, your Highness, we are back." She said politely, then stepped out and down, hurrying up the stairs and out of the weather.

It was a moment or two before the prince looked around, noticed where they were and got to his feet. "Ethrayne?" He reached out one hand to touch her forearm lightly. "We're home. Shall we go and find our parents?"

"Oh, dear Arven, Jerryn, what are we going to say to them?" She asked as he stepped down from the coach and turned to hand her down. "Thank you . . . This is -." She paused and sighed, shaking her head as they headed up the steps. "*You* can tell them, our parents." She declared stoutly. "I just don't know how to start."

"Thank you. Not at all . . . But you believe the Archpriests." It was not a question.

"Yes." Ethrayne answered levelly. "And you, your Highness?"

At the top of the steps, Jerryn stopped and gently took the scroll from her hand. "Yes, I do. How can I not?" He shrugged. "But, oh my word!"

"I know." Ethrayne flashed a smile that did not reach her eyes.

*

King Marrand, the Duke and Duchess of Clirensar and Lord Chamberlain Ferman were having luncheon whilst discussing certain details in advance of planning the expense that would provide the spectacle of the marriage between their children, so Jerryn and Ethrayne ate their own luncheon with their friends, neither saying very much of anything at all. They had left word that they would like a private meeting with their parents with Shan, the king's valet.

"You haven't been arguing, have you?" Lord Varlan asked bluntly, making Jerryn jump in his seat when he nudged him hard in the side, for he had completely ignored Varlan's latest joke.

"Don't be silly, Varlan." Ethrayne countered with mild indignation. "It's just . . . it's been an unsettling morning."

Someone else sniggered derisively.

"There's no need to laugh." Jerryn said, patting his left hand to his right breast, where he had secreted the copy of the prophecy in his doublet, safe and out of sight. "Come on, Ethrayne, Shan should be able to tell us when father is able to see us. We'll see you later, thank you." He said abruptly, his tone sharp, before hurrying her from the room with almost indecent haste.

"Are you all right?" She asked in concern as he sank down in a window seat further along that corridor. "You look just how I think I felt after that ride." Jerryn usually was polite and well mannered, he hardly ever let his emotions take control.

He glanced up at her, his eyes dark, and shivered slightly. "Ethrayne, what are we going to do?"

"Your Highness, my Lady Ethrayne." A voice said from Jerryn's left before she could answer; Shan, Marrand's personal servant, was approaching quickly along the corridor, halting and bowing low. "Your honoured parents will join you in your suite shortly, Prince Jerryn. Is that privacy enough?" His tone was faintly disapproving; he spent a lot of each day protecting the king's free time from myriad, desperate, calls for his attention.

"Yes, thank you Shan." Jerryn replied, rising to his feet. "We won't keep my father or the duke long from their business, I hope."

Jerryn's private sitting room was decorated with the royal colours of blue and green, but the walls were of plain stone covered with old, rather faded tapestries, whilst the furniture was all at least a century or so newer. Ethrayne went over to the window, as he and his valet, Karne, tidied furnishings which were neat, and plumped cushions vigorously. She stared out over the palace rooftops towards the city below but focussed more on the grey sky above and paid no attention as Karne assured his master that refreshments were ready if required.

"Do calm down, Jerryn, there isn't any need to panic." She said then, denying her own feelings as she turned back to take a seat as the prince was straightening ornaments on a blocky sideboard. "You quite startled Varlan and the rest, you know. And we saw our parents this morning, after all -."

The outer door opened and Duchess Riyala swept in, followed by King Marrand and Duke Sarant.

"Jerryn, Ethrayne, you have been having a busy few days, haven't you?" The duchess kissed them both affectionately, sinking down in a chair with her usual grace, her earrings sparkling. "What made you ask Lord Shan to ask us to visit you, when we will see you later at dinner? You have not decided to do anything precipitous, have you?"

"Mother!" Ethrayne blushed, then paled, completely unaware that she had clasped her hands tightly before her, her fingers moving nervously as she got back to her feet and began pacing. The enormity of what they had been told seemed to be sinking in, most uncomfortably. "We met with Archpriest Lurco and, and a colleague of his as requested this morning . . . His Grace didn't mention anything, well, anything unusual to you when he visited, did he?" She asked, glaring a little, simply because she could not think of any other way to broach the subject; she had forgotten that she had encouraged Jerryn to speak first.

"He did, surprisingly, mention a prophecy that has been discovered, but only briefly. Something about the Flame of Arven emerging." The king said easily. "How remarkable is that? Is this what you want to speak to us about?" He asked, looking from Ethrayne to his son. "What is amiss?"

"At least he referred to it, how very sensible of the Archpriest." Jerryn muttered. "Would it be considered *very* rude if I were to throw all his bloody books at him, when we next meet, do you think?"

"Ethrayne, Jerryn, will you *please* sit down and start talking sense?" Marrand grated, sounding exasperated.

"Your Majesty. Your Graces. Have you ever heard of Arven's Book of Days? Archpriest Lurco and ex-archpriest Bahlien of Orbain showed us a page, you see . . ." Jerryn had plunged on in headlong, but paused, perching on the edge of a seat, swallowing with a gulp, taking a breath. "A prophecy; it's about *us*, Ethrayne and I, but -."

"Oh, give me the scroll." Ethrayne had ignored the request to be seated and had been pacing near the window, but now she strode across the room, yanked the scroll firmly from Jerryn's hand and cracked the wax seal, pulling it open. "'*And behold, my loyal servants –*.'" She declaimed crisply, and the three adults sat up straighter, listening. When she reached the end of the passage, she passed the scroll to King Marrand with a curtsy. "Please excuse my peculiar mood, your Majesty." She snapped with a flash of her eyes. "I admit that I am a little disconcerted."

Sarant got to his feet and silently took her in his arms, holding her tight as Marrand and Riyala both leaned over the scroll, reading it quietly, their expressions suddenly grim.

"You are scared." He noted, looking down at her pale face, kissing her on her brow, his arms warm and strong around her for a moment before he sat back down beside her mother.

"Yes, yes I am. Do you know, Father, quite ridiculously, I had already asked Jerryn and Pualyn to teach me how to wield a sword, yesterday? But-but ex-archpriest Bahlien said that I should begin training as soon as possible, just in case."

"He did, your Grace." Jerryn confirmed gravely. "On my life, sir."

"I haven't heard of Archpriest Bahlien." The king said coolly. "Did you say that he was from Orbain, Jerryn?"

"He was, I mean, he is, Father." The young man sat up straighter, his face also pale, his expression resolute. "He is razine and he was Archpriest in Lerat. He, he said that he would explain, but-but he said that he was *there*, there at Car'Agasse, when the Betrayer imprisoned our God . . . We-we are to wield Arven's Flame against the jajozeli-razine!" Then finally Jerryn slumped back into the chair, his eyes wild. "Us!" And he laughed in a slightly brittle manner.

"Oh, my word!" Duchess Riyala murmured in dismay. "My word, Marrand!"

* * *

CHAPTER 4

The courtiers assembling in the dining hall were rather shocked when the announcement was made that King Marrand would be dining privately that evening. When everyone realised that the Duke of Clirensar's family, Lady Lyria and Prince Jerryn were also to be absent, certain stories were fabricated out of thin air whilst the servants, naturally knowing far more, were dutifully silent.

From Jerryn's rooms, the king sent Karne for Pualyn and Lyria, then escorted Ethrayne, her parents and Jerryn to his own suite, with its private dining room.

"We will eat here." Marrand instructed Shan. "Lord Pualyn and his betrothed will be arriving momentarily but no one else will be admitted this evening."

When Pualyn and Lyria arrived soon after, they found the two younger people being poured glasses of a much stronger wine than was usually served and his parents and the king were hovering around them with openly worried expressions on their faces.

"What has happened now?" Her brother asked his lady with what seemed a flash of childish envy. "Why does she always get all the attention?"

"Pualyn, honestly! You couldn't wed Jerryn after all!" Lyria chided him with a smile for that resentment. "It's hardly Ethrayne's fault -."

"Oh yes, it probably is my fault!" Ethrayne snapped back, having caught their quiet exchange but sounding more frustrated than annoyed. "I think pretty much everything that has happened recently is my fault, brother!" She didn't notice their families startled expressions: none of them had ever seen her behave so erratically.

"I'm sorry." Jerryn offered then. "But don't let Ethrayne confuse you – it is not our fault. Something has happened, Pualyn and it-it's frankly breath-taking -."

Pualyn's disgruntlement faded almost instantly at the news, and hs sister noted his contribution to the evening's discussion then was in a more subsidiary role, supporting his best friend and herself. All of them were struggling to make their minds encompass the fact of *prophecy* and just what it might mean to them, to everyone else and to the kingdom at large. The explanation haltingly provided – of them leading not only Tenarum but other kingdoms to war in the name of their frozen God – was met with shock. Not a great deal of the excellent meal was eaten, to the cooks' chagrin, but quite a lot of wine was drunk throughout the evening.

"We must speak to Lurco and this ex-archpriest Bahlien as soon as possible, to coordinate our announcements on this matter." Duke Sarant said gravely. "I am sure that the crown has never had to work so closely with the Church since our God was imprisoned. Perhaps the Archpriest needs to speak first on this matter, rather than you, Sire."

"Our children are not the property of the Church of Arven!" Marrand snapped back. "Any religious obligations must be secondary to their roles within our realm! They are prince and noblewoman, soon to be wed; they are not priests!"

"We know, Marrand." Riyala soothed him, patting his hand resting on the table top. "But apparently this prophecy is ancient. Lurco might expect precedence."

"What do you think, Ethie?" Pualyn asked quietly.

"Me?" The girl looked up with dull eyes, a frown, not at all her usual demeanour. The enormity of the issue alarmed her. "I don't really believe anything that we think or say matters at all. The prophecy is ancient, as mother said. Is everything predetermined? Are we doomed?"

"Well of course we're not doomed, Ethrayne." Jerryn disagreed with a short, insincere laugh.

"But what, excuse me your Majesty, Mother, Father, what the-the *hell* are we meant to do?" Ethrayne demanded forcefully, in answer to his denial. "Are we meant to somehow free Arven from that ancient ice, or destroy the Betrayer, or something else entirely? I only wanted to learn some sort of basic self-protection, you know – not become a-a warrior!"

"I think that we should stop speculating, my dear and wait until we can speak to the Archpriests." Duke Sarant suggested soothingly. "It's getting late, Marrand."

"Yes, you're right, old friend." The king acknowledged with a nod. "Let's leave this for now. Jerryn, Ethrayne, I'm sorry that this has landed on you in this way. Please report here at noon tomorrow. I suggest that you do begin weapons training in the morning and if the exercise doesn't clear your mind, my dear Ethrayne, then nothing will."

*

Early the next morning, Ethrayne was staring at the pile of clothes arranged neatly on her bed with some trepidation: two crisp new shirts, leggings and a well-worn leather jerkin. Part of her wanted to abandon the whole idea as ludicrous – she never wanted to become a soldier! But King Marrand himself had approved her request for training, as had Archpriest Bahlien, and she could not back out now.

"Right, let's give everyone a laugh." She said, smiling at Lyria before she took the pile into the dressing room, discarding her nightgown and reaching for a chemise.

A short while later, dressed and after her hair had been braided, coiled and pinned securely around her head, Ethrayne went to meet her mother and Lyria feeling both horribly self-conscious and strangely light: free of the weight and confinement of all those skirts and the tight corsetry that usually bound up her ribs and her legs. Wearing her own riding boots with the borrowed male clothing – a pair of tight leggings, a shirt and jerkin which were not too baggy, she stepped slowly and self-consciously into the sitting room where she knew the others waited; she had worn trousers occasionally on South Vale Farm as a child – but not for about six years at least, and never in public.

"I look ridiculous, don't I?" She asked ruefully.

Her family stared for a moment, then strove to collectively recover their composure quickly.

"No, of course you don't." Riyala replied crisply. "But I must say that you do look ever so much like your brother, Ethrayne."

"Really?" Pualyn asked, sounding surprised. "But Ethrayne is pretty – I'm certainly not."

"No, but you are handsome, my Lord. And you seem taller, too, Ethrayne." Lyria stated, smiling.

"So, shall we go and scandalise the entire palace, my Lady Ethrayne?" Duke Sarant asked with rather a mischievous smile on his lips and in his eyes.

"After you, your Grace." Ethrayne responded, greatly heartened by their support. She bowed deeply with a flourish, as she had seen countless men behave and her mother laughed as her father bowed in response.

Bolstered by her family, breakfast proved to be much more light-hearted than any of them expected, before Ethrayne strolled down to the enclosed combat hall with Jerryn and Pualyn, now unconcerned at the shocked expressions on the faces of courtiers and servants alike. Awaiting the three of them in the half-basement hall in the north wing were Private Tymain and Commander Vedeigne. Seeing them both, armed professionals, bulky men, business-like in their uniforms, Ethrayne felt a return of all her fears as a tight knot in her stomach.

"His Majesty has assured me that this exercise is no mere frivolity on your part, my Lady." Vedeigne snapped the statement out startlingly, his gaze stern as he looked her up and down.

"No, Commander." She agreed a little nervously. "The original idea was perhaps stupid to begin with, I admit, but not since his Highness and I spoke with Archpriest Lurco yesterday. I want to learn how to defend myself; and apparently I *need* to know how to defend myself." She shrugged and grimaced. "And, yes, I realise that fighting also includes attack and that I might well eventually have to kill someone, to possibly save myself or others." She stood up straighter quite unconsciously as he continued to stare at her.

"Humph. That possibility will not occur for a good while, my Lady. And I will warn you now that the whole business will include an awful lot of hot, hard work, my Lady Ethrayne; you'll work up a proper sweat here." Vedeigne quirked his lips into what might be construed a slight smile as she held his gaze. "Well, young lady, you're tall enough, and these three young men are certainly experienced, so I'll just stand over here out of the way." He grinned momentarily as Ethrayne sighed audibly. "His Majesty and their Graces, your honoured parents, want regular reports, I'm afraid."

That first lesson was far more a tutorial than a practical lesson, Ethrayne found, as she was introduced to a vast array of weaponry, from massive five-foot bladed broadswords to equally huge and impossible to wield longbows, and practically every other weapon in the armoury, as their usage was briefly explained. Then, with Pualyn and Jerryn providing a quick demonstration, she finally picked up a medium-length wooden sword and started to learn the first basic moves, the positioning of feet, body and weapon. All too soon, it seemed, it was noon, and she had to almost run to get back to her rooms to get washed and changed. Properly attired in her usual long gown and petticoats, her stride limited, she made her way to the king's apartment, still feeling most overheated.

"Ah, Ethrayne, come in, luncheon will be served shortly." King Marrand greeted her with a kiss on her cheek as she was admitted to the private, green-draped dining room. "How does the exercise suit you, eh?"

The girl smiled a little ruefully. "I can definitely feel my shoulders, your Majesty." She admitted, and he chuckled.

"Yes, we know what you mean, and it will feel strange for a while." The king led her past her parents to where the two representatives of Arven were stood watching her approach and both bowed politely to her when she curtsied.

"Your Graces."

"Ah, here are our young men and the lovely Lady Lyria; do come in, please." Marrand greeted them also as the doors were quietly closed behind Jerryn. He, Pualyn and Lyria all paid their respects. "Please, come and sit down, everyone; who would like wine? Ale? Water?" He gestured to the silver jugs on the sideboard. "I hope you are all hungry."

Ethrayne and Jerryn found themselves sitting opposite Lurco and Bahlien and exchanged quick, nervous glances as the servants came around with the first course before departing, leaving them alone around the large table.

"Your Graces." Duke Sarant said quietly after Lurco gave the usual blessing and everyone had sampled the layered terrine that adorned their plates. "Perhaps you should tell Jerryn and Ethrayne some of the details of the early history of Iullyn, and the founding of-of Car'Agasse."

"Most certainly, your Grace." Archpriest Lurco agreed and smiled at them as he set down his cutlery. "Do not worry, there are no tests at the end of this and we are certainly not expecting any signs of excess piety or devotion on your part, your Highness, my Lady . . . nothing beyond what you have always believed. So, to begin, Bahlien?"

The Creation of Iullyn, naturally, was familiar to all of them, but Bahlien's account of the pre-eminence of the razine as the oldest intelligent race of Arven's world was far more detailed than the brief paragraphs usually shown to members of the laity who might peruse the annals of the Church.

"During that period, the razine resided on the continent of Mendor, north of Selith and Jaece, learning from Arven, for he was eager to teach us all that we could learn; those were wonderful times, it is said; he walked with us, before travelling throughout the world, studying what he had made; and coming back to us when he created humans. That was a great many millennia before I was born, of course; and then your ancestors dwelled alongside mine for thousands more." The ex-archpriest said. "We all learned philosophy; farming; writing; art; plumbing; sailing, even town planning, I think, at Arven's knee. Time passed, and many humans moved to the Selithian and Enlath continents and then the outlying islands, for your birth rate has ever outstripped ours and, of course, there was always the lure of exploration and a new vista.

"Arven set up a Hall at Car'Agasse, there in the perpetual snows of the northern land, Piyan, simply because he could make a hall of ice that was comfortable for all, where food and drink and heat were arranged by his Will alone. It is at the roof of the world, with a rough island chain leading south-west to Enlath. It was a beautiful palace. Children would beg to attend him, both razine and human, for a period of three moons; he loved children: their innocence and their joy in the world. Then, some decades before my birth, some who had been present as children began to attend Arven as adults, learning more from him . . . In that way a formal discipleship was finally set up in the organisation of the Church.

"A year or so before I was born, a young man called Gregnor went to Car'Agasse. Handsome, brilliant at everything he turned his hand or mind to, charismatic in his own right, with power already greater than most razine; and he was as devoted to Arven as our God was to him and the others there. I wonder if even Gregnor himself knows what changed in him, leading up to that fateful night." Bahlien paused and sighed. Everyone else in the room was completely silent, staring at him.

"Of course, most of this is pure speculation, you understand. But at some point towards the end of the first decade of my childhood, Gregnor's heart changed and no-one, not even Arven himself, ever realised that fact. I had been there in the hall for two moons, one of many children chosen randomly to serve there, but it was rather more a school: we sat and listened to Arven and his disciples discuss – oh, any matter; then we cleared up with them, and helped serve them food and drink, soaking up the serene atmosphere of the place." He grinned. "Once, we even had a snowball fight, right there in the Iullyn Hall, oh, it was wonderful!

"That day, the disciples had been discussing power with Arven: the differences between razine and human and the vastness of our God's power over all of us, continuing a topic which had been followed for a while, I recall. Arven had gifted some of his power to Gregnor, apparently as part of the discussion – I remember seeing him look so . . . majestic, as I served lunch, before anything occurrred. He had shone with power. The entire situation, the discussion, might even have been planned by him; I do not know it for the truth, but I admit that I am tentatively supposing that this is so in hindsight. My reasoning is based on the devastating speed with which Gregnor acted later on;

Lord Arven, on his disciple's innocuous-seeming urgings, made a hexagonal crystal casket, a little less than two feet high and across, and physically took from his own chest a double-fist sized mass of almost incandescent, white-hot flame that seemed to grow in the open air. Thereby our God removed almost all his native might and power, it seems. He placed this flame within the casket, although it seemed far too large to fit inside, but the lid closed with a snap, locked; and the moment, it seems, had come." Bahlien stopped, noticing everyone's rapt, entranced attention, and took a sip of wine before continuing.

"Still, there was nothing amiss – nothing alarming, or so I recall. It was later that night, after dinner, when Gregnor attacked our God and abruptly encased Arven in an unbreakable pillar of ice, in the vast majestic central hall, the Iullyn Hall; we could call it the throne room, but there were no thrones, fancy paraphenalia or altars, only the image of Iullyn in its entirety in the ice of the floor. Arven had, on occasion, gifted power to Gregnor and many other disciples, both human and razine; many had dispersed throughout Iullyn, serving the people as best they could and devoting themselves to Arven's purpose. Many in Car'Agasse were asleep, at first. Arven was imprisoned in that ice; he was helpless, frozen and completely unable to break free, for his power was encased in that crystal casket gleaming in the centre of the hall. The imprisoning of our God woke everyone – a horrible, jarring jolt of *wrongness*, I suppose.

"Instead of just taking the casket and fleeing, Gregnor acted ruthlessly; he had a scheme of elimination in mind: of course, by killing the other disciples, he would remove all those who could seriously oppose him, even amongst the razine. No-one expected treachery. There were no weapons at all in the place, never had been. Gregnor, however, had secreted his weapons somewhere out of sight. He killed his lover, Holy Ayline, and everyone else in Car'Agasse, even the children! I managed to flee, at the violence; some instinct made me first hide for a while, before I raced back to the Iullyn Hall, just ahead of Gregnor. Somehow, I believe, Arven protected me as it's the only possible explanation for my survival. I ran across the hall, past Ayline's butchered body and hugged the casket tight in terror. I couldn't lift it and the Betrayer was screaming at me madly, racing towards me with a blazing sword in his hands, covered in blood . . .

"And we vanished, as he extended the blade. The Iullyn Hall was gone and I appeared in the Cathedral in Lerat, the capital of Orbain. I caused quite a stir: screaming, crying, somehow with my arms almost locked to the casket." Finally, he fell silent and took a slow sip of wine.

"Oh, my word!" Ethrayne breathed, not even realising that she had gripped Jerryn's hand tightly in her own during his recitation. It was fantastic, yet clearly the truth, the pain on the old razine man's face was genuine.

"Some years later, when Bahlien was fifteen, war descended on Iullyn, centred throughout the Mendor continent where most of the razine dwelt. Gregnor preached of his might in imprisoning our God: of taking control, becoming master; of riches and of slavery, oh, you can imagine. He possesses to this day the power which Arven had gifted to him before the attack." Archpriest Lurco took up the story. "The Betrayer wanted the rest of our God's power, but on his own terms. Humans he viewed as tools, inferior. He had always been eloquent, and he certainly used his gift to the best effect; by it he gained many followers and not a few of them were razine. They proclaimed him Emperor in the end, after he and his army had destroyed all the disciples of Arven still living. They brutally invaded the Enlath continent, far to the west, taking it as his realm and Empire. But this process took a century or so to be finalised."

"What of Arven's Casket, your Grace?" Prince Jerryn asked quietly. "And what happened to you, after you were transported across Iullyn to Orbain. Surely the Betrayer was searching for you?"

Ethrayne was glad he had asked – she hated the depths of her ignorance here. He was very good at asking questions, probably had had the method drilled in to him by his tutors: to always strive to gain information

"Oh, indeed he was, most assuredly. He lay waste to the city of Lerat with his troops and killed untold thousands in the process. I was schooled there in the monastery, I swore to serve our God when I became a priest. But of the priesthood in the Cathedral, many of their number came from those who had learned from Arven, before the Betrayer killed the last of them; they spirited the casket and I away by sea before he reached the city and we came to Selith. I travelled nervously throughout the continent for some years, before we settled here and Arven's casket was hidden in its present location, deep beneath this city's cathedral." Bahlien laughed aloud at the looks on their faces. "Gregnor has searched Selith, Mendor, Piyan and even Enlath in vain; it has been here all along."

Silence filled the room as, completely unnoticed by the diners, the servants cleared the table and sideboard of the main course dishes and served dessert before they vanished again. The wonderful aroma of spiced apple and rhubarb pie with thick cream proved a temptation even above the history they had been hearing, or any questions they had intended to ask. It wasn't until their plates had been scraped clean that anyone spoke.

"Excuse me." Pualyn said, taking a sip from his water goblet. "You mentioned Arven's Book of Days before, your Grace. These prophecies that Arven made . . . Well . . . surely there must have been one, a prophecy I mean, made about something so, as crucial as those awful events at Car'Agasse . . . was there?"

"Dear Arven! Was there a prophecy about the Betrayal?" Marrand demanded sharply. "And, if there was, why was our God not warned?"

"Yes, I thought you would ask that, your Majesty, my Lord Pualyn." Bahlien nodded approvingly. "The Book of Days was written in antiquity, but Arven never really considered it as worth any study!" He grimaced. "No-one did. It was one of Archpriest Lurco's predecessors who found the volume in the library here, locked in a box in the back of a storeroom, covered in cobwebs. I had resigned as Archpriest a few years before, certain that I was required here in Tenarum. That was twenty years ago. Trenayne showed me the book and we spent nearly four days reading it from cover to cover, reading Arven's own words. There is a prophecy that warns of the 'Disciple with the heart of blackness'; but, of course, the event had already occurred, unfortunately." He sighed and suddenly looked much older than he had before, for a moment, before he sighed for a second time and straightened his shoulders and back. "I will show you the prophecy but that is all in our past and perhaps the reason why the book exists at all. You two young people, together, are to take the Flame of Arven from the casket where it has been locked safe and secure for over eight centuries. You, together, will open the casket and the pair of you will Wield the Flame, Arven's power, for our God."

"Seriously? The – the power of our God? Us?" Ethrayne's voice quavered with some trepidation. The whole idea was terrifying. "But . . . we are only human, your Grace, we are nothing, certainly nothing particularly special -."

"Don't be ridiculous." Bahlien contradicted her jovially. "You are *everything* special, my Lady Ethrayne, your Highness, else the prophecy would refer to two other people, and not yourselves."

"Y-you really are sure about that, your Grace?" Jerryn asked levelly. "It's not that we are implying -." He faltered, fell silent then dropped his gaze to the empty plate on the table before him.

"I understand your concerns." The old razine said kindly. "And no-one would blame you for being frightened; you both understand what duty and responsibility means and we apologise for so abruptly increasing your duties. Arven's casket will open for you and only you. From that moment on, you will have to begin to learn how to use the Flame of Arven."

Ethrayne unclasped her hands and laid both palms flat on the table top. "You are certain that the Prophecy of Arven refers to us?" She asked quietly but intently and both old men nodded gravely. "You are sure, you are certain, that you all approve of this, your Majesty? Your Graces?" She asked of Marrand and her parents.

"I really don't think that even I as your ruler have the authority to disapprove, my dear Ethrayne. Nor your parents. This goes far beyond secular matters. Despite everything – his imprisonment – our God is paramount." Marrand answered after a pause, his tone and gaze troubled.

"We do not have any say at all in this, do we?" Jerryn laid his right hand over Ethrayne's left. "We cannot actually refuse, can we?"

"Because if we refused this responsibility; or ran away for example, there wouldn't really be anywhere to go." Ethrayne continued, glancing at her betrothed. "And if our God is demanding our help . . . well, it's only a continuation of those formal vows we will make when we are wed, Jerryn, to Lord Arven and your father the king; and, many years away, God willing, the vows made when you are crowned king to Arven and to Tenarum . . . Well, what do you think?" She asked the prince in a challenging tone.

"The Betrayer, his Empire and us?" Jerryn snorted, then spat a word that startled them all, graphic and to the point. "Excuse me. They already clearly know about us, though; about all this. I, they'll . . . oh, dear Arven, we have no idea what they'll do!" He let go of Ethrayne's hand, shoved back his chair and leapt to his feet, striding away from the table. "You'd better get married again, Father: you're going to need a few more children! Hell! I'll do it!"

"And I also." Ethrayne also rose to her feet. "I promise."

"Thank you. On behalf of all Iullyn, Bahlien and I earnestly thank you." Archpriest Lurco said, his tone heavy.

*

"Why did we agree?" Jerryn asked Ethrayne later that day, after the Archpriests had left. Recklessly, they had climbed to the top of the tallest tower in the palace. "We must be absolutely mad, Ethrayne!"

"I agree, it is mad, but it is necessary, can't you feel it?" Ethrayne replied, raising her arms wide. "Bahlien was right: Arven has called us, Jerryn. Us!" Her tone was stunned, she shuddered, as if at an icy blast, although the breeze through the open window was light and relatively warm, even two hundred feet above the ground. The countryside beyond the city walls below was green and vibrant with spring, but not even the sound of birdsong entering the space improved her mood.

Jerryn looked at her for a moment and then took her in his arms and hugged her tight. "It doesn't say that we will die, the prophecy just warns us to be careful, Ethrayne."

"The Archpriests have only showed us one page, you know!" She replied with an edge in her voice. "Bahlien said that there was a prophecy warning Lord Arven about the Betrayer. There might even be one saying that the Emperor of the Jajozeli slits our throats. And how would we know?"

"Then we will ask to read the whole book." The prince answered, his tone almost annoyingly calm; his equilibrium was returning, she noted. "Well, the Archpriests want us to attend them at the Cathedral a few more times, so we will study the Book of Days . . . Oh, Ethrayne, I can't believe it! You and I, chosen to wield the power of our God!"

"I have never been that good a person, you know." Ethrayne remarked, shrugging and stepping back from her betrothed's embrace, turning to stare out across the rooftops. "I have never been *bad*, yet I've never been like any of those helpful, selfless, benevolent characters in the parables, Jerryn." She sounded almost fretful, a lot younger than her years.

Jerryn cracked a rather lopsided smile. "I really don't think that many people are. From what I understand, well, rather as it *feels* to me, the Wielder of the Flame isn't meant to be a 'good' person, Ethrayne. The archpriests said we would lead our peoples . . . The Protectorates as well as the kingdoms of

Selith. I think we are meant to be, oh, I don't know, strong?"

"Strong? I'm a girl, Jerryn."

"But you are strong, Ethie: you are *amazing* when you are angry; you are sure of yourself and you were quite scary after luncheon, when you faced the Archpriests. You are not and could never be that mythical sort of timid girl who daren't ride a horse, or go out into town alone, or ever contradict her elders. And you're going to learn how to use weapons, too, so you are about as strong as anyone I've ever met; you never back down. I'm certainly going to have to watch my step when we are wed, you know." Jerryn managed a genuine grin at that point. "You're more than a match for Lord Ferman, or anyone else for that matter."

Surprised at his statement, Ethrayne felt a mixture of embarrassment and pleasure at being described so. "I thank you, Prince Jerryn." She said levelly. "But I have to admit that I am scared."

"Gosh, so am I and I'll shout it from the window, if you like. Even what we know so far is unnerving." Jerryn replied, grimacing. "I'm not afraid of admitting it. That man or jajozeli-razine, whatever he was, he scared the juice out of me."

"Yes, he felt completely different to how Bahlien does, didn't he? They were both so strong. I was amazed that no-one else could sense it. One, so cold and confident, giving out that level of hatred and power; whilst the Archpriest, whom I guess is at least his equal in power, feels friendly, safe, supporting . . . damn! I can't explain it." She shook her head in frustration. "But do you understand what I tried to define?"

"You explained it well, Ethie. It's something we don't really have the words to describe . . . I suppose we have to trust the Archpriests, at the end of the day, and pray." Jerryn held out one hand, and the girl clasped it. "But this means war, I suppose – I doubt there's any other way to try to free Lord Arven. I don't imagine the Betrayer will back down, given the history we know."

"I've never prayed so much. War? Oh, great heavens!" Ethrayne admitted in a whisper. "Oh, Jerryn, hold me tight for a moment, please?"

They kissed, quite naturally then, for some reassurance was required, brief yet proper, considering everything; Ethrayne wondered at the profound changes which had affected them so swiftly following their betrothal. Now, she realised, the feel of Jerryn's lips against hers was comforting as it had not been before, his body warm and strong against hers. She felt her heartbeat rising, but easily resisted temptation; this certainly was not what was required, she knew it. She and her betrothed would surely be far too busy to consider an early wedding! Especially if war was looming.

"We will all have to practise hard, not just you, Ethrayne." Her betrothed murmured, to her surprise.

"But you've been learning how to fight for years; I'm the novice." She objected.

"Yes, but only some of our soldiers have ever fought in real situations –

real fights. The guards here in the capital; Earl Orthen's men in Rothern; Lord Kierven's in Saremouth, those dealing with lawlessness and criminals around the kingdom. I suppose it's all theory, apart from tournaments . . . Dear Arven, Ethrayne, we must take care . . . even leading an army isn't safe." His arms tightened around her. "Especially against the Betrayer, I think."

"I'll do my best, I promise."

Their chaste yet comforting embrace only ended when a red-faced Tymain knocked politely on the half-open door to announce that they should descend for dinner, keeping his gaze averted.

* * *

CHAPTER 5

Across the city, a man moved unobtrusively through the Riverside, one of the poorer areas of the city that ran from behind the wharves and up either side of the Ayne River: a rather steep-sided valley with a slightly unhealthy atmosphere, since it received little direct sunlight and housed some very unsavoury inhabitants. The area angled to the south, separated from the hill that housed the Cathedral by an offshoot of the Artisans district.

No one took any notice of the man, and he appeared to be utterly different to how he had looked facing Lady Ethrayne on the lane above the city a few days before. Then, he had been very tall, blonde and chillingly handsome but he now looked like a thin man of only average height, with a head of sparse, greying black hair hanging around his ears; watery brown eyes; a loose-lipped mouth and a stooping gait. In the tatty cloak he wore over his clothing, he was unremarkable: a man, walking along Stonecutter's Street, one of thousands; perhaps a workman making his way home, perhaps a criminal, perhaps nobody.

But hardly anyone marked his passing, not even the eagle-eyed men and women of the local gangs, whose remit it was to identify and follow strangers, if not to simply rob them. He smiled to himself as he headed up a narrow alley, picking his way past a pile of refuse to a slightly battered door at the end, at the top of three dirty steps. He unlocked it with a sturdy iron key and stepped inside a dimly lit space, quickly locking the door again and securing it with a hefty oak bar. Whistling a few notes, he climbed three flights of creaking stairs to the top floor, unlocked a shabbily-peeling red-painted door and entered a large, surprisingly airy room, shaped almost like a triangle, the steeply angled ceiling meeting in the centre, forming the underside of the roof above, with a window in each gable end showing a great deal of sky and a view of jumbled rooftops in orange, red and greyish tiles, and darker grey slates, stepping haphazardly down the slopes of the valley towards the river below, and a distant glimpse of green fields beyond. There were other bedrooms below and even a kitchen, but he preferred being high, with the view across the city, however irrational that was.

The room contained a large, wooden-framed bed covered with white sheets and neatly folded blankets; an old plain chest; a rather battered and misused deal table containing a basket of food – eggs, some vegetables, cheese and a loaf of brown bread. In addition, there were two rickety chairs set one on each side of a dusty fireplace where a few embers smouldered amid a bed of grey ashes, around which were set a few iron pans and a skillet, brought up from the kitchen below.

He stretched as he cast off the cloak and the non-descript man was somehow replaced in the blink of an eye with the blonde, handsome figure who had so frightened Ethrayne there above the city, laying a large slab of meat and a wineskin on the table.

Since his arrival in Tenum a few days before, he had familiarised himself with the city in all its aspects, from the outer environs of the palace complex, to those much less salubrious areas where ordinary people avoided straying on towards evening, with no hindrance or concern. By a judicious use of his innate abilities, he had learned a great deal about the primitive little kingdom, its ruler and his council of noblemen and, most pertinently, he had discovered the name of one in the palace who might be amenable to divulging a few secrets concerning the young prince and his lady, if given the right inducements.

He had had to take the utmost care in his perambulations: the presence of the aged ex-archpriest Bahlien in the Cathedral complex was, of course, unknown to the general population, but as clear as the sun at noon to one such as him. Likewise, the old razine might also be aware of his arrival; yet, on balance, he assumed that he would be safe enough, unless he tried something recklessly stupid such as trying to enter the Cathedral or making a direct move against the young couple. Such recklessness, however, was not part of his remit here, or of his makeup.

Whistling again, he began to prepare a meal; he had a destination and a target in mind for that evening.

*

The Kings Arms was a spacious tavern of some standing, located directly below the palace wall on the steep north-facing slope that plunged down to the Benton district, where the richest merchants and nobles lived in luxury. The area was well-known for its fruit trees growing on wide verges along the main roads and in many little parks; the blossom here was beautiful in the spring.

The stranger now looked like a pale reflection of his real self, a mere six-foot-tall, with yellowy blonde hair and a bent nose, but his eyes were still that intense, sharp blue. It was not an actual physical change that he had affected, but a form of suggestion that he could project outwards and so alter what everyone else saw. It worked very well on humans, as a rule, for they lacked the regime of mental exercise and control that the razine and their enemies undertook from childhood. It did, however, take a lot of concentration to keep up for long periods; some people were better at complying with the suggestion emitted amongst them, whilst others just were naturally able to see the truth and not what he might want them to see.

There in the Kings Arms, however, people just accepted him for what he appeared to be: a well-dressed man of perhaps thirty at most, with money and good-quality, well-used weapons; probably a merchant, the tavern-keeper and his staff had decided. He had paid for one of the better rooms for the night and now sat quietly reading a scroll, a goblet of wine at his side.

"May I join you, sir?" A voice asked politely. "The other tables are all occupied, I'm afraid."

He looked up and suppressed a sigh. The person standing before him with an apologetic air was unknown: a paunchy, middle-aged man with a round nose and the most ridiculous comb-over from right to left of coarse, iron-grey hair which did nothing but highlight the bald area of scalp that he was so desperately vain to disguise; the slightest gust of wind would throw the ridiculously long strands every which way, for sure.

"Of course, sir, please do." He replied with a smile and a gesture of welcome. He was contemplating murder in his heart, however, as the one he had hoped to lure from across the room laughingly joined a larger group of acquaintances closer to the fireplace, a mixed collection of well-dressed and well-behaved senior staff-members from the palace.

"Thank you so much. I've just got in: settled my staff down at the Old Keys and I'll be off to the guild tomorrow." The man sat down, chuckling, and thanked the young maid with her pristine apron who promptly laid a plate of food and a tankard of ale before him. "M'name's Galton, by the way, Galton of Tenasse, you know. I deal in fine cloth and furs in all the main towns and cities of the kingdom."

"I am Kesta from Saremouth, trading ironware; I am just starting to expand north." He replied, adding a mental nudge to suggest to Galton that it was a boring subject.

"Saremouth, hey? Was there only last autumn." And Galton began a pretty-much one-sided conversation in between relishing his mouthfuls of dinner, so that 'Kesta' did not really have to do much more than nod his head every now and then and add the occasional 'yes' and 'no', as he in turn watched the group by the fire, relaxing merrily on their evening off.

He recognised the man to his target's left as the king's valet and indeed it seemed that Shan was the very embodiment of decorum: he hardly said a word and drank sparingly as some of the others chattered and supped as if it was going out of fashion.

"- And I've noticed that the roads over the Eppleton Hills are most unusually rutted this spring -." Galton continued his monologue, as 'Kesta' nodded his agreement.

"- The Prince and his Lady are spending a great deal of time together, I heard tell." One man remarked with a leer, nudging his neighbour at the other table. "Think he's tasting forbidden fruit? She's certainly a pretty little thing."

"Rannon!" Karne, the prince's valet, hissed, shocked. "Don't be disgusting!"

"Ah, c'mon, Karne, she's just -." He moved his hands out, in and out again in the most eloquent hourglass representation indeed and some of the others sniggered. "You couldn't blame him, could you?"

"They are all spending a great deal of time with the Archpriest, actually; they are not alone." Shan corrected him primly, backing up the younger man's statement.

"And that's in between the lady learning some self defence." Karne said with a low laugh, clearly ignoring his master's command to be circumspect.

"Never thought I'd see the day when a little bit of a thing like her would seriously pick up such weapons, yet his Highness says she is quick and strong."

'Kesta' pretended drowsiness, nodding slightly as he sat nursing his wine and Galton fell silent and drank his ale, so the imposter could clearly hear the other conversation. So, she had begun weapons training already: he must have seriously scared the brat; whilst she and her betrothed were conducting meetings with the Archpriest. An interesting development. Inwardly he smiled, listening on as the conversation turned to other matters.

*

The next evening, the palace servants did not attend the Kings Arms, but some of the Palace Guard did, including Tymain, looking serious beyond his years as he colleagues ribbed him mercilessly about teaching a girl how to use weapons. 'Kesta' had extended his stay and recognised him, briefly considering using the young man as his contact, until Tymain met his eyes across the room, frowned and automatically laid his hand on his sword hilt, a reflex action that the stranger acknowledged with an inner sigh: the young man, so well placed that he would have been ideal, had just enough power of his own to recognise his own difference and strength. A moment later, the soldier shivered – and noticeably relaxed, as 'Kesta' suppressed his aura slightly, so as to seem much less threatening.

It was not a common occurrence. Humans generally lacked those skills of the mind he had been trained in since childhood, but natural ability sometimes won out and it was an effect that he should have expected: that the young couple, brimming with perhaps an enormous potential for power and strength, would attract those with similar if lesser abilities to themselves, subconsciously drawn in like moths to a flame. Prophecy or no prophecy, both the prince and the lady had that potential and, as such, his master would have marked them out from the other side of the world, regardless . . . But he wondered whether that potential would have existed at all, if not for the prophecy.

"Foolishness!" He murmured to himself. "That is not your concern." But it was an interesting concept, one he might mention, once he had returned to civilisation.

"So, how does it feel, teaching a mere girl to fight?" One of the other privates demanded with a snigger. "Dear Arven, what a waste of time! I can't believe the king even approved such a thing!"

"No, actually I am not strictly doing so, Calle." Tymain answered with a calm smile. "Prince Jerryn and Lord Pualyn are teaching her, I'm merely one of their advisers -."

"Adviser!" The youth named Calle snorted and swore graphically. "You're only a private, Tymain. Women have no place using weapons, she'd be better placed in a bedroom! The prince and his father the king shouldn't have agreed to it!"

"You weren't there on that ride, fool!" Tymain replied with a little more heat. “All right, I agree, Prince Jerryn always seemed a complete, pampered idiot, but that afternoon, he behaved so differently to anything I’ve seen before; that stranger who appeared, he was really dangerous, I’m sure. It could have been an absolute disaster, although Lady Ethrayne hardly did anything reckless, only raced his Highness. Somehow, all our horses were slow, I think that’s how she was so far ahead. Thank Arven that stranger only talked to her! Prince Jerryn has surely grown up because of it. Oh, shut up! No, really.” He waved down the derogatory responses from some of the others, but he still wasn’t smiling, Ackat noted. “With regard to her ability, the lady has good reflexes and his majesty, *and* her parents approved this. If they say so and Commander Vedeigne agrees, who am I to object?”

“Ha! He’s fallen for her -!” Calle sneered, laughing raucously, but Tymain reached out, grabbed him by the collar and dragged him half across the table. “The prince’s lady! Hey -!”

“Lady Ethrayne is the prince’s betrothed, you fool!” Tymain growled, a sudden rush of anger roaring in his head. “Don’t insult her, or the prince, in my hearing again! Whatever else might be going on isn’t our concern and you might not believe it, but I’ve given them both my complete loyalty! Times have changed, Calle!” Glaring, he contemptuously released one of his oldest friends in the troop, pushed back his chair and stalked out of the tavern as if mightily offended.

Watching him go, ‘Kesta’ marked him down as a far more significant personality in the future than he had previously supposed and wondered, smiling wryly to himself, whether the young man would remain a private for long.

Striding up the street, Tymain felt his flare of anger ebb away and began to wonder at the differences that only a handful of days could make. At the start of that fateful ride out, the very day before of their betrothal, he had thought of Jerryn with little more than vague contempt mixed with a certain amount of jealousy for his rank and life of privilege; he had considered Lady Ethrayne not at all, really, except as a very pretty girl and far beyond his reach! But now . . . now, as he had said, everything had shifted monumentally and changed completely, with the appearance of that blonde man. The prince was becoming a man and was pleasant company; the lady also had an interesting, complex personality and the young couple, together, were apparently at the very heart of this strange prophecy which he would never mention here in public . . . Dear Arven, what was happening to the world?

He shivered, and the bland face of the stranger who had been sat opposite him on the corner table suddenly came into his head, with those deep, intense blue eyes. Something about the man bothered him, but he had no idea what, or why that should be: a blonde man perhaps ten years or so older than he; a merchant, by the look of him. He would keep his eyes open for that one, anyway.

*

With her mornings now filled with weapons' training and afternoons increasingly spent attending Council meetings, not forgetting the other meetings often scheduled for her and Jerryn with the Archpriests; King Marrand and her family, Ethrayne now found that her days were racing by as spring advanced.

Archpriest Lurco had issued a bland statement that acknowledged her and Jerryn's now singular status as the subject of a prophecy by Arven himself; it was so bland that it almost seemed to turn the fact into a non-event; which, ex-archpriest Bahlien admitted with a raffish grin, was the whole point: not to concern the population overmuch with such odd portents. Jerryn; his father; her family and she merely attended an incense-fogged ceremony of blessing at the Cathedral where she and Jerryn knelt and swore to carry out Arven's will regarding the prophecy, to the best of their ability. Lurco seemed deliberately vague on the details of the prophecy itself as he spoke there before the altar, but they could both sense that Bahlien viewed the blessing with mingled trepidation and triumph.

"I can only apologise again." The old razine said quietly after the ceremony, at the celebratory feast served afterwards. "I know for a fact that the one who accosted you is lurking around the city but, of course, I have no idea where. I am certain that he is only watching and trying to gain information about you. We can only wait and watch and take care."

"You have no idea what they, the jajozeli, intend?" The prince asked.

Ethrayne felt a peculiar jolt of unease, recalling how strange, how alarming that encounter had been. Even at ten days' distance, it still disturbed her.

"The jajozeli's emperor is a law unto himself." Was all that the old razine acknowledged, in reply. "Now, how is your training progressing, my Lady?" He changed subjects so quickly that the young couple exchanged glances and glared at him rather intently; Bahlien had the grace to look a little embarrassed.

"Please don't *ever* think that we are stupid, your Grace." Ethrayne stated quietly.

"You certainly are not stupid, my Lady, I apologise." Bahlien agreed with a grimace. "Neither of you could ever be considered so, I can only ask that you please forgive me. It's, well, I just -." He paused. "I cannot very well give you a list of their atrocities over the past centuries, can I? On one level, most would say that for you two young people to be chosen like this, to wield the Flame of Arven is wrong: you are far too young, far too inexperienced and far too vulnerable, which would be the view of most of the razine in Orbain, I must admit. I can only apologise for that statement, for clearly you are not. Our people age much more slowly and to us, you are children but, please, I ask you, do not take offence, your Highness, my Lady. On behalf of the High-King, all our peoples in the Protectorates and our God, I must help you prepare, but we must be careful: the enemy are watching and waiting and probably ready to release thousands of troops at short notice into Selith, if we razine seem to be getting too involved." The elderly man sighed deeply.

"An army? Against the kingdom?" Ethrayne asked quietly with a shiver.

"Armies in the plural, my dear. And marching against many of the kingdoms of Selith and Mendor, not just Tenarum alone." Bahlien admitted. "We don't want that, any of us, I am sure you agree? As an alternative, we can cope with them watching and waiting, can't we?"

"Yes, your Grace. Do you believe that they might try to abduct us, your Grace, before war descends?" Jerryn asked, frowning. "You believe that the Betrayer will want the Flame of Arven?"

"We do believe that perhaps at some point in the future, yes, he will seek your capture, because you will hold Arven's power." He replied. "In fact, Lurco is suggesting that we return to the Cathedral later tonight for a rather more meaningful ceremony." And, for the first time that day, Bahlien smiled.

Ethrayne glanced at Jerryn, seeing the concern in his eyes and managed a quick, spurious smile of her own. "If you believe that the time is right, your Grace, then who are we to argue? It is so strange, being named – designated – as the Wielders of the Flame!"

Jerryn took her hand in his and she noticed that his palm was chilly to the touch, although his face looked calm. She found his outward serenity and confidence hugely reassuring; this matter just seemed to be getting more and more complicated and dangerous, the reality of learning how to use weapons was now very daunting, especially in the face of war.

*

Kesta walked boldly through the night-shrouded corridors of the palace, covered in a plain soldier's cloak and completely unremarkable. This was his second visit to the virtual labyrinth that was this range of buildings; the first, two nights before, had been to orientate himself, a brief walk around the outer reaches of the main building in the early evening had been enough. He had perfect recall, which ensured that the confusing range of corridors would prove no obstacle at all and, with his ability to hide in plain sight, nowhere was barred from him.

Now, hearing a distant chime of bells, he slipped through one of the plain doors and into the store room beyond, where a solitary candle burned on a scrubbed table top, casting angles of warm light and deep black shadow on the neat lines of crockery and silverware stacked neatly on the shelves which lined the walls. As he shut the door behind him, he saw the man who waited for him visibly jump at his appearance.

"You startled me." He said with a nervous laugh. "You move quietly, Master Kesta."

"Yes." Kesta replied with a smile, watching as the man's eyes became a little less focussed as he released his own power. "What can you tell me?"

"King Marrand, his son, Duke Sarant and his family left the palace earlier, after dinner; I was not informed where they have gone, but they will not be back until later tonight." He reported levelly. "They went by carriage, however, so I guess they are visiting out in the city."

"That is excellent news, thank you." Kesta sighed inwardly at the man's lack of detail, but he already knew that the prince and his lady had returned to the Cathedral, for he had asked one of the grooms earlier that evening, loitering in the stables, posing as a temporary servant and admiring the duke's horses as he had shovelled manure into a barrow.

He had made a definite contact with the palace servant eight days previously, hooking his mind and interest easily with a hint of sexual regard and a jug of wine, there at the Kings Arms. It had been quiet, that night; the inn largely empty, whilst the owner and his staff were obviously discreet, he had noted. Getting the man upstairs, staggering a little for effect and singing slightly off colour songs, he had used his innate power to nudge ideas into his head, taking plenty of time to lay controls and commands in his victim's mind, so that they would lie deep and unnoticed by everyone else as well as the man himself as he filled him with ecstasy; he would remember nothing but the pleasure of the night, of that the jajozeli-razine was sure. There, in bed with the man, he had laid his plans: pre-setting their first meeting at the palace gates for the next night at moonrise in his head without any need for explanation: it was not necessary to give any spurious reason for their meeting, just the fact that it would happen.

He had smiled: humans were so wonderfully easy to work with! No ridiculous complications to get in his way; most of the time, anyway. Simple commands and simple pleasures held sway. As he had lain there with him, he had considered that the young couple who were the subject of his scrutiny might possibly prove more challenging to manipulate, and the chance of bedding either of them would be so utterly remote as to be completely unobtainable, although both were very handsome.

The controls on his victim had set and held, naturally; the man was no simpleton, but far from a genius and Kesta had walked around the palace in the dead of night, unnoticed by everyone including the guards as he had planned, easily locating the places he had wanted to find without any fear of discovery, as if he walked through his own home.

Now, he mused, he could proceed: he could do what he had intended to do without interruption and depart the complex to melt back into the shadows after enjoying his contact again. It would be quite a novelty, he acknowledged with a smile, to just leave the man none the wiser as to who or what he was, and he considered the matter gravely with its pros and cons.

Dealing with a being with the complexities of appetites he and many of his peers had, was usually a huge shock and a frighteningly abrupt education to the victim concerned. Most of those targeted and so used never survived the experience, in the end.

"Come." He urged quietly, his bland mask smiling pleasantly, banishing the courtier's unformed fears of discovery and illegality before they could rise and be voiced. "Show me the wonders of this magnificent palace, my friend."

*

It had been easy to gain the agreement of the two families to return to the Cathedral, at the end of their meeting; their relations were curious as to what this event might entail, after the largely meaningless preamble of the earlier ceremony, not just Jerryn and herself, Ethrayne considered. Their families were also intrigued by the private nature of this meeting in the middle of the night. The underlying serious nature of the prophecy was beginning to loom higher in their awareness: the danger of the jajozeli could not be denied. Ethrayne dressed in deep red velvet, her mother wore blue and Lyria was beautiful in soft purple, whilst she noted that the men wore comfortable clothes and boots, the king and Jerryn in their usual blue and green for their private dinner before they would leave; all of them seemed interested, their conversation light and wide-ranging.

The Cathedral was mostly shrouded in a comforting darkness which was lifted by widely spaced, crystal-walled lamps set along the plain corridor which Archpriest Lurco led them along, heading towards the monastery complex, as far has his guests could surmise, having left the main courtyard by a small, ancient gate into a night-shrouded loam-smelling garden and past twisted apple trees.

They moved quietly; it didn't seem appropriate to ask questions, Ethrayne thought, although her curiosity was high; at Lurco's direction, they all turned left into a slightly narrower side passage and, ahead of them, they could now see the taller form of the old razine waiting for them with a smile of greeting, standing beside a plain arched doorway. Bahlien held a glowing lamp in his hand, highlighting the most formal robe that they had yet seen him wear, of white silk, embroidered with shimmering gold and silver that, due to the intricate differences in the twist and thickness of the thread and the many different styles of stitching, formed various shades that delineated the hands, globe and flame of Arven.

"Your Majesty; your Graces; my lord and lady." He greeted their families, bowing politely to each of them in turn. "Am'maiya." He bowed very formally to Jerryn and Ethrayne, who had walked along at the rear of the group, both looking very sober, considering their years.

"Am'maiya? What does that mean?" The prince queried the unknown word as he bowed in return.

"It is an old mendor title. It means 'Wielder of the Flame'." Lurco provided the translation with a smile. "It is a title which you share your Highness, my Lady. Now, we must apologise for the next stage of our journey: the entrance is concealed through some of our storerooms, your Majesty."

"Storerooms?" Sarant snorted with amusement. "I bet you've not entered anything so humble as a storeroom since you were a prince, old friend!"

"Of course not, Sarant, that's what you're for." King Marrand replied with a hearty guffaw, slapping his friend hard on the shoulder. "Lead on, please; I am intrigued, and I am not ashamed to admit it, your Graces."

Bahlien opened the plain door and they filed through a square room with shelving set from floor to ceiling to left and right, full of variously sized candles and many wooden boxes; the air was thick with the scents of beeswax and incense, almost overpoweringly strong, and Lyria sneezed. The elderly razine man went to the rear wall where a second door led into a narrower room that was almost a corridor: fifteen feet long and only six feet wide, also shelved, the air sharp with the mingled aroma of herbs and spices, mostly neatly packaged and boxed, whilst bunches of lavender and rosemary hung from the ceiling.

Half-hidden at the far right-hand corner of the room, behind a stack of barrels, was a further doorway, but the already opened door seemed to be constructed of stone, not wood, and might be pretty-much invisible when closed.

"Here we are." Bahlien said cheerfully, heading through this doorway with the lamp in his hand, his voice becoming slightly muffled as he continued. "There is a short passage and then we descend a staircase; there are some lamps and the footing is secure. Please, follow me, ladies and gentlemen."

The staircase was about thirty steps deep, traditionally curved and it opened into a square area with a number of doors leading off it; more storerooms, they guessed, but the ex-archpriest touched one of a number of carved circles in the midst of some rather poor engraving on the straight, central spine of the staircase and, slowly, smoothly and silently, an aperture opened on the opposite wall to where the steps had ended.

"Oh, my goodness!" The Duchess remarked, the first of them to speak for a while. "This is very well hidden, your Grace – it reminds me of stories I read when I was young, of mysterious houses with hidden rooms and so on."

"Really?" Lyria asked, smiling as she followed her future mother-in-law. "I love those stories, Madam."

"That is quite a strange pastime." Marrand grunted. "I get quite enough entertainment from the tax reports and so on with the Council, Riyala. I don't have time for fiction, my dear duchess."

"Oh, but they fill a quiet, rainy afternoon quite well." Riyala answered and both Lyria and Ethrayne agreed with her, laughing for a moment; but the strangeness of the evening was still a fact, their destination was beyond mythical, somewhere deep below the Cathedral housing the Flame of Arven.

An arched doorway about two and a half feet wide and seven feet high was revealed which opened directly onto a second spiral staircase that descended out of sight. A dim but warm light was just visible below, the small group all glad of the lamps held by Bahlien at the head and Lurco at the rear of the line, as they followed quickly and quietly downwards.

* * *

CHAPTER 6

The stairs led downwards, seemingly endlessly until, as her legs began to tire, Ethrayne noted that the light coming from below began to brighten beyond the glow of Bahlien's lamp; near the rear of the line, ahead of Jerryn and Pualyn, she stepped into a hexagonal chamber some fifty feet wide and moved forward, startled. There was a high vaulted stone ceiling nearly thirty feet above and glowing lamps hung on the four walls without doors; facing them, a short corridor led to an ancient blackened-oak door thickly bound with iron and studded with massive nail-heads. It was very well constructed, she thought.

"We must be a long way below ground level." King Marrand said, sounding quite surprised. "This must have taken some committed work to excavate, your Grace."

"Oh indeed, your Majesty." Bahlien replied. "And all in a very good cause, I assure you. My Lady Ethrayne, Prince Jerryn, if you can please lead your families onwards? That would be best as we go forward. Thank you." He stepped back as the brightly dressed group milled about for a moment, catching their breath after the descent.

"Is any ritual or ceremony involved in this night's event, your Grace?" Ethrayne asked intently. "This place, well, it feels -." She stopped speaking, struggling to find words to describe what she sensed. Ever since they had started down the long spiral staircase, she had sensed . . . a power, a force awaiting them: there was a slight tingle on the skin; in the nerves; a slight pressure in the mind. It was subtle and certainly not painful, but it was noticeable. "It feels quite strange." She ended, rather lamely.

"Yes." Jerryn agreed. "I can sense it too . . . and I think it knows that we are here, whatever it is."

"Oh, my word." Duke Sarant murmured to the Duchess beside him. "I don't feel anything different at all, do you, dearest?" He sounded almost worried.

"Don't be concerned, Father." Ethrayne reassured him and flashed a smile at them all. "We are all perfectly safe."

"But I wouldn't touch anything." Jerryn added as he reached out to take the girl's hand in his. "Shall we?" He asked and, together, they led their families along the short passage and opened the heavy door with a shove.

The space beyond was brilliantly lit with beautiful golden oil lamps burning a delicately fragranced oil; some were set on ornate stands, whilst others rested low on the floor around the edge of the room, shining so brightly that the group all halted in the doorway, blinking for a moment.

"Heavens!" Ethrayne said, and her exclamation and her clear surprise was repeated by King Marrand, her mother and her brother. They had all descended here at Bahlien's request, but he had given them no details of what to expect; perhaps he had wanted to surprise them, she guessed with an inner smile. Certainly, his brief mention of an underground vault had not given them any clues of what to expect.

The hall was also hexagonal in shape, but it was some five or six times larger than the foyer at the bottom of the stairs. The walls were covered in a uniformly pristine white painted plaster; the floor a beautifully multi-coloured and elaborately designed mosaic where patterns flowed into other patterns, framing depictions of trees, birds, animals and the sun, moon and stars, all large and breathtakingly beautiful. Crowning this was a great vaulted ceiling, high above, where the carved stone was picked out in delicate-looking gold leaf and more white paint between the pale stone trusses. Around the edge of the walls were low stone blocks carved to show animal faces staring across the hall: a mouse, a hawk, a fox, a horse, a deer and an otter amongst them, all set at regular intervals; some of them held oil lamps on their flat tops, others were empty.

At the centre of the hall, in the middle of the floor, was a large mosaic of the sun, shining with tiles of what looked like gold as well as myriad shades of orange and yellow edged with white and, rising from this, was a four-foot tall column of fine white marble on which lay a hexagonal gleaming crystal casket.

A strange abstraction had filled Ethrayne as she and the prince crossed the space. She could definitely feel that other *presence* which Jerryn had described so lamely, understanding that ordinary words just could not do justice to the aura so obvious here. She considered it, but it did not make any sense that she could find, although, peculiarly, she felt slightly removed from her family, although they were all standing close together behind them. The exception to this abstraction was Jerryn. Tonight, here, she felt a greater affinity for him than she had ever before, a regard that came from deep within her; it was strange, although the feeling made that well-used phrase 'soul-mates' very real, for some reason. For the first time, the prospect of becoming Jerryn's wife did not alarm her as it had on their betrothal.

"So, Jerryn, what do you think?" She asked lightly. "I've never seen an object that so wanted us to open it before, have you?"

"No, I agree." The prince said with a chuckle. "It certainly wants to be released." He considered the casket with a slight frown and shook his head a little. "Well, this certainly proves the truth of the prophecy that Bahlien read to us and I suppose we must trust Arven and his servants."

Together, hand in hand, they stepped forward, crossing the magnificent floor, as their families and the two priests watched, still clustered by the entrance to the hall. The golden glow from the lamps seemed to focus about the pillar and the casket, a strange effect: it almost looked as if the light was solidifying as the group watched it, into a peculiar golden gel and Ethrayne and Jerryn stepped into it without any hesitation.

"Have we lost our children, Bahlien?" King Marrand asked intently as the golden light started to swirl, spiralling delicately around the young people. "Has Lord Arven claimed the only heir I have?"

"Claimed?" Lurco answered for the old razine, and grinned. "Nay, your Majesty. Jerryn is and remains your heir, and Ethrayne will be his princess. This role is, well, not secondary I must agree, but certainly additional to those other duties."

"Yet we have enemies in our midst, your Grace." Duke Sarant added, blinking rapidly against the increasing brilliance of the light. "And they are both so very young. Forgive us if we seem sceptical."

"I am sure that their age will prove to be of no consequence, your Grace. The Flame of Arven will gift them with many things and not even we two could possibly guess or predict as to what. Oh!" Bahlien gasped suddenly. "Oh, watch -."

They all stared at the centre of the hall, but the golden light had now formed a sort of hazy mist that slightly obscured Jerryn and Ethrayne, although it seemed that the crystal casket had vanished from the pillar and, suddenly, it looked almost as though the young couple were both crowned with bright flames.

Simultaneously, Ethrayne and Jerryn reached out to the casket, but Ethrayne was startled to find that there was no surface to touch. Her hands plunged into the thing as if the surface was less than smoke, meeting no resistance at all, as if the entire thing was merely illusion. Then the pale shape of the casket faded away from her sight and she could see that her and Jerryn's hands now rested on what appeared to be thin air, on an invisible surface some inches above the flat top of the column.

"Great heavens!" Jerryn murmured, as surprised as she.

Then, in a heartbeat, making her jump on the spot, there was fire blazing there on the column, surrounding their hands and lower arms. Flames! She and Jerryn could see fire, burning in intense shades of red, orange, yellow and nearly white, blazing upwards some four feet into the air, well above their heads. It also spread steadily outwards over the two of them, but Ethrayne realised that the heat of it was contained somehow and did not consume anything or hurt them. Her heart thudded wildly even so and, her eyes wide, stared, amazed, but oddly not frightened, feeling a tingling sensation coursing through her, increasing as the fire flickered about her and her betrothed.

<*Welcome!*> A voice whispered quietly in her head, for she definitely did not hear it with her ears; Jerryn was as startled as she – clearly he could also hear the disembodied voice. <*Taking this Flame, you can begin to redress the balance upset by my Betrayer . . . Will you do this for the peoples of this world? Will you be the Wielders of my Flame?*>

"Lord . . . are you sure?" Ethrayne asked, concern breaking through that calm certainty that had filled her up to this moment. Now, she felt awe fill her, an icy touch down her spine.

"W-we are not at all special." Jerryn added, his tone earnest, and Ethrayne felt him shudder deeply. "Are you certain?"

The voice laughed a little. <*You are both young in years, that is true, but only you, Ethrayne, and you, Jerryn, have the strength that will be required, and you will gain experience . . . Will you Wield my Flame?>*

Ethrayne exchanged a glance across and through the fire with Jerryn, recognising the mixed look of fear and determination on his face, before she focussed back on the column. "I will." She said clearly at the same moment that the prince spoke the same words.

The flames suddenly sprang upwards, turning white and gold, then dropped down almost like a sheet of water from the blade of a watermill and she felt an indescribable strength fill her . . . and fill her . . . and fill her . . . and fill her even more! Uneasy, exhilarated, Ethrayne realised that more power than they believed could exist, let alone that they could ever hold, was soaking into the very fibre of both her and Jerryn's bodies. It was making her teeth ache slightly, as if at eating rhubarb or sharp apple, and her skin tingled sharply, as well. She and Jerryn were, amazingly, stood in the centre of a gleaming, stunning vortex and . . . absorbing it all – the fire, the energy, the power . . .

Ethrayne then found that she was thinking as two people, not just herself! She and Jerryn – both of them! Now, it felt as though they were jugs being filled with water; she thought that that was perhaps a little like what the pouring in of power felt like. Hand in hand, mind touching mind, they stood there, wondering what would happen to all that remaining power of the Flame when they could hold no more of it . . . But, amazingly, they found that the force, the power sank down into the very matter of their bodies, from the tips of their fingers and toes to the very ends of the hair on their heads.

<I think I am going to explode!> Jerryn's voice rang suddenly in Ethrayne's head, which was very peculiar, but also somehow entirely natural. The power that poured into them contained some information within it; and at that singular happening, the knowledge of mind-speech opened within their heads.

<Heavens! We're so different to how we were earlier!> Ethrayne thought the words and felt her betrothed's amusement clearly, bubbling in his mind and so into hers. *<Isn't this peculiar?>*

"Yes, it's very strange indeed." Jerryn whispered the words. "I wonder just how we can hold so much power in check." And he shivered, affected by the slow, gradual slackening off in the amount of power and strength around them; the vortex had mostly vanished and the glow about them was fading fast as they absorbed the last portions of Arven's strength.

<Ethrayne, dearest, I really don't think that many people are going to be able to understand any of this. I don't think we will be able to talk freely, even to our parents.> He added silently, his tone and thoughts uncertain at this so personal form of communication.

Ethrayne acknowledged that her emotions matched his and turned slightly to glance behind them to where their families waited, staring with wide eyes: her parents, so dear to her; her brother and her best friend, so wonderful;

and King Marrand, who had always been as close as a blood relative and who would soon be as her father-in-law as well as her king. At some level, she could sense their mingled awe and concern at this singular event.

<No, you are right, my love.> She agreed with him and blushed slightly as Jerryn smiled, his eyes shining, his mind radiating a clear, strange amazement at her beauty - *<Oh, please don't! . . . We are going to have to be careful with this, aren't we?>*

"Yes." He replied and suddenly started laughing, as humour won over all the other feelings that swirled through him. "Well, I never imaged a night like *this*, my Lady."

They stood there, hand in hand, leaning on the half column that had supported the casket that had vanished, giggling together like a pair of children, as the unique strangeness which had consumed them slowly faded away and eased their tender, hidden nerves. The others watched them laugh, a little bemused.

*

"Your Majesty your Grace, I would like to ask a favour of you." Ex-archpriest Bahlien asked as they watched the strange fire flowing around the young couple in the centre of the hall and smiled ruefully. "This is not for Arven so much, I must admit: this is partly for me or, rather, for the razine in Orbain. A member of your Council would be invaluable to send as an envoy to the Razine Protectorates and, I must say, that Lord Pualyn would be ideal."

"You would take both my children from me, your Grace?" Sarant demanded rather sharply. "In little more than a span of days you would remove them both?"

"Sarant, we can hardly blame the priesthood for this prophecy and, well, all of this." King Marrand said, gesturing, his eyes wide, his tone quietly reverential.

"We do not intend to take this young couple anywhere, I assure you." Bahlien answered calmly. "The reason why your son would be the best envoy, your Grace, is that he has been included in this singular meeting of fate and he naturally knows his sister and Prince Jerryn really well. I understand that certain other members of the Council are more sceptical of what has been reported, and dismissive of your children, perhaps because of their youth -."

"That is certainly true, look at Galton!" Sarant muttered, rolling his eyes and sighing. "All right, your Grace, I agree with your logic there. But may I ask why you need an envoy from Tenarum to your realms?"

Bahlien shrugged. "It is simple expediency, your Grace. We strongly suspect that the jajozeli are spying out your lands from the sea and may also well be engaged in piracy. Our ships patrol the seas widely in their pursuit of trade and profit, and they naturally protect others where they possibly can; but there will be far more legitimacy, shall we say? if your official envoy, for example, would convey an open request for assistance to the High-King in Lerat."

Marrand and Sarant exchanged looks of great surprise at this statement. “But you don’t have any relations, diplomatic or otherwise with the jajozeli, your Grace, so why do you need such an excuse?” The king asked levelly.

“We are generally peace-loving and there is a faction amongst the razine in the Protectorates that would rather withdraw entirely from the world, if such a thing was at all possible, than even strive to stop our enemies destroying the world. Some of them profess to be religious, though I don’t understand how they can equate hiding to avoid war with what the Betrayer did so brutally to Lord Arven.” The old razine frowned. “People can be incredibly foolish, as I am sure you are aware. If your representative is knowledgeable regarding the history; and especially if he were the brother of a Wielder of the Flame, then the High-King will definitely be able to give that group short shrift.”

Duke Sarant snorted. “Politics! It stains everything it touches!”

“You and your High-King have thought this matter through very well, your Grace, haven’t you?” Marrand noted dryly.

“Yes, of course. A great deal may eventually depend upon cooperation between us, your Majesty. It would be most foolish for our peoples not to work together. And where Orbain leads, the other kingdoms which form the Protectorates will naturally follow.” Bahlien said. “The razine ship the Lerat Pearl will dock at Rothern soon, probably in fifteen days or so, depending on the winds. I believe that it would be most beneficial for Lord Pualyn to board her there. But I must stress that he and the young Lady Lyria must be formally betrothed before this.” He smiled. “As a dedicated servant of our Church, I always strive towards supporting marriage between our young people as a boon to society.”

“Well, I can actually raise no legitimate objections, your Grace.” Sarant conceded with a sigh. “And I must wholeheartedly concur with you regarding Pualyn and Lyria’s betrothal.” He glanced sideways away from the vortex of fire and light to where the tall young man now under discussion stood, hand in hand with Lyria, close to his mother. The three of them were totally enthralled at what was happening around Jerryn and Ethrayne, with Lurco standing rapt beside them.

“Pualyn is indeed a most sensible and gifted young man. I agree, your Grace, if you believe that he is the man you need.” The king said and grinned in return. “You have manipulated us very easily, ex-archpriest Bahlien. I am very glad that I am not your enemy and that we are all on the side of Lord Arven.”

Bahlien grimaced rather dramatically at that. “I agree. I apologise profusely, but I cannot help but wonder, on occasion, whether Arven himself would approve of some of the things I have done during my life to counter our enemies. Dedication is all very well, but over the years, perhaps, I have abandoned some tenets of which our God would never approve.” His tone was a little sad as if he considered awful acts committed in his youth, but his next words were delivered more cheerfully. “Look: our young champions are taking the Flame of Arven into themselves. This is a most remarkable end to any day in the history of Iullyn."

The three of them returned their attention to Ethrayne and Jerryn standing hand in hand as the flickerig flames swirled about them. The two of them were glowing gently as if lit from within.

"Oh my!" Sarant breathed with a shiver. "Is this safe?"

"Yes indeed, your Grace. The couple are still absorbing the Flame of Arven into their being: the power of our God. They might feel a little peculiar for a short while, but this is not dangerous."

*

"Are you feeling better now?" Archpriest Lurco asked, as Jerryn and Ethrayne finally turned back to them, no longer laughing or glowing, but still smiling broadly.

"Yes, we are quite well, thank you, your Grace." Ethrayne replied honestly. "It must be ever so late by now, I am sorry -."

"My dear Lady, your Highness, tonight's events are quite unique, unprecedented and amazing!" The old man said, waving his arms as if only the movement could give vent to the depths of his emotions. "We had no idea at all how long this might take, you know."

"Oh, Ethrayne, you look weary." Duchess Riyala exclaimed, taking her daughter in a tight embrace and looking deep into her eyes before freeing one arm to embrace Jerryn too. "Are you *sure* that you are all right?"

Together, the young couple hugged her back. "Honestly, your Grace, we are." The prince assured her, kissing her gently on the cheek. "But I admit that it has been a very long day. I am looking forward to getting into bed at some point tonight." He looked at Bahlien and Lurco and smiled. "I imagine that you are also weary, your Graces."

"Yes, I am, despite my inner excitement." The old razine admitted. "And now we must slowly begin our climb back up to ground level. After you, your Majesty."

"Oh, heavens, no! Let the young people lead the way, please." Marrand demurred.

As they climbed the stairs, her brother, following behind them, curiously asked Jerryn and herself what exactly had happened and how they felt.

"At the moment, I just want to rest and review in my own mind what we experienced." Ethrayne said.

"But do you *feel* different, Ethryane?" Pualyn asked the question directly of his sister. "It looked as though you both soaked up that golden fire. I've never imagined such an amazing sight! I mean, Ethrayne, it's hardly a normal everyday occurrence, is it?"

His words made them both laugh again, as they climbed the spiral staircase up and up. "Likely not and we'll let you know, Pualyn." Jerryn said lightly. "Come on, don't dawdle -." And he strode out ahead, his boots ringing on the stone.

The priests bid the group farewell at the entrance to the main courtyard where the coach waited in the cool darkness, and they began to step up into the dimly lit interior, where she and Jerryn lingered until everyone was seated.

"We will come at once if you ever need us, Am'maiya." Bahlien said earnestly, bowing deeply to them both. "Rest is the best thing for you and, apart from your combat exercises, I suggest that you take the next few days easily."

"Oh, we will, I assure you. I feel rather crammed full of, of stuff, or power, but it's only very, very peculiar." Ethrayne wrinkled her nose as she struggled to find the words to describe who she felt. "Thank you, your Graces." And she curtsied as Jerryn bowed. "Good night." They both said that at the same time, as Jerryn handed his lady politely into the carriage, and they sank down, sighing, as the groom quickly shut the door and the carriage driver urged the horses into motion.

Nobody spoke much on their return to the palace and the night-shrouded, empty streets only served to emphasise the fact that the night was at least half over.

"You know, I'm heartily sick of stairs tonight." Marrand commented with a deep sigh as they ascended towards their private rooms, a while later. "My knees are waving a flag of surrender, good night, all of you." He kissed the ladies and shook the hands of the men, as they separated and headed off towards bed.

*

Ethrayne closed the door to the bedroom with relief, once Fionn and Sallie, wearing warm robes over their nightgowns, had helped her and Lyria into their own nightgowns and brushed and re-braided their long hair; the girls were dull-eyed and tousled from being woken up and she felt a little guilty at disturbing their rest, although she knew that it was not entirely her fault that it was so late. But she had ushered them back to their beds, Lyria as well, for she too longed to sleep, and to try and begin to make sense of all that had happened, hopefully in her dreams.

"Goodnight, Ethrayne." Lyria murmured, her eyes already closed, sighing deeply.

"Sleep tight, Lyria." She whispered.

The covers on her bed had been folded back neatly with the sheet at one corner and, in her opinion, it had never looked so appealing, it had been a *very* long day. She pulled the covers down and stared. There, in the centre of the sheet, in the centre of the bed, rested a folded piece of parchment. Ethrayne felt a sudden shiver of unease run down her spine as she leaned forward and picked it up; quietly she moved over to the fireplace, studying it in its low glow; the sheet was sealed shut with the honey shade of beeswax, pressed down with what looked like a thumb print. But who on Iullyn had left it here?

<Ethrayne?> She dimly heard Jerryn's voice inside her head, despite the distance between their rooms. *<Have you found a letter, perchance?>* His

outrage was clear, even so.

<*Yes.*> Ethrayne concentrated on sending her silent reply, unsure of how to succeed. It felt such a strange method of communicating, but also oddly natural. <*Just now, in my bed. Have you?*> As she thought the words, she broke the seal, opened it, and read:

> *'With this note, Lady Ethrayne, I can confirm that no part of your realm, nor any fortress that you may inhabit, is beyond the reach of either myself or my colleagues.*
>
> *'You need not fear for your safety, however. I have been commanded to only observe you and your prince and not to interfere. I wish you both well in your encounter with the Flame of Arven.*
>
> *'Do not doubt, however, that we will meet again soon.'*

<*That's what my note said.*> The prince said, his tone grim. <*But to find them right here, in our own bedrooms -.*>

<*I can feel your worries and mine are the same, Jerryn.*> Ethrayne confirmed. <*I dread to think how he crept in here, through the palace. Dear Arven, he could have killed our maids, or Karne!*> She shivered again and quickly scanned the clearly empty room, glad that Lyria already seemed almost asleep and unaware of her unease.

<*Well, he won't be hanging around here now.*> Jerryn's tone had turned sombre. He also was tired, she could tell. <*He'll be somewhere at a safe distance, watching us.*>

<*So damn him!*> Ethrayne snapped back, anger warring with her concerns and with tiredness. Decorum could go hang, at this time of night. <*It's probably nearly dawn, Jerryn; we'll discuss this tomorrow, agreed?*>

<*Agreed. And we will suggest an increase in security, as well. How* dare *he intrude and threaten us like this? . . . Sleep well, darling Ethrayne.*>

<*Sleep well, my prince.*> She sent back, smiling.

*

Across the city, the man known as Kesta had sensed some of what had occurred in the Cathedral complex, channelling the Flame of Arven to the young couple. He had shivered at the strength of it. He had been awed by it. Now, however, he smiled to himself: the prince and his lady surely must have discovered his letters by now and he hoped that they would take his warning to heart.

* * *

CHAPTER 7

After their very late night below the Cathedral, nobody was up early the next morning and both families, except the king and the duke, congregated to eat a leisurely late breakfast in the knowledge that they were, temporarily at least, excused duties. Jerryn, Ethrayne and Lyria said that they were going to go and play Stepping Stones with the Duchess, for Pualyn was to join the king and his father.

"We'll see you later, old friend." The prince said with a smirk, when the duke came to fetch the young man. "Your sister and I did far too much brain-storming last night, with everything that was happening, so now it's your turn."

"Thanks for that, Jerryn." Pualyn replied sarcastically, heading for the door with his father, who laughed a little. "See you later."

Marrand was sat in his private office with Lords Gorman and Ferman, both large men of late middle age; but whilst Lord Gorman was portly, with a jowly face and pepper-and-salt hair, Lord Ferman was still clearly a muscular, physical man who worked quite hard to combat the effects of his age. They sat one on either side of their king at a respectful distance and slightly behind him, both dressed in their smartest clothes, wearing their most forbidding expressions as the duke and his son and heir entered. As senior members of the Council, they were often intimately involved in important matters, alongside Duke Sarant, although they were not personally as close to their king as the duke.

"Sit down, sit down." The king urged them, smiling broadly. "I'm not sure that such late nights are for me, you know; I woke up ridiculously early, and my head feels as if it's been stuffed tight with wool, but I'm sure *you* feel sprightly, Pualyn. The gift of youth is so quickly missed." He grinned and his advisors both laughed briefly in agreement. "Now." He continued with the barest wink at Sarant, who was sat directly opposite him. "We require a special kind of envoy, Pualyn, to travel to Orbain in Mendor and liaise with those in the Protectorate Kingdoms who are apparently keen to ally themselves with Tenarum. We need someone well and broadly educated, and also flexible in attitude and beliefs, for they are rather different people to us, it seems. And since their rulers have been informed about the Prophecy concerning Jerryn and Ethrayne, and you yourself have been privy to all that has occurred, it is obvious to us that *you* would be ideal for the task."

Pualyn blinked, completely stunned. "M-me, your Majesty?" He asked, feeling as though he had been hit over the head with one of the hard, wooden swords in the combat hall. "I am greatly honoured, Sire, but, are you sure? I am not yet twenty-two -."

"Pualyn, I am fully aware that recent events seem to have pushed Ethrayne into the forefront of the court's attention." Sarant interrupted his son. "But you are my heir, and I must proudly acknowledge that you do have both the qualities and the knowledge that his Majesty is looking for."

"We trade with the Protectorates, and their merchant ships seem to reach every port in the kingdom, if not the entire continent, but we do not really know much about the razine themselves, beyond ancient legend, although they seem fine people." Lord Ferman said in a bombastic tone. "The kingdoms of the Mendor continent are extensive, inhabited by both men and razine, but they have largely kept themselves apart from us in diplomatic terms. His Majesty is correct in that your closeness to your sister and the prince, and even your youth will be central to opening the proper channels of communication: you are level-headed Pualyn, despite your age. We do not wish for war with the Betrayer, Arven forbid!" He shivered slightly. "Yet, if that were to happen, the razine and men of the Protectorate Kingdoms would probably make excellent allies and they do seem to have kept an eye on the enemy."

Pualyn could hear the scepticism in the older man's voice and he noted the frown on Lord Gorman's face; experience told him that such scepticism would not be suitable for any serious dealings with folk who had worked to protect their kingdoms and Arven's Flame for over eight hundred years. This, then, was why the king and his father wanted him to agree: they needed an envoy who *believed* in the Prophecy, one who supported the Wielders of the Flame, not one who would support the kingdom alone. After watching the golden fire eddying endlessly around his sister and Jerryn, early this morning, far beneath the Cathedral, he knew that he certainly believed. It would be impossible to deny the truth of what he had seen!

"I will do everything I can to fulfil your remit, your Majesty." He finally replied gravely. "I am honoured that you judge me capable of this important task."

"Excellent!" Marrand exclaimed, smiling broadly, but his smile faded a little after a moment and he sighed. "I appreciate that you will be loath to leave the lovely Lady Lyria, so the official announcement of your betrothal will be made later today, and we will hold the ceremony tomorrow evening. Unfortunately, events are progressing too swiftly for us to consider holding your wedding – for we have no way of ensuring that the Lord and Lady of Callorton can attend. Yet, as part of your fee for travelling so far, you may pick a suitable gift for your lady from the royal treasury."

"On behalf of, of my lady and myself, I am greatly honoured, your Majesty." Pualyn got to his feet and bowed formally.

"We will all be greatly in your debt, Pualyn for the future is most uncertain." The king replied. "You have four days to get packed before you will leave for Rothern by barge, for a razine ship will be awaiting you there at the port."

"Ex-archpriest Bahlien will, of course be able to give you the names of the razine royal family and other highly ranking individuals and I imagine that he will have communications of his own for you to convey." Duke Sarant continued with a smile. "It was he who told us about the razine ship heading to

our shores, by the by."

"Ah, that explains a great deal." Pualyn murmured and both his father and the king grinned broadly. Why was that not a surprise? He thought wryly.

"Go and speak with Lady Lyria, young man." Marrand said reprovingly. "I am sure that you and she will need to get used to your impending separation – whilst you must must review the suitability of your outfits at this sudden escalation of events. We will see you both at dinner, Lord Pualyn."

"At once, your Majesty, Father, my Lords. Thank you." Pualyn bowed to them all politely before hurrying from the room.

"The youth of today are far too frivolous." Lord Gorman declared, shaking his head.

"He is a steady young man." Lord Ferman countered firmly. "Lord Pualyn will do his Majesty and the kingdom proud."

*

The others were halfway through their second game when Pualyn arrived, slightly breathless and brim-full of mingled excitement and fear.

"Excuse me, Mother, may I ruin the game and please steal away Lyria?" He asked, taking the girl's hand in his, and bowing to her. "We won't be long, honestly -." And he helped her to her feet with a broad smile on his face without waiting for a reply from the duchess.

"Pualyn?" Lyria asked, but he said nothing as they left the room, quietly closing the door.

"What is going on?" Jerryn asked, then laughed aloud. "Do you think that we might have a second official betrothal on the way?"

"It might well be, I do hope so." Ethrayne said.

"Yes, as do I. It would be wonderful to have the four of you all safely married." Duchess Riyala confirmed, smiling.

"What is it, Pualyn?" Lyria asked, laughing, as he drew her along the broad corridor. "Your mother and I were beating Ethrayne and Jerryn, you know, and they make a really good team."

"Never mind the game, Lyria. I have just spoken with the king. He wants to send me as an envoy to the razine, but first he wants us betrothed. Tomorrow evening, in fact!"

"What? Oh, never! Really?" Lyria stuttered, stunned, as he lifted her up off her feet and spun her about in a circle, kissing her on both cheeks, then on her lips. "But, you said, *tomorrow*! Pualyn, oh, my! What shall I wear?"

"His Majesty thought you might want to discuss that with Ethrayne and mother, dear." Pualyn said, setting her down. "Shall we go and tell them?"

The reaction of his family was all that anyone could have wished and Pualyn and Lyria basked, just a little, at the centre of the entire court's attention; in fact, the young man realised that Jerryn and Ethrayne seemed pleased to relinquish that place as the women of the palace spent an inordinate amount of time running backwards and forwards with gowns and jewellery and ideas for hairstyles, so that Pualyn was quite content to sit back and watch his modest, shy, beautiful bride-to-be the absolute focus of the entire complex. The downside, of course, was that he would be leaving Tenum City so soon, although he could not deny that the thrill of the unknown was exciting.

At dinner that evening, Lyria and Pualyn were seated either side of the king and Marrand made the announcement of their betrothal in a ringing tone, to hearty cheers and applause throughout the hall.

Next morning, Duchess Riyala, Ethrayne and the other ladies continued their complex designs upon Lyria's wardrobe, whilst Pualyn was closeted with his father and ex-archpriest Bahlien from just after breakfast.

"Are my sister and Jerryn in real danger, then, your Grace?" Pualyn asked levelly. "They, they *absorbed*?" He made the word a question and Bahlien nodded slightly at its relevance. "They absorbed the Flame of Arven into themselves and all our teachings tell us that the Betrayer wishes to destroy our God . . . Will he try to destroy Ethrayne and Jerryn too? And will he try to take their power?" He shuddered and stared from Bahlien to his father. "They are so young!"

"There is that possibility, yes, in the future." Bahlien agreed seriously.

"Father!" Pualyn was aghast at that confirmation. It had been a shock to discover that that singular encounter which his sister had had with that stranger had been by design, yet this confirmation was far more alarming: they were both only sixteen!

"His Grace and ex-archpriest Bahlien have explained all of this to the Wielders of the Flame, the *Am'maiya*." His father stumbled slightly over the strange-sounding title, emphasising the odd name. "Ethrayne and Jerryn made a fully informed choice, Pualyn, and who are we to refuse prophecy, my son?"

"And that is why you are heading to Lerat in a few days, young man. You are the first vital contact in our endeavour to set up a united front against whatever the jajozeli-razine will send against us in the future." The ex-archpriest replied. "It will take some considerable time before the young couple can begin to command what they now possess; they have absorbed much of the power of our God into themselves and they must learn how to wield it. We certainly have time on our side for the knowledge to come to them."

"I hope so!" Pualyn muttered.

"Now, you will have heard rumours and old tales about razine 'magic'. I know it's a part of your folklore, as well as being mentioned in our liturgy. We call it 'power' sometimes or 'talent' when we refer to it. We razine have some abilities beyond those of humans: some predictive ability perhaps, being closer to hunches or intuition; some may be able to read the emotions of others, say; others have some healing talents, or can move objects from one place to another for it varies as greatly as, say, being good at drawing or mathematics or even hair or eye colour and also varies in strength: some people are very strong, and others are not."

<I'm quite powerful, probably because I have dedicated myself to Arven's service since those awful events in Car'Agasse, so long ago.> His voice continued but within Pualyn and Sarant's minds, echoing slightly it seemed, with a touch of humour clearly colouring his tone; flashes of pink and orange they thought, wondering how exactly speech could be colour as well as words. *<Ethrayne and Jerryn will probably find that these sorts of abilities will quickly make themselves known, and such skills will be invaluable.>*

"Great heavens! It's true!" Sarant murmured, his eyes wide. "Magic!"

"Heavens! To be able to hold entire conversations in complete silence? That would be amazing!" Pualyn stated, stunned. "My word!"

Bahlien grinned. "Yes, it has its uses. But I don't want you to feel inferior or less important, young man, not in any way! We are just a little different, after all, so don't let us intimidate you; you are talented as a politician, a rider of horses and a master of arms. You represent your king, his kingdom, your family and the Am'maiya: your sister and the prince." His tone was earnest; it seemed that his words were genuine.

"Very well, your Grace." He whispered, whilst feeling exactly that: inferior and very small.

"And don't forget that there are many thousands of humans living in the Razine Protectorates. Many more than there are razine. Orbain is the only mostly razine kingdom, with a razine ruler. We are not and never have been a sort of overlord class, not by any means. Humans command the other realms with their own kings within the whole, but by common consent we all look to the High-King, Mhezal, as our chief. He is the one who will formally assemble the armies of Mendor, should they be required."

"It seems a very enlightened form of government, your Grace." Duke Sarant commented approvingly. "It sounds rather like his Majesty's own council, except with kings attending."

"Yes. It was something that Arven himself encouraged, actually and it has worked very well for us all. I imagine that if the Betrayer had not acted that fateful day, we would all be dwelling together, even if thousands of leagues apart, in peace under our God's care." The old razine sighed deeply. "Ah well, one can dream." His tone had turned a little sad, but he managed a quirk of a smile. "Anyway, enough of that: you have a betrothal to prepare for, my Lord Pualyn. Shall we speak again tomorrow, at noon, say?" He asked politely.

"Of course, your Grace. I must say, this is all fascinating." Pualyn answered, rising politely as Bahlien stood and made his farewells.

"I am pleased you find it so, young man." The old razine answered, bowing slightly to them.

"He is a good man, razine, priest." Pualyn commented, once he and his father were alone, stumbling slightly over the proper description.

"Yes, I agree. Marrand and I believe that we can trust him, but never let your guard down, even so: not until we really know just what is going on." The duke replied. "Now, come along: you're in for a busy evening, young man."

*

Pualyn and Lyria's betrothal ceremony was accompanied by a hastily arranged banquet and lots of dancing, but it was noticeably less formal in tone than Jerryn and Ethrayne's evening of feasting had been, and the prince and his lady enjoyed it much more than they had their own glittering party, sat together out of the way, enjoying the music and trying to ignore Lyria's attempts to make them both dance and failing cheerfully.

It was a pleasant evening, all in all, although Pualyn would be leaving Tenum in a few days; the betrothed couple felt that separation looming over them and their smiles and laughter were a little forced for they were trying their utmost to act as any happy young couple would. Not all members of the court were yet aware of the young lord's impending mission to a far, foreign land. Lyria glowed as never before in amethyst silk, expertly embroidered and swiftly altered, to be enhanced with exquisite jewellery consisting of beautifully cut, graduated, glowing amethysts set in white gold, consisting of a deceptively simple tiara, drop earrings and choker: the jewellery chosen from King Marrand's treasury, gleaming in the lamplight, whilst her betrothed wore deep blue.

Many of the assembled, especially those who had not deigned to acknowledge the young woman before when she had been merely the duchess's lady in waiting, after all, sighed and remarked favourably on her beauty and her attributes, now that her betrothal to the heir of Clirensar was official and she had been 'noticed' by the king. It was entirely vacuous.

Listening to some of the compliments paid and invitations planned, Ethrayne sighed inwardly and kept her face neutral. *<Ridiculous!>* She remarked silently, and Jerryn grinned.

<But of course, my love.> He agreed. *<These people are of very little importance -.>*

<But they believe that they are, and they run around the palace like mice, sticking their noses into everything and getting in the way of all the folk who really do the work!> Ethrayne smiled wickedly. *<Squeaking.>*

It was strange, finding that she now shared her mind with Jerryn, at some general level; personal privacy was assured, of course at a deeper point inside, but the 'upper' parts of their thoughts were now freely shared between them. It would take some getting used to and Ethrayne realised that they were both lucky, in that they were close friends and had been since childhood; exploring this new ability would be quite challenging enough, apart from any other matters! She imaged it could be very embarrassing.

<Oh, don't -.> Jerryn broke off his silent words and covered a burst of laughter with a coughing fit at her description.

<I'm sorry.> Ethrayne said quickly, trying to keep her own amusement under control. *<Oh, don't they both look lovely?>*

<They're a fine couple, but Lyria will never be as beautiful as you are in my eyes.>

Ethrayne found that she could not reply to that but knowing that Jerryn could read her surface thoughts as easily as she could was slowly becoming a little less of a worry, a little more natural. Then they were both distracted by the music of the orchestra and finally joined the dancing, in complementing pearl grey and deep green.

*

The next day was a whirlwind of activity, mostly consisting of endless lists to be ticked off, in addition to an inordinate amount of packing to be done. Pualyn could only gaze on in amazement as his own clothing and accoutrements were added to by the king, Lord Ferman and his father; and Bahlien also added items. The number of bags and boxes grew, as if breeding quietly when no one was watching. The duchess proved invaluable, he discovered, as she had a wealth of experience and advice on how to pack properly and safely that no one except her husband had ever known of.

There was an official surcoat, the material thick and stiff with intricate embroidery, delineating the king's device on midnight blue velvet; smart clothes; new clothes; travelling clothes; various boots and shoes; his mail shirt and other gear for combat practice; hose, socks and underclothes, a number of cloaks; there was also an empty leather-bound book for him to use as an official journal, with a silver inkwell and a number of quills stored safely in a handsome box. Pualyn would also bear a few small tasteful gifts from King Marrand to the High-King of the razine and some missives from the ex-archpriest in addition to a set of scrolls titled 'A History of Iullyn', for his own perusal.

"Well, I'm going to need a herd of horses just to get me down to the wharves." Pualyn joked as he finally felt able to leave his rooms, once most of his possessions had been packed, with an increasingly quiet Lyria at his side. She had begun the day laughing as she helped with the piling and packing, directed by his mother, but her mood had changed as the sun had moved relentlessly westward and, now, she looked rather sad. "Oh, Lyria, I'm going to miss you so much!"

"I am going to miss you. Oh, take care of yourself, Pualyn, do!" And she threw herself into his arms with an uncharacteristic recklessness. "I love you so much!"

This admission bolstered the young man's courage: he would prove his worth to his love by undertaking this task resolutely, relishing this step into the unknown. Gently he kissed her. "I love you too, Lyria, with all my heart and soul." He said quietly, for a couple of servants and their guards were watching their exchange with great interest. "I hope I won't be away for too long and I promise that I will write to you when I can . . . But I must admit that this chance to travel is exciting." A smile made his eyes sparkle. "Come on, my love, let's join the others for dinner."

"Yes, let's do that, I bet you're hungry, aren't you?"

"Gosh, I am. Why are you laughing, Lyria?"

"You've hardly eaten all day, Pualyn. You've been fretting over your packing since breakfast."

"Well you try and arrange that lot sensibly and quickly, Lyria." He complained.

*

Ethrayne enjoyed the fact that her oh-so-modest friend and companion had been thrust right into the very heart of the court, for as the youngest child of a rather poor, minor lord, such notice had been lacking, until now. Even the daughter of a close friend of her parents counted for nothing in the heady atmosphere of the palace, yet her friend had handled the situation with admirable dignity and ability, even to the surprise of her betrothed's impending departure.

Because of this hurried rush and its associated near chaos, neither she nor Jerryn had told even Bahlien about the notes left in their beds. Strangely, they believed what their enemy had written, and found that his terse words were made clearer as they considered what Bahlien had explained about their history: that war had engulfed Iullyn in the past, might engulf the world again; but as the enemy razine were hardly about to act, why worry everyone else unnecessarily? They had burned the notes to pale ash and Ethrayne was resolved to excel at her sessions with the bulky wooden sword, the shorter wooden knife and now the hand-to-hand combat which filled her mornings.

Most lessons were conducted with Jerryn as her opponent, or the very correct Private Tymain, explaining some detail or mistake respectfully and clearly; sometimes, Commander Vedeigne or one of the other officers took a hand. It was not at all an easy concept to learn at first, fighting; she must learn how to fall properly, how to balance herself safely and how use her own strength as she had never done before, except when riding horses. It was awful, in one regard, knowing that she was learning how to become proficient at the mechanics of killing an enemy, a fellow human or razine. The enemy stranger's foray into the palace, brazenly walking into their bedrooms, did serve, however, as an excellent focus.

She contemplated this as she toyed with her dinner that evening in the dining hall, on the eve of her brother's departure. She and Jerryn were near the centre of the top table and the ex-archpriest was sat to their left at the end, beside Archpriest Lurco.

<Something is troubling you, my dear Lady Ethrayne.> Bahlien said very quietly in her mind, and he smiled as she started, hearing his voice. *<The prince and you have been brooding over something for a few days now; may I be so bold as to ask what is concerning you? Perhaps I may be able to help?>*

The girl glanced across at Jerryn and wondered if she looked as foolish and guilty as her betrothed now did. *<You can read our minds?>* He asked bluntly.

<Well, I could, but it would be considered exceedingly rude, the height or depths of bad manners, to do so.> The old razine assured them. *<I have felt*

that you have concerns, but you do not have to tell me anything, honestly.>

<Thank you, your Grace . . . this is all so new to us, I imagine that we are making heaps of mistakes.> Ethrayne communicated with a quick grimace. *<We feel like young children, faced with this strange ability. But we did not want to worry you, or our families.>* She broke off, the tone and feel of her mind somehow a little darker. *<They have been worried enough, faced with all this newness and they just wouldn't understand.>* She shrugged slightly. *<They are dealing with quite enough.>*

<When we returned from the Cathedral so late, with the Flame, we both found, separately -.> Jerryn emphasised that point rather defensively. *<Sealed letters in our beds, under the covers, from* him*: the-the jajozeli-razine. It said, 'I can confirm that no part of your realm, nor any fortress that you inhabit, is beyond the reach of either myself or my colleagues. You need not fear for your safety, however. I have been commanded only to observe you and your lady, and not to interfere. I wish you both well in your encounter with the Flame of Arven. Do not doubt, however, that we will meet again.'>*

<That damned arrogant bastard!>

They felt Bahlien's blast of anger almost like a blow that just missed contact, strong in their heads and he quickly and contritely apologised for a series of graphic curses as the two young people struggled to master and control both their shock and their laughter; feeling such emotions so clearly was utterly peculiar and they would never have expected the venerable former Archpriest to descend to such coarseness.

<I knew we should have kept it to ourselves, Jerryn.> Ethrayne thought rather weakly, a napkin clutched to her mouth as she fought that burst of laughter. *<Oh, my word!>*

<I sincerely apologise. Honestly, I should not actually even be surprised at our enemy's audaciousness, but -.> He shook his head. *<May he be struck by lightning! There is nothing I can say to fully express my shock and anger, but, well, he has done all that he wanted: he has startled us severely and he has frightened us, but are we going to jump at shadows?>* Bahlien's mental tone was cold, and he shook his head.

<Like hell we will!> Jerryn growled. *<Our world is turning upside down, but they won't defeat us by scaring us, your Grace! And our security has been tightened. I just hope it will be enough.>*

*

Breakfast for the Terarean Royal Envoy, his family and that of King Marrand was arranged for early the next morning; the royal barge would set off downstream almost as soon as Pualyn, his valet Lennarn, and their baggage were loaded.

"Have you ever travelled by sea, Pualyn?" Marrand asked with a smile. The young man was rather pale and quiet. "We both did in our youth, your father, my father the king and I, from Rothern to Saremouth, one summer. It was rather interesting."

Sarant grinned at his drawling tone. “There was a huge storm which hit the ship, I still remember it, oh, dear Arven!” He laughed aloud. “I think even the captain was ill, for your father was, wasn’t he, Marrand?”

“Oh yes.” Marrand essayed a huge shudder. “But that was a bad storm; you’ll be fine, Pualyn, you’re a lot more sensible than we were. I think part of your father’s and my problem was that wine we drank.”

“Sarant!” Duchess Riyala exclaimed with fake horror. “Oh, you didn’t!” And she laughed merrily. “You wouldn’t think it to look at them now, but they were both quite reckless youths, you know!”

“Pualyn’s far too sensible to sink most of a wineskin in one sitting, as we did.” Sarant said with high dignity, winking at Lyria and Ethrayne as he shook his head at his wife. “And I’ll thank you not to tell tales to the children, dearest.” Everyone chuckled at that and the tension was lessened for a short time.

“Now, are you sure that you have packed everything?” King Marrand asked seriously.

“Yes, your Majesty and Master Lennarn has made me check for a third time this morning.” Pualyn replied, grinning at his valet with a wicked gleam in his eyes. “I’ve got money, the signet ring, oh, everything.” He patted his jerkin.

“Please take care, Pualyn; you will, won’t you?” Lyria asked in a subdued tone, pushing her breakfast plate aside almost untouched. “I know that you’re going to have a wonderful adventure, yet, oh dear -.”

“I promise you that I will be most careful, dearest Lyria.” The young lord replied earnestly, taking both her hands in his and leaning forward to lightly kiss her on the nose. “Oh, gosh!” He straightened, his eyes shining still, excitement clear throughout his body and demeanour. “I’ve never felt like this: I’m so scared, yet so excited, I can’t tell which is strongest. I will keep that journal daily and I will write when I can. Oh, my!” He gulped as the door opened and Lord Ferman came in, smiling.

“All the luggage is on board the barge, Lord Pualyn and the horses are saddled and awaiting you in the courtyard.” He reported with a bow to them all. “My word, young man, part of me really is envious of you at this moment: few people have travelled officially to the Protectorates in the last century or so, except priests, I suppose. I urge you to make the most of your time there, please; such experiences will enrich your whole life.”

“I will Lord Ferman and thank you.” It was a general thank you to everyone in the room. “I promise that I will conduct myself properly, your Majesty, Mother and Lyria.” He assured the three whom would worry most and bowed deeply as he rose to his feet, glancing across at Lennarn. “Are you ready, Master Lennarn?”

“Yes, my Lord. Shall we go?” His valet moved politely to the door along with Lord Ferman, as Pualyn shook hands and kissed his family farewell, enveloping Lyria in a bear-hug and then spinning her around, kissing her soundly and repeatedly before setting her down and picking up his long travelling cloak. The two young men departed with a final bow, their footfalls loud as they set off down the corridor.

*

As master of the royal barge, the Tenarean Crown, Captain Zecherry was quietly resigned to, generally, having to wait for his passengers to deign to arrive and he was quietly relieved that Lord Pualyn, his man and the guards accompanying them to the wharf were free of hangers-on; and early. Even the city streets had been relatively quiet and the soldiers on duty at the Wharf Gate had cleared the normal dock traffic at their approach.

With little more than a wave of thanks to Captain Nash of the Palace Guard who would return their horses to the stables, the two young men boarded by the obligatory bouncing plank, as the crew almost simultaneously cast off and even before they could speak to the tall man in charge of the tiller, the oars below were moving steadily into the dark water and the fifty-foot craft was moving smoothly out of the wharves and into the deceptively slow-looking current in the centre of the river that coiled around the south side of the city. They shot under the South Gate Bridge, passed the narrow mouth of the river Ayne and turned east to face the fresh, bright sun in what seemed like moments. Pualyn and Lennarn stood at the rail, out of the way, gazing back at the jumble of their capital city, catching glimpses through the rooftops of the towers of the palace and then the great rooftops and bell tower of the cathedral, now receding rapidly as the barge moved downstream.

"Well, that's that, my Lord: we're off and we should make Rothern in three days. Shall I show you your cabin?" The Captain said with a friendly smile and a bow, now that they had left the danger of the city waters. "I am Captain Zecherry. All your gear is stowed safely, and you're guaranteed a smooth trip to the coast."

"Thank you, Captain. I'm Pualyn, this is Lennarn. Please direct us, I admit that neither of us know anything at all about boats or sailing, so we don't want to get in your way." Pualyn answered with a nod of his head. "This is a lovely craft."

"Aye, commissioned by his Majesty's father; we keep her in tip-top condition for his majesty and the court's use. Please come this way."

*

Their journey downstream was indeed swift and smooth, the broad river's current augmented by the twenty oarsmen sweating through the day. Pualyn had been placed in the royal cabin, which was much larger than expected and opulent with gold leaf and well carved wood, a well-lit space for travelling. The two young men spent a lot of the next few days standing or sitting on deck watching the land that seemed to slip swiftly by, a whole new view of the world.

It was not yet mid-morning on the third day since they had left Tenum City when the Tenarean Crown approached the massive, bustling wharves of the port city of Rothern, that seemed to eat back into the land, although the width of the estuary made the actual demarcation between land and water most unclear. The barge was making slow headway, dodging the throng of traffic from tiny boats to laden craft twice its size and actual sea-worthy fishing boats on the river, making for the Royal Dock set aside for official travellers at the western edge of the city.

"Commander Vedeigne said that you were awaiting a foreign ship, my Lord?" Captain Zecherry asked politely. "If you give me the name, I'll send a man to inform them that you've arrived, which should save you traipsing across to the wharves and back." He grinned, as he expertly guided the craft towards the stone wharf. "I know you get expenses on the king's business, but Lord Ferman makes every penny squeak, they say. Tie up, Lorn!" He yelled, casting out one of the thick ropes towards the man who had leapt onto the dock.

"Thank you, Captain. The ship is the Lerat Pearl, but that's all I know." Pualyn answered and looked about with interest. "You know, I've not been here since I was child, so my memories will not be much use in getting us about. Have you, Lennarn?"

"I know the Golden Anchor, my Lord, but not the wharves." The other man admitted. "I had forgotten how vast the docks are here in Rothern. I will appropriate a porter ready for when we need to move our bags: there's far too much luggage for us to carry." He grinned.

"That's a good idea." Pualyn approved, gazing out across the surprisingly clean water, dark and opaque, for the day was cloudy. He could smell sewage, smoke and salt, along with spices and myriad other scents; some were pleasant, some not, but this was what he remembered about Rothern and Saremouth to the south: the melting pot of the docks, where land and sea merged, handling and trading goods from all around the known world. Excitement filled him, driving out the nervousness at the vast tracts of ignorance that he knew filled him, especially regarding the razine and the whole strange business surrounding his sister and the prince. He hoped that he would soon be filled with knowledge and smiled to himself at the thought, before going to help the respectful crewmen moving his and Lennarn's baggage to the deck, ignoring the captain's protests with a wave of his hand and a grin, continuing until Lennarn returned with some rather shabbily dressed porters.

"It's good seeing you doing some real work, my Lord." He said with mock seriousness.

"Thanks, Lennarn."

Pualyn and Lennarn were enjoying a small glass of wine and a nice lunch, courtesy of Captain Zecherry, once the crew had been dismissed for the rest of the afternoon, sat at the cheaper yet still presentable Kings Arms on the landward side of the wharves when the first mate, Lorn, entered the dining room with a stranger with him.

He was around six-and-a-half feet tall, with a muscular build that denoted a high level of fitness and a gait that spoke of years of combat training.

He had short, wavy, dark brown hair, a slight tan to his skin, and pleasant features: large, almond-shaped eyes; a slightly bent, long nose and high cheekbones, plus a wide-lipped mouth that smiled, matching the shine in his long-lashed, dark eyes. He wore a plain linen shirt embroidered in grey and green about the collar, black leather leggings and boots; there was a long broadsword at his hips.

"Ah, you must be Lord Pualyn of Clirensar, Captain Zecherry and Master Lennarn." The stranger said with a low bow, to their astonishment. He spoke perfect selithian with a slight accent. "We are pleased that you are here in such excellent time. My name is Kerrenan, from the Lerat Pearl. Please, don't get up gentlemen, do carry on eating, I know that a good lunch should not be rushed: I'll just join you, if I may? Then, we will get you over to the Pearl."

* * *

CHAPTER 8

Days turned into a moon; her life quickly returned to a familiar pattern, yet Ethrayne could not deny that it was one completely different to how her life had been before her betrothal to Jerryn. That one event, so formal, formed a sizeable rift, a break, between old and new. Early mornings now were devoted almost completely to combat training; then there were Council meetings, or else instruction in economics or the intricacies of law, delivered by Lord Ferman; then, after a light luncheon she often spent some time with her parents and Lyria, if she and Jerryn were not meeting with Lurco and Bahlien. There hardly seemed to be any remaining time, now, for those traditional and previously familiar feminine tasks of embroidery and tapestry making and she smiled, recalling her fear of those 'golden chains' that had seemed to be wrapping about her, so stifling.

Of course, despite her shared and exalted status of Wielder of the Flame, much was still the same, regardless: the older men of the court and some of the younger ones, as well, were still set against her learning how to use weapons, despite the approval of the king, the Archpriests, both active and retired, and her own family.

It was peculiar, Ethrayne considered. As well as learning about this unique, peculiar power, she was becoming daily more practised at the noble arts of diplomacy and politics and, most especially, at keeping a dignified silence and smiling, no matter the sort of semi-polite jibe or veiled insult thrown her way at gatherings or mealtimes.

<*Don't listen to them, they know nothing, my love.*> Jerryn said silently to her, after another rather barbed, criticism-filled dinner. <*Their only defence is ignorance for they just can't get their minds around the role which the Archpriests passed to us . . . not that I'm finding it very easy myself.*> He joked.

<*I suppose you are right, Jerryn.*> The young woman conceded. <*I imagine that we really ought to behave better than they, if only to show that we are – worthy? of this honour and the responsibility that goes with it . . . But I can't help worrying more than a little about the enemy: that man lurking around, the Betrayer. . .* > Her tone faded into silence and they both considered those innocent yet menacing notes that had been left in their beds.

<*Yes, it's strange, knowing that we might be the catalyst for great change, even war.*> Jerryn's doubt was clear. <*Frightening, too.*>

<*Very. Well, I don't care what the fools think: everyone who matters has approved my training and, I must say, I'm certainly finding it easier to get to sleep nowadays.*>

Jerryn laughed. <*You must be the stongest noblewoman in Selith, Ethrayne . . . I wish I could sleep soundly. I find myself fretting about Pualyn, amongst other things.*>

But he had clearly forgotten that his surface thoughts were no longer private, and Ethrayne could sense and read his fears: for Pualyn, setting off into the unknown; for herself, having to learn something so dangerous as weapons-craft, let alone ever having to wield a sword or whatever in earnest; for his father and the realm in general, facing potential war against the jajozeli empire . . . As Bahlien had said, they were, in a way, staring down into an abyss.

<We can only do our best, Jerryn, as with everything we may face in the future.> Ethrayne answered stoutly to those comprehensive fears.

*

Reports began to trickle up to the garrisons and then slowly coalesced towards the Council table. Reports of strange ships seen offshore to the south of Saremouth; of acts of piracy against Tenarean vessels; but it was some time before these rumours could be confirmed as fact, despite the details of the letter sent by the razine, Kerrenan and delivered by Captain Zecherry on his return from Rothern. Pualyn's letters to Lyria, of course, were private.

Addressed to King Marrand and ostensibly signed by the razine High-King of Orbain, Mhezal, this offered the usual polite felicitations and diplomatic greetings, but these were followed by a rather worrying paragraph detailing the possibility of incursions by the Betrayer's forces, especially off the coast of Tenarum. The High-King then declared that the ships of the Protectorates might also be espied out to sea, as well as coming in to port to trade; these ships would always identify themselves with crimson and blue pennons and would deal directly with any piracy by the Jajozeli without mercy, when they could intervene.

"Well, it's good to know that we have allies." King Marrand said doubtfully at the next Council meeting.

"Allies we know nothing about!" Lord Gorman grunted.

"You know that that is not so, my Lord." Jerryn countered mildly. "We have not had much official contact with them, but we have traded with them for years; we all worship Arven and, obviously, Archpriest Lurco and his predecessors have maintained close links with their counterparts in the Protectorates. I must say, I envy Pualyn his opportunity to visit such an unfamiliar part of the world."

"Well yes, you are correct, your Highness." Gorman conceded, but perhaps a little reluctantly. "But they are different -."

"We are all different, Gorman." Duke Sarant said with a laugh. "As his Highness says, we have always had trading links with the realms of the Protectorates, don't forget. They trade for the wines of Rothern and the iron and steel shipped downstream to Saremouth, bringing many items in exchange as you know. I've never heard of any trouble with any of them."

"Trade notwithstanding, we need to alert our garrisons and the ports both large and small." The king said gravely. "There are descriptions and drawings here of the enemy ships and their pennons, as well as those of our allies. We'll put together an announcement to be disseminated along all settlements along the coasts and rivermouths, requesting that any news be sent to the local garrison or town officials so that it can be collated when it is delivered here to the palace." He pointed down to the tabletop. "Security is vital, across the realm."

"Perhaps we could utilise the old beacons in case of emergencies, your Majesty?" Lady Celia suggested tentatively. "I know there is one above Pellerton Court and another on the ridge above Oldene; you can see one from the other quite clearly, depending on the weather. I am sure that my father told me that they were used when he was young, as warnings when there was a terrible storm and some ships were wrecked."

"Brilliant!" Earl Bennard exclaimed, and the young woman blushed slightly at his approval. "Should've thought of that myself, very good, Madam.

"We all should have, my Lord." Marrand sighed. "The manning and stocking of combustibles at the beacon sites has certainly dropped off in recent decades, I admit, but they span the entire realm. See to it that they are readied and that soldiers are detailed to man them in sequence, the usual arrangements made."

"Your Majesty." Various members of the Council agreed, some scribbling on parchment.

"Is there a beacon near Tenum?" Ethrayne asked Jerryn quietly. "I know there's one north-east of Clirensar, above Black Fell."

"We'll go for a ride with the court and some soldiers on our next free day, Ethrayne and I'll show you one or more; that is, if we're allowed. I think they'd be overgrown these days." The prince replied with a smile, then he shrugged. "If they were lit, it would speed up our response, certainly."

*

"I'll be taking you off your regular duties, young man." Commander Vedeigne said to the young soldier whom he had called to his office, set between the main barracks and the kitchen store rooms on the lower ground floor of the northern range of service buildings. It wasn't spacious, but it had a window looking out over the courtyard, towards the stables, if one stretched upwards. It was just afternoon, after another early practice session with Lady Ethrayne, Prince Jerryn and Captain Garane, then a period of guard duty on the main gates. He had been relieved by Private Murne a short time before.

"I beg your pardon, sir?" Tymain asked, stunned, a sudden, terrible fear filling him which was based on nothing logical at all: that he was going to be ejected from the job that he had always longed to undertake, ever since he had been a young boy, years before his father had died.

"No, lad, calm yourself." Vedeigne flashed him a grin as he shook his head reprovingly. "His majesty has become aware that you have been pivotal in instructing Lady Ethrayne and Prince Jerryn recently. You've earned yourself a promotion. Congratulations, Corporal Tymain."

"I, well, thank you, sir!" The stunned expression on his face remained, but a very foolish grin was spreading over it. "I -." He stopped there, guessing that he was now starting to sound stupid, stuttering like that.

"Events since Lady Ethrayne and Prince Jerryn's betrothal have been tumultuous and you have matured admirably, from a youth who completely irrationally and ridiculously seemed to hate the prince, to a man willing to see the wider connotations of all that has occurred. You know what's been happening here in Tenum City?"

Tymain frowned and rubbed at his chin with one hand. "Concerning the man who accosted Lady Ethrayne that day? It was very strange, sir, as if he knew we would ride that way: he was certainly waiting for her in that orchard; and to tell you the truth, sir, some how he felt . . . peculiar. I've had that same slight feeling a few times since then round about the city. I'm not sure if that man's lurking about still, watching the palace, perhaps watching the, the Am'maiya." His tone was stern as he thought about it, someone who might be an enemy, loose in the city. "The prince and his lady are the Wielders of the Flame, Commander. They represent Arven, whilst these others are a threat to everyone."

"But doesn't that sound overly mystical for a soldier and a lad who grew up in Riverside? And what on Iullyn do you mean by '*he felt peculiar*'?" The Commander asked rather testily, as if such feelings were hardly important in the real world.

Tymain moved slightly; he had meant to shrug but then decided against it, considering it unprofessional. "It doesn't matter where we were born, sir, but what we make of our lives. Arven is our god. We all have heard that prophecy, sir. His highness and Lady Ethrayne are his servants at some level, as are the priests and priestesses who guide us. Perhaps we are destined to live in interesting times, though the Betrayer is not the sort of opponent one would choose to face. And there was that man in the inn, some days later. He did feel . . . strange, for a moment. I can't -." He struggled to find the words to describe it, for he wasn't even sure what he was trying to define. "I could feel some sort of difference in him, in my head. It faded very quickly, but my disagreement with Calle knocked it out of my mind. Actually, I feel something similar but much less threatening from Archpriest Bahlien." He admitted.

"That is very interesting. A few other soldiers have had odd reactions to the archpriest." The Commander said, to Tymain's surprise and shook his head. "So, Corporal, you have faith enough to stand up with Prince Jerryn and Lady Ethrayne against the Betrayer?"

"Yes sir, I hope I would prove strong enough. I was young and stupid, before the Am'maiyas' betrothal; and I was also most stupid when I took exception to Calle's snide comments on our evening off. I regret it, sir. But, I must admit I've completely changed my position and my view of the world from what it was before the betrothal of the prince and his lady."

"Good to hear it. You will be part of the young couple's guard, Tymain, reporting to Captain Garane. You will work with Antan, Ferle and Murne, to begin with. Between you, you will work out a sensible system of guarding the

Wielders of the Flame and when the rota is organised, I will present it to his Majesty. I still want regular training for you all, not just for the prince and his lady." Vedeigne frowned, gazing down at a piece of parchment before him. "Go and report to Captain Garane immediately and I suggest you get rid of that stupid grin, Tymain, before someone trips you up along the corridor."

"Yes sir, thank you, sir." Tymain saluted smartly, turned and marched out of the office, trying to remove the smile from his face but failing dismally.

His friends and colleagues reacted predictably to the announcement, but the young man did his best to live up to the commander's faith in him and refused to rise to the baiting they subjected him to. Tymain still felt embarrassed at attacking his old comrade like that, taking insult where none had been intended.

Truth to tell, however, the guards and soldiers generally were rather impressed by Lady Ethrayne's dedication to her training regime and even more so by the news that she and Prince Jerryn were the Wielders of the Flame of Arven. Soldiers generally were a religiously minded group, due to the risks inherent in their chosen profession and to discover that they had two visible focuses of their god right there before them was somehow heartening as well as awe-inspiring.

*

The new Flame Guard, as the group of soldiers quickly became known, expanded by Don and Nate's appointment to their ranks, began to seem quite ordinary as a job after half a moon, even after taking delivery of newly designed surcoats which had been hand-stitched in part by Duchess Riyala and the ladies Ethrayne, Lyria and Celia, along with Fionn and Sallie's expert touch. In truth, Ethrayne had not done an awful lot of the embroidery due to her other commitments, but she had sat with her family, chatting and sewing when she could, for such occupation never detracted from a good conversation. Two of the guards were always assigned to accompany both Jerryn and herself, from when they left their rooms to bedtime, their duties augmented by the ordinary Palace Guard as required.

"So, what do you think of your new roles and responsibilities, my dear?" Duke Sarant asked seriously, although there was a twinkle in his eyes. "Was it only just over a moon ago that you were feeling sorry for yourself at being somehow figuratively imprisoned, never to leave the palace again?" Her parents both laughed at his gentle teasing.

"That's not fair, Father, throwing my words back at me." Ethrayne complained, pretending to cover her face with embarrassment and chuckling. "Oh, wasn't I childish?"

"No, not at all, Ethie." Her mother said cheerfully. "We always have known that the world favours men and highborn women lead very constrained lives. But who could ever have imagined that our world would change so, so completely?"

"It has changed so quickly, too." Lyria added with a sigh.

"For certain, Lyria, it has." Ethrayne agreed with a smile, briefly clasping her friend's hand. "Pualyn has been sent right across the ocean to the Razine Protectorates as Royal Envoy and Jerryn and I have become, oh I don't know, some sort of figurehead for the followers of Arven."

"Is that how you see yourself, Ethrayne dearest, as a figurehead?" Her mother asked intently, worry suddenly apparent on her face. "It has all been rushed, certainly, to my mind. But that ceremony at the Cathedral seemed a great deal more serious and formal to me than just you and dear Jerryn becoming figureheads."

Ethrayne exchanged a sober glance with her father. The sort of look, she realised with a sudden brief chill, that men usually exchanged when faced with questions from women; questions that they were generally most reluctant to answer fully.

"Yes, Mother, I also think that it is more serious." She stated quietly. "Apparently, the servants of the Betrayer might be out there, watching us." She gestured with a sweep of her hand. "There might well be a war against the Jajozeli starting in the future. And that's why Archpriest Bahlien wanted Pualyn to go to the Protectorates as our Envoy."

"Sarant! You didn't tell me this." The Duchess exclaimed, shocked. "War! Oh, great heavens, no!"

"My dear Riyala, nothing is certain in life. The razine ex-archpriest wanted to ensure that we are prepared, that's really all that's happened." Sarant said, trying to soothe his wife.

"The ceremony there below the Cathedral was not symbolic, you see, Mother, Father." Ethrayne finally decided to tell them. "Jerryn and I really do hold the Flame of Arven inside us and I have a feeling that we are going to change in a great many ways. In fact, I think we *are* changing already. The problem is that he, the Betrayer, tried to destroy our God at Car'Agasse and succeeded in stealing a lot of his strength. Bahlien and the other priests hid the casket, but the Betrayer has always wanted the power it contained for himself. There was a stranger lurking around the city, watching us, you realise: the man who spoke to me on our ride. He was one of the Betrayer's servants -."

"What?" Riyala almost screeched this, abandoning her usual poise and elegance. "Ethrayne! Darling, I -."

"But this is our destiny, Mother, mine and Jerryn's. At some point we will have to face them." She continued to explain, surprised at her own sense of calm.

"Aren't you scared, Ethrayne?" Lyria asked.

Ethrayne thought for a moment. "Yes and no, but I expect actual war will frighten me into fits; it's all very well, learning how to use a sword or knife or bow, but to know that I really might have to stick them hard and lethally into an enemy?" She shrugged. "I suppose I won't know until that moment comes. What we do know is that the Betrayer has always yearned for the Flame and since *we* now hold it, Jerryn and I, his forces may well concentrate on us."

"Said as honestly and true as any young soldier could." Sarant said approvingly. "My word, Ethie, I am very proud of you."

"You are not alone in your admiration, your Grace." Jerryn added unexpectedly, sticking his head around the door. "Excuse me, but I couldn't help overhearing you -."

"As if you need to listen at doors, your Highness." Ethrayne said with false shock. "Why didn't you just come in?"

"Jerryn, my dear, is Ethrayne correct in what she said?" Riyala asked him almost imploringly, clearly hoping for him to refute her words.

"Yes, pretty much, your Grace, I am sorry. But we didn't really know how to tell you this, you see. Bahlien said that the words would come to us in time, however and it seems that he was right yet again." The prince sat down on an empty chair, his tone slightly contrite.

"I'm going to have words with that duplicitous priest!" The duchess muttered with heat.

"No, Mother, please don't, he is also doing what he must; Bahlien isn't here by chance any more than we are. Please. I suppose that it would be rather difficult, doing what he has? How do you tell people that they will spend their lives fulfilling some ancient prophecy without being laughed out of town? It sounds so silly, doesn't it?" Ethrayne said with a wry smile. "Can you imagine how awkward it must have been to work out just how to tell us all of this?" She waved her hands expressively. "So, you have explained matters to your father also, Jerryn? I hope he is not too cross with us."

The prince sighed but offered a shrug and a brief flash of a grin. "No. I believe that Bahlien's words with father and his Grace here has made our fathers seriously consider matters such as the realm's security since we were there below the Cathedral."

"We have suspected something such as you suggest, Ethrayne, my dear." The Duke answered easily. "It was Bahlien's request to send someone sympathetic to you both as Envoy that alerted us. It seems that we will indeed see interesting times ahead, but I'm not really sure that I'm looking forward to them."

"Amen to that, my dear." Riyala said intently and suddenly embraced her daughter tightly. "You must take care, Ethrayne!" She commanded.

"Yes, Mother." The girl answered levelly. "I will, I promise."

*

Kesta had watched as Pualyn set off for the coast on the royal barge and had smiled at the young man's obvious enthusiasm and excitement. The razine of the Protectorates could try to interfere all they liked, but his Master had had his plans set up and ready to implement for over two years, after decades of work; and everyone involved would be in place ahead of time, poised. Bahlien, the old fool, was circumscribed by custom, politics and the proprieties involved between allies, whilst his master commanded an empire.

His time in Tenum City was coming to an end, however: he had received orders to head elsewhere but, for those such as himself, the order was rather fluid: he had a mocn or so to reach his destination.

Prowling around the palace compound, in far more disguises than his contact here could have imaged possible, he had noted the creation of the Flame Guard as an entity within the palace guard and he had listened to far too many conversations conducted by brainless sycophants. He had even been able to watch one of the girl's practice sessions, for his contact had shown him a storeroom and he had lingered there, cramped, amongst boxes and supplies, his strength pulled inward and so pretty-much undetectable, watching almost invisibly that early morning. The young woman's technique was terrible, but he acknowledged that she had been training for only a moon and she *did* show some degree of promise. As a professional himself, he thought that she certainly had a great deal of determination, for a girl who had never held any form of weapon before in her life, probably fully expecting a continuation of her life of idleness and tedium before becoming the prince's bride. He wondered if she might even be enjoying the challenge thrust her way so unexpectedly. He didn't believe the women of his own family would have been up to the challenge presented to her, not that such ability was generally required of females of any rank in jajozeli society!

Another few days passed as Kesta took stock of the information still being passed on by his tightly controlled contact, considering how best to take his leave. Some of his colleagues would just have left quietly, but that was not his way: after leaving the notes for the young couple, he abandoned the idea of just sneaking away. He wanted to make everyone involved here with the young couple in the capital more than a little frightened of his kind and, of course, to disgust that holier-than-thou meddling razine who had haunted his master's cause for centuries.

After moving his baggage to the Golden Star, the most expensive inn in the city, set across the tree-lined Cathedral Square and directly opposite his protagonist's base, Kesta invited his contact to a private supper in the most expensive, very well-appointed suite in the place. The man had kept quiet about his meetings with the supposed merchant, encouraged by Kesta's controls that were set deep into his mind, so nobody in the palace was aware of where he went on his evenings off, or that anything might be amiss. Cheerfully expecting a pleasant evening's conversation, company and excellent food, he made his way to the second floor sitting room of the suite.

"Good evening." Kesta greeted him with a large goblet of wine and a broad smile. "The kitchen staff will be pleased that you are on time, my friend, they seem to have been wcrking on dinner all afternoon."

The meal was indeed exquisite, as good as anything served in the palace, he assured the waiters when they cleared the table of everything but the liqueur, fruit and cheese and departed most professionally.

"My word, you know how to treat your guests, Kesta."

"Such is my intention, since I must depart in the morning, my friend."

Kesta replied easily.

"So suddenly?" He asked with evident dismay. "Oh, that's terrible."

"Yes, which is why I moved to this inn: this suite is being paid for by my sponsor. Come and see the other rooms and then we can relax and chat."

The four-posted bed was easily large enough for the dalliance of the two men and the silken cushions and coverlets made a pretty litter across the priceless carpets in a short time. It was getting late and the Tenarean lay back in the plump pillows, goblet in hand and sighed appreciably.

"My, this is the way to live!"

His companion laughed, but the sound was mocking; he turned to Kesta, laid close beside him, in surprise at the tone.

"This place is a pigsty, man! The city is a cesspit and you people are so primitive that living amongst you has been disgusting!" Kesta answered languidly, which confused the man further. "Yet I must admit that you have been a pleasant diversion and the information you have given me has proved useful. For that reason, you idiotic little man, I will be merciful: you will be dead before sunrise." He smiled at the incredulity on the other's face, winked; and Kesta vanished, turning instantly into a taller, muscular, more handsome and blonde-haired person with chillingly cold blue eyes that shone disconcertingly.

"What the hell?" Relaxed and more than slightly drunk, the man laughed loudly, blinking. "Dear Arven, how did you do that, Kesta?"

"Oh, I'm full of all sorts of tricks and surprises." He replied, sitting up and yanking the crystal goblet from the man's loose grip. "Let me show you a few."

"But who are you?" The man asked, quavering a little now at the look in the hard, blue eyes holding his gaze. "I don't understand -."

"No, you wouldn't." The General grinned and the other shivered with a sudden chill. "You're a complete imbecile my very foolish friend, but you will prove an excellent object lesson for the Am'maiya!"

"Me, me? B-but -." He tried to retreat across the bed, but the other man's presence and expression somehow paralysed him: he could not move a muscle, no matter how he tried. "But I'll shout, Kesta. I'll alert the guard -."

"No, you won't." He chuckled. "But you will want to, believe me and you'll wish you could scream, too . . . Now, where shall we start?"

*

In his disguise as the human merchant, Kesta left the inn at dawn as arranged, carrying his own bags and tipping the polite innkeeper as he said farewell in pleasant tones. It took only a moment to change his appearance, a short distance away and he strode on down to a well-arranged stable closer to the main gates where his horses, saddle and other equipment had been housed. He was out of the city and riding south not long after.

*

The two maids who entered the bedroom of Kesta's vacated suite to change the bedding and clean up after breakfast succumbed to hysterics at what they found there. Only the innkeeper's desire to keep his business running kept the girls quiet for a few crucial moments, which at least stopped the other guests from learning the awful truth and leaving in droves.

Finding the girls screaming in shock in the bedroom, their voices loud from the sittig room where he had been cleaning the fireplace, he slapped them into silence in desperation and dragged them out of the room with its awful content; he quickly locked the outer door, dragged them up a level towards the back of the building where his private rooms were situated and shoved them bodily at his startled wife with curt orders to dose them up with strong drink. Then, taking a deep breath, he went in search of aid; he approached the city guards, initially, but the captain on duty entered the bedroom very reluctantly, took one look at the polite note that was laid on the corpse and requested that the palace take charge as he retreated, his face almost as pale as that of the dead man.

Consequently, it was nearly midmorning by the time that Commander Vedeigne, Captain Garane and a most reluctant Lord Ferman arrived, pushing through a curious crowd that filled a good proportion of the square. To their surprise they found ex-archpriest Bahlien awaiting them at the foot of the stairs, dressed anonymously in a dark grey tunic and black leggings. They sent two of the soldiers who had accompanied them to gather more city guards to calm and disperse the crowd and left the others at the main door to the inn.

"Your Grace!" Lord Ferman greeted him, clearly stunned to see him. "May we help you? We are here -."

"You have come to investigate a rather nasty murder, my Lord Chamberlain." The tall, elderly razine finished their sentence, his tone heavy. "But I suspect that the perpetrator will be known to me, although he will be many leagues away by now."

"Oh, please my Lords, let us resolve this quickly: this is so bad for business! I really don't know what to do." Master Pellarse, the innkeeper, blustered almost tearfully. "Please, come up I beg you -."

"Yes, Master, we will, do not distress yourself any further. We will speak further with you shortly about your guest." Commander Vedeigne patted his arm smartly and shooed him towards the kitchens. "Come along, gentlemen, let's get on with it." And he led them upstairs, their boots muffled on the deep carpets.

Shan lay spread wide upon the expensive sheets of the massive bed and his blood had stained and pooled all over the fine linen and silk. He had been expertly butchered, and the frozen agony evident on his handsome, unmarked face proved that he had been alive and helpless during most of the grizzly process.

Lord Ferman fled to the bathroom to throw up as soon as the stink of blood and excrement hit them, for it filled the room; the two soldiers and the ex-archpriest took a firm grip of their own disgust and sickness to move closer to the bed.

"Dear Arven!" Garane breathed in horror. "What sort of man could do this to anyone?"

"Don't be naïve, Captain." Vedeigne snapped in a crisp tone that disguised his own reactions. "You wouldn't believe just how sadistic some people are, but I admit that this is the worst outrage I've ever seen. Poor Shan!"

"Aye, he is indeed a most unfortunate man to have ever met his murderer." Bahlien said, carefully reaching across to pick up the letter that was resting on the one remaining pristine embroidered cushion beside the victim's head. "Here, this is addressed to King Marrand. You had better make sure you tell him what has occurred here before he opens it, however." He straightened, passing the parchment to the Commander. "And this is surely the work of one of the Betrayer's Generals, likely the same one who spoke to Lady Ethrayne last moon." The disapproval in Bahlien's voice deepened his tone. "They are notorious for their rather exotic perversions and punishments."

"But-but Lord Shan! Oh, dear Arven, I never thought that he, well -." Captain Garane spluttered, clearly still overwhelmed.

"Favoured men over women?" Bahlien laughed quite lightly, considering what lay before them. "Why should it really matter whom he slept with, Captain? And don't forget that Jajozeli Generals are notoriously adept at turning people, their victims, any which way they please for their own purposes. Clearly, this is how the enemy managed to sneak into the palace: by confusing poor Shan with a disguise, lulling him with supposed affection and finding out all sorts of information we would rather our enemy would never discover. Even with this horrible killing, the murderer clearly conducted it with evident pleasure, turning it into an object lesson -."

"He got into the royal palace! When? That-that evil creature actually got into our palace?" Vedeigne demanded furiously, shock in his tone, catching up with what Bahlien had been saying. "But, but our security, your Grace -."

"Prince Jerryn and Lady Ethrayne decided not to worry anyone overtly, Commander. He left mildly insulting notes for them in their bedrooms, that was all. Apart from the obvious, there is no need to worry about your security levels, man; the most excellent levels of protection would be inadequate to keep out a determined General, if he wanted to get inside." Bahlien sighed. "I suppose we are lucky only one man has died here."

The experienced soldiers both shuddered deeply at his matter-of-fact tone, his knowledge of such atrocities and they dimly heard Lord Ferman groan expressively from the bathroom.

"But to die like this!" Vedeigne's voice shook a little, straightening as he stared down.

Shan had been raped with a very large, ornate silver candlestick and the tendons in his limbs expertly severed to render him immobile. His torso had been sliced open from the hollow of his throat to his groin, the sternum broken, the ribcage opened, and his major organs lifted carefully, laid out neatly around his body.

"Dear Arven!" Garane muttered. "My father was a butcher – even he couldn't've done a better job!"

"It's precise, certainly. War doesn't sicken the soul like this torture!" The commander said bleakly, clearly concerned. "Lord Shan has served our king faithfully for years, your Grace. King Marrand will be devastated! And what might Shan have revealed to this murderer? Captain, please send someone to the palace – have them tighten security immediately. Send for more guards – four, to assist us. He'll not get past our gates again!"

"Sir." The captain saluted and hurried away to quickly return, his face pale, his jaw set.

"Aye, that's a question . . . Your king. We can tell his majesty together, if you'd prefer some support." Bahlien offered calmly. "It is a nasty business, and we can hedge around the gory details. Why don't you send Lord Ferman to speak to the innkeeper? I will pray for Shan's immortal soul and we then can get everything out of here through some back-door."

"Dear Arven, yes!" Vedeigne prayed. "Thank you, your Grace. I'm sorry, this has shocked me." He grimaced and lifted his hands helplessly before covering the dead man with a sheet to his chin.

"You are not the first to react so, Commander." The elderly razine said, standing straight at the side of the ruined bed, raising his arms and hands wide over Shan's body and beginning a prayer in a ringing tone. Vedeigne watched him for a moment, then went to the bathroom door, glancing in to see Lord Ferman wiping his pallid face with a towel.

"My Lord, we want you to go down and question Master Pellarse about the man who took these rooms." He said bracingly. "We will sort this mess out. You go downstairs and have a little restorative drink. We will be down soon."

"Oh, th-thanks Vedeigne." The Lord Chamberlain said rather hoarsely. "I'm so sorry -."

"Don't apologise, my Lord. It's revolting, there's no avoiding that fact."

"Yes, it truly is. I, I'll see what Pellarse can tell me." And, keeping his gaze fixed determinedly on the far door, Ferman edged around the room as if on a crumbling precipice and escaped almost at a run.

"- Amen. May his soul reside with you forever, Lord Arven." Bahlien concluded his prayer, bowed slightly to the desecrated body and sighed deeply. "Well, this will be messy." He commented, shaking his head dubiously.

"How about we bundle the body tight in the covers and wrap it in oilcloth, perhaps, your Grace?" Captain Garane suggested diffidently, sounding as though he had been puzzling how to shift the mess for a while. "Trouble is, the whole bed will be ruined."

"Let's start with Shan and progress from there." Vedeigne decided.

*

It took time, but the vast amount of ruined evidence of Shan's death was out of the inn before nightfall, and a group of less vapourish and well-paid women were hired to scrub away at any remaining blood from the bedroom and bathroom; there was surprisingly little of this, due to the murderer's expertise. Master Pellarse bitterly mourned the loss of half of the suite's mattresses, the expensive bed linen, and upholstery, but they were all relieved that the atrocity had been so well contained, in every way.

Shan's body was washed and wrapped tightly by priests under Archpriest Lurco's direction and placed in a coffin, his eyes closed, so the horrific facts of his death were hidden; everything else was taken out of the city and burned that night under Captain Garane's gaze, whilst Commander Vedeigne and the ex-archpriest finally returned to the palace to report on the day's events. The compound had been rife with rumours, most of which were leagues wide of the mark, but it could not be disguised that something awful had occurred.

"Shan is *dead*?" Marrand repeated the words with shock, there in his private sitting room. "Dead?" He shook his head. "I missed him this morning, for sure and he has never been late in all his years serving me! But, dead?"

"He was murdered last night, your Majesty. Unfortunately, it has taken most of the day t-to sort everything out, but his body is now respectfully laid in the Small Chapel in the Cathedral. We found this letter beside the body, Sire." Vedeigne handed his king the sealed and folded parchment sheet with a low bow. "We realise that this is a great shock and it was a horrific way to die, but Archpriest Bahlien suspects that the perpetrator was an agent of the Betrayer."

"But Shan has served me faultlessly for years!" Marrand countered, still hardly able to believe what he heard. "How on Iullyn -?"

"These Generals, or so his Grace named them, Sire, seem to have a strange ability to, to twist and confuse their victims, your Majesty -." Vedeigne tried to explain what was so difficult to describe.

"They have the power and strength to turn loyal men into traitors without the victims even being aware of it; the most trusted servants of the Betrayer are very skilled. It seems that he did this very thing to poor Shan; he befriended him perhaps, asked questions about the palace and Shan would never have been aware of any threat or danger. Even the best people can be subverted, your Majesty." Bahlien said gently.

"So how on Iullyn are any of us ever going to be able to defend ourselves?" The king demanded sharply, but both men shook their heads soberly. "This is an outrage! I want his murderer found, d'you hear me? I want him in chains! Dear Arven, Commander Vedeigne, Archpriest Bahlien! This is – criminal! Damn, he must have died horribly if you won't tell me how." He sighed. "What does this mean? What now?"

"The letter, your Majesty?" Bahlien prompted him gently, for he had been waving the sheet about rather wildly.

"Dear Arven, I'm too scared to read it!" But Marrand broke the red seal impatiently and shook the sheet straighter as he opened it, scanning its contents quickly, his expression hardening before he read aloud:

> "'To Marrand, King of Tenarum, greetings and thank you for the use of your manservant, he has been most entertaining company.
>
> "'On behalf of my Master, I would warn you and yours against meddling in matters far beyond your collective comprehension, yet the promises made by your only son and his pretty young lady have now dragged you closer to a future conflict which you can only lose.
>
> "'You will be relieved to know that I have left your backwards little city. But be assured that we will meet again at a time and a place of our choosing.
>
> "'Respectfully. General Ackat.'"

"That is a truly offensive letter, your Majesty." Vedeigne breathed, shaking his head.

"It's quite chilling, isn't it?" Marrand's tone was still angry. "They're obviously experienced politicians, trying to scare us like this, the bastards! This is sick! Shan was completely loyal! He served me well! If they are so powerful how on Iullyn can we possibly stand against them? . . . If there is a way to arrest the murderer, I want him apprehended, Commander!"

"That is an admirable goal, your Majesty, but I doubt that it will be attainable against a General." The old razine stated coolly, sounding far too – not smug, Marrand decided, but certainly superior to himself; not that he likely meant it. "Lady Ethrayne can give you a good description of the man, but he probably looks completely different now, considering his abilities. You need a more achievable goal, King Marrand."

"A goal?" The king snorted and shook his head, then swore expressively. "Excuse me, please. I have a feeling that this prophecy is dragging us all on a road we would never have expected, your Grace. I want this compound safe for the Am'maiya!"

"As you command, your Majesty." Vedeigne bowed. "I ordered security increased earlier this morning. I have already called for my officers and we will address the lapse, our error, when I leave you. I can assure you that we will do all we can, and I will report to you in the morning – or even later tonight, Sire. I can only apologise – offer my resignation -."

"Don't be ridiculous, Commander, this is not your fault." Marrand said at once, his tone a little quieter. "As Bahlien states, it seems very difficult to guard against such enemies – I am sorry. Report to me after dinner. I wish the palace – the city – secure."

"Yes, your Majesty."

* * *

CHAPTER 9

The Lerat Pearl was a merchant vessel which plied between ports within the Razine Protectorates, usually far to the north of the Selithian continent and across the Hessarth Channel, but occasionally calling at Rothern to trade fine oils and so forth for the wines of the region. She and her sister ships had been commissioned by the High-King of Orbain, who was fully aware of the imminence of the Prophecy and was not prepared to see the unprepared kingdoms of Selith fall to the enemy if there was anything he could do. The Pearl professed to be a normal cargo ship, but her construction was far different to what was usual in the kingdoms of Selith. The razine vessel was considerably larger than most craft that plied the continental waters, with a reinforced hull; its three masts towered above the rigging of the other ships in the docks and the main deck was higher above the waterline, which meant that the stern deck, where the wheel was situated, was at least a good seven feet higher than on any other ship that Pualyn had seen.

"Our ships venture into the deep ocean, my Lord Pualyn." Captain Lowther explained simply, during a brief lull in the organised confusion that presaged departure, due at high tide late that evening. "We have found that the bigger the ship, the more likely it is to survive adverse weather." He was a tall, grey-haired man with weather-beaten skin and a lantern jaw plus clear blue-green eyes that seemed to stare directly at a person's soul.

Kerrenan, however, snorted at that explanation. "Lowther, my friend, tell Lord Pualyn the truth, please." He said easily. "The Tenareans are our allies, you know."

"*Your Highness*." Captain Lowther laid some emphasis on the title and seemed to glare frostily, although perhaps there was a slight twitching of his lips as if he suppressed a smile. The younger razine man's look was mild. "I have a ship to prepare for sailing here. Please take our guests down below and *you* can explain matters. I will join you at dinner."

"Very well, Captain. Come, I will show you to your cabin, my Lord Pualyn, Master Lennarn, it's not large, but it's cosy enough; I'll give you a bit of a tour, show you the resting room and the galley." Kerrenan said, grinning at the dismissal, ignoring their surprise, heading across the deck and through a doorway and down some very steep steps into a rather dim passageway less than three feet wide; after thanking the captain, the two men quickly followed him. "Then I'll tell you what I imagine that old rascal Bahlien couldn't."

"An ex-archpriest is 'an old rascal'?" Pualyn asked, astounded, as their host headed down a second ladder and along a further, darker passage lit by a line of small lanterns hanging from the ceiling and stopped to open the second door on the left to reveal a cabin about nine feet by eight feet, with a bank of small, square, nearly opaque glass panes forming windows rather than port holes set in the port wall. There was a narrow bunk to either side of the central doorway, with storage cupboards beneath, built in as part of the construction like the bunks and walls. The men's baggage had been piled neatly on the plank floor in front of the windows, filling the space between the bunks.

"I have known our revered ex-archpriest since I was a small child, my Lord and he *is* an old rascal." Kerrenan laughed aloud. "You should see your face, Pualyn! He is also the oldest razine in existence, other than Gregnor the Betrayer and maybe Doreth, who is his second in command." His smile faded, but then returned just as brightly. "So, this is your cabin with this figure on the door," it was a bronze shape a little different to how a Selithian *sh* was scribed, "and I'm next door, in here." He went out, advanced a few steps to the next door on the right and opened it to reveal a cabin of about the same size, with only one bunk made up with sheets and blankets set in the stern of the ship. "The sitting area is above, the steps are more like a ladder, as you see, so do take care until you're used to it, please. Come this way. Let's go up and we can have a drink and I'll do my best to explain."

They rather gingerly clambered back up the narrow, steep rungs to the level below the main deck, Pualyn certainly using his hands as well as his feet for balance, then they followed Kerrenan into a stern-facing cabin about twice as wide as the one they would sleep in, furnished with some comfortably cushioned seats built in around the window, plus plain benches, a built-in table in the centre of the cabin and a full-height cupboard.

"Is the matter so complicated, sir?" Pualyn asked a little nervously, taking a seat before the wide bank of windows as the razine gestured politely. He grinned at Lennarn, hovering by the door. "Sit, Lennarn, please, this is no time for formality."

"My Lord." His servant said gravely, sinking down, clearly ill-at-ease.

"Have some wine, gentlemen." Kerrenan opened the cupboard and lifted out a wineskin andthree silver goblets, pouring generous amounts into each and handing them out before he sat down with a sigh.

"So, sir, what has the revered Archpriest not told us?" Pualyn asked directly, raising the goblet to their host and taking a sip, tasting the familiar fruity tang of Rothern red and it went down very pleasantly.

"The Lerat Pearl is a merchant ship, true enough and Lowther is both an excellent captain and an instinctive merchant, trading back and forth between your continent and ours, but it and the other 'Pearls' and 'Opals' out there, ten in total, are actually owned by my father, the High-King."

"The – the High-King?" Pualyn stuttered, feeling that his head was stuffed full of wool fresh from a fleece. "Your Highness -."

"Don't you dare bow!" Kerrenan pointed at him with an intense look in his eyes as Pualyn made to rise. "I *hate* all that high ceremony, you know! That's why I'm out here on board this ship , bringing you safe to Orbain, Pualyn. I'm sorry we've dragged you away before you could wed your lady, by the way but, well, when my father and Bahlien realised that their betrothal was imminent and that the Flame might transfer itself to your sister and the prince so quickly, we were dispatched at once to fetch you to Lerat." He laid his free hand on his chest and inclined his head politely.

"So swiftly? But, forgive me my stupidity, Highness, how could people hundreds of leagues apart across the ocean possibly communicate effectively on such an immediate scale?" He asked, confused.

"We razine have those so-called magical abilities, Pualyn and my father and Bahlien can speak mind-to-mind even over such distances, utilising other razine church members as intermediaries." Kerrenan explained almost apologetically. "It's not at all easy, even for them, in fact it's exhausting, but they can do it in real emergencies, if the conditions are right." *<Like this, you see.>*

Pualyn jumped in his seat, even though he had experienced this with Bahlien, as the razine's voice rang in his mind so *intimately*, was the only description that seemed partly adequate. "Oh, my word!"

"I apologise for the intrusion, but it is a very useful tool at our disposal." Kerrenan grinned at his surprise. "Well, to explain more fully, the 'Pearl' and 'Opal' ships are our eyes and ears, especially here to the south: our spy ships and marine fighters against the Betrayer's forces. The Orbain Pearl and Mador Opal are further to the south, keeping their eyes open for the enemy there, for there have been sightings of their ships running up the coast from Cal'Badon, their only port on this side of the continent; we fear them attacking Tenarean ships and isolated settlements." The tall razine grimaced and took a gulp of wine. "Actually, they are the *second* Orbain Pearl, for the enemy destroyed the first ship nearly a century ago and killed my older brother Khalassan and his crew."

"Dear Arven, I am sorry, that's awful!" The young man said quite automatically, even as the full statement sank into his brain and he sat up straighter, frowning. "I'm sorry, did you say a, a *century* ago?" He enquired, his tone stunned rather than disbelieving.

"Yes indeed, Pualyn, I was a very junior cadet in training then, only in my late twenties. I idolised my brother. Don't forget that we live a lot longer than humans, lad I've no idea why, though. I'm a hundred and thirty-two, though I don't look much older than you do." He shrugged and grinned. "Khalassan was forty-six when he died, seven years into his first official duty as first mate, with a General's sword in his vitals." Kerrenan's tone had darkened considerably as if even the passing of a century had not lessened the pain of loss. "My parents were not happy and even Bahlien was against it, with the view that the pursuit of vengeance can stifle the soul quite severely, but I have dedicated myself to the age-long struggle to stop the Betrayer ever since: he's got to be stopped!"

"Great heavens!" Lennarn quietly murmured, gulping at his wine; the High-Prince looked younger than he did.

Kerrenan laughed aloud. "That's very diplomatic of you." He offered, and his inner darkness seemed to have retreated in the face of what seemed to be his usual cheerfulness. "So, when the ex-archpriest told us about the prophecy and then, later, that the prince and your sister had been born -." He paused as their mouths literally dropped open and the men exchanged stunned glances. "Yes, I know, that was over sixteen years ago. That was when Bahlien resigned, packed up and returned here to Tenarum, to wait. But it is certain that there will be war at some point."

"And I don't suppose it would have been at all sensible to speak to our parents when they were both babies." Pualyn himself answered the question that he had been about to ask. "Hello there. Did you know that your daughter, your Graces, and your son, your Majesties, are destined to take the Flame of Arven; it'd have been bloody mad, even for a respected priest!" He shook his head and shivered a little. "Bloody hell!"

"Yes, exactly. You might be able to raise some excellent armies from your own population and even the other kingdoms of Selith, but time is against us. We did not dare warn you, for we know that the enemy are watching – and any action on our part might drive them to something unpleasant, you understand. The Protectorate Kingdoms have at least been quietly preparing for war and stocking up on foodstuffs, equipment and so on. You are the envoy of the Wielders of the Flame as much as of your honourable king, my Lord Pualyn."

"Oh, my word!" Pualyn murmured, stunned at the older man's declaration.

The conversation moved, then, to less vital matters, as they heard the crew shouting and occasionally banging above their heads and Kerrenan had a pleasant way of getting his guests to talk; at his encouragement, Lennarn ventured the information that he had grown up in an ore-smelting village some twenty leagues downstream from Clirensar and had been able to get a good education because of his father's hard work in the forge, determined that his only son would not have to work so hard to earn a crust. Even Pualyn had never heard that fact before.

"I'm not surprised." Pualyn said respectfully. "Father had me working in Master Queyt's forge for six months straight, two years ago and I slept like a baby each night, once I'd got used to the aching muscles." He raised his goblet to his valet. "Here's to our iron and steel and the men and women who shape it so very well."

"Amen to that." Kerrenan agreed and got to his feet. "Come on, we'll go and watch the traffic on the docks, it's getting a little warm in here, isn't it? If we keep out of his way, Lowther shouldn't shout at us too much."

*

The rest of the afternoon passed quickly and pleasantly until, finally, the Port Authority waved the green flag from the hefty thirty-oared boat that would organise the three others tasked to haul them safely into the channel of the estuary. The hawsers were pulled in from the dock, the ones to the tugs were secured and the huge ship moved almost at a snail's pace forward, the current and the tide swirling eddies of silt-laden water about the sharp bow; the docks and the city beyond oh-so-slowly retreating.

Pualyn, stood safely out of the way, halfway along the port rail with Kerrenan and Lennarn, watched their slow advance with growing excitement, despite all the uncertainties raised by their earlier discussion. The future might be bleak, but he was heading out into the unknown with a light heart, although he wished that Lyria was here at his side. He couldn't wait to get to his journal and add this day's events to its crisp pages, as soon as he could find the words.

"Goodbye for now, Tenarum." He murmured under his breath when the lead tug waved the yellow flags that denoted that the lines were being released and the ship could raise its sails as the oared boats sculled quickly off towards the docks to port and starboard.

The captain gave orders, backed up by his huge voiced first officer. The wet ropes were hauled in and coiled neatly, as the sailors shinnied up precipitous rigging and hurried across the huge cross braces far above to release the massive sails; these cracked loudly in the rising breeze as they came down, huge sheets of dark blue canvas. The ship slid out into the wide channel of the river mouth, facing the endless blue-grey ocean scintillating endlessly to some undetermined point ahead, the great port city sinking behind them.

"Arven take care of all of them, please, especially my darling Lyria." He added as a prayer in his head, aware that he was grinning like a fool.

*

Pualyn found that sea travel mostly agreed with him, or at least it seemed to by the afternoon of the second day, when his queasiness at the motion of the ship on the ever-moving vast ocean finally subsided. Lennarn, however, seemed to have no such trouble at finding his own sea-legs.

Watching the coastline recede and pass by, dimmed by the miles of water that separated them, Pualyn felt decidedly peculiar at the movement of the ship and hung around the rail for as long as he could, glad that the horrible nausea seemed to have largely faded away. Despite the sympathies of Kerrenan and Lennarn, he could not face dinner that evening after they had left Rothern, nor breakfast the next morning: he had raced desperately for the open deck despite the rain that poured down.

"Here, Pualyn, this might help a little, it's ginger tea." Lennarn came up onto the deck after breakfast bearing a tin mug of steaming yellowy water that made his eyes smart as he sniffed it dubiously. "His Highness says it eases nausea and upset stomachs."

Pualyn took his first sip with a polite smile, coughed at the strength of it and then drank it down manfully; he was thirsty, and the liquid felt good going down, but he was fully braced against its return. Yet that horrid roiling and sickness gradually began to ease, although he had no idea whether it was in fact due to the medicinal nature of the tincture. That evening, ravenous, he ate his first full meal, clearing his plate with indecent haste and then finally felt able to interact with the others properly, joining in with their conversation and the respect he felt for the High-Prince seemed likely, very soon, to turn to friendship.

The days passed quickly as they rode the rolling waves until one day dawned bright and early on, Captain Lowther turned the wheel and the Lerat Pearl swung to the east, the wind full in her sails, and they turned away from the distant view of the coastline, heading out into the deep ocean, one ship, tiny and alone, in the vastness of the waters, until, curving from the left and fading out ahead of them to the north, they saw solid land, which must be the isthmus that joined the Selithian continent to Jaece, Pualyn realised, extending much further to the east than Tenarum's coastline. They veered north-east again, keeping the land far distant until it vanished in huge banks of misty cloud. The ship travelled alone, bothered by nothing but the wind and waves, seeing only wide-winged seabirds soaring or diving; the occasional strange creature in the sea that occasionally broke the surface to the world of air, sometimes seeming to stare at them with large, black eyes. Then, safely past the dangers of shoaling rocks or islands in to shore, the ship turned back to the north, shooting forward with the wind belling the sails. Often sat comfortably in the sitting room, the three passengers gazed out of the open windows and talked idly, for the day seemed to pass at a very different rate out here on the ocean.

"How many lands are there in the Protectorates?" Pualyn asked.

"There are seven, in all." The High Prince replied. "Zoillan, Jaece, Rhastten, Orbain, Mador, Cheass and Veddock. Jaece is the northernmost realm in Selith as you know; Rhastten is a large island to the west and the other five kingdoms form the Mendor Continent. Orbain, you may know, is where my father rules; the other realms are all equal with Orbain, but their kings always swear fealty to the High-King traditionally as First King under Arven." Kerrenan clicked his fingers and a scroll appeared in his hand.

"What is that?" Lennarn asked, still amazed by the razine's casual use of 'magic'.

"Only a map." Kerrenan unrolled it on the table and anchored the four corners with a couple of table knives, a tin mug and a salt cellar. "I know we have discussed the Protectorates before, but a map will make it all easier to understand. Here." He pointed out the various kingdoms delineated in the very well-drawn map of the northern continent.

"You said that there is a King's Council similar to the one in Tenarum?" Pualyn asked, looking at the various landmasses spread out north of Selith, it looked so far away! Iullyn was vast!

"Indeed, and all the kings attend, but I bet our version predates yours by a few centuries, even if I suspect that some of our arguments are at least as tedious as any you have been involved with." Kerrenan remarked drily and shook his head. "Get so many rulers in one place, you're bound to have a few clashes of personality."

"Heavens, I can imagine, with seven kings!" Pualyn agreed, recalling a few intransigent souls who had caused awful disagreements, not least of which, a year or more ago, was a most spectacular war of words which had taken a great deal to resolve. "You should have been there when King Marrand elevated Lady Celia to inherit Pellerton Court over her male cousin, a complete rake and then to a seat on the Council." He shook his head; he had been quite amazed at the terrible disagreement that had ensued.

"Awful?" Kerrenan asked.

"Oh yes, indeed. And then there was just as much trouble when the lords learned that Ethrayne wanted to learn how to use weapons, after meeting that stranger up above the city. It's just not customary, you see: a woman, especially a high-born woman who's betrothed to the prince, learning how to fight? That was before they met the Archpriests and learned of the prophecy, as well; I don't even know what made her say it, not really: no noblewoman will have to look to her own security, after all. Everyone was shocked, I can tell you, but then the Archpriests agreed that it was a very good idea and that pulled the carpet from beneath them, figuratively speaking." He grinned, remembering those intense, angry conversations.

"Hmm, yes and I'm sure an awful lot of people in the Protectorates would agree with your traditionalists, Pualyn. Fortunately, *most* razine, being talented, see that when people have a desire to learn or a gift for a craft or skill, you should do all you can to help them achieve it. Well, generally so, anyway. Emotions can cloud even our judgements, of course. We have a few female fighters in our ranks, but not that many. How was your sister faring at learning such skills?"

"Ethrayne was quite impressive, really, considering that I don't think she had ever even held a sword before. She's strong for a girl: she can ride any horse our father has had trained, so that must help, and she is quick on her feet and pays attention." He said rather proudly, having considered the matter for a short time. "She's determined to do well. Jerryn is going to have his hands full with her as his wife."

"And what of your young lady, mmm?" The High Prince asked mischievously. "I'm sure she will not let you always get your own way either, Pualyn: that's the nature of women."

"Oh yes." Pualyn agreed. "Are you married, Kerr?"

"Yes, to an equally wonderful lady, Arialle. She is beautiful, talented and quite wonderful in every way, so I assure you that I speak from experience." And they all laughed at his deliberately rueful tone.

*

"Please, tell me about your sister and the prince." Kerrenan asked on the evening of their fifteenth day on board ship as they met for dinner. "I have known of them only as 'those-who-will-wield-the-flame-of-Arven' for so long." He grimaced at the string of words, even as he made it a chanted title of sorts and shrugged. "I imagine that they were stunned when they found out what Bahlien and your Archpriest had to tell them."

"Oh my, yes!" Pualyn shook his head and laughed a little. "My earliest memory is when she was a little baby. Maybe I saw them both newborn – I was almost five then. Ethrayne and I fought when we were children, as siblings often do; the three of us all grew up together in each other's homes from babyhood: our fathers are the best of friends, mother was very close to the dead queen and our father is the king's right hand.

"My sister was always trying to emulate what I did, and I do remember, when I was about eight, she just seemed to follow me everywhere; it quite annoyed me. Then, she and Jerryn would gang up on me: once, when they were young, they pelted me with most of a tree worth of unripe apples; a complete barrage it was, and I felt the indignity hugely." He laughed again. "I was covered in bruises for ages: green apples are bloody hard. In fact, I recall they both fell out seriously a year or so later, they wouldn't even speak to each other for moons, it seemed. Jerryn said it was over his knife and her necklace, I think. But, mostly, they have been very close friends, along with Lyria, of course."

"Yes, it's funny how the fallings-out of childhood can completely reverse again when the youngsters start to grow up, isn't it?"

Pualyn made a half-smile, half-grimace at that as the sailors-cum-servants served dinner. "Yes, I suppose. Our parents had been considering a union between them for years. They are both very handsome; Jerryn is everything a prince should be, tall, strong, determined, rather like yourself." He complimented the High-Prince, who smiled. "My sister is pretty. But no, she's beautiful; feminine but strong and she was quickly confident wearing male clothing, sparring. They're very intelligent and well educated, of course, but everything just seemed to happen so, so horribly swiftly even before they were betrothed. First, Ethrayne met that stranger who threatened and frightened her; they were betrothed; then she joined the Council and, a day later, they were told about the Prophecy by the Archpriests. A few days later we trooped to the Cathedral one late night, when Ethrayne and Jerryn received the Flame of Arven in a hall hewn out of the rock far beneath the Cathedral! It was so unique." And, slowly, encouraged by Kerrenan, he tried to describe that evening's events and the setting aloud, although he found that his words were not even remotely adequate to voice what he had seen and felt that night. Saying it aloud made the speed of it all even more startling.

"The world is a far more complicated place than I had ever imagined, that's certain; actually, I'm not really sure if I like it. Ethrayne learning to fight with sword and bow with serious intent; strangers lurking about wishing she and Jerryn ill, on behalf of one we practically all assumed was a mere myth -." Pualyn shuddered, although the temperature in the cabin was comfortably warm. "It scares me that there are people out there, the jajozeli, who really seem to hate them!"

"Yes, and by extension, they hate all of us equally intensely. I know what you mean." Kerrenan agreed gravely. "My parents tried to keep me innocent, as the younger son and, of course, you and your family have all protected your young sister from the evils loose in the world. Yet I *chose* this path and I believe that she and Prince Jerryn know instinctively that their path is clear before them . . . And although the jajozeli are our avowed enemies and powerful in so many ways, Arven will ensure that the young couple are powerful too. They have to be, afterall, to ever destroy the Betrayer!"

"Amen to that, Kerrenan!" Pualyn said as fervently as any prayer was ever uttered. "But they are so young."

*

Days passed, of middling quality, as the ship sped north, aided by gusty winds from the south and Pualyn, Kerrenan and Lennarn became fast friends, spending much of their time together, talking, playing and learning either mendor or selithian games; Pualyn was determinedly trying to learn the Mendor language which took up a good part of the day, along with watching the endless play of the waves that bore them onwards, or fishing.

On the afternoon of the thirty-fifth day out of Rothern, they saw the first glimpse of land since they had left Selith and Jaece behind. It was low on the horizon, as vague as a cloud to Pualyn's gaze, yet Captain Lowther barked out orders instantly: the sailors hurried to adjust the sails as he turned the wheel so that the vessel turned her prow further to the east to skirt along, all the rest of the day, just barely within sight of the coast.

"There, that's Zoillan you can see, with its low hills and olive groves. We are perhaps nine days from Lerat, if the winds hold fair." Lowther said to them with good cheer. "It's a good season for sailing."

It was far more pleasant to continue along within sight of land, for they were more aware of their swift progress for the next two days as they passed barely visible towns and farmland, woodland and even one large, white-walled and red-roofed city set around a deep river mouth that the captain identified as Cerris, capital of Zoillan.

"Very pretty." Lennarn remarked. "Those white walls and those thin trees edging up the hillsides are most picturesque."

"Don't tell King Rase, but I've always thought it's a bit contrived." Kerrenan said quietly. "The walls are whitewashed every year by decree before the spring festival, but it's a nice city, well planned."

Pualyn laughed. "We don't have the climate for whitewash in the south and Clirensar is definitely too smoky by far, with the charcoal burners working over such a large area, along with all the ore smelting all around the region. It's a good job our local stone is pale limestone, but it's grey. Planning and aesthetics are all very well, but they do fail around industry I believe."

The High Prince grinned. "Most definitely, Pualyn. Cerris is the centre of the olive industry so there's no smoke or excavation to contend with, you see, whilst Hessarth, the capital of Jaece, frankly *stinks* as the centre of the dried and smoked fish trade in this part of Iullyn."

"Yes, there's a market for their fish all over Tenarum and in the other kingdoms, I imagine." Lennarn said. "Smoked and dried fish are staples in every marketplace."

"And that helps us to keep an eye out for the enemy yet again." Kerrenan said and grimaced. "My wife says that I spend far too much time concentrating on them and I have to admit that she's probably right, but I won't stand by and permit Gregnor and his servants to destroy us all!" His face and tone were both fierce, revealing the depth of his conviction.

"Well, I don't know what we can do, your Highness, but we won't let you face the enemy on your own." The young lord assured him. "As you said, Kerr, the kingdoms of Selith would have no hope at all against them and, if the realm was alone, Tenarum would be lost in days." A draught touched the back of his neck and Pualyn told himself that he shivered at it, not at the thought of the ancient rumours and myths about the Jajozeli. "Actually, I'm just glad that they seem to have pretty much ignored us until now; from your accounts, they are implacable."

"Implacable is what *we* will be, determinedly working together." Kerrenan stated. "Armed with Clirensar's steel, we will be hopefully unbeatable."

But the reminder of the enemy had darkened Pualyn's mood; the forces answering to the Betrayer must be vast beyond imagining and it was terrifying to acknowledge yet again, and always with a jolt of real fear, that the focus of the emperor's attention was his own little sister and her betrothed.

Kerrenan and Lennarn saw his abstraction and moved apart.

"It will hard for your lord, now separated from his family most particular; and for the kingdom as a whole." Kerrenan said seriously. "But if there was a better way to break the news about all this, I would have found it, Master Lennarn."

A medium goblet of Rothern red did much to improve their moods as the ship continued, passing fishing boats and other traders, sometimes within shouting distance.

Cerris had vanished into the haze that descended as the afternoon turned into a balmy evening and the wind that had filled their sails all the way from Rothern faded away, leaving the Lerat Pearl motionless in the rocking swell. Captain Lowther grumbled about this for a while, even as he admitted that the weather ruled sea travel mercilessly at times. He then regaled them with stories of his life which had been spent mostly on ships since the age of fifteen, nearly fifty years before. This kept them all amused until late.

Next morning dawned just as frustratingly windless and the haze had become a fog so thick that it could nearly be cut with a knife. The quiet ship was disturbed by the rhythmic striking of the bronze bell in the bow, as one of the crew hit it every hundred heartbeats to warn of their presence, on and on.

"Oh well, I'll have to continue teaching you our language, won't I?" Kerrenan suggested. "If this weather continues, you'll both be completely fluent by the time we reach Lerat."

The Lerat Pearl, however, was becalmed only until the next day when, before noon, the fog began to thin and lift, becoming almost a line of murky grey ribbon that seemed to move sinuously before them as the barest hint of a breeze touched their faces and moved the sails a little. It blew fitfully for ages, then to a purpose, a wind from the east that dispelled the fog and cloud, leaving a clearing sky, as the captain gave crisp orders, his crew trimmed the sails and they raced on anew over the brilliant blue sea.

It was late evening, seven days later, when the lookout atop the main mast gave an almighty cheer and a massive wave of his arms, which Kerrenan cheerfully translated as confirmation that their destination was in sight.

"We'll sail around the headland in the morning." He said with a grin. "The tide is against us now and the channel is narrow from the south."

"And at least we'll have time to smarten up and shave." Pualyn remarked, feeling the bristles on his face with a slightly shaky hand as unexpected fear filled him for a moment.

"You will if you want to give everyone the best impression to our hosts, my Lord." Lennarn added dryly, with a wink.

* * *

CHAPTER 10

The horrific murder of Master Shan was city-wide news for longer than the palace really hoped, but Master Pellarse, the landlord of the Golden Anchor, was quietly amazed that custom increased substantially on the back of the sometimes-ridiculous rumours that circulated the palace, the city and the countryside beyond. Those who considered themselves to be at the cutting-edge of elegant fashion and considerable importance, on the very outer fringes of the court and desperately aware of the fact, beat a path to his door, to 'partake of the atmosphere', or some such nonsense.

Neither the palace nor the cathedral made comments of any kind regarding Shan's death, other than to state that they all mourned the loss of a much-loved and respected man and servant. The Palace Guard issued a carefully worded warning about the movements of a sadly deranged, ill escapee from a church hospital, after they had found his body floating in the river. And Shan's tragic befriending of the mad patient explained both deaths: the king's manservant the unwitting victim of the unnamed maniac and the madman drowning himself in remorse.

Still, those who thought themselves the best of Tenarean society and many more without any such pretensions, favoured the Golden Anchor with their custom and the genial barman, Farn, was permitted to hold court in the bar, tutting at the nasty but unspecified death that Shan had suffered, following up with many discussions on the terrible nature of man; the goodness of the church; and the intricacies of the local hood-ball teams, on which he was an authority: the Cathedral Square team was currently third in the city-wide league of six, behind High Market and the presently formidable Fountain Court teams. It was Farn's dream to see hood-ball's attraction spread far beyond the city, a major source of amusement and activity amongst the young; but the attraction of the air-filled bladders, hoods and the misuse of them, was still rather confined to the city environs or, at least, to the side of the archery field just outside the walls.

Thus, most expertly and quietly, was worry and panic averted, which was not at all what Kesta had intended by his acts.

*

Archpriest Lurco and ex-archpriest Bahlien met with Jerryn and Ethrayne after Shan's quiet funeral, two days after the discovery of his body, in the Palace chapel. The details had been arranged assiduously by a grim-faced Lord Ferman and led by Lurco, commending the poor man's soul to Arven and his body to the earth of the main graveyard to the north of the city, with his elderly mother and two younger brothers attending from Chielton, twenty miles north-east of the capital.

"I've known Shan since I was eight or nine, it seems so strange, not seeing him there tending my father." Jerryn said, once he, Ethrayne and both representatives of their God were ensconced in his private sitting room. "We've heard all sorts of horrible rumours, your Grace, but what *really* happened?"

"That blonde-haired General happened, your Highness, the self-same one who accosted you on your ride the day after your betrothal, my Lady." Bahlien explained heavily. "He lured poor Shan along, probably commanded his will to gain access to the palace and killed him most brutally three nights ago. He left at dawn the next day. I doubt he's within forty leagues of the city by now." He sighed, the sound most weary.

"Is that why Lord Ferman has been so completely silent?" Jerryn asked uneasily. "I've never known him to behave like he has; it must really have been shocking."

"Yes, indeed it was." Bahlien acknowledged, saying no more.

"And that man, the General, was wandering about in, in our *rooms*, Jerryn!" Ethrayne snapped. "Here." She pointed to the floor. "Right here in the palace, close to our dear servants, and yet you did not tell us that he was so dangerous, your Grace!" She accused the old razine, glaring.

"Ah, well." Lurco said, sounding slightly uneasy. "No, we didn't. Yes, they are certainly unpredictable."

"We did not expect him to single out and murder Shan." Bahlien said calmly. "He left an insulting note for his Majesty, as he did for you both, and Shan's death was intended as a direct provocation to me: that he believed himself to be beyond my control. I prayed that no one would die, that he would just watch and gain information, but the jajozeli-razine Generals apparently still enjoy making such object lessons."

"Urgh!" Ethrayne shivered. "What a monster!"

"I suppose this is the reason why you encouraged Commander Vedeigne to create our very own troop of guards?" Jerryn wondered heavily. "Now we are starting to understand the truth of what you told us: that our enemies are much, much worse than the old stories portray."

"Yes, that is exactly why." The ancient priest confirmed with a sigh. "I am sorry." He apologised with clear sincerity. "It's not what you want to hear, I know, but I must urge you that your task is to learn to understand the Flame of Arven that has been gifted to you and to begin to learn how the power of it may be used. This is far more important than anything else, even combat."

"To stand against the Betrayer, yes." Ethrayne acknowledged. "I am sorry I snapped at you, your Grace, I was rude and ignorant, forgive me -."

"Never, Ethrayne!" Bahlien countered immediately, to her surprise. "It was a shocking murder and another reason for his brutality was, ultimately, to frighten you. We have prayed for his souls and you must both learn how to harness the Flame of Arven as easily as you wield a sword."

The young couple exchanged glances. "We *have* tried." Ethrayne said uneasily.

"But it, it feels too strange, your Grace. It feels well, most peculiar, actually." Jerryn expanded slightly, shrugging slightly.

"It is oddly different, alien – and strange." Ethrayne continued.

"But you must understand your own natures first, my dears, before the Flame will feel natural to you and that will take time, just as much as learning to use weapons effectively." Bahlien assured them with a smile. "I can only suggest that you begin by meditating." He smiled at the question clear in their expressions. "Find a quiet evening, close your eyes or maybe focus on something like a flower or a design, a picture, then focus your thoughts inward, into your own mind, your centre. Then you breathe slowly and deeply, concentrating."

"That sounds complicated." Jerryn commented doubtfully.

"It's actually an integral part of prayer, your Highness; if you asked any priest he or she would tell you that prayer and meditation are closely intertwined. It will take time and all sorts of thoughts will distract you in sequence, I am sure. But at some point, if you work at it regularly, you will move your focus inwards towards that figurative place within you where the Flame now resides." Archpriest Lurco stated confidently. "We all learn meditation as part of our training and some people just get to the right result faster than others." He chuckled at their expressions. "You will complain that this sounds mystical, but we must admit that you are now an integral part of the mysticism and ceremony of the church of Arven."

"Hmm." Ethrayne uttered thoughtfully. "Concentration and quiet? Well, we can only try."

<We managed to find out how this works, after all.> She continued silently. *<And it was most strange.>*

<Yes, we can at least start to learn meditation, your Graces.> Jerryn agreed. *<But it might be difficult to find the time to practice, for we just have so much to do in every day.>* His tone was doubtful.

"You really must find the time, Am'maiya, there is no alternative." Bahlien said levelly. "You must both, separately, find a particular point in the day when you can be completely alone and undisturbed so that you can meditate daily. The process may well prove difficult, or perhaps you will find it simple to achieve, but this is the only way in which you can discover how the Flame within you can be wielded."

Ethrayne could tell that the old razine was serious and that he was probably correct: since they had absorbed the Flame, she had felt its presence only dimly, there deep inside and largely out of reach, as it was beyond all her experience; Jerryn had agreed with her: it felt so strange! A different kind of force within her, spiralling endlessly somewhere near her spine; unthreatening, just very bizarre.

"We do need to know how to Wield the Flame." Jerryn remarked rather heavily. "Especially since that spy killed Shan, for whom else will his servants slaughter, whilst we lounge here in safety?"

"We are not training you so that you can murder Generals, Prince

Jerryn!" Lurco disagreed firmly. "Great heavens -."

"But you are, in the end, your Grace." Ethrayne countered, looking from face to face, her expression firm, exasperated by the old man's strange obtuseness. "If you eventually do want to stop the Betrayer, surely there will be murder involved somewhere along the way and I'd rather it was them dying, than us!"

"Yes, I think you have our purpose, my Lady Ethrayne!" Bahlien admitted with a sigh.

"Monster!" The prince remarked lightly.

"Simply practical, your Highness." She answered with a toss of her head.

"Oh, dear Arven, protect us all!" Bahlien almost prayed. "Kerrenan is going to love meeting the two of you: he's been thirsting to attack the jajozeli for a very long time."

"Who is Kerrenan?"

A detailed image of a handsome, dark-haired man came into their heads. "He is the High-Prince of the razine; he's the one who is taking Pualyn to Lerat." The old razine said. "He has been yearning for you to reach adulthood ever since I told him that you had both been born."

"That prescience is incredibly peculiar, your Grace." Jerryn marvelled, his tone uneasy.

"Mythical, mystical and mysterious, my dears. But, please, I urge you to learn to look inwards. I'm not expecting miracles in how you advance, but a little progress before our next meeting would be heartening for you especially." Bahlien smiled. "This is how razine of about your age begin to learn about themselves and their abilities, however limited. You two young people, taking Arven's strength into yourselves, will be learning to control much more than you can presently imagine."

They looked at him seriously, their fears reawakened by his words.

"You will help us to understand all this, won't you, your Graces?" Jerryn asked. "It is so far beyond all of our experience."

"On our honour we will, whenever you need our input, but don't be alarmed: we have the utmost confidence in you both." Lurco assured them, patting their hands gently. Then, he and Bahlien bowed and departed.

*

Their mornings were now almost exclusively taken up with combat training and what command of forces entailed; both Jerryn and Ethrayne were now being coached mercilessly by Captain Garane and his equals, usually in one of the lower halls off from the barracks in the palace.

Ethrayne was still a novice, though she had advanced from a basic, short wooden sword to a short, blunt steel sword; as well as fencing, she was learning how to manage a bow and arrows in addition, although she would never be strong enough to use a longbow; unarmed combat, and knife fighting, which meant she was again using wooden sticks as a weapon, in addition to more varieties of useful footwork and defensive arts. She had never realised just how much work was involved in the simple phrase '*combat practice*'; it was sometimes tiring, and she was sleeping very well because of it and although her previously beautiful pale hands were ruined by callouses, her posture and muscle-tone had improved vastly. She thought that she looked so different to how she had appeared only a few moons before, but all this hard work and exercise would ultimately prove worthwhile, if it saved her life, or someone else's.

Day after day, on and on and on – step, thrust, reverse, step – over and over. Sometimes, her opponent was Jerryn, concentrating as much as she, occasionally Corporal Tymain or Private Calle. It was certainly repetitive, doing the same things time after time until the captains were happy with her movements, but Ethrayne never found it boring; she learned how to fall, how to roll and leap, until it seemed that she was turning into a sort of tumbler, such as was seen occasionally at town fairs and palace events. It seemed that she was only existing, now, to absorb information: from the power of the Flame of Arven; to the steps involved in sword-fighting, as intricate as any court dance; to battle tactics; and, occasionally, subjects such as economics and law in the Royal Council.

Jerryn was being worked just as hard as she, although he was much more advanced, fighting with his own weapons, drawing a massive longbow that was as tall as himself; and the young woman was learning just as much watching him fight with the soldiers as during her own sessions: how a move looked, what that a thrust or footstep would result in. He – all of them – were also learning, seeing how the soldiers decided to alter some long-established movements for the smaller, lighter body of a woman. Flexibility seemed to be the word of the season.

And now they had their evenings taken up, as well. By enlisting their parents' help, Ethrayne and Jerryn were excused from some of the post-dinner get-togethers without extended explanations or fabricated stories: undertaking a measure of religious training at the Archpriests' behest sounded wholesome and tedious enough to halt any questioning and, of course, it was the truth.

The evening after their meeting with Bahlien and Lurco, the young couple retired separately to their apartments with their guards, leaving the courtiers to plan a picnic lunch; they were quite unaware that their parents and Lady Lyria were watching them closely.

Ethrayne changed out of her formal gown and pulled on a light dressing gown before curling up in her favourite armchair, having dismissed her maids until bedtime; with the guards outside her door, she was guaranteed not to be disturbed at least.

<*This seems strange.*> She thought, slightly embarrassed for some unknown reason, speaking across the palace with far more ease now.

<*Yes, I agree, but we did promise to try our best.*> Jerryn replied silently. <*And we can do* this *now, so why not that?*>

<I know, but it feels very odd, Jerryn. Oh, let's compare notes at breakfast.> Ethrayne broke the connection between them, pulled herself out of embarrassment with a chuckle, took a deep breath to steady herself and closed her eyes.

Thoughts kept intruding, no matter how assiduously she cleared her mind; thoughts of the excellent dinner served earlier, for example; followed by others as random: how happy Jerryn had looked when she had finally mastered a complicated jump and thrust that morning; Captain Garane's quiet respect; the roses in the old Queens Garden below, odd snatches of conversation . . . *Stop it!* She scolded herself, trying not to laugh, blinking, before trying again, searching (but how?) inside herself for . . . well, Bahlien had not really described it, so she could only hope that she would recognise it if she ever found it!

More thoughts, many random thoughts, followed each other, keeping her from any sensible level of concentration until, in frustration and completely at random, Ethrayne counted slowly as she breathed, intoning one to five as she breathed in, and again as she breathed out. Somehow, this felt correct although nothing much happened until, after a while, she brought in a third count of five, holding her breath between inhalation and exhalation and then, strangely, her mind began to clear . . . "Done it!" She said aloud, immensely proud at her discovery and her calm mood vanished instantly. This was no bad thing, she found on opening her eyes, for the sun had set, so she had been wrestling with her thoughts for most of the evening. She sat there in a rather pensive mood until her maids returned and she began to get ready for bed and then, a little later, comfortable under the bedcovers in her bed, she found that sleep came very quickly.

*

Breakfast, however, proved much too busy for a meaningful discussion, for Lyria was a little melancholy, missing Pualyn, so Ethrayne and Jerryn devoted their attention to her cheerfully and even made her laugh a little. Promising to have luncheon with her and leaving her with Duchess Riyala, for they were planning a shopping trip down into the city that morning, the couple headed off to combat practice.

"So, Ethie, how did you do?" Jerryn asked cheerily.

Ethrayne snorted. "Awfully, I think, but it seemed to take all evening . . . I did find that *breathing* seems to be a key."

"Breathing? How?" Jerryn asked. "I just couldn't get my head clear at all actually, it was so frustrating." He shook his head ruefully.

"I was sure you would have managed it, Jerryn." Ethrayne admitted with a laugh as they descended the first of many flights of stairs that led to the most direct route to the combat hall, one of the service routes, plain and whitewashed, where the passing servants stopped and moved aside for them to hurry along, bowing politely and getting smiles and thanks in return.

"Me? No."

Quickly, she explained about breathing deeply, pausing and counting all the way through. The prince was dubious, and their discussion continued during the fencing lesson and the hand-to-hand combat that followed it, leaving them aching, red faced and tired, but Corporal Tymain and Captain Garane were both politely complimentary by the girl's steady progress.

"You can only try it, Jerryn and if it works, the Archpriests will be pleased with our advancement in that, too." Ethrayne concluded, having noted the small smiles of the taciturn soldiers. She wore one of the plain shirts, lace-fronted jerkins and leggings that had become her usual morning attire, along with her old, comfortable boots, sturdy enough to cope with whatever they called of her. "We did promise to practice you know and it won't hurt, not like landing badly. I found it very restful and I slept really well."

"All right Ethie, I agree, we promised; and I'll try it, but it does sound peculiar." He held up his hands in surrender, abandoning the argument.

"Good, hurry up, we've a lunch appointment with Lyria soon." And the girl rushed off ahead, glancing back quickly and grinning. "Come on, don't dawdle, your Highness."

Corporal Tymain, who was also one of their official guards that day; tried and failed to suppress a quick burst of laughter at that.

"I heard you, Corporal." Jerryn said. "You don't have to laugh at me too, you know." His tone was slightly injured.

"Oh, I think I do, Highness, my apologies." He replied with a grin and a low bow.

Pretending offence, the prince stalked off after Ethrayne, but he was grinning as he strode out of the hall ahead of the guards.

*

There was no Council meeting that afternoon, as the king was undertaking legal business, so the young couple spent it with Lyria, Duchess Riyala and Lady Celia in the sort of female-centred occasion that Jerryn was getting quite practised at; he did not view such events with the horror that had previously filled him, anyway and he found that sometimes the female viewpoint was refreshingly different on many matters.

After a nicer afternoon than he had expected, Jerryn viewed the onset of a quiet evening's meditation with better grace than he had the previous day; his mood was lighter and with Ethrayne's suggestion in mind, he sank back against the mound of pillows that he had arranged on his bed and closed his eyes, starting to attempt to seek that inner sense of peace which seemed impossible to attain and, of course, Ethrayne's image filled his head: her lithe grace as she fenced with him and the soldiers, the seldom-used rapier becoming quite a weapon in her hand . . .

Concentrate on your breathing! He told himself sternly, recalling what Ethrayne had said and starting to count even as he slowed his breathing, not for any real reason other than it felt somehow oddly right to him.

In . . . hold . . . out . . . hold . . . in. Jerryn could feel his lungs filling and emptying as never before and even his heartbeat was loud in his ears as he sat there. Strangely, it seemed that he almost *floated*, and his mind was clear but for the slow count . . . The world was open to him, it seemed: he could go anywhere . . .

Something tickled his nose and he sneezed suddenly, a loud explosion, and most of the calmness that had enveloped him vanished instantly, except for a part of it that (even now his eyes were wide open, and he could see that night had fallen) he could now feel as *part* of himself.

My word! Is this what Bahlien meant? He asked himself. Across the wing of the palace, he could sense that Ethrayne was already asleep, so he could not share his thoughts and excitement with her. A picture came into his head, of the girl curled up amid her covers, her lovely hair constrained in a long plait; she was breathing slowly and deeply. Moving pillows about and leaving his dressing gown on a chair, Jerryn soon laid down himself and, that image of Ethrayne sleeping foremost in his mind, he soon joined her in sleep.

*

Shan's family were awarded a stipend, with regards to his murder; the bereaved family were heartened, to meet the king and prince as well as Archpriest Lurco, before they departed with his possessions, leaving the danger of the capital behind, returning to their quiet lives.

Earl Orthen of Rothern, an enthusiastic rider and hunter in his late twenties, was duly announced as the king's personal servant, an honour that he and his family were very glad to receive, although it would probably cut deeply into the time that he could spend both out of doors and trying to wheedle a stallion out of Duke Sarant, as King Marrand himself joked. The appointment seemed to work well; Marrand found the younger man to be hard-working, with a great attention to detail and the days passed relentlessly.

The midsummer celebrations were a little more muted than was usual, but the commoners both within the palace and in the kingdom at large enjoyed themselves as was traditional and the long days of summer continued.

Jerryn and Ethrayne slowly improved at their meditation exercises, for the deep, slow breathing and counting in tandem seemed to help, winning them the Archpriests approval, Bahlien especially. He talked of 'centring' themselves; of 'holding' the Flame within; of 'opening their souls' to Arven and, laughing at their expressions of bemusement, advised them to ignore his complicated words and just to continue as they had begun for now; they might well progress quite naturally to those 'other' states and time was on their side.

"It is strange, however, that we seem to be receiving mixed messages." Jerryn noted coolly, one afternoon. "Ethrayne, and even I, I've noticed, are being pushed to learn and master more advanced combat techniques, your Grace, but you seem reluctant to push us to master this power that has been gifted to us. Why is that?"

Bahlien looked rather embarrassed at his words. "Well, at one level, I imagine that the enemy will be watching and waiting for you to learn how to control yourselves and your power. They will make their move, I am sure, at some point. Send out forces. You are both rather young to learn all that you will have to, for these are the sorts of skills that many razine three times your age would have difficulty mastering. We do not know our enemy's mind – his intentions – and so we are doing our best to address as much as we possibly can. I admit that I am torn by the whole situation and I sincerely apologise."

<An honest answer.> Ethrayne noted, silently. *<We will do our best, your Grace, as we have begun. You are right: we cannot know what he plans, or when his forces might strike, so we really must work at learning and honing all these new skills.>*

"And that is all that any of us can do in life. Thank you for your forbearance." The old razine answered with a smile.

*

Their parents were interested in what their children were discussing during their regular meetings with the Archpriests and they *did* try to explain for, after all, that night deep below the Cathedral had been an unique event, when they had absorbed the Flame of Arven into themselves, but Jerryn and Ethrayne found that they did not have the words to describe what they were learning or what they must begin to master. They were reduced to saying that they were meditating, learning mind-speech and studying history, philosophy and ethics with the old priests.

"Philosophy?" The king retorted once. "Great heavens, it sounds almost as though he's trying to turn you both into priests!"

"No, your Majesty, I don't really think so, but -." Ethrayne answered slowly, to be interrupted.

"But it's a little complicated hey?" Marrand repeated one of their stock sayings of the past moons, one they used frequently, and he smiled sympathetically. "You don't need to worry at the matter, Ethrayne, you both have our full support, even if we don't understand it."

"I know what you mean, Father." Jerryn replied with a rueful chuckle. "Most of what the Archpriests talk about is way over my head."

Ethrayne smiled. "You are exaggerating, Jerryn." She said gently. "As are you, Sire, but it is not easy to explain."

*

Announcements released from the palace and church, regarding the Wielders of the Flame, made much of an unspecified threat from the Betrayer and encouraged men and boys to attend to their skills with spear, sword and bow, even as Ethrayne was. The youth of the city and probably of hundreds of other towns and villages took to weapons practice with great enthusiasm on rest days and holidays, for the legendary Betrayer would, naturally, fall at *their* hand, with no danger or loss of life, as they conveniently ignored the reputed perils of dealing with the jajozeli.

War, even the merest threat of it, proved both exhilarating and frightening, for the realm was largely peaceful, as were Tenarum's relations with Derravale and Amorry; there was a small standing army, mostly concerned with keeping the peace in settlements; investigating occasional crimes and dealing with a usually very low level of banditry; but landowners and the civic dignitaries of towns and cities could raise troops, at least figuratively, in the king's name, even if it had never happened before.

The Council of Tenarum set down in legal statutes the revised procedures for calling up troops, sending envoys out across the realm for landowners, mayors and priests to inform the people in their areas. In fact, many folks were already registering their names for any army required, and the local churches in many villages had been forced to obtain fresh supplies of parchment, to cope with the pages already filled with lists.

These lists were copied and sent to the regional capitals and the numbers, collated by church administrators and sent to Tenum City, were heartening: if it was necessary, there were potentially thousands of men prepared to fight. King Marrand and many of the lords were pleased at this, but Jerryn and Ethrayne were quietly alarmed.

It was quite shocking to realise that people would volunteer to possibly die in their names as Wielders of the Flame of Arven. The responsibility of what they had agreed to was sobering and both grew quietly more serious in manner as the days passed. Even Lord Gorman, however, grew slightly more accepting of the young couple as a political and religious force. They both studied diligently at everything required, from politics and law and history and the daily requirement for meditation, with slow progress, to their eyes, although both Lurco and Bahlien approved of their improvement despite their fears that they were impossibly slow.

"Don't try to run before you can walk." Lurco reassured them, after another few days of evening meditation exercises. "You are learning very well, my dears."

"They are training men for war!" Ethrayne countered, almost angrily.

"Yes, because it might take a year or more to train, equip and amass so large a force adequately, my dear Ethrayne." Bahlien explained politely. "That is what the High-King told me, before I came here. It takes a great deal of time."

She sighed deeply. "Yes, Commander Vedeigne said so, but it is, it is."

"Daunting." Jerryn finished with a shrug.

"Yes, it is." The old Archpriests agreed gravely, nodding in unison.

"Oh damn!" Ethrayne shuddered. "War!"

"This is not your fault, you know." Archpriest Lurco said gently. The prophecy exists, and *you* are its subjects, but the kingdoms can only prepare and gird their loins, so to speak, just in case. That is surely better for everyone concerned that doing nothing and maybe seeing the slaughter of folk with no training or provision at all."

"Oh, I agree, your Grace." Ethrayne said. "I do, but, well, it *is* frightening." She sighed deeply. "But I agreed to this, swore to this and I know I can't back out or run away and, honestly, most of me doesn't really want to."

"Gracious, you are wonderful, Ethrayne!" Jerryn said with a laugh. "You are so determined."

The girl blushed slightly at his approval and the priests smiled tolerantly as they exchanged glances.

"Well, my dears, we can only urge you to carry on with all your lessons until our next meeting." Bahlien's tone was jovial. "And hard work will reduce all our fears, I assure you."

* * *

CHAPTER 11

The walled port of Cal'Badon was situated to the east and south of the towering peaks of the vast Lerracon and Astoln mountain ranges, which had ensured Zanezli's isolation from the rest of the Selithian continent for well over five hundred years, since its founding. It was known to the sailors of the eastern coast of the continent as a location to avoid; the area around the Badon Inlet and indeed, from within the furthest sight of the snow-peaked mountains that edged the coast leading to the peninsula and the inlet beyond were deemed out-of-bounds. Out of the earliest histories there were tales of piracy, murder and ships vanishing, no matter if they were merchant vessels or little fishing boats perhaps blown off course.

Such had been the intent of the Emperor of the Jajozeli when he had founded the realm, early in the third century after the war in Mendor, leading his forces by ship into the empty lands in the moutainous south of Selith. Having discovered that the razine of Mendor were allying themselves once again with the puny humans in the southern continent, he wanted to keep an eye on them and especially for any sight of Bahlien, that meddling youngster (for so he designated him) who had dared to evade him, taking the Casket holding Arven's Flame beyond his reach.

Cal'Itase, on the western coast, had been Gregnor's first base; it was ideally placed to receive ships from Enlath and his servants, both jajozeli and human, had laboured assiduously to ensure first that port city and then the starkly beautiful Ban'Lerracon, his mountain-girt castle and capital city, were impregnable. Their infrastructure was designed from the foundations up, with an attention to detail that the kingdoms to the north could only have dreamed of. With his fanatically loyal jajozeli-razine and millions of men eager to obey his every command, Emperor Gregnor hardly needed his vast wealth to see that every amenity from well-metalled roads to piped hot and cold water and sewerage were properly constructed, despite the icy winters that blanketed the region in feet of snow for almost all the season.

The well-nigh impenetrable Lerracon Mountains; the distance from the southern borders of the more northern kingdoms and those freezing winters helped to ensure that most ordinary hunters, fur-trappers and adventurers in search of gold, precious stones and silver, religiously avoided the region. Those who did continue to venture into the far south were normally quickly eliminated by the forces that were spaced throughout the mountains. Led by jajozeli-razine Generals, their abilities ensured that almost all trespassers were captured. The few who were not were razine spies, risking far more than their lives to gather all the information they possibly could about Gregnor's expansion into the vast area known as Zanezli.

To the razine, Zanezli's existence was most unwelcome, giving their bitter enemies a foothold on the continent where Arven's Casket had been concealed at Bahlien's behest, but it was impossible to seriously consider removing them, without enveloping the world in a second conflict when it had taken centuries for them to recover from the first of the Betrayer's punitive actions, after he had imprisoned their God in ice. The razine set watchers where they could, north-east of Cal'Itase in the foothills of the Lerracon Mountains; trusted to the courageous few who dared to try to bypass the border forts, secreting themselves in the remote landscape; and they could only wait.

The founding of Cal'Badon was even more unwelcome, overall, as it gave the Betrayer access to both oceans and thus to the world at large, for the Southern Ocean that was Zanezli's southern border, was generally too storm-swept and ice-bound to be safely navigated by even the most intrepid sailors. All who had attempted it had drowned, over the centuries. But, with a port on both oceans, the jajozeli could circle the world back to Enlath and so, eventually, they would threaten Selith and Mendor beyond.

*

And so, nearly six hundred years after its founding, the unique city in the far south-east was finally going to fulfil its purpose as devised by the emperor. Warmed to an acceptable degree by hot springs from deep underground, the port had thrived in a harsh mountainous landscape where it would have been frozen for most of the year, otherwise; the inlet a harbour for only icebergs. Yet the volcanic vents provided a vital lifeline and kept the land and the sea ice-free.

For well over a year, troops had been shipped in across the Faell Ocean, a journey of many moons from the west coast of Enlath; or had marched across the continent from Cal'Itase, through Ban'Lerracon during the few more clement moons of summer, along with supplies ranging from foodstuffs to arrows; chain mail to boots. The store houses and warehouses of the port were packed to the rafters yet General Tequan, who was in overall command, could have located any individual item within a short amount of time, so wide-ranging was his assistants' filing system. Elsewhere within the city, hidden by the high walls that protected it, the hundreds of buildings that had been largely empty since their construction were now occupied by the thousands of soldiers that Tequan would command in the name of his master. The extensive, deep-water wharves at the head of the long inlet, also so strategically warmed by the volcanic activity of the region, were full of ships; large, fast craft that outmanoeuvred the vessels built by the men of the Selithian continent at every confrontation.

The spies of the Protectorates knew well that their enemies were quietly mobilising, yet there was little that they could do but warn the kingdoms of Selith; as the spring advanced, even in these southern regions they could only watch and wait, for the jajozeli were otherwise peaceful and the armies of Mendor were limited.

Ships sailed from the port, vanishing into the vastness of the ocean on most occasions although the Orbain Pearl and her sister ships managed to track a few, arriving too late to save the crews of two merchantmen that had been boarded and emptied, before being torched; yet the razine ships had destroyed three ships from Cal'Badon in return.

The taking of prisoners, however, was not an option: they had tried the merciful approach on many occasions in the past, but the fanatical devotion of the jajozeli soldiers and the jajozeli-razine to their emperor was absolute: they only strove to slaughter even more of their enemies during any skirmish and, also, the Protectorate crews had uneasily realised that they did not have anywhere on board their ships to secure prisoners intent on killing them at any cost.

The destruction of the jajozeli ships was generally kept from the wider public of the Protectorates for it was deemed that the population was too far removed from the grim reality of a situation that was closer to a blood-feud than war. Unlike their enemies, however, most of the sailors and soldiers of the Protectorates actively hated the slaughter they partook in and consigned the souls of their foes to Arven, although he was still trapped in unbreakable ice, even as they watched the jajozeli ships sink or burn.

*

General Tequan gazed out over the sea, sparkling pewter-like in the first light presaging dawn, that morning; the sight of the houses of the village of Newventure Bay with their smoking chimneys was clear, despite the league or more that separated his ship from the land. The upper stories and roofs of the houses were poking out of a thin layer of grey mist that glowed pearl-like in the light, extending out over the smooth seashore and out to sea for a good distance and which would reduce visibility on the land.

He led two warships and three smaller craft, bearing three thousand soldiers in all, armed and eager for the fight. By sending in two separate ships selling foodstuff but bearing scouts over the past moon, General Tequan had obtained a detailed map of the village and the number of inhabitants; he knew that there were fewer than two thousand Tenareans dwelling in the vicinity and less than half of those were men of fighting age. It was six days after the summer solstice.

Newventure Bay was the southern-most fishing village in Tenarum, isolated from the rest of the kingdom by towering cliffs curving to the south, a pre-cursor of the Astoln Mountains that formed a formidable border at the southern edge of Tenarum, and by practically impenetrable marshy lagoons to the west and north. It possessed a surprising wealth for such a modest settlement because of its trade in sea salt and fishing, and the only realistic way to reach the village was by ship.

From its founding some fifty years before, Newventure Bay had flourished. It had been built by a close-knit group of younger sons who hailed from two towns further up the coast, far-sighted men who had gambled on their hard work and basic living conditions in the first few years paying a good return; and won. Now, their homes were solidly constructed of stone, furnished as well as any in the kingdom, on the profits of the fine, white salt panned during the summer months; and an almost limitless supply of large, oily shoaling fish that frequented the rich, deep seas thereabouts. Both fish, salted and dried, and salt were sold in many markets of the kingdom and even in Tenum City, at a handsome profit; the villagers had constructed a modest but well-made harbour wall and wharf off the steeply shelving shingle beach that fronted the bay, with the village set on higher ground beyond, protected from the sea by gnarled, ancient pines and mountain ashes, incongruous but striking. A line of dunes heaped up on the right, spiky with marran grass and sea buckthorn, protecting the lagoons beyond, always full of the sound of birdsong, even this late in the breeding season.

The General nodded and the captain's mate waved a red flag vigorously so that the three smaller boats rowed swiftly ahead, one heading towards the left of the harbour, the other two north, to beach quietly before the dunes. Meanwhile, the crews of the warships raised flags in the colours of Tenarum's trading fleet, blue and green stripes prominent; their extensive weaponry hidden and sailed straight into Newventure Bay's harbour. With the rising sun directly behind the ships, the look-out from the village could see little detail and the jajozeli had been careful not to attack any Tenarean villages in the vicinity, so they were not alert to any danger.

The fishing boats were soon burning, along with the lines of nets, barrels and so on, at the hands of the advance troops. Then, the General led his soldiers towards the village beyond, even as the urgently rung warning bells ceased suddenly, the ropes cut down with the terrified folk who had rung them, the initial shouts ceased. Doors to houses had opened and some men rushed out with weapons in hands, but most of them were confused, half-dressed and unarmed, for it was rest-day in Newventure Bay. The villagers didn't stand a chance as the slaughter extended. Tequan himself entered the largest house in the village, striding into a comfortable kitchen to face a burly man armed with a double-headed axe, which proved utterly ineffective: the middle-aged man was not very skilled, the axe lacked the reach of his own sword; he died in moments, gutted, almost dismembered, and his screaming wife and several children, all cowering by the hearth, followed him quickly.

"Who are you?" One teenage girl asked in panic, backed into one corner of the kitchen and still holding a pan, spilling water inattentively, too frightened even to cry, her pretty face pallid despite her spots.

He enjoyed it when he scared people so greatly, Tequan acknowledged privately; sometimes, it was better than sex, the power of it! He didn't even bother to answer, smiling broadly, and ran her through. Then, pausing only to eat a fresh, warm roll from the table, he emptied half the fire onto the kitchen floor, watched the embers set fire to the dead family's clothes and left the house, whistling.

By midmorning, Newventure Bay was no more. The boats were ash; the men folk killed; the surviving women and children herded together, some for the brutal enjoyment of the jajozeli, the rest just to be slaughtered as a group. Still, it was well before noon when all the villagers were dead, their houses and workplaces stripped of all useful or valuable items, including the barrels of salt and salted fish that had founded their wealth, before the settlement was put to the torch. As the five ships set off back out to sea, they deliberately left behind the burning ruins as a beacon.

*

That evening, the Orbain Pearl approached the village with an almost reckless disregard for her own safety, having steered towards the coast of Tenarum mainly based on their captain's razine talents. Captain Ashanner's mental abilities had warned him of *'death/trouble'* earlier that day and he had urged his crew on, shouting his orders and praying to Arven that he had received warning enough to save innocent lives.

Now, stood at the wheel and staring out over the blackened, slightly smouldering ruins of the prosperous little village, he cursed aloud.

"We'll make fast, you all know the drill." He snapped. "Keep alert, watch out for enemy troops and search for survivors, but I've no real hope of any: those bastards look to have done a very good job of destruction!"

"Aye, sir." His second-in-command said, frowning as the massive ship swept towards the outer wall of the harbour; the villagers had been proud of the depth of their little harbour and their captain's skill had the ship just kissing the massive stones with their fenders that hung there protectively. "But it doesn't feel good, does it?"

The crew of the razine vessel were split practically half-and-half, razine and human, with the officers' ratio skewed slightly in favour of humans. Ashanner and Kellen, his first officer, were mature veterans of the on-going conflict with the jajozeli, but most of the rest of the hundred and twenty were young, especially the razine; for a period of duty on one of the 'Pearls' was a good way of working towards promotion, if one survived the experience.

They took the usual precautions for their defence, but their weapons and chainmail were unnecessary as they searched the village from end to end, from loft to cellar, where possible, after the fires. They found only dead bodies, a few frightened cats and dogs that fled at their appearance and some domestic fowl.

Some of the sailors set about collecting firewood for a pyre, whilst the others attempted to restore a little dignity to the dead as they gathered them all together, laying them within the still smouldering shell of their modest Trade Hall, men, women and children. Even the older, experienced members of the crew paled at the atrocities committed on the helpless fisher-folk and they were glad to set the fire, pray for the souls of the victims and depart, poling away from the harbour until the wind caught their sails, heading for the open sea as night descended.

"Well, that was singularly unpleasant. Shit! I've heard of attacks on land, sir." First Officer Kellen said, as the officers gathered briefly in the captain's office. "But the bastards don't usually attack villages. I mean, sir, what would be the point? I doubt they were raiding for slaves, or there would've been fewer bodies."

"The High-King warned in our last communication that the enemy's focus might well change abruptly. The last I saw like this was in the north of Mador, over twenty years ago – nearly as sickening." Captain Ashanner said heavily. "Apparently, the newly revealed prophecy concerning the Wielders of the Flame of Arven is pertinent to this kingdom now. That's why we have been patrolling closer to land and further south."

There was a chorus of surprised exclamations at the news; they had been told about the changes to their orders on setting out from Lerat four months before, but not why they had altered.

"Prophecy!" Lieutenant Hachorn murmured derisively. "The Book of Days is many millennia old, sir, how can it probably have any relevance in this day and age?"

Ashanner shrugged. "I'll have to refer you to the Archpriestess, Hachorn, for an answer to that, but the Wielders of the Flame are known, and it's our task to help protect Tenarum and assist the kingdom." The Captain looked around. "We set sail for Saremouth. The king here needs to know of Newventure Bay's fate; we can refit and get fresh supplies anyway. That's all, gentlemen. Thank you."

Fortunately, when the Orbain Pearl sailed into the harbour at Saremouth on the afternoon high tide, some days later, there was a berth free at the wharf designed a century before for the larger razine vessels, and they were greeted cordially by the crew of the Mador Opal who were loading oil-filled casks of iron and steel, tools and weapons both, for finishing in the Protectorates.

Captain Ashanner sent an officer to notify the local Garrison Commander that he would visit him when convenient, then crossed to the Opal, another merchantman–spy vessel, where Captain Phellos toasted him with Rothern red.

"I didn't expect to see you here, Ashanner." She said, grinning.

"There's been trouble, Captain." He said tersely to the vivacious red-haired razine woman who had commanded the ship for decades, the daughter of a family of traders who had been captained a ship and flourished in business for half a millennium before she had switched trades to this riskier cause; Phellos was respected and successful over half the world. "Those bastards butchered the village of Newventure Bay six days ago. I'd say war is brewing; take care out on the ocean, trust your instincts."

"I *always* trust my instincts, Ashanner, which is why I always notch up a healthy profit." She assured him lightly, then sighed and shook her head. "Newventure Bay? We transported building supplies there when they constructed that harbour wall a decade ago; such an insignificant place, that's tragic. When I next run across the enemy, I'll take payment for those people from their stinking hides!" She raised her goblet, saluted the dead solemnly and gulped down the contents in one. "So, the change has happened: the enemy are starting to alter their methods and focus."

"I only hope we can help the Tenareans." Ashanner said quietly. "The ocean is vast, their coastline long, and unfortunately we can't be everywhere." He raised his goblet to the woman, took a drink and set it down. "I have to tell the local commander. Sail with Arven, Phellos, may we all live to see victory."

"Amen to that, sail with Arven, Captain Ashanner. Thanks for the warning." Phellos replied. "At the very least, we'll take some of those jajozeli monsters with us before we die!"

The woman's fierce smile haunted Ashanner as he made his way through the crowded streets to the Port Administration building that housed the office of the Garrison Commander, on the port side of Church Square, not far from the wharves.

"Ah, Captain Ashanner, how nice to see you again it's been, oh, a couple of years since you were last in Saremouth." Commander Taess was a grizzled former local policeman who had waged war against local smugglers for years; he knew the port city like the back of his hand and kept a firm hand on both the soldiers in his command, the citizens of the city, the sailors and the local criminal fraternity. "Are you here to trade, perhaps? You will have seen the Mador Opal of course; I am sure Captain Phellos has made a handsome profit, as always, on this leg of her route." The man grinned and poured two modest goblets of wine from a plain flask: he had a tight budget.

"Yes, she has marvellous business instincts." Ashanner answered, then sighed deeply. "No trade, unfortunately, Commander, I have come with grim news; you will want to warn your lord, the communities along the coast, especially to the south, and send a messenger to your king as swiftly as possible. Those -." He broke off and changed the word he had been about to use. "Pirates from Cal'Badon destroyed the village of Newventure Bay, utterly and completely: they killed everyone, took no prisoners as far as we could tell."

"Newventure Bay? But it's so small! Only fish and salt! Oh, I suppose they had some money, of course, from their trade." The Commander interrupted, startled. "But-but, why?" He stopped there, took a gulp of wine and shook his head helplessly.

"You have information on the jajozeli in Cal'Badon, Commander: they have plundered and destroyed shipping at the southern edge of Tenarum's range for centuries. My guess is that it's happened simply because Newventure Bay is, was, the southern-most settlement in the land, closest to the border and Zanezli."

Taess paled at the mention of that name. "Lord Kierven and I have received missives from his majesty, King Marrand, regarding Prince Jerryn and his betrothed, the Lady Ethrayne of Clirensar, Captain." He admitted quietly, setting his rather battered goblet aside. "One mentioned the fleet of ships called 'Pearl' and 'Opal'; it seems that we must thank you and your colleagues for protecting us, Captain Ashanner . . . But what are we going to do?"

"Set soldiers in the villages and towns. Forewarned, they will have considerable defence against attack. Mend the watch fires ready for lighting: those beacons are a tried and tested method of sending out warnings. Arm your fishermen and sailors. We can describe the flagships that General Tequan masters, and our own ships too; any Protectorate vessel will aid your people when the need exists." Ashanner grinned at the Commander's expression at his ready answers. "I'm sorry, but we have been planning for this eventuality since your prince and his lady were babies, Taess. I might suggest sending a letter to your king with Captain Phellos, for she's heading north, and a diversion to Rothern won't inconvenience her at all, since she is also part of our network."

"A woman?" Commander Taess objected, without thinking and grimaced. "I apologise, that was stupid, she is a formidable captain and leader."

"And she's damned good with her weapons, too." Ashanner remarked.

"I'll start writing a letter, Captain, thank you. Private!" He shouted to the youth standing politely outside the door who stepped into the office and came to attention.

"Sir?"

"Run down to the Mador Opal and politely enquire of Captain Phellos if she will consent to bear an official letter to be delivered to the Garrison Commander in Rothern, addressed to King Marrand."

"At once, sir." He replied, before saluting and hurrying off.

"You've got them well trained, Commander." The captain said levelly.

Taess snorted. "It's a busy port, Captain and those of us in charge of law and order need to be well disciplined. I don't know if simple discipline and training will be enough against Zanezli, however. I will go swiftly and explain all this to Lord Kierven and his advisors when Captain Phellos has the letter, but it's more important to get the details out to King Marrand, of course. Oh, dear Arven! And Lady Ethrayne and Prince Jerryn are the subjects of Arven's Prophecy? What is the world coming to?"

"Challenging times, Commander Taess, we are entering challenging times, may Arven bless us all."

The letter to King Marrand was as detailed as Taess and Ashanner together could make it and included a copy of Ashanner's best map showing the southern border of Tenarum and the inlet leading to Cal'Badon.

*

Captain Phellos set sail at first light, sailing some leagues out to sea, then heading north within sight of the coast with a strong following wind, coming to the south of the Rothern Estuary late in the day, as the tide was falling. Quickly, the sails were neatly furled, and the anchor lowered with a rattle and splash.

"Hey the fishing boat!" First Officer Lunde waved vigorously at a thirty-foot fishing boat with a bright blue bow that was heading into port under oar, moving steadily against the tide; it was just coming level with the much larger ship, at a sensible distance.

"We hear you, Opal, how can we assist you?" Shouted an elderly, grey-haired and bearded man at the boat's tiller, ordering his men to slow their strokes; he had a reddened, wrinkled face clearly visible between the wind-tangled grey. "Looks like you missed the tide today." His tone was matter of fact, it was a hazard of sea-travel, gauging the tides in new ports.

"We bear an urgent letter to the King of Tenarum, sir; could you set our captain down at the wharf, please?"

The four other men stared up at the ship with awe-struck expressions, but the captain showed no fear or any other emotion as he looked at the first officer. "Razine, are you?" He grunted and nodded a greeting.

"As you see, Captain." Lunde replied politely. "We're men and razine of the Protectorates. We have been charged to deliver these messages to the capital. If you could deliver her to land, the Garrison Commander can have those letters sent upriver tonight -."

"*She?*" The Captain started, then guffawed with good cheer. "'T'wouldn't be that strikin' red-headed lady, eh?"

"Could there be two such?" Captain Phellos asked with laugh, coming up to the rail. "Captain Dhell, you look very well, how's the boat these days?"

"Ah, she's holdin' up well, thank-ee Ma'am. Men, ship those oars; Varro, toss up a line smartish. Stop gawpin' you loon!"

Captain Phellos was about six feet tall, lithe and long-limbed; she was a beautiful, pale-skinned, hazel-eyed woman; and she stood out even more for she had long, wavy red hair that seemed to shimmer uniquely with energy and life in all light, which she generally wore contained in a workable plait. As ship's captain, she wore leggings and shirts almost all the time, which made her seem somehow taller and more graceful; as a skilled fighter, she moved most gracefully, and people had been known to stop and stare at her just walking along, not even noticing the weapons she usually bore, so unknown for Tenarean women, for her entire attitude and approach were unconsciously confident, the equal of everyone she met.

"You know these men, Captain?" Lunde asked, stunned, as his Captain caught the rope cast from the fishing boat below. "Dear Arven!"

Phellos laughed aloud at his surprise as she handed him the rope. "It can be a very small world, Lunde and I've been sailing these waters for over a decade. Captain Dhell's boat had sprung a nasty leak some seven years ago and we on the Opal were within reach. I'll see you tomorrow for breakfast at the usual inn; take care, Lunde -." And she looped her carry-bag's rope handle around her wrist, stepped over the rail and onto the netting that extended down the outside of the hull, descending in moments with the skill of many years' practice.

"Steady, Ma'am. Here -."

Below her, she felt the net tighten as the fishermen took a firmer hold of its bottom and then one hand tapped politely on her left boot.

"Just one step down, Ma'am, we're right under you." Captain Dhell said respectfully. "There, but mind those baskets, that's it. We'll take the captain straight to the garrison, never fear, young man. Then we'll see her safe to the Golden Anchor, good night to y'll."

The smaller boat shoved smoothly away from the much larger vessel, rocking slightly in the swells as they extended their oars again and turned, heading unerringly for the current of the estuary that pushed relentlessly against the waves of the sea, moving steadily inland towards the port city.

"Good night, Captain." Lunde called, seeing a brief wave from Phellos in answer as she sat now in the bow, out of the way of the oarsmen and catch, seemingly as comfortable on the little boat as ever she was on board her Opal. He gave commands for the netting to be hauled up, the watch set, and the lanterns lit as evening began to descend.

"It's good to see you lookin' so well, Ma'am and your ship is a very fine vessel." Captain Dhell said as the fishing boat continued her route, tossed over the waves formed by the sea's melding with the river water, which seemed to want to slow their advance, although the oars were moving strongly in the fishermen's gnarled hands. The city was drawing closer now and they passed other small boats coming in after a long day's work, the buildings getting larger and closer. The older man sighed. "Must be lovely, sailin' the wide ocean." He sounded almost curious and Phellos laughed.

"She's a good ship, but mishaps affect even the best, out beyond the shore, Captain." She said calmly from where she sat. "Sailing is half luck and instinct anyway and the rest is love. The oceans are perilous, but we all love them. We left Saremouth eight days ago, and the day after tomorrow we will set sail for Orbain. The wines and the iron and steel of Tenarum are legendary in the Protectorates."

"You're a very lucky lady, Captain Ma'am." Dhell said and shouted without warning. "Oi! Mind out, Lee! Carryin' Lady Phellos here!" He bellowed, waving one arm urgently.

"Sorry, Dhell, Ma'am, sorry. Arven go with you." The middle-aged man in the boat that had briefly tried to cut ahead of them at the wharf, raised his oars and saluted them politely as he let them go on. "See you at the Sea Star later, Dhell?" He called after them.

"If we can, Lee, thanks."

The little Brighteye was soon fast in her berth, and Captain Phellos did some serious talking to convince the crusty old fisherman to accept the coins she laid in his callused palm, followed by a quick peck on the cheek that would have stunned everyone in the Protectorates who knew her: Phellos *never* showed physical affection for anyone. Then she climbed the ladder to the wharf, waved and smiled at them and set off alone through the crowded dockside as evening deepened.

Her fiery hair fastened tight in the braids wound around her head like a crown, striking and unique in her razine-styled outfit, she made a very direct route through the crowds with no trouble at all. The Lady Captain of the Mador Opal was known and respected, even by the criminal fraternity, since it was well known that the razine were practically impossible to steal from or bamboozle. She strode along, attracting only cheery greetings as she advanced.

Day or night, there was always activity in the docks and wharves of Rothern as in any port city and the garrison offices were manned likewise. A young corporal met the captain in the hallway of the brightly lit law-enforcement section of the plain building and bowed politely.

"Captain Phellos? Captain Kelbourn is expecting you, Ma'am." He said politely. "Welcome to Rothern."

"Thank you, Corporal." She answered.

"Please, follow me." And he led the woman past some plain wooden chairs lined up beside a small table and tapped on a door, opening it to reveal a small, cramped office dominated by an old oak desk, behind which a man was rising to his feet.

"This is Captain Phellos from the Mador Opal, Captain Kelbourn." The young man said, saluting smartly.

"Thank you Allun." Kelbourn was maybe thirty-five, tall and muscular, with an unremarkable face, but for his bright, long-lashed, greenish eyes. He bowed politely. "The famous Captain Phellos, I am honoured, Ma'am. What can I do for you? Are you safely moored?"

"The Opal is anchored off-shore tonight, Captain; we missed the tide, so I came in with Captain Dhell. I bear a letter for King Marrand and his Council from Commander Taess in Saremouth that must leave for the capital tonight." She said, pulling the sealed parchment scroll from her canvas bag and handing it to Kelbourn. "We were the fastest ship available." And she grinned. "Always up for a challenge."

"My word!" The Captain breathed, taking in her confidence and bluff manner and realising that everything he had heard about the woman was true, which somehow shook him to the heart of his being. "Well, may I offer you a drink, Captain, after your voyage?"

"No, but I thank you, Captain Kelbourn, I am due at the Anchor." She declined graciously, smiling genuinely. "A fishing village was obliterated by the jajozeli a few days ago; they killed everyone, I heard. It seems that they have moved beyond their usual predilection towards piracy. Please ensure that the letter goes tonight."

"Oh, dear Arven! I didn't ever expect the warning to be carried out! Yes of course. Corporal!" Kelbourn shouted and managed a wry smile as he scrubbed at his hair briefly with his hands; the news from the palace had been disseminated, of course, but this was the first time that it seemed *real*: that heightened threat from the jajozeli. "I'm afraid you have quite disarmed me, Ma'am." He admitted, as the younger man returned. "On behalf of my superiors and his Majesty, King Marrand, Captain Phellos, I give you and your colleagues our heartfelt thanks."

“And on behalf of his Majesty, High-King Mhezal of Orbain, I accept, Captain.” Phellos bowed slightly and winked as the door opened to admit the Corporal. “I will leave you both to sort out your courier this evening whilst I head for a hot bath and a lavish supper at the Anchor, good night, gentlemen. Arven go with you.”

“That is cruel, Captain Phellos.” Kelbourn accused her, shaking his head. “Have a pleasant evening and Arven go with you and your countrymen too.” And both men bowed her out.

* * *

CHAPTER 12

The royal couriers, changing men and horses at every outpost upriver from Rothern, reached Tenum City by early morning on the third day from the moment when Captain Kelbourn had handed over the scroll to the already mounted rider.

The last travel-worn courier was passed efficiently from point to point from his arrival at the city gates, quickly entering the palace complex where one of the uniformed guards led him quickly to the Council Hall, where everyone around the polished table, whether grey-haired men or two surprisingly young and pretty ladies, stared at him, his uniform dusty from his swift travel along the king's highways.

"Your Majesty." He bowed low and handed over the scroll, explaining quickly. "This message was delivered to Rothern from Saremouth by Captain Phellos of the Mador Opal, acting as courier to Commander Taess."

"We thank you for your swift arrival. Corporal, take him over to the barracks, make sure he eats a good meal before he sleeps; we may call for you later, Courier. Thank you." Marrand said gravely.

"As you command, your Majesty." And both men bowed low before they strode out.

"From Saremouth, hey?" Marrand muttered quietly, almost to himself, his gaze meeting that of Sarant opposite as he broke the seal and unrolled the parchment, before he looked down at the scroll, a frown hardening his expression as he read it once, then a second time more slowly, as the Council sat watching him silently.

"The 'Orbain Pearl', one of those dual-purpose razine ships, was alerted to an atrocity quite deliberately, it appears. The village of Newventure Bay has been obliterated." He said finally in a heavy tone, then started swearing quietly, but intently.

"Newventure Bay?" Lord Gorman made the name a question.

"It is, it was, the most southerly village in Tenarum, isolated." Marrand expanded briefly, having passed the scroll to Lord Ferman. "It was only approachable from the sea, we've been buying their salt and preserved fish for some years now."

"And they were of an excellent quality." Ferman agreed as he read the message, shaking his head. "The people who took the time and effort to carve out a home and livelihood there were most hardworking."

"Honestly, even I know that you don't set fire to a place where you've slaughtered everyone there unless you want everyone passing by for miles to know about it. The men, women and children: all killed for no reason!" The king's voice was cold. "Read it aloud." He ordered.

The report made by Captain Ashanner and Commander Taess was detailed on the actual destruction of the village and it also included all interactions between the razine and the jajozeli since the start of the year; the garrison commander had added all that he knew locally about jajozeli piracy, and both had made suggestions for the protection of ships and settlements.

"They've come up with some good proposals." Duke Sarant said approvingly, scanning the list. "Taess is a good leader, he knows how important the ocean is to all our trade . . . It is chilling that Archpriest's Bahlien's prediction has already come to pass, however."

"Attacks by the jajozeli have been happening for a long time, I suspect." Marrand mused. "I doubt that those jajozeli from Cal'Badon would ever allow other parties to encroach on their territory. Ships have always been lost at sea, but that region around the coast of the Astoln Mountains has accounted for far more losses than could really be considered natural, however cruel the ocean. Damn them!"

"But to attack a defenceless village, that is horrific!" Lady Celia shivered. "They must be evil, or quite mad, your Majesty."

"Possibly they are both, my Lady. And in response, ladies and gentlemen, let us discuss and implement all that we can do to increase the safety of all our people. The lives of every man, woman and child must be dearly bought by our enemies!" Marrand reached for parchment, quill and ink, to their surprise, glaring at everyone around him. "I want Newventure Bay to be the only settlement lost to such evil!"

"Amen!" Jerryn said fervently, as chilled as the rest of them.

It took until late that evening for the Council to agree to the defensive strategy, even eating there in the Painted Hall, to the servants' displeasure. The document produced was hurriedly written up by scribes and was due to be announced publicly the next morning in the city; copies would be sent downstream to Rothern, for wider dissemination up and down the coast; it would also be copied and was due to be sent out to every garrison and government office in the land.

*

The next day, Jerryn and Ethrayne made their way to the Cathedral after combat practice, continuing their instruction with the two aged priests and passing on the news of the fate of Newventure Bay. By now, there was little formality in their private meetings, other than that which exists naturally between young and old, but the cold brutality of the world beyond the protection of palace and church kept intruding, as it did that morning.

"I don't understand, I have to admit it." Jerryn said, raising his hands helplessly. "I know you told us that the jajozeli sank ships and stole their cargoes, but why attack such a tiny village? And why did they kill everyone? Are they really so cruel?"

Lurco sighed deeply. "Yes, they really are, Jerryn. They attacked Newventure Bay because they did not have to risk many lives to achieve the most impact, so slaughtering everyone at first light or whenever it occurred was easy. By setting fire to the buildings, they perhaps counted on the fact that the

Pearls and Opals try to patrol along the coast of Tenarum and took a chance that someone on our side might discover what they had done and report it."

"The Fleet captains are razine, trained as well as they can be, so that their power can warn them of threats – instinct is important, as it will be for you, Am'maiya." Bahlien stated.

"Oh. So, might it be considered a warning to the Protectorates as a whole, rather than to just our kingdom?" Ethrayne asked. "Is that what you mean?"

"It was a warning to us all, my Lady, I am sure. We must be united against the Betrayer, Selith and Mendor together. Newventure Bay was the southern-most village in Tenarum, isolated, the closest to that unclear border; they were no threat, of course, but I imagine that the jajozeli desire to alarm us, as well as wishing free-rein in the vicinity of Cal'Badon." Bahlien said, but in a questioning tone as if he was thinking through the idea aloud; he shrugged then shook his head. "Actually, of course, they want free rein in all the oceans all over the world, it's all part of the Emperor's larger plan, of course to own Iullyn completely."

Ethrayne shuddered and Jerryn grunted expressively as he grimaced.

"Father was worried that the enemy would land an army and try to take over the kingdom from a base on the coast." He said quietly. "I mean, Zanezli must be vast, and we know so little about it."

"It is a large realm, yes, but an awful lot of it is mountainous or ice-covered for much of the year." The old razine said. "As far as anyone knows, it was mostly empty land for millennia, with only a few explorers trapping for furs or searching for gems or precious metals; there are always folk drawn to the unknown, the wilds. No one had mapped it properly, or even thought to use its unknown miles to expand Tenarum or Derravale southwards or create a new kingdom entirely; it's a land defined by the harsh snows of winter."

"But isn't Cal'Badon a very long way south of the border, in the Astoln Mountains? Doesn't the ocean freeze down there sometimes? Ethrayne asked, puzzled. "I'm sure my tutor once told me about ice floating up from the south after winter, even north of Saremouth."

"Yes, it does indeed, and floating ice is a phenomenon that also occurs to the north of the Protectorates. Apparently, the floes can be a real hazard to shipping. Cal'Badon, however, lies at the head of a deep inlet south of the Astoln Mountains and the region is volcanic; there are hot springs and volcanic activity around the city, meaning that winter cannot get a grip on the city or the inlet, the water is too warm to freeze. That's probably why the place was occupied: it's a prime location, despite being situated in such an inhospitable region. Though I'd personally be very wary of living practically on top of such a dangerous force."

"Volcanoes?" Jerryn asked, sitting up straighter in his seat. "Oh, I've always wanted to see a fire mountain!"

Ethrayne laughed aloud at his enthusiasm. "We are facing war, Jerryn

and you're thinking about volcanoes?"

"Well -." A slight annoyance warred with embarrassment in his voice. "I know, but they're fascinating, I'm sorry -." The Archpriests and Ethrayne all laughed and, after a moment, Jerryn joined in with them.

*

The general enthusiasm for weapons training amongst the population did not abate as summer continued; the defensive strategies to protect the coastline and ships were implemented and improved locally where required. Yet, as the long summer days began to shorten, there were few sightings of the enemy, although the razine ships reported tell-tale debris well out to sea on two occasions. Those in command were relieved, but not reassured; the watchers along Tenarum's shore were alert, but jumpy.

The Archpriests' extensive communications with their counterparts in the neighbouring realms of Amorry and Derravale were answered within a moon and a half, when the citizens of the capital viewed the arrival of foreign churchmen and their extensive entourage with cheers and a huge procession followed the visitors almost to the Cathedral Square one sunny morning.

The Cathedral and Palace had been forewarned of their imminent arrival and King Marrand and Archpriest Lurco had ordered their servants to arrange an innocuous public meeting before the Cathedral doors, to be followed by a banquet in the palace.

Lurco, Bahlien, the ambassadors of Derravale and Amorry and King Marrand were all assembled to greet the dignitaries as a great trumpet fanfare blasted a welcome throughout the square. The members of the Council and Archpriest Lurco's staff took up a lot of space in their separate positions, but the prince and his lady were not formally introduced; that was scheduled to take place at the formal banquet which would occur in as much privacy as could be arranged.

They could see the arriving group clearly; lots of soldiers and servants for the basic work, of course, and various well-dressed folk, mostly unfamiliar, their accents strange, their voices overloud with slight unease. Ethrayne recalled what Bahlien and Lurco had told them both earlier: that they were at least the equal of any ranking churchman or lord in Selith or Mendor and, although some might sneer because of their age or Ethrayne's femininity, they should respond politely but firmly to establish their status within this much larger group of religious personages and ordinary men.

"That will go down well." Ethrayne had commented dryly.

"My dear young lady, you have his Majesty's backing and ours as well, so who will dare to try to demean you?" Archpriest Lurco had replied with a smile. "Just please be polite when you attack, that's all we ask."

It was strange, she mused: at her betrothal, she had been so ridiculously fearful of being shut up in the palace, nobody, a queen who was only a face. Yet now, as half of the Am'maiya, she was at least the equal of everyone, perhaps even kings! It was so, so peculiar.

The Archpriests had clearly brought secular representatives of their kings as well as their own retinues and there were bright colours visible amid the sombre robes of the priests, as the visitors were graciously welcomed to the heart of the oldest cathedral on the continent. The speeches were a little flowery but not too lengthy and were concluded by the invitation to the evening's festivities, to mark the centuries of the cooperation and alliance between the kingdoms of Selith. Then, after prayers, the visitors were able to retreat to rest in comfort, either within the expansive complex of the cathedral, or their own well-appointed embassies.

*

Archpriest Eduard was fifty-one, the spiritual leader of Derravale, a largely pastoral realm where sheep, flax and weaving ran the economy. He was five foot six or so, with short, iron-grey, wispy hair, pale eyes and a long nose. Crown Prince Tarlan and Colonel Varle had accompanied him, the latter a man of forty or so, clearly a career soldier, with an old scar down his left cheek; nearly six feet tall, the colonel was lantern jawed, with a huge frame to match.

From Amorry, Archpriest Ghorhant was seventy-two, with thin white hair, rheumy eyes, a stooped five-foot eight, and quite rotund. His assistant was Canon Rayse, in his mid-forties, six feet tall, blonde, chisel jawed with bright brown eyes and a ready smile. Duke Agamn represented the throne, a cousin of the king; he was in everyday charge of the army of Amorry, a man of thirty-five, six foot two, with a long nose, wavy reddish hair and freckles, green eyes and a big frame that also attested to his day job of soldiering.

They had gathered after breakfast the next morning, in one of the meeting halls of the cathedral, where one of the huge sideboards was nevertheless groaning with food and drink. The church took hospitality very seriously, even after the sumptuous feast served the evening before in the palace.

"Please, everyone, get whatever you please and then we'll get down to business, your Majesty, your Highnesses, your Graces, my Lords, Ladies and gentlemen." Archpriest Lurco urged as the last of those summoned milled about the sideboard, pouring tea, ale or fruit juice, or picking a pastry or two. King Marrand was deep in conversation with Crown Prince Tarlan about advances in weaving and sheep breeding, the everyday intruding, as always, in important matters. The representatives of the three kingdoms did not get together very often, and they had to seize every opportunity to discuss trade, taxation or whatever, whenever they gathered.

The seats at the large table were filled and a few seats set at a second table also, designated for lower-ranking staff. Lurco and Bahlien watched as the polite conversations faded into silence.

"Thank you for attending." Lurco said crisply. "We are living at a landmark moment for the world. Earlier this year, Prince Jerryn and his betrothed, Lady Ethrayne, were Chosen as the Wielders of the Flame of Arven, witnessed by my colleague, myself, King Marrand and the Duke and Duchess of Clirensar and their family. After centuries of waiting, we will soon be able to act against the Betrayer and set Arven free!"

Silence followed his words as almost all the strangers gazed long and hard at the young couple who were sat together, dressed rather soberly for their apparent ages, their faces solemn, but even those looking askance at them could tell that they were displaying what seemed to be a very natural air of confidence.

"Yes, they are young." Bahlien continued as Lurco inclined his head and sat down, grinning. "But as the one who has protected the Flame Casket for over eight hundred years, I can assure you that oldest is not necessarily the best." A ripple of amusement ran around the hall. "Prince Jerryn is the heir of Tenarum, the Eastern Realm in the Prophecy and Lady Ethrayne is the daughter of the Iron Duke; the Betrayer is fully aware of this: his servants have been lurking and snooping around the city and engaging in wanton murder and piracy further afield. The lands south of the Astoln and Lerracon Mountains are wide, and the ships of his empire could easily reach your shorelines -."

"What sort of threat is this?" Colonel Varle from Derravale spluttered angrily.

"Oh, there is a threat to all the followers of Lord Arven, whether human or razine, Colonel, and equally within Selith or Mendor." Bahlien said smoothly. "But all we are doing is acknowledging it and warning you that it exists."

"If the Betrayer deems that the moment is right then, yes, we are all in danger." Archpriest Eduard's voice was mellow, despite the topic of conversation. "He has been waiting for the opportunity to try and claim the power in that Casket for centuries, Varle."

"Which is all very well, but was it wise to choose two so young?" Crown Prince Tarlan of Derravale objected. He was thirty, stocky, reasonably handsome and kept his gaze on Jerryn, exclusively. "I mean no disrespect, your Highness." He added in a rather condescending tone.

Bahlien and Lurco both laughed merrily at that, which made most of the group stare in consternation.

<Are you going to answer that, Ethrayne?> Jerryn asked her and she gave him the barest wink in reply.

"Your Highness, your Majesty, my Lords, your Graces, you are very much mistaken if you believe that the Archpriest of Tenarum and the ex-archpriest of Orbain actually had any part in the choosing." Ethrayne stated calmly. "Events have raced along since Jerryn and I were betrothed in the spring, but it seems that Holy Arven chose us in infancy and that we are fated to face the Betrayer at some point, whatever our age. We agreed to this, yes, but we certainly did not go out of our way to volunteer! It seems that his highness and I must lead all our realms, here in Selith and the Protectorate kingdoms in Mendor, against the Betrayer."

The Crown Prince finally looked right at her in shock, but some of the others, Duke Agamn and Duke Werhend from Amorry especially, were visibly stifling amusement.

"Is there anything humorous about my assessment, your Graces?" She asked them coolly and the look in her eyes was measuring.

"Excuse us, Madam." Duke Agamn rose to his feet and bowed low. "We were just appreciating your answer, I assure you; we would never intend any disrespect."

"Arven chose us and we must presume that our God knows what he was doing: the Book of Days is his creation, after all." Jerryn stated. "We might all wish that we lived in a quiet century, but it appears that we have no say in the matter."

"Unfortunately, as some of you are aware, the Betrayer has been preparing for the emergence of the Wielders of the Flame for some decades." Archpriest Lurco said calmly. "We must get organised in many ways and quickly!"

"On my word!" Colonel Varle muttered, shaking his head. "Excuse me, your Grace, but-but the Betrayer? Honestly?"

"Varle, you are not thinking clearly." Archpriest Eduard said, rather shortly. "We in the church have always known that the Am'maiya would come and that there would be war between ourselves and the jajozeli."

"This will bankrupt the kingdoms!" Crown Prince Tarlan objected.

"It'll bankrupt the kingdoms for sure, if the Betrayer lays waste to our cities and tries to take over Iullyn." Earl Rhane, the Derravale ambassador to Tenarum snapped. "We have to counter his forces, your Highness, there is no other option. So, what must we do, your Grace?"

*

With so many knowledgeable people involved, they thrashed out an advance agreement of an expansion of the Council of Tenarum's mobilisation plan; it proved a useful base on which to work. They were also greatly relieved by Bahlien's assurance that the Protectorate Kingdoms under the High-King's direction had large stockpiles of non-perishable food. It was evening before they had finished, and the cathedral staff provided a sumptuous dinner for them all as Canon Rayse, Archpriest Ghorhant's assistant, made notes in a clear, steady hand. The evening was well along before they had finished putting together the preliminary document. Finally, they separated, generally satisfied with the agreement produced.

Returning to the palace in a carriage with Jerryn, the king and her father, Ethrayne sighed deeply and sank back in the corner of the seat, suddenly exhausted.

"Are you tired Ethrayne?" Duke Sarant asked, leaning forward to take her hands in his, laid in her lap. "You look strained, my dear."

"I am, I admit it, Father." She agreed; talking and trying to find agreement and common ground for so much of the day was at least as tiring as combat.

“It has been a very intense day and you have both done very well. These sorts of discussions can be much worse; we managed to be reasonably focussed today.” The king said, grinning. “What do you think of our noble visitors, hmm?”

Jerryn snorted. “I know you told me that the royal family of Derravale are, well, quite old fashioned, father, but I did not believe just how much until Tarlan opened his mouth.” He shook his head.

“Tarlan learned it all at his father’s knee and Nemeth at his father’s.” Marrand said with a laugh. “I’m very glad that you startled him and his companions, Ethrayne. That sort of attitude in this day and age is quite ridiculous in educated men.”

“The Archpriests suggested that we attack right back if anyone took impertinences, father.” Jerryn acknowledged then. “I think Ethrayne took the right note there.”

“Thank you, your Highness, your Majesty.” Ethrayne said graciously and smiled. “But, really, they accepted correction from their Archpriest and Ambassador quickly enough and were not too offended about it -.”

“I liked Duke Agamn’s amusement best.” Jerryn admitted with a chuckle. “It disarmed everyone.”

“I agree, it was very well done.” Sarant agreed and covered his mouth suddenly as he yawned widely. “Excuse me, please.”

“Heavens, Sarant, don’t apologise, we’ve been talking and hammering at words for most of the day, with more to follow tomorrow.” Marrand said with mock dismay. “None of us has any chance to complain of boredom, though.”

“No, your Majesty. My complaints around our betrothal ceremony seem self-centred and selfish, now.” Ethrayne shrugged.

“Don’t apologise, they seemed true at the time, Ethie but look at your life now!” Jerryn spread his hands wide. “I mean, who could expect their lives to alter so completely? We’ve shaken up most of the world, I think.”

“Yes, haven’t we just?”

*

Over the next eight days, the four Archpriests led daily meetings with the civilian and military representatives of the three kingdoms, the Am’maiya and King Marrand. The religious leaders smoothed the occasional disagreements and damaged male pride as required. There were also a few meetings where Jerryn and Ethrayne met only with the Archpriests, where they sat and discussed the Book of Days; the sort of power that might be at their disposal as they grew to understand what they had taken into themselves, and ancient history. It was interesting to discover that their collective support was genuine, and even the elderly Archpriest Ghorhant was kind and positive in his dealing with the two young Wielders of the Flame, whom they might have assumed to be set against two such young representatives exactly as the Crown Prince of Derravale was. In fact, he thanked them both for lighting up the sunset of his years.

"It will be wonderful, when you can free Arven from that ice which has imprisoned him for so long, Am'maiya." He said eagerly.

"We will certainly do our best, your Grace." Ethrayne affirmed with a smile.

*

Spending so much time together, the rather disparate group found that they were not so different after all, although the representatives of King Nemeth of Derravale always stayed a little more aloof from the rest of them, even of Lord Gorman whose mind-set was similar to theirs, as if the liberal tendencies of Tenarum and Amorry might be catching.

During this period, evenings were the best time, Ethrayne found. Early mornings were busy with combat practice, before their meetings; yet, after dinner, she and Jerryn were still free to leave the gathering and retire to meditate. It certainly helped her keep calm, considering how different they all were, clearing her mind, ignoring Crown Prince Tarlan's manner especially.

Their last meeting was the shortest, as ex-archpriest Bahlien read through the treaty that they had all wrestled into existence; it included the coordination of the kingdoms of Selith in any future war, with Bahlien's own addition that their efforts would always be supported by the seven kingdoms of the Razine Protectorates.

Hearing the call-to-arms spelled out so calmly, Ethrayne and Jerryn felt again the enormity of what their elevation meant to be named as Arven's Saviours, or whatever they were as Wielders of the Flame. It made the role of king seem quite tame and manageable in comparison.

<It isn't our fault all this has happened.> Ethrayne said silently to her betrothed, stoutly. *<And we know that the Archpriests have not lied . . . But isn't this strange, for all of us? The kingdoms of Selith have not officially gone to war – well, ever, really . . . The razine and men of the Protectorates mostly struggled against the jajozeli alone during that ancient struggle, or so we understand.>*

<Yes, but I feel horribly guilty about turning the world upside down, with Shan's death and the sacking of Newventure Bay.> Jerryn replied uneasily. *<Yet it's not our fault, you are right of course!>*

The copies of the treaty were signed and witnessed by the men of government and the men of religion before the scrolls were sealed and handed to Duke Agamn and Crown Prince Tarlan, for delivery to their kings. Then after even more speeches, the group dispersed for a farewell banquet at the palace, prepared for that evening. The visitors from Derravale and Amore would leave Tenum City on the morrow and the intensity of the past nine or ten days would hopefully return to normal.

* * *

CHAPTER 13

Ethrayne considered the merest feelings, the lightest touch of surface thoughts that she could now begin to sense from the people who surrounded her in the palace of Tenum. It had been disconcerting, at first, to begin to 'hear' as a very quiet, whispering sound rather like a rustling breeze, something of what people around them were thinking or feeling at that moment, however superficial, and she had been greatly relieved when Prince Jerryn had told her how shocked he had been to hear his father's internal grumbling about finding time to rest, on top of all the meetings scheduled into his day.

They had taken their concerns to Bahlien and Lurco at their next meeting, of course, for whom else could they approach? And the elderly razine had laughed aloud, risen to his feet, and bowed low to them both, grinning broadly.

"Congratulations, Am'maiya. You are advancing with your understanding of the power that you have absorbed; you are now beginning to sense what I and many other razine can feel every day. What you will have to learn now is how to make a barrier to block these emotions."

"But I don't understand, your Grace." Jerryn acknowledged, frowning deeply. "You've been urging us to become at one with this, this power that Lord Arven has gifted us, yet now you are telling us to block it?"

"Oh no, your Highness, I was not very clear, I admit it, forgive me." Bahlien acknowledged. "You are learning how to use many different forms of ability, but such gifts also have responsibilities, as with all power and duty."

"Yes, I understand that." The young man said, nodding.

"Along with possessing such strengths and abilities, you must know when it is appropriate to turn them off, in effect, for it would be rude to be able to read peoples' minds in most social occasions; it would be most impolite and indecent. The next step is to form a barrier, a shield in effect which would keep other peoples' thoughts and feelings out of your minds, just as you have been learning to control your own surface thoughts. Amongst nearly all razine and humans in the Protectorates, such learning begins in childhood, along with basic schooling, whether they may gain power or not. You, of course, don't need to be told not to read other people's thoughts, considering the protocols of your positions; there will undoubtedly be occasions when it's necessary or useful, especially in the future when events might be uncertain, but in everyday interactions, you don't want or need to know that such and such lusts after someone else or dislikes them for whatever reason, and ordinary folk are not aware at all that they are effectively broadcasting widely."

"Yes, I see what you mean." Ethrayne grimaced a little. "This is very complicated, your Grace." It was, now, a common complaint.

"Many things in life are complicated, my Lady and you have already mastered most of the challenges that you have faced." Archpriest Lurco countered with a broad smile and a reassuring tone. “We are very pleased at the maturity that you both display and, as you may be aware, not a few of our colleagues from Derravale and Amorry agreed, including both Archpriests, which was quite a surprise, considering. Even Crown Prince Tarlan’s men were with us.” He chuckled a little. “Your presence amongst us as the Am’maiya rather than as prince and lady has already been disseminated to every kingdom, you know, to their secular kings and church leaders. That was one reason why Pualyn went to Orbain, you know – to represent you, guided by High-King Mhezal.”

“Oh my, really? You are very kind your Grace, but there is just so much to deal with now!” Jerryn made his comment half a complaint by its tone, then sighed a little. “And all this is necessary?” He seemed far more serious, now, to her mind than he had even a few moons before – frowning a great deal, listening hard and thinking before speaking. As was she, of course.

“Oh yes indeed, your Highness.” Bahlien agreed. “Actually, the forming of a barrier is quite a simple act and once you have mastered it, the basic form will stand you in good stead in most situations: you are forming a mental shield, an invisible helmet above and around your own head, that blocks your thoughts *outward* and any thoughts penetrating *inwards*.” He grinned at the dubious looks on their faces. “Look with your minds to see what I am doing.”

He clearly visualised a version of a far-too-large helmet that did not actually touch his head, but began at the tips of his hair, and extended outwards and around like an over-thick cloth helmet, perhaps made of greyish felt, all around his head from above his eyebrows to the nape of his neck. Whilst it was there, they could not sense his thoughts at all. Then, in a moment, it vanished.

<*There, that’s what I mean.*> He said silently.

“Well, it certainly seemed to work, your Grace.” Ethrayne said, straightening the hem of her sleeve. “We could not hear you at all.”

“That is what it will do when you have both mastered it: you can think, simply, ‘block’ or maybe ‘helmet’ and your form of defence and protection will be there in a moment, keeping your thoughts and feelings safe and keeping the minds of others safe from your inadvertent reading.”

“And you want us to practice this, as well, your Grace?” Jerryn asked evenly.

“Yes, if you please, but it isn’t arduous, you will soon get the basic idea formulated and fixed in your heads, I’m sure.” Bahlien reassured them, smiling at the prince’s clear, but silent, sigh.

*

The lessons and exercises continued, designed to bring home to them the fear that had consumed so much of the Protectorates after Gregnor’s depredations throughout the kingdoms: some people, frightened and traumatised, clearly would rather have had peace at any price, even the destruction of their way of life, the abandonment of Arven, the triumph of Gregnor. Whilst others, chief amongst them, the razine royal family, had simply set out their own view uncompromisingly and had stuck to it ever since: the restoration of Arven, even from the unbreakable ice that had imprisoned him for so many centuries; and the destruction of the jajozeli.

A large number of survivors had fled Mendor after the war, sailing away to inhabit the Bertaan Islands, even abandoning their worship of Arven, so traumatised had they been at the Betrayer's war.

From their studies, Ethrayne and Jerryn had grown used to ideas that had deeply shocked them at first, chiefly, that of surrender. Discussing it privately, they had acknowledged that they were young and idealistic to a fault, but surely, when faced with such a war of ideologies, one must fight one's enemies? The Betrayer had brought death and murder to his previous compatriots, his war had been against Arven, after all. War was evil, horrible and destructive, yet surely it was better to fight, in the long run, than to ever let tyranny and evil win?

They had many discussions with the Archpriests and, indeed, with their parents, on this sort of matter and still, despite all arguments to the contrary, the young couple were adamant that their duty was to destroy Gregnor, or at least to stop his advancement and empire, as well as free Arven at some point.

"Just because he's stronger doesn't mean that he should win and grind the world down to his desires." Jerryn stated stubbornly. "Father, you've always taught me how to be a good leader of men and a good, fair king, and what the Betrayer has done completely turns all of that on its head. Arven is our God and we must help him break free somehow and stop the jajozeli."

"I cannot argue with you, you have paid attention, my son." Marrand agreed, smiling. "But it is pertinent to realise just how fear and the threat of war can affect even well-educated and sensible people in very many odd and unexpected ways."

"Yes, your Majesty." Ethrayne agreed. "I suppose that shock can have many unforeseen consequences."

But, alone that evening, she sat back in bed and considered just how many privations and terrors people might have to endure under an occupying army or violent force and, if so, just how easy it would be then, to find the courage to stand up and fight. She hoped and prayed that, if she was faced with such an awful future, she would prove strong enough.

<Well, of course you would, Ethie.> Jerryn's voice sounded in her mind, his tone matter of fact and calm. *<You are one of the strongest people I know. I have every faith in you.>*

<Thank you, Jerryn and I have in you, yet -.> Ethrayne allowed him to see some of her fears, the questions spinning in her head.

Jerryn's mind, now, was a familiar as his handsome face, his wavy, dark brown hair. The whole, Ethrayne found, was even more attractive than just his physical aspects; he was, completely, by far the nicest, most generous but strong-minded person she knew – and, he loved her.

It was another aspect of the growing power they could use; now they could see thoughts and emotions in each other's heads just as clearly as having an ordinary conversation, after the last few moons of meditation, practice and conversation. It had been hard work and deep breathing to numbers had only been the very start of the process. They had both embarrassed themselves and each other with thoughts and ideas and even their own very personal view, their own selves. Until they had gained this power, this ability, their minds and thoughts had been totally private; yet now they had access to memories such as puberty and thoughts concerning physical love and, of course, young betrothed couples do not generally share those incredibly private thoughts and feelings before marriage, especially so completely.

They had both quickly backed away from such revelations, rather than talking about it; an apology and the other's hurried mental retreat from such contact seemed the best approach at first. For some couples, faced with such things, it might have been very difficult to address the differences and concepts concerned. Ethrayne and Jerryn, however, had actually known each other all their lives and the support of the Archpriests was important; Bahlien and Lurco had been very kind and utterly correct in their suggestions on how to progress – they were betrothed, promised to each other in the eyes of the church and their families so therefore the usual constraints could no longer apply as they did to couples who only dealt with 'ordinary' feelings and emotions.

"I am not suggesting any, hum, exploration of the differences and similarities between you." Bahlien suggested mildly, using the sort of sermonising tone that they had come to understand meant that he was personally distancing himself from their predicament and speaking as Arven's representative. It was a reassuring way of telling them that their revelations and confidences would always remain private. "This is a common problem between boys and girls, as I'm sure you understand; in fact, amongst the razine, the slow maturity of children is an advantage in that emotional education and maturity occurs first and off-sets the awkwardness of puberty. You are both dealing with this exceptionally well, my dears."

"Thank you, your Grace." Ethrayne murmured, trying to hold in the blush that she had been attempting to contain for quite a while, not entirely successfully, her gaze fixed on the old razine's shoulder as a safe point of focus.

He patted her gently on one hand. "I know this is awkward and I am sorry, my dear Ethrayne, but we will do our best to assist you through the mire of possible problems and you have our promise on Arven that all that we discuss is completely private."

"We are grateful for your assistance, your Grace." Jerryn said honestly.

*

"That's right, Lady, keep your attention on his eyes, foremost." Captain Garane said, raising his voice above the sound of steel on steel. "But, really, how many times have we asked you to move your feet properly? You have to be swift of movement, my Lady." They were outside, in a large courtyard behind the barracks, part of the palace defences; the only way into it, apart from one narrow, secure ground-floor gateway from the next level towards the outer walls, was up two flights of narrow steps that were covered from all angles by arrow slits and walkways above. It was a space that was generally only used in spring and summer, proving useful for archery and combat practice when required.

"Yes, I know, but it's rather hard to dance in mail, Captain." Ethrayne growled, but it was half a sigh and she winced slightly as she flexed her arm and adjusted her grip. She had been fencing in real chain mail for about a moon, now and was still finding it hard work, it was just so heavy! But at least the ache was starting to lessen, all in all, as she gradually got used to its weight. As a result of her exercise and improved muscle tone, many of her clothes had had to be adjusted accordingly: her shoulders were broader, her upper arms more muscular, her midriff taut and her whole body toned from these almost daily exercises. She did not always fence, of course; she was using different types of sword, for a start: some for thrusting, some for slashing and, of course, she was also learning how to defend herself with so many recently acquired associated skills, that sometimes it was bewildering.

"This dance will save your life, my Lady." Corporal Tymain said reassuringly. "You are doing very well, but you have to learn the lessons so deeply that it's instinct, rather than thinking, that coordinates you."

"Bloody hell! Honestly, why fighting hasn't simply died out because it's so much awful hard work, I don't know!" She complained. Ethrayne acknowledged that she had also inadvertently acquired a soldier's blunt vocabulary since the spring.

"Men like competition, Ethrayne." Jerryn suggested with a laugh. "Tymain is right, you are doing better than you think you are." He was not taking part yet, but was unstringing his long bow, after archery practice against Nate and Antan; he had been marginally closer to the gold than they, but only just.

"Yes, strange creatures." Ethrayne agreed and flashed a grin. *<Oh, well, I can't really complain since I asked for this.>* She added silently.

<They are always critical, for they expect perfection: just think how they criticise me, Ethrayne.> The prince reassured her, wrapping his bowstring neatly. *<Concentrate - and look: if you do this, he'll be disarmed -.>* He showed her a sidestep and change of angle of her sword, that looked quite straightforward, passed directly from mind to mind. "Try it, Ethie."

"Oh, all right. Thank you." Ethrayne stepped backwards three steps, moving lightly on her feet, frowning a little as she considered Jerryn's suggestion, then took two steps forward towards Don, her opponent in this bout; he was a tall, curly haired young man with a strong, muscular frame and a quiet respect for the Am'maiya. She slipped to the left, switched the angle of her sword and that, amazingly, worked as Jerryn had said: the soldier was not expecting her to thrust from his right and so, his posture and approach unchanged, the sword was knocked easily from Don's hand, hitting the cobbles with an almost bell-like sound.

"Brilliant, my Lady!" The Captain exclaimed. "Oh, that was very well done. I told you you could do it! That was very well done indeed."

"Thank you." Ethrayne inclined her head and turned to Jerryn. "Now I understand just what you've all been telling me: my thinking and acting ahead, proactively, outsmarts my opponent in different ways; sorry, Private Don. So, if I am always thinking ahead and prepared, I can disarm or even disable an enemy, sometimes." There was excitement in her voice as another layer of combat was laid clear to her and there had already been many of these. Fighting effectively was certainly not simple, she had learned.

"I'm glad you approve, Ethrayne." Jerryn said, grinning.

"Excuse me, Lady Ethrayne. Now, Corporal Tymain, attack me! Lady, watch me; please, pay attention: this is what you tried, but if you had done this." And Captain Garane knocked the extended blade from the tall young man's hand, then continued with his own sword and stopped his thrust when his sword-point was almost at Tymain's mail-covered chest, heading towards his heart. "You would likely have injured or even killed your enemy."

"I see, thank you." Ethrayne nodded, and her expression moved from a frown to a quick grin. "Can we do that again, please?" She asked eagerly.

"But of course. Let's start again, men, pair up, please." Garane ordered crisply.

And the more she learned, the better she got, however slowly; oddly it became a more fun, despite the pain, discomfort and accidents that occasionally occurred – such as when Jerryn nearly knocked her out with the hilt of his sword, one bright summer's day, and she was sporting a massive bruise on her temple for six days. Her mother and many other ladies, both titled and untitled, nobles and servants both, were horrified at first, but King Marrand, her father and Commander Vedeigne were very reassuring.

In fact, Ethrayne began to find the concerns of her female friends and the older male courtiers a little wearing. She had asked to learn these skills; the Archpriests had urged her to master them and, as the Wielder of the Flame, the common protest of unladylike behaviour on her behalf was trivial in the extreme.

"I'm sorry, your Grace, but shouldn't someone remind them just what is at stake here?" She demanded, one afternoon, when she, Jerryn and the Archpriests were gathered again. "I can't win, can I?" She flung up her arms and glared indiscriminately at the men.

"Yes, but patience is to be exercised, my dear young lady." Archpriest Lurco urged with a smile. "You are uniquely placed, Ethrayne, Jerryn, as icons to your peers and you have been magnanimous and gracious throughout, so please don't fall into bad habits now."

<Bad habits?> Jerryn asked silently. *<We wouldn't dare, your*

Graces!> His mental tone was mildly sarcastic.

"You are bridging a divide that has largely existed since the creation of Iullyn, Ethrayne." Bahlien said after pouring more tea. "The lives of women have been largely constrained throughout history, simply because of society's needs and values; by that, men and women have had different roles, of course you know what I mean." He grinned at Ethrayne as she rolled her eyes expressively. "But even amongst the razine and in the Protectorates at large, most girls and women conform to the same role models that constrain your sisters here in Selith, but not all, by all means." He paused for a moment. "There is a most unique lady razine sea captain who has confounded every usual convention: she is an expert with weapons and is one of those keeping watch on the jajozeli in the eastern seas. No one except the High-King tells Captain Phellos what to do, and she is viewed with the utmost respect throughout the Protectorates and at the seaports down your eastern coast. I am sure your fathers will have heard her name and her reputation, for she delivered the report concerning Newventure Bay. As well as guarding the seas, she trades back and forth between Lerat, Horann and Saremouth and other ports, probably making a tidy profit as well."

"She sounds amazing." Ethrayne said, clearly a little nonplussed.

"You would probably like each other, but she's a little too formidable for some people." The old razine said. "It is a lonely path, leaving the well-worn ways of one's peers, but you are already well on the way to that; as future king and queen, you will be always apart from the rest of the world. Now, however, that distance is greater in different ways."

"Yes, that is true." Jerryn nodded. "I have been trying this helmet mind-block, your Grace, it sometimes works quite well, I think." He shrugged. "But people just think so many ridiculous things and it's a little hard to achieve all the time, I admit."

"You will soon find that it is simply second nature to you and you will always have a good means of finding truth, loyalty and lies amongst your courtiers in the future." Lurco stated. "It's an ability that a lot of folk in high position would perhaps give their left arms for."

"Gosh, yes, I can imagine." Ethrayne smiled. "It's probably a very good thing that such abilities are not universal, really, some people would definitely abuse them."

"But if everyone had such powers, such abuse would be impossible, wouldn't it?" Jerryn wondered and frowned. "I can feel one of those large discussions starting on ethics and power and responsibility, you know."

"Surely not, your Highness!" Lurco exclaimed, smiling.

*

It was hard, considering her busy days, but Ethrayne now tried to spend a great deal of her remaining free time with her mother and Lyria, for she now realised just how much the changes and revelations of the past moons had pulled her away from the one person who had spent all her time caring for her daughter and was now watching, regretful but perhaps proud also, as she strove to master such innovative and rule-breaking concepts and training.

She had always considered Riyala, her mother, to be simply beautiful, calm and always perfectly presented; supporting her husband, the duke and always at his side, just part of the whole. That realisation of her own view shook her, for, of course, her mother had been the absolute centre of her own world until she herself had grown out of the nursery. When had her mother begun to seem just an adjunct? Not even considering that she personally managed their home entirely. Ethrayne had somehow found herself with the blinkered view of the servants, perhaps, spending more time with her maids rather than her mother, a vision that she realised was utterly mistaken.

It wasn't until the Flame of Arven began to awaken talents that had been previously far beyond her understanding, that Ethrayne understood that Sarant discussed every single matter that came before him with his wife. All right, so this was done privately, rather than publicly, as Jerryn proposed to make her his equal as queen, ruling at his side. Yet every single issue that was raised to the duke was raised to the duchess: in the end, her opinion was just as important as her husband's and she, their daughter, had never realised it.

Ethrayne felt quite ashamed of herself, for her ignorance and assumption that her mother was simply a wife and mother, rather than a politically aware person in her own right, with her own fully developed opinions, political acumen and logic. She would be horrified if people considered herself to be so limited, so how had she been so stupid to consider her mother so?

"Mother, can I ask: why on Iullyn haven't you ever told me that you have supported father so much, all these years?" She asked meekly, one sunny afternoon when they were all sat in the shade of an old oak in the Queen's Garden.

Riyala smiled. "You have realised the truth, then?" She asked in reply and her daughter blushed a little. "Age is bringing you wisdom, Ethie dear."

"Mother!" Ethrayne protested and grinned in a rather embarrassed manner. "I admit it, I was most inattentive not to realise, but -."

"You faced all that opposition from the lords when Marrand asked you to join the Council, dear. That was why your father has never publicly announced my; well, let's call it my advisory capacity, shall we?" She laughed aloud at the mirrored expressions of surprise on Ethrayne and Lyria's faces. "If you had not been singled out by the Archpriests and thrust into the front of the court so completely after your betrothal, dear Ethrayne, we would have told you that this is how many women fill such a role in many situations, but it seemed rather superfluous at that point. Marrand's wife also assisted him in this way . . . oh, the long discussions we all had, when you were little, Ethrayne. Poor, dear Tanallyse." Riyala sighed deeply. "But Marrand, your father and Jerryn all wanted to shake up the kingdom, after the Council's reluctant acceptance of Lady Celia's inheritance and look at you!" She exclaimed, gesturing. "Not only are you the foremost woman in the kingdom, you are now central to the church as well, oh my dear Ethrayne!"

"And look what happened to throw the world sideways." Ethrayne said ruefully. "It's still rather a shock, Mother."

"You are managing well, my darling." Riyala assured her. "And even the older men in the court have come to terms with the changes we have rushed in."

"Yes, but they struggled against it, your Grace." Lyria noted, in her characteristic calm manner, smiling.

"Men do; even if the changes are vital or desirable, they can fight tooth and nail against it." Riyala remarked drily. "Fortunately, the king and the duke have never been so obtuse, and we all did our best to bring up Pualyn and Jerryn sensibly. Well, you saw how the Crown Prince of Derravale behaved when you met Tarlan and he is, apparently, a well-educated man." She shook her head disapprovingly.

"Oh, Mother, what would we do without you?" Ethrayne sighed.

"Well, let's hope we never have to find out!" Lyria said prayerfully.

"Amen!" The three of them said together and laughed aloud.

*

Lyria was quieter than usual, of course, missing her betrothed much more than she would admit; it did feel strange to all of them, not having Pualyn around, even though he would have been back and forth between the capital city and Clirensar, usually on business for his father, or travelling further afield through the kingdom for the Council as required to represent the king. It seemed that the actual knowledge of the great sea voyage that had swept him so far away had somehow reinforced the distance between them in a peculiar way.

Ethrayne was pleased that her friend was coping so valiantly, in the quiet, dignified manner that the court would have expected of one who would one day become the Duchess of Clirensar. The capricious nature of people proved rather baffling, she agreed, pleased that neither of them really had to worry about the vagaries of public opinion again! The approval of the king and the duke and duchess was armour far exceeding the strength of the best chain mail.

Yet, still, the existence of the Betrayer lurked at the edge of her awareness; the possibility of war at some point in the future was unsettling, as she strove to master her lessons. History; philosphy; combat training and learning how to manage the slowly surfacing power that was just starting to feel as if it might really belong to her . . . yet despite so readily agreeing to the responsibility of accepting the Flame of Arven, Ethrayne wished, in a way, that she and Jerryn were not the ones Chosen – that void of the unknown just seemed too vast to accept.

* * *

CHAPTER 14

Pualyn had appreciated the efforts that the people of Lerat had made, for when viewed from the vantage point of a ship's deck, the city was all but unassailable, without what would probably be a huge loss of life for the forces of an attacking army.

The capital city of Orbain was a beautiful city spread out above the sea; it was well planned, with a gridiron layout of roads and old walls that towered massively over all the structures nearby, thick and solid. As High-Prince Kerrenan had said, although it had been sorely damaged by the jajozeli after the Betrayer's imprisonment of Arven, the inhabitants had had over eight hundred years to plan and build effective defences and they had done it well, even cutting away the coastline in one area to utilise the bedrock, so that now a massive circular watchtower jutted, impregnable, above the boulder-filled shoreline with panoramic views.

"My word!" He said, stunned, as the Lerat Pearl headed for the wharves that extended into the estuary channel, the city walls looming high above them, a smooth, cunning, slightly outward-curving wave of stone, stark in the midmorning sunlight. "Most impressive, your Highness."

"It's best to be obvious in the matter of defence, my Lord for it reduces complications in the long-run." Kerrenan said.

"That's true." Pualyn glanced at Lennarn. "You'd have to be suicidal to try and attack, wouldn't you?"

"Oh, indeed you would. I wonder how long it took to construct?" Lennarn asked.

"Apparently they were building off and on for nearly five hundred years." The razine said. "I'm just glad it's there, but the effort involved in building it all; well, it would have been bloody tedious work, wouldn't it? I don't think I would make a good stonemason."

Pualyn laughed. After over a moon of travel, he was pleased to have found their host so excellent and friendly a man, despite his great age and strange abilities. Still, he acknowledged that the sight of Lerat's defences had reawakened his inner concerns at the very great differences he would face here, in a society already old when the Betrayer had imprisoned Arven.

The ship docked smoothly and a stocky man with spiky strawberry-blonde hair came aboard almost immediately; Harbour Master Souden was briefly introduced to Pualyn and Lennarn. He bowed, shook their hands and that of High-Prince Kerrenan, then made his way astern to where the Captain was giving orders.

"Souden helps coordinate sightings of the enemy, in case there are any suspicious patterns of behaviour." Kerrenan explained. "Now come along gentlemen, they don't need us here, we'll head on up to the palace. Our luggage will follow." He flashed a grin. "Don't look so worried. Look, there's our transport."

Some distance away, close to a huge stack of bales and barrels, a carriage of a strange design, pulled by two large horses, had come to a stop, having manoeuvred in a tight circle to facilitate its leaving of the bustling dockside. It was constructed of plain, deep brown wood clear against dark blue paint on the edges and decoration; the coachman wore a matching blue coat, whilst the proud horses were gleaming chestnut geldings, Pualyn noted, professionally.

The High-Prince led them down the gangplank and through the mass of labourers and sailors. Pualyn caught a polite chorus of 'hello, sir' as they advanced and Kerrenan replied in kind, it seemed rather informal. The coachman saluted as they came up to him. "Good afternoon, gentlemen." He greeted them in razine.

"Afternoon, Donnal, can you drive steadily, please? I want to show our visitors some sights of the city as we go." Kerrenan said in selithian.

"Of course, sir, we don't have a schedule as such." Donnal replied in the same language.

"Thank you." Kerrenan said, opening the coach door himself and ushering his companions inside.

The interior was understated but well-crafted, deep-blue upholstered leather seats and a light-blue paint on the walls and ceiling, with space enough between both sets of seats for the longest legs. As the door was latched shut, Donnal set the horses moving and they all sat back, swaying slightly as they set off along the cobbles.

The gated entrance to the city was a tunnel leading right through the bottom of the wall, a good fifty feet long, filled with portcullises, gates and defensive positions. Sharp eyed soldiers patrolled both ends of the tunnel in groups of four, all of whom came to a brisk, brief attention as the coach passed. The tunnel climbed slightly at its inner extent and the coach emerged between twin curving towers with arrow slits strategically placed; they were inside the city, entering a large paved area that extended a good few hundred yards to left, right and ahead, before the buildings began; most of the square was taken up by a large, busy marketplace, a great number of brightly covered stalls and kiosks were laid out neatly, either side of the thoroughfare, leaving a broad path. Markets were universal of course, but the speech and sights and smells that alerted their senses here were subtly different, the two Tenareans realised as they passed. Even the clothing worn by the people were different, in odd ways.

Kerrenan told them that the plain, blocky buildings fronting the square were mostly military, matching the ones facing the Land Gate on the far side of the city. Beyond those, the road ran straight between a mixture of private houses and shops filling the ground-floor of other buildings, with a glimpse of gardens beyond. There was a smell of cooking fires, food stuffs, horse manure and even flowers, but there was none of the reek of night-soil that tended to permeate Tenarean towns and cities, even those with some sewerage.

“Our ancestors constructed an underground sewage system as well as a piped fresh-water supply.” The High Prince explained. “It makes things a lot more pleasant, doesn’t it?” He laughed. “Miscreants are tasked with keeping everything working properly and we have a relatively low rate of criminality overall.”

“I would have thought that you would not even have criminals, Kerr.” Pualyn said with surprise. “I mean -.”

“Dear Arven, we’re not perfect, Pualyn! There are always going to be those who thieve, or fight, or whatever. Most of us who are drawn to such distasteful activities join the army!” Kerrenan winked. “Life here can be tedious whilst training to defend the world against a maniac who desires to destroy our God and then take his place, keeps us busy enough.”

The city was large, the main road as straight as an arrow. They passed houses, parks, businesses, tenements and warehouses before finally nearing a second great defensive wall, this one only a hundred feet tall, again curving outwards at its top and faced with fine white limestone, bright against the grass at its base, sloping down steeply to a wide moat that cut across the road. Twelve guards in chain mail and deep blue surcoats embroidered with a golden sun, holding long spears in their hands and swords at their side, stood in groups of three stood at either end of the drawbridge. One of them lifted a horn and blew a series of notes that rang in the air as the coach passed, rattled over the wooden drawbridge and on through the gateway beyond into another tunnel, this one only about thirty feet long.

Beyond, the road crossed a rising slope of grass to a large complex of buildings that put Pualyn in mind of the Cathedral in Tenum; there were external buttresses, a variety of styles of tower and lots of windows, shining in the late autumn sunlight. Banks of trees were dotted about, many showing a beautiful but thinning range of colours from pale yellow to deep crimson, with dark evergreen types in between. There were ranges of other buildings across the lawns within the walls for the size of the area was vast, but all eyes were drawn to the palace ahead, where standards atop the tallest tower flashed the golden sun emblem.

The road before them finally began a graceful, sweeping curve that brought the coach around to a canopied entrance edifice, where people were waiting.

A servant stepped forward to open the coach door facing the elegant portico and steps as the horses came to a decorous stop and the High-Prince descended first, embracing one pretty, young woman tightly, then bowing to an older man and woman, his left hand entwined in the younger lady’s, before turning back to Pualyn and Lennarn who had stepped down almost fearfully.

“Father, Mother, Arialle, may I present Lord Pualyn of Clirensar, and Lennarn, his assistant.” Kerrenan said formally and all three nodded politely, smiling. “Pualyn, I have the honour of introducing my father, High-King Mhezal, my honoured mother, High-Queen Nicail and my most precious wife,

High-Princess Arialle."

"Your Majesties. Your Highness. I am deeply honoured." Pualyn managed to say in the mendor, bowing very formally.

"My Lord Pualyn, welcome to Lerat." The High-King said, taking his hand and shaking it heartily, speaking in selithian. "I have to say that we have been eagerly awaiting your arrival. Come along inside, gentlemen. You will be guided to your rooms and you may bathe and rest, as you like, until tonight."

"Unfortunately, my Lord Pualyn, many local dignitaries wish to meet you and a banquet has been arranged for this evening in your honour." High-Queen Nicail said, her voice surprisingly deep for a woman and very melodious. She was as tall as Pualyn, a beautiful woman with luminous skin and green eyes, her light grey hair arranged simply but stylishly with the sort of jewelled pins his mother and sister used. The gowns that she and princess Arialle wore were very different to the fashions in Tenarum, but elegant, comprising of a long-sleeved under-gown of a single colour and a sleeveless, almost sheer silk over-gown that spread wide from the hips, girded with simple belts of beautifully worked patterned silk in a complementary shade. The princess wore deep green beneath a lighter shade of sea green, whilst the queen was striking in crimson with rose pink on top. High-King Mhezal was dressed rather as Pualyn and Kerrenan, in deep grey, black and white, whilst the servants were rather uniform in maroon.

"I am honoured, your Majesties." Pualyn said, bowing again.

"Excellent, let's go inside." Mhezal said and glanced sideways at his son, standing close to his wife, speaking quietly. "Kerr, come on." He added with a chuckle.

"Yes, Father." The High Prince winked at Pualyn and followed the guests as they climbed the steps to the imposingly massive doors above, hand in hand with Arialle.

*

A polite, middle-aged servant showed the two Tenareans to a sunlit suite on the second floor, equipped with a bell-pull to call for assistance in the sitting room. There were also two bedrooms and a bathroom, all very well equipped and spacious. They were shown huge closets for clothes and storage, the arrangements for filling the bath and a covered tray holding cold cuts, salad, bread and fruit in addition to cakes, wines, ale and fruit juice.

"Please, my Lords, refresh yourselves and rest. If you require anything at all, please ring the bell, else I will return later with your baggage. My name is Cenrayn." The servant said in flawless selithian, bowing politely.

"Thank you, Cenrayn." Pualyn said.

The two men made full use of the facilities and Pualyn then Lennarn enjoyed a leisurely bath, after he and Lennarn had eaten and his servant had trimmed his hair. Then, they sat in the sitting room, chatting idly, until Cenrayn knocked on the outer door and waved in several youths bearing their luggage.

"I will leave you to get your possessions straight, my Lord." He said with a smile. "Tea will be brought shortly, if you would like some?" He gestured to one of the youths and the tray that had held lunch was removed.

"Yes, please." Pualyn looked at the chests and bags with dismay. "Dear Arven, I'd forgotten we had brought all this, Lennarn!" He exclaimed, and his valet laughed aloud as Cenrayn smiled.

"Could I have access to a hot iron please, Master Cenrayn? I imagine that an awful lot of my lord's formal clothes will be creased." Lennarn asked.

"Yes of course, Master Lennarn. I will send a young man along presently with your refreshments and he will be able to show you the laundry; it is the problem with travel, of course: it does not do fabrics any good at all. Please, excuse me."

"Thank you for your assistance, Cenrayn." Pualyn said gratefully as the man bowed and turned to leave. "Right, Lennarn, let's see what's where, I simply can't remember."

By late afternoon, they had unpacked their baggage and Lennarn had rescued some of his master's finery from the demon creases, visiting the extensive palace laundry located somewhere to the rear of the vast complex and telling Pualyn of the many differences he had noted, even in so quick a visit.

"This palace has been here for a thousand years at least, Lennarn, although it was extensively damaged in that war." Pualyn remarked, donning the formal tabard of his rank as Tenarean envoy over a fine but plain silk shirt. "Gosh, I'd forgotten how heavy this thing is! Am I straight?" He frowned into the large silver mirror in the bedroom.

"Hang on." His valet lifted the neck and shoulders, pulling slightly and flattening the thickly embroidered fabric here and there. "There, perfect."

"I don't want perfect, Lennarn, that's for ladies, Ethrayne and Lyria. Just so long as I don't disgrace the king and our family, I'll be all right." He grimaced.

"You look elegant and sophisticated, Pualyn and I'm sure you'll dazzle everyone you meet with your wit; don't worry, the High-King and High-Queen seemed very pleasant and I'm sure they would never spring some travesty of a ceremony on your shoulders without warning." Lennarn assured him.

"Gosh, I hope not!" The young lord's answer was almost prayerful.

High-Prince Kerrenan arrived not long after as the sun sank into the west, striking in green and white and smiling at his guests.

"Here we are, all properly dressed and Lennarn can go and rest, whilst we have to smile and make small-talk." He said easily. "I've always thought that sometimes the servants have a better time of it than we do."

"Perhaps we do, your Highness, on occasion." Lennarn agreed, bowing deeply. "But certainly not all the time; and not with all the chores of cooking, cleaning and preparations for a banquet, certainly."

"Kerrenan, King Marrand sent a number of small gifts for your family in friendship, but should I present them this evening?" Pualyn asked fretfully, frowning.

"Heavens no!" Kerrenan interrupted. "No, such gifts are better presented at a later, private occasion. The other guests would only want gifts as well if you did." He sighed. "Unfortunately for you, word got out that you were arriving and apparently every king in the Protectorates is here, desperate to make your acquaintance."

"What, all of them? Not just your family?"

"So Arialle says, which is why I'm here and protocol be damned! At least dinner will be superb." His tone was exaggeratedly droll.

In retrospect, the evening went as pleasantly and as smoothly as he could have wished, Pualyn acknowledged, late that night: none of his fears came to pass and his inner nervousness had faded a little; he had been introduced to five more kings and queens, some with crown princes with them; in addition to a queen-regent and her eleven-year-old son, the King of Jaece. All of these were human and, amazingly, everyone he met, whether razine or human, seemed both genuinely pleased to meet him and rather over-awed that he was the brother of one of the Wielders of the Flame.

The conversations, by-play and interactions were surprisingly similar to how such an evening would have proceeded in Tenum City; once or twice, the young lord looked around for his parents, or King Marrand, but the only familiar face was High-Prince Kerrenan who kindly stayed at his side, introducing him to the guests and providing information on them. High-Princess Arialle kept coming to join them, elegant in pale lilac and silver, her blonde hair arranged beautifully and so providing her with even more height; she added quiet observations that were rather witty and Pualyn realised that politics was actually the same anywhere in the world and started to relax a little as they all went into the banqueting hall.

"Don't worry at trying to remember who everyone is, my Lord Pualyn." The High-King advised him privately, part way through the excellent feast. "You will be meeting all the important players again in less formal circumstances." He grinned and winked. "Some people have a gift at recalling names and faces instantly, but I confess I am worse at it than my son, for example. I imagine that you find these occasions just as tedious as we do."

"Yes indeed, your Majesty, but if your court here has not managed to find an alternative after all these years, then I suppose that these magnificent banquets are just a part of our lives." He replied politely, then tried a smile in return. "And at least it gives us a chance to show off our best clothes and our staff a chance to show their wonderful arrangement and cooking abilities."

"Ha! Yes, you're right there." Mhezal burst into laughter. "Else what's the point of them? Well, my Lord, I hope that this has not been too great an ordeal. We can start normal meetings the day after tomorrow. Nicail thought you might like to look around the city in the morning, get yourself a feel for the place? What do you think?"

"Thank you, your Majesty, for making me feel so welcome." Pualyn answered gratefully.

*

The next morning, he was summoned to breakfast with the royal family, where Mhezal jovially gave him a purse full of Protectorate money in exchange for his Tenarean coins; Pualyn felt far too unsure to question the exchange-rate, he just hoped that the High- King wasn't being too generous; then the High-Queen, High-Prince and -Princess took Pualyn on a tour of the beautiful city beyond the palace walls. It was a nice, quiet interlude after the formality and stuffiness of the previous evening and gave them all the chance to stretch their legs, something that Kerrenan seemed to relish, striding ahead with a grin as he seemed to shake off the inactivity of their long voyage and Pualyn quickly felt better for it.

Wandering through a bright, bustling market in the imposing, tree-lined central square, Pualyn spent a little of his money on small, pretty trinkets for Lyria, Ethrayne and his mother and the vendors, seeing his companions, politely offered excellent discounts. They headed back up to the palace the best of friends.

That evening, after a private dinner with the royal family, Pualyn handed over the letters from Bahlien and the polite letter and gifts from King Marrand; these consisted of the finest weapons from Clirensar's craftsmen for Mhezal and Kerrenan and jewellery for their wives: pearls and diamonds for the High-Queen and diamonds and emeralds for Arialle; the best that the treasury could offer, re-worked by the master-craftsmen who had been commissioned to assemble Ethrayne's betrothal jewellery.

"Dear Arven, Pualyn, we are most honoured!" The High-King said enthusiastically, as he and his son examined the swords rather as Jerryn had done on receiving his betrothal gifts and the resemblance made the young man smile to himself: people were not so different.

"My word, Pualyn, thank you!" High-Queen Nicail exclaimed, holding up the earrings to Arialle's ears. "These are beautiful, Tenarum has some exceptional craftsmen. You will have to visit again, bring your new wife when you have wed and *do* bring more gifts, please -." And she laughed merrily. For a woman of mature years, (Pualyn balked slightly at the two or three centuries that marked those years) the High-Queen was a warm, approachable, beautiful woman with a well-developed sense of understated humour.

"I will certainly return, your Majesty, if my king and my duties allow." He replied with a bow and a chuckle at their approval. "But it might bankrupt the treasury in the long-run."

"My word, yes it might, and we will all need all our resources and our revenue to pay for the soldiers we might require the aid of in the future." Mhezal said soberly and glanced around at his family, sighing deeply. "It is awful for your family, your king's, your kingdom and especially for the young couple concerned, suddenly having to make such a decision: to accept Arven's Flame after discovering the danger posed by the Betrayer, but we had no sensible way of alerting you to what might happen; we have agonised about it."

"That's true." Kerr said in a heavy tone. "I've been on the verge of coming up-river to Tenum City on more than a few occasions over the past few years."

"But would King Marrand even have believed you if you had, Kerr?" His father continued with a shrug and essayed a fake smile that did not reach his eyes, he looked rather tired, now. "I mean, Pualyn, who on Iullyn would have believed such a tale?"

"I understand, your Majesty and we have held the same conversations a number of times in Tenum City with ex-archpriest Bahlien and neither you nor he should feel guilty, sir, if I may be so bold." Pualyn replied confidently. "You have summoned me here to hopefully address the situation and to provide the kingdoms with an organised approach to deal with the threat of the jajozeli." He smiled at the rather worried faces across the room. "Unless this is some sort of elaborate farce and we all face total annihilation?"

"Dear Arven, I hope not!" Kerrenan spat with feeling and a shudder.

"Our God would not treat us so cruelly, my Lord Pualyn." The High-King asserted gravely. "And none of us, least of all ex-archpriest Bahlien, would ever have been party to such a monstrous concept!"

"Excuse me, your Majesty, I intended no disrespect." The young man apologised, getting to his feet and bowing low.

"We understand your concerns, Pualyn." The High-Queen said soothingly. "Our world has been shaken significantly and we are gazing into the unknown, except for that passage in the Book of Days. Your young sister and her betrothed are vital to Arven in some significant way that none of us yet understand. We must gird ourselves for war, or whatever may develop from this point on. We will certainly never abandon Selith."

"Thank you, your Majesty." He bowed again, subtly reassured by her earnest words and those of her husband and son.

"We have gathered our allies, the rulers of the other realms of the Protectorates; the Archpriestess and her staff for they are the most knowledgeable concerning the Book of Days; we also have experts on the enemy, both civilian and military, along with logisticians for it is always useful hearing from those who understand the movements of people and supply chains and so on." The High King said more calmly. "Together, we will prevail."

*

Over the next two moons, as winter took a firm, chilly grip over the land and Pualyn thought rather wistfully, now and again, of the summer that he was missing, he spent a great deal of time learning an awful lot about a great deal, as well as educating his hosts and the other rulers in return. There were many misunderstandings on both sides, including not a few concepts and beliefs that were utterly alien, which needed more explanation or discussion; Archpriestess Gailla was always central to these sorts of talks, for the tall, grey-haired woman (plain of face and short-haired, the opposite of High Queen Nicail) was expert in mediation and soothing stung personalities.

Pualyn earnestly thanked his life-long education and his place on the Council of Tenarum, for he found that his grounding there, learning of the running of Clirensar from his father and the managing of the kingdom from King Marrand, was a firm basis on which to build. His poise impressed everyone and especially the razine with his maturity and knowledge and his willingness to both question and learn.

Of course, he did not spend every day in discussion and meetings. There were rides out, hunting and hawking; banquets and religious ceremonies and even just rest days, in between, when he could sit and think, or read or rest and chat with his now firm friends, or Lennarn.

Gradually, he grew to understand the nature of the people of the Protectorates, both razine and human and how their society worked. He also came to know an awful lot more about the eight-hundred-year schism created by the Betrayer's actions in Car'Agasse, and the atrocities committed in his name against Arven's faithful worshippers across the Protectorates. The High-Prince's eagerness to hear about his sister and her betrothed was now understandable; he and his people had been awaiting the long-promised Wielders of the Flame for centuries.

"You have known that they would come, the Am'maiya, Ethrayne and Jerryn, but you really do not know what will happen now that they have been Chosen?" He asked once of Archpriestess Gailla and Kerrenan, having spent a day studying the Book of Days; it hadn't made much sense to him at all . "That's not very helpful."

"I agree, Pualyn." Kerrenan said, nodding.

"Kerrenan." Gailla was rather a serious person, but frivolity would not have worked within her role as spiritual leader of Orbain, and she tended to calm down some of the more volatile members of the main group during their meetings. "At the end of the day, Pualyn, would you rather know that your future is of your own making, or that it is all pre-ordained? How would you feel?" She asked, fixing the young man with her large hazel eyes, and smiled a little as silence filled the room and both males considered her words.

"Dear Arven, your Grace, I see what you mean." Pualyn said quietly, after a while. "But the Betrayer sounds so-so inimical, I fear for my sister and the prince, I admit it."

"As do we all, but we will strive with all our strength to prevail." Gailla said, bowing her head prayerfully.

*

News from Tenarum arrived with the captains of the various Pearls and Opals, but it was the arrival of Captain Phellos with her cargo of Clirensar's iron, that really made Pualyn both considerably homesick and worried for his countrymen. Kerrenan brought Phellos to meet Pualyn one rainy, winter's day and the young Tenarean lord grilled the vibrant woman about the events at Newventure Bay, but she held up her hands in surrender.

"Forgive me, my Lord Pualyn, but it was not I who found those poor souls, but Ashanner of the Orbain Pearl. He said that the enemy set fire to the houses quite deliberately, ensuring that the village would be approached and so the finders would then broadcast the news and tell everyone of their power and their evil -." She added a salty phrase that greatly surprised Pualyn, for he was not used to ladies swearing, but he kept his reaction from his face. "Those bastards are evil, Kerr!"

"That's why they try to shock us, Phellos, the killing of Newventure Bay's inhabitants was hardly necessary." Kerrenan replied with a sigh.

"I've been there, it's tiny and isolated. You'd hardly think it would be worth it!" Pualyn shook his head, recalling the faces of the people he had met there: fishermen, the women folk and children who had crowded around the dock to greet the ship he had been on. It was bewildering, sickening, to realise that they were all dead now! "The only feasible way out is by sea; they were fishermen, by Arven! What sort of threat could they possibly be to great ocean-going ships?"

"And that's the point, lad." Kerr muttered glumly. "General Tequan's in charge of Cal'Badon and he's probably the one who killed my brother and destroyed the original Orbain Pearl all those years ago; dear Arven, I'd love to kill him slowly!"

"I'll hold your shield, Kerr." Phellos offered, grinning fiercely.

"And I'll hold your cloak, if you'd like a hand." Pualyn added. "You haven't met my sister, Ethrayne, have you Captain?"

"No, but I would be honoured, my Lord."

"She has been learning weapons craft since late spring, after encountering . . . General Ackat?" He asked and Kerrenan nodded gravely. "She's enjoying it; I think you would like her and she you." But then he sighed. "Gosh, I'm missing home, suddenly."

"We'll be heading to Tenarum in a few more days, Pualyn, I'm sure the ship will be ready by then; the logistics always take the most time and you need those figures we have been compiling for your king and your allies."

"Aye that's true, there's no avoiding it." The young man agreed. "I am sorry if I seem ungrateful, Kerr, but I am really missing Lyria."

"I definitely can't compete with your betrothed, my Lord Pualyn and I would not try." The High-Prince admitted with a laugh.

"If you have any letters for your kinsfolk, my Lord, I would be honoured to deliver them to Rothern for you – I'll be heading back out to sea tomorrow." Captain Phellos offered. "I never stay on land for long at a time, except occasionally and only if it's really stormy."

"Thank you, Captain; well then I will leave your exalted presences, if you do not mind and write a few letters for them." He got to his feet, bowed politely and hurried away.

* * *

CHAPTER 15

The afternoon following the departure of the delegates from Amorry and Derravale saw Duke Sarant, some of the household servants set off for Clirensar with his guards, leaving the Duchess, his daughter and Lady Lyria in the capital. Ethrayne's maids, Fionn and Sallie were returning with the latest plain copy of the outfit, to continue the assembly of their lady's wedding gown, as traditional, for Ethrayne would return home later in the year, before her wedding to Jerryn took place on the first day of Instur. Finally, the families had all agreed to wait for Pualyn's return before the young couple were wed.

Sarant's trusted Reeve, Thomur, generally managed the duchy in his absence, but the duke had never left Clirensar in Thomur's hands for so long since Queen Tanallyse had died, all those years before. Of course, the region had not been abandoned. Thomur was trusted and well-liked by the citizens of the city and its environs, and he ensured that local matters and business were dealt with promptly; taxes collected and paid; criminals punished; charity for the needy distributed; the castle, the city and region all running smoothly. Reports were sent every few days to the Duke and written approvals and advice returned by swift couriers.

It was a system that the Duke had been using for years, since Pualyn and Ethrayne were small children, without any major problems and, this summer, Sarant thanked Arven that it worked so well. Events since the betrothal of his daughter to the prince had spiralled dizzily; nothing was out of control, certainly, but never had so many things consumed so much of his time consecutively, delaying his departure on three or four occasions. The Council had never been so busy, it seemed and the enormity of what they faced in the jajozeli was sobering. With all that they had learned, regarding the threat to the new Wielders of the Flame, Sarant had not dared to leave the palace until the talks with Derravale and Amorry had been concluded.

King Marrand and he had had to resort to early morning meetings just to talk privately together, meeting not long after dawn in the palace chapel where they could discuss the most recent events and issues frankly and without interruption. They were conscious of the honour to their children, to their families and of the responsibilities that such honour entailed, certainly. But they were aware of the danger in a way that Jerryn and Ethrayne could not see, perhaps because of their youth; and they initialised plans of their own quite separate to their alliances with their neighbouring rulers, only informing the Archpriests of their decisions. In furtherance of some of these, Sarant travelled a lot faster than he would have done with his family in the entourage, apologising to the weary maids, reaching Clirensar in ten long days.

"Your Grace I am pleased to see you." Reeve Thomur said, bowing low as he greeted his master in the tapestry draped entrance hall of the castle, as the evening sunlight finally faded from the sky. "You look very well." He smiled sympathetically at the group of servants who made their way to the plain entrance to their domain, looking very tired and dusty.

"Well?" Sarant laughed at the ordinary looking scholar who had proved such an asset to his duchy. "I've returned for a rest and a change of diet, Thomur!" He said, pulling off his cloak. "Too much rich food destroys the digestion and there have been far too many banquets and far too little exercise recently."

"I can send to the kitchens, your Grace and have the cooks serve you gruel for supper, if you prefer? I'm sure your chefs could rustle some up in a short time." The slightly older man enquired, smiling mischievously and Sarant snorted expressively at that. "I hope that her Grace and your children are well?"

"Yes, thank you and Ethrayne really is quite enjoying all the combat training that she's undertaken." The duke replied, laying his cloak and his gloves on an ornate chair to one side of the hall, leading the way through the castle. "She's rather good, actually, for a complete beginner."

Thomur raised one eyebrow eloquently, knowing that Sarant was deliberately understating his pride in his daughter. "Excellent news. There is a hot bath waiting for you, your Grace and supper in your suite."

"Ah, the benefits of civilisation, thank you, Thomur. Come along, you can tell me what's been happening since I was here last." Sarant suggested, grinning.

*

Local gossip notwithstanding, life in the duchy was progressing perfectly well without the daily input of the duke, although there was a great deal of signing of scrolls and pages, stamping of seals and the shaking of hands, as Sarant verified what required his confirmation, and met with those few who had not been content to deal with even so trusted a servant as Thomur. It was early on the third day when he was able to leave the castle and ride for Black Fell, where he had an appointment with the Master Armourer.

Black Fell was a bustling town some four leagues north-east of Clirensar, set in the wooded hills where centuries of mining had carved out what almost looked like a rocky gorge, hence the name: for the remaining rocky cliffs, although less than a hundred feet high, were dark and ominous amid the scenery; the smoke from the furnaces and kilns had stained the grey crags that were topped with tall, dark evergreen trees. In winter, the town did not receive a great deal of direct daylight.

As the source of some of the purest ore in the region, the smiths of Black Fell had been specialising in forging weapons and armour for many years, with the Duke's requirements and his royal and noble contacts across the kingdom in mind, and the associated ancillary trades had expanded as the demand had increased.

Sarant rode up the main road with his guards, passing the stinking tannery that was set a good three hundred yards from the wooden palisade that surrounded the town to the south and about half this from the road; even so, the smell was all pervading. Entering through the narrow gateway, the duke was instantly hailed by the innkeeper of the Crossed Keys, who was polishing the outside of the windows of his establishment vigorously, despite his advanced age.

"Good morning, Master Richon, you look well." Sarant called back. "How's the family?"

"All fine, all well, your Grace, thank you for asking. Please give my humble regards to your lady wife and children, not that they are children now." The white-haired man chuckled. "Congratulations on such auspicious events, sir."

"Thank you, Richon, I'll call in on my return." The duke answered and rode on up the street. Richon had been his valet until the man's retirement, six years before.

Master Armourer Queyt was waiting at his substantial forge as Sarant walked across the cobbled yard and shook his hand with a grip of iron. As tall as the Duke, he was ruggedly built, with a highly muscled upper body, arms and neck clearly showing his vast strength. Wearing an old but clean linen shirt covered with a thick, burn-marked leather apron, he had old scars and burns on his arms and massive hands, a shock of iron-grey hair and deep brown eyes in a plain, ruddy face.

"Your Grace, I hear that the prince greatly likes his betrothal gift." He said in a booming voice that a sergeant major would have been proud of.

"So much so, Master Queyt, that his Majesty and I want to commission similar weapons for my daughter, Ethrayne and chain mail for she and Jerryn." Sarant replied gravely. "You have heard about her weapons training and such like, I imagine?"

Queyt grinned. "My, the news flew through the region, your Grace, but though many people disapprove mightily, we -." He stuck a thumb into his own chest. "Know you an' his majesty would hardly agree to it if it wasn't necessary. Little Ethrayne's takin' to it well, then?"

"Yes, frighteningly well, really. With her and Jerryn now the Wielders of the Flame of Arven, it seemed sensible to ensure that she can also defend herself . . . But the jajozeli -." Sarant broke off and shook his head, trying to dispel the sudden rush of fear that gripped him. "Anyway, I got Vedeigne and the others to narrow down the size and weight of sword that suits her best and I've measurements for them both for mail; something a little finer than ordinary, of course, with this small device over the left breast -." He pulled out a small scroll from a pocket in his doublet and handed it over. Queyt unrolled it to reveal a drawing of a diamond emblem where Arven's device was laid over and amongst that of the Tenarean crown along with various figures and other details and nodded once, decisively. "Is that workable, Master Queyt?"

"Should be, your Grace; I might tweak the drawing slightly, but the two crests are well known and should be easy to amalgamate. Now, about the weapons, what d'you want?"

"I imagine you've still got the designs of Jerryn's weapons?" Sarant asked, smiling. Master Armourer Queyt was well known for his extensive archives.

"Naturally, your Grace, but you won't want me to copy them, will you?" The Master asked.

"Of course not, but you are brilliant at adapting everything you set your mind to. Something just a little more refined maybe, in terms of decoration, but only very slightly – certainly nothing frivolous: they are weapons to be used, after all, to kill and maim." Sarant sighed, this prospect hung over everything and it scared him. "A little lighter, just as sharp; double or single bladed as you see fit, no fancy ostentation, using the Tenarean colours and a three-foot blade, a two-foot blade and a dagger."

Queyt nodded, frowning down at the parchment in his hands then flashed a grin at the Duke. "Now that's a challenge, your Grace!" He said enthusiastically and laughed a little. "But it won't be cheap, mind."

"We know. Marrand and I will split the fee and here is gold and gems." The Duke handed over a small, heavy box of black iron. "I think the treasury is rather down on sapphires and emeralds now." And he smiled. "Thank you, Master Queyt."

"Thank you, your Grace, for your commission. I will be as economical as I can, I promise." The Master Armourer answered, bowing deeply. "I'm looking forward to getting started, I admit it."

"I just hope it doesn't impact on all the manufacturing we now require." Sarant said with a sigh. "A possible conflict with the jajozeli, the Betrayer, is not at all what any of us want!"

"We've forges, ore, charcoal, limestone and iron pigs ready enough across the region to cope, your Grace and it would be very good to eliminate that betraying bastard and restore Arven; only good can come of it in the end, you'll see." Queyt answered confidently. "We're not warlike, but the enemy have always been a threat, looming over us. You'll have heard about Newventure Bay." He shook his head. "A nasty business . . . Now, a drink, your Grace, to seal our business?"

"As is the custom, Master Queyt, I thank you."

Queyt unlocked a stout cabinet in the parchment littered room next to the forge, producing two small crystal glasses and a decanter of a pale, clear liqueur which he poured carefully into the glasses. A faint scent of honey wafted around them for a moment.

"Your good health, your Grace and especially to your honoured daughter and Prince Jerryn also. May they destroy our enemy and restore Arven." He made the toast seriously.

"Amen to that. To Ethrayne and Jerryn." Sarant raised his glass then downed the drink in one gulp. "May our God protect you all." He added quietly. "Well, thank you, Master Queyt. I will be here in Clirensar for a few more days, but Thomur will be charge, of course, when I return to Tenum City; if you have any questions, which I know you probably won't, being the Master Armourer, you know where we will be."

"Indeed, your Grace. I am grateful for your trust." Queyt said, pouring a second drink for them with a flourish.

"You are the best, Master Queyt." The Duke replied, grinned, inclining his head in thanks as he accepted the second drink. "Your health." Then he set down his glass. "Well, I had best be on my way. Master Richon has probably encouraged his staff at the inn to rustle up an entire banquet for my delectation. For some reason, he seems to think that no one else feeds me, which is obviously a fallacy." He patted his stomach ruefully, but it was impressively lean. "I think I had better get back to combat practice myself."

"Aye, you'll find an awful lot of folk at it nowadays. I've got my hammer." Queyt managed a fierce grin as he patted the handle of the huge, rather battered sledge laying on the table top, one of number of well-used tools. "I will be in touch, your Grace and please give my regards to Richon."

"I will, Master Queyt and a good day to you." Sarant bowed slightly as he departed, remounting his horse and thanking the soldiers for waiting, before riding back through the town to the Crossed Keys; where the entire group of them were indeed served with a sumptuous meal by Master Richon before they headed back to the city.

*

The duke enjoyed the six days he spent in Clirensar, although he was very busy. The pomp and ceremony that defined every movement in the royal palace was absent and he was surrounded by people and servants whom he had known for many years. He even managed to visit Callorton, the small estate owned by Lord Terfylls and Lady Allara that adjoined Clirensar South Vale Farm, two leagues or so south of the city.

Terfylls and Allara were Lyria's parents, a couple in their late fifties, who were more farmers of three hundred and fifty acres of prime land, than nobles, despite their titles; with the aid of their two oldest sons Dettar and Heldor and their families, they produced meat, milk, fruit and vegetables for the castle complex. Their third son, Salyr, managed the day-to-day business of the castle's South Vale Farm and stud, whilst Sevanter, their fourth, served in the army.

"Sarant, how wonderful it is to see you!" Allara cried, as the duke entered the pristine dairy that rainy morning and kissed her cheek as he hugged her. She was busily churning butter, a clean apron over her well-worn, blue linen gown. The large room was well scrubbed, with rounds of cheese stacked up on stone shelves that climbed the far wall, and jugs and bowls lined up neatly. "Salyr told us that you were due back, but you left the family in Tenum City?"

He grinned at the woman, small and beautiful with luminous blonde hair; it was clear from whom Lyria had inherited her beauty. "I know, it's tragic, Allara, but although she is missing Pualyn greatly, Lyria is rather coming to enjoy life in the palace."

"My word yes, so it seems. My word, she described her betrothal gifts in her last letter, Sarant! So fine! You must all have spent far too much. Just let me call Dymia -." Allara was getting flustered – the cost of such gifts worried her, for they were far beyond the family's means. "You must be thirsty, Sarant -."

"I'll do it, dear. Dymia!" The Duke shouted out of the doorway, and Allara smiled her thanks as she carried on churning. In a short time, a sturdy girl of eight or nine years old, with mid-brown hair in thick plaits came in, wearing an apron that matched the older woman's exactly over her plain dress.

"Your Grace, Grandmother?" She gasped from running, a wide bright smile lighting up her freckled face. "I've fed the fowl, and Serren is collecting eggs."

"Thank you, Dymia; we will be in the kitchen if you can carry on making butter, dear." Allara gestured for the eight-year-old to take her place at the churn and stepped out of the way to remove her apron, hanging it neatly behind the outer door. Then the lady led their guest towards the sturdy farmhouse on the far side of the tidy, cobbled yard.

"It's so nice to be back, Allara; it's been frantic in the capital, I've really missed the farm." Sarant admitted, following her and breathing deeply of the redolent air. "I do feel rather guilty, leaving the family and your own dear Lyria behind, but Ethrayne must remain in the palace for now, with Jerryn, concentrating on everything there, and she needs Lyria and her mother close by. It's been very unsettling. We are planning to return home in a moon or so, before she and Jerryn are wed, and Fionn and Sallie have come back to complete her bridal gown."

"Oh, I can't wait to see it!" Allara said enthusiastically. "Those girls are so talented with their needles."

The kitchen was large, a fire was blazing in the hearth to the right of the door where a woman in her late twenties was pouring tea into two fine cups, whilst a second, a little younger, cut a rich brown cake into slices, two tiny children hiding amid her skirts.

"Your Grace." Hella, Dettar's wife, curtsied deeply, followed by Jenfer, with the two small twins and they all swept off further into the house, leaving their elders alone. The sounds of small children chattering and a baby crying fitfully could be heard elsewhere through that doorway.

"Please, sit down, Sarant." Allara gestured, setting the cups of tea on the fire side of the scrubbed table and Sarant sank into one of the handmade chairs in front of the fire place as she took the other. "You look tense, your Grace, please tell me what's been happening. Most of the news we have had has been rather garbled."

"I'm not surprised." He replied drily. "It's been quite ridiculous since the day before Ethrayne and Jerryn were betrothed, frankly -." And he began to try and explain pertinent points, between sips of tea and bites of cake. "It's been a great honour, Allara, but the responsibility is vast, to my mind; and the razine Archpriest, ex-archpriest I mean, was far too quick to support training Ethie in using weapons, I think." He concluded, a while later, after a second cup of tea.

"But have you asked this Archpriest why? He is a servant of Arven, Sarant: he would not lie to you." Allara stated confidently.

"Oh, I know, Allara, dear, I know . . . but they are both so young. The old tales of the jajozeli Generals make the blood run cold, don't they?"

"Yes indeed." She agreed with a sigh. "But if everything is prophesied, imagine! What sort of world do we live in?" She asked wonderingly and shook her head. "Our God would hardly choose to place his champions in mortal danger, would he? Or there would be no point to it at all; the Betrayer would have won all those centuries ago and we'd probably be worshipping him instead!"

"Arven protect us all!" Sarant prayed intensely and shuddered. "I am sorry to burden you, Allara -."

"That's what friends are for, sometimes, Sarant my dear. Now, tell me about both of those betrothals, do; I want to know what our girls wore, how they looked: I want every detail, your Grace, I warn you."

Before Sarant could begin, however, the outer door opened wide and Lord Terfylls strode in with his eldest son, Dettar, both looking rather hot and mud stained after their hard morning's work.

"Sarant, this is a pleasant surprise. What could have dragged you away from the comfortable capital, hey?" The large, strong man rocked on his heels with a booming laugh. "Still, you are looking well, your Grace."

"Thank you and I'm cleaner than you, certainly, my Lord Terfylls." Sarant commented dryly at once.

"When was the last time you ever exerted yourself, unless it's over your beloved horses, hey?" Terfylls responded easily. The men were such firm friends that such mild insults were somehow customary in their everyday conversations. "Have you visited South Vale Farm yet, hmm? I'm amazed you weren't there at dawn, counting your horses and bushels of grain."

"I'm calling in there after I leave you, my Lord, to see whether Salyr is coping without me. I knew you would want many more details on how Lyria is finding the capital." Sarant replied. "I think this extra time in the palace, which has been so unexpected, along with everything else, is bringing your daughter out of her shell, although she is sorely missing Pualyn."

"It would hardly have been appropriate for their wedding to be rushed through." Terfylls asserted gravely. "He is your heir, representing the entire kingdom, gallivanting far across the ocean; I hope he's enjoying himself, it must be amazing, travelling so far. Yes, it is far better to have delayed their wedding, Sarant."

"I am very glad that you both agree, old friend. Lyria has conducted herself so very properly and it seems that even some of the lower members of the court have finally deigned to notice her existence." Sarant shook his head. "The fact that she was simply a lovely young woman obviously didn't count for much before, which we have never understood!" He commented on those who seemed to view the world in such a frivolous way. "I am hoping to bring the family back certainly before the end of Vhisson and you can return to Tenum with us for both weddings, it's only right."

"Oh, that would be lovely!" Allara said with a sigh. "It's been years since we were in the capital, Terfylls; gosh, it must have been Jerryn's Naming Day! We could not attend the queen's funeral because half the children had measles."

"Yes, I remember: practically all at once, wasn't it?" Sarant answered. "Well, it's time you returned, old friends, at least to see your daughter dazzle the court with her beauty and then Ethrayne I imagine, as long as you can clean him up a little, Allara."

Dettar, who was drying his hands on a towel, laughed aloud at that, but his father nobly ignored the dig.

*

Duke Sarant took his luncheon with his friends and their extended family and his guards were fed alongside the farm hands. It was early afternoon before he reached South Vale Farm and heading on for dinner time when he left to return to the city, very well pleased with how the crops and usual tasks were progressing; the stud was expanding with new foals gambolling in the fields and new orders for trained mounts; and Salyr's family was expanding likewise, for Terfylls's third son was clearly trying to match his brothers and their wives fecundity, for Deanne was expecting her third child. The stud was definitely proving to be a profitable side-line, which was fortunate, with two weddings due before the end of the year. Despite the confusion elsewhere in his life and the world, it was immensely reassuring to discover that certain parts were succeeding without his direct input.

"I'm not sure you even need me at all." He grumbled rather wistfully to Thomur, whilst they ate the excellent meal served by the castle kitchens later that evening. "Salyr is running South Vale Farm far better than I was managing it all and here you are, with everything oiled and running smoothly. I might as well resign."

"Ah, but do not forget that the efficiency of your staff throws a marvellous glowing light upon you as Duke, your Grace, for you hired us all and trained us." Thomur answered with a grin. "You can consider on how the successes of the Council similarly reflects upon his majesty."

"Are you trying to be funny?" Sarant asked, smiling.

"Of course, Sarant, you have hardly smiled at all since you've been home." The man commented and grimaced. "Everyone's feeling it, of course, but I'm sure the future won't prove as fearful as you suggest; Ethrayne and Jerryn are both very sensible. And young people always seem to be eminently adaptable as a species."

"You are right, Thomur but, you know -." Sarant shrugged and offered a grimace of his own. "I'll be glad when Ethie's got her own arms and mail; the thought of powerful, magical enemies bent on destroying Arven fills me with horror . . . I know we trust the Archpriests and Arven too, yet I admit that it's bloody hard sometimes!"

"You need less thinking and more action, your Grace, more combat practice will ease your worries." The reeve advised calmly.

"Only if you join me, old friend, us old men have to stick together in the face of all those youngsters."

"What, me? You're joking!" Thomur protested, then sighed and shook his head, sighing deeply. "Dear Arven, Sarant, I'm too old!"

"If Ethie can do it, so must you, Thomur; Marrand and I have started exercises again, you know. I'll see you at breakfast, all ready to start." Sarant said, smiling, yet it wasn't a command. "And I've got to lose a little weight for I really don't want to have to be measured for new clothes for the weddings."

Oh, all right, Sarant, you speak too much sense, but I've no idea where my weapons have been stored." Thomur conceded with a sigh.

*

The exercise proved vigorous, but it did serve to improve the duke's mood anew before he faced the next bale of paperwork, scrolls and agreements that required his ratification, however formal or informal, all signed for by Thomur over the spring months. That work, along with the numerous meetings that Sarant had to organise with various tenants, businessmen and the local military headquarters; advancing the King's request for combat training, the amalgamation of stores of food and equipment, plus general preparations for any action. It was just as intense as all the meetings he had attended in Tenum City and just as important.

Sarant did manage to invite Terfylls and Allara to dinner on two occasions, including Thomur and some other local dignitaries and continuing the discussions regarding their daughter and his own, but they were short interludes amid all the work. Three days passed before he could finally bid farewell to his friends and servants and set off back to Tenum City with a lighter heart.

* * *

CHAPTER 16

The forces that had been amassed in Cal'Badon were well on their way northward by the time that General Tequan had returned from the carefully orchestrated attack on Newventure Bay; the demanding preparations he and his subordinates had made, had ensured that large amounts of foodstuffs and equipment were already stockpiled along the well-defined route through the steep, winding valleys of the Astoln and Lerracon Mountains and across the Chellason Plateau to N'Astoln, the large fortress-city which guarded the lands bordering the south-west extent of Tenarum.

With excellent food supplies, clothing and footwear, in addition to their extensive training, the companies of the jajozeli army made their individual way to N'Astoln for a few days of rest, before continuing on their way. The considerable journey they undertook was concluded with very few problems, overall; such was the scale of the army's superior logistics, barring the occasional accidents, of course, such as avalanches and rock-falls. Even the notoriously harsh weather of the mountainous regions, storms and blizzards almost as likely in summer as any other season, seemed to cooperate with their advance and their master's wishes.

Moving each thousand as an individual unit was easier by far than trying to coordinate the advance of larger numbers together and it might have taken less time, overall, than trying to cram snaking miles of troops past the harsh icy peaks and treacherous ravines and valleys; spring had barely made much of an impression at all on the harsh landscape when the first group had set out, carting the extra supplies allotted to them.

And so, by mid Kharsare, the eighth moon, thirty thousand men had passed through N'Astoln, their passing engraved into the very ground they had crossed, leaving a snaking, earth-coloured scar through the plateau and the empty hills beyond, north and east.

The soldiers were now amassed in six stoutly constructed forts of strong wooden palisades, living in dun-coloured tents, in the largely uninhabited lands on the southern border of Tenarum, far beyond Clirensar's bounds, a region of wide forests and grassland, where wildlife teemed, beyond the scope of the villages and farms of the region. Patrols now ranged through the countryside both by day and night, eliminating every person they came across: the occasional, hunter or miner; the jajozeli explored the countryside assiduously, ensuring that no one could possibly raise the alarm that an army was encamped on their very doorstep. Morale was high: they were well sheltered, well fed and they were eagerly anticipating the action ahead, confident of their abilities and dismissive in the extreme of the native humans of this land.

General Tequan rode in to the central fort on a drizzly afternoon with four thousand cavalry at his back, to huge enthusiasm from the troops at large, and he turned in his saddle to grin at the two Generals who accompanied him;

one, the blonde, blue-eyed razine who had sought to frighten the Wielders of the Flame in Tenum City, the second a tall, slender, pretty woman with short cropped white-blonde hair and sparkling hazel eyes, all wearing long, dark cloaks stained from long travel over their plain, dusty clothing, their weapons prominent.

"They seem pleased to see you, my Lord Tequan." She said quite respectfully.

"They're just glad they've stopped marching, Cavaln." Ackat offered with a laugh. "Of course, we've still some distance to travel -."

"General Ackat, *must* you turn everything into a joke?" Tequan asked rather shortly, but chuckled. "The roads are not too muddy, the camps look well built, they're neatly arranged. You've done well, Jaike." He complimented the thin-faced and skinny, green-eyed General who had come out to meet them, as he dismounted and turned towards the pavilion ahead.

"Thank you, my Lord Tequan." He answered politely. "Did you have a good journey?" He included the other Generals in the query and grinned at the woman's grimace.

"I'm sick of riding, that's for sure, Jaike." She said, swinging down out of her saddle. "You look well, Zanezli agrees with you. I've not seen you since you left Ban'Ganleth, it must have been two years at least."

"Aye it is, and you've made General since I left. Congratulations, General Cavaln." He replied.

"Carry on the reunion later, youngsters." Ackat grumbled as he dismounted, tossing his reins to a soldier and striding after Tequan, followed by Cavaln and Jaike shoulder to shoulder, very much the juniors.

Tequan and Ackat moved in tandem to pause over a table, undoing their cloaks automatically and tossing them over one of the folding chairs, gazing down at a large, detailed map of Zanezli, showing the broad lands that they had crossed, but the wide portion north of the Astoln Mountains was mostly empty of detail, descending towards the Vale of Clirensar.

"How are the preparations coming on?" Tequan asked, stretching massively. He was a large razine, at least six foot eight tall and bulky at chest and shoulders with hard muscle. His skin was slightly browner in tone than the other three razine and he had shaggy dark brown hair and a far redder, coarse-haired beard and moustache, which was not usual amongst the jajozeli-razine, who tended to be clean shaven as a group. Even in plain travelling clothes, shirt, jerkin and leggings, dusty and creased, he was imposing.

"Everything is in place, my Lord Commander and our daily rounds of scouts are updating the map, as you ordered –." The younger male General assured him as he moved to a second table and began to pour three silver goblets of dark wine from a skin, then handing them out. "Would you like the full briefing now? Or would you prefer a bath first and something to eat, sir?"

Tequan sipped the wine, nodded at the flavour, then glanced first at Cavaln and then at Ackat, grinning toothily. "Well, put like that, Jaike, I must say that a hot bath would be most pleasant." He agreed.

"Then, if you will follow me through here, I will show you our domestic arrangements." Jaike said, smiling back. "We've not quite got the amenities of Ban'Lerracon, or even N'Astoln, but it's comfortable." He led them through a covered doorway at the back of that room into a pleasantly furnished sitting room with folding chairs, cushions, carpets woven in bright colours and a few low tables. There were further cloth-covered doorways to the left and right walls. "Lady Cavaln, if you please?" Jaike bowed and gestured to the right, so the woman strode through that doorway, her cloak over one arm, the wine goblet in her other hand. "Gentlemen, this way to your baths." Jaike headed to the left, the two older Generals behind him.

The tent room they entered was carpeted and held two camp beds, a small table, two stools and two wooden tubs, not large, but nicely full of steaming water, with soap, ewers full of more hot water and two piles of towels all arranged within reach.

"Acceptable." Tequan growled, nodding.

"I will return when you request, Commander." Jaike said, bowing slightly and pulling the curtain over the door closed as he left them.

In a short space of time, the Generals had stripped off their travel-stained clothes and immersed themselves in the baths with sighs of enjoyment, relishing the touch of hot water after eight days of hard riding from N'Astoln, then fishing for the soap.

Behind them, two soldiers bustled about quietly, setting out the items from their luggage; shaking out their packed clothes, removing their worn items and dusty boots. After a while, they returned with covered platters which they set on a table and quickly departed, as the Generals chatted, rinsed, and soaked. Then, sheeting water, first Tequan and then Ackat emerged, rejuvenated.

<Jaike, Cavaln, we will meet in the next room when you're ready.> Tequan sent silently, rubbing himself down quickly with a towel, then at his wet hair before he started pulling on clean clothes. Ackat was already starting on his plate of fragrant stew, still wrapped in his towel. In addition to stew there was fresh bread and sharp cheese.

"Good cooks." Ackat remarked, devouring his food quickly before getting back to drying himself and dressing.

"Yes, they certainly are, the troops would be most upset if they had to eat mediocre food as well as sleep in tents for moons." The Commander replied easily, spooning up his own meal just as quickly. "Are you ready?"

"I'll bring these -." Ackat picked up a plate of fruited honey cake with a grin. "And this, of course." With plate and goblet, he led the way through the door and into the main central sitting room where the two young Generals were already sat waiting, Cavaln now in a loose linen shirt and leggings, her damp hair stuck up. Ackat and Tequan were similarly attired in plain, comfortable clothing perfect for camp.

"Right let's talk; we'll disseminate it to the others tomorrow." General

Tequan said, reaching for the pile of maps that Jaike had set on the central table, sitting down.

The four of them spent the evening until darkness had fallen outside the then lamp-lit tent, going over their original itinerary and plans; discussing recent developments and local events and scrutinising reports. Fortified by more wine and the occasional slice of honey cake, they refined their purpose, ready for the large meeting due the next morning and retired late.

*

The day dawned and General Tequan and his staff breakfasted on steaks, scrambled eggs and fresh bread as they reviewed the updated portions of the maps of the region, north of the foothills of the Astoln Mountains; an area of wilderness it seemed, at first glance.

"What is the countryside like?" He enquired. "It appeared quite rugged, riding through."

"It is sparsely populated, this far south of the Vale of Clirensar, but there are pockets of hamlets and villages dotted about, a few farms; charcoal makers and some rough mines, both iron ore and coal, very randomly spaced, of course." Captain Reddessor reported. He was the head of the scouts that were ranging through the land, a thin man of middle height, with a weather-beaten face. "The countryside is a little wild, but the woods and hills will provide excellent cover and the few roads are well constructed and they all lead to Clirensar." He chuckled.

"Yes, they do, don't they?" Commander Tequan agreed, grinning. "But I want many more details about these settlements before we can advance, and I want them quickly!"

"The latest groups of scouts are scheduled to return throughout today and on into tomorrow, my Lord General." Reddessor assured him. "I am confident that we will be able to put together the beginnings of a final approach for your campaign by tomorrow evening."

"Then see that it is so." The General answered. "How are we for supplies, Colonel?" He demanded of Colonel Macasse, who was in overall charge of logistics, under General Jaike.

"We have stockpiled food enough for six months, my Lord General and there are warehouses full in N'Astoln and Cal'Badon as contingencies; the supplies from Cal'Badon are being brought steadily north to the border. Also, my Lord General, it is practically harvest time here. If we advance carefully and do not stamp rough-shod over the fields, the local farms should be able to support us very well."

"Carefully is certainly what we intend." Tequan confirmed, scanning the faces around him. "It may take a little longer but consider the glory if we succeed – and the horror of the folk of this land and the razine!" And he laughed as if in anticipation of such success.

*

The camps were spread out along a broad, shallow valley that had a narrow river meandering through its centre, through rough stands of willows, hazel, alder and thick undergrowth. There was plenty of land above the river level so that they could have comfortably constructed two or three more forts in the available space, and none of the sites was small; there was plenty of space for the soldiers camping there.

All the forts were intrinsically identical, neatly laid out and well-spaced, with straight lanes between the lines of tents that were set almost precisely throughout and large fenced paddocks had been constructed to contain the horses that they had brought with them, close to the central points of each wall; those outer walls were uniform and there were even watch towers set some five feet above their tops at the corners, the wooden frameworks very well built of logs. Even the storage for the massive piles of supplies was planned, set in a fenced area in the centre of each fort, neatly arranged, marked and closely guarded. Security was very much in evidence: there were constant patrols on the outer edges of the valley and sentries on every possible approach. Thus, Commander Tequan had deliberately chosen this area for his purpose, because its remoteness was ideal: the valley was at least six leagues from any known habitation.

Even after at least two thousand years of occupation, despite the relatively recent expansion of settlers because of the iron and steel industry, the countryside two days travel south and west of the city of Clirensar was largely empty.

The jajozeli patrols, accompanied by Generals who could sense the presence of any native human intruders, were circling the area to ensure that any travellers vanished without a trace. And, since the local population was mostly almost entirely focussed on getting in the harvest during the good weather, there were relatively few of these; the movement of the harvest to market would occur later, of course.

When they were not on duty, the jajozeli soldiers rested. They gambled a little for small coins or duties; wrestled; practised their sparring skills, or archery – ate large meals, expertly prepared; and slept, regaining their energy and bulk after their long march from Cal'Badon. The patrols kept changing, engaging the ordinary soldiers in sequence along with the expert trackers. Consequently, morale and discipline were high in all the camps. The days passed slowly but steadily as the late summer days continued, mostly bright and sunny; it was better weather than anyone could have hoped for, all in all.

*

General Cavaln joined one of the patrols out of a mixture of boredom and curiosity. Only two years previously, she had been a senior cadet in Ban'Ganleth, one of fifty razine youngsters who had excelled in their year at the very exacting training regime undertaken by all aspirants to the rank of General; she was the first ever woman to have sought to succeed in such a supremely masculine role. A General was the emperor's representative right across his empire: commander of soldiers; civic governors or mayors; always leaders. They were exclusively razine, and all very able, although their abilities might range from healing to mind-reading and every talent in-between. Cavaln's speciality was healing. She had far surpassed everyone's expectations, including her own, apart from her great uncle, Lord Governor Doreth, the emperor's second-in-command.

Having spent her childhood in the highest levels of society in Ban'Ganleth, with many rough older brothers and surrounded by far more men than women, perhaps it was inevitable that the young woman, on discovering her predisposition for healing, would throw convention to the wind, abandon the usual rather easy and elegant life of jajozeli-razine femininity and strive to succeed in the hardest training regime on Iullyn. She had not wanted to be an ornament, or a plaything or even a conventional healer. She wanted the sort of life, the sort of excitement, that the males enjoyed.

The emperor had viewed her determination, dedication and hard work with amusement, but there had been no concessions at all made in her training: she had had to compete directly in every subject with all the youths who had been accepted as cadets. It had been hard work. Still, she had finished at the top of the school in every discipline except hand-to-hand combat and there she had still been second in the year.

On attaining the rank of General; wined, dined and feted throughout the city, Cavaln had imagined that her life would be transformed, and she would swiftly embark on risky missions on behalf of her ruler, despite all logic. Instead, she had been working there in the infirmary in Ban'Ganleth for nearly a year, before his Majesty's order had come through, commanding her to sail here. Cavaln had been in Zanezli for three moons now and, following her brief interview with the emperor, had immediately travelled for another, to N'Astoln in the back-of-beyond and then across the border into their enemy's realm. Despite her presence here on the edge of civilisation with her colleagues, she was bored stiff, with the remit clear: a return to waiting.

Riding out with six burly men, the young General ignored their behaviour: their sideways glances and elaborate courtesy. She was easily far older than all of them and better trained in every form of combat they could imagine; the natural arrogance of her race could never be easily erased; her rank and all that it entailed and meant, was paramount. Simply because she might be the first female General in history, it meant nothing at all.

The countryside north and east of the hidden camps was mostly wooded and rather beautiful, in an unkempt sort of way. They rode until noon, through hills and valleys, through woodland and meadows stuffed with wildlife, going steadily rather than rushing, alert for anything at all; yet all they saw were animals and birds, all vanishing quickly into the undergrowth or treetops ahead of them. As the sun began its slow descent towards the distant west, they stopped by a purling stream to eat a lunch of cold meat between slices of bread, dried fruit, honey cake and cold water; simple, but sustaining.

General Cavaln led them in a rough loop back towards their hidden valley, circling further away from the foothills to the south that climbed relentlessly towards the distant wall of the Astoln Mountains, heading north. They passed some evidence of human habitation: tumbled walls covered in moss, ferns and undergrowth and many equally tangled holes in the ground, some quite large; clear evidence of the long-standing search for iron ore. In this place, the seam had obviously all been removed and the miners long-since moved on. At one point, the group struck what seemed to be the overgrown remnants of a track and paused.

"We had better follow it." Cavaln said, frowning a little. "I don't recall seeing this from the map that Lord Commander Tequan is amalgamating."

"Aye, Ma'am." The corporal agreed. "And we'll need some meat to add to our meal later if we're out overnight."

"Yes, set one of the men to bring down game, Corporal." She answered and marked the rough position of the track on her own copy of the chart, using a charcoal stick, glancing up and down, orienting herself with the sun's position. "I'm not even sure if this was ever a road, it's very winding. Let's move on." She did not add the rejoinder 'advance carefully' for it had been ingrained deep in every soldier; she led the soldiers roughly northward, the men spaced out behind and advancing through the undergrowth as well as along the faint trail, whilst one man moved out to the right on foot, stringing up his bow.

<We have located what may be an old road, Lord General.> Cavaln reported to Tequan as they continued through the afternoon, her eyes constantly moving, scanning and assessing, her mind probing. *<I will contact you this evening, if we have not returned.>*

<Thank you. Good hunting.> The Commander replied and returned his attention to what he had been concentrating on, back in the command centre.

The further they advanced, through the rough undergrowth and old woodland, moving up and down hills and along little valleys, the more convinced Cavaln became that they were riding along a road, or at least a lane, for they had passed a few places where the ground had been cut away on slopes to provide a flatter surface, as would be wanted for building houses; once, they crossed a stream where parts of mostly rotten logs were still visible, resting on squared-off stones, some neatly stacked one on another, the rest tumbled into the stream and onto the steep banks, the remains of a bridge.

It was nearly sunset when the group made camp, in a copse of the almost ubiquitous sweet chestnut that seemed to thrive in this sheltered, low-lying area north of the mountains, situated close to a bubbling spring surrounded by grazing. One man was collecting firewood, whilst the corporal started a fire with his sparker, in a protected hollow; two soldiers were unsaddling the horses and checking them over, whilst the fifth sorted their food supplies and the last, who had gone hunting, was dressing the double-brace of pheasants that he had shot. General Cavaln seemed to be resting, leaning against a smooth tree trunk, relaying exactly what they had seen that day to General Ackat, having travelled a good ten leagues or so through the tumbled land.

<So, are there any signs of people?> Ackat asked.

<No, not really, my Lord, only a few ruins spaced out and the remains of ore mines. I think the locals abandoned the area at least half a century ago, perhaps, the ore seams proved sparser than they hoped. Shall we continue to follow the road in the morning?> Cavaln asked. She knew that, technically, she was his equal, but the habits of over a decade's diffidence in training were hard to break.

<You're in charge, General Cavaln. We're not going anywhere in a hurry; see you when you get back.> He replied easily, with amusement in his voice.

After toasting the fowl on green sticks and eating it with the last of their fresh bread, making tea, they let the fire die; the weather was warm enough, they were well sheltered and hidden in the copse. As darkness settled in, they lay down to sleep, wrapped in their cloaks, one soldier standing guard.

Cavaln slept soundly until before dawn, despite the relieving of the guard by his fellow, waking fully alert before the eastern horizon had even begun to lighten. She stepped away from the motionless forms of the soldiers, passed the man on guard and climbed up the hill north of the camp, her eyesight good enough even in the night to find a clear way through the woodland. She stopped by an ancient oak, stretched out the kinks of sleeping on the ground and reached out with her power to sense any lucid minds beyond where she stood, easing outwards very gently as she had been taught, as the first light of dawn sent the darkness suddenly fleeing towards the west and the stars faded . . . And, yes . . . there! Cavaln smiled, for the touch of minds was quite unmistakeable, only a few leagues ahead: humans, undoubtedly Tenareans. She concentrated on them and assessed the number as between three and five, conscious that others might still be asleep, then put a fix in her mind to their rough location; this group of natives would be quickly eliminated.

She returned to the group, now stirring, and began to eat her breakfast of dried meat and fruit, quickly planning her strategy.

*

The barely distinguishable trail now ran through more managed woodland; coppicing was much in evidence and there were clear tracks where the cut wood had been dragged out by horses. After nearly two leagues of gently rolling hills, the two scouts that she had sent out returned, grinning.

"There's a valley ahead holding twelve cottages, fields and a shrine of some sort, plus plenty of cover, Ma'am. There're belts of trees between some of the fields." The older of the two reported crisply.

"Very good." Cavaln nodded. "Let's go and have a look-see and coordinate; with only twelve little cottages there might only be a handful of men, but there could be more. Huillear, circle the valley, you know what we require."

"Yes Madam." The older man bowed his head formally. "I won't be long."

The six of them moved slowly forward, the General again using her talent to check that they were alone in the woods, until the group were hidden behind an overgrown mass of hazel, ivy and bramble at least twenty feet across that was close enough to the edge of the wood that they could see the hamlet, but not all that clearly: the buildings were hidden behind orchard trees and each other and although some people were visible in the fields in the valley, there was also the strident clang of iron on the air. Children darted about between chickens and geese, shrieking, playing, as two women hung up washing on lines strung between some of the apple trees. It looked very peaceful and the villagers were in no way aware of the presence of hostile forces.

Huillear returned, leading his horse and made a concise report. The village was pretty much as they had seen: twelve little cottages; storage buildings; byres and pigsties and a blacksmith rather than a foundry or smelting pit; Cavaln's initial assessment on the number of men around was probably accurate.

It did not take long to finalise their plans, although the Corporal suggested diffidently that General Cavaln ride in alone and take their attention for the few vital moments required, which she rejected.

"These are farmers and their families. They might have tools that they can use as weapons, but we have weapons enough and many years of training and the element of surprise. Remember to leave the fields and animals: we will take the stores back to camp." She ordered. "And watch out for pitchforks and sledgehammers!" She added, remounting her horse. "Farm tools are always lethal in the wrong hands!"

"Yes, Ma'am."

Seven riders appearing out of the thick woodland at a gallop, three from the left and four from the right without any warning at all, presaged the end of the hamlet before noon. As in Newventure Bay, the jajozeli was merciless. The only saving grace was that they killed everyone there, man, woman and child, quickly; only the blacksmith really tried to defend himself, hefting a four-foot length of wrought iron like a club. The unexpected attack stunned everyone and the ten or eleven other men in the settlement were slaughtered, as they tried and failed to rally themselves to fight and the rest were easily rounded up from field and cottage; their helpless terror and bewilderment very pleasant to see, as the attackers wielded their sharp weapons to devastating effect, especially when they saw the pretty, blonde woman enjoying the slaughter as much as any of the others.

General Cavaln then ordered the soldiers to gather up the food stocks from the houses and the iron from the forge; they loaded up the few horses in the hamlet with this, then set off back towards the south. She had already given the hamlet's location to General Tequan and a larger group of soldiers would be on their way to collect the farm produce and animals, whilst a second patrol would follow the lane from this valley back towards the north and civilisation.

Cavaln was quietly pleased as they rode back into the wooded hills, for this was her first trip out as a leader since becoming a General and she had found something that the other Generals had missed. She hoped, inwardly, that her success would continue, and the commander would give her a favourable report.

Much later that evening, back in the command centre and hiding a few ridiculous nerves, Cavaln made her report to Tequan and his staff, even before removing her cloak. The other Generals asked pertinent questions and she answered promptly.

"You clearly have inherited good instincts, Cavaln, thank you." Tequan said with a nod of approval. "Sit down."

"Thank you, sir." Cavaln sank onto a camp stool and took the goblet of wine that Ackat handed to her with a quick smile.

"Jaike is leading the group that will follow that trail back towards the city and you have obtained some useful stores, Cavaln. I suggest that you eat, rest and then you can take out another patrol either tomorrow or the day after, as you prefer." Tequan said easily. "You are a credit to our rank, young woman."

"Thank you, sir." She repeated and finally relaxed a little, taking a sip of wine, privately elated.

* * *

CHAPTER 17

General Tequan's delay was deliberate, as he waited there in that long valley south of Clirensar, for he was waiting for a specific day on which to begin the advance. He and the sea-borne troops left behind in Cal'Badon had arranged for a diversionary attack on the port of Saremouth, which would get the full attention of everyone in the realm.

A fleet of six ships had set out from Cal'Badon, carrying crews of soldiers and Generals, sailing with no identifying features. Although they were plainly jajozeli craft, out on the open ocean they had passed largely unseen, except at great distance, their provenance unclear as they headed north. Then, the ships had turned westward towards the wide mouth of the estuary, finally nearing their target as the sun had set. It was the night of the last day of Jawell, one most luckily thick with moon- and star-blocking clouds, so the ships had continued without lights, unnoticed, sliding towards the well-lit city. Clear across the water came the accumulated noise of the taverns and inns close to the waterfront, although it was late; ports all over Iullyn tended, as a rule, to be a great deal rowdier than the far more staid settlements inland.

Three ships ran in close to the old jetties just downstream on the northern side of the estuary, where the ancient wooden structures were rotting slowly into the estuarine mud. From them, three hundred soldiers scrambled down, moving carefully but quickly towards the modern stone-built wharves, their weapons already in their hands, bearing flasks of lamp oil and unlit torches as part of their arsenal. The ships tied up, simply hidden by the darkness, waiting for the signal that would tell them that their men had reached their goal; presently, a small, bright flame flared up and was waved widely back and forth three times.

Even the most alert guards would have been hard-pressed to raise the alarm, for the black-clad, sooty-faced attackers simply appeared before them out of the night to cut them down in near silence, apparently at one with the shadows, as the other three ships advanced and separated, casting quickly-ignited balls of fire from slingshots right over the front ranks of fishing boats and other craft tied up, a wealth of vessels which separated the open water from the wharves. The fire appeared as if from nowhere, soaring into the night in beautiful, deadly parabolas, as the wooden machinery banged loudly, suddenly, the sling arms crashing back down, echoing strangely.

In moments, horror descended onto the banks of the river. There were screams, shouts and ships and boats of every description were soon ablaze, the flames spreading quickly. Those caught on the boats or the lower wharves screamed with a different pitch of horror as the fire caught them, fanned by an on-shore breeze. The black-clad soldiers already on the riverbank threw oil and torches at the warehouses and other buildings that formed the backdrop to the wharves, their disguise now rendered pretty useless as the night took fire; then they used their weapons with deadly effect on all and sundry they encountered in the area.

Confusion reigned. The air was soon full of smoke and sparks, fanned by that fateful breeze, pushing it inland and into the faces of the frightened people who attempted some sort of hurried, uncoordinated defence. The shouts and screams continued and only increased in volume; chaos quickly spread beyond the docks and into the city beyond, as Generals blasted the gates into Saremouth wide open with their power.

The soldiers arriving from the garrison and the castle found it hard to advance to the scene of conflict, simply because of the milling crowds which filled the streets and lanes, desperate to escape the spreading conflagration and the fighting. It took a little time, time that they could not afford, but the defenders did rally to some effect, organising themselves, getting the panicked populace out of their way; many civilians joined them, forming a defensive cordon that they tried to push towards the riverside, denying the attackers any further advance along the streets. As they pushed onwards others, especially those with their livelihoods going up in flames, organised lines to get desperately needed water to the seat of the fires, moving around the fighting largely concentrated on the main streets.

A number of jajozeli were killed, for not all the locals or sailors who had been forced out of the taverns were inebriated or unarmed, but, after some time, the vast majority of the attackers quite suddenly stepped back and vanished into the darkness, for their task had been achieved: to cause mayhem and carnage before leaving as quickly as they had arrived. Their disappearance cause confusion as they returned to the wharves in short order, dodging around the remaining fires and back to the sagging old jetties to the east. As the soldiers and civilians desperately searched for them and tried to restore order, the six ships tacked back out to sea, aided by the current, their mission accomplished at least as well as it's architect could have wished.

The first light of dawn only served to highlight the destruction: boats burned and sunk; wharves, dwellings, businesses, warehouses and stock reduced to smouldering ash, or at the least damaged by smoke and water. Perhaps hundreds killed. The beacon fire had been lit shortly after the attack had begun, and the alerts had quickly spread inland: Saremouth attacked!

Lord Kierven had taken charge from Garrison Commander Taess shortly after the defenders had realised that their attackers had fled, the young man having had to overrule his advisors, outraged that this had occurred, already trying to figure out how to defend the port in the future and how to make the portside fireproof, as he walked through the ruins, as blackened by soot and smoke as everyone else, offering condolences and the assurance that such an attack could never succeed again.

All eyes turned to the threat that loomed from the coast, especially as two other fishing towns were burned to the ground simultaneously, two nights later, one ten leagues north of Saremouth, the other six leagues or so south past the mouth of the estuary.

*

Five days after this, on the seventh day of Vhisson, General Tequan finally released his troops but, again, in a controlled manner. He led a three-pronged advance northward, using the updated maps to their best effect, utilising lanes and roads as arterial routes and the settlements along them as staging points. By the end of that first day, they had crushed all resistance in a rough line nearly eight leagues from the valley where they had been encamped; with the added benefit that the highly wooded landscape, the mainstay of the local iron smelting industry, hid their advance. By the end of the eighth day, the army was gathered on the edge of the great vale that surrounded the city of Clirensar, still enshrouded in the forests that protected the farmland bordering the river valley.

It was the early afternoon of the ninth of Vhisson and Lord Terfylls was discussing the sale of pigs with his second son, Heldor, and Lady Allara when they heard the distant sound of a hunting horn from across the fields and woods towards Clirensar South Vale Farm. The sound, two short blasts repeated four times, was a warning call that was one of a code traditional in the region, dating back to when a band of outlaws had tried to carve out a niche of their own, whilst causing a great deal of trouble to the duke's ancestors. Terfylls' sons, amongst many others, had learned the horn code and had used it on occasion; usually the warning entailed three short blasts repeated twice, the code used when livestock had escaped. This call, practised quietly and unused otherwise for centuries, as far as tradition knew, meant 'danger, get families out now!'

"Oh, dear Arven!" Heldor cried out, just ahead of his parents.

"What on Iullyn is going on?" Allara asked, puzzled, looking about the nearly empty farmyard in surprise.

Terfylls, however, being taller, could see above the pigsty to his left and noticed an approaching group of horsemen which had just emerged from the woodland that covered the hilltop beyond, riding quickly; men in dark gear, with the bright flash of steel in their hands.

"Run, Allara! Get the children!" He shouted, brandishing his belt knife, whilst Heldor ran across to grab the pitchfork that had been left at the front of the barn doorway and Allara got up on the front step to look at what had taken her husband's attention. Confused, amazed, the three of them stared at the riders, over twenty strong, as they raced across the turnip and carrot fields towards them; then they noticed that there were more men, on foot, marching behind the riders, more than could be counted quickly.

The taking of Callorton and South Vale Farm cost only three jajozeli lives, two killed by Heldor wielding the pitchfork with deadly accuracy, and third by Dettar at the farmhouse, using a hastily grabbed scythe, but it was the most resistance that the enemy had yet faced in their advance.

General Cavaln, as the most junior of them, was charged with searching the buildings of both farms, for both were clearly far above the average type of rural dwellings that the jajozeli Generals had yet encountered. After reading the documentation gathered together by the group and handed to her, she reported to General Tequan later that evening in the South Vale Farm farmhouse; the soldiers accompanying the Generals had removed all the corpses to the barn for neatness.

"So, Cavaln, what have you discovered about these prosperous-seeming farmers?" The Commander asked, lounging by the hearth in the well-appointed kitchen, wine goblet in hand.

"This farm is owned by the Duke of Clirensar, sir. This is South Vale Farm, a farm and stud run by Salyon, third son of the minor noble who owned the farm across the fields; their daughter and youngest child is betrothed to the Duke's son and heir, Pualyn." Cavaln waved the parchment sheet that was Lyria's letter to her parents. "Lyria is the Duchess's lady-in-waiting and, apart from the details about clothes and jewels, there's quite a lot of information about the daughter, Ethrayne and the prince." She grinned widely, offering the sheet. "Shall I -."

"No, read it to me, I hate that selithian scrawl." Tequan ordered dismissively and smiled. "It's a good job we didn't just kill everyone we found here immediately, isn't it? We'll question her later."

"Of course, well . . . I'll condense what it says . . ." She frowned, scanning the page. "Lyria writes that Ethrayne is apparently enjoying her combat lessons, although her friend is worried that she isn't sleeping well . . . the young couple's days are full of combat and meetings with the Archpriests, the Council of Tenarum, the king and representatives of the western Selithian realms . . . The news of Newventure Bay's destruction is well-known and the warning beacons and messaging system across the kingdom seems to be well organised . . . Ethrayne has been elevated to the highest councils in the continent . . . Lyria is party to a great deal of information in and has passed it on rather well . . . the rest is mostly just personal."

"We saw the effectiveness of the beacons after Saremouth was hit a few days ago." Tequan agreed, nodding his head. "It was good to hear it and know that our presence has had such a positive effect upon their meagre defences." He grinned broadly, his eyes glittering maliciously. "And now all their attention will be on the coast, fatally so. All we have to do is get inside those high city walls without raising a general alarm, any ideas?"

Cavaln shook her head. "No, sir, not yet."

"The problem is solved!" Ackat's voice sounded unexpectedly and exultantly from the doorway behind them and they turned. "We'll use the duke's excellent horses, of course. I'll explain during dinner, it's brilliantly simple, Tequan." And he vanished back outside.

"Does he do that very often?" Cavaln asked drily, folding the parchment carefully.

"Just often enough to be bloody irritating." Tequan replied with a sigh. "And don't look impressed when he announces his idea, he'll only get worse."

Cavaln smothered a laugh at both his words and his tired tone.

"Oh, shut up and get yourself a drink, woman."

General Ackat's deceptively simple plan, related with a grin during a very nice meal that had been prepared by Salyon's wife that morning, was received with grudging approval by the Commander. In fact, he smiled, nodded his respect and actually congratulated his colleague, toasting him with a goblet of the wine that had been appropriated from the farm's cellar.

"I like it, Ackat." He admitted, finally. "Get it arranged."

"Of course, Commander, I'm glad you approve." And Ackat sat back, laughing merrily.

*

The next afternoon, it seemed that Salyon and six men entered Clirensar, riding ten of the Duke's fine horses up through the city and, without any questioning and only a hearty 'hello' from the guards, to the castle's stable courtyard, bearing baskets of soft fruits and fresh vegetables picked that morning from the fields. Ackat had ruthlessly questioned one of the few surviving people from South Vale Farm and Callorton for Tequan had decided, arbitrarily, that a few of the screaming, helpless women would make good prisoners; on discovering which of the dead bodies was Salyon's he had made himself look identical to the man, to the hostages' horror.

"Oh, thank you, Master Salyon!" Gushed a large woman in a plain grey gown, who was crossing the courtyard with a milk pail in her hand, as he and his men dismounted at an empty section of railing close to the lower range of buildings that climbed high above their heads, merging into the towering castle. "I want to make jam and these raspberries will be perfect; and if you can possibly send more fruit in seven days, the family should be nearly home and your sister too, isn't that wonderful?"

"The Duke's family?" Ackat asked in odd-sounding Selithian and coughed two or three times. "Excuse me, I've got a bad throat, I sound awful. Now, that is good news!" And he smiled broadly, his eyes dancing as he explained his voice, which likely did not sound much like the dead man's.

"Come on in, Master and we will serve you and your men with ale. Steward Pellarse will be here shortly. Now, how is your lovely Deanne?"

"Oh, she and the children are fine, thank you." Ackat followed the woman through the doorway ahead and into a wide corridor that had doors off to both sides, with a larger door ahead leading into a massive kitchen where men and women, boys and girls, all wearing green, worked industriously around large deal tables or at the huge fires. One man with greying brown hair, deep green eyes and a paunch tight under his deep green doublet, gave him cheerful greetings and a second man poured a huge tankard of foamy-topped ale. "Thank you, Pellarse and good health."

He recalled his time in Tenum City, coughing again to explain his voice. The mannerisms he had noted in the people in the capital, how they had spoken and how they had behaved, helped him stay in character; he had not dared to bring his weapons with him and he certainly didn't want to rouse anyone's suspicions. Fortunately, the servants who actually knew the man that he was impersonating accepted him as he seemed, although he knew that he was probably not doing a very good job of it.

The ale was pleasant: cool, refreshing and with a nice bite of flavour; the jajozeli he had brought with him enjoyed it as they loitered around the courtyard, like workmen everywhere, taking a break where they could; 'Salyon' had just described them as farmhands, dressed in plain tunics and jerkins from the farms, ordinary-looking soldiers from Tequan's ranks, whom Ackat had chosen because they spoke fluent selithian. They exchanged a little banter with passing servants and whistled appreciatively at the maids.

Leaning against one side table, surrounded by people who were comfortable in his presence – Salyon's presence – Ackat slowly sipped his ale and fished for details, thoroughly enjoying himself. The knowledgeable servants simply assumed that he was finding out as much as he could for the edification of his parents, since Duke Sarant had departed, and were happy to oblige. As the afternoon progressed, he found out rather a lot of information and managed to arrange a private dinner with Reeve Thomur besides; Salyon was practically a member of the ducal family, after all. He wandered about for a while, visiting the privy, ostensibly, then carefully poured a sleeping drug into the main part of the meal being prepared for the hundreds of staff in the castle. Then he slipped outside and quietly directed his patiently waiting men to disperse into the city, but with orders to congregate together by the tavern that they had passed earlier, a large establishment rather unimaginatively called The Duke's Arms, at sunset. Then, laughing as if at a joke, he returned to the kitchen where Thomur was giving directions to the staff.

Reeve Thomur was the perfect host, he found and the man was pleased to dominate the conversation, filling 'Master Salyon' in on recent developments; the weapons and chain mail made for Ethrayne which were awaiting the Duke's approval in Dark Fell; the latest news from the razine aboard the Pearl and Opal ships; information regarding the terrible night-time assaults on Saremouth, Elport and Arnaport. Ackat appreciated the meal, including the dessert featuring the raspberries that he had picked that morning, answering and commenting as appropriate to Thomur's conversation; he hardly needed to think at all.

As the evening advanced, he gently used his innate power to tire the talkative Reeve, nudging him mentally towards the idea that he really wanted to go off to bed; he actually helped the man up to his bedroom, using his power to knock him into sleep even though it was so early. Then, unobtrusively, even as he had done in Tenum's palace, he slipped silently and unnoticed through the castle, pouring a second sleeping draught into the ale jugs set out for evening refreshment: this was a well-provisioned kitchen in a prosperous castle; even the servants were well looked after here, it seemed. The night darkened, the servants retired.

The jajozelis' purpose was conquest, but conquest with a difference; an invasion which would go hopefully entirely unnoticed beyond the northern fringes of the broad Vale of Clirensar, at least for the time it would take to see the army well established and well protected in the area. That was Commander Tequan's intent, with his master's approval, and his fellow Generals would follow his lead to the end.

Walking with purpose, the General used his power again to send those men on guard duty into a deep sleep. He cut the throats of those sleeping soldiers who had been stood at the main entrance, their threat eliminated; then quietly unlocked the two main sets of gates that led out into the city, as full night fell, the darkness hiding and muffling the slight differences that he wanted unnoticed, although he left them closed. Only then did Ackat finally change his appearance back to his original form and walked quietly down the steep, nearly empty streets; there were night-watchmen marching around the city, but he avoided them easily, heading to the huge square and the tavern where he had ordered his men to meet up together at sunset.

He slipped past the dark tavern into the wide, unlit alley that led to a slightly run-down but spacious stable yard secreted behind it's cramped rear yard and his men were waiting here, out of sight, but not alone. Seventy men had wandered in during the day, singly or in twos, unchallenged, at the main gates, and had just made their way through the city, walking idly, looking around for important landmarks and the barracks, plainly dressed and unarmed. Thirty other jajozeli soldiers had entered the city throughout the day in small groups, bringing in six purloined carts between them that were loaded with more farm produce from Callorton and South Vale Farm. Under the eggs and fruit and vegetables, however, all their weapons had been hidden beneath close-packed straw in the beds of the carts. At General Cavaln's suggestion, they had ranged about the city markets and had sold their stolen harvest, bartering with housewives and innkeepers, making a tidy sum. They had used their selling to be quietly prominent, looking for their fellows and giving them quiet directions to the stable as a safehouse for meeting later.

After concluding their business, the disguised soldiers had stowed the carts securely in the stable near to sunset, offering the trusting owner a few un-sold vegetables and a few coins, before, having ascertained that his family lived above the stable and his assistants had left for the day, they had efficiently slaughtered the family; then they had simply waited for darkness, having latched the stable doors shut, feeding and watering the horses.

Ackat rapped on the door and the lock was undone with a scrape of iron before one wide door swung slightly open. "Are you ready?" He asked simply, slipping inside and scanning the space that was dimly lit with a few horn lanterns, where the men got quickly to their feet. "Has there been any trouble?"

"No, Lord General." His captain replied with a salute, rather incongruous in his farm tunic. "It's been quiet, there's been no interference and no alarms have been raised."

"Excellent. Let's get prepared." He moved to the nearest cart, where their bundles of clothing and the weapons were now laid neatly out. Ackat simply stripped off the garb of a moderately wealthy farmer that did not fit his true frame, replacing them with the grey silk tunic and black leather jerkin and leggings, the workaday uniform of a General, whilst his men changed into their plain black padded tunics, ranged around the space out of his way, ignoring the snorts of the horses in the stalls.

Ackat pulled his own weapons from the pile, buckling on his sword belt, settling it comfortably at his hips. He didn't bother with chain mail or any ordinary personal protection, although the soldiers rang and made scraping noises as they hauled their own mail shirts on, puffing slightly.

"Well, you know what to do, men: eliminate the sentries on the city walls and the gates; open the city gates; neutralise any barracks; secure the city and castle gates." He ordered crisply. "There are only about a hundred of you, so move carefully: if they don't know we're here, we have free-rein. Silence is the watchword. The last thing the commander wants is the population alerted to our presence until dawn breaks and by then it will be far too late!"

"Yes, sir." They chorused.

"Lieutenant Ejas." Ackat looked at the officer, a burly man with grey hair and a scarred face with flat eyes. "You're with me. We will hold the castle gates until Tequan's forces are inside the city walls."

"Aye, my Lord General." The man grinned briefly. "They're going to have a big shock come morning."

"Oh yes." Ackat agreed, his eyes glittering coldly. "Let's move out."

Ackat took about twenty soldiers with him, and the remaining group of eighty split up under the captain, their purposes clear: the sentries on the outer walls, the guards on the gates, their fellows on duty around their barracks, all unaware of the lethal force advancing in their midst; the taking of Clirensar occurred with a surprising minimum of reaction from the natives. Moving silently, or as near as possible, the jajozeli eliminated all opposition with their characteristic brutality.

* * *

CHAPTER 18

General Tequan led a force of ten thousand men who filed into the city shortly after the taking of the city gates in the south wall, having advanced from the cover of the woods around South Vale Farm after dark, sure of their invisibility due to the soldiers scouting ahead in small groups who had killed those in the farms and hamlets along the main roads. The rest of the army were now ranged out in the woods and farmland, likewise, hiding until their presence was required. With this significant army behind him, he was confident of success. Some soldiers took up position on the vacated walls, at the open gates; others patrolled, quietly killing the night-watchmen they came across, for whom amongst them expected attack? Others were detailed to set up guard posts at significant junctions, whilst the rest walked into the two barracks, one in the centre of the city, the other in the castle complex on the crag far above and killed the remaining soldiers.

Of course, some competent citizens were awake, sufficiently forewarned to fight back or shout warnings, but Ackat's sleeping draught and his encouragement for the castle residents to sleep deeply, reinforced by the effect of the other Generals' power, had succeeded beyond any realistic expectations: most of the soldiers had been asleep, or drowsy and now would never wake again. Those who did reach for their weapons, those who fought, were ruthlessly cut down.

General Cavaln led two hundred men through the city towards the citadel above the city, excitement pulsing through her. It was proving to be an exhilarating night, not least because the commander had explained her presence in Tenarum, as the emperor had not. Grinning, she joined Ackat and Lieutenant Ejas at the massive but ultimately useless castle gates, slipping inside. It was still some hours until dawn, the night was black.

"Shall we take the seat of Clirensar, Lord General?" She asked lightly, saluting him with her sword.

"Yes, why not? After you, Madam." Ackat bowed slightly. "I think you will find the doors unlocked."

*

Reeve Thomur was woken roughly from deep sleep, a cold blade laid hard against his throat. He opened his eyes in a mixture of confusion and alarm to see a dark-clad woman with cold eyes stood over him, a long, sharp sword steady in her right hand, a burning torch in her left.

"Wha'-?" He began, blurrily.

"If you value your life, man, you will be silent." The woman ordered harshly in accented selithian. "On your feet and don't try anything: I am armed as you see, and I'll react much faster than you!" Her face was an odd mixture of pale skin and deep shadow, but her eyes were clear, the look in them deadly.

Scrambling out of bed in his nightshirt, Thomur did not seriously consider arguing, his mind frozen with fear. He just could not believe this how could this have happened? Who was this deadly woman, and where had she come from, in the middle of the night? The woman moved back lightly in her utilitarian male garb and held the weapon with practised ease in her gloved hand, keeping a good distance away from him. And he found his realisation that the woman was about his own height even more unnerving.

His bedroom door opened and an even taller blond, blue-eyed man entered, staring at him as if he was a pile of filth, wearing clothes identical to the woman's.

"Ah, Reeve Thomur, thank you so much for all the details of the duke's family at dinner." He said with a mocking smile at the frightened man. "I am General Ackat. You may remember me from last evening, looking like Master Salyon." Thomur staggered, awed and stunned, when the tall figure suddenly seemed to shrink into a smaller, stockier, brown-haired man who was completely familiar to him, before shimmering back into the blonde stranger.

"Oh, dear Arven! Who-who are you?" Thomur dared to stammer, despite the sword blade still so cold at his throat, the need for some sort of answer taking precedence over personal safety.

"I am General Ackat." He repeated coolly. "This is my colleague, General Cavaln. Clirensar is ours and you now belong to the Emperor of the Jajozeli. You will accompany General Cavaln to the Lady Ethrayne's rooms, understand?" Ackat's own sword flashed in the torchlight as the point was laid, with a slight push, against his groin. "She loves slaughter, so I strongly suggest that you cooperate with her every word. Go!"

Thomur gulped. Barefoot, his legs pale and thin below the edge of the nightshirt in the light of the torch, his heart beating with terrible fear, he led Cavaln along the empty corridor from his modest room in the staff quarters, up some stairs and along a rather convoluted route that led to a far wider, more elegantly decorated passage where the doorframes were made of carefully carved stone arches, the doors of oak, the plain white walls covered in bright hangings, some parts standing out starkly in the torchlight, whilst other areas were black and shadowed. It was unnerving, walking along corridors when he knew the castle guards had been eliminated but, of course, many of the internal guards had been mostly stood down to normal duties, since the family were absent. It was unbelievable yet, strangely, the castle felt alien and unfriendly, as it had never done before.

"This is Lady Ethrayne's suite, m-my lady." The Reeve said in a shivering voice, pointing at the last door on the right and gazing at the woman behind him with trepidation, with the sword still steady in her hand; he guessed with yet another jolt of unease that she probably was a lot quicker at sword fighting than he was.

"You will open the door carefully, fool, or I'll end your life in a breath!" The General ordered coldly. "Does anyone sleep here?"

"Well, er, y-yes, Lady, they do . . . Sallie and Fionn, actually, they sleep in the room next to Lady Ethrayne's bedroom -." The man replied quickly, reaching one shaking hand to the ornate latch, lifting it and pushing open the door to reveal a night-shrouded room that came suddenly into life as Cavaln entered on his heels. A pleasant, almost square sitting room was revealed, with deep blue velvet curtains at the windows; a thick, multi-coloured carpet on the floor; there were well-upholstered chairs and a settee arranged around a wide fireplace in the centre of one long wall; a sideboard and circular table and chairs to the left, and high shelving to the right, containing a range of books, scrolls, quills, an ink pot and ornaments.

"Hmm." The woman said. "Through there?" She pointed with the sword to a door in the opposite wall.

"Lady E-Ethrayne's bed-bedroom is that way, lady." Thomur stammered, inching forward uncertainly.

"Lead on, fool." She ordered shortly, pausing to light a pair of lamps and a candle as she passed the table and glanced quickly at the well-worn, polished sideboard that held obviously personal items.

There was a smaller, still comfortable-looking room containing other items of furniture and two large windows, beyond, where a beautiful gown sat on a roughly body-shaped dummy, ornate, with gold and silver embroidery gleaming on the pale blue silk of the bodice, sleeves and hemline, surrounded by a wealth of sewing equipment, threads and fabrics. A further door led to a large bedroom containing a massive four posted bed with old tapestry hangings, white bed linen, colourful cushions and a neatly folded, patchwork coverlet that looked to be made of many handstitched triangles of bright dress fabric, backed with green velvet. The carpet was nearly as ornate as the one in the sitting room and there was an old, rather battered padded chair before a fireplace, holding a floppy old rag doll in a red dress.

"Comfortable." Cavaln remarked, scanning the room, reading the obvious signs that the occupant was female, young and well loved, from the three-foot square silver mirror on the low table to the left, flanked by a pair of large beeswax candles, to the carved jewellery box on the large old chest against the right-hand wall. Everything breathed luxury and privilege.

There were two further doors leading from the bedroom on either side of the large fireplace. Thomur opened one to show a rather well-appointed bathroom and closed the door nervously, before approaching the one on the right, which opened into a chamber containing two low beds, covered with plain linen sheets and clearly handmade coverlets, both occupied.

Roused by the sudden torchlight, the movement, one girl awoke quickly, clearly accustomed to waking when called; a simple nightgown was revealed as she sat up, her pretty face still slack from sleep, her dark blonde braids hanging down her shoulders. "My Lord Thomur!" She gasped, rubbing her eyes quickly, focussing on the Reeve first, before noticing the woman behind him, her gleaming sword so prominent -.

"Don't scream, girl." Cavaln warned coldly. "Wake your friend but move slowly." There were always some people, the young General reflected ruefully, who could apparently sleep through even earthquakes or their homes collapsing around them!

Shortly, both girls and the Reeve were stood in the centre of the sitting room, shivering in their nightclothes under the woman's cold, sharp, appraising glare, frightened and confused. Now and again, distantly, they could hear an occasional muffled shout, scream or even footfalls outside the door, moving elsewhere along the corridor, but no one disturbed them until after the sun had risen, the sky lightening outside the windows, the sunlight visible on the distant walls opposite that faced east.

"Excellent work, General Cavaln." Tequan's deep voice sounded from the outer doorway and the three prisoners all turned in alarm, the maids squealing piteously at his appearance. "The Wielder's rooms are secure?"

"They are secure, General Tequan." She replied.

"Good. Take the man down to the great hall, if you please; check with Jaike there, then return. I will instruct these brats on the necessity for instant obedience until you get back up here." He grinned slowly and winked and Cavaln smiled in return; she could read his surface thoughts clearly, as he intended. "After that, I believe the kitchen staff is preparing rather a nice breakfast for us."

"As you command, enjoy yourself." She answered lightly, jerking her head at Thomur, and then pushing him into motion towards the door, past the tall, reddish-haired male.

"Oh, I will." He assured her as she headed into the corridor, closing the door on him.

*

In the light of day, the massive castle proved to be rather an attractive structure, solidly constructed of the local pale limestone that seemed to glow a little in the warm sunshine. The corridors held only patrolling jajozeli who saluted her politely as she headed down to what the man called the High Hall, guided by the unwilling but helpless Reeve; the route was complex, she considered.

This high hall was a large, vaulted space on the first floor of the building, its size diminished somewhat as it was crammed full of prisoners in various states of undress, matched by various degrees of distress and fear. It was interesting to see just how many people it took to run a castle; the laundry, stables, barracks, brewery, bakery, kitchens, dormitories and all the bedrooms and suites had been emptied. Many of the women and girls were sobbing, whilst some of the men were clearly injured. General Jaike was sat comfortably in the duke's large seat in the centre of the dais and at least a hundred cold-faced soldiers stood to attention around the walls and at the doors, swords and spears in hand, ready to subdue any wild uprising.

Everyone in the hall turned to stare at General Cavaln as she brusquely shoved the Reeve hard in the back, so that he staggered helplessly into the rear ranks of the prisoners.

"Look! A woman! Dear Arven, she's armed! She's one of them! A woman soldier!" And other exclamations were clearly audible as the prisoners shrank away yet again.

"Silence!" She commanded in selithian, the word echoing harshly from the walls and the prisoners cowered meekly, leaving a long corridor through the centre of them as she advanced through them to the dais, her boots ringing on the bright patterned tiles.

"You look comfortable." Cavaln remarked to Jaike in jajozeli. "Pirris! I'm parched, have you got any water?"

"Here." He offered her an ornate silver goblet that had been set down by the legs of the chair and she drank gratefully. "How's it going?"

"All right. General Tequan is having a great deal of fun." Cavaln replied, handing back the goblet. "Thank you, Jaike."

"My pleasure." General Jaike weighed the object in his hand before he also drank. "I wouldn't mind some of that myself, later: some of the women are pretty. And this is a wealthy duchy, look at this workmanship." He sounded rather surprised, then grinned. "Yet all their defences and walls and gates have proved less than useless against our myriad talents." He chuckled.

"It'll be interesting to see what will happen to the kingdom beyond Clirensar's valley, won't it?" The woman remarked. "I'll see you at breakfast, General Jaike, keep the rabble suitably subdued."

"As you command, General Cavaln."

*

Rape, violence and murder were the stock-in-trade of the jajozeli Generals, when necessary and General Tequan employed two of them to excellent effect during his intense questioning of the maids, whose world had fallen into ruins overnight. Having wrung every single drop of information on their young mistress out of them, he callously used his power to loosen their vocal chords so that they could no longer speak. Then, having taken the time to rather inexplicably tear the beautiful wedding dress into rags, he set them to packing up the lady's possessions, locking them into the suite, bruised, battered and tearful.

"There you are, come on." Tequan said jovially from the top of the wide, sweeping stairs that led down the public areas as Cavaln climbed towards him; she stopped dead, four steps below, glaring. *<Ackat!>* He sent silently. *<Breakfast, we need to talk.>*

"Pirris!" Cavaln grumbled, but not seriously. "All these bloody stairs!"

"Oh, stop moaning, we need to pool all we know to better coordinate our actions here and it's been a long night: I'm hungry." He countered.

Breakfast, served in the family's private north-facing dining room, was very good indeed, but their conversation was perhaps much better.

"The Duke and his family are on their way back here." Tequan said, cutting up ham and eggs with relish.

"They're halfway here, Tequan." Ackat amended with a grin, spooning kidneys and mushrooms onto his plate. "Reeve Thomur was most effusive yesterday evening at dinner." He chuckled a little.

"That is most fortuitous, my Lords." Cavaln remarked, enjoying a bowl of strawberries and raspberries with a plate of warm, freshly baked bread and honey.

"I don't believe that fortune has anything to do with it, young woman: I thank our master. He sent us here at this time to begin our campaign." Tequan countered. "It is excellent news. So, Ackat, what else did the Reeve tell you?"

"The Duke was here during Kharsare, checking his duchy's workings, and actually commissioning weapons and mail for his daughter. It seems that there are two weddings planned for the end of the year: that of the Wielders of the Flame and also of her brother to the sister of those we killed yesterday at Callorton -." He barked a laugh. "It's a shame we have to ruin their well-laid organisation, for such royal and noble weddings must cost a fortune. Also, the brother, Pualyn, the heir of this place, is presently with the razine in Orbain as envoy. So, hopefully, all this will blow away their good intentions and scupper the Protectorates' plans to assist the kingdom."

"Excellent. I want the servants questioned extensively, even so. I want every scrap of news or gossip available." Tequan growled. "Well, let's eat up, we've got a city to control."

*

The citizens of Clirensar had woken to the horror of an occupying army pacing their streets, the troops ruthlessly slaughtering anyone who stood up to them. Overnight, their situation had turned totally upside down. The corpses of the Clirensar soldiers and sentries lay where they had fallen in the streets or dropped from the walls which they had been patrolling so uselessly. The screams of women being raped could be heard from many points. The city gates were all locked, there were enemy soldiers patrolling in wide loops around the outside of the walls and across the valley, killing the farmers and villagers in the vicinity, collecting the harvest. Clirensar was locked down and the shops, businesses and inns were all closed.

No one could comprehend quite how the jajozeli had arrived overnight and simply taken total control, but mastery they had. The soldiers began house-to-house searches at dawn, bringing out weapons, large kitchen knives and every male aged over approximately ten years of age; all were rounded up and marched into the Cathedral, whilst the ancient, venerated space was abruptly and forcibly abandoned by the priests and priestesses of Arven who were all murdered out of hand in the cathedral square, which soon ran with their blood. Surrounded by grim-faced strangers speaking an unknown language, bristling with weapons and seeing the bloody consequences of any argument or disobedience so plainly the men and boys of the city shrank down, terrified, beaten.

"As of this morning, you are the property of the Emperor of the Jajozeli Empire." General Owenn announced, glaring indiscriminately across the cathedral, leaning against the smashed altar, scanning quickly over the prisoners, on their knees. “You can thank your little Lady Ethrayne and her prince for this -.”

A few men hissed or booed -. “Bastard!” Was shouted. The jajozeli soldiers stormed into the mass of prisoners and simply slaughtered a good number of them, whether rebellious or not. There were screams, shouts and not a few sobs -.

“You will obey, or you will die.” Owenn finished dispassionately.

*

Ackat and Tequan made a midmorning visit to Black Fell, backed up by three thousand soldiers who had advanced through the covering woodland to the east of the city. The farmers and townsfolk there were simply murdered; the finished chain mail shirts and the jewel-embellished weapons constructed for Ethrayne were confiscated by the Generals, whilst as before, any foodstuffs, the other weapons in the town, pig iron and ingots were loaded onto carts to be taken back to the city. They set fire to the buildings and left the village smouldering in its gorge.

The occupation of Clirensar was going to plan and in ways that none of them could have imagined or expected, even a few days before.

* * *

CHAPTER 19

Autumn was almost upon them, for Vhisson had arrived, heralding later dawns, earlier sunsets and slightly cooler temperatures as the farmers continued harvesting their crops. Ethrayne marvelled that the year was passing so swiftly. Although, considering just how full her days were now, it was not surprising that the seasons had turned so fast.

Now, sat on her horse, following her father and mother down the main street towards the South Gate, she was quite looking forward to a short period containing no interminable meetings; no study and no combat, unless she chose it; which, considering how organised her days had been, Ethrayne thought that she might well continue the practice of the past moons, after a few days' rest. Turning in her saddle, she saw the tallest tower of the palace vanish behind the ordinary buildings that lined the street and sighed slightly as she turned back and straightened.

"Oh, it will be lovely to see mother again!" Lyria said, riding beside her. "And Deanne should have had the baby by now. I can't wait to see them, I wonder if it's a boy or a girl?"

Ethrayne laughed at her enthusiasm. "It's been moons since we left, all your little nieces and nephews will have grown so much, you won't recognise them, dear. And you're so sophisticated, they won't recognise you either, Lyria."

"I've just got a new wardrobe, Ethie, I've not changed at all. But I have missed them all, mother and father especially. It's been a very strange year, since we arrived in Tenum City in Staipe, hasn't it?"

"Yes, I agree, it's been unexpected, yet it seemed so normal until the day before his highness and I were betrothed. Then it changed completely." The younger girl agreed, smiling, shrugging.

"I just can hardly believe that we are finally leaving Tenum and heading home, despite the latest news from Saremouth that came in last night." Lyria continued, shaking her head. "It's terrible to have had the city attacked like that with no warning!"

"Father nearly called off the trip, but King Marrand overruled him." Ethrayne said. "It's just awful to hear that the wharves and lower city were burned; none of us can really sleep safe in our beds, can we? How on Iullyn can we possibly guard against such attacks?" She frowned deeply at her hands on the reins, continuing to ponder that conundrum, for the sheer unpredictability of the attacks so far made by the jajozeli was worrying. It would be impossible to patrol every coastal town and city completely!

Seeing her expression, Lyria did not interrupt her reverie, but rode quietly, enjoying the prospect of the return to Clirensar and, with it, enjoying the changing view of the city and the exercise. The main roads were full of the usual crowds, but the people stopped to waved and cheered to see the group pass and they quickly reached the gate and exited the crowded city, entering the farmland that filled the countryside beyond, the King's Road arrow straight before them, the stones that surfaced it dustily grey in the late summer sunshine.

Worries filled Ethrayne for a while; she considered, again, that this was all her and Jerryn's fault: yet another attack had occurred which had led to the deaths of innocent people. An attack that the excellent soldiers of the city clearly seemed incapable of preventing, although they had checked the enemy's advance into the city of Saremouth before the enemy had progressed too far. After the sinking of ships and blatant piracy which had happened even in view of the coast; the destruction of Newventure Bay; it seemed that the enemy was deliberately targeting the kingdom, causing murder and mayhem but in oddly minor ways. From what she had learned about the Jajozeli Empire in the past moons, it seemed that their emperor commanded vast armies that could potentially overrun this part of the continent with relative ease. Why they were moving on such small targets, using such small forces, was a puzzle not even ex-archpriest Bahlien could understand.

Of course, she shook herself mentally, it was not their personal fault; she and Jerryn were the focus of the enemy's action, not the perpetrators, their parents, Commander Vedeigne and the Archpriests had stated this often. Yet it was awful to know that people were dying, their homes and livelihoods destroyed, simply because she and her betrothed had agreed to become the Wielders of the Flame . . . Not that either of them would really be wielding any power any time soon; and the snail's pace of their progress rankled, with the many long evenings she and Jerryn had spent meditating, concentrating and practising as required.

The old razine had assured them repeatedly that they were doing very well with the 'visualisation', which involved trying to hold on to pictures or images in their minds, which proved difficult, after the relative ease of the initial meditation. She and Jerryn both viewed their slow progress with impatience, but Bahlien simply told them that they needed strong, well-trained minds before they could realistically start to learn to use the power that had been gifted to them.

"I know this seems tedious and slow, but you will be commanding power far greater than any razine, but one, has ever possessed." Bahlien had said, the evening before. "Human or razine, we must all work hard and train to use our minds properly. Commander Vedeigne would not let you loose with sharpened steel without ensuring that you have a good degree of competence: both swords and power can be easily and quickly fatal."

And now, riding away from Tenum City, leaving the bustling corridors of the palace behind, where her days had been so full of important meetings and decisions, she felt the worries that constrained her suddenly begin to loosen; with nothing taxing to occupy her immediate attention, she could simply ride and think and . . . recuperate.

<You need to get out of the city, Jerryn; go riding with your friends and rest a little.> She sent back to her betrothed, at the very limit of her strength; the range between which she and Jerryn could 'talk' mentally had grown to further than a mile, perhaps nearly half a league. *<I think that Bahlien is correct about our training, and a rest will clear you mind. Oh, I wish you could come too!>* She said honestly.

<Yes, so do I, but my father needs me here. Take care my love and I will see you in Thurton. I love you, Ethrayne.> His tone very dim, but still clear in her mind.

<I love you, Jerryn, my Prince, farewell.> Ethrayne sent him a kiss with her reply. It was wonderful, they had both agreed, that their mental abilities had rendered the love between them so obvious; neither of them now embarrassed by that fact, at least.

Then she abandoned contemplation for conversation with Lyria and her parents; the leagues began to pass more quickly as the group rode on, their possessions drawn behind them on a series of carts behind them and a huge group of soldiers around them, jingling, their weapons shining, in the warm sunshine of a fair Vhisson day.

*

The entourage was beginning the long descent from the ridge top down the winding route through the North Coppice; collectively, the nobles, soldiers and servants all seemed to stretch and sit up straighter, more alert in their seats and saddles, and even the horses pulling the heavy carts seemed to prick up their ears and their pace as if they realised that they were nearly home. The wide road ran through a partly dappled shade, even though the forest trees formed a border at least twenty yards back on both sides; the swift-growing sweet chestnuts so loved by the charcoal burners dominated the woodlands here, forming a dense shade that was beginning to show bright yellow or orange splashing bright amid the deep green leaves. Only low growth was permitted along the road itself, the grass and shrubbery curtailed by the charcoal burners: they scythed the undergrowth back periodically throughout the growing year. Clearly the chore was nearly due again for the elders, brambles, nettles and bracken were burgeoning.

"There, we'll be home well before evening, my Duchess Riyala." Sarant said with a broad sweep of his arms, grinning widely at his wife, his daughter and his prospective daughter-in-law. "We've had very good weather, all in all, but I'll be glad to get out of the saddle, I admit. I must be getting old." He chuckled and slapped Letwar's neck appreciatively as if in apology. His black stallion did not take insult, however.

"Oh, my husband, you will not ever get old." Riyala exclaimed, also chuckling. "After a long hot bath and a short rest, you'll be rushing about the countryside as usual, I'm sure." She reached across to clasp his hand in hers and squeezed it tightly. "You are still only eighteen in my eyes, my dear Sarant."

Behind the couple, Ethrayne and Lyria exchanged looks, both young women silently hoping that their marriages would be as loving as this one, despite the uncertainties that had arisen since the spring. True and long-lasting regard, after all, was hard to find and hard to retain, sometimes, amid the vagaries of the world.

"It will be lovely to be home and away from the court completely." Ethrayne admitted with a smile. "I'm missing Jerryn, of course, but, gosh, it was wearing, wasn't it?"

"Yes, but your castle is hardly a farmhouse, is it?" Lyria laughed aloud. "Oh, Ethie! If you want informal, you can come home to Callorton with me; sometimes father hardly changes for dinner."

"I know, the lucky things! Such informality! And fewer clothes to wash, too. Just good food and conversation and no banquets and stuffy get-togethers, I can't wait; I haven't seen your mother since late winter, you know." And they both laughed; Ethrayne and her family had frequently dined at the farm, just as Lyria and her family had dined in the castle, and all were used to the peculiarities of the others.

Their armed guard rode all around them, the servants brought up the rear with the carts; the unsubstantiated reports of attacks inland from the coast along with the raids on Saremouth and other ports were of concern. Clirensar's thousand troops rode with five hundred Royal Guardsmen, including some of the best scouts and soldiers in the kingdom, at Marrand's insistence. The professionals had ranged out in every direction during the fourteen days of their journey and they had all been relieved that no danger had emerged from the busily harvesting countryside. Duke Sarant had breathed a little easier with each league that they passed, for he had been privately concerned for their collective safety. And now only a league or so separated them from home.

Ahead, the descending road took a wide sweep to the left along the slope, the vista of the Vale still hidden by the woodland, although a few glimpses of far distant hills and tiny hints of haze-covered peaks were espied between trunks, here and there, far beyond the city. The group continued, perhaps relaxing slightly as they rode finally out of the trees, leaving the forest behind as a great curve of hillside spread off to both left and right. Sun-lit, summer-browned grass dominating the view ahead, the broad Vale of Clirensar stretching bowl-like around them, its jumbled southern edge at least eight leagues beyond the city, its closest extent curving off to the west on their right where, hidden in more woodland, some four leagues beyond the city, the vale formed a long arc where the three valleys cut up into the highlands, south-west, west and north-west, their tumbling, vigorous streams forming the river that sparkled below. The Sare curved around the north side of of the city walls, not much more than a league or so away in a straight line, the tops of the highest towers of the castle almost at the same height as they themselves, for the castle was stepped far higher above the city than the royal palace was above Tenum; the pale crag its buildings stood on was stark to the left of the defensive walls:

an almost sheer cliff climbing above the left hand edge of the wharves far below, clear despite the distance, boats and barges lined up as usual. Off to the east the vale continued in a straight ridgeline for some leagues, the river meandering through it, heading towards the lowlands and, eventually, the coast and Saremouth. All around there were little farms and villages, and tame woodland, the fields mostly cleared as harvest continued.

Home! Ethrayne said silently to herself in sudden contentment, smiling at the view she knew best, looking for the tiny suggestion of the knife-shaped peak that she could see from her own bedchamber window, how many leagues away she could not guess; it had just always been there like everything else, a mere hint of the wider world which had come crashing down to affect them all.

The commander of the troops barked some orders and the soldiers all began to form up, splitting; half the group wheeled smartly to the rear, as the people all straightened in their saddles and seats, exchanging a quiet banter as they started on down the sweeping slope –.

A blast from a horn, a deep, harsh but brassy sound, came from nowhere. It sounded nothing at all like the sort of fanfare of greeting that occurred at official homecomings, echoing harshly from the dark woods. It came again, loud, raucous. Several things seemed to occur at once. In retrospect, it was undoubtedly due to meticulous planning –.

The bright flags of Tenarum and Clirensar were pulled down from the flagpoles over the north gate and the castle; different standards were quickly run up to replace them, displaying an unknown device that unfurled swiftly and whipped in the wind, showing black, silver and red; the field as black as night, with a bright red circle in the centre, both split by a pair of silver lightning bolts, stark and clear in the sunlight, the silver glittering in the sunlight.

The city gates facing them below slammed open with a crash, as the massive leaves hit the sturdy stone sides of the archway, and a great number of mounted soldiers galloped out across the bridge over the Sare, all in black.

"Oh! Dear Arven, no!" Sarant cried in disbelief, even as the captain of the troop with them shouted their orders, sudden shock and surprise being discarded quickly for professionalism, automatically fulfilling their purpose.

As the force from their own home city thundered up the slope towards them, ignoring the sweeping road for a direct route across the grass, advancing awfully quickly, Ethrayne saw, aghast, that yet more soldiers in black were approaching quickly from both left and right, only a few hundred yards distant from the edge of the concealing woodland. Obviously, the enemy had expertly hidden from the concerted efforts of the kingdom's best scouts; their origin, after all, had been the city of Clirensar, not the north or east.

Confusion reigned amongst the servants, and some of the carthorses threatened to kick out against their fellows, the harnesses, but the soldiers and duke were grim-faced and calm, united. Ethrayne could feel fear, sharp and uncomfortable, her own as strong as anyone else's.

"You must go, your Grace!" Captain Callin shouted, as their mounts tossed their heads nervously, sidestepping. "Go, all of you!"

"Go where, exactly?" Sarant countered curtly, his face as pale as the rest. The two groups from the woods were closing fast, the force from the city not far behind, galloping hard uphill. Their black garb was stark, somehow highlighting the mirror-brightness of the weapons they brandished. "Oh, Arven protect us! Ethrayne – Riyala – Lyria -!" He turned to look at his womenfolk.

"Don't be ridiculous, Sarant, what would be the point of fleeing when they're so close?" The Duchess snapped rather waspishly, fear clearly making her sharp. There was an almighty crash and yelling as the front ranks of the hastily collected soldiers met the enemy, weapons clanging, forming an awful cacophony of noise that filled the air, sending all the birds in the area fleeing, squawking warnings. "It's three leagues to Foston, and they'd catch us within a mile."

"You couldn't spare a soul to send with us, Father." Ethrayne added, as her mother flinched at the sounds, her own heart in her mouth. Despite all the training she had undergone, this was new, completely unlooked for, unwelcome. Lyria, beside her, clung suddenly at her hand, clearly shaking in terror.

Fear filled her, growing, but Ethrayne fought against it. She noted that the soldiers were holding their own against the enemy, but also supposed that the enemy outnumbered them at least two or three to one, although there was so much movement ahead, she could not be certain. She could see more men in black than their own. A strange analysis was occupying part of her mind, perhaps a result of her moons of training, but the fact that it pushed back her fear was welcome. There was no way to escape when there were so many against them, it was certainly true; and just what had happened? What had happened to the city? When had the enemy occupied it? And why was she unable to warn Archpriest Bahlien or Jerryn? Her range was still so limited! It was so frustrating when the old razine had said that he and others could touch, however briefly, other minds across hundreds of leagues, when necessary!

"Dismount." Sarant ordered quickly, for all their mounts were snorting, sidling nervously at the chaos. "Get on the ground, all of you, before you're thrown."

So Ethrayne, Riyala, Lyria and the servants behind them obeyed, all crowding together naturally against the first of the carts, trying to shrink down, to be ignored. The fighting had intensified as the third group had arrived, larger by far than the other two, and the soldiers protecting them had to work ever harder in the face of the violence. The Duke had drawn his own weapons and, making sure that his family were as safe as he could make them he glanced once, hard, at his daughter.

<I love you, Father. I'll try to escape with them.> She answered his own clear order to flee. *<Oh, Father, I'm sorry -.>*

"Ethrayne!" He exclaimed in answer to her silent apology. "It's certainly not your fault, my dear child." And he turned with a grimace that took in the group of them and rode Letwar forward, straight towards the struggling mass nearly a hundred yards ahead, his sword in his hand.

Abruptly, as if a door had swung open, Ethrayne could suddenly feel other emotions than her own and her friends and family. She flinched as a mixture of exhilaration and hatred struck her hard and she recalled that long-ago outing and picnic above Tenum City, the day before her and Jerryn's betrothal . . . Yet, this time, this time she realised that she could clearly sense emotions from at least two or three individuals!

That blond jajozeli-razine who had threatened her so smoothly had been a General, one of the Betrayer's servants. Remembering that made her cold to the bone, for she must suppose that there were more of them here, now! Bahlien had confidently asserted that their enemies would likely watch and wait, yet he had admitted that this was only based on sound logic, not on the knowledge of any possible agenda that the Betrayer might have. So, obviously, logic had utterly failed them. Whatever it meant to them, that she and Jerryn had been made the Wielders of the Flame, the enemy had set up a course of action involving attack. She struggled against fear, desperate to keep control of herself.

There were shouts, screams, the massive clash of weapons seeming to reverberate through the very ground and the woodland to behind them, making their ears ache. The defenders manfully tried to protect the civilians in their midst, but they were badly outnumbered by the enemy. Ethrayne, her mother, Lyria and all the servants cowered, stunned by the awful reality of the terrible violence that surrounded them.

This is it! Ethrayne thought to herself, hugging her mother and Lyria tight, the maids also huddled up against them, the unarmed male servants just beyond, all shaking in terror. *Somehow, they've taken Clirensar, but when? Oh, how many poor people died? And-and, all to capture me? Oh, this is just terrible! Will, will I ever see Jerryn again? What of my family?* The thoughts ran in circles in her head. After the last few moons of intense tuition and the strange reality of the Flame becoming part of her, the girl was not frightened of dying; somehow, she knew that whatever might happen, her death was not going to be part of it, not now, but she was deeply worried for the others. Now, the knowledge that they would die to try to keep her from capture was the worst possible thing! *This is all my fault!* She shouted at the universe, irrationally. *Oh, dear Arven, I'm so sorry!*

There was a pulse of reassurance from deep within her, and Ethrayne started; it was rare for the Flame to interact directly, or so Bahlien had said, and that sense of comfort did somewhat lessen her rising fear. Breathing deeply, she looked around, trying to make sense of the melee, the chaos. Men were dying everywhere, both jajozeli and Tenarean, and the various knots of combat were coming closer all the time. Lyria and her mother tightened their hold on her, their fear huge, of course, and some of the maids were screaming, crying -.

There did not seem to be any way that she could see that she could possibly run! They were pretty-much surrounded. That seemed plain enough.

Ethrayne found her attention caught as her father came back into view, standing out in his emerald green doublet, but now on foot. He must have discarded his cloak and his mount, somewhere during the fighting, bright against the black garbed enemy, grim in a way that she had never seen before. The sword was bright in his right hand, his dagger effective in his left as he made the enemy pay again and again in blood for their occupation of Clirensar. But the soldiers around him were also dying, leaving him exposed. The brutal reality of war, of gruesome injuries and death, was indeed far beyond what anyone could describe.

"Oh, dear Arven, we're going to die!" Lyria quavered, flinching away, only voicing, of course, what all of them were thinking.

"Ethrayne, you must flee!" Duchess Riyala shouted, struggling to make her voice heard above the cacophony of battle. "Take a horse, darling, ride!"

"But, Mother -." She started to reply but fell silent and shuddered as the projected feelings of malice and hatred seemed to reach a peak, somehow matched by a lull in the fighting and noise, which faded somewhat.

A hugely tall, reddish bearded and shaggy haired male strode into view, imposing in black and grey, an outfit which was completely unlike the workaday uniform of the soldiers around him. He held a massive broadsword in his left hand and he towered above everyone around him, practically a full head taller than her father, who was six feet three. The duke raised his sword without hesitation as the enemy approached.

"You must be the duke." The stranger said, his accent chillingly familiar to Ethrayne, like that of the male who had accosted her so many moons before, although she had heard it only once. "I would welcome you home, your Grace, but this, unfortunately perhaps, is as far as you will go!"

"And who might you be?" Sarant demanded coolly. "Why has your army dared to invade our lands? What is your purpose here?"

The stranger laughed coldly, his dark eyes glittering with the malice that choked Ethrayne. "Our purpose is conquest, your Grace. Oh, and we desire ownership of your iron, and your daughter, of course." Then, with a leap, he moved, attacked at speed. Sarant brought up his blade in defence, then swung back; sparks flew –.

Ethrayne's fixed, appalled attention was broken as someone suddenly grabbed her from behind, lifting her -.

"What the -?" She struggled in alarm, but found that Evvan, the head groom, was lifting her up, his face pale, fear in his eyes.

"Excuse me, my Lady, but look." He ventured, then jerked his head. Letwar stood there, close to the cart, froth around his mouth, splashes of blood on his coat, his eyes wide, circling, moving nervously. Her father's stallion had somehow made his way back to safety from out of the battle. "Get on Letwar and may he carry you to safety, Lady. Please, go!" His voice quavered. "Please!" He repeated.

Tally, his apprentice, a skinny lad of fifteen who had hardly ever dared to even look at her before, did his best to help her up into the saddle; it was not easy in such a tight space next to the carts, with so many people around; and her skirts were bunched up around her legs, her rear, but the stirrups were out of reach, once she had been boosted up and there was no time -.

"Go, Lady!" They urged, turning Letwar away from the battle.

Ethrayne was all too aware that she was dithering like a complete idiot. She glanced at the frightened men, the other servants, then at her mother and Lyria, realising that there were so many things choking her that she wanted to say, but she couldn't; she had to at least try to get away! Finally, she looked across the battlefield to where her father and the General were exchanging blows with furious energy. As she stared the stranger somehow reversed his stroke, grinned toothily and rammed his long blade right to the hilt through her father's ribcage. The point, and a foot at least of steel beyond it emerged, dripping blood, from his back.

Her mother screamed at the sight of her husband's death.

"Don't bloody-well move, girl!" The reddish haired General ordered curtly, gazing right up into her horrified eyes, pointing at her with his free right hand even as he yanked the sword out of her father. Sarant dropped -.

Yelling incoherently, Evvan and some of the other servants raced forward, catching his attention, and Ethrayne shuddered at the power that had held her frozen for that instant. Finally, she kicked Letwar into movement, urging him around in a curve past a couple of pockets of fighting. She managed to kick out at a couple of black-garbed soldiers as she went past and one of the men spun down, dazed, to be finished by the Tenarean soldier he had faced. The huge horse sped up and she gazed about with renewed purpose, looking for any possible way out of this place, walling back that awful shocking reality that her father, her beloved father, had died trying to protect her! If she let that realisation take hold, she guessed that she would not be much use for anything.

"Go, Letwar! Go!" She cried and let him get the bit between his teeth. The stallion took over, his hooves pounding on the turf like drums, racing away from the noise and chaos.

"Stop, you fool!" A male voice yelled from behind, far clearer than the melee by the road, and Ethrayne turned her head to glance quickly behind, seeing two other figures on horseback on the city side of the battlefield, coming towards her. Quickly she returned her attention to her galloping mount and tightened her grip on the reins, her face grim. That short glance had told her all she needed to know: although wearing plain cloaks, both riders were jajozeli-razine, not human, like the one who had murdered her father -.

Ethrayne blocked that thought instantly. They were Generals; having spent so much time with Bahlien, she was sure. Fiercely she urged Letwar faster and faster along the slope and he headed westward pretty much in a straight line, a few hundred yards below the edge of the woodland; she could not direct him, now, to the right and uphill towards the dubious safety of the trees, though she tried: Letwar was set on his course. She had to glance behind to the left to see the distant city walls falling behind and began to swear forcefully in her head, leaning even lower over his neck as the wind of their passage buffeted her head, face and clothes.

"Go, Letwar, go!" She shouted into that gale. The need to get away from the death, the fighting, the enemies was foremost in her mind, however vain that chance might be, alone against an entire army.

"Stop!" The voice shouted again in a commanding tone, sounding much closer than before.

Ethrayne ignored it, though she could now hear the following hoof-beats, despite the wind in her ears, and she supposed that her pursuer was trying to draw level, to grab either her, the bridle or the reins. She grinned. Let them try! And managed to steer Letwar to the right and then to the left, up the slope a little then down again; dancing him, despite his speed, out of reach. Letwar was one of the prizes of her father's stud: faster, stronger, cleverer and no one could catch him easily. As if in agreement, she heard foreign words uttered harshly, perhaps curses. She urged the stallion uphill and he obeyed more willingly, heading towards the forest's verge, dark and forbidding.

"Go, you wonder!" She shouted eagerly, feeling her hat spinning off her head suddenly at a lurch in his gait. "Go, boy!"

Something flashed through her mind. Strong, it was a blow of sorts, but mental rather than physical. Nor was it aimed at her -. As that thought came to her, Letwar collapsed from beneath her. Dead, between one breath and the next!

"No!" That was a shriek of panic, for she found that her damned skirts were caught in the saddle somehow, the fabric imprisoning her. She couldn't free herself. Lift herself. Leap away . . . In less than a moment, Ethrayne was dragged down utterly helpless, slammed into the grass with force enough to knock the breath from her lungs. It was like hitting stone rather than grass and jarring pain filled her from head to foot, all along the left-hand-side of her body. She was unable to even gasp, let alone scream, as the dead weight of the horse crushed her left leg. Then, for the first time in her life, she fainted.

*

Duchess Riyala, Lyria and the servants shrank back in terror as Evvan and the other servants rushed at the enemy, armed only with belt knives or their fists. The tall, bearded commander laughed coldly, cutting them all down as if they were a crop being scythed, his movements showing a brutal efficiency. Finally, he decapitated Evvan with a flourish, so that the man collapsed close to the legs of his dead master, the duke.

"Murderer!" Riyala spat the word, drawing herself up regally to glare at the tall male, hiding the fear that choked her. "You will be hunted down -."

"Who by, exactly? Your puny, inexperienced forces, your Grace?" He replied in a coldly contemptuous tone. "The vast might of our emperor supports me and this little realm and the continent it sits on will be in his control soon enough, Duchess!"

"But what of our daughter and the prince? What of the Prophecy that we were told of?" Riyala demanded, her hands shaking as she held tight to Lyria, her emotions striving to escape her control.

"Prophecy?" He laughed loudly, contemptuous again, and spat in derision. "Prophecy be damned! Our emperor is merely claiming what is his: the Flame which was hidden by Bahlien! Your daughter will be safe enough."

"Liar!" Riyala retorted imperiously. She gasped, once, as the point of the commander's massive sword slid slowly but inexorably into her throat, blood spilling around the edges of the blade and down the front of her dark green gown. All the women around her were frozen in absolute terror, except for Lyria, shaking like a leaf, as she felt the duchess's hand go suddenly limp in her grasp, just before she slowly crumpled to the ground.

Lyria stumbled, sobbing in shock and horror, fighting hysteria, then shrank back as the tall, cruel-faced man stared down at her with a dark, mesmerising gaze; he was a ghoul, but living! He raised the bloodstained sword again and waved the point right in her face before he laid it gently against her throat. It was icy cold to the touch. She flinched. And he smiled!

"And who are you, girl?" He asked calmly, then lowered the blade so that it rested on Riyala's body below her.

"M-me?" She squeaked, panic taking over for a breath. "I-I Lyria . . . Lyria, sir. Lady-in-waiting." She managed to force the words out past the massive lump of rock in her ribcage that was her fear.

"Pshaw!" He exclaimed. "You must be the absent brother's betrothed, yes?" He demanded chillingly. "The king knows you?"

Lyria nodded frantically as her head strove to understand just exactly what he was saying.

"Hmm. Of course, you wrote that insightful letter we found at Callorton. You might make an adequate messenger, girl. Stay there and don't move a muscle." He ordered with a frown, so that she quickly shook her head with as much energy as she had nodded, faint with fear, horror and revulsion. Frozen. They had found her letter to her mother! They had been there, destroying her family! She couldn't get the names and faces of her little nieces and nephews from her mind.

The battle was over. There were windrows of Tenarean corpses piled up all around the front of the group, ahead of the carts, along the road but the sun still shone with sparkling afternoon sunlight, only slightly lower than it had been when the enemy had begun their attack. There were also enemy dead, not a few by any means, laid dark amongst the natives. None of the duke's troops remained alive, only a scant handful of servants in addition to Lyria; and all were women apart from Tally, who had been held back from the desperate last attack by the maids; one boy of fifteen, six maid servants, and she. Uneasily, she wondered where Ethrayne was, if she had escaped, by some miracle.

The enemy commander wiped his sword calmly on Riyala's skirts, unconcerned at the revulsion this raised in the prisoners, then turned and gave out crisp orders in an unknown language to the hard-faced soldiers who were stood around, alert and dangerous. Temporarily ignored, the prisoners huddled even closer together by the first cart, trembling and weeping in fear, as the enemy started to gather together the horses and the discarded weapons from the battle. But Lyria stood still as ordered, her back straight, shivering in dread.

* * *

CHAPTER 20

Ethrayne came to with a jolt of agony so great that it felt as though molten iron raced along her nerves, in her blood, through every single part of her body. Momentarily confused, her breathing laboured, she opened her eyes to an extremely close-up view of the summer-browned grass and a spread of tiny yellow flowers amid them, bright like the sun, but each bloom smaller than a child's fingernail. Dry stems tickled her nose; she could smell the grass, wet, maybe marshy ground and blood; she could taste blood in her mouth, too. It felt as though she lay on waterlogged ground, for a cold dampness seemed to be spreading through her clothes. She lay as she had fallen, crushed into the very earth by the dead weight of the horse on her left leg, a mountain of black flesh blocking most of her view. It felt as though that leg was broken and the entire left-hand side of her body and head throbbed in sympathy.

Behind her, close, she could hear the creak of leather, the jingle of buckles and realised that perhaps only a moment or two had passed since Letwar had collapsed, dead and she had blacked out. It sounded as though those who had pursued her were only just dismounting. Ethrayne started, jarring all those nasty, sharp pains, as shadows blocked out the sun above her and she tried to lift herself, but only her right arm seemed to be working properly and she slumped back down with an involuntary groan.

"Don't try to move." An accented female voice said, to her surprise, causing Ethrayne to squint upwards against the sunlight to see more clearly. Two figures stood over her: one, the blond, blue-eyed male who had walked out of the orchard so many moons before: there could not be two so identical; the other was a young woman with short, striking, pale-blond hair, hazel eyes, pretty features and an identical aura of strength. They also wore the same outfits as the one who had killed her father: black and grey tunic and leggings, full-length black cloaks and the woman looked confident and comfortable in the leather leggings and sturdy boots, an array of weapons at her hip.

"You should have stopped when I commanded it, idiot!" The male General snapped, bending down to study her and the carcass imprisoning her. "Let's get you out of there." He laughed a little. "And if you remember, I did warn you that you'd never make your wedding, girl, back in the spring."

"Why would I remember that?" Ethrayne retorted, startled, frowning up at him. "I was hardly going to surrender!" Her words were sharp with fear, it was choking her, and her voice quavered. He was so close, his gaze sharp; she felt a surge of relief as he moved away. "Why have your forces attacked us?" She tried hard not to think about the deaths that she had witnessed already that afternoon.

"We have come for you, brat." The woman answered simply, her eyes flashing as she moved around the dead horse and knelt on one knee, laying her hands just below its neck, as the man crouched by his back legs. To Ethrayne's amazement, with very little effort, the pair of them lifted Letwar's huge body right up into the air and set it down a few feet further down the slope.

The girl shuddered as she sensed the power they expended, for it stung oddly within her aching head. She had thought that the loss of the massive weight would be an improvement, but the crushing pain was replaced with a sensation like red-hot pokers stabbing through the length of her left leg, especially below her knee. Ethrayne had to stifle a sob at that discomfort as the pair turned back to her, lying helpless on the grass; she wiped away a few errant tears with her shaking right hand, then saw blood on the palm of her glove, too, a sharp ache on her left cheek.

"Don't touch me!" She muttered with futile defiance, and the two simply ignored her. The woman lightly ran one hand up and down her left leg and foot, then up over her body generally to her head as she flinched.

"How seriously is she injured, Cavaln?"

"Fortunately, it seems that nothing is dislocated or broken, my Lord." She answered and passed her hand up and down over the girl's left leg again, frowning. "But this is not going to be an easy journey."

He snorted. "No, not for any of us I'm sure; which we knew anyway, Cavaln, since that's the reason you're here. And *please* stop using my title. Mount, I'll pass her up to you. We'll get her a horse back at the road."

Laid there, Ethrayne wished that she could understand their language and steeled herself as the male knelt beside her, put one arm under her back, lifting her upper body, his right arm moving carefully under her knees; she grimaced at the pain increasing within her as he raised her easily off the ground, getting quickly to his feet. There was a strange tingle/ache within her at his touch even through her clothes; she froze, for even that slight movement set all the pains to a deeper level of discomfort. She noted that the left-hand side of her gown from her feet to past her waist was indeed wet, a darker blue, her underclothes chilly against her skin and grimly thanked the boggy ground which had broken her fall, saving her from broken bones.

"Don't wriggle, or I might drop you." He advised in selithian, moving across the slope and lifting her higher in his arms; she heard the snort of a horse behind her.

"Here you are." The woman's voice was also behind her. Ethrayne felt the front of a saddle against her right hip for a moment, then another arm was strong and sturdy around her, steadying her as the General set her down reasonably gently before the woman in the saddle, lodged roughly sideways, her aching left side against the horse's neck. "I won't let you fall, girl."

"Ow!" Ethrayne muttered, flinching at her touch; it also raised that strange tingle/ache, so that probably proved her theory at the power of her captors and equally at the pain of her body. It was so different to how Archpriest Bahlien made her feel.

The woman turned the horse and nudged it from a walk to a trot, then a canter, her arm still holding Ethrayne steady, heading back the way they had come. The girl gritted her teeth and tensed her body even more as the movements sent waves of discomfort through her, determined not to complain; but she found herself slightly distracted from the pain, when she looked up and realised just how far her mad ride on Letwar had taken her from the road: perhaps two miles distant. As they came closer, returning to the clear scene of the battle, she noted that the people milling about the carts and horses were nearly all enemy soldiers, and only in one place did she see a few bits of colour other than black and grey. Surely, they had not killed almost everyone! But who was still alive? She wondered fearfully as the last few hundred yards vanished under the horse's hooves. The bodies were spread out over a much wider area than she had imagined.

Oh, dear Arven! How many lives have been wasted? She mourned silently. Then, far worse, as the horse came to a halt almost exactly where she had fled from, by the head cart, she could see the deep-green clad form of her mother lying with a horrible, unnatural stillness on the blood-soaked ground!

"Oh, Ethrayne!" Lyria's terrified voice broke through her tight focus and the girl blinked and looked up with a face suddenly mask-like to meet the gaze of her closest friend. There was blood down the front of her gown, a mark by her throat, her face ashen. "Dear Arven, your face! Are-you all right?"

Slowly, she raised her right hand, pulled off her glove and ran her fingers lightly over her face, wincing: the left-hand side felt cut and swollen to the touch, as well as generally uncomfortable, her head pounding. "He killed Letwar and I fell . . . I-I'm all right . . . Are you-you injured?

"N-no, honestly -." Lyria hiccupped.

Ethrayne shuddered with both relief and dread, then her attention was caught by the shocking, ragged wound in her mother's neck, the blood staining her gown, far too much of it! "Oh, Mother!"

The woman had hold of her right arm but, without thinking, Ethrayne pulled herself free from her grip and let herself slip from the horse, a movement she had completed innumerable times, after all, but never whilst injured. She had turned slightly to set her right hand on the horse's flank, but even though she only extended her right leg and foot to take her weight, the drop was too great. Pain shot through her anew, and she crumpled to the ground with a groan. Mocking laughter filled her ears as her discomfort rose to a whole new level, and Lyria cried her name, sobbing.

Damn it! She spat silently, taking a couple of deep breaths before, recklessly, starting a half-crawl, half-drag movement across the stony, bloodstained ground to where her mother lay, shaking with emotions and the effort of keeping a check on them. Every inch hurt, but she ignored that. "Oh, Mamma!" She said quietly, weeping as she leaned forward to kiss her mother's pale, cooling cheek, laying one hand there. "Oh, I'm so, so sorry!"

How could all these awful events have occurred in the space of one afternoon? Part of her mind wondered, as the rest of her mourned the deaths of her parents, the soldiers and friends; let alone what might have happened to the inhabitants of the castle, the city and the region since the arrival of these bastards from the south! And she couldn't warn Bahlien or Jerryn; she, Lyria and the few others were on their own, surrounded by enemies! What would happen to the kingdom? What would happen to her and her friends? Fear choked her as much as the tears. How could her mother and father possibly be dead?

She glanced backwards and saw a sword amid the bodies that had stained the ground so deeply with blood, lying a few feet away. Despite her injuries, Ethrayne shuffled, wincing again, as a completely ridiculous idea came to her -.

"Don't be stupid, girl, you can't even crawl properly, let alone get up and fight!" The shaggy haired and bearded General who had killed her father bent down before her, his accent strange, his tone contemptuous. He took hold of her right arm and hauled her roughly upright and Ethrayne gasped in pain as he shook her roughly. "Cavaln, take her -."

She hated that she did not understand their language. She didn't like the way they all loomed over her, fully armed, so tall, so menacing. She hated the sharp discomfort of his touch. But she guessed what he had said, when the blond woman strode across and took her arm from his grasp, supporting her when she sagged: her left leg and foot were only agony, she couldn't even rest it on the ground. The rest of her ached as well. The male General gazed at her, grinning maliciously as the female General slowly walked her away from her mother's body; she had to hop to advance and she was aware that Lyria was watching her anxiously, weeping and pale faced, whilst Tally also seemed to be in tears. Beyond them, in a group, the maids were huddled, terrified, surrounded by soldiers.

"Wh- what are you going to do with us?" Ethrayne asked, her mind still reeling, horrified, as the man who had slaughtered her father and probably her mother as well, now casually began to remove her mother's jewellery, kneeling beside her corpse, dropping the earrings, necklace, rings and so on into a canvas bag. "What are you doing?" She asked this more shrilly, shocked. "You can't do that!"

"Shut up!" He replied coolly, getting up and striding over to her to begin pulling the silver and pearl hairnet and pins roughly out of her hair, uncaring of the knots and snarls that pulled painfully, so that the weight of her hair fell down over her shoulders; then he jerked the ring from her fingers, her earrings, the necklace from her throat – simply yanking it free, so that the chain broke, her neck smarting. Everything was added to the canvas bag. A soldier came forward, his hands cupped with the few jewels from her father, his weapons secure in their sheaths in his belt which was slung over his shoulder.

"What on Iullyn -."

"I told you to shut your mouth!" The General ordered and cuffed her smartly across the back of the head, nearly knocking her back to the ground and raising her headache to a whole new level of discomfort. The places on her skull that had hit the ground throbbed agonisingly. "These two will require proof of your presence, girl." He thrust the bag of personal items and the duke's sword belt at a startled Lyria, and Ethrayne saw that her hands were trembling as she struggled at first to tighten her grip.

"Get them horses, food, water and blankets." He ordered his soldiers as the prisoners wondered what he was saying, then switched instantly to selithian. "Take the north road to Foston, girl, I assume it's the closest guard post." He instructed Lyria, with only the barest glance at the shivering youth beside her. "Make sure they know not to venture through these forests: Clirensar is ours, it no longer belongs to your little kingdom! Inform the king and his son that Lady Ethrayne is guarded safely and appropriately for who and what she is and continuing on her way to Ban'Lerracon."

"Ban'Lerracon?" Ethrayne repeated the name in dull horror. "But who *are* you?"

"General Tequan, I am the Commander here." He touched his own chest. "General Ackat." Gesturing to the blonde male General. "And General Cavaln." He indicated the woman supporting the girl and grinned at the expression on her face. "I believe you may remember Ackat from earlier this year; and why are you behaving as if we are bad dreams come to life? We are some of the most trusted servants of King Gregnor, the Emperor of the Jajozeli Empire."

"Enough introductions, Tequan let's get going." Ackat said brusquely, clapping his hands sharply.

"Good luck, Ackat, Cavaln." The commander said levelly.

"Thank you, Commander and you also." Ackat shook his hand briefly and grinned toothily.

"Good luck, Commander." The woman said, her tone musical, the words unfamiliar to Ethrayne. "Let's get going."

A number of soldiers moved about; some were laden with baggage as Lyria and Tally were hustled quickly onto horses, the bags set behind their saddles as Lyria paused to quickly juggle the bag of personal items on the saddle, taking the awkward, heavy sword belt, which she quickly looped over one shoulder, then tying the treasures onto the belt at her front, wiping tears from her face. Ethrayne was relieved to see that her friend was sitting on Oxalla, even though it was wrong to be concerned about a bloody horse when so many had died this afternoon!

"Take care, Lyria, Tally -." She ventured quickly.

"Silence!" The female General shook her hard.

Ethrayne did not dare to challenge her. Helpless, she could only stare as her best friend and the stableboy turned their mounts and slowly made their way through the prisoners, enemy soldiers and carts to the north side of the road, and headed back towards the forest above, Lyria managing one last frightened look backward and raised her right hand in farewell before the mass of soldiers closed back around the remains of the entourage, hiding her and

Tally from sight.

"How do you feel?" General Ackat demanded, glaring at her. Ethrayne only stared at him and shrugged slightly in reply, guessing that any protestation of discomfort or weakness would only count against her. "You look terrible. Excellent, let's go." He said with a quick grin.

Ethrayne looked back at General Tequan, who had killed her father; she was startled to discover that he was staring intently at her in return. "I will kill you, you bastard." She stated quietly as Ackat lifted her onto a horse, pulling the reins out of her reach with a smirk. "If it takes the rest of my life, I will kill you, Tequan!" And, to her amazement, none of the three Generals mocked her pronouncement in any way. Drawing herself up as straight as she could, wincing slightly as she strove to set her right leg over the saddle, uncaring that it bunched up her skirts ; she pulled her cloak a little straighter around her as she was led away from the battleground, shivering a little, trying to hide her discomfort and fear from both her captors and the few remaining prisoners who watched her leave. Nor would she look at Clirensar, now a nest of the enemy! She fixed her gaze on the grey mane and ears of her horse and tried to control her pain, although her leg, foot and hip were hurting even more.

*

By nightfall, at least four leagues from Clirensar and deep in the wooded hills at the western end of the vale, Ethrayne was upright in the saddle through sheer willpower alone. The two blonde Generals led the way and six soldiers followed behind her. They had travelled swiftly, eating up the miles, and the sun was close to the horizon ahead of them. By now, the pain of her injuries from her left foot to her head was sheer agony at every stride the horse made, matching the headache that was far beyond anything she had ever experienced before. She was trembling uncontrollably, her right hand holding tight to the horse's mane, her left resting as well as she could in her lap, her whole side throbbing with pain, useless.

The Generals stopped in a grassy dell amid the thick woodland, not far from a stream that Ethrayne could hear bubbling over its bed off to the left, as fiery sunset colours briefly touched the clouds above. The soldiers swiftly dismounted and set about tasks; fetching firewood, clearing the ground and starting a fire with practised efficiency; others went off to fetch water in buckets and so on. The Generals moved in a more leisurely fashion, stretching with relish. Still in the saddle, unable to move, Ethrayne could only watch, trying to hide the fact that her left arm and leg were both frozen, cramped from sitting, aching abominably. She was sore and exhausted, her head pounding, her clothes stained with mud and far too much blood.

"You look worse than you did earlier, girl." General Ackat remarked lightly with cold laughter dancing in his eyes. There was a leather water bottle slung over his shoulder. "Down you get."

It was the first time that anyone had spoken to her since they had ridden away from the battlefield at the road.

"I-I can't move . . . Every-everything hurts." Ethrayne admitted in a whisper, only now realising how thirsty she was.

He laughed, rather maliciously, she thought, but he did lift her carefully out of the saddle from the right-hand side, set her down on the grass nearby and handed her the water bottle.

"Just rest, my lady, don't run away." He said, but his tone was menacing, despite his joke.

Ethrayne seriously considered replying with something cutting but decided against it: these might be her enemies, but she was helpless and in a great deal of discomfort. She also recalled Tequan's quick slap, his violence and murders, all too clearly. All she knew about the Generals she had learned from the archpriests and from legend, after all. There was little enough fact. It would be stupid beyond belief to antagonise them.

And she was their prisoner, being taken south to Ban'Lerracon . . .

That realisation woke her from a near doze, to find that the fire was burning heartily; strange globes of pale light were floating in the air as the last light faded from the sky and the two Generals were stood nearby, talking as they looked at her and the woman was hefting a large leather bag by its strap.

Dear Arven, I feel awful! Ethrayne acknowledged to herself, trying to fend off misery and despair, with only partial success. Her mind kept coming up with all sorts of awful events and concerns and the images of her father's sudden death and his and her mother's bodies on the ground, their blood drying in shocking pools . . . those and many other concerns just wheeled, unstoppable, in her head -.

"Are you hungry?" Cavaln asked, walking over and the girl shook her head slightly with a grimace. "Alright, well, you will drink this." She had a leather bottle in her left hand, a horn cup in her right and crouched down beside Ethrayne. "It's not poison I assure you." She said, pouring a measure of liquid into the cup and offering it to her.

"Wish it was." Ethrayne retorted, shivering, uncertainly taking the small cup and sniffing at the stuff inside, but it seemed innocuous enough, a little flowery in scent, perhaps. "Everything, everything hurts awfully." She admitted in a bare whisper.

"Drink it, it won't hurt you." Cavaln urged patiently. "I'm a healer as well as a General."

"Humph!" Ethrayne managed with as much contempt as she could muster, but she did take a sip; it was nothing like the strong drink some people enjoyed, for it was smooth, with no evident bite, a slightly sweet flavour remaining in her mouth -.

"Drink all of it." The woman's tone was firm and Ethrayne obeyed, taking the dose in two quick swallows.

She didn't feel any different at all but, gradually, a strange lassitude was pushing back her pain, the fear and discomfort . . . Ethrayne sighed, her head lolled, and she slumped slightly as her eyes closed against her will. It was so pleasant, so nice, to lose the pain -.

Ackat laid out some blankets on the grass and lifted the unconscious girl onto them, covering her with another blanket, two of the pale light globes descending to hang closer, providing a surprisingly clear light, whilst Cavaln began cutting away the boot that covered her left leg, carefully easing the leather away and cutting off the stocking beneath.

"That doesn't look good." He remarked, wincing slightly, looking at the mess of bruised, swollen flesh that began at Ethrayne's toes and continued past her knee, the result of the horse's impact.

"It looks worse than it is, honestly; as I said, nothing is broken." The female General replied calmly. "Thank you, I'll take over from here."

"I'll get one of the men to cut a stick for the brat – I'm certainly not carrying her everywhere." Ackat added, frowning.

"Well, you killed her mount, Ackat so her injuries are down to you." Cavaln grinned at his expression. "Though I agree with what you did: that horse was fast, I don't know how else we could have captured her before she reached the cover of the trees."

*

Ethrayne awoke to deep darkness, instantly alert. She could feel no pain anywhere, but her head was feeling strangely thick, as if stuffed with fleece. To her left, the dying fire cast hardly any light and the forms lying around her in the camp were still, blanketed lumps, barely visible. The wind was gusting, making trees creak not far away, but the feel of it was oddly warm.

Got to get out of here! She thought to herself, sitting up abruptly and throwing off the blanket that covered her. Her left hand touched a long stick, laid close beside her and part of her wondered if it was a crutch, for there was a definite fork at one end, she discovered a moment later. Reaching down, she could feel that her left leg was swathed in bandages from above her knee to her toes, although she couldn't remember why. *Very nice of them.* She decided dryly. *I bet they didn't expect me to wake up, so I'll go right now before any of them do.*

It was certainly like a dream, fuzzy and unclear, with huge gaps replacing full sense; yet Ethrayne could, nevertheless, clearly recall that she was amid enemies. She slowly got to her feet, finding that her left leg only just held her weight and something there seemed to *twinge* urgently, even if she did not feel any pain; she tried to bunch up her skirts out of the way but with only partial success, tried to knot up her loose hair, to fail, and attempted to slowly straighten up. The crutch was almost perfect in length, and sturdy. Somehow, her heart in her mouth, she managed to hobble quietly through the camp, past the Generals and soldiers, without disturbing any of them, the ground relatively smooth. She saw no sign of the sentry she supposed must be somewhere about. Thanking Arven for that miracle, Ethrayne focussed only on escape and simply headed for the route of least resistance, angling downhill and into the forest, wobbling as she went, moving very slowly.

The first light of day, that faint wash that somehow banished night within the blink of an eye, making shapes and colour where all had been dark and unclear a moment before, was most welcome to her exhausted gaze, for Ethrayne had come to deeply regret her impulsive break for freedom during her limping, hopping struggle through the woods. Only sheer bloody-mindedness, desperation and the crutch now kept her moving, although her advance had long since slowed to a snail's pace. Without that stick supporting her useless left leg, certainly, she would have collapsed into the brambles and nettles long before and given up in agonising despair.

Whatever drug Cavaln had given her to numb her pain so effectively, which had, bizarrely, given her the strength and impetus to flee her captors, had completely left her body well before this faint light, whilst she had struggled through endless tangles of thorny undergrowth and trees, where only the terribly slow pace of her advance had let her through, her clothes and hair catching on the brambles and twigs and so on, jolted with every stumbling step; her left leg knocked even more times as she fought to keep going, the pain refilling her as the drug left her, the whole of the left hand side of her body hurting even more than before she had slept. Now, fighting to continue, Ethrayne wondered fearfully whether this idiocy on her part might mean that she had crippled herself for life. She had been moving relentlessly for at least half the night, uncaring of the chilly wind, crashing into trees and bushes that she had not been able to see, damp from occasional flurries of rain, or the streams that she had splashed through, falling over once as she had slid helplessly down a muddy bank. Now, the agony that pulsed through her body with each step was frightful. She had probably covered much less than a league through the woods and now she was at the utter limit of her strength.

Unexpectedly, off to her right, came the clear call of a cockerel, raucously loud amid the quieter beginning of the encircling, woodland dawn chorus. It took a moment for the realisation to sink in past her exhaustion that, by some mad chance, she had reached civilisation! The girl took a gasping breath and lurched on; a little further, pushing slowly through more nettles, the sharp reek of manure was strong on the air. Ethrayne felt a tiny spark of hope flare deep inside, dispelling a miniscule amount of the fear and despair -.

"You've only managed a mile or two, if that!" She snapped to herself sternly. "They'll be right behind you, you fool! And only Arven knows what those Generals will do to you!" She shuddered at that realisation.

Ethrayne forced herself onward in the increasing light of dawn and, just past a stand of pines, saw brighter light ahead: a clearing, different entirely to the darker, green-hued light of the autumn-filled woods. More nettles and brambles made an effective barrier before her and she wobbled through them, swearing quietly. Ahead, she could now see buildings, cottages and barns, some thatched, some roofed with stone, with fields and apple trees beyond. Somehow, incongruously, it was familiar to her! A man wearing an old smock was moving across the cobbled yard, a large shaggy dog at his side; he glanced up as he walked and saw her, a girl in a stained, deep-blue gown, fighting through the undergrowth from the forest. He stared, aghast, as she collapsed, finally beyond endurance. Both he and the dog rushed towards her, one shouting out, the other barking in defensive excitement.

The next few moments were a confusing mass of images, until Ethrayne found herself seated in an old rocking chair in a farmhouse kitchen, with a bowl of porridge and a cup of milk before her. A good number of women were bustling about to some purpose and a group of small children were clustered around the far side of the well-scrubbed table, staring at her with sober expressions, some of them sucking thumbs or fingers as they considered her sudden appearance. The farmer had vanished back outside to his chores.

"Honestly, good people, I can-cannot stay." She found herself repeating. "They will be searching for me. They killed my parents . . . Clirensar is taken by jajozeli forces. Oh, I must go!"

"And where will you go and how, my Lady?" A rather stout, short lady asked her, thrusting a bowl of hot water to another woman, then kneeling to unwrap the stained, tattered bandage from about her leg. "You cannot walk, Lady, you cannot set out alone. The nearest garrison is at Foston and that's a day's journey from here."

"Yes, I know. Oh, I've been so stupid! Look at me!" Ethrayne quavered as the woman with the water began to gently dab at her face. She was almost crying, then realised that she sounded stupidly hysterical too, sniffed, took a deep breath and tried to regain some control. "I've put you all in danger. Oh, I'm so sorry -." Another deep breath, a third and then her mind seemed to start working a little more clearly. "This is Applegarth, isn't it?" She asked in a more level tone. "I remember coming here with father and mother; you send us cider and apple brandy every year -." She stopped there abruptly for it was almost a physical blow: the knowledge that her beloved parents were dead!

"Yes, but you need to eat, Lady." The woman washing her face and hands so carefully with fresh warm water and lavender scented soap urged.

"Ethie -." The lady of the house, unwrapping the last of the linen from about her leg, spoke to a tall, dark-haired girl of about eleven, who had been stood apart from the little children, beside a boy a year or so younger. Ethrayne started at the familiar shortening of her name. "Fetch my herbs. Ianto, fetch me a clean sheet from the basket. I'll make a poultice. Oh, my word!" She rocked back on her heels as she wadded the discarded bandage up and threw it into the fire, aiming off to the left, away from the kettle.

Ethrayne looked down at her exclamation but wished she hadn't: her leg was bruised and swollen from above the knee to her toes, mottled with garish shades of red, purple, yellow, green and deep blue; even her foot was at least twice the size it should be. No wonder it hurt so much!

"The horse was killed, it landed on my leg." She said simply with a grimace.

"Just eat your breakfast, Lady." The woman commanded seriously.

"Rosie, can you help me please? Support her leg whist I make a poultice?" She nodded at the boy with the linen sheet. "Rip strips about a hand's width, Ianto please; yes, that's perfect, keep going."

Someone else thrust the porridge into her hands, as another woman started gently combing her hair as if she were a tiny child or ill. "Yes, Mistress. Thank you." She acknowledged, holding the bowl against her chest with her injured left hand and wrist, trying to ignore the swelling and bruising evident there, vanishing into her sleeve. She was spooning the warm stuff desperately into her mouth, for food had never tasted so good, she decided. "Thank you so much -."

"Pshaw! We'll do all we can, Lady and call me Jess, my Lady . . . You said the city was overrun? What on Iullyn has happened?"

"We were riding home; my parents, Lyria from Callorton, soldiers and servants . . . We had just emerged from the woods on the road from Foston, it's such a lovely view . . ." She faltered and shivered. Every woman in the room stared at her, except for the one combing her hair until it was stick and knot free, quickly tying it back with a cord. "There were horns sounding and-and soldiers rode out of the woods on either side of the road and up from the city . . . Yesterday afternoon. Oh, dear Arven, only yesterday! They outnumbered the soldiers . . . the General killed my father, my mother . . . all the soldiers, only a few servants still live, and they sent Lyria to warn King Marrand . . . They're taking me to Ban'Lerracon, they said . . ."

"Mmm." Jess's soothing tone was automatic; she was stirring a small pan containing what smelled like a very pungent mixture of herbs and things, before moving back to her injured leg, spooning green stuff onto a large, square piece of linen spread out by one of the other ladies, folding it, then laying it around Ethrayne's foot and ankle; it felt surprisingly warm against her skin. "We grieve for your loss, my Lady, I can't believe it! Your honoured parents? Dead!" Her voice quivered slightly. "We will do all we can, I promise you. Ethie, have your father saddle three horses. Marta, pack some food. We will get you to safety, never fear and Foston has a garrison, of course. First, we've got to dress your leg."

"Thank you, Mistress Jess!" Ethrayne felt a surge of relief wash through her, as comforting as the food that she had gobbled so quickly. Then, in just a heartbeat, that comfort was dispelled as a sense of approaching menace came into her mind; immediately, instinctively she knew that the enemy were closing in; they must have tracked her route through the woods.

It was strange. She would have welcomed this increased insight into her abilities two days ago but, now, now it marked the point where her life had been irretrievably broken apart.

"They are coming! The jajozeli! Please, take the children and go, hide somewhere!" She blurted in desperate fear. "Oh, you must hide, Jess. It's me they're after, and too many people have already died!"

Jess, however, calmly continued wrapping more bandages around the cloth stained a garish green by the poultice, a smelly concoction which was soothing about her foot and lower leg. "Cassie, Rosie, Marta, please take the children and hide down in the hazel brakes, stay there quietly, no matter what. Go, quickly!" She urged. "Lady Ethrayne speaks the truth. Go, take bread and cheese and apples, go on. And warn the men!"

With a small amount of confusion, the room was quickly cleared, the women and older children herding the tots out of the kitchen and running quickly across the farmyard in the direction of the orchards.

"Thank Arven!" Ethrayne breathed. "Oh, Jess, please go too; you've been so kind, I would hate anything to happen -."

"Nay, Lady, you are our responsibility, and you need my help. Finish your milk, I've nearly done here; would you like some bread and cheese? Oh, you look better than you did at dawn." The woman managed a little laugh, but it was shrill.

"I'm a complete mess, Mistress." The girl replied with an attempt at humour, glancing down at her ripped, filthy gown, her one, muddy boot. "Thank you, Jess." That sensation of danger closing in was an unpleasant tingling akin to the feeling that the Generals' touch had caused, growing stronger as the young woman sat there, waiting, as Jess continued her chores, clearing the remains of the poultice, folding up the bandages ripped out of the sheet, moving the porridge bowls and so on towards the old stone sink. Ethrayne could feel her fear rising. "I bet Jerryn would never recognise me!" She continued. "Oh, Jess -."

"Get out here now, Ethrayne!" Ackat's accented voice shouted from outside and they both started. "We know you're here. You've wasted quite enough of our time!"

"Look at you, sitting at ease after leading us a fine chase!" Cavaln spat, stepping through the doorway from the farmyard, her eyes flashing as she glared, her thumbs hooked in her sword belt, tall and slender. "On your feet, brat!"

The woman dealt her a ringing blow across her right ear which stung and smarted, but Ethrayne felt angrier at the extra pain than tearful; she winced, ducking nervously in case of a second blow, but carefully rose to her feet, hanging on to the table top, balancing on her right foot, as Jess handed her that life-saving crutch. "I -." She began an apology but stopped at once when she realised that she *wasn't* sorry, despite her injuries. The Generals certainly didn't deserve any apologies on her part: they had abducted her, after all and caused her injuries! But their anger was clear to her. "I-I-I will try, Madam General . . . please don't-don't hurt anyone." She started again.

"Shut up and walk!" Cavaln retorted, then frowned as the girl unsteadily worked her way forward, the middle-aged woman watching anxiously at every thump of the crutch on the flagstone floor. "Char'hase, child, you look even worse than you did last night!" She exclaimed. "Outside, now!"

Each step made her wince, feeling utterly unsafe, however useful the crutch had been during her night-time excursion. On her feet, she could feel the bone-deep weariness within which had been hidden during her quick breakfast, but advanced to the kitchen door, puffing.

"You have tended her leg, woman?" Cavaln demanded of Jess shortly.

"Aye, Lady." The woman answered warily. "Bathed, poulticed and re-bandaged, but Lady Ethrayne must rest -."

"I am a healer, woman. Do not concern yourself." The General said dismissively, putting her left arm around the girl's shoulders. "Thank you for your care."

"Thank you, Jess . . . I am sorry." Ethrayne said earnestly, as Cavaln helped her down the two steps there and across the yard. But, looking ahead, her gaze was caught by General Ackat's dark glare. He sat in his saddle in the centre of the yard, the middle-aged farmer (Kethar, she suddenly recalled his name) at sword-point beside him, pale-faced and sweating. "Oh, please -."

"Get on with you." Cavaln interrupted her brusquely, trying to hurry her across the forty or so feet of cobbles that lay before them. Behind the General, Ethrayne now saw the six soldiers ranged about, weapons in hand, alert.

"So, still lame and still stupid, hey?" General Ackat called mockingly as she advanced. "Your antics will delay us by nearly half a day, brat, yet you ask for mercy? I really don't believe that you have thought through your situation properly, child, or that of your people. These lands are *ours* and you are also ours, or, to be specific, you belong to our emperor."

"I am Ethrayne of Clirensar, General. I belong to no one!" Ethrayne retorted instantly, recklessly.

"Silence!" He bellowed, leaning forward, his left hand extended and slapped her hard across the face, knocking her out of Cavaln's grasp and hard to the dirty stones. "One way or another, you stupid little girl, you will obey us!" He swung his sword at the trembling farmer in what was clearly a killing strike -.

"No!" Ethrayne screamed in mingled horror and fury, reaching up with her hands into mid-air as if to grab that sharp, shining, lethal blade and, oddly, in addition to her exhaustion and fear, she felt an expulsion of *something*, an odd kind of strength, she supposed, that jarred throughout her mind and body like steel being beaten on an anvil. Her head was suddenly lighter, spinning -. No one else was going to die! She was determined on that, even if the way to ensure that eluded her.

Ackat grunted, his hand cramping, his swing blocked dead as if by a shield and the sword was knocked out of his grip to land, ringing, close to where Ethrayne was laid. The farmer staggered backwards, his hands clutching his neck, his eyes wide in shock, clearly wondering just how he was still alive. Keeping his gaze on the horse's hooves, he dropped to the ground and crawled off to the side, as fast as he could, away from the General and his soldiers.

"Get her on her horse, now!" Ackat commanded shortly after a moment, ignoring the farmer. "Pass me my sword. Move, Cavaln!"

Ethrayne's head was reeling at that explosion of energy, as Cavaln hauled her upright, Ackat's sword and the crutch in her other hand. The weapon was passed quickly to the glowering male on his horse, the crutch thrust back into her shaking hands to improve the girl's stability. Whatever had just happened, Ethrayne realised that she was far less stable on her feet now than even a few moments before, clutching at the thing with desperation. Shoved roughly up onto the horse (Ackat assisted with a hiss of anger, his grip painfully tight on her upper right arm as he hauled her off the ground), Ethrayne struggled then to get herself properly into the saddle, her left leg and hip protesting mightily, her face grey. She bit her lip, guessing from the expression on his face that Ackat didn't think that one blow had been enough punishment, although she certainly did.

In a moment, she found herself drawn along behind Cavaln's horse, as they rode quickly back towards the dark woodlands above the farm yard, leaving the stunned farmer and his wife standing there, watching them go.

* * *

CHAPTER 21

Apart from a brief rest for the horses' benefit sometime after noon, when Ethrayne was handed a water bottle and helped into the undergrowth by Cavaln, she was ignored. The two Generals spoke quietly together, some way ahead, turning frequently to look at her, following at the end of the piece of rope by which Ackat led her horse. She was unsure whether her imagination was working overtime, but their expressions were stern, their eyes dark; but what did she know of Generals? Had she done something else to anger them, or were they worried, perhaps? Why were their gazes almost measuring her? Or was it only her imagination? But they did not deign to speak to her, riding on at the head of the group with a clear determination to cover as many leagues as possible before nightfall, from their start at Applegarth. Ethrayne didn't really know this, but it was what she thought: she was just a passenger, baggage; everything hurt far too much, today, for her to pay much attention to the countryside they rode through, the parts that might have been familiar, giving way to land that surely was not, heading west and south.

The sun was hovering close to the far horizon when Ackat called a halt, dismounting quickly to inspect the site that he had deemed suitable for their camp, a flat area of land set between low limestone cliffs that protected it from the west, and slightly above the thick mixed woodland that they had been climbing through for most of the afternoon.

Looking around, with slightly more interest, Ethrayne wondered if this was the Perotan Forest, those the Perotan Hills ahead, that were west and south of the Vale; this meant that they must have crossed another of the feeder rivers for the Sare, without her noticing at all! They could be only a few days from the border of Tenarum. It was frightening, that realisation, and she shivered.

Ackat strode over to where she sat, slouching uncharacteristically in intense discomfort on the horse as the soldiers separated to their tasks and Ethrayne flinched slightly, without meaning to. He laughed a little, the sound cold, as he lifted her down from the saddle and sat her on the damp grass. "Perhaps you are starting to learn, brat!"

"I am the Lady of Clirensar and betrothed to the Prince of Tenarum!" Ethrayne struck out verbally only because his mocking words mirrored her own thoughts at her helplessness. "I hardly need to take lessons from the servants of some, some foreign king!"

He had turned away, but the look on his face, burning in his eyes when he bent over her, his face only inches from hers, was terrifying and Ethrayne realised, her heart sinking, that she might have gone too far.

"You little bitch!" He spat furiously, raising his fist -.

"Stop, Ackat!" Cavaln interjected firmly, stepping right up to the pair of them, her hand extended. "She is injured and ignorant -."

"Ignorant and reckless!" He snarled. From nowhere, there was a long knife in his right hand as he stepped around Cavaln and took hold of Ethrayne's long weight of hair, pulling hard as he went down on one knee beside her. "You insolent, ignorant, self-important little brat!" He continued, his breath hot on her face. "We are the servants of our master, the emperor, yes, but only in so far as you could be considered a servant of your little king! We are his tools, his eyes, ears and hands across Iullyn. If you were naked, bitch, you could trust any General of the Empire to deliver you safely to our emperor's presence anywhere in Iullyn, untouched! Cavaln is here, true, but your state of virginity, if it exists, would be safe throughout the world with any of us! You will learn to think before you speak and to guard your tongue, brat, or you will suffer the consequences!" And he raised the blade, shining bright in the light of the setting sun and sliced through the length of her hair below the bow that Bess's friend had tied, so that about half its weight fell behind her.

"What are you doing?" Ethrayne cried in horror, lifting her right hand -.

"I suggest that you sit still, brat." Cavaln advised with laughter in her voice. "If you irritate my colleague any more, he might decide to remove your clothes next, simply to prove his trustworthiness, no doubt!"

"Ha!" Was all that he said, pitilessly cutting away at her hair until there was a startlingly large pile of light brown, wavy hair in her lap and little more than varied lengths of stubble left on a head suddenly very cold. Ethrayne did not dare to move a muscle as he cut and hacked roughly at her head, sat frozen in horror and fear, tears pouring down her face, shivering; the blade had scraped painfully against her scalp more than a few times, yet she had not dared move, shocked; only when he stood up and stepped back, slipping the knife into its sheath, did she slowly raise her right hand to feel her denuded, stubbly, painful scalp, where the places that had hit the ground the previous day were very tender. "There you are, a haircut worthy of nobility. What do you think, is it an improvement?"

The laughter of Cavaln and the soldiers, raucous and mocking, was answer enough and Ethrayne hid her face in her hands and sobbed. The evening wind, gusting, caused the cut and bruised areas and most of her scalp to smart; had his knife cut her skin, too? She flinched again as Cavaln leaned down, taking the pile of hair, to drop it over by a stand of browning bracken and set it on fire with a flash of power – in a few moments, with a harsh smell of burning, it was nothing but ash.

"And that's not all, brat." Ackat continued, his tone still uncompromising as he strode away across the camp that had been set up around them. "You're not getting a bite to eat tonight until you have apologised and asked me *very* politely for supper. You will learn your place, Ethrayne, if it kills you!"

*

It was much later and Ethrayne shivered, although General Cavaln had given her two blankets earlier which did provide some protection against the weather. The night had turned gusty and the stars were hiding behind thick clouds, peeping out now and again for a moment, whilst the fire sparked. She had at least eaten, for her humble pleading with General Ackat had been genuine enough: he terrified her, and the hollow feeling of desperate hunger inside her had been awful. She had also recalled that he had killed Shan in cold blood, which chilled her – no one had told her exactly how the poor man had died, but the men had all looked grim enough, stating only that he had been butchered!

General Ackat had laughed at her request and finally relented, quite some time after the others had finished eating; she had eaten what they had given her with real need, not even tasting it, only vaguely aware that it wasn't even warm, but her nerves were stretched as tight as a bowstring; the pain of her injured leg and the entire left side of her body worried her far more than hunger had. She lay there, cold despite the blankets, lying on her right side on the hard ground, trying to get comfortable, just glad to be ignored.

"What happened, there at the farm, Ackat?" Cavaln asked her colleague, taking a wine sack from him. They were sat further around the fire, but still within earshot of their prisoner. The woman took a swallow. "I really thought the farmer was dead."

"Yes, he would be, but for our troublesome little prisoner." Ackat answered with a sideways glare at the girl, his eyes reflecting the fire. "Somehow, she blocked my blade, shielded him; that's why I dropped it, it was like hitting a bloody wall. Didn't you see her suddenly glow? She expended a lot of strength."

"I was watching you." Cavaln admitted.

"It was only for a moment. It seems that she does have some talent, even if she doesn't know how to harness it or use it consciously yet. D'you know, Cavaln? I'll be really very bloody pleased to get the girl back to civilisation."

Listening, Ethrayne wondered what the General meant, for she was sure she hadn't done anything at Applegarth, she had only screamed like an idiot and acted like a mindless fool. It was awful, she was now completely helpless: even more crippled than she had been the previous day. The two Generals terrified her, for their power abraded her nerves, their manner and their ready violence scared her.

Dully she reflected that the damned Prophecy had not mentioned the taking of Clirensar or the murder of her parents and friends . . . If she had known of this, she probably would not have agreed so confidently to take the Flame . . . It had seemed so simple, there in Tenum City, so straightforward . . .

And now here she lay, aching from head to toe, her left arm and hand stiff, weak, bruised and swollen so she could hardly handle the crutch; her ribs, hip and leg agonising. The Generals had certainly ensured compliance simply because she could hardly move a yard without requiring assistance!

How can the monsters be stopped? She asked silently, and tears began to well up again as the realisation hit home as hard as Ackat's earlier blow: *Mamma and Papa are dead! Dead! I'll never see Jerryn again! A-and so many innocent people have died, and more will die! We're doomed! And what of Jerryn? We were meant to be married in a moon!* She sniffed hard, and somehow controlled herself, but horrible thoughts and fears filled her head. It was a very long time before exhaustion finally let her find solace in sleep.

*

Three days passed. Three long, hard days of intense discomfort and teeth-gritting bloody-mindedness, during which Ethrayne very privately agreed with her brusque captors that she was weak, useless and pampered beyond belief. Even if she had been uninjured, she would probably have found the constant travelling hard work, for they were setting off soon after dawn and riding almost nonstop until sunset, every day. Hampered as she was, it was terrible. Travelling with her family had never been so intense, despite her familiarity with horses. She suspected that it was mainly due to her own fragility that General Ackat led them on mostly at a canter, rather than racing across the unpopulated region of the Perotan Hills and beyond, into the south.

The border lands south and west of the Perotan Hills were mostly virgin forest, with wide meadows between that seemed stuffed with wildlife, game birds, deer-like creatures and so on, which formed many of the meals prepared by the soldiers. There were no signs that people had ever dwelled here. Ethrayne had caught occasional glimpses of wolves and even a bear at a great distance, busy on their own business. Consequently, it was a shock when the small group came to a wide muddy scar that obviously marked the route the jajozeli had taken; it angled off to the north-east behind them, vanishing around a hill and into the woodland, but led south-west, a massive ruin of rutted brown mud some fifty or more yards wide, stark across the pristine landscape.

Frustration marked her days; frustration mixed with liberal amounts of embarrassment and anger at the help that she was forced to accept from Cavaln for even the most intimate things. After five days, her left leg was still badly swollen and bruised and could not support any weight at all; but at least her arm and hand were slowly returning to usefulness. It was awful, but Ethrayne did thank Arven that Cavaln was there, for the prospect of having had to rely on General Ackat or a soldier for assistance would be simply unbearable; the woman's healing skills were excellent, as she checked and re-bandaged her injured leg each evening. It was strange to think that a General could also be a healer, although Bahlien had said that their talents moved in as many ways as any Protectorate razine.

The southern Tenarean border was uncertain, but antiquated standing stones stood like sentinels across one ridge top, huge, grey and lichen covered, set at odd intervals; these huge, roughly hewn rectangular blocks over seven feet high were generally accepted as border markers, whether it was fact or not.

This land was higher, and summer here was only a memory; the windswept, largely coniferous woods and rough heath land which had replaced the fading, brown meadows of lower altitudes showed autumn to be at a much more advanced and cooler stage. Gazing westward towards the fading colours of sunset, that fifth evening from Clirensar, Ethrayne shuddered at the chilly, rain-laden wind that cut through her tattered travelling cloak and gown; fine silk was not designed for hard travelling. She assumed that she looked a complete fright, looking down at the stained, ripped hemline and the filthy state of her gown and petticoats. She tried hard not to think about how many more days might pass before she might possibly feel the touch of clean, hot water to wash in; before she was warm. The vast realm of Zanezli was upmapped territory, and she had no idea how many more leagues they still had to travel.

All Ethrayne knew was that she was heartily sick of it. The despair and horror of Clirensar's fate and her parents' deaths cut at her emotions terribly, but the fear, pain, privations and hard exertion of this forced journeying were never-ending, it seemed. Four more days passed, their rate of travel increased at the Generals' urging, whilst the weather was worsening. The last of the warmish, sunny days vanished abruptly behind dark clouds, propelled by cold winds from the south-east, out of the mountains, bringing almost constant hard, cold rain.

Since that first night, General Cavaln never offered her any medicine to lessen the pain she suffered from her injuries, yet she took pity on the girl when the rain began to fall in earnest and had taken an almost full-length, thick, amazingly waterproof cloak almost identical to the ones she and Ackat wore from one of her packs and given it to Ethrayne. She was immensely glad of it: it was very warm and excellent protection against the weather; but she still felt horribly weak every night, useless and emotional. She was usually fighting tears at some point in the darkness, trying to hide her mourning from her captors.

The tenth morning of their journey began, identical to the rest: with rude remarks from the soldiers and General Ackat, which she had learned to ignore without any reaction. She was surprised, after the usual hurried breakfast, to find that she could put a little bit of weight on her left leg, for a moment anyway, although she was still hugely dependant on the crutch and General Cavaln. It hurt, was still tender, but it was nowhere near as painful as it had been a day or two before.

"You're doing rather well, considering." The woman said unexpectedly, helping her back to the campsite where the soldiers were loading the last of the baggage onto the horses.

"Thank you." Ethrayne answered shortly, her right hand running quickly over her bald scalp in a newly established nervous habit. She *had* learned to think before speaking and the thought of antagonising either General again brought her out in a cold sweat: the feel of their power in her head, their strength and authority were frightening. She was being drawn helplessly to a place that had existed only in myth, to an unknown fate; and she wondered what, if anything, her abduction had meant to the prophecy that Lurco and Bahlien had explained to them so many moons ago.

Oh, dear Arven, poor Lyria! Pualyn! Jerryn! King Marrand! She mourned, yet again; her near sister-in-law must have lost all her family at Callorton, even the babies, as they had likely lost so many who were friends as well as servants! And Pualyn, where was he? He would be heartbroken, to learn of their parents' deaths. That he was now the duke! . . . And what would Jerryn think? . . . She deliberately tried not to think about her betrothed or the city very much, as she had skirted around the cold, brutal deaths of her parents, the shock and raw grief too great to deal with. She should have been riding north again with her wedding gown, by now . . . What was happening in Clirensar? She wondered uneasily. *Dear Arven, please take care of them!* And, feeling tears welling up yet again, she quickly turned her thoughts elsewhere, dwelling on just how much she hated her captors, using anger to control her fear and despair.

That morning, the clouds blew off as the group rode fast along the road beside the scar of the jajozeli army's passing; a beautiful blue sky and a much colder wind were left, the latter blowing hard in their faces. Ethrayne pulled her borrowed cloak tighter around her body and shivered. The countryside had suddenly changed not more than a mile from their campsite beside the road, which, the previous morning, had emerged from out of the rough grass, beyond a pair of tall, lichen-dotted standing stones. At that point, as if set out with a rule, farmland replaced the woodland and scrub; fallow fields and paddocks which would not have looked out of place in Tenarum. It looked surprisingly ordinary in the sunlight, although no workers were in evidence; of course, the grey clouds and rain returned soon enough, and the afternoon seemed to pass in a chilly storm of cold rain as the horses climbed a long slope out of a shallow valley, finally reaching a rough ridge which stood out amid the landscape, blocking the view to the south apart from a distant view of high, grey-green slopes that seemed to climb towards the distant mountains.

Ethrayne wondered where the farmers lived and who they were, for they passed mainly fields since they had set out that day. It had kept her from worrying, a very little, until, reaching that vantage point of the hilltop, Ethrayne felt a jolt of shock. There, completely unexpectedly and only a couple of miles away, if that, was a great complex of dark-roofed buildings surrounded by a high wall that was clearly designed for defence atop an open slope, with many more wide fields laid out as far as the eye could see, across the valley which separated the hilltops. The Betrayer's distinctive black, red and silver flags cracked in the wind on poles on the tops of the towers.

"N'Astoln." General Ackat said succinctly, turning and grinning at her with apparent good humour before he urged his horse on down the steep slope before them and she was drawn on behind as the evening deepened, although it had become so gloomy with the thick clouds, it didn't really make much difference.

From her first view as they rode through the surprisingly narrow gate and along a straight, cobbled street, Ethrayne thought that the settlement was more a military fort than a normal city, despite the farmland surrounding the place. The buildings all seemed nearly identical: blocky, tall, steep roofed and plainly constructed of brick and stone with small windows; the people they passed were male and all wore the same black uniform as the soldiers behind her; smartly, each of them stopped where they stood and saluted the Generals respectfully. Also, there were no shops to be seen. The streets were quite narrow and straight, excellent for defence. Ackat and Cavaln led the group through the streets, finally reaching the first wide space that Ethrayne had seen here, a broad empty square bordered by more plain ranks of buildings. There was a massive flagpole in its centre, also bearing the large black, crimson and silver standard that had been run up over Clirensar. One building ahead was taller than the others, with five levels of windows and the roof surmounted by two more lightning flags, whilst the entrance was reached by three broad steps.

"Halt." Ackat ordered. "Dismount and disperse."

"Sir." The soldiers saluted, dismounted, and strode off with their equipment and bags, talking quietly.

"By the ice of Car'Agasse, is *that* your prisoner, Ackat?" A loud voice boomed from the top of the steps. A tall, black-haired General stood in the newly opened doorway, staring at Ethrayne with a look of exaggerated horror on his face as she strove to dismount without anyone's help. "Pirris! What a mess! Did you drag her through the mud the entire journey?"

Ackat laughed aloud as he watched the girl reach the ground, holding tight to the saddle as she fumbled with the crutch that was looped over her back, not really daring to set her left foot down properly yet; after another long day, her injuries still ached.

"I cut off her hair and the mess on her face is mostly bruising from her capture. It's been an interesting journey." He explained, waving the girl on towards the steps. "I'll tell you all about it when I've bathed; Cavaln, can you sort the brat out?"

As the woman came up beside her, Ethrayne saw Cavaln's eyes flash with a moment's anger, although her expression was neutral. "Of course, Ackat." She said calmly, catching a large key which the black-haired man tossed to her. "Come along, girl."

It was noticeably warmer inside, as Ethrayne hopped along behind the woman, heading along a plain, torch-lined corridor, up two flights of tall steps which were challenging, and she had to use her damaged leg to ascend them; she gritted her teeth at the top, following the General along a second corridor lined with doors, to one the same as all the rest, which Cavaln unlocked with the key. The door opened to reveal a square, grey-walled room lit by a few large candles, containing a scarred table and a low stool; she saw a long, narrow bed along the right-hand wall, a surprisingly large hearth containing a blazing fire, and, bliss! There was a wooden bath next to it like a large half-barrel, nearly full of steaming water.

"Oh, dear Arven!" Ethrayne felt suddenly giddy at the sight of the bath and the bed and had to fight back a sudden rush of tears from nowhere.

"I'll lock you in here. I've got the only key, girl." Cavaln waved it in front of her face. "Get washed. I'll return later with hot food and some clean clothes." She advised as she left, slamming the door hard, the sound of the lock turning clear.

"Thank you very bloody much!" Ethrayne retorted. This was the first slight return of spirit that she had dared show since Ackat had cut off her hair, probably raised by the realisation that her leg was getting better, although it throbbed considerably from having to climb the stairs. She set the crutch and cloak aside by the door after checking that it *was* locked, then scanned the room properly, limping a little.

There was a simple bi-fold wooden screen by one wall, which she slowly pulled across to set between the bath and the door. A second door led to a little room containing a privy; a shuttered window was in the right-hand wall, beyond the neatly made bed on which there were adequate towels laid out, whilst the bedding smelled of lavender, which was surprising; there was soap, a mat on the wooden floor and a large basket of dry logs for the fire. Only then did Ethrayne feel secure enough to strip off her tattered gown and underclothes, all too aware that she was a complete wreck; the lacing of the gown practically gave way at her touch. She unwound the latest bandage from her leg and was slightly encouraged to see that, although it was still horribly bruised, the swelling had pretty-much gone: her foot and ankle especially were practically back to normal size. This matched the faded mass of bruising that covered all her left side and her arm from her shoulder down; no wonder she had found the journey so hard! Finally, she stepped into the bath and reached for the soap.

It felt that this was the first time that she had been properly warm since the battle above Clirensar and she was thankful to be out of the ever-watchful gazes of the Generals. Ethrayne almost felt that some of her constricting emotions loosen a little as she washed, for they had choked her for so long, it felt strange but wonderful to be temporarily free of grief, fear, anger and the rest, even though she supposed that they would quickly return.

By the time that Cavaln strode back in to the room, Ethrayne was securely wrapped in plain brown towels and striving to scrub some of her own clothes clean, to turn her muddy and bloodstained petticoats and underclothes white. She had not been able to just sit there waiting idly: that way lay fear and horrible imaginings of the vast unknown. She jumped as the door opened with a click.

"Here's your dinner." Cavaln said, pointing to a tray that a soldier behind her laid on the table; the woman glared as he tried to ogle the girl knelt by the bath tub. He headed back to the door, brought in a large pail and hurried away with a salute. "And some clothes." She placed a pile of stuff beside the tray. "It's sensible, washing your clothes: I've not been able to find underclothes, so adapt what you can. Here's twine and my knife." She held it up, plain, with a six-inch blade, smiling at Ethrayne's start of surprise. "I'll have that back in the morning, of course. Don't bother trying to escape with it, or even think of hurting yourself. I'll be very, very annoyed, girl, if you do and my colleagues will be furious. Come in here." She beckoned, and the girl followed her into the privy, where she tapped on a grey metal faucet in a pipe. "Turn this for fresh hot water, tip the dirty water down the privy." Water gushed into the bucket set below it for a moment as she demonstrated. "The clothes I've brought will need taking in, I imagine. Eat first." She glared at the girl. "Now."

Ethrayne blinked and considered arguing, but the smell of hot food had made her stomach rumble, it was a long time since breakfast. She headed for the main room and the table, keeping a firm hold on the towels; she was glad when the General left and the lock snapped shut again.

The tray held a mug of milk, making her wonder where the cows were in this bleak landscape; there was dark bread and cheese and what seemed to be a sort of stew, an ample helping of meat, vegetables and some sort of grain, oddly flavoured. Ethrayne devoured the food so quickly, she had to rest for a while before starting to rinse her clothes. She had eaten regularly, twice a day, during the journey, of course, but her emotions and injuries had meant that she had had difficulty finishing meals as well as with sleeping properly. Now, it was her desire to be safely and appropriately dressed that overrode her need for sleep.

She emptied some of the cooling bathwater, added some clean hot water, then scrubbed and rinsed what she could, finally draping it over the screen and made up the fire to dry it. Then she blew out the candles, got into bed, pulled the covers up over the towels she still wore and quickly fell into sleep.

Ethrayne awoke to a loud bang and broad daylight, for the shutters were wide open. The noise brought her upright, clutching the bedclothes tight to her body, staring at the black-haired General in dismay, edging as far back into the wall behind her as she could, pulling the blankets right up to her chin. He was stood over by the fireplace; she wondered if he had been re-lighting it, for the room felt chilly and the fire was crackling loudly as it burned through kindling and a few larger pieces of wood.

"Hmm. You look a little better than you did on your arrival." He said, raking her with his gaze. "Obviously Cavaln is no fool: you've slept half the day away."

"I, I have?" She was amazed: it felt as though only moments had passed since her head had hit the pillow, apart from the fact that some of the bone-deep exhaustion that had plagued her since Applegarth had vanished. "I -." But she stopped speaking and the grin that the General gave her made it obvious that he knew she had deliberately not added an apology.

"There's no help for it." He said easily, still studying her closely. "Breakfast is there. Eat and get yourself dressed. We'll be setting off by dawn tomorrow."

"Yes, sir." Ethrayne muttered.

"Not sir, girl." He corrected her, but his tone was deceptively mild, whilst the feeling of danger she received from him increased. "The correct form of address is *yes, my Lord General* and don't you forget it." And he turned and left, locking the door again.

Breakfast was an odd sort of porridge, which was filling, and scrambled eggs with bread, again with peculiar seasoning. Ethrayne enjoyed it, knowing that she would never have eaten so much at one meal at home; but she had noticeably lost weight on her journey, and those times during it when she had been almost starving hungry filled her with horror.

Full, she mended the fire then turned to the pile of clothes and slowly fashioned an outfit that would hopefully prove both warm and robust enough for the next stage of her journey; Cavaln's knife and the twine proved invaluable indeed: over her own crumpled, clean things she pulled on a thick tunic in faded green, then a pair of black leggings, the smallest in the pile which still swamped her, needing twine for a belt. Next, she took a felted red wool jacket, turned up its sleeves as she had turned up the trouser legs and used more twine to fasten it tighter; it was so long that it came halfway down her thighs. Two pairs of baggy socks meant that the pair of well-worn short boots were not *too* loose, and the turned-up leggings helped pad the boots around her ankles. Looking down, Ethrayne supposed that she must look ridiculous, but at least she was warm, and she would find it easier to get on and off horses. There was even a rough pair of mittens and a baggy woollen hat amongst the clothing, rather old and tatty.

Time passed slowly, so she emptied the bath of the cold water and stood at the locked window that she had ignored until now, staring down a narrow street three floors below, watching men in cloaks walking about to some purpose or other. The sky was a mass of deep grey cloud, dotted with a few areas of clear blue; rain fell at intervals, she saw a few distant dark birds flying and nothing else.

At least, she thought at once point, she was recovering her strength, and she was relieved that she was no longer sunk into that abject fear and upset which had seen her weeping far too often since her capture: helpless in every way, and mourning.

At some point, Cavaln reappeared with two soldiers; the muscular men easily removed the wooden bath tub, rolling it out of the room on its side. The woman only stood there, staring at the girl.

"You'll do." She allowed after some study. "Knife?"

"Here." Ethrayne gestured, then moved to the old table and picked up the weapon, offering it to the General hilt first. "Thank you, Lady."

Cavaln slipped it into a sheath on her belt. "I suggest you pack these other clothes and bring them with you, it gets bitter in the mountains. And how will you deal with menses, girl?"

"What?" Ethrayne stared, then sank, blushing, onto the stool beside her. "Well -."

Cavaln snorted. "You need a nursemaid, girl! You are not a child, even if my esteemed colleagues seem to think that you are. Sort yourself out, brat, no-one else will do it for you!"

"I never asked you to murder everyone in my home city and drag me here!" The girl retorted resentfully. "He killed my parents! I won't apologise for being who and what I am! And I won't apologise for trying to escape!"

Cavaln flashed a brief grin. "Fair enough. Don't answer back again, however. Get organised, girl. Saddle bags will be brought later; don't forget the other clothes, you will need them, bring a couple of blankets too." Then she departed, sweeping out as regally as any queen despite her manly garb.

They make me feel so stupid! So childish! She muttered resentfully to herself later, ripping the remains of her clothing into useful sized rags and shivering – *Still, at least* she *said it, and not any of the men!* She acknowledged; that would have been completely unbearable.

She stayed there beside the fire as the light faded from the sky, glad of the chance to rest, to appreciate time spent alone, puzzling over the myriad questions that had been stuck inside her since her capture. She wondered at the nature of the power within her, the Flame of Arven and how helpless she was despite it, although she had somehow saved the farmer's life in Applegarth from Ackat's sword stroke; she wondered about the Betrayer and his servants, and her role and Jerryn's. A million questions, but with no answers!

She had no idea if there was a way in which she could have warned Jerryn or Bahlien of the forces that had attacked them across the many leagues between them; she didn't have a clue how she had stopped Ackat's murder of Kethar; she did not know anything at all, it seemed! What sort of Wielder of the Flame could she possibly be, when she was so ignorant that the Generals had laughed at her? Ethrayne's thoughts span almost sickeningly towards despair, until she welcomed the interruption of a soldier after sunset who brought a meal on a tray and a pair of saddlebags, halting her increasingly depressing thoughts. Swearing under her breath, she ate the food quickly and then packed the spare clothes neatly away as Cavaln had suggested. Then, to hopefully prevent herself from returning to those awfully spiralling thoughts, she got into bed and tried to force herself to sleep, but it was late when she finally did so.

*

A banging on the door woke Ethrayne abruptly from a dream where she and Jerryn were walking together through a field at South Vale Farm, past the horses. She leapt up in momentary confusion as General Cavaln strode into the room, her uniform pristine, her boots shining, with cup and bowl on a tray. "Be quick, we set off at dawn, don't forget the blankets." She ordered crisply, her boots sounding loud on the floorboards as she left.

The sky outside was still black, Ethrayne found, opening the shutters when she had lit candles from the fire; she quickly ate, then washed and dressed, pulling on the ill-fitting clothes and tying them securely. She rolled two of the thick blankets up and packed them in the other saddlebag, then finally pulled on the loose boots, wriggling her toes experimentally, then smiling slightly: her left foot still hurt, but noticeably less even than the day before. Then, she waited with a strange mixture of feelings, a dichotomy: unease and fear at heading into the heart of Zanezli and pleasure at leaving this prison, however nice it had been to be apart from her captors. Being locked in an empty room was, she had found the previous day, a peculiar torture.

A pair of soldiers opened the outer door a short time later; a quick glance out of the window had shown her a few windows glowing with lamp light in the surrounding buildings, but the sky had not lightened at all. Ethrayne picked up the saddlebags and the thick black cloak and headed towards them, limping slightly but ignoring the crutch that had been so vital until now. She could walk, if slowly and she would only improve and get better quickly now, please Arven!

The soldiers flanked her, marching her back down to the bare entrance hall, where the massive doors were already open to an icy wind which tore down the corridor with teeth. Still carrying her cloak, she shivered.

"What an ugly little creature she is!" One of the sentries at the entrance remarked with a derisive snort. The courtyard was badly lit with spluttering torches, but the sky to the east was just lightening now, so dawn was approaching. "Looks more like a half-starved boy than a girl!"

A sudden fury flashed through Ethrayne from nowhere: she might have to accept the cold superiority of the Generals, but she did not have to cower before mere soldiers! Dropping the cloak and saddlebags on the top step she recalled her lessons, took a breath and spun around, grabbed the hilt of the soldier's sword with her right hand and punched him in the stomach with her left, just as Jerryn, Pualyn and the rest had taught her. To her satisfaction, he fell backwards off the top step, his arms windmilling, swearing wildly as he hit the cobbles below. The other guards all stared at her, clearly stunned.

"I am the Lady of Clirensar, betrothed to the Prince of Tenarum and Wielder of the Flame of Arven. I might not look my best, but I am hardly an *ugly little creature*!" She replied with all the icy hauteur of her rank, a mannerism she had hardly ever used before in her life, raising the sword. "Keep out of my way -."

"Or what will you do, brat?" General Ackat asked from behind her in a tone of polite interest. The soldiers who had guarded her had not even drawn their own weapons and they quickly edged away from the tall jajozeli-razine. "Get out of my way, fucking idiots!" He growled as the downed sentry got to his feet, pale and angry.

"Oh -." Ethrayne added one of the curses that would have brought shock and disapproval from her parents; Ackat, Cavaln and the black-haired General all grinned, grouped formidably in the doorway.

"Tut, tut, Ethrayne, how very rude." Ackat scolded her and she tried to keep her grip on the sword steady despite her rising fear. "Do you actually know what to do with that long, sharp, dangerous piece of steel, mmm?" There was cold laughter in his eyes again.

"Jerryn, Pualyn and the commanders in Tenum City were teaching me, yes, Lord General." She replied as assuredly as she could manage, despite her unease. "Surely you heard about my combat practice whilst you were lurking about the fringes of the city, sir? Some courtiers were shocked at it. I am not completely untrained, sir."

"Excellent." He did not answer her question. "Then I will assess your ability, girl. Although we are on a tight schedule today, we can just about make space for a quick lesson. Come along." Still smiling, he gestured and passed her, stepping down into the courtyard where the wide-eyed soldiers quickly moved away again.

Behind, helpless, Ethrayne followed him, praying desperately to Arven, all too aware that Cavaln and the other were laughing aloud at her predicament. Limping towards the blonde General, she realised again just how very tall he was and remembered how frightening, furious and formidable he had been when he had cut off her hair. He stood there in the gradually increasing grey daylight, his sword already in his hand, point down, watching her, grinning and poised.

"Are you ready, my lady?" He asked lightly, bowing elegantly and Ethrayne bowed too; the basic manners from her combat lessons were deeply ingrained, but she did not trust herself to speak. "And begin."

Ackat moved with lethal speed and his blade sliced through the air. Unexpectedly, Ethrayne's fear vanished as six moons of lessons meshed together in her mind: her blade met his with a ring of steel, although she knew that her defence was rather clumsy, the collision hard in her grip; she stepped quickly, forgetting her aching left leg, yet awfully aware that the boots she was wearing were too big, that she might slip up at any moment; she shifted her shoulders and her swing, then thrust with her arm -.

"Not bad." The General commented, easily blocking her move, forcing her backwards. "Ha, that's better!" He sounded almost approving as she recklessly attacked for a second time. Rather unnecessarily he retreated a few steps, his sword held wide, his body exposed. "Come on, girl, move your feet."

"You're playing with me, Lord General!" She growled. He laughed and shifted, hitting her blade so hard that she nearly lost her grip on it. Ethrayne danced awkwardly aside, crouched and attacked again, but Ackat span with acrobatic grace and was on the offensive, leaving her wrong-footed, clumsy and desperately trying to block him . . . It was as if this was her first lesson, that the sword in her hand was made of wood . . . Any one move could have disarmed her in a moment, but he was holding back . . . After far too long, a short, humiliating period which felt like a complete lifetime, he finally brought the session to an end. Her hand was empty, her arm numb almost to the elbow and she landed hard on the cold, wet cobbles on her rear, hardly daring to breathe as Ackat laid the edge of the sword that he had knocked from her grasp across her throat. The blade was very, very cold. Then he withdrew it and grinned anew.

"You may show some promise, Ethrayne." He commended her, to her amazement, then leaned forward to crack her hard across the face with one hand, before tossing the sword back to the soldier she had disarmed and sheathing his own weapon smoothly; he reached down to pull the pale-faced girl to her feet and wrapped a length of finely woven rope firmly about her wrists, checking that it was tight before he secured it with a couple of intricate knots.

"But -." Ethrayne quavered, feeling the rope already pinching at her skin. This alarmed her more than his slap, to her surprise. His blow hurt, but that made her angry, not tearful, thank Arven! She was so sick of crying, although she supposed her tears had been more a result of her injuries and grieving than cowardice on her part!

"Shut your mouth, brat!" Ackat advised coldly, his expression once again a forbidding glare. He grabbed her by the collar of her jacket and tightened his grip, shaking her. "If you ever defy us again on this journey, I'll beat you black and blue!" He warned her, quietly. "I suggest you keep that in mind."

"Can we leave now?" The black-haired General asked in an amused tone, negligently dropping her cloak and saddle bags at Ethrayne's feet as he passed. "The sun is rising. Let's go." The cold wind made Ethrayne shiver, despite the weight of the felted jacket that had made her feel far too hot a short time before; constrained, she fumbled with both items with her tied hands, almost dropping the cloak. Cavaln snorted and deigned to take pity on her; she quickly fastened the cloak about the girl's throat, then walked across to set the bags level behind the saddle of the nearest of the horses that had been brought over, but she was smiling rather nastily as she did so.

Ackat also strode to the horses but turned back and gazed at Ethrayne rather coolly. She had stayed where she was, for she wasn't sure if she should move or not. She knew that he wanted her to realise that he had been deliberately holding back, as she now meekly followed them: she knew that she had got off much more lightly than she could ever have hoped in his *lesson*. She supposed that being tied up like this was not as bad as things might get, remembering his violence before, although it felt bloody awful and very humiliating.

"Right, girl we're riding fast." The unnamed General stated, swinging up into his saddle. "You can cooperate, or we can rope you over the saddle and give you a really unpleasant day, followed of course by my colleague's beating." He chuckled maliciously and Ethrayne quickly shut her open mouth. "So, which is it going to be?"

The girl glared at him and was up in the saddle of the huge, badly groomed grey that held her bags, trying to ignore her already hurting, confined wrists, damp rear and her actively aching left leg before Cavaln and Ackat were mounted.

* * *

CHAPTER 22

Lyria's desperate journey north to Tenum City took eight long days from her and Tally's arrival in Foston, after nightfall; side by side, they had ridden along the clear road as fast as they could, away, away from the massacre, terrified, weighted down with the family's treasures and Duke Sarant's weapons. She had hardly dared to speak, stunned at surviving the murders they had seen, guilty at her relief at living, and frightened for Ethrayne and the city.

The sight of the young lady and the stable boy, both blood-stained, the girl bearing the huge sword across her back; pale, alone, riding back into the little town caused considerable consternation. As a garrison town on the crossroads of two main highways, Foston was active far later than was normal in rural communities: the guards at the gates were alert, for opportunistic thievery from caravans travelling through the woodlands was not unknown, although highly discouraged. The guards quickly called on the local civic leaders and ushered Lyria and the stableboy into a private parlour at the spacious inn where the party had stayed only the previous night. Lyria had been surprised how much more quickly she and Tally had been able to ride than they usually could in a large group, covering the leagues at a gallop when they had been able to, but careful not to exhaust their mounts.

Then, sat by a comfortable fire, surrounded by concerned locals, Lyria hurriedly related the awful events that had occurred above Clirensar, her voice shaking with emotion as she spoke, then growing uncharacteristically annoyed at the horror and disbelief of her questioners.

"Dear Arven, Captain!" She shouted, pulling away from the well-meaning servant who was trying to wrap a blanket around her. "You must send some fast riders immediately – to warn his majesty! I must leave for Tenum City as soon as possible! Tally and I are the only ones who can tell the king exactly what has happened. The duke and duchess are dead! Lady Ethrayne has been taken!" Lyria had battled with her fear, grief and horror during their terrible ride and now anger filled her.

The town mayor was waffling something to no purpose at all, as the garrison captain finally pulled himself together and got to his feet.

"Send Seplar and Foukes as King's Messengers. We need to write the basic information down; find me ink, a quill and parchment, please. Thank you, Master." Captain Chasson said, nodding as he took a quill from Banley, the inn keeper and spread out the palimpsest. "They will be your heralds, Lady Lyria." The scratch of the nib on the parchment was loud as he quickly wrote a summary of what the young woman had reported and repeated it. "Is there anything else you want me to add, Lady?" He asked. "Is there anything you require?" He scattered sand over the inked words, shook it off back into the bowl and rolled up the message, sealing it with a blob of molten wax from one of the expensive beeswax candles on the table and his thumb print. "It is far too late to carry on your journey now, you cannot leave tonight; you must rest, my Lady, if you can."

Lyria sighed. Her mind was a mess of confusion, but she acknowledged that the captain was correct: she was exhausted, her head was pounding, and Tally looked ready to fall asleep where he sat. "Dear Arven! . . . I-I don't know." She admitted, sounding weak and small. "Perhaps you are right, Captain; perhaps we should rest a while -."

"But what are we going to do?" Mayor Fergus demanded in a fearful tone. "Clirensar taken! Clirensar! The Duke and Duchess dead! An enemy army –."

"Shut up, Fergus, we'll sort that out after Lady Lyria has been settled for tonight. We'll need to patrol the roads south and keep watch, you know. Now, Mistress Ellysa -."

"I'll take care of the Lady and her servant, Chasson; you lot shift out of my way and get organised." The inn keeper's wife declared decisively, shooing the locals out of the room, and ushering in more servants. "Lady, you must eat. There is plenty of hot water for a bath and I'll find you some more clothes . . . oh, it's tragic! Such a terrible thing! Eat, both of you, then bathe and rest and we'll see you safely on your way in the morning. Greta, Issy, ensure that there are clean clothes from my wardrobe and towels in the bathhouse!"

"Thank you, Mistress." Lyria acceded. "Forgive me -."

"Honestly, Lady, it's our pleasure, our duty: you need our assistance, to get back to Tenum City. We will do all we can, I promise you."

*

Night was drawing in, dark and starlit where the clouds had parted, but for the very edge of the western horizon where the last orange of sunset faded, as Lyria and her escort, comprising the stable-boy, Tally; Greta, who was the fourteen-year-old daughter of Mistress Ellysa, and fifteen well-armed and watchful soldiers under Lieutenant Barnd, finally rode into Tenum City. The ancient but sturdy gates creaked shut behind them, as ten men in the livery of the Royal Guard formed up ahead of the group and led them through the largely deserted, rain-swept streets and up through the city; halting, strangely, in the Cathedral compound, having entered through the Penitents' Gate.

"Lady Lyria." A man stepped out of the deep shadows that pooled around the buildings, close to the great doors, as the Lieutenant helped Lyria out of her saddle. She started but realised almost instantly that the man was Corporal Tymain and he bowed politely. "I am commanded to bring you to the king immediately. Please, lean on me, you look weary, my Lady."

At the concern in his voice, Lyria pulled herself up straight and, clutching the plain, grey soldier's cloak tight around her, glanced around at her companions: the soldiers, Tally and Greta, all probably as exhausted as she. "Thank you, Tymain, I am fine; please lead on." She said clearly. "Come on, you two and thank you for your care, Lieutenant Barnd. Please make sure these men from Foston are fed and rested, Captain, we have travelled hard."

"As you command, my Lady." The Captain of the Royal Guard saluted precisely.

The young people followed close behind her as Tymain led them into the vast building; the cathedral seemed empty, the corridors quiet and only dimly lit, the enormous hall, the focus of the worship of Arven cloaked in darkness, with only a few torches casting a light that picked out an occasional flash of gold, crimson or emerald. The young Flame Guardsman, however, strode confidently along a plain corridor to an old oak door of almost normal proportions, set in one diagonal wall of what Lyria supposed was the base of a tower. He flung open the door and ushered her into an ancient, oak-panelled octagonal room beyond -.

"Thank Arven!" King Marrand exclaimed, pushing through the knot of people who seemed to fill the space before the door and unexpectedly folded the young woman in a tight embrace; then he quickly released her and took her hand, leading her towards a large circular table, pulling out a chair for her, but Lyria did not sit down immediately. "Please, my dear, sit down; everyone, business. Jerryn, Tymain, please pour the lady and her companions some wine; you two can sit there, at that table." He pointed towards a small table with chairs, noticing the fear on the faces of the young servants. "You look weary, my dear Lyria; you have made very good time from Foston."

"We had reason enough, your Majesty." Lyria replied, clumsily removing the sword belt that she had carried almost continuously since the battle from around her left shoulder before she sat down, laying the sword and the canvas bag carefully on the tabletop, glad to be rid of the weight and the tragic responsibility of them. Silence filled the room as everyone there stared at Sarant's sword. "Thank you, your Highness." She said gratefully, when Jerryn set a large goblet of wine and a plate containing bite-sized nibbles before her and smiled when Tymain set similar viands before Tally and Greta.

In addition to Marrand and Jerryn, the two Archpriests were present; Commander Vedeigne; Lord Chamberlain Ferman; Lord Gorman; Lady Celia and Earls Orthen and Bennard, as well as Tymain.

"So, my dear Lady Lyria, the riders from Foston arrived yesterday morning and they were admirably terse. Judging by that description and the state of your clothes, events have been gruesome. Can you please tell us exactly what happened there above Clirensar?" Marrand asked gently.

"Yes, your Majesty . . . Well, we had just come out of the North Coppice, heading down into the valley and the city was ahead and below, nothing was out of the ordinary. The soldiers formed up neatly and then, then a great blast on a horn rang out . . ." The young woman coldly described everything, from the advancing black-clad enemy soldiers closing in on three fronts; to her own freezing fear; the Duchess's murder and her and Tally's almost miraculous survival, leaving the maids huddled together and Ethrayne, shocked and injured, by the side of the road, surrounded by the Generals.

"The one who murdered the Duke and Duchess, the General, did he give you his name, my dear?" Archpriest Bahlien asked intently.

"Aye, m'Lord." Tally finally dared to stutter, getting quickly to his feet and bowing low. He had been glowering at the plate and goblet before him. "Identified hisself an' the other two, who rode back with m'Lady Ethrayne: he was Tequan, the Commander; the blonde man, Ackat; an' the armed woman was Cavaln." He shuddered, bowed again and fell back into his seat. "Dear Arven, m'Lord, they scared the spit out o' me!"

"She, the female General, was Ethrayne's protection, your Majesty." Lyria confirmed with a glance at Jerryn, who was frowning deeply, his fists clenched before him on the tabletop. "She looked as dangerous as the males. Poor Ethrayne! Injured, mocked, her parents killed so brutally! Oh, I hope she is all right. The horse was killed beneath her: she must have hit the ground hard . . . She was red all down the left side of her face." Then, she took a sip of wine, a second, although she could not eat a thing: she was too tired, too upset for food.

"You named Ackat when Shan was murdered." Jerryn interjected harshly. "I saw you nod at the names, Bahlien. Is Ethrayne safe?"

"Tequan, Ackat and Cavaln." The old razine repeated the names. "She I know the least about, although we had heard rumours of a female cadet in training, so she must be quite newly elevated. I believe she may be Lord Governor Doreth's great-niece; she is young, maybe less than fifty years old." He broke off as Earl Bennarn snorted. "Remember, we live many, many years longer than you, my Lord. She is very young by our standards. Tequan was Commander of Cal'Baden and he will have coordinated the attacks on your settlements. Now he commands Clirensar, which is a tragedy for everyone concerned. And Ackat, of course, was lurking about the city here after your betrothal. They are some of the Betrayer's most trusted servants. Ethrayne is safe, but far from safety."

"I must admit that I don't really understand, your Grace." Lord Gorman growled, frowning. "A female General? It's quite ridiculous!"

"Why should her sex limit her in life, my Lord?" Lurco countered in a mild tone. "All Generals have extraordinary abilities; they are all razine, remember. Their loyalty, their very lives, are in the hands of their master -."

"I'm a little startled that Selithian proprieties have been taken into consideration, actually." Bahlien added with a tired sigh. "For Lady Ethrayne would be equally safe with any male General as with Cavaln as her guard –."

"That's revolting!" Jerryn spat with furious intensity. "That-that damned prophecy! I mean, there's poor Ethrayne, perhaps gravely injured, orphaned and alone amid her enemies! And what can we do?" He demanded, glaring from face to face, returning at last to Bahlien. "We've got to be able to do something, surely?" He entreated. "And, dear Arven, Lyria, there's your family to consider at Callorton and South Vale Farm, as well as all the citizens, the villagers and farmers in the area!"

"It is hardly your fault, your Highness." Lyria murmured. She had been trying to block out any thoughts of her own probable losses. Her mad race across Tenarum had been a boon, since she had been too tired and entirely focussed on reaching the capital to really think about the wider ramifications of the jajozeli invasion on her own family.

"Lord Pualyn and the High-King of the razine should already be on their way to Rothern by ship; at least, that was how I understood your betrothed's visit to conclude: that he would be here before the late autumn storms. With the Protectorate kingdoms, Derravale and Amorry, we should be able to pool our resources and our expertise and come up with something decisive and effective." Bahlien said gravely.

King Marrand grunted. "Well your countrymen will certainly know an awful lot more about how to deal with the Jajozeli Empire. This means war, you realise. They have taken Clirensar, with all its infrastructure and its resources! Oh, dear Arven! The iron and the steel they were preparing!" He groaned a curse.

"The attacks on Saremouth and the other coastal towns are explained, your Majesty." Commander Vedeigne stated levelly, his arms folded. "Every single one has been a massive diversion from their advance on Clirensar. We must regain the region as soon as possible."

"Winter is not far off, Commander." Jerryn added fiercely. "I want to attack immediately, but it would be stupid to try anything right now; we'd never get anything properly organised until Umtearn or even Instur, and by then the winter to the south will be terrible, we all know how bitter the weather is off the southern mountains, even if the Vale is relatively well protected."

"The winter has ever been a time for planning." Bahlien agreed, nodding. "Yet any campaign against Clirensar is only a diversion, you understand Prince Jerryn. They took the city for one purpose: to capture Ethrayne if she headed home before your wedding. She might well have remained here, your Highness, or you might have joined them on their journey to that fateful battleground."

"What are you saying, your Grace?" Marrand asked rather heatedly.

"The focus of this turmoil has not changed, your Majesty: it is all about the Flame of Arven, Prince Jerryn, Lady Ethrayne and their enemy, Gregnor, the Betrayer." The old razine said.

Lyria felt a sob rise uncontrollably within her and it burst out, harsh and loud in the room. She paled as everyone turned to stare at her and fixed her tired gaze upon the tabletop. "Excuse me, your Majesty." She murmured meekly, then picked up the canvas bag, opened the fastening, and tipped out its contents onto the table; the rings, earrings and other items forming a glowing pile of scintillating colour in the lamplight. "Here you are, gentlemen: this must be reason enough to make war!" She challenged them all, rising to her feet. "I don't really care how long it takes, but you bloody-well have to kill them! They killed the Duke and Duchess; they must have killed all my family as well, and s-so many others . . ." She shuddered. "And what of Pualyn?"

Jerryn picked up Ethrayne's betrothal ring and slid it onto the little finger on his left hand, where it only just fit. "Amen to that, Lyria." He answered fiercely, a nasty grin on his face, no humour there nor in his eyes. "Death is too good for them! I can't believe it! Arven only knows how they managed to get control of Clirensar, but we've got to get them out of there!"

"Yes, I agree, but we aren't in any position to be hasty, Jerryn." The king replied as he began carefully placing the treasures pulled from Sarant, Riyala and Ethrayne back into the bag and it was clear that the sight of the jewellery, some stained with blood, affected him deeply. "Oh, dear Arven!"

"Forgive us, Lady Lyria, you must be as tired as you are heart-broken. It is very late, and you have ridden hard. You might want to return to the palace, where you can bathe and rest. Tomorrow, we will meet with the ambassadors of our neighbours and I assure you that you will be central to this, my dear."

"I am, am honoured, your Majesty, but I must admit that-that I am having difficulty concentrating tonight; I really hope that I can remember more details tomorrow." She admitted, shuddering.

"Come along, Lyria, Tally and who are you, dear? Greta?" Lady Celia said, getting to her feet, her tone decisive. "I will see Lyria back to the palace and settled, your Majesty. Rest is certainly what she needs, after travelling so swiftly."

"Yes, very well my Lady, we will follow shortly. Thank you. Corporal Tymain, have a carriage brought around and escort these ladies to the safety of the palace, see that this young man is settled also, please, with the palace grooms."

"Your Majesty." The young Flame Guard bowed and hurried from the room.

"Thank you, your Majesty." Lyria curtsied politely, but both young servants were frozen in place.

"Go on along with you all; no, don't worry about bowing, go with Lady Lyria. We'll see you at breakfast, dear Lyria." He said gently, ignoring their fear.

"I-I hope you sleep well, Lyria." Jerryn added, opening the door for them and the young woman noted the dark circles under his eyes. "Thank you for getting back as quickly as you have." The words were formulaic; he looked weary and very upset.

"We are incredibly lucky the Generals didn't just kill the lot of us, but I would have travelled to the ends of Iullyn if required, your Highness." She answered simply, feeling deep sympathy for him. "Good night."

*

Conversation swirled around him like eddies in a stream as the group got ready to leave the Cathedral in Lyria's wake, but Jerryn found that he could not concentrate on any of them. Since that awful moment so early the previous morning, when the two soldiers from Foston had delivered their terrible news, his desperate fear for Ethrayne and the kingdom at large had warred with a terrifyingly intense fury. Ever since, he had been struggling with an almost overwhelming need to physically *do* something, chiefly destroy things and shout in fury. The news brought so unexpectedly had had an immediate effect upon the palace, rather like that of kicking an anthill: people were scurrying about in panic. Lyria's more detailed report would perhaps calm the ants, but her words had left the prince fighting an urge to grab his weapons, saddle his horse and immediately ride south in fury. The world was falling to pieces. He was struggling to stay in control.

<*Jerryn, you will have to lock away your fear and work through your anger.*> A voice said quietly inside his head, sympathetic but firm. Startled, he looked up to meet Bahlien's gaze. <*Your father will need your support now more than ever and you must continue to master yourself: you must learn to use the power that Arven has bestowed upon you -.*>

<*I . . . But-but this is disastrous!*> He replied,, and a thought struck him hard like a blow. <*Are we doomed?*>

The old razine grinned and shook his head. "Of course, we are not doomed, Jerryn. You are the Wielder of the Flame of Arven as equally as Ethrayne and Tenarum does not stand alone against the enemy. I imagine, also, that the jajozeli-razine will find young Ethrayne a little difficult to handle." He said aloud, his tone reassuring.

"I really hope so, your Grace." The king said darkly. "She owes them! I hope she makes the journey really uncomfortable!"

*

Next morning, Jerryn was up before dawn. He had tossed and turned, and his dreams, when he had eventually drifted into sleep, had been unclear but with an undercurrent of fear and worry; late the previous night, after the shock of Lyria's recount of what she had seen, he had paced his bedroom in the grip of unrelenting fury for a long time. Now, that fury and the fear that was wrapped up with it, together with a deep underlying weariness, were making a whole that matched the sombre black garb he had chosen. He felt terrible.

Deliberately, he folded up his smart, embroidered wedding clothes in midnight blue and stuffed them in the closet – even the sight of it made him angrier, more worried, for he and Ethrayne had been due to be married . . . He recalled what the General had said to Ethrayne in the spring and shivered.

There was a brisk knock at the sitting room door and he walked over to pull it open, for who would be visiting at this time of day when it wasn't even light? He wondered, and stared at Tymain, who bore a laden tray.

"Dear Arven, you're up early." He said. "Come in."

"And you. I thought that royalty didn't rise before noon." The young man returned with a bare-toothed grin.

"That was last year, Tymain. Nowadays, we're far too busy trying to think of any way to save the kingdom." Jerryn's reply was as dark as his tone, his expression a frown. "Anyway, why are you here? A few moons ago, you wouldn't have exchanged the time of day with me, Corporal."

"I grew up, Highness, as did you." His visitor answered soberly, laying the tray on the table between the fireplace and the window. "I've brought something to eat, Jerryn, I know you sent Karne away last night -." He held up his hand as the prince opened his mouth to snap back. "Look, you're frightened and angry, Jerryn. Just please sit down and have some breakfast. Please feel free to talk, or even shout at me, if it's going to make you feel better." He met Jerryn's rather stunned gaze that had replaced the frown and smiled in a friendly fashion.

"Bahlien and Lurco sent you, didn't they?" The prince asked pointedly.

"Yes, their Graces did. And, as a dutiful son of Arven, here I am. Everyone needs you to be able to think clearly, Jerryn, because standing there planning wholesale murder isn't appropriate, not now. Here is your breakfast, Am'maiya." He bowed low, then lifted a plate of neatly rolled-up pancakes, gleaming with honey and fruit stewed with spices.

"How on Iullyn did you find out pancakes were my favourite breakfast as a child?" Jerryn asked curiously, finally unfolding his arms, feeling a tiny smile hitching at his lips.

"I asked the kitchen staff, of course, I'm not stupid." Tymain retorted mildly. "Even the servants are worried about you, you know, so eat up before it goes cold."

"Thank you." Jerryn sat down at the table and Tymain set the plate before him. He did eat, enjoying the pancakes as he had not enjoyed any food or drink since he had heard the news from Clirensar. Sat opposite, also eating heartily, Tymain watched him closely. After they had finished, Jerryn poured fresh cups of tea and piled the plates neatly on the tray.

"It's an appalling turn of events." Tymain said quietly as Jerryn sank back in his chair with a sigh. "Clirensar overrun . . . thousands could have died, as well as the duke and duchess!" He shook his head. "Those bastards have caught everyone unprepared -."

"What bloody use are prophecies?" Jerryn asked bitterly. "How could we be chosen, or appointed, or whatever it is, yet no warnings be given to guard our families or our people better? Bahlien and Lurco knew nothing of their advance into our lands! We've been protecting and concentrating on the coast, to little effect, obviously and it was all a bloody bluff! All the mayhem and murder they instigated in Saremouth and the other ports, to disguise their purpose!"

"Look, I know what you mean, Jerryn, but you've lost me there. I've not had that extensive education you've been blessed with, but how could anything written down hundreds of years ago possibly predict how the Enemy of Arven will act against you?" Tymain asked. "I mean no disrespect, but surely describing the betrothal of a couple who will come to Wield Arven's Flame is one thing, but the Betrayer's thoughts and preparations are completely his own, aren't they? Arven could hardly be expected to know how the one who is trying to destroy him will think *this* year, from centuries ago, could he?"

"I -." Jerryn began, stopped, set down his teacup and frowned. "D'you know, Tymain, that's a very good distinction. I'm not at all sure." He said after a period of silent thinking. "Are you quite sure you gave up schooling when you became a private?"

The other young man snorted. "I can read, write badly and reckon up, your Highness, I promise you. But, I don't know, I just trust our God and I know he would not have Chosen you and Lady Ethrayne and then simply abandon you to the Betrayer . . . It isn't Arven you have to blame, or yourself even, it's that bastard who locked our God in ice!" His tone was low, but full of conviction, then he shook his head. "It must be terrible, worrying for your lady."

"I remember the blonde man, jajozeli-razine, who accosted Ethrayne that day on our ride, Tymain. He was General Ackat. He was lurking about the city and even sneaked into the palace, leaving notes for Ethrayne and I in our bedrooms, before he killed Shan so horribly. We could *feel* him, you know, that day: sense his animosity and power, although we didn't know what it was or even what he was -." Jerryn finally admitted what had been concealed from everyone but their families: the changes within Ethrayne and himself.

"I've felt it too, Jerryn." Tymain admitted quietly, sounding rather embarrassed. "In the inn one evening in the spring when we were off duty; it wasn't clear, really, but *something* strange seemed to affect me for a moment, and it was *weird*! . . . And killing Shan like that was a nasty business."

"I-I don't want to know the details! They wouldn't tell us. And that bastard, and some female General, are taking Ethrayne south and she is injured, Lyria said!" Jerryn threw out the words, took a breath and looked at Tymain. "Oh, I hope and pray she is all right! . . . So you're sensitive, too. Bahlien said that some people are affected by that sort of power or strength in odd ways, like we are."

"It's certainly odd, but *you* don't make my nerves scream just yet."

"At the rate I'm learning how to use this, this power I've been gifted with, soldier, I'll be an old man before I can *ever* use it!" He answered grimly, feeling like a complete failure.

"No, I'm sure you'll master it a lot quicker than that, Jerryn. I trust Arven, I trust the Archpriests and I trust you and Lady Ethrayne." Tymain answered calmly. "It's alarming, but ex-archpriest Bahlien did assure us that your lady will be cared for. Now, *your* focus must be learning your strength whilst we amass the armies we will need to free the south and face the Betrayer, your Highness."

But Jerryn laughed at the confidence of his words and felt a tiny part of that debilitating knot of misery within him loosen slightly. "Thanks, Tymain."

"I meant what I said, Highness: I trust you, and I believe in you both, and I would give my life to ensure you destroy the Betrayer and restore Arven."

The soldier stated.

"I-I am honoured to have your support, Tymain. Are you up for a second helping of breakfast? I want you in on our meetings, if you'll accept another duty. The soldiers of the Flame Guard should be included, and I think I need your common-sense behind me. Will you?"

"Well . . . I'd be honoured, Highness, if you'll join me for practice in the hall later: work off your anger in some exercise and work off that second breakfast, too, else you'll get fat."

Jerryn answered with a few choice curses that made the soldier laugh.

*

Lyria slept rather better than she had thought she would, ensconced in a suite in a different area of the palace from that traditionally occupied by the Duke and Duchess, but the rooms were still full of her own possessions, brought across quickly at Lady Celia's command. These reminded her strongly, sharply, of her own family, as well as Sarant, Riyala, Ethrayne and Pualyn. She woke early, refreshed by sleep and rose to find herself wondering desperately as to her parents' fate – her brothers, sisters-in-lawn, all her nieces and nephews . . . were they all dead? It was a while before she could motivate herself to start looking through her own mostly modest clothes to find some that was suitably plain; the quite old deep-blue gown that she finally decided upon was all that she wished.

Young Greta, who had volunteered to help care for her, having been pressed upon her by a shocked Mistress Ellysa in Foston, fiercely determined that a titled lady should not travel alone with men even on such a desperate mission, carefully helped her to dress and added a black velvet ribbon to her hair.

"Thank you, Greta. I suppose you want to explore the palace now, don't you? I know I did, when I first came here; oh, good morning, my Lady." She rose and curtsied to Celia, pale in her own black gown, nervousness warring with her sense of loss.

"Lyria, you are grieving, you have lost your family. You will also be a necessary part of our Council now, representing the south, so *please* don't curtsy." The older woman said, giving her a tight hug. "You will need some more suitable gowns, I suppose. Mallie, please start preparing those with Greta here after breakfast. Greta, go with Mallie, she will take you for breakfast, show where things are, and we will see you later, thank you." She smiled as both girls curtsied. "Go on with you."

The East Dining Hall seemed full of men, mostly but not entirely dressed soberly. Lyria and Celia were greeted by Marrand and Jerryn, and the Prince and Tymain set to bringing breakfast for the ladies, as the Archpriests asked after Lyria's general health and she quickly assured them that she was rested and well able to continue her narrative from the night before.

It was not the most pleasant of breakfast meetings, despite the quality of the dishes provided; the subject under discussion saw to that, but Lyria's account, backed up by Tally's as written down by Captain Garane of the Flame Guard that morning, was clear and detailed; the events were stuck in her mind so clearly that she thought she would never forget them. The cheeriest news she had for them was that Oxalla, Ethrayne's mare, was following on safely from Foston in the care of two of the guards.

The group were released for a while, but due to reconvene in the same hall for luncheon with the ambassadors of Derravale and Amorry. Restless, Lyria went for a walk about the public corridors of the palace and was surprised, despite her introspection, just how many servants and courtiers paid her their respects; as Riyala's lady-in-waiting she had only been a very minor player in the affairs of the palace; yet now, now she realised that she was virtually the most powerful woman in the kingdom by default, since Ethrayne's abduction. All sorts of people were sorry for her losses, it seemed, their words hopefully heartfelt . . . yet she would never see her parents or the rest of them again . . .

She was officially betrothed to Pualyn, so they were practically the duke and duchess even if they didn't actually hold Clirensar . . . if Pualyn would still have her . . . She stopped in a corner, half-hidden by an old tapestry and fought against tears, for weeping would do no good at all.

"Are you all right, Lyria?" Jerryn's voice intruded on her conflicting emotions and the young woman quickly wiped her face and lifted her chin. "I'm sorry, my Lady, it's this, this power we have now: I could feel your distress." He said in an apologetic tone and shrugged.

"I didn't want to be duchess for decades yet, your Highness!" She answered brokenly. "I've known Pualyn's family all my life, they were *friends*, and it is awful, losing both our families – I can't believe it! E-e-everyone I knew at home has brutally murdered I'm sure . . . How could it happen, Jerryn? How could Arven allow so many people to die?"

The young man sighed and leaned against the opposite wall, his expression serious, but his eyes at least were not showing quite the fury he had been full of the previous night. "I've discussed this with the Archpriests, my father and even Tymain, you know, and I must say I like his answer best: it's short and sensible."

"Really?" A hint of a smile moved her lips slightly, but her eyes were dark.

"Arven is locked in ice, isn't he?" He asked and Lyria nodded. "And the Betrayer stole some of his power. Ethrayne and I seem to have been gifted with the remainder of that strength, so Arven is powerless, imprisoned as he is."

"Well, yes, I suppose so. Gosh, that's a horrible responsibility, isn't it?" Lyria shivered slightly. "Holding the power of God! You are both so brave, Jerryn!"

"But it was right, it is meant to be. Bravery hasn't anything to do with it, it just is meant to be part of us . . . Doesn't that sound arrogant?" He shrugged. “But Tymain said that no one could possibly predict the Betrayer’s actions, because not even Arven could know in advance how he might move against us and if he had known, if it had been in the Book of Days, I suppose it would have been preventable . . . the Archpriests are devastated as much as the rest of us -.”

“And how are you, Jerryn?” She asked him directly, meeting his gaze. “You look, well -.”

“Terrible, I know.” He grimaced. “I have a-a great need to smash things. Shout. Attack people. I’ve not slept properly of course, it all just goes ‘round and ‘round in my head: them all dying so horribly, Ethie, so hurt and frightened –.” He stopped there and took a long breath. “I’m going to have a long training session later with Tymain and work off some of this anger I hope.” He admitted, feeling suddenly better for saying it. “Oh, dear Arven, Lyria: we’ve all completely forgotten about your brother, in the army!”

“Oh, damn it!” Lyria spat that and groaned, slumping down onto the floor in despair. “Oh no! Sevanter, poor Sevanter! He’s . . . dear Arven, I don’t even know where he’s serving, Jerryn!” She was almost crying, but managed to hold her distress in, although her insides hurt with her pain. “He needs to know! I can’t believe I’ve been so selfish!”

Jerryn countered that at once. “You only just arrived last night, Lyria and you’ve been travelling nonstop for days. We should have thought of this – father and I; I am sorry. Come on, let’s go and tell father: he will send people to find Sevanter and bring him here quickly.” He held out his hands to help her up.

“Oh, thank you.” Lyria hiccupped, thankful for his assistance, aware just how much she was trembling. Jerryn was right: she had not had time for anything yet except explaining what had occurred. Bells rang out, then and she stiffened with upset and fear. “Oh, no! Here we go again!”

The prince hugged her quickly and shook her with playful roughness, as they had used to as children; dealing with her intense distress somehow was lessening his own, at least for a while. “I know, but there’s no way to avoid it, I’m afraid: we need our allies, though we never expected to have to call upon their aid so soon after we united against the Betrayer. Father will do most of the talking, I’m sure: it would be cruel to expect you to go through it all yet again.” His tone was placating, but she appreciated his sympathy: it must be nearly as hard for him.

She shook her head fiercely, wiping away a few tears. “Please don’t say another word, Jerryn else I’ll fall apart like a fool. I’m trying to be steel, like Ethie and-and my Lady Riyala.” She said and set off back along the corridor towards the hall.

“Me too.” Jerryn agreed quietly.

*

The ambassadors from Tenarum’s neighbouring kingdoms arrived together, Duke Werhend of Amorry and Earl Rhane of Derravale, expecting an excellent luncheon along with an afternoon of business. The luncheon was indeed as fine as anyone could have wished, but the business that followed it, the visitors slightly alerted by the sombre clothing and stern faces of the Tenareans around the table, was likely to lead to indigestion.

"On behalf of my king -." Duke Wherhend said with a bow.

"And mine also, your Majesty, your Highness, my Lady." Earl Rhane interjected.

"We extend you every sympathy at this tragic news, these deaths." Wherhend looked from grim face to grim face and shook his head as if trying to get it to absorb the news. "Well we never expected a direct attack, after learning of that prophecy a few moons ago!"

"No, not at all." Jerryn agreed.

"This does not bode well for any of the kingdoms of Selith." Earl Rhane muttered. "Derravale's border with Zanezli is also extensive and there have been incursions in the past." He shuddered. "But we were planning a completely different type of conflict. Now, everything has changed."

"My intention, my Lord, was to retake Clirensar and kill General Tequan." Jerryn said drily, but his expression was fierce. "We must get the jajozeli out of our kingdom before we can attempt to rescue Ethrayne from the unknown vastness of Zanezli!"

"But what of Ethrayne? You can't abandon her!" Lyria blurted in a tone of shocked disbelief, jumping to her feet and blushing crimson as everyone turned to stare at her. "I . . . You can't! Oh, excuse me." She apologised lamely. "B-but I don't understand." There was a great measure of hurt and confusion in her voice.

"Lyria, my dear -." Marrand himself left his seat and came right around the table to embrace her reassuringly and handed her a crisp handkerchief as she suddenly started crying. "Ethrayne is in the hands of our enemies, but at least she is safe. Yes, she is safe: she is priceless to the Betrayer." He repeated as she reacted with horror to his words. "There is no way that we could, any or all of us, invade Zanezli, especially in the winter, my dear; the region is vast and largely unknown! We know that they must have thousands upon thousands of troops in the lands they control."

"And we can't do a thing until we have regained our territory, that's for certain, my Lady. We can't let our enemies keep a foothold in our lands: it leaves us terribly vulnerable, although winter is coming on; we are stymied there, for sure." Jerryn continued when his father fell silent. "We must prepare to wage war in the spring, kill the bastards and retake Clirensar, wiping them out in our lands. Ethrayne will be rescued, we promise and your families and so many others will be avenged. But even I cannot hope that we can act quickly."

"But act we will." Archpriest Bahlien stated firmly.

* * *

CHAPTER 23

Captain Chasson sent messengers out from Foston almost as soon as Lady Lyria and her escort had set out for Tenum City along the King's Road, north, east and west. His men moved as quickly as possible from farm, to village, to town, calling upon hunters, charcoal makers, farmers and any other males willing to patrol the woodland and forests on the northern edge of the Vale to prevent any incursion by the enemy.

The news of Clirensar's taking was unimaginable, yet it had happened, with hardly anyone outside the city's immediate vicinity even noticing, so carefully had the jajozeli proceeded, hiding in plain sight in plain clothes for days, whilst awaiting the return of the ruling family.

Small groups of men began to move through the countryside, edging cautiously through woods, fields and wild meadows, using their local intimacy with the landscape to locate hamlets set deep in the hills and forests; there was a broad network of narrow lanes far from the main roads that they could use, many barely more than footpaths.

Master Kethar and his wife, Mistress Jess, reached Foston early in the afternoon on the day after Lyria's departure from the Duke's Arms; the farmer still bore a faint mark on his throat from the General's sword, when Ackat had tried to kill him. Having left their children in the care of their concerned neighbours once they were sure that the enemy group had left the area, they had set out on two of the farm horses, grim faced but determined, riding slowly along the woodland lanes which ensured that they were nearly always out of sight of the vale and the city beyond.

"Excuse me, sir." Kethar approached one of the farmers milling about in front of the inn. "We're looking for the man in charge -."

"We're organising patrols, man. The captain's a busy -." The burly, grey-headed and grey-bearded man answered dismissively, turning away.

"But it's about Lady Ethrayne: she's been abducted." Kethar said in a louder tone.

"What? You've seen her? Lady Ethrayne of Clirensar? Where's the captain? Hey! They've seen the Lady!" The grey farmer's demeanour changed instantly. "Come on, man! M'name's Effran. Mistress, if you please."

Captain Chasson was in his small office, ignoring the people crowded in the room around him, studying a map and frowning. He looked up at the couple behind Master Effran and ordered everyone out of the place, ordering drinks for his guests. "Please, do sit down. Who are you? Where are you from? What do you know?" He asked, pulling a grey sheet of parchment towards him, picking up a quill.

"I'm Kethar, this is my wife, Mistress Jess and we're from Applegarth, sir. It's directly west of Clirensar but deep in the woods, north of the Robin

River." He said politely, thinking that the captain looked as tired as he felt, after travelling almost without a halt. "Yesterday at firs' light, Lady Ethrayne limped down into our hamlet from the forest up on the west."

"I – *what*?" Chasson demanded, staring wide eyed from one to the other. "But-but Lady Lyria reported that she was severely injured! How on Iullyn? Oh, dear Arven!" He spluttered, almost incoherent.

"Lady Ethrayne's leg is a real mess, captain, but it'll heal, you don't need to worry, there's a great deal of swelling and bruising, but nothing broken." Jess announced calmly. "They, her captors I mean, gave her something before they tended it, that first night, some drug or strong medicine and the lady said that she woke with no pain in the depths of the night, got up and limped with a crutch down through the woods . . . Oh, she was such a mess: her clothes torn by the brambles and covered with bruises; her left arm and hand, her face, her left leg as well; she's not going to be mobile for days, sir. She just burst out of the woods at first light, as Kethar said and then we washed her, bandaged her leg and fed her . . . She told us what has happened!" The woman broke off quickly and sniffed. "We sold most of our cider and brandy to the castle, you see; his Grace'd come every autumn with Reeve Thomur, sometimes the children . . . Oh, to think that we should live to see such evil here, in the Vale!" She continued brokenly.

"But-but what of the lady?" The Captain demanded rather shrilly.

"It wasn't that long afterwards, sir, when a group rode out of the woods to the west: six soldiers, two, two Generals, one female." The farmer said with a shudder. "Jess'd sent the women an' children from the house at the lady's urgin'. Thank Arven! The General, he laid a sword to my neck whilst the armed woman went into our house."

"They took her away southward. The woman said that she was a healer, despite her weapons. They were rough with the poor lady, yet she was so brave. Thought the General was going to kill Kethar, but he somehow didn't, only dropped his sword after he'd struck the lady and that was strange. They got her on a horse a-and rode off." Jess said. "We can only thank Arven we're still alive to tell you, Captain."

"Applegarth? You're on the western edge of the Vale." Chasson glared down at his map, aware of its lack of information and clarity. "Can you mark it? We're trying to set up a cordon of sorts, for we've got to keep the enemy in the city if we possibly can. Your lands might mark the boundary there in the west. How many houses and men do you have there?"

"Oh, it's a tiny place, Captain; five houses plus our farm, seven men includin' me, four boys aged eleven to fifteen, the rest are women, girls and small boys. We farm most of our food as well as makin' cider and brandy for the Duke. Arven bless their souls! He was such a good man, such an honourable, fine family." Kethar said sadly, shaking his head.

"Named our eldest Ethrayne, we did." Jess murmured quietly, a tone of pride in her voice. "Oh, that poor child! Arven protect her!"

"Right, good people." Chasson said, pressing their drinks into their hands with gratitude. "I'll arrange Mistress Ellysa to give you something hot to eat and I'll send a sergeant back with you this afternoon. I'm sorry to rush you, Master Kethar, but we've got to keep those bastards in the city if we possibly can!"

"No, that's all right, isn't it Jess?"

"Yes, Captain, we'll manage." The woman said stoutly. "Besides, I want to get back to the children."

Fortified by a mug of ale and a substantial meal at the inn, they were presently on their way back out of town, alongside a grizzled sergeant with a limp and a wary eye, mounted on an old nag; plus, an unexpected bonus, an order for cider from Mistress Ellysa who had heard of the produce of Applegarth and guessed that she would certainly sell it, if Foston continued to buzz with activity in the moons ahead.

Leaving the King's Road for a barely visible lane to the right, which began by a browning hazel thicket, looking like nothing more than an animal track, they rode on until evening and made camp probably a third of the distance into their roundabout route, supping on cold victuals in the dubious shelter of a charcoal-burners shack, unused for a few seasons at least, amid the thick, autumnal branches of coppiced sweet chestnut and other species. They set out again not long after dawn and reached Applegarth during late afternoon; travelling carefully was far more important than travelling quickly, considering the threat from the jajozeli.

"Humph, a nice place." Sergeant Remmen spoke for about the second time since they had set out that morning, as they came out of the woods through which Ethrayne had emerged, a mixture of deciduous and coniferous trees, into the broad valley that held acres of apple trees amid small fields and pasture, edged by more forest. "Well sheltered, too. Are those all the houses? Where's the lane to Clirensar?" He swung down from his horse, ignoring the cluster of men, women and children who had congregated in the farmyard, displacing the chickens.

"You are not going to rest, sir?" Mistress Jess asked, rubbing her lower back; it was years since she had ridden a horse for so long and her body was protesting.

"No, Mistress." Remmen stated blandly. "I want to know how well this settlement is hidden, work out how we're goin' to hide the road from the Vale and set up the cordon: it's only a few leagues to Clirensar, after all an' we don't want those bastards comin' here." He managed a crooked smile at the expressions of fear that suddenly marked their faces. "I won't be long, Master. Now, who can show me the way?"

"Me. I will." A couple of the younger men offered at once and the three of them walked off down the valley, whilst Mistress Jess glared at her eldest son, who had also volunteered.

"You will do as you're told, lad!" She warned him fiercely. "Go and help your father with the horses, make sure they're groomed and watered."

*

The message detailing Applegarth's encounter with Lady Ethrayne went north with a willing young man, a lot faster than the four ox-drawn carts loaded with pig iron, steel and charcoal which had been brought back to Foston from some of the local smithies and foundries, north of the Vale. Captain Chasson had argued that it wasn't sensible to leave their greatest commodity within easy reach of their enemies and the local priest, Fenton and Master Banley, the innkeeper, who both could figure and write well, had been given the task of recording the movements by founder, weight and quality. The kingdom needed the metal, but they all hoped for payment somewhere down the line. Banley's wife, the doughty Ellysa, ran the inn with her usual flair, unfazed.

Little by little, their patrols went further, the area still in Tenarean hands slowly grew in definition on Captain's Chasson's map; but all the soldiers and trackers kept away from the edge of the forests on the north and west side of the Vale, hoping to avoid confrontation and trouble.

*

Secure in the ancient, tall castle atop the crag in the centre of the city on the curve on the Sare, General Tequan was consolidating his position with the assistance of his Generals, under Jaike. He had lost nearly five hundred men in the battle to take Clirensar, including walking wounded; two thousand more were detailed with managing the wagon-train that had set off on the long journey back to Ban'Lerracon two days after he had taken command, loaded with goods and prisoners.

The farms, villages and industrial centres within approximately a day's ride of the city were stripped of everything with brutal efficiency: the inhabitants killed or enslaved, whilst barn-loads of harvested produce, useful equipment and the components of the ever-present iron and steel industry were all brought into the city, and farm animals of all types were herded to the fields south the city itself. These would be managed through the winter that would arrive all too soon: an army requires a vast amount of food and the local farms were quickly manned with chained-up, terrified slaves and patrolled by soldiers, detailed to work the farms and plant winter crops, even if only temporarily.

Other slaves were sent out to begin digging defences around the city, starting at the far side of the bridge over the Sare and just to the north of Dark Fell. The iron industry within the commander's reach would be tightly controlled, for the resulting steel would boost the jajozelis' weapons. Digging ditches and ramparts would not be a fast process, no matter how brutal the overseers, but it would serve to keep both prisoners and soldiers occupied and make any advance by the Tenareans and their allies a much slower business.

Still, with almost thirty thousand troops, his task now that Ethrayne had been captured was simply to remain there. His army was a menace in the south that Tenarum and her allies could not dare to ignore, but one that they could do nothing at all about in the shortening days of autumn. General Tequan knew that his purpose here was diversionary: *he* was the focus that his master wanted the followers of Arven to concentrate on. Whatever happened to the city of Clirensar beyond the end of winter did not matter, for the vale would be the setting for battle and, in the meantime, the jajozeli were free to benefit from the high-quality iron ore and the smelting and processing expertise of the captured local craftsmen. The loss of even nearly thirty-thousand troops would not affect the Empire at all in the long run. Emperor Gregnor had had his plans laid for well over two years and his enemies would always be running in a vain attempt to catch up.

Life for the surviving prisoners in the castle and city, of course, could only worsen, day on day; and it did. He, his fellow Generals and the soldiers they commanded were nothing but brutal: rape, beatings and murder occurring daily.

*

Jerryn suffered a great conflict of emotions when the news from the hamlet of Applegarth reached the palace. He felt proud that, even injured, Ethrayne had tried to escape; yet he was shocked and appalled that the General had struck her and knocked her down, and the description of her injured leg and bruising worried him, for how on Iullyn was she going to manage, riding south, virtually crippled?

He had left his father's office with a bleak expression and had made his way directly to the practice hall, to be met by Captain Cheyrn, one of the men who had supervised Ethrayne's combat training.

"You don't look happy, your Highness." He said sympathetically. "Has there been more bad news?"

Jerryn related the news in as few words as possible, then sighed and shook his head. "But she *tried* to escape, I'm so proud of her!"

"Aye, Lady Ethrayne is brave, there's no denying it." Cheyrn agreed and smiled. "And we were fearing that every settlement in the area had been destroyed; so that is very good news too, your Highness: that not every village has been overrun."

"But how on Iullyn can we protect the region, Captain?" He asked darkly. "We have no idea how many soldiers are now based in Clirensar, or how good their route is to and from their lands to the south; there could be many thousands of men ranged against us and we're so very far from being organised for war!"

"Yet we will be, your Highness." The Captain replied. "Come on, leave your worries for a while: have a bout of practice; hey, Catron!"

"Well, if nothing else, Captain, we'll all be amazingly fit and expert fighters by spring." Jerryn said with a sigh.

"Whatever it takes to kill the bastards, your Highness." Cheyrn agreed fiercely.

*

The razine had explained the cyclical current that, each spring in the northern hemisphere, changed direction to sweep in a most useful arc down past the east coast of the Selithian continent before it turned eastward some distance north of Rothern, heading far out into the ocean before it swung back north. Pualyn had found the concept fascinating. Unfortunately, it did not work in the other direction, south to north, and it generally only lasted for a moon and a half, until about the middle of Thurton.

The voyage from Orbain was consequently faster than their outward journey from Rothern had been, but time on board the ship still seemed to stop; the temperature around them warming up as they approached the equator and then cooling steadily as they sped south on the river that miraculously ran amid the very ocean. Vhisson was drawing down.

Pualyn found that he was more homesick now than at any point since he had left Rothern, although he knew that it was completely irrational. He and Lennarn spent as much time as possible on deck when the weather was good enough, at least, talking of home, both of Tenarum generally and Clirensar specifically.

His companions, especially the High-King and the High-Prince were excellent company, however; he was pleased to be associated with such knowledgeable and well-placed people and to be able to hold his own in conversation with them. But, many times a day, he found himself watching for the first sign of land, that would prove that they were nearly 'home' and the distant glimpse of grey-brown-green close to the horizon, twenty days out from Lerat, was heartening. The captain then angled carefully south-westward out of the current and they sailed on at a more normal speed, subject to the world's winds, closing gradually on the uneven coastline until they were heading southward at a rough distance of ten miles from land, towns and villages barely visible across the sea.

*

<*Sire! Ah, it is good to know that you are nearly here!*> Bahlien's voice rang in Mhezal's head, one night as the ship continued south-west from the visible coast of Jaece. <*Please forgive me for disturbing your rest -.*> His tone sounded very distant, rather muffled. Such communication over so many leagues was impossible for most razine, for it took a great deal of effort, both physical and mental, to achieve; and managing it across the ocean was even more difficult, for some reason.

<*What has happened, old friend?*> The High King cut through the old Archpriest's apology. <*You would never contact me just for a chat when we will reach Rothern in a few days, if the winds blow right, anyway!*> The winds had been blowing straight out of the south since the day before, seriously slowing their advance.

<The *enemy took Clirensar. General Tequan has captured Clirensar. He slaughtered the duke and duchess twenty-one days ago and Lady Ethrayne was abducted; she will probably be in Ban'Lerracon by now!*> Bahlien

announced coldly, but Mhezal could feel the emotions that he was containing, and very similar emotions suddenly boiled up within himself.

<*Oh, hell take them all!*> He spat back, sitting up in his bed quickly. <*May the Betrayer's balls wither and his teeth fall out! Damn it all, Bahlien!*>

<*She was travelling back hone with her family and Pualyn's betrothed; those usual conventions of society: the weddings of both couples were due before the prince's birthday . . . How could I or anyone know or expect that an entire army seems to have sneaked out of Zanezli? There is nothing in the Book of Days; no warnings; no dreams . . . Absolutely bloody nothing!*> The old razine was the closest to despair that the High-King had ever sensed. <*I am so, so sorry. I have failed you all! So many have died!*>

Mhezal began to swear graphically. <*Those bastards! Those evil -! The Am'maiya should have been safe, by anyone's logic! So young; so inexperienced; so-so innocent!*> He abruptly sighed deeply, discarding the insults against the enemy as useless. <*You want me to break the news to Pualyn, I imagine.*> It was not a question.

<*Please, Mhezal, if you will; and emphasise that Lady Lyria is safe, although most of her family is suspected to have been murdered as they dwelled close to Clirensar. There is one remaining brother in the Tenarean army whom they have contacted. The King, Prince Jerryn, Lady Lyria and I will head for Rothern first thing tomorrow to meet you . . . I can't believe that I've been so remiss -.*>

<*Do not blame yourself, Bahlien. If there were no warning, old friend, how could anyone suspect such a turn of events? I will go and wake our new duke to give him the terrible news.*>

*

Pualyn was sound asleep when the cabin door was rapped upon and opened; he and Lennarn awoke quickly, staring up at the frowning, globe-lit visage of the High-King in the doorway.

"I am sorry to disturb you, Pualyn, but can you both come to the main cabin as soon as possible? I'll get Kerr; it'll be best to get this all done in one go." He sighed and left the strange form of light to hover by the ceiling.

The two men exchanged glances as the High-King left, his footfalls clear on the planks and each swung his legs out of his bunk, wondering what could have happened in the middle of the night, in the middle of the ocean. Quickly and quietly they rose and reached for their clothes. In a short while, yawning, they had made their way to the main cabin where Mhezal was standing by the liquor cupboard built into one wall, pouring four large goblets of wine. The High-Prince entered the cabin on Lennarn's heels as they made for seats around the table; he was straightening his shirt with one hand, scratching at his head with the other.

"What has happened, Father?" He asked bluntly, walking across the room to pick up two goblets and handing them to the men with a flourish before sitting down. "Good morning, gentlemen." He said with a tense, brief smile before yawning widely.

"Archpriest Bahlien just reached me, speaking mind to mind." Mhezal stated, the other two goblets in his hands as he took the remaining seat, thrusting one at Kerrenan. "There . . . there have been developments . . . events. Oh, damn it all to hell! There's no good way to say it!" And the urbane, poised, dignified High-King of the Razine Protectorates cursed crudely before taking a gulp of wine. "Pualyn, I am most sincerely sorry, but your honoured parents are dead -."

"What?" The young man leapt to his feet, his goblet falling, wine spraying outwards to soak him. "No! No, surely not!"

"Forgive me, my Lord, but it is so: your parents have been murdered." Mhezal looked up at the agitated man with sympathy and pain.

"Oh, dear Arven, no! But, how? What on Iullyn has happened?" Pualyn asked brokenly, his hands gripping the back of the chair, his knuckles white as he tried to hold in the rage that was rising relentlessly within him.

"A jajozeli army somehow took Clirensar. Your family was riding home and were intercepted on the edge of the Vale." Mhezal said.

"Lyria?" He quavered. "Oh, dear Arven, is Lyria -?"

"Your Lady is safe, my Lord; she was released to notify the king of what occurred. Lady Lyria is safe and unharmed . . . Ethrayne . . . your sister was captured by the jajozeli. I . . . I am sorry to have to tell you –."

"Oh -." And Kerrenan, stunned, released a whole river of curses in what seemed a variety of languages, finishing in gutter selithian; foul, but to the point.

"Exactly." Pualyn nodded to the High-Prince. "That is just what I mean. Thank you, your Highness . . . Oh, dear Arven -." He shook his head helplessly, then sank back down into his chair and hid his face in trembling hands.

"Forgive me, my Lord, we we will leave you . . . But if you wish to talk, please do -."

"Just- just go!" Pualyn interrupted the High-King abruptly. "Please."

*

The wind continued to blow contrarily, and it was mid-morning five days later when the Lerat Pearl finally approached the wharves of Rothern. The passengers stood together out of the way on the main deck as the captain brought them in, the crew busy at their allotted tasks; Pualyn stood apart from the others, only a foot or so away, but every part of him evidence that he considered himself separate, his face set, his eyes dark.

The terrible news and all its ramifications haunted him. Wearing the darkest clothes that were in his wardrobe, with the heavy envoy's surcoat bright when the sunshine broke through the gusting clouds, he fought against anger at practically everyone, including himself, and the accompanying fear and despair. He had avoided the three others since the High-King had imparted the terrible news. He had hardly slept, or eaten a bite; pacing the deck in all weathers, or staring out over the rail, trying to make some sense of it all . . . He was just grateful that Lennarn and the razine were leaving him alone and that they were not offended.

There were armed soldiers down on the dockside below as the ship moved slowly to the edge of the stonework; the ropes were cast down and tied to the great metal posts. Pualyn noted the number of them, men bearing the standards of both Tenarum and Clirensar, the flags cracking in the wind. He also saw King Marrand, Jerryn, the Archpriests and Lyria, her hair shining in the flashes of sunlight. She and the rest of them wore black; elegant, correct, but also forbidding. Her hair was plaited neatly under her hood. She looked beautiful, but awfully pale and his heart leapt with both fear and his love for her.

Sailors set down the ramp to the solid flagstones and stepped quickly aside as Lyria hurried up the slope and onto the deck with totally uncharacteristic haste and threw herself into her beloved's arms.

"Oh, Pualyn!" She cried out and started to sob, burying her face in his shoulder.

"Lyria, my darling. Please excuse me, your Majesty, Highness -." Pualyn said with natural awkwardness to Marrand and Jerryn who had followed the young woman, holding her tenderly.

"It is starting to rain; please bring your lady below, your Grace; I think it would be better for you all to speak together out of the weather." Lennarn suggested with a light cough and a low bow. "Please, your Majesty, follow me."

"That's a good idea, Lennarn." Marrand agreed, glancing up with a slight frown at the clouds above. "Good morning, sirs." He politely greeted the pair of tall razine males who led the way and followed Lennarn, glancing quickly back to see Pualyn easily supporting Lyria, with Jerryn behind, his face solemn.

The main cabin below the deck was a little cramped, holding so many people and their titles, but there were seats enough as Pualyn helped Lyria to one by the bank of windows, as she fished for a handkerchief to wipe her face and blow her nose.

"Please forgive me, your Majesty -." She began a meek apology.

"My dear Lyria! We would join you in weeping, but convention prevents it." Marrand said quickly, grimacing. "You are distraught -."

"Do please sit down, gentlemen. Perhaps the lady and yourselves might enjoy a restorative glass of wine, your Majesty?" The tall, grey haired razine suggested smoothly. "Let convention go hang, I am Mhezal, my son, Kerr – Kerrenan. We grieve deeply for your loss. It is simply evil!"

"Indeed, your Majesty, thank you." Marrand bowed his head politely. "Mhezal, I am Marrand, this is Jerryn, my son and Pualyn's betrothed, Lyria. Oh, dear Arven, Pualyn, forgive us. If we had had any inkling . . . Your father had been in Clirensar less than a moon before the attack! I am so sorry!"

Pualyn felt his insides roil with conflicting emotion and straightened, quickly wiping his face as he did so and breathed deeply in, out and in again. "There has been enough grief and sorrow, your Majesties." He said decisively. "Now we must make plans in earnest to repair the damage the enemy has caused . . . But I must confess I can't think of anything useful at all -." His voice cracked slightly, betraying him.

"I am sure that, together, we can all come up with something workable, your Grace." Jerryn laid his hand on his friend's upper arm for a moment. "We've had some days to get used to this, whilst your head will be spinning, and you won't really believe it yet." His tone was rueful, and he shrugged. "I was denying it for ages, Pualyn."

"That's very prescient, Jerryn, it's pretty much exactly what I feel." The younger razine stated, essaying a false smile as he handed around small goblets of wine. "And for those of us with some talent, such feelings can be dangerous."

"I wouldn't know, Kerrenan. All this chaos has just made any control I had weaker than ever!" Jerryn's tone was slightly bitter.

"Yes, it will, Am'maiya. Shock is a problem, but you are expecting too much from yourself too fast -."

"Archpriest Bahlien said so, but I can only think of Ethrayne, alone with them -." His voice cracked, he shuddered and Pualyn groaned a curse. "I've got to be able to do *something*!"

"We will work with you and your abilities, Am'maiya, do not despair." Kerrenan assured him gravely. "Soon enough it will seem natural to you, easy, I am sure."

"The High-Prince is correct, Jerryn. You must not let your fears command you, however hard that is to achieve." Archpriest Lurco advised him with a sigh.

"It's simply impossible, your Grace." Jerryn admitted. "I keep trying, but uselessly."

"These circumstances are definitely not how we wished to meet you, Marrand." The High-King said. "We can only hope and pray that we, as part of the Protectorates, can provide useful assistance; we must prepare for war." He frowned. "I have warned the priests in Horann, as we sailed – using my power of course. By now, the news will be winging across the kingdoms."

"Yes, thank you, seems a useful gift. War is something the kingdoms of Selith know almost nothing about." The King of Tenarum replied with a shrug. "But the enthusiasm of our volunteer soldiers has been very heartening, I admit."

"Enthusiasm will count, I am sure, along with dedication and simple hard work." Mhezal was being very polite indeed, to match the gravity of the situation, glancing quickly at the younger people grouped closer together, Jerryn sat at an angle from Pualyn and Lyria, who were hand in hand. "If your people are all as earnest and hardworking as Duke Pualyn, you are blessed,

Marrand; he has been a most conscientious envoy, a true asset."

"Thank you, Mhezal." Marrand said gratefully. "Shall we disembark, gentlemen, my Lady?" He raised his voice slightly. "The quicker we return to Tenum City, the quicker we can start acting."

*

The Royal Barge was swiftly loaded with baggage and passengers and the crew set off rowing upstream; as the nobles and priests sat quietly, Pualyn learnt from Lyria just what had happened on that awful afternoon. It was not pleasant, least of all for the young woman who had had to repeat the tale far too many times for comfort. Yet, viewing this as her duty, she fulfilled it admirably, sustained by the fact that this was probably the last time that she would be forced to relive that terrifying period. After her narration, they spoke of everything and anything but that event, as the afternoon passed.

On the fourth day out from Rothern, they reached the wide docks of the capital, the two kings and their sons now as close friends as the razine and Pualyn had been, and the new duke and Lyria were almost inseparable, brought even closer by their mutual grief and loss.

Pualyn didn't talk of it but found that he spent a great deal of time repeating in his head what Lyria had told him of the attack and murder of his parents and the abduction of Ethrayne, hurting acutely, but somehow proving that he was alive. He still found it hard to believe, however: thousands were dead! His ancestral home in enemy hands! His sister imprisoned somewhere in the uncharted vastness of Zanezli, surrounded by enemies. And he, he was Duke of Clirensar! Fury seethed within him, mixed equally with icy fear, for it was only by some fluke or quirk of wholly uncharacteristic mercy on the jajozelis' part, he knew, that Lyria and Tally had been spared to travel to Tenum City. The thought of them standing there, frozen in terror as the violence streamed all around them, of long blades and far too much blood haunted his dreams, although he did his best to disguise his nightmares and was very attentive to Lyria.

Watching them, as the young duke handed his lady into the carriage at the wharf at the riverside in Tenum City, Mhezel, Bahlien and Marrand exchanged benevolent smiles.

I hope that the wedding is planned, Marrand." Mhezal said drily.

"Indeed, your Majesty, in ten days." Marrand confirmed with a sigh. "There are a few formalities, of course, but once they're out of the way, they can wed. Arven knows we need something to smile about, before we start planning war."

The greeting of the court to their razine guests was a little muted, of course and limited to a fine banquet in the great hall, which was all to their taste. Pualyn was tied up with the Council for a greater part of every day following, along with their royal guests, working through the official confirmation of his status as Sarant's heir, followed by his investiture; and then the framework of the alliance between Tenarum and the Protectorates was couched in the formal language of the scribes, as the young duke became slowly used to sitting where his father had been sat for all his life.

But still, quietly, beneath the surface, fury and the urge to unleash violence upon their enemies seethed within him.

Lennarn woke the duke early, on the appointed day of their wedding, bullying him with threats of a cold bath and no breakfast, which made Pualyn smile a little; a rare expression anywhere within the palace, these days.

Lyria wore a magnificent pale lavender gown that, highlighted with delicate lace, set off her betrothal amethysts to the best effect whilst the serious Pualyn was stern but handsome in black and white, plain and unadorned. Archpriest Lurco married them in the traditional ceremony in the heart of the Cathedral, watched by dignitaries from the palace and residents from the Vale of Clirensar who had, by good fortune and business, been absent from the city when Clirensar was attacked. The traditional kiss between bride and groom raised a cheer that echoed through the vast, ancient space.

Archpriest Lurco stepped back and King Marrand took his place as Lyria was invested as the Duchess of Clirensar and Sarant's son was ceremonially presented with his father's ancient sword, newly cleaned and polished, and the highly embroidered formal surcoat. Together, duke and duchess swore fealty to their king and yet more cheers were raised to the vaulted ceiling.

The following banquet was a political event more than a true celebration, for neither Lyria nor Pualyn were comfortable with mirth and gaiety, although they understood that many around them needed the excuse for frivolity. All the laughter was a little brittle and the wine and ale provided, drunk so enthusiastically, were watered.

At the high table, conversations were carefully managed, deliberately light, but nevertheless sincere. As the new duke and duchess left the great hall, the wishes for a long, happy marriage and many children were shouted along with the traditional scattering of grain and flower petals. Finally, after processing past nearly every servant in the palace who all wished them good fortune, they entered their newly appointed suite in the west wing and were alone.

* * *

CHAPTER 24

Ethrayne and her captors had ridden hard since leaving N'Astoln at daybreak, following that gash in the ground beside the road which showed exactly where the massive army had passed, a depressing reminder of the fact of the invasion into Tenarum. The three Generals and their prisoner climbed upwards through a wide area of farmland in which the arable fields now lay ready for ploughing in the spring, their produce long-since harvested, whilst large cattle, pigs and horses occupied others, passing sheltering belts of wind-swept pine trees and wider stretches of scrubby coniferous woodland that gradually gave way to the heights of the vast, bleak, treeless slope, the steppes she had seen from a distance; this was covered with heather, reeds and rank grass, with an occasional scrawny, misshaped pine tree visible, sheltering within a dubious fold of land, a grotesque caricature of true trees in this strange, cold, unfriendly land, so completely different to what they had travelled through on their way to N'Astoln. The land climbed steadily, upwards towards the mountains. The vista behind, to the north, was indistinct amid low cloud, however, as Ethrayne glanced back once towards Tenarum.

The girl had been inwardly pleased with her returning stamina; although her left ankle still ached acutely after her impromptu combat session that morning, she had felt rested and was well able to keep up with the pace demanded by the Generals. After her horrible weakness on the previous stage of her journey, this was a definite bonus, although she still wished she had been able to escape them. Ethrayne tried to ignore her powerlessness and the increasing discomfort of her bound wrists, but the rope was increasingly feeling like it was cutting into her flesh and she could only pray that they would remove it eventually.

Now, after riding relentlessly with hardly a halt, the sun was hovering just a finger's breadth above the horizon behind their right shoulders as the unknown General, now leading, headed into a crinkle of a valley that had been hidden amid the featureless plateau. Ethrayne frowned as her horse came up behind the others, for she had not expected to see anything much, and certainly not the building she could see ahead, which was, strangely, roofed with grass. The walls of the structure were of fieldstone, a single- storey building some hundred feet wide nestled against a rising slope to the south, with two windows either side of one dark door, whilst a second set of wider, double doors was positioned further to the right. The Generals rode on and halted on a bricked surface which covered the ground before the building.

"Dismount." The black-haired General ordered curtly. It was the first time since leaving the fort that any of them had spoken to her. "Can you cook, girl?" He demanded.

"Cook? Dear Arven, no, sir!" Ethrayne replied earnestly and truthfully as she swung her leg over the saddle, wincing as she stepped down, hampered by her bound, aching wrists but determined not to complain, not yet.

"My name is General Garrtnor, brat." He said mildly, stepping up to untie the rope on her wrists with a look that clearly dared her to speak when he coiled it and stowed the rope in a pocket. As surreptitiously as she could, Ethrayne rubbed at her wrists, trying not to react. "So, make yourself useful and take the horses through there -." He pointed to the double doors. "Unsaddle them, water them and feed them. Go!" He dropped the reins of his mount negligently, then strode to the packhorses and started lifting off bags and bundles.

Ethrayne stared at him for a moment, but when the other two Generals simply went to assist him with unloading, she frowned slightly and started gathering the reins of the horses together, her swollen hands feeling oddly heavy at first, pins-and-needles stinging, loosened from the constraining rope, rubbing them again whilst she waited for the animals to be unburdened before claiming them. She moved forward carefully, so thankful that her ankle was only aching dully now, but the looseness of the boots on her feet was uncomfortable, inhibiting her stride. Her wrists then began to hurt much more, she found, throbbing as her other injuries had done; they had been rubbed red raw where the rope had chafed, with some bruising and swelling after this long confinement. Frowning, she carefully flexed her hands and fingers, a flash of anger slightly counteracting her discomfort and upset.

They had ridden out of N'Astoln alone, with three packhorses and four extra mounts; there were no soldiers to undertake the chores of setting up camp, so perhaps she should have expected to be called upon to help; Ethrayne didn't expect that a refusal would be accepted, although she certainly did not want to cooperate with them. So long as they didn't insist that she cooked!

The wind was cold, blowing down from the heights to the south, the sky darkening from the east as clouds blew back in and Ethrayne shivered, taking up the lead rope of the pack-horses and guiding all of them towards the double doors, wondering what was behind them and keen to get out of the weather, heading up a shallow ramp, reaching up to struggle to unlatch the left-hand door which swung outwards to reveal a dim area beyond -.

"Oh, you'll need some light, I suppose." Cavaln said coolly from the doorway to her left, moving one hand slightly; Ethrayne shivered, feeling the woman's power flare, and a globe of light appeared from empty air to hover a couple of feet above her head, pale, but useful, stationery despite the wind.

"Thank you." She thought she must be polite after Ackat's warning, the rope which had bound her. Heading into the space, Ethrayne found herself walking into a rectangular stable with a blocky, smooth brick floor and a vaulted ceiling, somewhat over thirty feet wide and leading away into darkness, as the globe of light moved above her obligingly, revealing lines of stalls to left and right, behind empty benches above which were nails for tack, some common equipment and other familiar things arranged neatly.

"Well!" She allowed, pushing the lead horses off to the right whilst she guided the rest in behind them, pulling the wide door shut with surprising ease. The horses were a bit nervous, but she was well-used to dealing with the animals, so her confidence was more than a match for them, even though her hands felt heavy and cumbersome; she removed tack, her own baggage, saddles and so on easily enough, glad to stretch herself after being stuck in the saddle all day, then was busy hauling water to long troughs from the creaky pump at the rear of the stable, locating feed in stooks and great metal bins: hay and oats, stored against vermin. It was easy, repetitive work that didn't require any hard thought and she moved through the tasks as slowly as possible: horses were much better company than three Generals! They were just unbearable. She dreaded having to join them and seriously considered mounting a horse and setting off north into the night, now that she could walk again!

But common-sense was reasserted even as she thought it: she was already deep within Zanezli; she suspected that the Generals could sense her just as much as she could sense their power, so she probably wouldn't get more than a mile; also, most pressing, she had no food or water and, the most pertinent point was that they would naturally be alert in case she tried anything reckless. The way they watched her made her skin crawl. Sighing deeply, Ethrayne wondered whether to ride away anyway, before completely abandoning the idea: her bare head and the bruises on her wrists certainly warned her of the inadvisability of defiance. Ackat's curt warning earlier, his cold violence at Clirensar and their skill with weapons, as well as their power thrilling through her nerves told her that such action would be utterly stupid.

Slowly she continued her work and when the eleven beasts were settled, she sorted out the tack and saddles, laying them all neat ready for morning, just as she had done for years, helping at South Vale Farm . . . The memory hurt.

Finally, however, she had done everything; she couldn't linger there with the horses forever, although she wanted to, with all her heart. Carrying her bags over one shoulder, Ethrayne emerged from the stable and carefully closed the door, the ball of light still lighting her way into a blast of cold, rain-laden wind which caused her to shiver; the globe faded gradually in the air above her to vanish, leaving the small valley dark, but for squares of lamplight that spilled out from the windows of the building the Generals had entered . . . Now and again on the wind she could smell wood smoke, a fire. Taking a breath, garnering her courage, she tried to ignore the next blast of chilly, wet wind that threw back the hood of her cloak and seemed to freeze her bald head and headed reluctantly towards the dark doorway, climbing the three sturdy steps and lifting the latch, slipping inside -.

"Finally. I thought you were going to stand outside all night." Black-haired Garrtnor remarked from where he leaned over a fireplace in the right-hand wall, stirring a large, steaming pot. "Come over here. Sit down."

"My Lord General." Ethrayne murmured, closing the door before quickly scanning the space. It was wider than the stable, but just as deep, a nearly square room with doors at the rear, and large fireplaces in both side walls. There were folded-back shutters on either side of the windows. The lighting of one fire had filled the room with warmth and interesting smells from whatever was cooking. Light globes floated near the ceiling, providing plenty of light. Along the walls around both fireplaces were shelves, some holding boxes, whilst there were piles of long grey fat bags, which she supposed were thin mattresses for sleeping; otherwise, there were four large tables, two near each fireplace, with chairs, some benches and stools, but the room was bare, otherwise. Ackat and Cavaln were sat at one table, cloaks removed and hanging on hooks that hung from the wall, with a wine bag close to hand, both watching her closely and, yet again, she felt a touch of fear.

"Didn't you hear me?"

The girl shivered at the edge in Garrtnor's voice and quickly crossed the space to sink down deliberately at the empty table, dropping her bags underneath it as the three Generals all stared at her, their power assaulting her senses.

Garrtnor stirred the pot again then turned his back on the fire and strode over to sit down opposite her, whilst Cavaln rose to take his place minding their dinner. Ethrayne felt cold, even though she now was too hot in her cloak and fumbled to unfasten it, trying to disguise her dismay -.

"I have some questions for you and I strongly suggest that you answer honestly: we jajozeli-razine can usually tell when people are lying, you see, and you know that we do not suffer fools at all." Garrtnor said, grasping one of her hands and pulling her arm outwards, so that her wrist was free of the over-long sleeve, clearly showing the bruised, red marks of the rope.

"Yes, my Lord General." She acknowledged unwillingly, pulling her hand back quickly when he released it, folding her hands together down in her lap.

"That little episode you instigated this morning." The General continued, as of course he would refer to, she thought, her heart sinking. "It was a very interesting diversion; most entertaining, actually. But do you even realise that the soldier was insulting you in jajozeli, not selithian?"

Ethrayne listened to his words, but could not take them in at first, they just swirled, senseless, in her head, which she shook. "No. No, he wasn't." She disagreed confidently, it was ridiculous!

"Was he not? Would you care to stake something valuable on that, Wielder of the Flame?" Ackat asked in a low voice.

Ethrayne stared at him in consternation. He had spoken in his own language and she had understood him! That was – impossible! "I . . ."

"You understand my colleague and I, don't you?" Garrtnor pressed her, also speaking jajozeli.

"I . . . y-yes, my Lord General, I do." Ethrayne admitted unwillingly, her voice barely a whisper.

"Considering the fact that you have only known of our existence for a few moons, child, I find it hard to believe that you have so quickly learned our language?" Garrtnor turned it into a question, his eyes dark in his calm, expressionless face.

"I. No-no I'm not -." She forced out the words, hoping for deliverance in some ridiculous way. "I mean . . . no one taught me to speak . . . Well, I-I don't think anyone in Tenarum even knows your tongue -." She broke off as General Cavaln snorted and flinched at the glare that Garrtnor was now directing at her, quickly burying her face in her hands, trying to make sense of it. Dear Arven, when would she stop cringing from them? "Oh, damn you!" She muttered, forcing her hands away, making herself look up at them as some sort of understanding unexpectedly rose inside her.

"Stop dithering and explain." The General urged, but his tone was still calm and quiet, seemingly unbothered by her hesitation, whereas she realised that Ackat would probably have lost all patience with her, and likely would be shouting. "Tell me girl, then you can eat and rest."

Which was probably the best offer she could expect; it was a very long time since breakfast. Still, Ethrayne was afraid to speak, the silence continuing despite the crackling of the fire and the sound of the spoon stirring the stew pot.

"I-I suppose it must have been the morning after . . . after the massacre above Clirensar, after I had escaped. When General Ackat -." She finally said in a mere whisper, her hands clasped quietly in her lap. "B-but I don't know -."

"General Ackat?" Garrtnor prompted.

Quickly, Ethrayne looked up and away, his gaze was cold, measuring, and alarming.

"When I would have killed that idiot, interfering farmer?" Ackat asked with interest, but Garrtnor jumped to his feet.

"Quiet, Ackat, *she* tells us." He snapped, a strange excitement in his voice; his face, when Ethrayne glanced up for a moment, was cruel, despite his shining eyes. "Speak."

"I . . . annoyed General Ackat, escaping, and he-he swung his sword to kill Master Kethar . . . I-I don't know what I did or how, how I stopped him . . . it felt so peculiar and General Ackat dropped his sword . . . They both discussed it later that night, he and General Cavaln; something about power. I did not understand . . . I wasn't sure if they were speaking selithian, now, but I thought they were. Perhaps they spoke jajozeli, I don't know . . . I'm sorry, I don't understand . . . my Lord General." She added lamely and lapsed into silence, staring fixedly at the battered edge of the tabletop.

She tensed when both males got to their feet and heard them stride towards the outer door; there was a blast of cold air when it opened and then the door was closed, leaving her alone with General Cavaln.

Oh, dear Arven, I feel awful! She thought miserably, pulling the thick cloak back around herself, fighting sudden tears, sick of worry and fear and, somehow, she battled the tears to her relief, resting her face in her cold hands.

"Here, eat." Cavaln said after a while and laid a metal plate and mug on the table before her and handing her a spoon when she looked up, startled.

Fear had wiped out her hunger again, but Ethrayne obeyed anyway, eating the meal through necessity, without enjoyment.

*

The Generals threw up a couple of light globes as they strode towards the stables, thankfully escaping from the night, for the weather had deteriorated since their arrival. They scanned the space and Garrtnor leaned back against one of the benches, frowning at his colleague.

"She's left the stables neat enough." Ackat said approvingly, noting the lean lines of tack, the carefully fastened food bags and bins. "Still, her father ran one of the best studs I've seen anywhere, she clearly knows the work. I think Tequan wants to get the rest of the breeding stock south as quickly as possible -."

"I'm not interested in bloody horses, Ackat." Garrtnor stated crisply. "I want to know how a little girl of, what? Sixteen? How she could instinctively raise power enough to block you and gain a complete and instant understanding of our language, with no training." His tone was tense. "She's only human, after all."

"Well, she is the Wielder of the Flame." The blond jajozeli razine replied and reddened noticeably as he realised how ridiculous his statement had been. "Unnecessary, I know."

"Quite." Garrtnor said and sighed. "Lord Governor Doreth told us that it would be wise to capture one or both of the young people before the razine could begin to train them, that their mental and physical maturity were some years in the future: they are, after all, not razine. So, either both he and our revered emperor are talking out of their arses, which I doubt. Or what is going on here?"

"I wouldn't like to guess, Garrtnor." Ackat shook his head. "She's been an annoying little brat, I told you. Yet, considering how injured she was when we captured her – and she could have seriously crippled herself, trying to escape whilst under the influence of Settalyin – she was completely helpless. Yet she has healed faster than we've expected: it's been less than fifteen days and she doesn't even walk with much of a limp now. She's recovered her spirit quickly. She also threatened Tequan above the city, promised to kill him and there was power behind her words: it wasn't an idle threat. And her parents were dead on the ground only feet away . . . She's certainly not your usual sixteen-year-old."

"Mmm. Well, it's a good job you scared her by just cutting off her hair, rather than punishing her any other way, else pure fear and no training might have proved deadly even for you!" Garrtnor noted dryly. "She acted on instinct alone; perhaps her fear proved a focus, it does happen. We've got to get her to Ban'Lerracon quickly: I'll feel much happier and secure when the girl is safely locked away."

"You'll get no argument from me there." Ackat agreed. "She's certainly starting to get interesting, now she isn't crippled."

"We all will emphasise the threat of violence, it should keep her mindful of her place. Hopefully, we won't have to administer it."

The two Generals came back into the main room as Ethrayne was finishing her mug of tea and she watched surreptitiously as they brushed water out of their hair in the doorway, their faces grave. She felt the meal she had eaten sitting heavily in her stomach.

"It's an unpleasant night out there." Garrtnor stated, moving towards the fire. "Let's eat."

Cavaln was already ladling stew onto plates, adding hot water to tea leaves. "Back already?" She asked coldly.

"What's up with you, Cavaln?" Ackat asked innocently, picking up a plate and spoon. "Thanks."

"The honourable Lady General probably feels disgruntled, acting as your prisoner's nursemaid and guard rather than being considered a full member of your so exclusive elite." Ethrayne found herself replying without consciously thinking about the ramifications of her words; the words were correct, as far as she was aware, for she could sense the older woman's inner anger with surprising clarity. Part of her feared that they would take offence; she was relieved when they all looked surprised at her words and she was startled when Garrtnor chuckled slightly. Was this certainty connected to her ability to speak jajozeli? She wondered. "And since we are many leagues inside your realm, and the three of you alone could probably defeat an army, surely you don't need to guard me so closely, sir."

"Thank you *so* much for your valued input, child." Ackat said, deliberately sitting beside her at the table and Cavaln and Garrtnor followed him, so that she was surrounded by them, her dismay obvious.

"When we want your opinion, girl, we'll ask for it, else hold your tongue." Garrtnor added. "Have you had enough to eat?" He glanced from her face to her plate and back again. "And since you so masterfully speak our language, discard that clumsy selithian, speak jajozeli."

"Yes, my Lord General." She acceded unwillingly after a pause in which she deliberately pushed her chair backwards away from the table, the syllables sounding and feeling strange in her mouth, in addition to an adjustment in her thinking to accommodate the change of language.

"Well, Cavaln, since you were wondering, we were discussing this surprisingly disrespectful brat and we've decided to head to Ban'Lerracon with all speed." Garrtnor said with a grin. "The weather is against us, for sure, but at least we don't have to cross too many mountains to get there."

"Thank you for your confidence, Garrtnor." Cavaln said drily, sitting back in her chair, sipping her tea. "It's only Thurton, we'll get through with no trouble, I'm sure."

"You've only been in Zanezli half a year or so, and you'll be surprised just how uncooperative the weather can be here: even in Thurton, the roads can be blocked by winter storms. You had better behave, girl." Garrtnor glared at the prisoner. “Keep your opinions to yourself, understand?”

It was bad enough having to endure their presence and their needling, but it was somehow worse in jajozeli, Ethrayne decided then. Pale faced, she picked up her mug, went over to the fire to fill it with more hot water and fresh tea leaves, then quickly turned away from the three. The proximity of the Generals was playing havoc with her nerves; she wished she dared flee back to the stables but supposed they wouldn’t allow it.

“Don’t go far, brat, you’re washing up.” Cavaln sent after her with a cool laugh.

Ethrayne shot an uneasy glance at them as she moved away across the empty room towards the rear where the closed doors broke up the wall, leaving her cloak and bags where they were; she was startled when one of the globes seemed to follow her, reducing the deep shadows when she opened the left hand door that led, she discovered, to a well-designed set of privies and a wash room, where a large copper was stood above a empty fireplace, so hot water would be available. That room was very usefully equipped, she thought, washing her face and hands with cold water afterwards. The next three doors led to separate bedrooms; none were large, but they were equipped with fireplaces, beds, empty shelves, a small table and chair.

Thinking about it, Ethrayne guessed that these private rooms were probably for leaders, when a group of soldiers were staying here. She briefly considered bringing her bags in and staying in one of the rooms alone, but the rooms were cold, and she didn’t really want to start an argument with the Generals; she supposed that it wouldn’t take much for them to decide to tie her up again or something equally unnecessary.

Sitting down briefly on the unmade bed in the last chilly room, Ethrayne considered her situation here. She certainly didn’t want to obey the Generals, after Cavaln’s order to wash up for them like a servant, but they just filled her with fear and she certainly didn’t feel secure enough to argue; they were all taller than she, stronger, armed and much, much nastier with the power of their master to back them up. And she found the realisation that she somehow had instantly gained the entire jajozeli language, as part of her power, to be equally encouraging and alarming – she had never believed Bahlien’s assurance of her advancing ability.

Emerging from the bedroom and closing the door quietly, she realised just how cosy the main room was, even with just the one fire lit. Slowly she went over to the pile of bed pads, dragged one off and carried it over to the left-hand side of the fire close to the wall, out of the way of the Generals who were talking quietly and ignoring her presence now, passing the wine skin between them. Dutifully, she checked the pot of water by the edge of the fire; it was certainly hot enough for purpose and she used her too-long sleeves to lift it carefully to the large stone sink in the corner to the right, against the front wall, checking; there was scouring sand in a pot beside it, standing on a small shelf.

“We might teach her some humility yet.” Ackat noted with a harsh laugh. "She was worse than useless all the days to N'Astoln, Garrtnor!"

"She was injured, Ackat, she couldn't even stand up alone." Cavaln noted. "Perhaps now she is learning her place."

"Excellent, children should be obedient." Garrtnor answered lightly. "I'm glad to find that Tenarean brats can be useful."

Ethrayne ignored their words, their auras, their clear menace. Quickly she pulled off the jacket, folded up the sleeves on the tunic to keep them dry. Washing up didn't take too long, although the hot water and the sand left her hands and wrists smarting and throbbing. Then, leaving the metal plates and mugs to drain, she politely apologised to the Generals for disturbing them, darting between Garrtnor and Ackat to quickly grab her things and move them to the thin pad, where she folded up the red felted jacket for a pillow; she pulled off the boots, set them aside neatly along with her travel bags and unfolded the blankets. It took only a moment to make a bed and she lay down and turned away, ignoring the Generals, pulling the blankets up almost over her face; she was tired, alone and scared. It was a long time before she slept, and she shivered, but not with cold: for the hundredth time, it seemed, she remembered the awful attack above Clirensar and her father's death . . . the shrill screams of the soldiers dying . . . seeing his and her mother's bodies, bloodied and lifeless.

*

Ethrayne dreamed that she was walking through a vast, pillared hall unlike any other she had even imagined, seemingly built of ice or glass: walls, columns and an amazingly vaulted roof in various shades of crystal-clear stuff, opaque white and many shades of blue, beautiful but stark. She was walking alone, silently, across a floor of opaque white that looked rather like fine marble tiles but when she paused, looking down, her gaze was caught, and she stared, awed- for just below the surface of the floor seemed to be delineated a map the size of the hall itself. From somewhere came the knowledge that this was a representation of Iullyn which was far more detailed than she could ever have imagined. It seemed that she stood directly far above a gleaming blue ocean between continents of varied greens and browns, mountains rising steeply, with small islands scattered like pebbles in the sea between. As she looked, it almost looked as if the seas moved, tiny wave lines advancing endlessly forwards and a tiny, gleaming silvery back curved upwards out of the water with beautiful grace, to vanish again, a sharp-edged tail the last thing she saw there.

"So beautiful . . ." A voice whispered, a mere breath of sound, echoing strangely throughout the hall.

"I-I beg your pardon?" Ethrayne asked, looking up from the mesmerising movement of the sea below her feet, turning in a circle where she stood; but she was still the only person in the hall. "Hello? Is there anyone there? Where are you?"

"That is quite a question, dear child." The voice sounded slightly louder, a little less ethereal. Now, it seemed that she could tell that it was coming from her left and there was amusement in the tone. "Come closer, my child, my Lady, we have but little time."

Puzzled, for part of her mind was pondering this peculiar event far beyond what was usual in a dream, Ethrayne walked from the centre of the hall towards the dais that stood empty at the far end of the space. As she moved, she found that she now wore a robe of silvery silk, soft and comforting, a robe that any king would covet.

A figure stood on the dais, where there had been nothing and no one a moment before; a tall figure, maybe approaching eight feet and well-proportioned with golden hair, a handsome face and huge blue-green eyes beneath shapely brows. He was robed in simple grey and completely encased in water-clear ice that formed a cylindrical ten-foot-tall pillar some four-feet thick around him.

"How strange." Ethrayne reached out with both hands but found that she could not touch the pillar. A peculiar tingle, like pins-and-needles, ran through her when she tried and both the pillar and the figure it contained faded a little from her sight. "Who are you? Are you a prisoner? Where are we?"

"This is Car'Agasse, my Wielder, my Sword." He said. The girl heard his words clearly and ordinarily, although his lips did not move. "I have striven with all the strength remaining to me, to gather the two of you here this once, to humbly apologise and to warn you."

"The two of us?" Ethrayne focussed on those words and turned in another circle, staring around desperately. "Jerryn is here too? Where is he?"

"Alas, he is within his own dream, dearest Ethrayne. I have wrought as well as I can but orchestrating a meeting between you both is far beyond my strength and I am very sorry for my weakness." He spoke with great sadness in his voice, yet Ethrayne thought that, for a moment, she could see a vague figure standing to her right: she could clearly see his eyes and the rather worried, pale face was Jerryn's; he looked as startled as she felt, before he faded away into invisibility.

"I just hope he couldn't see me, I'd hate him to see the mess that General Ackat made of my hair!" Ethrayne admitted uneasily, reaching up to feel her shorn, slightly spiked scalp, then glared at the ice-encased figure. "This is not a normal dream, is it?" Her tone was accusatory. "If it were, I would surely imagine myself with hair and without these marks on my wrists, since I haven't even seen myself like this, thank heavens! Who are you? Where is this place?"

"This is Car'Agasse, Ethrayne, the place where Gregnor betrayed me, killed his closest friends and imprisoned me, so very long ago. Oh, do not be afraid, my dear -."

"I . . . You . . . You are Arven?" Ethrayne stuttered, suddenly awestruck. "I, oh, my . . . my Lord, please excuse me -."

The sound of his laughter was clear and as musical as the chime of bells throughout the hall and served to dispel that sudden burst of fear; it was a very different kind of fear than she felt when close to the Generals, she noted absently. "My dearest Ethrayne, neither you nor your betrothed have been Chosen for your shy, retiring natures; please do not apologise, you are my Wielders, my Champions, my Sword -."

"A sword?" The girl retorted sharply. "Me? You surely jest, sir. They laughed at me, wielding a sword this morning. He could have killed me in less than a heartbeat, Lord. I am useless! Their prisoner! I can't do a thing to stop them taking me south!" That other, icy fear was rising although she tried to block it.

"You are guarded with the greatest care, my dear Ethrayne, else why the need for *three* Generals? You must be very wary of your high-ranking guards; do not trust them, dearest child. They are Gregnor's tools indeed: his most trusted tools and weapons and servants, most certainly not to be trusted. They wish you ill, child; they wish you compliant and biddable and easily influenced, never not forget that, Ethrayne. Speak their language when they insist. Obey their orders when they speak. But their sympathy, any concern they show, any interest in yourself or your wellbeing, it will only ever be false!" His tone was sombre. "That is how they are trained from childhood: they are wholly their master's. In fact, they are most to be trusted when they threaten you and are cold and unconcerned. When they smile and show any interest in you, my dear, beware -."

"I am alone with three Generals, Lord. They are terrifying." She admitted quietly with a shiver. "What the, the – do please excuse me, Lord . . . Do you really expect me to defy them?" Quickly she rephrased what she had been about to say. "I am not even seventeen, so they call me *child* and *brat*. They are – are horrible!" Her tone was a mixture of fear and outrage. "They slaughtered my parents and killed thousands of others to take Clirensar! I, I can't fight them!"

"On the contrary, my dearest Ethrayne, I believe that you will be happily surprised to find just how much you will fight them. I can only warn you again and please do not forget it: do not ever trust them, however friendly and sympathetic they might seem, especially the woman. She is the first female General ever and why else would she be elevated, no matter her skills and arts, except to try and influence *you*?"

"Oh, Lord, honestly, I will try . . . Please can you tell Jerryn that I am sorry; that I love him so much -." Ethrayne spoke quickly and earnestly, wanting to add so much more, but she could already feel herself emerging from the dream and the ice-wrought grandeur of the hall was already fading from her sight.

"Jerryn, your prince, assures you that he loves you with all his heart and soul, dearest Ethrayne and he says that they will all do their utmost to free Clirensar and yourself . . . Please forgive me, my Wielder . . ."

The voice receded into silence and Ethrayne opened her eyes to the light of a globe, the crackle of a burning fire. She could clearly recall every part of her strange dream, from the shock and sorrow on the trapped God's face, to every single word of their conversation . . . How strange! Slowly she sat up, stretching, to find Garrtnor setting pots over the fire and pouring meal of some type into one, stirring vigorously. It was still dark outside.

"Awake, are you? The General gave her a brief glance. "Get yourself organised girl, the wash room's empty and there's hot water here." He indicated the side of the fire. "My colleagues are seeing to the horses."

She nodded, acknowledging the information grudgingly and did as Garrtnor suggested, packing her blankets, setting the mattress back on the pile, then retreating to wash before a quick breakfast and the continuation of their journey even before the sun had risen.

*

The pattern of the next ten days of their journey were fixed by that first day: days of long hard riding, spending each night in roughly similar way stations; only the vista gradually changed as the land became steeper, whilst the mountains loomed larger and higher each day across their path.

Ethrayne used the strange dream to bolster her strength and separateness from the Generals and their command over her; that brief glimpse of Jerryn, so unexpected, and the actual presence of Arven himself was just simply . . . wonderful! Never would she have expected that their God, frozen in ice as he still was, could ever have manipulated anything enough to enter her dream and give both reassurance and advice! It was awe-inspiring and frightening; it was amazing that it had happened, and she cherished the knowledge she had gained, even though the advice that Arven had given her was hardly comforting: to never trust the jajozeli-razine! After her complete helplessness on the first half of their journey, the fact that she had had to rely on Cavaln for so much assistance, she cradled that warning close in her heart and was immensely thankful that she had not been beguiled into much interaction or cooperation with her captors . . . And Lord Arven had approved of her! Apologised to her! . . . No matter how awful the weather became; no matter how tired she became, travelling so hard through that unforgiving terrain, she could draw strength from the dream, from Arven, even though she was heading towards his enemy's stronghold. She would do her utmost to live up to his approval, Ethrayne decided: she would continue to fight, if she possibly could. She was a Wielder of the Flame and she was their enemy, not just a frightened girl. Please Arven!

The first five days, they crossed the windswept plateau, always ascending, which ended in a midday climb over a steep saddle between mountains that were huge enough to frighten Ethrayne; but they were tiny, she found, when compared with the peaks that she could see in the far distance from the top of the ridge which, ahead and below, became a bleak scree-strewn slope that descended steeply into a narrow, shadowed ravine, their route barely visible as it curved across the slope, especially since cold sleet was blowing stingingly into their faces.

Ethrayne shuddered as they descended in the teeth of the gale, immensely glad of the mittens and baggy hat in addition to the spare clothes that Cavaln had told her to bring, every scrap of which would be worn, she decided, the next morning: she had never been so cold in her life before. The weather had worsened as they grew ever closer to the mountains; it snowed at some point every day now and there was ice on the ground each morning.

She was glad that they were not forced to camp outside; the way stations provided vital shelter, and the separate stables gave her a brief respite each evening of tending the horses away from the presence of the Generals, which provided some much-needed balance against their unwelcome authority. After this, trying to ignore them, wrapped in her blankets, she tried to meditate for the first time since leaving Tenum City – but something about her state of mind, or their closeness, meant that she could not even clear her mind properly. All her progress from moons of work had vanished, it seemed.

That night, they took shelter in a building very different to the ones on the plateau, this one a two-storey building with the stable below and accommodation above, set beneath a steeply sided roof in the shelter of some bent, scrawny fir trees in the ravine.

The land seemed empty of people, apart from the road and the shelters, but it was full of wildlife. Ackat had hunted on a few occasions, and today he provided a brace of grouse and three hares that were showing their winter coats, to improve the staples that had dominated their diet in the past few days, beans, dried meat, meal and so on.

Ethrayne wondered then, wearily, how far they still had to travel before they reached Ban'Lerracon; they were still following the tracks of the army, although now the road was rocky, and the passage of the masses was mostly hidden. It seemed that they had been travelling forever, she was starting to sometimes believe; they were deep in Zanezli, but it seemed so unfriendly, so bleak; the mountains were just getting higher and more massive, blocking their advance.

For four more days they followed a series of steep-sided ravines in a generally southerly direction, the sound of tumbling streams occasionally loud despite a covering of ice beside or below the road they followed, the four of them seemingly shrunk to the size of insects against the mountains that loomed thousands of feet above them, blocking out nearly all the natural light and most of the sky.

That night, the ninth from N'Astoln, was a great deal different again: they rode late into the night, ignoring the howling wind that promised but, surprisingly, had not provided snow, finishing up at a huge walled structure that blocked the width of the valley they were traversing, entering through a gate into a large, cobbled courtyard where Ethrayne tiredly dismounted. She was guided by the Generals through a narrow gate and doorways into a fort or castle, passing sentries and soldiers. She was exhausted, moving numbly, uncaring of anything but relief at getting out of the weather, finding herself, a while later, in a room by herself, with a bed, a small fire cracking on a grate and a hot meal. Alone, relishing it, she ate quickly and then retired; she tried to meditate, dutifully, but fell quickly into sleep.

The next morning, attuned to waking before dawn, the girl was up and ready for breakfast when the door opened to reveal a guard bringing breakfast; she ate, waiting only a short time before General Ackat appeared in the doorway. It was still dark, torches blazing in the corridor beyond him.

"Come on, girl, this is no time to dawdle." He said with mock cheerfulness.

"Humph." She replied with a small hint of rebellion, even as she got to her feet.

They set out in the pre-dawn darkness, the expanse of the keep barely visible in the dim light of the torches that shone around its outer structure, but it seemed to block the valley entirely, was tall with narrow windows. Other than that, Ethrayne could not be sure, as they rode away on fresh horses, the Generals smart in clean clothing, the men freshly shaven. The road was clear, a pale ribbon heading into the blackness of a stunted forest as it descended the valley, and nothing was visible until they finally emerged from the slowly lightening closeness of the pine and fir trees, to find that the sun had risen. They crested a smooth, strangely curved, massive hillock at the place where that ravine joined another, far larger valley. Ethrayne gazed out along a valley so vast that she could hardly believe her eyes. It was at least two miles wide where she stood, seemingly cut from the very roots of the mountains that sprang up from stark, vertical cliffs thousands of feet high, forming the valley sides, with white lines of waterfalls dropping towards the ground far, far below with reckless abandon. The peaks high above clawed at the cloudy sky, shimmering white or black in shadows as deep as new ink. The sky between was a deep blue in contrast with small, ice-white clouds dotted about; amazingly, although the wind was breathtakingly cold, the clouds just scudded north, the weather continued fine.

A wide, pale green almost milky-looking river ran swiftly past through brown grasslands and stunted coniferous woods from roughly east to west; the road they were on wound away to the right, westward, a pale line visible some distance above the river. The girl looked left, to see more of the strangely shaped and placed hillocks merging away into a hazy distance some miles away – a view of vast peaks and an awe inspiring, massive tongue of ice that appeared to descend from the shoulders of the mountains behind, cracked and folded; but how could ice possibly fold? It was brilliantly white, black, grey and, most surprisingly, shot through with shades of blue.

"The Lerracon Glacier." Ackat informed Ethrayne; the word translated itself as 'ice-maw' in her head, at being spoken aloud. "We should reach Ban'Lerracon tonight, hurry along."

Ban'Lerracon, 'Fortress of the Ice Maw'. Knowing now that their destination was so close, fear suddenly filled Ethrayne, strong, but irrational.

As Garrtnor left the rounded hillock, the others following, she cast one glance behind towards the north, briefly recalling her old life; sometimes it seemed like a dream . . .

Ben'Lerracon? Oh, dear Arven, help me! She prayed, staring westward down the gigantic, ice-carved valley; a curve to the left more than a league ahead, plus the huge cliffs and the slopes of the mountains above hid the view past that point.

"Wake up!" Cavaln called back, pausing in her advance, her tone sharp.

Reluctantly, the girl kicked her horse into movement, then urged it to a canter to catch them up.

After that sweeping left-hand bend, the valley widened noticeably, and massive outcrops of rock were visible, looking as though the very bones of the earth had been carved out by the ice. There wasn't much noticeable apart from the great, pale river, trees, brown grassland and the towering cliffs as far as the eye could see as they rode on until, on one of the rocky outcrops, she noted that a fort had been constructed, it's entrance far above the ground, reached by a steeply zig-zagging trail. Tiny soldiers were visible on the ramparts and the starkly bright jajozeli standard was cracking in the wind far above. It must have been nearly noon when the small group neared the fort, which was approached by a sturdy bridge across the river, but the group did not pause, except to dismount, transfer their bags across and then immediately mount the fresh horses that were being held by soldiers waiting at the edge of the bridge; although she was tired and thirsty, Ethrayne quickly obeyed Garrtnor's order to remount, his impatience sharp.

Relentlessly, they rode on, the Generals keeping their pace to at least a canter along the smooth road, not even stopping to eat; their determination to reach their destination was obvious. Ethrayne could tell when the sun set, for the snow-capped peaks towering far above them were briefly bathed in a brilliant wash of pinky-orange light that faded almost immediately, to be replaced with almost total darkness; it seemed as if a thick curtain had fallen. Finally, not long after this, the Generals paused, she was allowed a drink, but they quickly set off again; there were stars clear in the depths of the sky above, but no moon shone yet, hidden by the mountains. Even in the darkness, however, the pale road was clear to follow.

Exhausted, her body aching, Ethrayne kept her gaze mostly on the dimly seen shapes of her captors, just ahead. It seemed to her that time had stopped: they were running on the spot as the world sped past with a rush of icy air. This day seemed to have lasted a lifetime!

Then, without warning, there was a flare of orange firelight ahead; torches were visible, shining fitfully on buildings due to the gusty wind, yet not much was clear to her tired eyes, only stone walls and slate roofs, a glazed window sparkling here and there. Shortly afterwards, the endless sound of hooves on gravel became a ring on cobbles as the Generals ahead of her turned to the left. She sat up straighter, frowning to try and see more in the darkness as they crossed an arched bridge; there was the hollow rattle of a wide wooden drawbridge beneath, before they were moving through a massively constructed gateway, protected by black-clad soldiers, enormously thick oak gates and gleaming ironwork, picked out by the light of the torches.

There were many voices shouting, speaking; many people, most of them in uniform, as far as Ethrayne could tell in the uncertain flares of torchlight; it was a jumble of confusion that assaulted the girl's senses after so many days of quiet travelling. She shivered as the Generals led her onward, along a wide street with three more encompassing gateways, past large buildings and small; then up a steep, winding way with bare rock clearly visible either side of the roadway; she could see high walls above, more sentries; great gates creaking open at their advance, at the summit of the slope; two sets, either side of a virtual tunnel. Beyond this were a series of courtyards, also gated; the buildings seemed enormous.

"Halt." Garrtnor's voice broke through her tired abstraction and Ethrayne blinked rapidly, then scrubbed at her face with her mittened hands. Looking around a courtyard, then up at a well-lit, elegant, curved and balustrade–edged staircase to a massive, ornate entrance some fifteen feet above, terror gripped at her, trying to take control despite her exhaustion. Ethrayne forced it away, but she could feel herself trembling as she dismounted.

"After you, my Lady." Ackat said unexpectedly with a mocking bow. "Welcome to Ban'Lerracon."

* * *

CHAPTER 25

Ethrayne opened the shutter, folding it back against the bulk of the thick curtain that hung there and, standing on tiptoe, gazed out through the thick diamond-paned glass, past the inch-thick iron bars fixed about six inches apart just outside the window, preventing escape; although anyone who would dare to leap from this windowsill would find escape only in death, so high was the aperture above the rooftops of the city clustered below. She stared westward along the mountain-girded valley into the distance, her view mostly obscured by the flurries of thick snow being carried past on whistling, howling gales that originated somewhere far to the south. The fading daylight was hardly noticeable. Autumn, it seemed, had retreated hurriedly in the face of winter, here in the heart of Zanezli.

Staring out for a moment longer, the girl shuddered, very glad, suddenly, that she had been brought here to Ban'Lerracon, incarcerated, for six days now, glad that she was not still travelling. This storm had been raging now for two full days and was the second spell of winter weather that had encircled the city since her arrival. Despite their exposure to the full force of the howling gales, the windowsills in every room were almost a foot deep in packed snow. All that was visible now of the great city, she had found, standing on a stool to look almost straight down, were tiny rooftops, now just ruffled angles of snow, an uneven blanket covering amid vertical stone walls.

A hint of a cold draught touched her hand, close to the window pane; Ethrayne shivered again before reaching for the thick shutter and pulling it closed; latching it firmly to its other half, all traces of evening daylight were shut out with the blizzard, before she shut the curtains, leaving the sources of lamp, fire and candle to bathe the room in cosy, ruddy light.

Despite the warm glow and the deep warmth cast out from the large fire crackling merrily in its hearth, Ethrayne's heart and soul were as cold as the gales and ice hammering at the thick walls outside; she suppressed a sigh as she came around the thickly padded, upholstered chair and sat down.

Fionn and Sallie gazed at her with some reproach for letting in the cold, sat together on the velvet-covered settee, shawls tight around their bodies as they sewed diligently at different parts of a fine linen nightgown that had been marked ready for embroidery before they had all left Clirensar for Tenum City in the early spring.

Her maids; her own bed; her clothes; her sewing box; some tapestries; a chest full of her clothes and other items had somehow been hauled here from Clirensar to Ban'Lerracon by the jajozeli!

The awful night of her arrival, after that relentless ride along the huge glacial valley towards the citadel, Ethrayne had been far too tired to absorb much more information. She had stumbled up the ornate sweeping staircase with her saddlebags over her shoulder, the Generals at her back, to enter a bleakly formidable entrance hall, past eight halberd-bearing guards in gleaming black who were standing to attention in the fifteen-foot-wide doorway.

Four other guards formed up around her as she crossed into a large foyer, a torch-lit space that was full of people, all of whom were staring at her. The sight of the throng nearly caused her to halt in fear, assaulted as she was by their projected emotions, for she sensed antagonism, interest, distaste and hatred amongst them; every one of them strangers and enemies. Some seemed human, others were razine; some were uniformed, others wore unfamiliar forms of winter clothing in varying degrees of opulence. Hundreds of faces surrounded her, everyone stared and there was a ripple of conversation: they were clearly discussing her, probably disparagingly, considering her dishevelled appearance.

Opposite the outer doors, facing her as she slowed, uncertain of where she was meant to go, was a very grand doorway with carven pillars leading into a well-lit place beyond, but her view was blocked by the mass of the crowd. From that area, it seemed to her, that she could feel more power, a sense of strength much greater than that of the Generals who had brought her here . . . But Ethrayne was tired, scared and emotional, whilst the sensation seemed to diminish as the guards shoved her into movement, marching her to the right past more spectators.

A wide corridor, brightly lit with golden lamplight, led onward into the citadel. There were turns: left, right; stairs, rising gracefully; another, less showy corridor led to more stairs, narrower, to a plain corridor with grey walls. The doors changed from carved to plain oak; from arched to simple rectangular doorways. On and on she trudged, her legs aching. Finally, she saw two guards stood at a doorway ahead, one otherwise identical to the rest; this was opened to reveal a square area with only a relatively wide spiral staircase winding upward in its centre, and no other doors. Her guards took her to the stairs and forced her upwards, pushing her to move quickly, although her tiredness made her stumble in her ill-fitting boots.

Vaguely she counted twenty steps to a small landing with a door, but the men behind shoved her onward and upward to climb another hundred steps, four more levels passed; the sixth landing was the last: there was only one door opening off a small, square space, an oak door with an ornate key in a large ornate lock and two massive iron bolts to top and bottom to secure it.

Ethrayne sagged, gasping for breath, her legs trembling at the effect of climbing so far; one guard unlocked the door and she was simply pushed inside, the inch-thick door slamming shut almost on her heels as she turned, the sound of the lock and the bolts being applied, quiet but clear through the door.

"Oh, dear Arven!" Mingled fear and relief filled her: she was alone, she might be fed, she might be able to rest . . . Ethrayne turned back to the room, took a step forward and her fear, exhaustion and hunger were replaced with astonishment: the carpets and the armed chair on the floor of the large, almost hemispherical room were rather familiar, as were the curtains on the whitewashed walls; then, compounding her amazement, a door on the far side of the room was edged open to admit two cowering female figures dressed in rather tattered gowns, their faces even more familiar in the wealth of warm light that surrounded them, despite the fading bruises evident there. Fionn and Sallie, her maids who had returned to Clirensar with her father to finish her wedding gown, were here, in Ban'Lerracon!

Stunned, bewildered, Ethrayne greeted them warmly, hugging them tight, tears in her eyes, pulling them over to the fireplace, dropping the saddle bags, shrugging out of the cloak; she asked myriad questions, but both girls were silent as they wept, bobbing curtsies repeatedly and smiling waveringly. Then, still without a sound, they drew her through the door into a smaller but still substantial wedge-shaped chamber where, even more astoundingly, her own bed stood, the frame and curtains in place! Arven only knew how the jajozeli had managed to transport it across the endless leagues through the mountains! Through a second door, the girls led her into a plain, stone-walled and smaller, almost triangular bathroom that obviously completed the circle of the forty-something foot wide tower, containing a full bathtub before a crackling fire.

"Oh, my word, a bath!" She breathed. "You knew I was coming?" Fionn nodded her head, but still did not speak. "I've no idea what's happening . . . how you got here. Oh, dear Arven!" Ethrayne broke off, fighting an urge to weep as the two young women started removing her myriad layers of clothing, bits of strings and too-large socks as well; numb, she just let them get on with undressing her, her head spinning, overwhelmed, speechless. They bathed her as they had used to; got her into some of her very own nightclothes, smelling of lavender; all that was missing, the most vital part, was the conversation and laughter that had always marked their interactions. Their silence was ominous, and she wondered uneasily what had occurred to cause it.

Wrapped in her old dressing gown, they led her back through to the large sitting room that must take up nearly half the floor space of the tower and produced a meal as if by magic from a cupboard in the wall; there was plenty for three plus extras: roast meat, herbed vegetables, soft rolls, butter and a bowl of oddly spiced fruit compote. There was even tea, different again to others that she had tasted, yet light and refreshing.

Dazed, Ethrayne sat at the small dining table, eating and drinking with relish; it had been a very long day since she had quickly eaten breakfast in the fort before dawn. Again, she tried to get some conversation from her maids, asked a few questions, all without success. She wondered if the young women had somehow been rendered dumb – wondering, fearfully, how it might have been achieved.

It was horribly late, of that she was certain; although night fell early in the mountainous south in winter, it had been a long time after sunset when they had reached the citadel, the ache of her muscles and joints proved that. She was almost nodding where she sat and Fionn and Sallie looked tired as well;

they cleared up the plates and so on into the little cupboard in the wall, blew out the lamp and candles and hauled a basket of logs into the bedroom to stoke up the fire burning there, for there was a great stack of logs against the wall to the side of the outer door, that would serve to keep them warm for days, Ethrayne hoped. There was one small lamp they left lit in the bedroom, on the table to the right of the four-posted bed, then they helped Ethrayne into bed, pulling up the crisp linen sheet, blankets and coverlets, also smelling of lavender, kissing her gently.

"Thank you, Fionn, Sallie." She said, leaning up on her elbows to gaze down to see the lumpy mattress on the floor to her right, where her maids obviously slept, with plenty of blankets. Reassured, even though she was still confused, she leaned back into the pillows and slipped quickly into sleep.

*

For the first time since leaving N'Astoln, Ethrayne slept past dawn, waking refreshed and alert, her mind clear. Sitting up in the darkened room she yawned, stretched and got quietly out of bed. The lamp had burned out during the night, but the fire was still glowing, although it needed mending. Pulling the dressing gown around her shoulders, she fed the dying fire as carefully as she could, for her companions were still asleep; she placed smaller sticks on the embers, waiting for them to catch, for the room was growing slightly chilly, then laid larger pieces onto those, watching the flames grow, the heat return.

Then she made her way to the bathroom, with its empty tub, privy and ash-filled fireplace. There was a half-covered window in the curved outer wall and she pulled open the shutter to gaze out through a small, barred aperture in a wall at least four feet thick, seeing an astounding vista of sheer cliffs and a sunlit, snow-clad mountain, soaring into a brilliant azure sky, where small clouds like the whitest fleece imaginable floated as if only designed to enhance that blue. The window sill was about four feet above the floor and the wall so thick that she could not see much below, even craning her neck, except a glimpse of dark rooftops and what might be the city wall above the river edge, a very, very long way below her vantage point, here at the top of this tower.

No wonder my legs still ache. She thought grimly, stretching again, gazing out of the window one last time before pulling the shutter mostly closed again, for reflected sunlight was shining into the room thanks to the snow-cover on the mountain opposite. *But here I am, and this is so, so strange!*

A gentle, polite tap at the door ended her musings: her companions were awake and Ethrayne fixed a smile on her face before she opened it to bid her fellow prisoners a cheerful good morning.

*

The three rooms formed the entire top floor of the tower, half the space making the sitting room, with the bedroom and bathroom forming the rest of the circle. The rooms all had good-sized fireplaces, which surprisingly lacked any icy draughts from outside; the sitting room had two large barred windows, covered with close-fitting shutters and thick curtains and Ethrayne's first, amazed impression had been correct: the curtains, carpets and some furniture had all come from her home. She could not fathom how the huge pieces, especially her bed, had been transported, even dismantled, let alone why! And how on Iullyn had it all been carried up the spiral staircase? That was beyond any sense, as far as she could tell.

For a prison, it was extremely well appointed, but Ethrayne found herself most concerned at her friends' silence: neither could speak a word, it seemed, and she supposed that whatever had happened on the taking of Clirensar was horribly traumatic, for both girls reacted very badly to sudden noise or surprise; even the piling-up of the firewood every morning sent them running from the sitting room. She ignored their fear, the fading bruises, their dishevelled clothing and just hugged them tight, making them change into some of her own clothes, for the chest brought from Clirensar held masses of gowns, underclothes, shawls and so on.

As well as the six-foot-odd wide stack of split logs against the side wall, there were two large boxes of wood chips and smaller kindling, plus flint and tinder and, every morning, a fresh pile of wood was delivered to their door by a soldier, at about the time that breakfast was delivered in the little cupboard contraption that, Ethrayne discovered, was far too small to admit a young woman, because she tried to get in to it, and failed. It was an ingenious thing easily holding plenty of provisions for three, run on a pulley she assumed, from a kitchen far below, ensuring that at least the food arrived hot, which wouldn't be the case, she decided, climbing all those spiralling, six flights of stairs! In addition, there was a water pump in the bathroom and a copper to heat bathwater when required, or to wash clothing or bedding. They even had a couple of old, black pans, some metal mugs and a box of dried camomile for tea.

Ethrayne had had all sorts of worrying thoughts concerning her captivity. None of them had featured a cosy, warm set of rooms with fireplaces, running water or her own comfortable bed, let alone companionship from girls she knew well, even if she was the only one who could talk. The lack of sense of it all, to her mind, only increased her unease.

After breakfast that first morning, she let Fionn and Sallie dress her in deep blue velvet and the girls stroked her head sympathetically, as if mourning the loss of her hair; but she managed a laugh and said that it was sure to grow back and was already slightly longer, if a little uneven.

It was frustrating that the two could not talk, because they could not tell her how the city and the castle were taken by the enemy, no matter how she phrased the questions; it seemed that they did not know anything useful and just hung their heads, tears spilling down their cheeks; the episode had traumatised them greatly. All she learned was that they had been imprisoned here for six days before her own arrival; yet the number was offered tentatively, uncertainly, by Fionn and Sallie, when they silently counted on their fingers.

"I imagine that my wedding gown looked absolutely beautiful . . . And now I will never see your workmanship." She said uneasily, realising that fact with a jolt of unease. She would have been preparing for her wedding now, if this hell had not descended upon them all. "All your hard work . . . Damn! I note they didn't include the gown with everything else, however."

Tears on her cheeks, Fionn mimed ripping something up with her hands and Sallie nodded and did the same.

"They destroyed it! All your exquisite embroidery? Oh, I'm so sorry!" Ethrayne said, hugging them both. "I am so, so sorry!" There were tears in all their eyes for she had already told them how she was captured, how her parents had been killed. They sat together, sadly, for quite a while, just taking a little comfort in being close.

That first day passed slowly, but the three of them kept themselves occupied nicely: washing the clothes that Ethrayne had travelled in, including the thick cloak and blankets, stringing them up neatly on lines in the bathroom, with the fire lit and then making a rough inventory of the things that had been carted here from Clirensar. Other than the larger items of furniture, curtains and carpets, there were the clothing and other things stuffed in the chest, including slippers and a book of poetry as well as her sewing box, intact, with some items half-finished or not even begun; it was as if crows or magpies had randomly picked up things to stuff in the chest, she imagined.

After that work, they sat together and Ethrayne reluctantly related what had happened when the enemy attacked the soldiers above Clirensar, her journey south, carefully editing it as she went along, for the two frightened young women did not need graphic details, she was sure. Then, she spoke gently of the past: of warm summer days in the castle gardens, or of picnics at South Vale Farm; simple, carefree, but painful, nonetheless. She lapsed into silence and they all sat staring at the firelight, deep in their own thoughts until they retired.

This night, Ethrayne did not sleep so well; too many questions and worries span in her head; she considered Lord Arven's dream, as well as the unknown future before her and her acknowledgement of her deep regret that, now, she would not wed Jerryn . . . become princess . . . would be a prisoner forever, perhaps. Ethrayne missed her parents so much that it hurt physically, and she was aware that the power which had, before her capture, been an intrinsic part of her – spinning inside her being – had faded away into a shadowy presence, likely because she had not had any chance to meditate. Grief and fear were strong emotions, of course. She tried to meditate, lying there, but she could not achieve even the most basic level of control she had had at the start, when she and Jerryn had taken the Flame into them . . . She cursed her uselessness, it did nothing to help.

The second morning brought leaden skies with breakfast, it was lighter with all the shutters and curtains closed and the lamps lit. The girls set about cleaning the fireplaces of ash and dust, scooping it into large, lidded buckets, setting logs on the fires and piling more next to each hearth ready for night time; then they checked the rooms generally for tidiness, just for something to do, folding up the clean clothes that were already dry in the bathroom, but the cloak, blankets and felted jacket were still wet, of course.

The outer door opened without warning and Ethrayne straightened from where she knelt by the living room hearth, finishing wiping the stone, all too aware that her companions were hurriedly backing away, their faces pale and lined with fear as General Garrtnor and two soldiers strode in; the guards set down more lidded buckets and picked up the two full ones, departing with a smart salute; General Garrtnor stared down at her.

"This will not do, girl: go and dress in leggings and shirt, quickly." He ordered, shaking his head disapprovingly at her blue gown. "Hurry, you have an appointment."

Ethrayne forbade mentioning that that was news to her; her look probably told him what she thought, for he almost smiled, she decided; his lips twitched slightly, anyway, despite his glare. "My Lord General." She growled, getting to her feet and following Fionn and Sallie into the bedroom, shutting the door with a snap.

"Damn him!" She muttered, moving to the chest where she had earlier stowed the tunic, leggings and so on from her journey, all terribly crumpled, of course, with no hot iron to hand, but clean and dry at least. It felt so strange, moving from one language to the other like this; she never would have thought that Arven's power would affect her in such a basic way as communicating with different peoples so seamlessly. The shaking girls helped her change, locating the string that she had used for a belt and she pulled on the two pairs of socks necessary to keep the boots on. "Thank you; now, stay here: don't worry about me, either of you -." Ethrayne held them tight and emerged alone, her arms crossed defensively across her body, quietly alarmed and cross that the girls were now hiding in the corner of the bedroom, so traumatised were they by the mere presence of the jajozeli-razine.

Garrtnor looked her up and down, his face expressionless, then impatiently gestured to the outer door that still stood open, admitting a chilly breeze which was making the fire crackle. Biting back her questions, Ethrayne walked past him and started down the first curve of the long spiral, shivering at the cooler air, suppressing a comment on the sheer number of steps as they descended, the General having locked the door before he followed her, his boots ringing on the steps right behind her.

Reaching ground level, or at least the base of the tower, Garrtnor took the lead, passing the guards by the foyer and taking Ethrayne on a winding route through plain, unadorned corridors and steps that were certainly service passages and unnervingly identical, so it seemed that they didn't actually go anywhere; they passed a number of people, some soldiers and the rest mostly servants, all of whom stood aside respectfully for their superior, who ignored them. Ethrayne, unnerved, decided on a semblance of icy hauteur and passed all of them with a straight back and a cold glare. The walls were grey, the floors grey with flagstones or striped brown with thick planks, the torch brackets and doorframes and doors were all practically the same; even the palace in Tenum City didn't have quite so many identical doors, she decided.

They walked a long way, to Ethrayne's mind, until a high-ceilinged, green-painted corridor took them into a large, vaulted, wide windowed hall that might be near ground level, for she could clearly hear horses' hooves on cobbles not far away.

She slowed, just inside the space and turned in a slow circle to take in the place properly, her heart sinking a little as she did so: this was as plainly a space designed for combat as the hall in the base of the north wing of Tenum's palace. The bank of high windows along one wall let in grey daylight, augmented by torches that filled the many iron brackets on the walls, on this wintry day; there were large braziers along the walls and in the corners of the space, emitting a welcome heat; further along the same wall through which the door had admitted her, there were wooden benches for spectators, four tiers of them climbing up the wall and some places were occupied by plainly dressed Generals, plus a pair of dour-faced human soldiers in smart uniforms. The flagged floor was smooth from much use and the space was vast.

One figure stood alone in the hall, clearly waiting, for he had turned as Garrtnor and his prisoner entered and Ethrayne sensed an implacable will that was mirrored in the icy grey eyes that appraised her dispassionately. He was as tall as Garrtnor, lithe, with a tanned, lined face under iron-grey hair, wearing supple leather in silver-clasped black, with a long, narrow sword in a plain scabbard at his hip. He was also undoubtedly another General.

"You want me to evaluate *this*?" He demanded, his tone scathing, as if she were sub-human. "She's only a child, Garrtnor."

"The request comes from his majesty, Master Cheltor." The black-haired General replied mildly. "I agree, she is young, yes, but she does show some promise and potential -."

"Really? Well, I'll be the judge of that!" Master Cheltor retorted, glaring. "Come here, girl."

Still frowning, Ethrayne stepped forward, inwardly determined not to be intimidated by yet another oh-so-superior-General, even if he did appear to be the sort of professional bully who trained combatants; she apologised silently to the men who had begun her training in Tenarum. Everything about him, from his stance, his expression and his clothes to his demeanour screamed that fact.

"Could you have dressed her in a worse set of clothes, Garrtnor?" Cheltor asked incredulously, slowly circling the girl. "I mean, those trousers are held up with string, I ask you! The tunic's a disgrace: tatty, creased, baggy. She'll need things that fit, if she's worth the effort, and those boots are far too loose. Get it sorted!"

"We were forced to use the only clothes available in N'Astoln, Master Cheltor, but you are correct: nothing actually fits her." Garrtnor protested and grinned at Ethrayne as she turned her glare back on him.

“The boots are essential: she will not set foot in here again until they are made, so send for the cobbler to attend straight after this session.” Cheltor ordered. Garrtnor nodded and strode back past Ethrayne to the double doors, opened one so that a draught of cold air chilled her and spoke quietly to someone outside.

“Ignore my colleague.” Cheltor told the girl crisply as she naturally began to follow Garrtnor’s movement. “I’m the one you need to concentrate on, girl. They tell me you have had some training, yes?”

“Yes, sir, I began training mid-Rhellay and continued to the beginning of Vhisson, when we were travelling south to Clirensar. I was learning how to use a sword, bow, knife and unarmed combat in Tenum City.” She answered briskly, wondering just why her enemies could possibly want to continue her weapons’ training; it didn’t make any sense at all.

Master Cheltor snorted. “Barely five moons is a very short period.”

“I attended almost every morning until we set off for my home, except when other duties took precedence.” Ethrayne countered coolly. “After encountering General Ackat above the city, I was not there for idle amusement!”

He smiled very slightly at that and inclined his head. “So why don’t you show me, girl?” He unbuckled his sword belt and handed it to Garrtnor, who had come back over, then moved out further into the hall and beckoned so that Ethrayne sighed and followed.

Cheltor bowed slightly, she copied him warily and was able to step aside as he kicked at her rather obviously, then raised her right arm to block the punch he threw with his left. Despite her moon of inactivity, Ethrayne was pleasantly surprised to find that she could recall all that she had learned. Cheltor was pushing her, but he was moving with a care that she suspected she would not be accorded if he was the one supervising any normal training session. He could have disabled her instantly, knocked her flat, knocked her cold, but his movements were measured, his attacks slow, giving her time to react, she suspected, dancing as well as she could in her loose boots, avoiding his feet, legs, hands and arms, once or twice even feeling just about confident enough to thrust an elbow or fist back at him and he grinned as wolfishly as Commander Vedeigne had used to as his attacks came quicker and quicker; he was as fast as a striking adder!

It felt like forever. It certainly lasted longer than her combat against General Ackat at N’Astoln, but not really by much. The faster he attacked in his different style of fighting, the more difficulty she had evading his blows in whatever way she could until, unexpectedly, he hooked his foot about her ankle, yanked, grabbed her right wrist in a grip of steel, twisting it and Ethrayne somehow found herself flat on her front on the hard flagged floor, her arm and shoulder agonisingly locked in his hold which he kept up for a couple more heart-beats before releasing her.

“On your feet.” He ordered tersely at once, nudging her rather roughly in the ribs with one foot. "Don't dawdle, child."

"We told you, Master Cheltor." Garrtnor said, laughing quietly as Ethrayne got slowly to her feet, breathing heavily, straightening her clothes. "You didn't believe us. So, what d'you think?"

"She might develop a small level of skill, with supervision." The combat master conceded grudgingly after a pause during which he looked her up and down again. "She starts when the boots are ready."

Ethrayne bristled a little at being so dismissed, after such a tiring session, but didn't respond, limiting herself to a haughty sniff and her continued glare, despite her aching ribs and arm. It was stupid, but she was not quite brave enough to argue with them.

"As you wish." Garrtor continued, sounding well pleased with the situation. "Ah, the cobbler and tailor, come over here, girl."

"Lord General." She answered coldly, and he laughed again at her tone as he handed Master Cheltor his weapons and turned to lead her over towards the lowest tier of seating where the spectators were all talking together earnestly in low tones, staring at her. She saw General Cavaln, standing out as the only woman amongst the group.

Two men stood diffidently near the corner where the seating began, by the double doors, hurrying towards Garrtnor as he approached; both were dressed in ordinary work wear, the cobbler defined by his worn leather apron, both men with measuring tapes, parchment and charcoal sticks in their shirt pockets. They were also human, politely bowing to their superior.

Ethrayne stood there feeling slightly foolish as the tailor measured her from head to toe; he hurried through the business as if being close to the General terrified him. She sat down on a seat for the cobbler and his light touch on her feet (when she pulled off the socks briefly) tickled awfully, but she suppressed the twitching with all her will. Garrtnor and the others were watching her, as normal. Fortunately, he was quickly done as well, and she could pull the socks and boots on with haste as the craftsmen vanished.

"Got your breath back?" General Garrtnor asked when she had straightened, and she nodded. "I'll take you back, then."

"I would like to know just what atrocities have been committed against Fionn and Sallie, my Lord General." Ethrayne asked stiffly, choosing her words carefully as he led her back through the complex maze of the citadel. "They have been traumatised, but surely – they are only girls, my maids, they are helpless -."

This time, Garttnor's laughter was cold, his gaze challenging as he glanced across at her. "Helpless, yes. Very helpless." He said, one hand lashing out to catch her hard across her ear – it stung. "You forget yourself, girl. And they are slaves of the Jajozeli Empire. What is wrong, girl? Ha!" There were connotations in his voice she neither liked nor understood. His eyes clearly showed his opinion of her reaction.

"But they are my friends -." Ethrayne quavered.

"That will be why General Tequan sent them here, then: to ensure your obedience. They are merely slaves, nothing more. You have a safe, comfortable little eyrie there at the top of the tower, but there are many other places with much less comfort where you could be housed. Your timid little maids might not be there one day, and you will never know their fate! They hardly need to speak, to be useful companions, and I suggest that you progress with a good measure of their meekness, brat, for your own good!"

Ethrayne shivered. "Yes, my Lord General." She murmured fearfully. Her ear hurt; she was shaken by his blow, yes, but she was more concerned at his threat. The longer she had been in their hands, the more she was coming to realise just how truly helpless she was. Never could she put her maids at risk! She vowed. "Forgive me."

But, even so, the apology stuck in her throat, as did her humility. Still, she longed to argue – to shout – to fight! Although that would be far too dangerous, she knew it, and imperil her friends.

* * *

CHAPTER 26

The marriage of the new Duke and Duchess was a bittersweet event, but King Marrand thankfully welcomed the return of Sarant's son. Pualyn took naturally to the role that his father had occupied at the king's side: consideration and calm appraisal had been passed to the son and the young man had good sense. His familiarity with their high-ranking razine guests, as well as his unquestioning support of the Am'maiya rather disarmed some of the older members of the Council; Pualyn had relinquished his hereditary control of the remaining Clirensar City Guards to the king's command, and they were quickly sent to Foston to assist with the exploration of the area and the building of the defensive dykes and ramparts. So far, the jajozeli housed in Clirensar had been quiet, hardly to be seen beyond the boundary walls ditches they were constructing.

It was the evening of the twenty-eighth day of Thurton, his seventeenth birthday, which he had determinedly cancelled as an event, when Jerryn managed to instigate a private get-together with the Archpriests; his father; Pualyn, Lyria, and the High-King and his son. Jerryn had become ever more serious since the news from Clirensar – his fear for Ethrayne's wellbeing mixed up with a longstanding anger which simmered beneath the veneer of politeness he maintained. Over the summer and into autumn, he had come to realise just how much his betrothed meant to him: her good sense, her intelligence, her fearlessness as well as her beauty. This had certainly been enhanced by the power they shared, the presence of the other's thoughts in each other's minds. He had hated her leaving, to prepare for their wedding, but the physical loss of her, her family and the city had been like an actual blow. The fury he had displayed on Lyria's return had only just sunk to a manageable level, with the assistance of the Archpriests. He missed Ethrayne so much that it hurt. His fear for her safety was unmeasurable.

This evening, he had asked the kitchen staff for finger foods, ale and wine and they had certainly obliged, sending a huge arrangement of sweet and savoury delicacies and some of the best wines in the cellar. The staff clearly considered his birthday as still worthy of celebration, even if he did not.

"Thank you for coming, my lady, gentlemen." The prince said as the group entered as a single mass through his outer doors, bowing low. Privately, they had all discarded their cumbersome titles as being simply unworkable and, other than Pualyn and Lurco, he was probably the man most comfortable with the unmistakeable aura of Mhezal and Kerrenan. He had wondered if the power that resided deep within him would one day manifest itself in a similar way; it was not an entirely easy concept to deal with, along with all the others, recently.

"Since you refused any birthday celebrations, we are curious why you have invited us here, Jerryn." His father enquired.

“Well, this seemed a good time to talk together without everyone else sticking their pennyworth in, Father.” He replied with a tight smile. “Please, sit down, do and our helpers will pass around appetisers and drinks, thank you.” He said to Karne, his valet and Tymain. “You had better stay, if you would consent to, gentlemen; for the more minds the better, I’ve discovered.”

“You have good sense, Jerryn.” High-King Mhezal complimented him.

“Rubbish. If I had any good sense, your Majesty, I would have fled at the first hint of prophecy and mystery, along with Ethie.” Jerryn replied rather coolly. “If we’d been at all sensible, she would be safe, Pualyn’s parents and thousands of others would be alive and we-we would have been wed by now.” He grimaced. “So, I’m bloody stupid, but who can fight destiny?” Silence followed his words. “I’m sorry, I didn’t bring you here to shout and moan, but I had a very peculiar dream a few days after Duchess Lyria returned -.” He toasted her with a glass of wine. “Since I’ve spent long enough thinking about it alone and thought I would finally ask you wise people for your input.”

“Dreams usually fade in the light of morning, Jerryn, this does seem peculiar. Can you be more specific?” Archpriest Lurco asked.

“I certainly can, for I remember every single part of it clearly . . . I had fallen asleep as normal, then, from nowhere, I just appeared to walk into a huge hall of glistening glass or ice; it was beautiful but stark, yet it was warm not cold in the hall. Below the floor was a map of Iullyn as large as the hall itself and it seemed that I walked high above the earth, staring down at land and sea from an incredible height . . . I could have stayed there and stared at it forever . . . there were mountains, lakes, plains; oh, it was beautiful!” He shook his head at the memory.

“Yes, it has that effect upon visitors.” Bahlien agreed quietly, his tone sober.

Jerryn shot him a sharp look and nodded. “Someone spoke, but I was quite alone. ‘My beautiful creation.’ It said and sighed. ‘Please come closer Prince, my Wielder, time is short.’

“I turned and there was a dais to the right and it had not been there before, I swear. In the centre of it stood a very tall person with the largest blue-green eyes and golden hair, wearing a grey robe and completely frozen in water-clear ice. I went right up to it, but I couldn’t even touch the ice . . . I still couldn’t feel any icy cold, either. My mind went completely blank. I said, stupidly ‘Oh my God!’ and he chuckled, but he was frozen: he couldn’t move.

“‘Welcome to Car’Agasse, my Wielder, my Sword.’ He said, a little louder than before. ‘I have worked with all my remaining strength to gather both of you here in the safety of your dreams, to humbly apologise and to warn you -.”

“‘Ethrayne is here?’ I interrupted rudely. I know, I’m sorry.” He shook his head ruefully as they all stared at him. “‘Is she all right? Where is she?’ I looked around and I could see her then, a shaded figure, rather ghostly, wearing awful clothes, looking a little strained and thin-faced, but I couldn’t see any bruises, not as Lyria reported, thank Arven!" He paused then; he didn't want to announce to the room that Ethrayne had appeared bald, he didn't want to upset everyone.

"'Your beloved is within her own dream, Jerryn. Unfortunately, I could not exert any more power for I have used it all to bring you together, please forgive me my failures.' He said. Oh! His tone was so sad!

"'Ethrayne was injured, is she all right?' I asked nervously, and he said, mmm . . . what? oh yes: 'She is healing well, Jerryn; do not forget that you are both now much more robust physically than you were before you took in my Flame. She is guarded appropriately – she is physically safe enough. She will need to hold onto her strength, however: her guards are our enemy's most trusted servants and they have considerable strength of their own.'

"'You are not reassuring me, sir!' I snapped, then apologised, but that warning made my heart pound in fear, when he said it."

"It's making mine pound too, Jerryn!" Pualyn snapped, rising slowly from his seat, his left hand tight in Lyria's grip. "Jerryn! F-for God's sake -!"

"I'm sorry, Pualyn, honestly, I'm only repeating the conversation from the dream, what happened. Oh, I know how you feel -." Jerryn's voice faltered and the control that he had maintained to keep a semblance of calm slipped, revealing a haunted expression for a moment before he pulled the mask back in place. "I am deeply sorry."

Pualyn sank back down, his face pale. "Yes, well, oh -." He suppressed the sort of curses that might offend their elders and took a deep breath. "I'm sorry, Jerryn." He managed meekly.

"It's all right." The prince nodded and continued. "He, A-Arven said: 'The Generals are wholly the Betrayer's servants, body and soul. I can only apologise that their actions and those of their master are beyond my ability to foresee and, oh, how I have striven! To know that so many have died in the south of your lands . . . I am sorely diminished, my Wielder.'

"'We will avenge them all Lord. We will wipe out the jajozeli holding Clirensar, every one of them! And then we will march and rescue Ethrayne -." I said, but he interrupted.

"'Lead no army into Zanezli, my Sword, else the world will be plunged into darkness!' His tone was sharp. 'Destroy the forces that have ravaged your lands, then confine the rest behind their border, but do not enter into their territory! Their master has sent an army that can be destroyed, yet he commands millions, Jerryn -.'

"I asked 'Then how are we to possibly prevail, Lord?' I admit. I was angry and scared. 'Against his millions, we will all fail!'" Jerryn paused and sighed. "And he laughed, and the sound filled the hall like, like the ringing of bells . . . 'Fear not, my Wielder, my Sword: we will prevail . . . Learn to use your gifts, Jerryn and hold on to your faith, please, although I know that I have failed you all so badly.'

"And then I felt myself waking up. I asked Arven humbly to tell

Ethrayne that I love her with all my heart and soul, that we would do our utmost to free Clirensar. He said that Ethrayne passed on her love also and that she was sorry. His voice was fading, as was the hall. Car'Agasse . . ." Jerryn stopped speaking, coughed, and shrugged, nodding thanks at Tymain when he offered him his goblet of wine, his throat dry from so much talking. "Thank you, Tymain."

"I told you so." Tymain remarked then into the deep silence, nodding decisively, unaware that everyone was staring at him, his gaze fixed on the prince. "I told you that Lord Arven couldn't possibly know how those bastards would think or act, Jerryn -." He broke off then, meeting King Marrand's eye, paled awfully. "Ah, oh, please excuse me, your Majesties." He managed then, bowing low and quickly moving to the back of the room.

"I told you you had good sense, Tymain." Jerryn said. "Thank you."

"Sit down, Corporal, if you please." Marrand instructed him mildly. "His Highness arranged this meeting, and I must say that your input is equally as valuable as ours."

"Y-yes, your Majesty, thank you." He bowed again and sank down on the dining chair he had occupied before, looking rather foolish.

"He said that, did he, young Corporal Tymain?" Archpriest Bahlien asked the prince, who nodded and smiled slightly. "Hmm, a very insightful young man."

"Yes indeed." Archpriest Lurco agreed. "Excuse me, young man, you haven't ever considered the priesthood as a vocation, have you?"

"Who, me, your Grace?" Tymain asked in a sort of squeak that caused Lyria to hurriedly suppress a giggle. "Oh no, sir."

"Well, Jerryn, that was certainly a unique dream." The High-King remarked. "To speak with our God after so many centuries! My word!"

"Yet our God said that he had used all his strength to communicate with the both of you, Jerryn. Is that not dangerous?" Kerrenan asked rather formally; it seemed a habit of his when faced with complexities.

"It would have been far more dangerous, I deem, for Arven *not* to have spoken with them, Kerr." Bahlien replied. "Whatever he and Ethrayne discussed, Arven has given our champion here some valuable advice: concentrate on freeing Clirensar and avoid Zanezli."

"Surely, though, we cannot leave Ethrayne in their hands?" Lyria objected hotly. "We discussed this before. Pualyn -."

"My darling, you know that we will do everything we possibly can to rescue her." Her husband asserted and glanced from face to face, glaring. "Won't we, my Lords?"

"On my life, Pualyn." Jerryn said, getting to his feet, his hand on his heart, Ethrayne's betrothal ring shining on his finger. "We certainly will, we all want Ethrayne to be set free." He grimaced and continued in a much quieter, yet intense tone. "Dear Arven, we should have been wed by now! All our moons of planning have just been wiped out. Ethrayne has been taken hundreds of leagues away . . . and she's all alone."

*

"Your Majesty, we have received terrible news from King Marrand and Archpriest Lurco from Tenum City." Archpriest Eduard said, nodding his head politely to King Nemeth, a scroll in his hand. It was early, not long after breakfast and the Archpriest had insisted on abandoning the usual protocols of Larrand's court. "Clirensar has been occupied by the jajozeli; the duke and duchess are dead; Lady Ethrayne, the Am'maiya, has been abducted."

"What? I . . . your Grace, what is this?" The King of Derravale stared, shocked at the news. "That girl, abducted, where?" It took a moment for the information to sink in and he almost found it difficult to read the scroll that Eduard passed him. "She's the prince's betrothed; what the hell was she doing outside Tenum City?" He demanded.

Eduard sighed inwardly. "She was travelling to her home with her family to prepare for her wedding actually, your Majesty but enemy soldiers attacked them at the edge of the Vale -."

"Dear Arven, what if they come here?" Nemeth asked in icy fear.

"They hold Clirensar, Nemeth. They're hardly likely to head west right across the continent when there's nothing here in Derravale that they want." The Archpriest stated crisply. "But Lady Ethrayne has been taken south to Zanezli."

"Dear Arven, we're going to have to prepare for war for a *girl*?"

"No, Nemeth, we are going to war to destroy the enemy occupation of Clirensar; Lady Ethrayne is hardly a mere girl: she is the Am'maiya, beside the prince."

"Women have no place in politics!" The king retorted.

"She holds the Flame of Arven, your Majesty and this goes far beyond politics!" Eduard answered gravely. "She and her betrothedare integral to the church, to Iullyn, remember."

King Nemeth didn't snort, but he looked sceptical, none the less.

*

The news of Ethrayne's abduction and the foul murders of the inhabitants of the city and the duke and duchess by the jajozeli that now held Clirensar spread like awful ripples through the continent and beyond; Tenarum's neighbours, Derravale and Amorry, took the news with varying amounts of panic. The panic was averted by calm men, but some of the more nervous, especially in the southern realm of Derravale, started imagining invasion into their own lands.

Leskerthorpe was a comfortable little town near the eastern border of Derravale, on the high road that crossed the low mountains into Tenarum. With a thriving logging industry, plus the ubiquitous sheep herding, farming and weaving, it was a moderately prosperous settlement, rather nicely placed above the river and the road. Now, however, it's pretty outlook across the grasslands to the west and the woodlands of the foothills of the Perotan Hills to the east had changed forever, and many local residents were unhappy, although they fully understood why chaos was descending upon them in the shape of royal-appointed engineers who had arrived in mid Thurton, armed with mounds of equipment, carts, horses and assistants to mark out suitable sites for settlements designed to hold the volunteers and regular soldiers who were required to head into Tenarum in the future. They had spent many days marching over the open countryside surrounding the town, surveying the land and making detailed charts from the local maps before announcing their intentions.

Mayor Thwaite bemoaned, especially, the loss of his best pasture to what appeared to be an entire new town, but Captain Seston, head of the engineers who had marked out new roads, drainage and water channels and buildings, fixed him with a glare.

"You are a God-fearing man, Mayor?" He had asked.

"Well of course, Captain." Thwaite had replied indignantly. "But -."

"Then Arven will view you and yours with approval, for the slight sacrifice you are making towards furthering *his* plans." Seston kept his tone level and polite, although the local official had been trying to block his task for two days now. "There's a jajozeli army in Clirensar, man and they've got to be stopped, to block the Betrayer's actions; that's empty land to the south, Headman and only the enemy on the far side of the mountains!"

That made the tall, skinny man squeak a little and he looked at the smaller, squarer engineer helplessly.

"Look, there're endless leagues of grass and pasture and it will all grow back in the end, but we've got to house the soldiers somewhere when they march through to Tenarum and I didn't really think that you townsfolk would like to put them all up in your little houses, would you?" Seston pressed on relentlessly. "I am sorry, Thwaite, but that level ground is ideal, and I am only following orders you know." He added, slightly more sympathetically. "Look, instruct your brewers to brew and get in as many food supplies as you can: the army has food supplies, but beer and sausages will definitely make you a bit of a profit; winter won't close these mountains until Umttarn if at all: it's a reliable route through to Tenarum." He essayed a smile.

"Y'know, captain, I never thought of . . . well, thank you!" And Mayor Thwaite hurried off quickly.

"That was very well done, sir." Lieutenant Douglas said dryly from just behind his captain. They were stood together in the town square in the centre of Leskerthorpe that afternoon, given a wide berth by the townsfolk and market traders; they had clearly watched Thwaite hurry off with interest, knowing of his opposition to the proposals.

"Anything to get that fool out of the way: we've got to get the water pipes in and the drains dug as quickly as possible." Captain Seston said with a sigh, feeling the chill of the wind and mentally counting down towards mid-winter. Derravale was a realm of rolling grassland and forest; generally, winters even in the south were not too bitter, considering the steppes that climbed across the unclear border with Zanezli, the Lerracon Mountains stark to the south. The necessity of having to move troops into Tenarum, however, had scared the engineers mightily, and the setting of water and sewerage was vital.

"We're marking the lines, Captain; I've teams of men felling trees on the edge of the woods to the north and there's a marvellous source of gravel at the river a league east." Douglas reported cheerfully. "We're practically on schedule, sir."

"I want to be ahead by the end of the day, Lieutenant for the Crown Prince is due to inspect our efforts in seven days." Seston warned him.

"I will report on our progress this evening, sir." Douglas saluted and strode off.

Those in charge of the army in Derravale were particularly concerned at the advance of the jajozeli into Clirensar since the western kingdom extended south than her neighbour, the border only a line on a map across the countryside that climbed gradually from hill country to the steppes. No one really lived in the region, it was as empty as the wild countryside south of the Vale of Clirensar, although the countryside was fertile.

Another concern was that the high road skirted the supposed perimeter of the occupied area around Clirensar, before joining the King's Road at Foston; guards now patrolled the high road across the hill country and within sight of the Vale, but there were no sightings of the enemy, to their relief and, equally, their unease.

*

On hearing the terrible news, King Namayomn barely blinked, before he simply commanded that his court move to his eastern border, although it was not a quick process, by any stretch of the imagination. He agreed with Archpriest Ghorhant that the ramifications of the matter were far beyond his capabilities, but he fully intended to be right at the heart of the proposed campaign and, whittling down his staff and hangers-on to fit into a large manor farmhouse that was commandeered politely by Earl Agamn, closer to events and the training of the volunteers.

Denster was the border city that had been chosen as that kingdom's staging post for the amassing of armies, set on the broad, well-metalled high road that led straight from West Port on the coast, through the capital city, Ronlow and past the low range of the Tenasse Mountains on the edge of which Denster was nestled, and so on into Tenarum and on towards Tenum City.

*

The towns, villages and iron foundries that had been so-far untouched by the murderous tendencies of the occupying jajozeli, within an area closer than about fifteen leagues of the captured city of Clirensar all relocated their families, their equipment and their supplies to the north of the surrounding ditch and ramparts, where they strove to restart their rather alchemical business, once a great deal of wood had been sacrificed to housebuilding rather than charcoal making. The creation of iron from rock and bright steel out of pig-iron was taken with a single-minded intensity, aided by the welcome discovery of a new source of ironstone in the woodlands eight leagues north-east of Black Fell. Smoke and noise rather disturbed the area, but the necessity of their iron and steel was paramount. Those willing were taken on as apprentices, to assist in the creation of chain mail, buckles and whatever orders the Tenarean army put in. As late autumn took a firm hold, the whole realm became a hive of activity and industry with one aim in mind.

*

Couriers sped northward from Rothern to the kingdoms of the Protectorates and their leaders instigated long-standing procedures that had never been set into action and the vast fleet of Jaece spread out to begin ferrying soldiers, weapons and materials across the Hessarth Straits to the Selithian continent, for the weather to the north was milder, of course, where summer was now fast approaching.

There was fear and concern as the news spread that one of the young Am'maiya had been abducted, but also considerable excitement and relief that the long-unaddressed threat of the Jajozeli Empire might be finally dealt with, although even the greenest, most inexperienced volunteer (expecting glory and riches) realised that it would not be a quickly resolved business.

Reaching Horann, with its balmy climate, the Protectorate armies rested before a good number of them marched southward towards Tenarum in easy stages along the broad highway that ran through the Belseque Mountains, a slow but steady advance, marching with wagon trains full of supplies, their leaders with them, kings and professional soldiers of high rank, but with other titles than general, which was never used, usually replaced with colonel instead. Other groups were brought in by ship to Rothern or to Aithport, the only town with a harbour on Tenarum's north coast with the Meroltane Inlet.

The people of Tenarum viewed the thousands of foreign strangers marching down the King's Road with askance at first, but the troops from the kingdoms of the Protectorates were well-mannered, mostly fluent in Selithian – their accents exotic – and tidy, as far as that was possible.

Of course, there were plenty of misunderstandings, fights, and associated criminal activity but, generally, the allies were managing to coexist as the season progressed, setting up in the area north of Tenum City where the razine and human troops were housed.

Jerryn watched the forces collecting, sometimes rode through the area when the meetings were abandoned, now aware that he was worried all over again for these disparate soldiers from every kingdom under Arven, as well as Clirensar and Ethrayne. He was at least able to perfect the mask of calm professionalism which the Archpriests had guided him towards, but he trusted Mhezel, Kerrenan, Pualyn and Tymain enough to show them his true feelings. Talking about it did not achieve a great deal in the long run, but it did ease his knotted fear, for a short while.

The prince was determined to do everything he possibly could to stand up as the Am'maiya had been described in the prophecy, even alone. He would be the figurehead which was required in their future war. He would never let his fear command him.

* * *

CHAPTER 27

It took four days for three complete sets of plain, utilitarian clothing to be delivered: underclothes and socks; three plain shirts in knobbly-woven beige cloth; three pairs of woollen leggings which were rather imperfectly dyed a dark blue that would at least stay in place on her hips; and three short-sleeved tunics in a slightly darker shade of blue woollen cloth. The clothes fitted her well enough but had clearly been made quickly: the quality of the sewing would not have passed even a cursory inspection in any household in Tenarum for the cheapest type of servants clothing. The three young women set about rectifying the most glaring mistakes themselves, whilst Ethrayne rebelliously sewed Arven's emblem on the left breast of the black cloak that now hung on the back of the bedroom door.

Those days after Ethrayne's initial meeting with Master Cheltor passed without any interruption, other that the daily removal of the ash buckets and the arrival of logs. But, not trusting the Generals to leave her alone, Ethrayne could not relax although, with hindsight, she knew that she should have done. She busied herself with trying to ensure that poor, silent Fionn and Sallie were comfortable and reassured, assuming any weapons' practice that the Jajozeli insisted she attend would take up a great deal of her days.

Also, General Garrtnor's clear warning was quite enough to enforce her compliance. After all, she had imagined dank, windowless dungeons for her accommodation here and never a spacious, sunlit (if it had not been approaching winter), fire-lit, comfortable apartment.

The boots did not arrive until the evening of the sixth day, along with a pair of plain gloves and a robust, quilted, mid-green leather sleeveless jerkin that was fastened with black iron clasps. It fitted well, not too tight, and was obviously designed for her protection, which was a little ominous. The boots were a delight: polished black leather that fitted perfectly over a single pair of socks, with just enough wriggle-room for her toes, coming half-way up her calves.

"At least the cobbler takes pride in his work, unlike the tailor." She remarked. "I suppose I'll be climbing up and down this tower a lot – good boots will be vital, it's such a long way up!" Ethrayne sighed deeply. "Well, there's no help for it, I suppose, I'll get leg ache."

Her companions smiled sympathetically.

Two guards appeared, predictably, the next morning after breakfast and marched her down and through the citadel. Master Cheltor awaited her in the hall, his thin face expressionless and nodded slightly before he waved her guards out of the way. She tried to stand straight, to meet his gaze, but everything about him made her uneasy. Standing there, Ethrayne turned slightly to see more Generals seated in the observation area, all strangers and all staring at her. She frowned.

"Better." He said finally. "You look rested."

Ethrayne snorted at that, as if they cared! Arven's warning in that singular dream/vision was again at the front of her mind.

The training session began and continued much as she had feared: much harder, physically, than her respectful Tenarean instructors would have thought appropriate, using swords sharp enough to separate one's shadow, or so they seemed; there were no blunt-edged practice weapons in this hall. The Master made no concessions for her inexperience, whilst the system of combat here seemed completely different to anything she had seen in Tenarum. Ethrayne was forced, that morning, just to do the best she could to protect herself, against him; an unnamed burly male General, then finally a singularly fast, strong, unforgiving General Cavaln, until Master Cheltor eventually called a halt at what turned out to be past midday, his tone impatient, his glare forbidding.

"You will have to learn to think, girl! You're meant to be intelligent, so concentrate!" He ordered shortly. "Get out of here, but return the day after tomorrow and be prompt, understand? I do not condone tardiness." Ethrayne dared to keep silent for the length of a few rapid heartbeats, but Cheltor's huge fist tightened painfully over her right hand before he roughly wrenched the sword from her grip, his face a few inches from hers and repeated very quietly. "Do you understand?"

"Yes, Master Cheltor." She muttered, and he nodded once before gesturing and she turned to begin her guarded trudge back along the corridors and up the stairs to the tower, aching all over. It would not have been so bad, she thought, if she had not done her utmost – but the jajozeli training was utterly different to what she was used to . . . And, at the back of her mind, was the awareness that she simply did not want to comply with his brusque orders, although she knew she had no choice, not after General Garrtnor's warning.

*

And her days into winter were set out: every other day, she spent her mornings and early afternoons there in the combat hall, being shouted at; thumped; knocked down and generally mistreated by Master Cheltor or one of the other Generals, all of whom were just as exacting as he was. But Ethrayne was forced to admit that their violence was controlled, measured. She had sessions with Garrtnor, Ackat and Cavaln amongst the group and the woman was as fast and as strong as the males. Being flung about and disarmed and so on, the girl felt herself to be impossibly slow, stupid and useless; it was their collective lack of approval or praise that led to this impression. She was always pushed to the limit of her ability; unexpectedly, they even introduced her to quarterstaffs after a few days.

In actual fact, she was progressing faster and better than any of the Generals would have thought, though they kept their knowledge to themselves. They continued to watch her closely.

The rest of her time she spent locked up in the tower with Sallie and Fionn as the days grew ever shorter. After a few more peeps out of the shuttered windows at the worsening weather, the gloomy days, they did not even bother to open the curtains and shutters any more: it was lighter, warmer and much cosier in the tower with them closed, leaving the three of them bathed in the golden lamp- and candlelight while the fires blazed. They sat in the sitting room, sewing together as Ethrayne talked, telling stories from childhood, or of their previous lives, before this happened; she sang songs. Else, after combat and early on the rest days, they set about undertaking laundry. Perhaps at Master Cheltor's instruction, they had been provided with an odd washboard to scrub clothes on, cakes of soap and even a flat iron. Maybe he hated creases, Ethrayne surmised, for she had turned up for combat wearing deeply creased clothes for a few days before these items arrived.

Days passed, relentlessly, yet they were quite comfortable whilst, to her relief, Ethrayne only had to endure the Generals' presence in the combat hall. For the rest of the time, fortunately, they were alone, warm, well-fed and time passed bearably, but slowly. In her bed at night, hidden in the darkness, she found her sleep disturbed despite her deep weariness at undertaking so much intense exercise. The loss of her parents still loomed greatly in her mind. Worries for Jerryn, Pualyn and Lyria, Clirensar and the kingdom at large surfaced stronger than ever, once her immediate fears for herself and her maids had diminished. She tried to meditate, to concentrate on the power within her, but – still – it proved impossible to even maintain the control she had had in Tenum City, meditation had no effect at all. Discouraged, she prayed a great deal to Arven for the routine was comforting, speaking silently in her head and she tried to keep the image of Car'Agasse in her mind . . . sometimes it helped her to sleep, but not always . . . She gave thanks that she had the comforting companionship of Fionn and Sallie, knowing that this awful place would be so much worse without their presence.

*

Ethrayne found out, one grey morning in the combat hall as usual, that the next day would be the Winter Solstice only because Master Cheltor mentioned the planned festival celebrations to the Generals in conversation; they all pretty-much ignored her as usual. Ackat, Cavaln and the others laughed as he warned them that he would be expecting no slacking in their training schedules, no matter the lavish festivities prepared for their delectation. Ethrayne started, amazed: Jerryn's birthday and Umttarn were far past; the date they would have wed and likewise Instur was speeding towards a close; her birthday was done, she was already seventeen without even realising it! She had been imprisoned in this horrible citadel for over two moons! But where, she wondered, had the days gone? How could so long have sped by, unnoticed? It was depressing news. She missed Jerryn with every bit of her being, that was what she usually tried to ignore . . . She wondered if he was missing her as much, wishing that she could reassure him . . .

Her momentary, dismayed, lapse of concentration meant that General Shaille tripped her and she had to duck into a forward roll to spring back up, dodging his follow-up attack as best she could. But at least she was stronger than she had been on her arrival and rather more agile and acrobatic on her feet as well. Breathing heavily, sweating copiously, she put the unwelcome information out of her mind, determined to at least try to gain fewer bruises this day, but it was hard, as always. Her chances, she reflected ruefully, of returning a solid blow to any of the blasted Generals who worked her so hard was still less than miniscule.

Ackat, laughing, was assuring Master Cheltor that they would all certainly be on time after the festival. Glancing up, Ethrayne saw one young-looking jajozeli-razine male grinning toothily from the spectators' seating. She realised that she had seen him before, a young man who was obviously of some importance though he was not yet a General; he usually wore plain combat gear like the rest and she had passed him on occasion, in the endless corridors, he and his friends of a similar age (she supposed), and arrogance. He seemed young to her: there was a sort of adolescence about him that a General like Cavaln had long outgrown; she wondered idly, uncaring, just how old he was and what he was doing here in this snow-bound citadel, for a bare moment, before she had to pull her concentration back again, dodging Shaille's kick to her knee.

After noon, she returned, aching, to the tower and washed and changed as usual; each session left her so sweaty and wrung out that her clothes always required scrubbing afterwards. She put on one of her old gowns that did not really fit very well now, with her wider shoulders from all her exercise; she thought that she probably looked stupid, with her hair now long enough to pinch properly, over an inch long, her gowns somehow a little shorter and tight in odd places: thank Arven there were no mirrors here!

"Tomorrow is the Winter Solstice, Sallie, Fionn." Ethrayne told them, making up the fire in the wash room ready to dry the clothes they wrung out after rinsing. "We ought to hold the holiday, curse the Betrayer a bit -." She broke off as a thought came to her: he, the Emperor of the Jajozeli, the Betrayer, might even *be* here in Ban'Lerracon. He might be here, and he might not appreciate curses -. "I should be able to remember some of the Solstice service, if I try. Shall we?" She continued, determinedly dismissing her sudden rush of fear and unease, an icy shiver down her spine. The mere possibility that she might be sharing the vast citadel with the Betrayer, perhaps breathing the same air, had not actually even occurred to her before! But surely someone would have mentioned him before now, if he were? Wouldn't they?

They nodded agreement, so probably the lucky young women, she reflected, did not actually realise who was ultimately in charge of their lives here.

*

Whatever the jajozeli festivities taking place elsewhere in Ban'Lerracon (and Ethrayne thought that their celebrations were likely very, very different to the ones traditional since The Betrayal) their rest day continued as was usual now, wonderfully unbothered by their captors.

She had slept badly, although she was as tired as any other night after hours of combat practice, waking well before dawn. Alone, because Fionn and Sallie were still sleeping, she crept into the sitting room and, opening the shutter of one of the windows, sat there wrapped in a shawl, beginning the Solstice dawn prayer, more than a little surprised that she could recall most of the words to a ritual that had always been a vital part of every year all through her childhood, saying the words quietly aloud as the darkness slowly gave way to a dim grey pre-dawn light which gradually revealed a blizzard-covered scene where almost all the mountains surrounding the city were obscured. Later, she solemnly recited the noon and then the sunset prayers at the approximate times, holding hands with her friends and adding a few more personal prayers in addition, recalling her dream-cum-vision of Car'Agasse and Arven's frozen expression of horror all too clearly. Their freedom to observe their religion unbothered, the fact that they had meals and warmth and comfort, turned the day into a festival in Ethrayne's eyes: having *seen* Arven, imprisoned, even in a dream, made the ritual somehow immediate and pertinent in a way it had never been before.

Please look after Jerryn and his father and Pualyn and Lyria. Oh, I hope they are wed and safe! Please, please look after everybody, including those poor people in Clirensar, if they're still alive, please -. She begged late that night, curled up in her bed, hearing the quiet breathing of her sleeping companions, feeling awfully alone. *And please, I hope you can help me find the strength to survive this, oh, please, Lord!* It felt as though a lifetime had passed since that terrifying, revolting afternoon above Clirensar; two at least since she had bid Jerryn farewell to leave Tenum City . . . *Lord Arven please look after the souls of those so cruelly murdered . . . I promise I will do my utmost to fight them . . . And look after Sallie and Fionn . . . Oh, damn it! Sometimes I'm so frightened -.* She admitted.

For, despite her regular morning sessions, slowly expanding her range of combat skills far beyond anything she could have considered possible, she did not know why the Emperor of the Jajozeli-Razine had ordered her capture, if indeed there was a reason. She wondered just who she would be expected to do battle against now; she had begun to learn, simply to protect herself against the Generals, yet now those same Generals were her tutors.

Ethrayne wished she dared question them, but Garrtnor's threat to her maids was still in her mind. She had tried to climb into the food-delivery box which descended through the tower – but she had not fit at all and it had creaked alarmingly. She had tried to open the lock on the outer door, as well, but nothing she had tried worked at all! She was stuck here.

Lying there in the fire-tinged darkness of the longest night of the year, all the myriad questions came to the forefront of her mind that night and it was a long time before Ethrayne fell into a fitful sleep. Again, she woke long before dawn.

And again, days passed inexorably, marked by meals delivered; ash bins emptied; washing done, and combat sessions undertaken. Winter only seemed to tighten its grip on Ban'Lerracon and the mountainous landscape that surrounded it: snow froze, more snow settled atop the diamond-covered drifts and turned to ice in turn; the very air in the corridors was chilly and even the braziers in the combat hall were ineffective. Only, surprisingly, the tower-top apartment was free of icy blasts and the chimneys somehow repelled any cold gales, ensuring that the young women were snug and warm. Perhaps it was the sheer brutality of the southern winter that convinced Ethrayne that nothing would happen until spring's return melted the ice and snow and she almost yearned for the frozen weather and blizzards to continue. For all intents and purposes, it seemed to comply with her wishes.

*

Inajo watched the human girl leave the hall after yet another bruising morning at General Ackat's hands, sympathising slightly with her slow exit: she had spent a considerable part of the session on the stone-flagged floor, as the tall General had almost literally thrown her about at Master Cheltor impatiently delivered orders. Whoever she was, why-ever she was there, (and women generally didn't learn how to fight, but for General Cavaln) their superiors were merciless.

He had occasionally watched her walking through that part of the citadel, always guarded, and had shared space with her and many others, here in the combat hall on numerous occasions since the late autumn; always aware of this pretty, lean girl with the ridiculously short, ugly haircut and the dark glare in her eyes. She intrigued him. He had asked around, but he had not found out an awful lot about her, not even from his father, General Oxttyn. She was a political prisoner, closely confined, but subject to Master Cheltor's exacting tutelage. Inajo's heart yearned to speak with her. With every sighting, his yearnings increased.

*

Almost imperceptibly, the days gradually began to lengthen, but so grim were the storms, so low the clouds hiding the mountains that surrounded the city, that few noticed the progress of the seasons; it seemed that more torches than ever burned in the halls and corridors, to raise the light levels.

Ethrayne could tell that time was passing, however: her hair was now over two inches long and she was very glad that she was no longer just bald, though the new growth could not be much of a hairstyle. After yet another gruelling session of sword-practice and unarmed combat, she had enjoyed a hot bath and then a typical lunch of cold ham, dark bread, sharp cheese and wizened apples with Sallie and Fionn, her aching muscles starting to ease gradually. Wearing one of her old gowns in faded crimson, wrapped in a shawl that she thought had been handed down from her maternal grandmother, she was reading poetry aloud. Her sweaty fighting garb, now faded, slightly threadbare, had been scrubbed again and hung to dry before the bathroom fire.

As always, their small domestic arrangements filled their days adequately, but Ethrayne still worried at what her friends and maids could possibly do when she was absent, sitting silent and frightened -.

The outside door was unlocked with a snap and swung wide open, completely unexpectedly. All three young women exchanged startled glances, for no one had intruded upon them in an afternoon for nearly all the time Ethrayne had been imprisoned there. A young man, jajozeli-razine not human, wearing well-made clothes and an arrogant expression strode into the room, looking around at the furniture and the three of them, a little confusion showing in his face.

"Who are you? What do you want?" Ethrayne demanded imperiously, dropping the old book onto the settee, then realised that she had spoken in selithian, so she repeated the words in jajozeli. "Go away! You should not be here!"

"Rubbish!" He gestured arrogantly. "I go where I please. I want you, girl. I have been watching you for moons -."

"Me?" She quavered, battling a sudden burst of fear as she rose to her feet. "Don't be stupid, you can't bloody well have me, so get out!" She used a modicum of that always-simmering anger which underpinned the rest of her emotions to try and dominate the situation, but he smirked at her as any obtuse young male might; he wasn't listening. He slammed the door shut and stepped forward. "Get out, you fool!"

"Pirris! Why are you wearing such horrible clothes?" He asked contemptuously. "How dare you speak to me so, girl! You are only human! My father is a General! And you are merely a prisoner!"

"I am hardly just a prisoner, you idiot, get out of here!" Ethrayne shot back, moving around the furniture, still hoping to stop the fool: she was tall, trained and stronger than she had ever been before. He tried to grab her arm and she struck him hard. "Get out of here!"

"Bitch!" His arm lashed out, but his hand collided with the iron poker held in Sallie's trembling hands, rather than with Ethrayne's face and he cursed graphically. "Idiot!" He wrestled the crude weapon from the maid and directed a blow down on her blonde head instead. Shocked, Ethrayne screamed in horror and grabbed his arm desperately, trying to stop him, but he roughly shoved her away and carried on striking the girl before Ethrayne could move. Sallie collapsed silently in moments, blood covering her hair, whilst Ethrayne jumped forward, still trying desperately to stop him, though it was probably far too late; he thumped her hard in the chest, knocking her backwards into the settee before he dropped the poker beside Sallie's horribly still body.

"Murdering bastard!" She hissed, fear choking her, inhibiting thought. She knew that her very clothing would be a hindrance, voluminous and cumbersome. "Sallie was no threat to you! What sort of animal are you? Are you all trained to be monsters from birth?" Her anger flashed out, and she considered her moons of training, yet how much good would anything she might attempt be, against someone so obviously strong and well-trained? But she was going to damn-well stop him, whatever it took! "Bloody monster! Have you any idea who I am? Get out, you murderer!"

"She dared to strike me! A slave! How dare you disobey me?" He retorted, again closing the distance between them in a couple of steps.

They were distracted, however, as Fionn screamed horribly from where she cowered down by the log pile, screaming with a frightening, hoarse intensity, then started throwing firewood across the room at him. Ethrayne sidestepped, moving quickly behind the settee, but the stranger snarled, ducked a couple of sturdy logs and leapt across the carpet to make a grab for her, moving far too quickly for Ethrayne to retreat again. One large hand was hard and tight on her shoulder, whilst the other clawed at her throat, trying to encircle it, the sound of ripping fabric horribly loud as she struggled.

She slapped him across the face, beat at it, but to no effect. At the last possible moment, as she meant to knee him hard in the groin, Ethrayne suddenly discovered that core of white-hot strength that she had faded during her journey – and largely forgotten about since her capture, so immersed as she had been in the boring, repetitive, safe routine which had filled her days here in the citadel. Now, she realised that Ackat ruthlessly cutting off her hair had inhibited her use of her power as well as her confidence. The youth's grip had tightened, the shoulder of her gown ripped aside, and he leaned over her, trying to force her to the floor, trying to throttle her into submission, his nails cutting in to her skin -.

You have no idea at all of who I am, you bastard, have you?" She whispered the words, relaxing with some sort of instinct rather than common-sense. In less than a heartbeat there was a surge of might from deep within her that knocked him backwards and caused her to step away, wobbling, in the opposite direction. "How dare you touch me?"

Power flashed through the tower room like a lightning flash. There was, in a moment, far more power than Ethrayne could even comprehend or imagine, greater than any strength had been since that night far beneath the Cathedral, when she and Jerryn had slowly soaked up Arven's Flame. But this was like forked lightning around her, flaring with terrifying, blinding strength -.

Ethrayne was thrown backwards against the wall behind, pinned there, unable to move a muscle, every sense assaulted, overwrought -.

Another figure had suddenly appeared in the centre of the room and the large space shrank exponentially at his mere presence. He was very tall, his muscular physique obvious through his loose, white shirt. He had gleaming, wavy, short black hair. Between one breath and the next, he had somehow used his immeasurable strength to jump right to the top of the tallest tower in the castle. Frozen, Ethrayne found that she was gasping for air, terror choking her. The towering, hugely powerful figure turned to glance at her and she stared, transfixed, at the largest, long-lashed black eyes in a lean, handsome but ice-cold face. He commanded more power than all his Generals put together. This could only be the Betrayer. The Emperor of the Jajozeli-Razine Empire. Gregnor.

The unnamed young male who had attacked her lay prone and trembling at his emperor's feet.

"Well, well, well, what have we here?" He asked in a deep, melodious voice that thrilled her senses with menace, then turned to glance across the room, once, before the sound of thudding footsteps advancing up the stairs became audible despite the closed door; it then burst open with a crash to admit Master Cheltor, Ackat, Cavaln, Shaille and a General she only vaguely recognised by sight. "You took your time." Gregnor said with deceptive mildness.

"Sire! Inajo! What? Pirris!" The unknown, dark-haired General stuttered in obvious shock, taking in the figures in the room: one girl quivering in terror by the woodpile; another dead with a broken skull; the third pinned against the wall as if she was nailed there and the youth sprawled on the floor. "Sire, I -."

"I will enquire as to recent events, Oxttyn believe me." His master interrupted in a far colder tone and General Oxttyn shrank back visibly as the emperor moved one hand negligently. Unexpectedly, Ethrayne found that she could now move her tongue, jaw and turn her head a little, but nothing more. "Tell me, Lady Ethrayne: what has occurred here?"

There was no thought of refusing to answer and the girl again found her gaze held as remorselessly by his black eyes as her body was to the wall, as a butterfly to a board: helplessly.

"You-your Majesty . . . He-he just burst through the door." Ethrayne managed to whisper hoarsely, stuttering. "Sallie . . . she, she tried to stop him but he h-hit her with the poker . . . He g-grabbed me -."

"And you finally released your defences." The Emperor concluded. "Just in time, it seems; but why did you not shout, hmm?"

"S-shout, Majesty? From the top of this tower?" She asked in shivering confusion.

"Pirris! With your *mind*, child! I have heard most of your silent comments for moons now and they have been so *very* tiresome! Why did you not call for aid that way?" He demanded shortly, shaking his head.

"I – I . . ." But she had no answer, terrified and confused.

He snorted contemptuously. "Have you seen this boy before?"

"Y-y-yes, some-sometimes, your Majesty, in the combat hall, occasionally in passing -."

"Yes, Inajo has attended on those mornings, but not exclusively." Cheltor confirmed in a confident manner. "He asked questions about her, but so have all the other cadets, Majesty. We had no idea -."

"Obviously." Gregnor's tone was somehow even colder and all the Generals, even Master Cheltor, flinched slightly at it. He released Ethrayne from her position so that she slid helplessly down the wall and onto the floor, gasping at the sudden shock of pain that flared through her nerves at even such a minor use of his vast power. "Bring her here, Cavaln."

The woman was dressed in a long, strangely designed, beautiful green robe or gown, fastened with a deep purple sash, the most feminine clothing that Ethrayne had yet seen her wearing, although she still bore her sword in her hand, which she now handed to Garrtnor. She hauled the girl up by her left arm, shoved her forward and onto her knees, locking that arm tight behind her back in case she might, recklessly, stupidly, attempt to flee. Ethrayne knelt only a few feet from the king and less than that from the prone, wide-eyed, pale-faced and silent Inajo.

"Still, at least you thought to defend yourself, girl." Gregnor said, sounding almost amused. "What took you so long?"

The question completely stunned Ethrayne. She could only stutter to no purpose for a few moments, finally hesitantly managing to whisper -. "I-it only seemed mo-moments, your Majesty . . . panic a-and -."

"And you have no idea at all of what exactly you command, have you?" The emperor might well have read her mind as he finished her sentence. "Idiot child! So here you are with your attacker, the boy who would have violated you, the boy who killed your faithful maid. He is helpless now; go ahead and kill him!"

"What?" Ethrayne and General Oxttyn cried at the same moment in similar shocked tones, the General shrinking back as fearfully as Ethrayne longed to at the dark glare that struck him from his master's eyes. It seemed a few moments before he could get a grip upon his emotions, bowing his head deeply and the girl wondered if he was the boy's father.

"You have power, girl and, as Emperor, I say that you have the right to act against this reckless youth." Gregnor said, speaking slowly and clearly as if to a complete fool. "Carry on, Ethrayne, you will not be punished."

Ethrayne stared up at him in horror, glanced down at the young man laid on the floor before her and slowly, reluctantly, raised her frightened gaze back to meet the emperor's. Minutely, quivering with fear, she shook her head.

"Come, girl, you have the strength, even if it is untried and untrained. Go on, do it!" He urged in a tone of reasonable encouragement. "You would have done so if I had not intervened, after all. So, kill him!"

Her heartbeat thudded hard in her throat and Ethrayne stared, completely caught in the cruel maliciousness which she could read in the emperor's black gaze simply because he permitted her to do so. Slowly she shook her head for a second time.

"No? But why not?" He pressed, relentlessly.

Ethrayne winced as Cavaln's grip on her arm tightened. "Tha- that was then, you-your Majesty . . . I-I could not-not kill anyone in, in cold blood." She stammered in a fearful whisper.

"No?" Gregnor asked, towering above her. "Do it!" He shouted, his words echoing awfully around the room, deafening.

Assaulted by his power, his overpowering presence, his voice; completely overwhelmed, Ethrayne would simply have run from him, if Cavaln had not held her arm in a grip that threatened to break or dislocate it. "I-I c-can't, Sire." Ethrayne croaked, quite amazed that she dared refuse him.

The look on his face was terrifying to behold, his eyes blazing. Then, unexpectedly, he nodded his head once and grinned at her, producing a long knife from a sheath at his right hip; negligently, he used it to cut away at the cowering youth's clothing. Inajo didn't dare move an inch either. Gregnor grabbed one arm to roughly pull him over from his front to his back in the process. The youth made some sort of sound, almost a whimper, once. The others all simply stared, frozen perhaps, as Inajo was stripped. Ethrayne could not pull her eyes away, even though she felt nothing but embarrassment and pity for him as he lay there, shivering in extreme fear, naked in moments.

"So, watch, Ethrayne. Watch and learn." Gregnor said, took hold of Inajo's privates and sliced, once, with the sharp blade, excising them, dropping the bits of flesh to the floor. The victim screamed in agony, again and again; writhing -.

Ethrayne failed to suppress a scream of her own as Inajo's life blood hit her hard in the face. Unable to retreat, she was helpless as the king stood back up, wiping his knife on a piece of shirt, watching the horrified girl dispassionately as she stared, transfixed, as the young male, her attacker, bled to death, tears starting to streak through the blood that now covered her face. It seemed to take forever for Inajo to die, his blood pumping steadily out of his body; the thick carpet was covered in it, the thick liquid also seeping into Ethrayne's skirt where she knelt and painting the king and Cavaln's boots and clothes with crimson.

Far worse than watching him die, however, was *feeling* him die as the blood poured from his body, his agony transferred to her by her own power; Ethrayne did not know how to block that pain and terror. Nausea filled her. The horrible process of Inajo's dying was even worse because the king could read her disgust and fear and pity just as clearly and clearly was enjoying her emotions immensely.

"Kill the maid." Gregnor ordered dispassionately, his gaze again freezing the girl when she instinctively tried to protest. General Shaille strode towards Fionn, cowering on the floor, his sword in his hand. "You, Lady Ethrayne, will learn the sense of obedience, or you will suffer!"

His huge, awe-inspiring strength returned to wrap tightly around Ethrayne as Cavaln dragged her to her feet, the power was stifling, smothering, closing on her like a snake tightening its coils perhaps. It flashed, again as brilliant as lightning and the girl staggered as her badly wrenched arm was released. The warmly lit, cosy sitting room and the enemies surrounding her vanished in the blink of an eye. Seemingly in a breath, stunningly, she swayed unsteadily on her feet in an almost impenetrable darkness, alone.

Overwhelmed, appalled, she sank down onto cold stone and sobbed, then retched uncontrollably. All she could taste was blood. All she could smell was blood; and it was swiftly drying on her face, her hands and her clothes, although she desperately tried to wipe it away. All she could see and feel, still, was that poor, impetuous fool, dying . . .

*

Back in the blood-soaked living room, the Emperor of the Jajozeli-Razine turned to glare at his servants. "I want these rooms cleared and cleansed." He ordered shortly. "Keep only her clothes, oh, and that sewing box I suppose, it will serve to keep her occupied, later; she is rather skilled, I have noted." There was a cold brutality in his voice. "Have the bodies removed -." General Oxttyn made an involuntary cry and shrank back as his master frowned at him, his eyes blazing. "You, Oxttyn, will travel to Clirensar and assist Commander Tequan. Let's see if you can possibly redeem your family and your name in my eyes: I am most displeased!"

"F-forgive me, your Majesty -." Oxttyn blurted, bowing low, speaking almost as fearfully as Ethrayne had.

"Get out of my sight, Oxttyn! NOW!" Gregnor roared and, cringing, the General quickly knelt before him, then fled.

"Sire, it is snowing by the foot outside." Master Cheltor offered the fact diffidently. Seeing him, Ethrayne would have been amazed to see her relentless, cold, heartless instructor behave so humbly.

"So? Either he will get to N'Astoln or he will freeze to death. Either way, he will have many cold days and nights to think on his obvious mistakes in bringing up so, so *stupid* a son." The censure in the king's voice was burning; all of them stepped back in concern at it. "Get this mess out of here. Get it scrubbed. Now!"

"As you command, Master." General Cavalr said meekly, bowing low, as he raked them with one last fiery glare and made for the stairs. Once he had left the tower room and sound of his ringing boot soles had diminished as he descended, they all sighed deeply at once and relaxed slightly as a group.

"Well let's get started." Ackat advised, gazing around. "It should all make a good bonfire out in the courtyard."

* * *

CHAPTER 28

Ethrayne was locked in a dungeon. It seemed that all her nightmares had come to pass. The space was only very dimly lit by a faint wash of distant orange-tinged torchlight that only barely illuminated the upper third of the back and left-hand walls, coming through a narrow, barred aperture above the thick wooden door, at least eight feet above the ground. The rest of the cell was smothered in thick darkness.

She had hit the floor, her head spinning and had, helplessly, thrown up repeatedly, her body in knots, trying to purge the taste of blood and the horror. The girl had searched the dark place on hands and knees, at some point after her initial panic had passed, only then daring to get up, for what if there was a hole, somewhere, which would swallow her up? Ethrayne had discovered that the cell was constructed of uniformly smooth stone blocks: floor, walls and the raised bed-space to the right-hand side, set some distance above the ground. There was a small metal grate, set securely into the floor by the back wall, she assumed for drainage, but nothing else, except two blankets folded neatly on the platform; this was less than three feet wide, maybe seven feet long, the same length as the cell and perhaps its width, she guessed.

It was horrible; dark; insanitary; lonely. Ethrayne acknowledged these facts readily enough, still shivering in reaction to all that had happened in the tower. Most pertinently, however, she was a long way away from the Emperor of the Jajozeli-Razine, something that she was only able to appreciate an unknown length of time after her initial hysteria had passed, leaving her hoarse, thirsty and breathless. After sheer exhaustion had pushed back her misery and distress, she slept, wrapped tight in the blankets on the unyielding platform; although she could still only taste and smell blood and vomit, the need of her body and mind for rest was paramount, even over disgust and her overwrought imagination.

She mourned for Sallie and Fionn, to die so horribly, so suddenly . . . every moment taken up with their dying . . . theirs and that stupid Inajo! The king was merciless! Despair filled her.

Awakening to the same dark cell, the faintly flickering orangey light high above only serving to make the darkness blacker, Ethrayne was coldly clear-headed, perhaps because of thirst and hunger and she strove to concentrate on where she was, rather than dwell on all that had happened so shockingly, so swiftly; she knew that she would have to seriously, levelly *think* about the king of the jajozeli and his immense power . . . But not yet! Not yet. Any tiny thought that included *him* raised sickening panic within her. Most importantly, she must deal with this horrible place.

The light levels never seemed to change, only flickered, and she guessed that she was underground, never able to tell whether it was night or day, or how fast or slow time was passing when she was awake. Consequently, she never knew, and her captors certainly did not enlighten her, just how long she spent locked in that cell. The only fact was that the ache of her combat practice and the pain she had suffered from Inajo's attack on her arms and neck had all gone completely when she emerged.

The arrival of meals in the narrow slot she discovered in the base of the front wall where it met the bed platform was also random, or so it seemed. Some plate or surface span about, opening into the corridor, she supposed, taking away the used utensils, replacing them with fresh ones beyond her line of sight. It did not admit any light when it turned, and Ethrayne had only discovered the food and drink by the grating sound made by the turning of the hatch, then the smell of it, enticing her. She had inched forward slowly, one hand extended warily, and she had jerked her hand away in surprise and some fear at the touch of a warm bowl that had certainly not been there before. The bowl was of thick pottery, when she lifted it; the plate she found next was metal, as was the ewer. Their appearance was completely unexpected.

She could not even tell by the sort of food delivered what time of day it was the meals were always the same, she found: a large bowl of savoury soup containing what she decided were well diced pieces of meat and vegetables, plus hunks of bread and cheese and a large ewer of what smelled and tasted like fresh water.

For a very long time after the arrival of the first meal, Ethrayne was just grateful for its appearance: food and water had never been so welcome. But time continued, passed relentlessly and pitilessly and soup, bread and cheese were quickly consumed, no matter how she tried to eke them out.

She soon found that she was lying prone on the hard bed platform for longer and longer of her waking time, wrapped in the blankets, shivering; she usually was fighting against tears . . . and mostly failing. As before, she relived the battle above Clirensar, the horror of the deaths of the soldiers and her parents, her utter fear. She could not avoid the memories, they were burned into her mind, her grief immeasurable.

And, in addition, the horror of the young man's attack and his unnecessary murder of Sallie, was bad enough to recall, but her stupid, unthinking helplessness in the face of what he had intended gave her nightmares. What on Iullyn was the point of learning all those skills if she could not act? And, so much worse than freezing instead of gouging at his eyes or punching him hard in the groin, was everything that had followed on from her desperate, unthinking, defensive blast of power; this haunted her whether asleep or awake . . . the king's reasonable suggestion that she kill him: that she had the right, as the victim! . . . His command – so swiftly followed by his ice-cold brutality in butchering the youth so readily, right in front of her eyes. And, much more important and more terrifying than all else, the king's immeasurable, astounding, overwhelming power.

The reality of Gregnor's awe-inspiring strength simply terrified her: she could not even begin to imagine being ever strong enough to be anything but an insect under his heel. The mere thought of becoming that 'weapon' able to *destroy* the Betrayer, as she and Jerryn had asserted so naively and confidently the previous spring, now only filled her with near-hysterical laughter at her foolishness at believing that the one who had bent his purpose so single-mindedly to imprison Arven and command Iullyn, could ever be defeated!

*

Ethrayne had not realised just how much Inajo had damaged the bodice of her gown until she attempted to use some of the drinking water to scrub the long-dried blood from her face, using a piece of her petticoat to desperate effect. Then, she discovered that his violent actions had ripped away a large area of fabric, leaving some of her chest and torso exposed, the fabric flapping under her arm. It embarrassed her awfully that the king and the Generals had had such a clear view of her body and she had quickly used her grandmother's shawl to bind the bodice back over her breasts, thankful for its length and width to be so adaptable. It had taken a good while, to complete this in the darkness, but she was at least, finally, modestly covered.

The dungeon soon smelled, and the stench only worsened as time passed, but Ethrayne was glad that the space was at least dry and relatively warm, or at least not so cold to render the blankets inadequate to warm her, although they were completely unable to protect her from the solid stone of the platform.

Gregnor had sent her here in a moment, somehow using his power to transport her from tower top to dungeon, but clearly he did not desire her to be damaged, only frightened, intimidated and overwhelmed. That realisation served to dispel a little of the overriding misery which was dominating her mind, and she strove to push back the horror of the three deaths, although it was not easy to achieve; her success was very fragile.

The darkness; the silence; the loneliness; the fear, all worked on her mind, certainly weakening her . . . the girl prayed to Arven, but even that was difficult, for their God was locked in ice, frozen, helpless himself! No matter how she struggled against them, her misery and despair increased.

*

The cell door crashed open unexpectedly, hitting the wall behind with an echoing bang! The noise woke her from a doze and unclear dreams in a heartbeat. Ethrayne sat up, bewildered and half-blinded by the ruddy torchlight that stung, filling the cell with, to her eyes, far too harsh a light.

Hands grabbed her, hauling her to her feet when she hesitated, still trying to see clearly through the tears brought on by the sudden bright light, the blankets pulled from her, leaving her uncertain and shivering, for the air in the corridor outside was colder and noticeably cleaner than that in the cell.

"March." Cavaln's voice ordered coldly, so she did, the stone of the corridor floor cold under her bare feet, finally able to clearly see the General ahead and the four large black-uniformed, armed soldiers who accompanied her along the broad, empty corridor broken up only by regularly spaced, massive oak doors to left and right, all secured with equally large locks, until they came to a locked iron gate that blocked the corridor from the base of a stairwell, from which steps rose up and up; and Ethrayne, who had grown to hate the imposed idleness of her imprisonment, had to grit her teeth against the discomfort of relentless climbing, with feet and legs and lungs grown too used to inactivity. The stairs were long, three long flights past two more levels to ground level and daylight, on the far side of a second locked gate.

Ethrayne walked on at a hobble, the stone hard against her feet, along another corridor and then, unexpectedly, she recognised a corridor that stretched off to her left as one that led to the combat hall where she had spent so many mornings.

I really hope they don't want me to spar or fence today. She thought wearily, recalling Master Cheltor's unforgiving sessions with a grimace, but General Cavaln led her off to the right, into new territory, up another slightly more ornately decorated staircase and further corridor, another set of steps, on and on, until, when she was started to think about simply sitting down to rest, Cavaln opened a large door without a word, entered a space beyond, and she was shoved roughly inside after her -.

Ethrayne staggered and stared with wide eyes. The room beyond was large, floored and walled in the same stone as the dungeon, but graced with thick patterned carpets, luxuriously upholstered furniture and long, thick curtains at the windows, detailed tapestries on some of the walls. Cavaln had vanished, but two women stood there, wearing strange, plain blue dresses that came to mid-calf with their hair tightly braided and fastened up; frozen, she simply stared at them in fear, embarrassed at how awful she smelled and the disgusting state of her clothes: ripped, filthy and covered with brown-dried blood-stains -.

"Just look at you!" The taller of the two women said in jajozeli, shaking her head and tutting. "Come on, follow us."

She turned to open a door in the wall beyond, but Ethrayne could not move, all her distrust for her enemies filling her mind. The second woman came around behind her and gently pushed her into movement, crossing the living room, entering a foyer, then through another doorway into a large bathroom, the last place Ethrayne would have expected. There was a large sunken, marble bath set into the floor, some distance from a fireplace large enough to roast a sheep in, where a fire sparked and crackled; to her right was a large, green silk-covered tri-fold screen and a table beyond holding ewers, towels and so on. Cavaln was waiting there, glaring at her.

Ethrayne hated herself for her all-encompassing fear; she was heartily sick of the emotion weakening her, but she still could not move. She was stuck exactly where the woman had guided her to, and the servant sighed and locked the door that led to the foyer.

"Come along, girl." She said in a calm tone, taking her wrist and leading her firmly towards the fireplace, where the women started removing her disgusting clothes, simply casting them into the flames. Numb, Ethrayne could only endure it, trying to ignore the General's presence.

They poured hot water over her where she stood and scrubbed her from head to foot with soft, soap-laden brushes, the dirty water vanishing into a drain close by; the floor must slope slightly, she supposed dully. Then, more water was poured over her to rinse off the soap, hot and somehow comforting, before Ethrayne was immersed in the steaming bath, up one step and down three, to sink into rosemary-scented bliss up to her shoulders, where she rested, closing her eyes against the world, feeling the warmth seeping into her aching body most delightfully, the stink of ordure finally eliminated.

Presently, the water starting to cool, the women ushered her out, helped her get dry. Cavaln checked her over, asking brusque questions as to her wellbeing, her hands warm against her bare skin, causing that all-too familiar discomfort. "Well, you're as healthy as can be expected, girl." She stated, sitting down in a chair.

The servants trimmed her hair, before Ethrayne was laid face up on a padded divan, covered with warm towels and her face, body, limbs and shoulders were massaged with scented oils; then, turned on her front, they did the same to her back and down her arms and legs again. Ethrayne felt a few more of her aches and pains dissolve as they worked with skill, either physical or mental knots, she did not know. She felt a delightful languor steal through her as the four hands massaged expertly, so that she nearly fell asleep, feeling the most relaxed that she had so far experienced since her capture.

"Up you get." They instructed then, still surprisingly patient, before trimming her toenails, buffing her fingernails and started to dress her in a series of robes, comprising of two sleeveless silk undergarments, one short, the second long, an elbow-length, floor-length white silk robe which felt simply glorious against her skin, covered with another of thicker, deep-blue silk satin; finally, an elbow-length satin robe was arranged around her, embroidered around the neckline and wide sleeves with delicate stars, the silver thread gleaming against the mid-grey silk, the whole fastened with a very long blue sash knotted about her waist, the same colour as the under robe.

"Thank you." Ethrayne said earnestly, her head spinning as the completely unpredictable nature and commands of her captor confused her yet again -.

"Well, you'll do." Cavaln said gravely, looking her up and down. "Come along, girl."

Ethrayne slipped thin shoes on to her feet, nodded a brief thanks to the servants, followed the General into the sitting room and out into the corridor beyond, where two of the guards who had marched her up from the dungeons fell in behind.

After following that main corridor some distance, the woman led her through more decorated parts of the citadel, Ethrayne noted; there were plaster mouldings, marble tiles, expensive panelling, other marks of quality, and ornate lamps instead of torch brackets that, along with staircases that swept upward rather than simply going directly up and down, showed that this area was occupied by more important people. She trudged along in Cavaln's wake, wondering just where she was heading now and when she would get a meal, other than wishing that she was freezing in a blizzard in the mountains, rather than being here in Ban'Lerracon.

"Surely those are not tears on your cheeks?" Cavaln asked her maliciously as she led her along a wide corridor floored with emerald green and black tiles. "Oh, *child* -."

"Leave me alone!" Ethrayne snapped back in a mixture of embarrassment and bravado, hurriedly wiping at her face, wishing that her reaction to all that had occurred since that young man's appearance could have been delayed until she was safely alone; but she had no idea what might happen next . . .

"Fool!" The General stated contemptuously. "Your empathy will be your undoing."

Ethrayne shivered, biting her lip to keep in all her fury and fear, knowing that to give vent to her roiling emotions would only get her into even more trouble.

At the end of the corridor, a semi-circle of four steps led down to an arched entrance and into a large hall containing various sizes of tables, capable of holding anything from four to twenty or so diners, some of the larger refectory tables had both benches and backed chairs. There were high, narrow windows ranged along the right-hand wall and a series of hatches in the left-hand wall; the air smelled deliciously of fresh, warm bread and cooked food and there was a buzz of conversation coming from many points.

Taking one step into the space, Ethrayne stopped dead, reluctant both to advance and retreat: the hall was full of jajozeli-razine wearing Generals' uniforms, many whom she recognised from combat training.

"Don't dawdle, girl." Cavaln growled, striding out towards the serving hatches. "It's noon, you'll need your strength this afternoon. How long is it since you had a meal?"

"I-I have no idea, my Lady." Ethrayne answered, forcing herself into motion, trying to keep her gaze at around table height, to avoid meeting anyone's gaze: for the diners all glared at her, their animosity clear to her nerves.

The green-garbed servitors behind the hatches all stared openly at her, this unwelcome intruder and Ethrayne felt oddly small and skinny in her pristine silk clothing; two meals were quickly dished up and set on a wooden tray, which Cavaln carried off to the left, to one of the smaller tables, Ethrayne following with two large mugs of steaming tea.

"From now on, you will eat your meals here." The woman stated, sitting down and handing Ethrayne one plate, then cutlery; the girl discarded good manners for simple need, she had not realised just how hungry she was, spooning up the food as soon as she was seated. “Don’t eat your meal like that, you’ll just make yourself ill. Slow down, girl.” Her tone was coolly disapproving and Ethrayne paused, waiting for a sudden discomfort to ease. “Your mornings will probably be spent at combat practice, daily and your afternoons will pass in study.”

“Study?” Ethrayne asked, sipping at the tea in the mug. “What sort of study, my Lady?”

Cavaln gave her a flash of a smile, but it didn’t touch her eyes. “His Majesty has decreed that you will learn to read and write jajozeli, along with improving your knowledge of mathematics and so on.”

“You-you are sending me to *school*?” Ethrayne demanded rather indignantly. Was this to do with the prophecy or her power? What was going on? “I am not a child, General Cavaln -.”

“You *are* a child, and will you dare refuse his Majesty’s command?” Cavaln countered in a mild tone, at which Ethrayne quickly closed her mouth. “Good girl. Now eat up.”

Not daring to reply, she did so. Questions seethed inside her.

*

The General then left the dining hall and they collected the two guards who had remained outside the space, going back along the passage, up a level where, halfway along a corridor with widely spaced doors, Cavaln opened one on the right, leading Ethrayne into a small, square foyer with doors to the left and right; again, the guards remained in the corridor outside. Opening the right-hand door, the woman gestured and Ethrayne stepped into a very plain, small bedroom.

“This will be your room.”

The girl had already recognised her sewing box, set on the small table to the left, and the long oak chest on the floor next to it that had, once, lain at the foot of her bed in her rooms in Clirensar. The narrow bed was directly ahead, stuck out from the opposite wall beneath the small window.

“As you see: bed, table and chair for study and there is a washroom there to the right. Your clothes are in the chest, open it.” Cavaln ordered and Ethrayne did so, stooping down to lift the heavy lid, seeing the heavy black cloak they had given her, folded on top of everything else with the emblem of Arven which she had embroidered on it so defiantly, bright and clear. “You will unpick your work this evening and replace it with his majesty’s device.”

Anger flared upward with reckless abandon. “I will not! I am Arven’s servant.”

Cavaln did not argue, she stepped forward, only two strides, pulled Ethrayne up and around, slapped her hard across the face and twisted her fingers tightly in the girl’s short hair, her left arm was then in Cavaln’s other hand, locked in a hold that Ethrayne could not possibly break: she was helpless, yet again! She fought against uttering a cry of pain, biting her lip hard as Cavaln pushed her to the left.

"Walk, brat! Open the doors." She ordered shortly, marching her out of the room, through the foyer and into a very pleasant sitting room beyond the other door, pushing her on, towards a further pair of doors that opened on a surprisingly feminine bedroom draped in shades of green and pink which was much larger than Ethrayne's small space, with a large, highly polished silver mirror between elegant pieces of furniture, to which Ethrayne was forced. "Look, fool!"

The figure she could see in the mirror was a stranger, wearing beautiful, strangely styled clothes, but her eyes were shadowed, her face thin and pale, except where the General had struck her, leaving a red mark; her hair was ridiculously short, stuck up, oddly wavy, her ears sticking out stupidly whilst, she noted, there were still bruises and scratches visible around her throat above the neckline of the gown, fading, but clear. Ethrayne could not recognise herself at all.

"You will unpick your frozen God's emblem, stupid girl, and replace it with his majesty's. Tonight. Then you will sew his device on the left breast of all your clothes and I will inspect them, or you can go back to the dungeon, if you prefer?" Cavaln twisted Ethrayne's arm even tighter and she rose up onto her tiptoes and could not halt a small cry of protest, for it felt as though her shoulder was being dislocated. "Do I make myself clear, brat?"

"But I am Arven's -." She tried to explain, despite the discomfort she felt.

"Who feeds you? Clothes you, hmm? This is the Jajozeli Empire, child. Our emperor owns you! You can try to fight -." There was cool amusement in her voice as Ethrayne briefly tried to struggle, then ceased before losing the hair on her head to Cavaln's grip. "But you are still only an amateur in combat, my dear! It takes a decade to complete the training to become a General and there is no certainty of success; ten years, brat, after I had completed all the schooling available. You were what, four years of age, playing with rag dolls, a decade ago?" She sneered.

"I-I was seven a-and I had puppies and horses, actually, my Lady General." Ethrayne admitted quietly. There had been a few dolls too, of course, but she would have sooner died than say so. Ten whole years to qualify! It was daunting.

"You have an awful lot to learn, child, before you can hope to take on even the least of us and possibly win a bout. I want an apology, brat!" Cavaln continued.

The woman's tightening hold on both scalp and arm both shot even sharper pain through her. "I . . . Ow! I am sorry, My Lady General, please forgive my lack of manners." Ethrayne said quickly.

"And you will embroider as you have been instructed?" Cavaln insisted, still not releasing her, her grip still as unforgiving.

"I-I will." For what choice did she have?

"You have five days, then, to complete the task. I suggest you begin later, brat." Finally, Cavaln let her go, then cupped her chin to glare down into her pale face. "Remember the dungeon, Ethrayne, before you attempt rebellion here. Follow me." She warned quietly.

Back in the elegant sitting room, Ethrayne saw that the comfortable looking furniture was upholstered mainly in a deep green with crimson highlights, with polished tables close to hand, set around a large, black marble fireplace in which the fire was lit, blazing merrily in an ornate grate. Cavaln sank gracefully into a large armed chair and pointed to one almost directly opposite, raising one eyebrow elegantly as the girl paused, rolling her aching left arm slightly before obeying.

"You have had some sort of education, I suppose?" The General continued rather insultingly. "Tell me, is that traditional for girls of your rank?"

"I have had a wide-ranging education, my Lady General, including language, grammar, mathematics, law, economics and politics -." Ethrayne countered defensively, rather confused. "I also was meditating, before you captured me, learning how to control th-the Flame within me."

"You will learn what his majesty decrees. At least you know how to learn -."

"Of course, General Cavaln. I will be queen of Tenarum one day and I am a member of the Council of Tenarum -." She retorted, already finding it horribly difficult to behave meekly, despite the threat of dungeons and violence.

"Queen of Tenarum?" Cavaln's tone was derisive. "Ah yes, you were betrothed to the prince, were you not?" She smiled with clear mockery as the girl bristled at her use of the past tense. "My, if looks could kill, girl. Yet you are even further from achieving *that* milestone than you are at being able to defend yourself effectively in any fight. I have to report that Master Cheltor was *most* disappointed that you did not even try to disable the boy!"

Ethrayne flinched, recalling that awful afternoon all too clearly. "I, well, everything just happened so quickly, Madam General." She admitted lamely.

"Idiot! So, you understand, your days will no longer pass idly by and you will work hard, I promise you." The woman had got to her feet. "And stop trying to control your power alone – remember, his majesty will know if you disobey his command."

"But -." Ethrayne frowned. At the front of her mind, she recalled Lord Arven's stipulation of not complying with her enemy's wishes, but what else could she do, here, alone? She had suffered cuts and bruises enough just in combat practice, she certainly did not want to experience any punishment ordered by the Betrayer, at the Generals' hands.

"You will risk his majesty's displeasure? You, brat?" Cavaln glared down at her, coming closer, her manner assured. "I strongly suggest that you obey, girl."

“I will do my best.” Ethrayne agreed, but obviously unwillingly, causing Cavaln to tap her face in warning; it was almost a slap.

“Don’t be stupid! You’re not strong enough for the consequences! Now go and get on with removing that disgusting emblem. I will take you for dinner later, of course.” Cavaln gave her a hard look. “If you behave and work hard, girl, you should not find your time passing too uncomfortably.”

*

Ethrayne did replace one emblem for the other, as required, using a badge of Cavaln’s as a template, but she felt exceedingly uncomfortable sewing the Betrayer’s symbol over her heart, even on her nightgowns, as she was ordered. All her Tenarean clothing, other than her nightclothes and dressing gown, had disappeared and it took a few days for her to get used to constantly wearing trousers; the fine gown’s intricate layers she folded carefully away, for it was far too fine for normal wear and she still did not know why she had been given it, for it was hardly suitable for the lifestyle she was following now.

The changes all too soon became normal, however. She also did not wash her own clothes any more, they were taken away and returned, clean and pressed.

Days carried on, slowly lengthening and they were filled completely from early breakfast until dinnertime, her time spent exclusively with Generals who despised her without exception. Master Cheltor and his ilk, including Masson, Shaille and Thellor occupied her mornings, whilst Cavaln, Tynsyn and Dahne also schooled her separately during the afternoons. She now was learning how to read and write Jajozeli; learning the history of the Jajozeli-Razine Empire; mathematics, alongside other subjects that seemed to make little sense to the prisoner, for battle tactics, philosophy and even poetry were amongst them.

At least she was finding it easier to sleep now: her mind was so full of disparate information that the events which had led to her being locked up in the dungeon receded somewhat. Ethrayne could not forget the king, however: his cold, handsome face, his mesmeric gaze, his violence . . . He was awe-inspiring.

She kept Arven’s warning in the forefront of her mind: not to trust them; and although none of the Generals ever seriously tried to befriend her, other than having to endure Cavaln’s presence almost constantly as the lone, token woman guarding her, she was, she admitted sadly to herself, horribly lonely. Truly, she had not appreciated those almost idyllic days spent with Fionn and Sallie!

Ethrayne always breakfasted alone with the woman, but luncheon was generally endured with her combat instructors as well, sat uncomfortably surrounded by burly jajozeli-razine males, sometimes Cavaln as well, all discussing war or combat strategy or something distasteful. Her afternoons were spent in a large, panelled room not far from the dining hall which contained tables, chairs and shelves full of scrolls and massive, leather-bound books, where she struggled with slate and chalk, parchment, pen and ink to complete her lessons. Her General tutors even insisted that she wrote essays; yet writing in the jajozeli language's completely different letter set and rules of grammar gave her a headache, cramped fingers and glaring mistakes almost every day. They generally shouted at her for a very long time about those. Cavaln came at the close of these, if she was not conducting a lesson, to take her along to dinner, for yet another period of eating in the dining hall, uncomfortably aware of the antagonism of enemies on all sides.

Still, she thought to herself, at least she had not been faced with General Oxttyn since her part in his son's revolting death. Nor had she seen, or sensed, the Betrayer in her vicinity and she prayed thankfully to Arven for that, every night.

Her only time alone now was when Cavaln locked her in her small room every evening, wrestling with the wretched work they demanded from her and trying not to worry at what might be happening in Tenarum; how Jerryn, Pualyn and Lyria were coping; and what the future might hold, for all of them.

Spring was sure to dispel the ice of winter at some point; her moons spent here, confined in the citadel, seemed like a lifetime.

* * *

CHAPTER 29

Ethrayne's birthday on the seventeenth of Instur was marked by quiet celebrations in the palace, marked by a feast hosted by Duke Pualyn and Duchess Lyria, an event which was rather more noted for the wine and ale consumed, although the presence of the Archpriests and the High-King and High-Prince of the razine did curb much misbehaviour.

Jerryn was sat beside Lieutenant Sevanter at dinner; he was Lyria's only surviving relative, a sober twenty-six-year-old man of average height with spiky blonde hair, brown eyes and an ordinary but pleasant face. He had returned from Foston earlier that day after a moon of work and planning and had spent a greater part of the afternoon in Commander Vedeigne's office reporting to his military leaders, regarding the impending campaign to regain Clirensar and the surrounding region currently under Jajozeli control.

"How is the area north of the Vale, Lieutenant?" The prince asked politely.

"The soldiers, smelters and smiths are working very hard, your Highness." Sevanter said directly, after a quick drink of water. "But it's very strange that the enemy are only sat there in the city, keeping food animals to the south as far as our scouts can tell. They are digging miles of ramparts, however: high defences are cutting across the valley, it's a mess." He shook his head, his eyes showing his emotion at seeing the place he had grown up and where most of his family had died, so utterly changed. "And our defences are continuing apace opposite on the northern edge of the vale, despite the weather. They will not dare to ignore our presence there."

"Yes, we've worried about that; the bastards could so easily have advanced, couldn't they? We don't even know how many soldiers the enemy commands in Clirensar." Jerryn grimaced. "We are really bloody lucky in that regard, whatever their real motives . . . But I wish I could understand their reasons; they scare me, Lieutenant." He admitted.

"They scare us all, Jerryn." The High-King, sat on his left, said then in agreement. "But we will eliminate the threat they pose; it's a pity that the empty border lands towards Zanezli are so indefensible."

"But his Highness is correct, your Majesty -." Sevanter scowled: all the titles were fit to crack a man's jaw; he much preferred the all-encompassing *sir* of his professional career. "Their intelligence is flawed at the least and lunatic at worst, as far as we can gauge." He sighed deeply. The whole matter was crazy, in his opinion and the enemy's behaviour most of all.

"The enemy's logic is definitely beyond our ken, Lieutenant." Kerr agreed, on Sevanter's left. "Which is why this bloody mess happened -."

"*Don't* apologise again, Kerr!" Jerryn snapped shortly. "We need action, not sorrow!"

"Quite right, Jerryn!" The High-Prince grinned quickly but his eyes were dark. "Well, we have enough commanders here to really make our plans stick, ready for the start of spring. I'm struggling to keep patience myself, I admit it."

"Welcome to the exclusive guild of impatience, Kerr." Jerryn replied sourly, toasting him with his goblet of wine. Sevanter stared for a moment, then flashed a surprisingly genuine smile and raised his own glass also.

"Here's to impatience, my lords."

*

Instur turned into Penttar, then Staipe arrived and the gradually lengthening days gave all of them hope, although the weather towards the new year remained cold and wet, with rain in the north, and ice and blizzards in the Vale of Clirensar and hill-country to the south. Spring was on its way, unstoppable, yet advancing with delicate slow steps, after a winter which seemed to be lasting forever.

The farmland north of Tenum City was covered by groups of men not only from elsewhere in the kingdom, but also from Derravale, Amorry and the Protectorate Kingdoms; thousands of them with more companies arriving every few days, so that the tent towns extended for over four leagues, with roads, supply dumps and even sewerage organised.

As the weather slowly improved, the Pearl and Opal ships docked almost sequentially at Rothern, along with other Protectorate vessels of various lines, delivering men and seemingly endless supplies of food, along with clothing, boots and various types of more warlike equipment.

Captain Ashanner of the Orbain Pearl and Captain Phellos of the Mador Opal met at the Golden Anchor and hired a boat to head upstream to Tenum City; both were muffled in plain brown cloaks, but nothing could disguise the woman's singular appearance that afternoon as the pair of them strode up from the docks through the streets of the city, and a path cleared ahead of them. The sight of the razine was becoming more common and less startling to the ordinary man on the street, but Phellos was the first woman.

"Excuse me." Captain Ashanner said politely to the guards on the palace gate. "We have travelled from Rothern to see his Majesty, the king of this realm and our ruler the High-King; can you please advise them that Ashanner and Phellos have arrived?"

The men stared at them for a moment, before one hurried across the courtyard.

"Just a moment, m'lord m'lady." Stuttered the eldest of the three remaining guards, almost seeming to shake in his boots. "Please, come into the guard-room."

"Thank you." Phellos said, for the clouds had closed in to drop yet more water on the world and the wind was chill. The guardroom proved to be a bare, functional space but it was warm and dry, slotted into the space within the curtain wall next to the gate.

Jerryn, Tymain and Pualyn were walking back from a combat session, having skirted out via the kitchens, when the whey-faced guard appeared, wide-eyed and gasping about new visitors at the gate. Naturally, curiosity turned their footsteps that way, out into the coolness of a rainy day that might presage spring, if one was very optimistic.

Jerryn led the small group, entering the narrow doorway alone and seeing the two strangers stood by the bare table, watched over by one guard whilst the other two had returned to the gate. "Good afternoon, we can show you into the palace, whilst their Majesties are informed of your arrival, if you wish?" Jerryn asked, his power sparking as he met the two cloaked figures; he was almost getting used to the feeling, now, although it was clear that both visitors held some considerable strength of their own. "The servants will provide you with food and drink whist you wait and it's a little more comfortable than the guard room, I can assure you -." He smiled and gestured as the guard saluted and stepped politely outside.

"Am'maiya, we are greatly honoured." The tall woman threw back her hood and bowed her head. "I am Captain Phellos of the Mador Opal, Ashanner is Captain of the Orbain Pearl." He also bowed low.

"Captain? Ah yes, you both served to alert us regarding Newventure Bay, didn't you?" Jerryn was pleased that the fact appeared in his head; it had been moons ago now, of course. "We are honcured to meet you, please, join us. May I introduce Pualyn, Duke of Clirensar and Corporal Tymain? It's very kind of you to visit, but I imagine that this is hardly a social call?" He was already advancing quickly across the courtyard and the rest of the group easily kept up.

"No, I confess that it is not, your Highness." Phellos agreed. "We are here to hopefully further our designs against our enemy." She paused and laid one hand on the duke's shoulder. "It is lovely to meet you again, your Grace, but may we offer our sincere condolences at your loss? To hear of such shocking events was just terrible!"

"Thank you, Captain, I am grateful." The man replied shortly. "I just wish -." He scowled.

"Most certainly we wish, Pualyn." Jerryn agreed with a sigh. "Welcome to Tenum City." They continued in silence and the new arrivals were handed over to servants in the main entrance hall.

*

"How are the patrols advancing?" Mhezal enquired with interest, once refreshments had been provided to the visitors and they had been shown to rooms, left to rest and change or bathe as required; now, the Council and visiting dignitaries had been assembled. They had all been fully briefed on the side activities of the Pearl and Opal fleet around Iullyn over the years.

Escorted to the Painted Hall, the captains were presented to their High-King and High-Prince, King Marrand and King Namayomn, as well as the Archpriests, but Mhezal and his son were surprised to see them so far inland.

"We have seen little activity at all throughout the winter, your

Majesty." Phellos said gravely and sighed. "Of course, the weather is not conducive to campaigns and we've endured the usual cycle of storms. But now -." She sighed again, shrugged and glanced at Ashanner.

"We'd like your permission to destroy Cal'Badon, Sire." The tall razine captain explained in as few words as possible.

"When have you ever asked my permission for *anything*, Captain?" The High-King asked, seemingly caught between amusement and disapproval.

"Well, I mean. That one jajozeli port is singularly responsible for all the atrocities that have befallen the east coast of this continent, Sire, you must agree with that fact." Phellos said in a tone of polite earnest. "We and the kingdoms at large would be better off if they were wiped out."

"Murder!" Archpriest Lurco said with horror in his voice. "Oh, dear -."

"We have been planning murder for moons, your Grace." Jerryn replied dryly, as the older man continued to shake his head, aghast. "*They* have committed murder in the name of their leader for centuries, so why would it be any worse if, in Arven's name, we strove to make this part of Iullyn safer for the ordinary people who have suffered so badly at Newventure Bay and around Saremouth?"

"I think he's got you there, old friend." Bahlien admitted with a slow smile. "Logically it does make sense to try and destroy the port, but is it actually possible?" He looked around from face to face. "Cal'Badon will be very well protected, I'm sure."

"Oh, indeed it will." Captain Phellos confirmed seriously. "It is certainly going to be risky and very dangerous, but if you are all going to retake Clirensar, it definitely makes sense to try and permanently remove the threat of their port in the south-east."

"But surely it is not the only enemy base in Zanezli, Captain?" Lurco asked.

"Certainly, your Grace, it is not, but Cal'Badon was chosen for its guaranteed lack of winter ice, despite its situation so far south: it is their only position on the east coast, a strategic advantage giving them easy access to your seas." The High-Prince said, pulling out one sheet from amid a pile of maps that covered a table. "Here." He pointed. "It's a long way even from Ban'Lerracon . . . It's been a complete gift of a port for them. And they'll surely be expecting attack."

"But will they be expecting destruction, Highness?" Ashanner asked coolly. "We are the faithful children of Arven, we have never before even contemplated such annihilation."

"The captains are willing, and, between us, we hold a great deal of talent and knowledge, your Majesties." Phellos appealed directly of the kings before them, her words confident, her thumbs hooked in her belt. "We might even be able to harness the local volcanic activity in our cause?" This last was a query and she smiled at their surprise. "We've put out word to more earth-centred razine, hoping for an answer quickly."

"Magic?" Lord Ferman quavered, awed by the woman's vibrant presence. "Oh, dear Arven!"

"Our abilities are our tools, my Lord and we will use everything in the furtherance of our long-term designs to free Clirensar, free the Am'maiya and to free Arven, eventually. It isn't magic." She replied confidently.

"We have let them run amok in the south for far too long." Ashanner declared in only a slightly less forthright tone than his colleague. "They might have stolen away the Am'maiya, but they really need to know that we mean business and we are not to be underestimated!"

"Amen to that." Jerryn said earnestly in an undertone.

"How many captains are involved in this?" The High-King asked, and the two seafarers exchanged glances, shrugged and grinned in unison.

"Pretty much everyone, your Majesty, but of course it would be rank stupidity to try and sail a fleet into the Badon Inlet; it's narrow and bound to be guarded and watched. We were thinking of gathering a force ashore and filling a few ships with those with talent, something like the reverse of the attack on Saremouth; it worked there, to horrible effect, so why change the formula?" Ashanner said.

"Dear Arven, protect us!" Archpriest Bahlien uttered seriously and looked around at the group. "Will it even work, Captain Ashanner, Captain Phellos? I know very little about attacks by sea." He wondered.

"If we can maintain the element of surprise it will work." Phellos asserted.

"You need to make a proper plan, Captains; gather your facts and figures; and you need a hefty dose of pure luck!" The High-King sighed deeply and shook his head. "You have a few days, Captains. I suggest that you work with our military commanders of all realms and come up with something promising and workable, if you please."

"We will, your Majesties, your Highnesses, my Lords." Phellos said, grinning broadly as she bowed formally. "Thank you for your time."

*

It was the beginning of Staipe when the forces began their slow, steady advance towards the vast area north of Foston where, by clearing the woodland entirely for the efforts of the smelting and ironworking so vital for their required weapons, mail and other necessities, a huge area had been set out for the armies arrival. The ground would be muddy of course, for the weather was unrelentingly wet, but it would be adequate, now that the necessary roads, drainage and so on had been marked out, the defences constructed.

Staipe crept towards Ertam and the New Year at the Equinox, although hardly anyone within the palace was thinking of the typical celebrations currently being set out across the continent. Everyone there, it seemed, was concerned with the logistics of caring for the welfare of nearly one hundred thousand armed men, fifty thousand from the Protectorates; twenty thousand from Tenarum; over fifteen thousand from Amorry and fewer than fifteen thousand from Derravale, for many soldiers there were diverted to watch that long, unprotected border they shared to the south with Zanezli.

A certain nervous tension filled the palace in Tenum City, both collective and personal, for the leaders of the separate armies would be waiting longer before beginning their own journeys; they were still, with the great assistance of their commanders, coordinating and planning.

Pualyn and Lyria had their own trouble, however; separate from everything but, of course, its reasons and existence were right at the centre of the issues that circled them all. The young duke was not cold, precisely, but cool towards the young woman he was married to, and he was a lot less attentive towards her than he should have been. They both knew why: the spectres of his parents, the loss of his ancestral home, their fear for his sister; these and many other concerns made a very solid wedge between them. Pualyn was not rude or abusive in any way towards the young woman he had adored for years, but he was distant and spent an inordinate amount of time in the practice hall and in the endless planning meetings.

Miserable, worried and lonely, Lyria finally sought out Lady Celia for, hopefully, some womanly advice, even though Celia was not married. Officially, as the Duchess of Clirensar, she now outranked the Lady of Pellerton Court, but such niceties did not bother her, even though she knew that it was vitally important to their servants.

"Your Grace, we are honoured." Celia curtsied politely.

"Oh, please, Celia, don't -." And Lyria sank into the closest chair, fighting against tears. "Oh, I'm sorry -."

"Go on, shoo!" Celia firmly dismissed her attendants and sat down beside the young woman still dressed in black and took her in her arms. "Lyria, dear, oh, Lyria." And her embrace tightened as the duchess sobbed.

"He doesn't love me anymore!" She cried as if in terrible pain. "He, he hates me!"

"No Pualyn does not, he loves you with all his heart, but you are both grieving and angry and worried . . . and you saw his parents killed, his sister abducted whilst he was off enjoying himself in the Razine Protectorates . . ." Celia sighed deeply and produced a handkerchief for her friend.

"S-so he blames me too!"

"Oh Lyria, of course he doesn't; well, not seriously, I imagine -." Celia amended the sentence honestly and winced as the younger woman began sobbing anew. "Sshhh!" She held her tight, stroking her head, letting her cry herself out, until Lyria began to hiccup instead of crying.

"You need tea, Lyria, cake and biscuits." She declared, rang a bell and asked for those viands from her maid, Mallie.

"I'm so stupid." Lyria sniffed, hiccupped and muttered from behind the rather damp handkerchief. "Pualyn hates me, I know he does!"

"That's silly, Lyria, he loves you as greatly as he has always done, as you love him. You have both have survived some terrible moons, in such awful circumstances." Celia said with a sigh and got up to take the tray of refreshments when her maid swiftly returned. "Thank you. Here, dear, have something to eat and drink, you are terribly pale.

"You miss your families, you fear for Ethrayne and likely many other people you knew in Clirensar – and probably you feel guilty at living, whilst so many are dead. Also, you and your husband have been thrown into these new, vital roles – and I imagine they are stressful for both of you . . . I do believe, however, that you are doing very well, Lyria. At least having to be so busy gives you a focus, of course."

"Well, yes." Lyria allowed, astonished to hear most of what she felt delivered so succinctly by the woman.

They paused for tea and cake, Lyria's pallor slowly replaced with a slightly healthier colour. Suddenly, unexpectedly, she found that she was enjoying the repast more than she had enjoyed anything since, well, probably since the awful events that had happened moons before, which still disturbed her sleep.

"Are you feeling a little better?" Celia asked gently.

"Yes, a little, thank you, but -." Lyria set down her tea cup and threw out her arms wide. "I really don't know what to do, Celia!"

"There isn't really an awful lot you can do, but be patient and let time take its course . . . I remember losing my mother, six years ago and it was awful. I was permanently stuck within a horrible black cloud for, oh, dear Arven, it must have been a year at least!" Celia shuddered. "And mother was ill for a long time, so it was nothing at all like those sudden, shocking murders you were witness to. You are still in shock, still sleeping horribly I am sure because you saw Pualyn's parents die, all those soldiers and servants as well; and Ethrayne being taken away . . . But Pualyn was in the far north, knew nothing about it for nearly a moon and I am sure he is coping very badly indeed; his manner and Jerryn's as well, have changed so much, haven't they?"

"Oh gosh, yes, but, oh, Celia, what can I do? Pualyn, he just seems intent on the war, on killing as many of the enemy as possible: he spends more time at combat practice that he does with me!"

"Yes, Lyria; well, I had better admit that his Majesty has sought me out and he is also concerned, but he lost his wife many years ago now: he knows how much grief affects us all. There isn't really a cure, or much you can do to shake your husband out of it; it's not that sort of problem, after all. You must try and keep calm, work through your own grief at the loss of your families and support Pualyn as he will hopefully support you too . . . And, please excuse me, it might be well to try and get pregnant if you can before the men leave!"

Lyria stared at her friend, stunned, but eventually, slightly hysterical laughter won over outrage. "I'll do my best, you can assure his Majesty, but I can't promise any such results." She said finally, feeling better in herself than she had for moons. "Oh, Celia, thank you so much!"

*

Lyria took Celia's advice to heart and, watching her husband's behaviour in a slightly more objective fashion over the next few days, concluded that her friend was correct: grief and fury filled him; although Pualyn was functioning in day-to-day situations and those interminable meetings, he was certainly not *there*. Even Jerryn, affected in a slightly different manner, could tell that his closest friend was just going through the motions of normal behaviour. The young duchess took heart from the realisation that Pualyn's rage was wide-ranging and aimed towards the enemy and started planning, which pushed back a little of her own grief, but not for long, overall.

Three days before the men were due to leave Tenum City, Lyria firmly dismissed Lennarn, Greta and their other servants from their rooms after they had drawn a hot bath. She had enlisted Jerryn's assistance, although she had been rather embarrassed at doing so, but the necessity of requiring practical help ensured it, and Pualyn was duly delivered to their door after another long, aggressive combat session, without the following goblets of wine which had become customary; it was late afternoon.

"My, you do look hot and sweaty, Pualyn. It's well that the servants have a bath ready for you. Here, let me help you." Lyria greeted her husband with a smile, took his hand and led him through into their bedroom, firmly shutting the door. "Lennarn told Greta that you were suffering from a stiff neck, but I'm really not surprised, Pualyn, for you're always rushing about and wearing that heavy mail." And, keeping up a light monologue into which he did not really get the opportunity to reply, (he did look tired, for such a young man) Lyria gently unfastened his jerkin and shirt and pushed him gently back onto their bed to try and pull off his boots. When the second came off without warning, sending her hard onto the carpet on her rear, Pualyn smiled slightly at her surprise and got up to help her to her feet.

"You know, I was just going to get washed and changed for dinner, but that bath looks lovely." He said with rather more interest than he had shown in anything for ages, stripping off the rest of his sweaty clothes and stepping into the tub with a sigh.

"Now you relax, Pualyn and I'll scrub your back before I give your neck and shoulders a massage with scented oil. You'll be wearing mail almost constantly when you leave and it's my duty as your wife to make sure you set off rested and in the best condition -." Lyria broke off to collect together his discarded clothing, setting his boots neatly by the wall.

Best condition? I'm not a horse! . . . But it is bloody heavy, all that gear." Pualyn volunteered, sending wavelets of bathwater rippling at the edge of the tub as he stretched with a second sigh.

"Yes, I can imagine." Lyria knelt beside him, soap and sponge in her hands. "Now, let's get you clean, my love. Just relax, Pualyn." And she chuckled at his sigh at the touch of the sponge.

Perhaps it was a complete coincidence, or due to her careful ministrations with soap, sponge, hot water and soft, uncomplicated conversation, but the man who emerged from the bath seemed, on the surface at least, rather more like the one she had fallen in love with, than the one who had returned from the Razine Protectorates. He even had a renewed sparkle in his eyes.

"Dear Arven, Lyria, you are a fine woman!" He declared, wrapped in a large green towel.

"I'll be even finer in your eyes when I've worked those kinks out of your shoulders, dearest." But Lyria never got around to using the sweet-scented oil, for her husband picked her up, set her on the huge bed and kissed her passionately.

That evening at dinner, the absence of the Duke and Duchess was noted and Marrand, Mhezal, Jerryn and Celia exchanged grins, whilst Lord Gorman and Earl Brennan remarked at the inconstancy of the youth of today.

*

Pualyn's dour demeanour had returned the next morning but, with the input of intense relaxation and the best night's sleep he had had since hearing the terrible news, he did strive to make his remaining time with his wife good days, forcing away his despair and fury when they were together, putting on a semblance of normality with surprising ease.

"I am sorry Lyria, I've been a bad husband, my dearest." He said, late on their last night together, after having again proved that he was not, holding Lyria close in the huge canopied bed. "It's just -."

"I know, honestly, and you have just been horribly pressured . . . Oh please, Pualyn, you will take care won't you? I couldn't bear it if I lost you too!" She couldn't stop the words spilling out.

"We're heading off to make war upon the jajozeli, Lyria. I really can't promise anything of the sort: we are all in Arven's hands, if not the Betrayer's."

She held him tight, snuggled up under his left arm. "I know you're going to try and kill as many of them as you can, Pualyn, but I want my hero back, do you understand me?" And she kissed his chest above his heart, then his lips. "May Arven protect you all, but if anything happens to you, dearest -." Lyria shook her head.

Pualyn smiled lopsidedly. "I know, dearest Lyria. I will do my upmost to come back to you, I promise on my honour and my love." He kissed her intensely and one thing led to another quite naturally.

*

The farewells next morning were formal but relatively short, as the kings and commanders of the four forces knelt for formal prayers in the Cathedral, surrounded by their staff, family members and servants. The square outside was filled with solemn-faced townsfolk and some local farming families, again mostly consisting of the elderly, women and children; most men of fighting age were already on their way south.

Archpriests Lurco and Bahlien led the prayers, keeping them simple and to the point: freedom for the area around the beleaguered city; death to the enemy occupying it and long lives to the allied forces involved.

<*Aren't you rather hoping for a miracle or ten thousand?*> Jerryn asked rather facetiously of the old razine ex-archpriest. <*There's no way on Iullyn that all of us will return!*>

<*We can all hope and pray anyway, Am'maiya, however unlikely the result we long for.*> Bahlien answered. <*Please take care, Jerryn and remember your power will continue to develop as you practice those exercises we have been working on.*>

<*I should have some days to practice as we ride south, your Grace, with Kerr's assistance.*> Jerryn confirmed. <*Dear Arven, I'm scared!*>

<*You're not the only one who thinks so, by any means, Jerryn.*> The High-Prince joined the conversation then and grimaced, shrugging as he admitted. <*I'm terrified, and I've been in a few battles against the bastards!*>

<*That's not very reassuring, Kerr.*> His father growled with mock dismay.

<*Sorry, sir.*> And Kerrenan grinned and winked.

Those riding out were overly hearty as they bid farewell to those they would leave behind, and everyone smiled and hugged and shook hands in a very old-fashioned and formal manner, except for Pualyn and Lyria, who, having already lost so much, were now fully appreciating each other's presence as if they stood alone and not faced with so many interested spectators. Reluctantly, calmly, they kissed, to huge cheers from the crowds surging below the Cathedral steps. Pualyn bowed low, splendid in his mail and formal, heavy surcoat that bore the arms of Clirensar and descended the steps, clinking like the others and then swung up onto his mount rather more laboriously than usual: the mail and paraphernalia, of course, was heavy, but all of them were covered in it. Once they were a few miles from the city, out of view of people, they had resolved to stop and remove the weight to ride on in a great deal more comfort.

Forming up behind King Marrand and High-King Mhezal, they all rode slowly out of the square to more rousing cheers that continued all the way to the South Gate, the people standing three or four deep, on every street. Straight backed and dry-eyed, Lyria, Duchess of Clirensar, Lady Celia and the rest watched them go, before they got into their carriages and returned to the palace.

* * *

CHAPTER 30

From the fourth-floor window of her small, bare room, Ethrayne could watch the relentless but slow hints of spring arriving, as the snow melted gradually from the courtyard below and the rooftops above, finally leaving only the carefully spaded-up piles of grey ice along the walls which seemed unchanged, as far as she could tell. Through a gap between the buildings, offering a tiny vista beyond the city rooftops, she could, by looking every morning, see the lower slope of one mountainside changing from white to green, above the almost black shade of the forest covering the hills below it.

It had been twenty-five days since she had been brought up from the dungeon, nearly a moon of daily physical and mental exhaustion. That afternoon, however, Cavaln took her back to her prison instead of to the work room where she usually studied.

"You will pack." She informed the girl shortly, which explained the two pairs of saddlebags sat on the floor. "Wash those clothes you're wearing. You will need soap, towels, all your clothes; blankets and your sewing box, since you are handy with a needle."

Ethrayne shivered and frowned, trying to ignore her unease. "I am running low of thread, my Lady General." She admitted. Sewing was now her one real way of concentrating on something that did not involve fretting on her situation when alone. She had never really enjoyed needlework before, but it did focus her thoughts.

"I'll make sure some is brought." Cavaln said dismissively. "Don't forget anything, girl, we leave in the morning."

"Where are we going? Is it Staipe or Ertam? How long have I been here?" Ethrayne asked quickly, but the General left without answering, locking the door as always. Alone, swearing expressively in selithian, Ethrayne went to wash, then scrubbed her combat gear as ordered. Her wardrobe had slowly expanded since her arrival, but she did not own so many clothes to consider leaving any behind, even if they were all embroidered with the Betrayer's crest.

She was frightened; she admitted that to herself, although she would have completely denied it if any of them had asked. After so long imprisoned in the vast citadel, having not stepped outside since her arrival, she had got horribly used to her constrained routine, or at least the predictability of it, anyway, although certainly not the company she was forced to keep.

"I knew things would happen once winter passed." She muttered to herself, making up the small fire in her room to hopefully dry the dripping clothes that hung over the screen. "Oh, dear Arven, where will he send me now? And what's happening in Tenarum? Can it really be five moons since they took me and killed Mamma and Papa?" She then began to take the rest of her clothes out of the chest; keeping busy was preferable to sitting down and worrying and crying, which is what a part of her wanted to do. *Dear Arven, I hope everyone is safe!* She prayed silently. *I am sorry I haven't been any use at all, trying to control this power . . . They – he – scare me so much!* She apologised, for at least the twenty-sixth time. At least, praying, she could try to bolster her determination.

General Cavaln returned with small reels full of long lengths of well-turned threads in various colours and took Ethrayne along to the dining hall for dinner, but the girl only really picked at her food, sitting in a glum silence. After having her questions ignored earlier, she was not going to demean herself by asking again.

Cavaln smiled at her with good humour and kept silent until, after dinner and about to lock the prisoner back in her room, she said cheerily. "You will need to be up early, girl: we will be leaving at dawn, so make sure everything is packed, understand?"

"Yes, Lady Cavaln." Ethrayne replied politely.

*

She did not sleep, of course and sat up, dressed, fully packed and waiting by the dim light of the fire, well before the first hint of approaching dawn lit the sky. In fact, the stars were still bright when the door was unlocked, and the General stuck her head around it.

"Don't forget your washing, girl and you'll need your cloak." She suggested with a sigh. "Bring your bags out here, breakfast is ready."

Ethrayne leapt up, for she had completely forgotten her clothes hanging in front of the fire, and quickly stuffed the shirt, trousers and socks into the top of the closest bag, glad that they felt dry; she unhooked the cloak from behind the door and hefted the two pairs of bags, passing through the foyer and into Cavaln's lamp-lit sitting room rather nervously. She set her luggage next to the pile close to the outer door and stopped, feeling uncomfortable.

Cavaln pointed to the table where two bowls and mugs were set and Ethrayne, sitting uncertainly, picked up one mug to sip the tea; eating, not because she was hungry, although she was, but through necessity. Both porridge and tea sat uneasily within her when the woman got to her feet.

"Go and check your room quickly." Cavaln suggested. "It's time to go, you won't be returning."

Hurrying back to her room with a lighted candle, she made at once for the tiny bathroom, where Ethrayne threw up her breakfast from worry, quickly patting her face with dampened hands before scanning that space and the largely empty bedroom for discarded items; it wasn't more than a few heartbeats before she emerged and stepped through into Cavaln's sitting room, grey faced, to put on the cloak that she had not actually worn since her arrival. She was surprised, for it did not drag so much on the floor as she remembered it had before, then slung a pair of bags over each shoulder before following the more heavily laden General out and into the citadel's dimly lit corridors, finally emerging at the very same courtyard where she had first dismounted, so many moons before, the torchlight starting to look dim against the lightening sky.

"Oh no!" She muttered with a groan, staring down the sweeping staircase in dismay at those awaiting her: her combat teachers, Shaille, Masson and Thellor, along with her tutors Tynsyn and Dahne. Along with Cavaln, that made six Generals! Which made at least five too many, in her opinion.

"Don't dawdle, brat." Thellor ordered, mounting a large, white gelding. "Let's get going."

"Yes, my Lord General." Ethrayne replied quickly, hurrying down the steps. Thellor had always been particularly quick to land a blow during his lessons; a burly male at least six and a half feet tall, with shaggy mid-brown hair; he was not anything but ordinary to look at, but he was as fast as a striking snake at combat.

There was a chill breeze blowing that seemed to deny any approach of spring and she shivered at its icy touch, appreciating anew the castle's largely draught-free construction, where she had not had to endure the terrible blast of winter.

Cavaln was already loading her luggage onto a pack horse, so Ethrayne picked a mount at random, a scrubby chestnut was closest; she laid her two pairs of bags carefully behind its saddle, fastening them securely so that they would not slide off and that they wouldn't discomfort the horse. It was strange, for she felt totally out of practice, having not even seen a horse for months, but she got into the saddle easily enough, settled herself and straightened her cloak and her gloves.

"Move out." Thellor called as the others got into their saddles and he took up the lines of the packhorses.

The sky far above was now turning blue, dispelling the pre-dawn grey; Ethrayne looked hard, but she still did not get a very good impression of Ban'Lerracon, for her view was constrained by the castle's and then the city walls, the high buildings that lined the streets; it was massive, she knew that, but she finally could look back, once they crossed the great bridge over the roaring, pale, opaque river, to see a great, grey city that was even more formidable than her imagination had wrought: rise after rise of huge walls and blocky buildings and then, the tallest structure by far, the central tower where she had been first imprisoned. Remembering Fionn and Sallie, she shivered and did not look back again.

*

The Generals took their prisoner swiftly along that stupendous ice-carved valley into the west, following the bank-bursting, icy-green glacial river as it snaked through the landscape of bedraggled, snow-flattened grassland; the snow had melted in the lowlands, but it still dominated the landscape above and about them. From the well-built road they travelled, constructed some fifty or so feet above the raging waters, they passed many areas of floodwater; clearly the arrival of spring was a major event here in the south, although winter still had a very firm grip on the mountain slopes and, during the nine days of their journey, they faced quite a few blizzards amid the rain, gales and only very occasional sunshine which swept over them.

Ethrayne discovered, although she had suspected it, that the Generals were just as awful as guards and travelling companions as they were tutors; worse, in fact, because she had no way to escape their presence and six lots of needling, threats and nasty comments was an awful lot worse than she had received from Garrtnor, Ackat and Cavaln on her journey from Clirensar. She had tentatively volunteered to help look after the horses at their nightly camps but, once the other Generals had realised how much she enjoyed the work, she had been maliciously ordered to assist with cooking instead and, naturally, washing up afterwards. Not daring to protest, Ethrayne obeyed, but she actively hated every moment of that journey. The landscape was spectacular, it was wonderful to be outside again after so many moons confined; but her guards were almost unbearable, and she only spoke when she was spoken to, most politely. In some ways, it was worse than being locked up in the dungeon had been.

The road crossed the raging river three times on massive stone-constructed bridges, cutting a straighter route through the widening valley than the widely meandering watercourse, gradually leaving the mountains behind. For four nights they stayed in forts that were strategically placed along their route, staying in plain barrack blocks together, where meals were provided, yet she was still required to scrub dishes; the other four they stayed in waystations with stabling and dry accommodation and Ethrayne was glad that she did not have to help put up tents.

Leaving the stocky defensive structure which had given them shelter overnight, at dawn on the ninth day, and beginning their descent from the pale outcrop on which the fort had dominated the hillock-strewn landscape of farmland which had replaced the grassland the previous morning, Ethrayne looked out ahead, past the now-distant curve of the river and saw, tiny at the edge of the horizon, a flash of sparkling grey, catching a mere suggestion of movement. She squinted, but she wasn't sure if her sight was accurate. Had she caught a glimpse of the sea, or was it her imagination? Dully, weary, she rode on after the Generals.

It was later when Ethrayne could confirm that she could see the sea and realised that she could see a city too, for, emerging from a large forest that had filled that part of the vast plain which had replaced the valley, the road ran back towards a much wider, grey river channel that was now the upper reaches of an estuary, with mud banks evident above choppy water which now showed no hint at all of its icy green shade.

The Generals did not halt but continued at a quicker pace and the city grew closer, the buildings gradually larger. Above them, in places, could be seen stick-like masts.

The group reached the wharves well after noon, a bustling area smelling of fish, seaweed and effluent, but Ethrayne was not paying attention to anything around her, not even the simply gigantic ships that were berthed to her left.

Suddenly, without any warning, thrilling her nerves worse than acute toothache, she sensed the presence of the King of the Jajozeli as clear as if he was stood before her. Her fear rose to choke her all at once. She scanned the area desperately and found him: he was at the far end of the wharf ahead, a good sixty yards distant, talking to a group of people.

"Oh, dear Arven -."

She tried, intended, to turn her horse as sheer panic took over, but the Generals' had anticipated her action and she was blocked to both left and right: Dahne and Shaille's lower legs pressed tight against hers for a crucial moment, Shaille grabbed the bridle.

"Don't be stupid, brat!" Dahne snapped, taking hold of her left arm and shaking her roughly, but Ethrayne struggled, despite his warning. "Pirris!" He said in disgust.

The other Generals dismounted, but Dahne held the girl firmly in place until Thellor came over and pulled Ethrayne from the horse, laying her over his shoulder to her dismay, one massive hand clamped tightly around her wrists, the other confining her legs.

"Hold still or I'll drop you hard, brat!" He warned her, striding easily towards the huge ship closest to them, heading up a steeply sloping plank that bounced beneath his boots and Ethrayne stared down into dark, oily-looking water for a moment.

"You bastard!" Ethrayne spat without thinking as he dropped her roughly to the deck and he replied with a crack across the face that shocked her into silence.

"Get the brat below before I hit her again!" Thellor ordered shortly. Cavaln had just stepped off the gangplank with Ethrayne's baggage over her shoulders, but it was a stranger who grabbed her hair, twisting it roughly as the burly General strode angrily away.

Her cheek burning; acutely aware of this sharp new pain in her scalp, shocked, Ethrayne was shoved towards a dark doorway at the rear of the ship, set beneath the higher stern deck, into a largely lightless passage, down a fixed ladder lit by a dim lantern hanging from a beam above, along and down a second ladder, the steep, narrow way also lit by lantern light. There was another ladder – this time, the tall, grim-faced male made a light-globe, forcing her on and down into what seemed to be the very bottom of the ship – there were no more ladders, she noted, only narrow doors.

"Welcome to the King's Lightning." The General said coldly, opening one door and pushing her into an unlit space beyond, slamming the door closed behind her.

The sound of bolts hitting home was loud. "Damn all of you!" She yelled and kicked hard at the door, but it didn't budge. There was no handle – and she banged her head hard on the beams above. "Bastards! I hate you!" Then, her fear rising past her anger, Ethrayne sank down on the planks, shivering in dread . . . This was worse than the dungeon had been, she realised, for there was absolutely no light at all, it was as black as a cave. "Damn you! Let-let me out!" But her voice was now a whisper. She shivered and felt her fear rising . . . Surely, they would not lock her up here indefinitely? Would they?

If they demanded that she apologise, Ethrayne knew that she would do anything they wanted. Within reason . . . This was a good warning, she allowed . . . Please Arven it was only a warning, she prayed.

Time passed, horribly slowly. The space was small, airless. Ethrayne could smell the stink of dirt, sweat and horse on herself clearly after their journey; she could feel the movement of the ship, an odd sensation, and battled against tears. She could hear distant sounds, but nothing clear and no voices. Slowly, carefully, she moved sideways until the closest wall was behind her . . . waiting. Hoping that someone would come. It seemed that an age passed until Ethrayne heard footsteps approaching and she grimaced at the relief that washed through her as the bolts were unlocked, the door opened. Cavaln stood there, glaring, with a light-globe by her shoulder, the pale light revealing a space less than six feet wide or deep. "Well? Do you want to remain locked up in here?" She demanded.

"No-no, my Lady." Ethrayne admitted, scrambling to her feet. "I am sorry."

"Humph. You will be if you loose control again, brat!" Cavaln waved her out, directed her up most of the ladders, then ordered Ethrayne inside into a surprisingly well-lit space behind the ladder on a level where a lamp shone. The cabin had, surprisingly, windows in the wall to the left. The General pointed to Ethrayne's baggage on the nearest of the two narrow bunks that seemed built into the cabin. "There's storage underneath the bed for your clothes and a wash-room of sorts through there, with warm water ready for you -." She pointed at a narrow door ahead and grinned. "Just keep off *my* half of the cabin."

"Y-your half?" Ethrayne stammered.

"Would you rather share with General Thellor, brat?" Cavaln asked contemptuously.

"Now get washed and changed, girl and scrub the clothes you're wearing." She ordered briskly. It was clear that the General had bathed and changed her outfit in the interval since Ethrayne had been locked up, for she was neat and pristine in her fresh uniform; the girl supposed she had done this on land, for she didn't think that ships ran to proper bathrooms. "There should be a line for your clothes in the washroom; go on, the water won't stay hot forever." Cavaln then started unpacking her own items and ignored Ethrayne.

The washroom was the same length as the cabin, but only about three feet wide, with a built-in washstand containing the usual and a large metal bowl that hung from the wall; and there were buckets of quite hot water waiting for her.

With a towel and soap from her baggage, Ethrayne washed, then, changed into clean but very creased clothes, she scrubbed assiduously at the ones she had so glad to remove. The line had been strung up looped from one hook, but it stretched diagonally across the window-end of the space and was soon draped with those few gently dripping items which she tried to wring out with all her strength. Stepping back into the cabin, she found that she was again alone, the door locked.

Her inertia did not last very long, however; she turned to the bank of windows that formed a good third of the height of the back wall which admitted so much light, but there was little to see, other than a few boats moving up and down slightly in the swell and grey water below; the distant sounds of voices and heavy items being moved around the ship were oddly alien.

The cabin was about seven feet wide, the bunks built into the walls and nearly seven feet long, but they were only about two and a half feet wide, with a straw-filled bag for a mattress and a pillow each. There were two cupboards under her bunk, fixed with sliding bolts and surprisingly spacious, so Ethrayne began to empty her saddle bags with grim finality; the door was locked, and the windows were locked, the leaded glass fixed in an iron framework which formed, effectively, bars preventing escape; so she was stuck here, surrounded by Generals, with the dreaded Betrayer close by . . . They were going to take her from Selith, probably to Enlath, the centre of the Jajozeli Empire . . . But that was all she knew about the continent, other than it was half a world away.

There were more noises on the ship around her; creaks, muffled conversations, footsteps above, below and alongside, the slap of water, doors banging and all sounding strange. Ethrayne had never been on a ship before and the movement of it on the water felt most peculiar. Her clothes and sewing box and so on all packed neatly away, her cloak hung on the back of the door, she sank back down on her neatly made bed, her blankets from Ban'Lerracon folded at the foot. She sat back against the wall, resting her chin on her knees, trying to battle her fear. Only the shifting shadows outside told her that the afternoon had gone – a few sunset colours were visible across the sky.

Were they going to keep her locked up forever? She wondered uneasily, just before she heard footsteps and the cabin door swung inward to reveal General Ackat, uniformed but unarmed. Ethrayne was already trying to pull her boots back on.

"Dinner is served, brat, come along."

He led her up the ladder and to a large cabin that she supposed extended the whole width of the stern, with a full width of windows, a large table that, oddly, hung from thick ropes at the corners, and benches. Ethrayne did not see anything else, for the space was full of Generals; she stared and gulped, for she only recognised a few of them, including the man who had locked her up earlier.

"And here she is, Ethrayne, Lady of Clirensar and potential Wielder of the Flame." The king's smooth tones came from behind her and the girl's wary expression changed instantly to one of fear. She took one step back out of the doorway and sank, trembling, to her knees, staring fixedly at the dark planks and horribly aware of the forest of legs stretching up above her as he entered the cabin. "What, nothing to say?" There was amusement in his voice and she wished that the floor would open and swallow her. He laughed. "On your feet, girl."

Very slowly, still gazing at the floor, Ethrayne obeyed, feeling her heart beating so fast and so loud, part of her wondered if the sound filled the cabin.

"Excellent. Well, Ethrayne, we leave these shores on the high tide later tonight and I expect your full cooperation and good behaviour, do you understand?"

"Y-yes, your Majesty . . . Please forgive my-my rude behaviour earlier." She managed to whisper.

"If you remember your manners and are obedient, I am sure you will not find your time on board ship too arduous, as long as you remain in the areas you are permitted: exploring is expressly forbidden. Now, get yourself something to eat, keep out of the way and don't even think of stepping foot up on deck until morning. Understand? Crew, you are with me."

There was a chorus of "Your Majesty's" that drowned out Ethrayne's whisper of assent and fully half of the Generals filed out past her, leaving her facing the rest: nine, all male, apart from Cavaln. The girl turned to the table that she only just realised contained many dishes, plates and cups, mostly constructed of pewter or silver. The jajozeli-razine were all helping themselves to food and drink, chatting in a friendly manner. Watching them warily and surreptitiously, she did not start to hesitantly advance until they were all sat down or leaning against walls or posts. Yet again, she had lost her hunger to her fear, but she spooned meat, vegetables and a deliciously scented herb-filled sauce onto a plate, as well as a slice of bread, filled a cup with water and sank down onto the vacant end of a bench to eat.

"You've surpassed yourself, Whillan." Tynsyn complimented another General. "We never ate so well shipboard on our last voyage." There was laughter at his comment.

"You may mock, scholar, but you try producing a meal for so many in that cupboard of a galley, then you can judge my skill." A large, bushy-haired male replied easily. "In fact, you can cook breakfast if you'd like to attempt it. Naturally I was going to use the inn's kitchen, you fool"

"I'd sooner let Tynsyn near a kitchen than the brat!" Thellor said with a guffaw that rang across the cabin. "Pity we've no horses for her to groom."

Ethrayne tried to shrink where she sat, as more laughter sounded around her, chewing her food but starting to feel sick, yet again.

"We'd be knee-deep in shit, though that would keep the girl occupied, I suppose." Dahne continued. "Pirris, it's going to be a long voyage, this time!"

"And pity poor Cavaln here, having to share a cabin with her." Shaille's laughter was hearty.

"But at least she generally doesn't fart, or snore loudly and relentlessly all night long like a sty full of pigs, as most of you do." Cavaln retorted easily to more amusement and hearty agreement and she looked across at the pale-faced girl. "Are you done?"

Ethrayne nodded, longing to get out of there and rose at once when the female General got to her feet, following her from the cabin. On their short way back to the cabin below, Cavaln sternly explained that she must not explore forwards along either gloomy passage or down the next ladder that descended into the depths of the ship, warning her that King Gregnor would know instantly if she disobeyed, and such transgressions would result in her being incarcerated for the entire voyage in the tiny space she had been locked in on her arrival. It was a warning she took to heart.

It was later when, sleepless, Ethrayne felt definite movement in the ship and she quietly sat up in her bunk; by her breathing, Cavaln was sound asleep opposite. She turned to look out of the night-shrouded window to see that the ship had set sail, for she could see a line of wind-buffeted torches seemingly receding, with other lights behind them in the city. The ship was moving out into the estuary and Ethrayne felt it acutely when the winds caught the sails that had been run out; she heard muffled voices and noises from above, then the great craft started to plunge in the swell, and she felt suddenly queasy . . . She decided that it was nothing like riding a horse . . . It proved to be a very long night.

Staring out eastward through the wide window as the sun began to rise, Ethrayne could see that the coast was already out of sight, bar a possible hint of solid ground right at the horizon, exactly as the lights of the city they had sailed from had vanished long before first light. It was far too far to swim and she was a terrible swimmer anyway . . . She was stuck on this ship alongside the Betrayer, the King of the Jajozeli and his servants with no escape.

*

Six days later, far out in the S'lorn Ocean, Ethrayne was just glad to have got used to the unending motion of the ship; they had spent four days plunging through waves almost as large as two-storey houses, the aftermath of a nasty storm that had reduced her fear of her captors somewhat when faced with her new fear of the power of nature. Now, gazing out of the stern window and faced with small patches of blue sky amid huge deep-grey clouds and waves that did not threaten to topple the ship into the depths, Ethrayne rose, leaving Cavaln sleeping. She dressed quietly in the washroom, took up her cloak and boots and crept out of the cabin, making her way up to the main deck for some chilly fresh air. She pulled on boots and cloak quickly, for the wind was gusty and cold and stood up a little unsteadily, wrapping the cloak tight around her, moving to the port rail, where she could look back to the stern of the ship to watch the sun rise inexorably above the waves aft.

She was now learning some of the strange terminology associated with the mysteries of the ocean.

King Gregnor was effectively Captain, with apparently a huge knowledge and experience of ships and the oceans, but he shared command with Jallon and Bentham, whilst Khaen, Allun, Eduren, Ollyn, Harstyn and Unwynn led the crew and Ackat, Garrtnor and Masson added their assistance where required. Whillan and Sepphor were the chefs, working in a very small space, which left the rest of them effectively passengers: Shaille, Tynsyn, Dahne, Thellor, Cavaln and Harton; the last two with the vital skills of healers. In Ethrayne's opinion, there were twenty too many jajozeli-razine on board, in addition to the twenty-four men who apparently carried out the ordinary tasks on board the ship.

Combat sessions were scheduled for every morning, if the weather was not too dreadful, there on the main deck and Ethrayne was glad of the activity, for it was tiring and helped her to sleep; and the practice was easier than trying to keep out of everyone's way in the small area of the ship she was allowed in. What she didn't like was not being able to wash her sweaty clothes: fresh water was not to be wasted on such frivolities, apparently, although she still was tasked with washing up after almost every meal.

Waking so far at first light every morning, Ethrayne politely did her best to leave Cavaln alone in the small cabin they shared; she had sensed the woman's antagonism, been subjected to her eloquent abuse that first morning when she had disturbed her inadvertently, so that meant creeping out like a mouse and usually making her way to the galley for breakfast, taking it to the main cabin if it was raining and horrible, or up on the main deck to eat; for at daybreak only those on duty were generally up and about, so she had some welcome time to herself, so early.

It was unnerving to be always so close to the Betrayer. His power was vast and terrifying and she recalled every awful moment of his slaughter of that young man, which only increased her fear of him; yet, to her relief, King Gregnor spent a lot of his free time in his suite beneath the stern deck, rather than with his subordinates; but if he was on deck, steering his ship or whatever else was required, Ethrayne often fled to the main cabin, to endure the insults and nasty banter of the Generals. Although the ship was over two hundred feet long, nearly all its area below the main deck was banned to her.

With most of her mornings taken up, that generally left the afternoons and evenings where she was lashed by their tongues although, with her expertise frequently demanded to mend a wide variety of damaged clothing from all of them, she could largely try to ignore their comments whilst busy sewing . . . But the ocean was vast, the days lengthening . . . Sometimes she feared that she would scream out her tension and fear, but she restrained herself, trying to beat that in combat practice instead.

Days passed, slowly and strangely similar.

On the twenty-fifth day out from Cal'Itase the King's Lightning came in sight of land, docking at the foot of a well-fortified city that filled a rocky slope, which was identified as Sha'Jevhar, capital of the island of S'Lor, as the sun sank into the west. Locked in her cabin alone, Ethrayne relished the fact that probably everyone else had left the ship, having taken all the laundry with them, so at least she would not have to scrub all the wretched shirts and sheets and so on! She rested, just wishing for something to read, for staring out of the windows only alleviated some of the boredom, despite having the chance to relax. Hot meals were brought to her and even hot water for bathing again, late on the second evening, along with the warning from Garrtnor that the ship was setting out with the tide next morning.

With clean laundry and supplies of fresh food and water, their new direction was north by north west, with a strong following wind and only the occasional sight of some huge denizen of the ocean depths to perk her interest, some showed huge sharp teeth, or blasting air or water high into the sky and even one with amazingly large, seemingly intelligent and interested eyes that gazed up at the ship for a few moments before sinking effortlessly into the deep. Ethrayne now spent as much of her free time on deck as possible, glad that at least the weather was slightly warmer, trying yet failing to ignore the king's presence, huddling out of the wind and occasional rain as best she could.

*

Nine days from Sha'Jevhar, having been dismissed from yet another intense bout of unarmed combat by Shaille, her tutor on the main deck today, Ethrayne slowly made her way down the two ladders, thinking only of getting washed as well as she could and changing into clothes that were not soaked with sweat.

Opening the cabin door, however, she could only stare for one horrified moment at the completely unexpected sight of a totally naked Thellor, lying beneath the equally bare Cavaln, both gleaming with sweat, moving together.

Cavaln spat a curse, her eyes blazing as she turned her head, even as, shocked and embarrassed, Ethrayne hurriedly slammed the door shut, desperately trying to dismiss from her mind far too many instant details of their coupling.

Tears leaked from her eyes, stinging; suddenly, finding herself mentally assaulted in some way by the pair's aggressive passion and their enjoyment, desperately frightened, the girl fled; she was unable to block their lust from her mind. She stumbled up that ladder, around and up the second, finding her way through memory alone, her vision blurred as she made for the open air ahead, gasping as if she had run a mile; but Ethrayne bounced off someone, staggering backwards and down, hitting the planks on her rear and, horrified, stared up at the emperor in terror. He was so tall!

"You are distraught, child." Gregnor said in an even tone. "Up you get." He extended one hand and took hold of her wrist, hauling her easily to her feet, ignoring her instant flinching reaction to his touch: it was burning her skin as if he was made of fire.

"Sire, I -." But she could not speak further either to apologise or explain. Even her fear could not dispel her confusion and distress . . . and why could she still sense Cavaln and Thellor's passion? What was happening?

"Come along." He said, opening the door to the left that led to his suite below the stern deck. <*Tea!*> He ordered silently, causing Ethrayne to flinch at his mental as well as at his physical touch, pulling her into a large, light cabin. "Sit down, Ethrayne."

There were chairs near the window, she saw it as she tried, surreptitiously, to free her wrist from his grip to no avail and Gregnor simply ignored that attempt as he courteously guided Ethrayne to a seat, then let her free to produce a large handkerchief from a pocket, pressing it into her hands as they covered her face; her tears were falling faster, she was gulping now, feeling like an utter idiot, hunched up, sobbing helplessly, feeling dirty and smelly in her combat clothes . . . She was hardly aware when the overpowering ardour of the two Generals faded from her mind. Yet her immediate distress could not last forever and, presently, she was reduced to hiccups and sniffs, hiding her face in the soggy handkerchief, trembling.

Someone came in to the cabin, footsteps sounding despite the carpet on the floor, but Ethrayne was too wound up by her fear and misery to look up, although the sound of objects being placed on the table was clear.

"Your Majesty." General Sepphar said and the door was closed quietly.

"I would never have opened the cabin door if I'd known -." Ethrayne declared in sullen defence, around the hiccups. "Honestly, your Majesty -." And she shuddered, unable to continue, all too aware that his mind was touching her mind. His power was terrifying, just so vast! "Oh, please don't make me think -." But that single image filled her mind for a moment: the two Generals, the passion they shared and had been radiating, their naked bodies, Cavaln's curse. Crying out in protest, she pulled her feet up onto the seat, hiding as well as she could behind her knees and the emperor laughed aloud a little at her reaction, before that momentary memory was as quickly gone. "I would never have . . . I would have stayed on deck . . . I had no idea -."

"Here, child, have some tea. It was an innocent mistake, they will not blame you." Gregnor stated firmly.

"I always go to-to wash and change after combat . . . I did not intend to, to run into you so rudely, I am sorry -." She babbled fearfully.

"Ethrayne, drink your tea." Gregnor cut off her frightened apology. "Calm yourself."

Gulping, then blowing her nose and setting her booted feet back on the floor, Ethrayne glanced across, seeing ornate, shimmering gold mugs, an even finer teapot on the table and she slowly, nervously moved her hand to her right and picked up the gleaming, heavy mug which was gently steaming there, her other hand clenching the handkerchief in a death grip, her blood-shot gaze on the mug, then on the carpet and the planks of the floor. She was forced to place the handkerchief in her lap and support her grip on the mug, for her right hand was shaking terribly and it was still a precarious matter, lifting it to take a sip; the metal edge rattled gently against her teeth, but she swallowed, the cooling liquid fragrant and almost minty in her mouth; she sipped again, suddenly thirsty.

"Your culture and ours are very different in some regards." The emperor said lightly, gazing intently at the traumatised girl on the other side of the table. "But my servants should have thought a little before they allowed their passion to have free rein, shall we say? You are entering a delicate phase girl, and some complications are unwarranted."

Ethrayne frowned and briefly raised her gaze to his and away, wondering just what he meant, but not daring to ask.

"How is the tea?"

She jumped. "It's, it's very nice, th-thank you, your Majesty." She stammered, cringing back again, her heart thumping. "For-forgive me -."

"Oh, that was entirely my fault, girl." Gregnor admitted cheerfully. "We all learn to dampen our abilities as part of our early training and, of course, it's been the only way I can observe you without alerting you, for you can usually tell when I am close, naturally." He laughed aloud. "And I did not want you to."

<Oh!> That explained it, of course. Ethrayne decided that it was quite sensible on hearing the explanation, but it was chilling to realise that he *could* hide in plain sight and probably had done so in Ban'Lerracon, to watch her . . . Her fear rose even higher, her mouth went dry, so she drank more tea, the tremor returning with a vengeance to her hands. Why had he brought her here? Was it only to laugh at her, to mock her?

"You have been in my care for some moons now, Ethrayne and I know some of your history, but actually mostly only third-hand. I would like to hear about your life, your childhood in Clirensar and so on." Gregnor answered her silent question. "From a very sheltered childhood, a future mapped out so very securely: betrothal and marriage to your prince and then the prospect of one day becoming queen, you have been thrown into the very heart of uncertainty, prophecy and war. I would like you tell me about it, please."

"M-m–me? Oh, I . . ." Her voice faded away uncertainly, for how could she refuse without giving offence? To the *Betrayer*? Her head was empty, but for fear. Her heart raced anew. "Your Majesty . . . please, I . . ."

"We will have some more tea." He sent the silent order, his power sparking all around her and silence filled the rather nicely furnished sitting room until there was a tap at the door and Sepphar came in again with a tray bearing a fresh pot of tea, clean mugs and a plate holding freshly baked biscuits. He set these down with a flourish, collected up the used items and departed with a second low bow to his master.

Gregnor offered biscuits and poured more tea for his petrified guest, whilst Ethrayne desperately tried to think of something, anything, to say, but without success.

"You are how old, seventeen?" He prompted her after another silent period. "When was your birthday?"

"I . . . I was seventeen on-on the seventeenth of Instur, Sire. Jerryn, Prince Jerryn was seventeen at the close of Thurton, the-the twenty-eighth . . .

We have known each other all our lives, your Majesty." Ethrayne whispered, her gaze fixed on the mug in her hands. She politely took a biscuit, but she could not eat it. A while later, after that heart-stopping thrill of awful fear, most peculiarly, it was somehow reassuring to just sit there and talk about her childhood, even to her enemy . . . It did not cross her mind that he might have simply '*dampened his abilities*' somewhat, for his physical presence alone was overpowering, quite apart from the vast power and talent that he commanded. Everything about her captor was simply overwhelming, terrifiying, awe-inspiring.

Gradually, as the afternoon progressed, she nervously described a childhood of care, love and privilege in the very heart of Tenarean society, that had somehow exploded beyond all recognition after her betrothal to Jerryn. All the time, her gaze was fixed on the tabletop or on her hands, never on the Betrayer. At the point when she described how she and Jerryn first heard about Arven's Prophecy in the Book of Days, she fell silent with a nervous, very polite. "I imagine you know an awful lot more about the Prophecy than we do, your Majesty."

"Perhaps I do, at that, child." The king acknowledged with a smile.

Slowly, she described her meditation, the singular method initiated by Bahlien, which had meant that the Flame felt almost natural within her – then, hesitantly, her loss of that awareness, since her capture.

"Yes, I ensured that deliberately. I know you have tried repeatedly to regain the ability, child, yet all such attempts will fail until I allow it. Thank you for your cooperation today, Ethrayne, your conversation has been most insightful. Now, the evening is advancing; you may leave and get yourself some dinner."

Her heart leapt with huge relief at finally being dismissed, although she was unnerved by his words, his lack of explanation. What did it mean? She would never dare to ask! "Your Majesty." She got up, backed away, bowed low and tried not to run out of the cabin.

Wrung out, her head pounding, exhausted, she nevertheless found that she was starving hungry. The Generals in the main cabin below all glanced at her coolly, but did not speak to her, thankfully, as she cautiously edged through them, piled up a plate with food, eating quickly, perched on a stool in a corner and, having finished, quickly drinking one mug of water and noting, thankfully, that Cavaln was talking with the others, she refilled her mug and retreated down to their cabin.

It was blissful, being alone she acknowledged, after such a traumatic time. Had she *really* spent almost the entire afternoon in the king's presence? She wondered, shivering. After that awful afternoon that had led to the deaths of Inajo, Fionn and Sallie, she didn't even want to acknowledge it. He was more powerful than anyone else living; he had tried to destroy Arven, after all and he terrified her. He had, however, at least explained why she had been unable to control the Flame's power in any way; it was daunting to realise that it was not due to her own deficiencies but the Betrayer's strength. Shuddering, wishing that her head did not ache so much, she washed as well as she could in the cool water left in the washroom, changed into her nightgown, and lay down, but her head was so crammed with fear and confusion that it was very late when she finally fell asleep.

* * *

CHAPTER 31

Jerryn viewed the stark defensive works and vast camps around Foston as a monstrosity on their arrival at the garrison town, for the engineers' labour had heartbreakingly destroyed much of the native beauty of the area, including the vast coppiced woodlands that had swept south towards the Vale. They had ridden as fast as they could to this staging post, the centre point of highly coordinated moons of work and had rested for one day, meeting Master Banly, Mistress Ellysa and Mayor Fergus so that Duke Pualyn, King Marrand and he had been able to thank them for their efforts and hear the Mayor and Captain Chasson's nervously delivered reports on local developments since Lady Lyria had ridden north, so many moons before.

It had been emotive, a painful meeting that they had all been glad to conclude, although the duke had been glad to inform her parents that Greta was a blessing to their household and his wife's constant companion; but, of course, much worse was to come as the commanders rode the rest of the way to the northern edge of the Vale and they had all steeled themselves against the shock. Yet, to Pualyn, no matter the awful aftermath of his parents' murders, the actual initial sight of Clirensar, his childhood home, his city, so close and yet so unattainable beneath the stark, ever-flying flags of the Betrayer, caused an almost physical pain. It was apparent even from a distance that the city was in an increasingly worsening state: many of the visible roofs inside the walls were damaged or missing. It seemed that the Jajozeli were not bothered about protecting the infrastructure around them.

"Oh, shit!" Jerryn muttered. He had visited Clirensar probably at least once a year for most of his life; this place was very familiar to him and his father. "My apologies." He added. He had not meant to react like that, he had been concentrating on keeping a tight hold on his own unease, aware of Pualyn's own distress – to fail.

"It's – revolting!" Pualyn sighed and glanced across at the king, his face set, his eyes dark with emotion. "Sire, are you all right?"

Marrand shrugged. "No, not particularly, young man, this is a nightmare, isn't it? How can it be real?" It was not really a question, his tone was musing, but the king was pale. "I've been dreading this, I have to tell you, and I imagine you feel the same, Pualyn."

"Oh yes, your Majesty." Pualyn agreed heavily.

The Tenareans had constructed a wooden tower upon a hilltop before their massive defensive ditch and ramparts, where most of the armies were encamped; this was close to the King's Road and from it the guards and patrols set up by Captain Chasson kept a close watch over the occupied Vale beyond. As they had been north of Tenum City, the camps were organised like towns, with kitchens constructed at regular intervals, supplied with huge mounds of firewood and charcoal and dry supplies; and King Marrand's staff had arranged the distribution of troops according to nation and company, determinedly creating equal sites for Tenarean, Protectorate, Amorean or Derravane soldiers, the roads serving them as well metalled as any in the kingdom. It wouldn't be palatial, even for the kings or officers, but it would be as comfortable as they could manage.

Chasson, assisted by a couple of lieutenants from the royal staff, had made as detailed a set of maps of the Vale as the patrols could describe and the knowledge that their input was so vital, had spurred the guards of the perimeter area every day, no matter the weather or how depressing the news. Any approach to the city from the east was impossible, due to the massive limestone crag that set the castle far above Clirensar, practically a sheer cliff into the grassland there. They took note of the maps that detailed the massive defensive ditches and ramparts that surrounded the rest of the city, separated by the route of the river, constructed by the occupiers and their slaves during the winter; then collated by many daring scouts who had repeatedly risked their lives, circling the city at a safe distance.

Just after dawn on the morning after their arrival, Jerryn and his friends left the camp and rode to the watch tower which made a stark landmark on the hilltop, which they ascended to stare out with fresh dismay at Duke Pualyn's home and inheritance, a view that most of them knew well, but terribly altered; the clearest view they had yet had. The fact of the monstrously large ditch and rampart on the curving north bank of the Sare, was truly daunting; it was manned by a considerable force of black-garbed soldiers, with many more patrolling the city walls beyond, their weapons glinting in the weak spring sunshine that peeked through the gusting rain clouds.

"Dear Arven, what a mess!" Karne gasped.

"Yes." Lennarn declared, cleared distressed. His family also came from the area.

Pualyn grunted, his face paling rapidly as the sheer enormity of what they faced sank in. It was far different to looking at maps, he discovered at that moment. "Oh, they'll pay for this!" He muttered bitterly. "It might take years to repair all the damage, but we'll do it. And they will pay, by Arven, every single bloody one of them!"

"Amen." Jerryn said, finding the sight repugnant.

"Most certainly they will pay." Lieutenant Sevanter declared coldly. "Well, no matter how long it takes, Pualyn, we will support you. Those bastards won't win!"

"It's bloody scary." Tymain admitted in a bare whisper. "But I'm glad we're finally here and ready."

"Yes, I've been itching to attack since the Solstice." Pualyn said with a grimace. "I know the planning and so on was vital, but, oh, dear Arven, I've been so impatient."

"We've noticed, your Grace, believe me." Jerryn said tiredly and they all laughed, but his own smile was a little forced. "Now that I've got the five of you all alone, gentlemen, I want your promise that you will do your best to stay alive. Especially you, Pualyn: my father, your lady and the kingdom all need you."

"There are no certainties in war, Jerryn, we can't -." Pualyn began.

"That army over there was sent out on a strange, mad gamble, you know, and it damn-well paid off ." Jerryn interrupted him. "They stole Ethrayne away and have established a foothold that none of us can afford to ignore, not at all. Now we must destroy the entire lot of them." He continued relentlessly. "Don't forget that the High-King and Archpriests believe that the Betrayer sent that army here so that their leaders could hopefully catch both Ethrayne and myself!"

"What?" Tymain and Sevanter cried at the same moment and the lieutenant stated. "Then you must leave, your Highness."

"The bastards took Ethrayne and slaughtered thousands, Jerryn, they cannot imprison you too!" Pualyn declared hotly. "Sevanter's right: you must leave here."

"No. How can I deny the destiny that made Ethrayne and I the Wielders of the Flame?" The prince asked easily; he had considered this for moons now, both sides of the argument strong in his head. "You mustn't think that I'm going to surrender to them, far from it: I fully intend to kill as many of the enemy as possible, just like the rest of you . . . I'm just preparing you for all eventualities, my friends, and I want your promises made here and now, before we head back to camp. Logically, the Generals will focus on me, which ensures that the rest of you can concentrate on taking Clirensar back!"

"Dear Arven, Jerryn!" Karne appealed, sounding shocked, but his master glared from face to face in turn. "We-we can't -."

"If they take me, they might abandon the city, remember. Father and the kingdom will need all of you; especially you, Pualyn. Logically, you and your children will be my father's heirs, if anything happens to Ethrayne or myself. Yet I don't believe that Arven will have chosen us just to see us dead, and I don't believe that the Betrayer will see much beyond our youth and inexperience." Jerryn declared. "I want your oaths, gentlemen, that you will stand with my father and protect the realm."

Pualyn sighed deeply and spoke with obvious reluctance, laying his right hand over his heart. "I swear before Arven, Am'maiya, that I will not act recklessly; I commit my life to King Marrand, the kingdom and to my Lady . . . But you had better beat the bloody Betrayer, Jerryn!" He ended his declaration fiercely.

Tymain, Sevanter, Karne and Lerrand made their promises with equal solemnity, hands on hearts and Jerryn finally smiled a little.

"Excellent, thank you, gentlemen. Hopefully it won't be necessary, you know. Come on, it's nearly breakfast time and we've got a parley to finalise, for all the good it'll do." And he started down the rough ladders that would take them back to the ground, whistling.

*

The leaders of the allied armies had been working on their approach and their plans for moons, greatly assisted by the maps and local knowledge at their disposal, although they were aware that the layout and street-plan of Clirensar might well have changed significantly under the occupying army. The professionals had respectfully laid their proposal to their kings and the rest of that first day since the extensive royal party's arrival was spent in finalising those plans, as the soldiers settled in, readied their equipment and rested as much as they could.

Jerryn hurried out of the extended pavilion that served as headquarters, where they were all collected, the day before they expected the fighting to begin. It was late afternoon and they had been talking backwards and forwards since breakfast. Tymain, Sevanter and Pualyn all exited close behind him, concern on their faces, as he stood outside in the chilly breeze, leaning on a tent pole, breathing heavily, his face pale and sweaty. Kerrenan strode out of the doorway after them a moment later. "Are you all right, Jerryn?" Pualyn asked. "You look awful."

"Thanks. I suddenly feel sick, so sick. Arven only knows why." He accepted a cup of water from Sevanter and nodded his thanks quickly, taking a quick sip, extending his hands. "Look, I'm trembling, but I felt fine only a short while ago."

"Ah, you need to construct that protective wall within your mind, Jerryn." Kerrenan advised with a nod of understanding. "We discussed it during our journey: you need that buffer in place against the emotions filling this camp."

"Really? Are you sure I've not just eaten something bad?" Jerryn asked, puzzled. "It's right here, Kerr." He pressed his stomach and took another sip of water.

"I'm sure it is, Jerryn: the emotions of everyone here are very much stronger than usual: fear, anger and so on are running rife and with so many people involved, such strength of feelings can make one nauseous and you're getting more sensitive by the day, of course." The High-Prince said calmly.

"It just sounds weird to me." Pualyn commented, frowning. "I really don't think I'd like to read other peoples' thoughts. Dear Arven, you can't read mine, can you?" He asked with sudden nervousness.

"Not with the sheer number of people in this vicinity, no, Pualyn." Kerr assured him with a smile and a wink. "It's not common by any means, but it's not unknown amongst you humans, and Jerryn and Lady Ethrayne are certainly not unique, for Arven's Flame has gifted them with diverse abilities that will develop as they mature. This type of emotional mayhem can have such physical effects on us."

"Dear Arven, if this is affecting me, just think of Ethrayne, stuck alone with those monsters!" Jerryn said with a grimace. "So, if I concentrate on making that wall inside my head, it'll ease the sickness? Oh, I'm sorry, Pualyn

-." He added quickly as a single blast of fury and distress drowned out all the other emotions assailing his mind.

"Well, if you can read my mind, Jerryn, at least I don't have to shout it!" The young duke snapped and strode off, his shoulders hunched, his head lowered.

<I should have thought before I spoke.> Jerryn admitted guiltily. *<Oh, damn it! We need Pualyn -.>*

<I'll speak to him, reassure him, Jerryn. Pualyn is frightened and upset, along with the rest of you. This is his city, he probably knew most of the citizens who would have been captured and slain and it hurts acutely, as you know.> Kerrenan reassured him, his tone gentle. *<You all have a lot of responsibility heaped upon your young shoulders, but you are managing commendably well. Don't worry, Jerryn; go and meditate, block your mind against their fear.>* He advised and set off across the uneven ground after the retreating duke.

"Is Pualyn ill too?" Sevanter asked politely, looking concerned. He still seemed uncomfortable with his old childhood friend's rank and his own elevation, due to his sister's marriage and the unsettling events that had devastated the region.

"He just wants a moment alone: we're all worried, Sevanter." Tymain said, glancing at Jerryn and noting his distress. As a small group, they generally had discarded their titles when alone. "I mean, you grew up here as well, it must be horrifying to have lost almost all your family so suddenly."

"Yes!" Sevanter did not bother to elaborate and his face was sombre as he remembered them.

"Go and re-join the meeting, gentlemen, please give my father my apologies and I'll see you later." Jerryn set off towards his own gaudily striped pavilion, set close to his father's.

The small bedroom area was hung with carpets on the walls for extra warmth, but the furnishings were simple army fare: a narrow, collapsible bed, table and chair. He sat down in the chair and closed his eyes laying his hands on his knees, trying to rediscover the inner sense of peace and rightness which he had grown somewhat used to in his meditation . . . He had neglected his studies terribly since they had all left Tenum City.

Meditation, visualising that strong mental wall about himself, did help to greatly reduce the nausea affecting him, but although it was heartening to be able to control the power within him and stop the myriad emotions assaulting him, the sheer enormity of what they were undertaking was overwhelming, along with the simple fact that although justice and Arven were on their side, the enemy were formidable in the extreme, holding the city and its environs with an unknown number of troops, an extremely defensible position in anyone's book.

His fear for Ethrayne, however, was always present, no matter how the razine tried to help him block it. It had been moons now since he had seen her ride away. He just prayed that she was all right, even amongst their enemies. Now, of course, they were so close to where her parents and so many others had been slaughtered – although Captain Chasson's patrol had never found any remains, other than discarded equipment. The bodies had been removed, they assumed. It was hard to maintain any balance, he found, as he finally lay down.

Few of the officers and nobles slept that night within the allied camps and a great many officers and commons soldiers were up as early as the cooks preparing a hearty breakfast that few would be able to stomach. Everyone was jumpy; some were openly bad-tempered; some men were sick. Very few men from the selithian kingdoms had fought in a war, though some soldiers such as Sevanter had seen action against occasional bandits or criminal groups which had set themselves up for hoped-for but rarely realised profits, throughout their realms; a greater number from the Protectorate forces had seen action against the Jajozeli, serving on Pearl and Opal ships, or defending outposts under attack from pirates.

Jerryn certainly did not eat anything. Up well before dawn, he walked around the night-shrouded camp for a while with Tymain and Karne at his side, before they returned to the pavilion to start pulling on their padded tunics and chain mail and so on; checking pristine weapons, straps and kit for non-existent damage. Around them, outside the canvas walls that enclosed them, they could hear the murmur of quiet conversations; the ring of steel; the sound of hooves, the march of feet, all oddly loud in the peaceful air. Yet, at a distance, they could hear horns and drums echoing out from the city below – it startled him, and probably everyone else as well. The jajozeli were waiting for them.

As dawn lit the sky, revealing the tent-covered landscape anew, Jerryn, Tymain and Karne set off towards the command pavilion, leading their horses, exchanging greetings with many of the soldiers passing to join their own companies.

"Jerryn, I'm sorry I reacted like that." Pualyn said, as they were coming up on the lines where grooms were tying the horses' reins to long rails to the right; clearly, he had been waiting for them. He was pale faced, but his eyes were clear, tall and impressive in his mail and surcoat.

"No, I can only apologise, Pualyn; it was just crass and stupid of me: everything here must really hurt you." Jerryn answered, laying his hand lightly upon the duke's shoulder; they were all covered in hard mail, not a material conducive to affectionate, hearty slaps. "Just remember your promises, all of you: if I'm taken, though Arven protect us all, I at least should be able to find Ethrayne; you must all assist my father, protect the kingdom, please." His tone was stern and they all nodded agreement as he led them into the crowded pavilion.

*

It was not long before the decided-upon advance group of the amalgamated armies began their slow march from the camps, through the few remaining stands of budding trees, as their commanders made for the large, well-built gate that blocked the King's Road, the advance heralded by drumming and rather musical horn fanfares. From the great city in the valley to the south they could hear horns sounding in answer or defiance, the noise somehow deeper and less musical, echoing around them, almost sounding like it originated in the ground below their booted feet. Moving onto the hillside, it was clear that the

Jerryn found that his fear had receded somewhat, replaced with a cold excitement that he knew was perfectly illogical, as he rode behind his father and his fellow kings, their standards whipping in the gusty breeze, brightly lit by the sun when it escaped every so often from the large grey clouds scudding across the sky.

They halted just outside the gate of their own hilltop defences, but Duke Pualyn, Commander Vedeigne, King Marrand and High-Prince Kerrenan rode on under the flags of Clirensar and Tenarum, as the delegation for the allied forces, with a plain white flag in Pualyn's left fist. The four of them rode a few hundred yards down the road and the young man tried to ignore the evidence of burned and rutted ground, the few remains of broken weapons and equipment that marked the site of the battle where his parents had died. No bodies had been recovered, though their men had searched the area. Gritting his teeth, breathing deeply, trying to breathe slowly, he forced back the rage, mixed with fear, that threatened to consume him and kept silently repeating his promise to Jerryn and Arven.

"Courage, your Grace." Marrand said, his tone a strange mixture of brevity and unease and Pualyn realised that his king was also frightened, which made him feel better.

"Thank you, your Majesty." Pualyn answered, managing a crooked smile. "I think I'd rather face boars single-handed, you know."

"Yes, I know what you mean, your Grace." Vedeigne added, straightening in his saddle. "Look, here they come, the bastards."

A similar group under the Betrayer's distinctive standard had set out up the road, four men on horseback, wearing black cloaks, climbing quickly from the defensive ramparts that surrounded the city and the river, coming to a halt some sixty or so yards from the allies.

"Welcome home to Clirensar, your Grace." A huge man with brown hair and a thick reddish beard greeted Pualyn, bowing slightly in his saddle. His eyes were black, glittering and there was a cruel smile on his broad face. "I am General Tequan, Commander here. These are my associates, Generals Oxttyn, Owenn and Jaike. I see that you've taken up alliance with the razine, to your loss!" He sneered, gazing from face to face, discounting the king and commander's presence. "You're looking a little pale, Highness."

"Thank you for your opinion, Tequan." Kerrenan replied quietly, his tone calm but Pualyn was startled, realising that he could sense the undercurrent of intense hatred between the two powerful beings and he shivered at the animosity thrilling his nerves, realising how Jerryn had been so affected: it was distracting, to say the least.

"General Tequan, on behalf of his Majesty, King Marrand and my countrymen, in addition to our allies from around Iullyn, I give you formal warning to quit our city and its environs or face certain death." Pualyn declaimed coldly, his fear and unease keeping him tightly focussed.

"Retreat?" Tequan laughed expressively, throwing back his head as he did so, the sound almost like a roar. "Leave this prime, defensive site, Duke Pualyn? Don't be stupid, boy! We were ordered to take Clirensar and hold it to the last man and we will, I assure you! Call up your armies and avenge the deaths of your parents and your townsfolk if you can! Come!" And, with one curt gesture, he and his cohorts turned their horses smartly and thundered back down the pale road, to hoarse cheering from the jajozeli ranged below.

"An eloquent bastard, isn't he, your Majesty?" Kerrenan said with a sigh to King Marrand, almost apologetically. "Let's get back to the armies, shall we? We have observed the formalities, may Arven strike them all with pox!"

"And he was commander of Cal'Badon?" Marrand muttered. "A bully of a man, I deem; well, you and your father were right, your Highness." He shook his head as they rode steadily back to their companions. "He, their king, really would throw away thousands and thousands of lives to block us. Dear Arven, he must be a lunatic! . . . Surely he must be mad?"

"Aye, he might be." Kerrenan confirmed coldly. "Still, let's see how many of his lieutenants we can eliminate, hey? There's got to be more than four of the bastards in there!" He rubbed his hands together and grinned fiercely.

"You really hate them, don't you?" Vedeigne commented, surprised by the High-Prince's bitter tone.

"The Betrayer's servants are the descendants of those men and women who attempted to destroy our society once he had imprisoned Arven: there was open slaughter across many settlements and Lerat was razed. There might be blood relatives on both sides, Commander, but they are sworn to destroy us, and our God, and we are equally sworn to destroy them all." The High-Prince said shortly. "Our hatred is deeper than the roots of mountains!"

"That was a short discussion." Jerryn said gravely. "I thought that the formal introductions would take a little longer, actually -." He grinned as Mhezal snorted a laugh and some of the others smiled, the tension lessened slightly.

"It's what I expected." Marrand stated then. "Let's get this started, shall we, gentlemen? Forward!"

Their own men started the signals – blasts of horns around them, loud, shrill, whilst the horns and drums in Clirensar began again, a rhythmic beat, as the commanders moved aside so that the soldiers, both mounted and on foot, could advance and spread out across the sloping curve of the valley. The Tenareans formed the centre, backed up by the Protectorate forces, with the Amoreans to the western flank and the Derravane troops to the left, eastern side, beyond the line of the road. As they took their pre-arranged positions, the black-clad Jajozeli were continuing to spill through the huge gate in their rampart, their weapons clashing harshly against their shields, loud across the vale.

"Good luck, gentlemen, may Arven protect us all! Advance!" Marrand shouted, backed up by horns and, inexorably, the front ranks moved steadily down the side of the valley.

The sound of the impact of the two forces was unbelievable as the front ranks of the allies punched on through the enemy lines and the jajozeli seemed to be overwhelmed by the numbers descending relentlessly upon them.

It was complete chaos, Pualyn discovered, even though he and his cohorts were not very close to the van: the noise of battle was unbelievable, the shouts of his companions only a few feet away could not be heard; the sheer brutality of having to hack at the enemy, whilst the enemy hacked back in return was shocking and all his years of practice, of course, meant nothing when trying to cope with the horror of having to kill people. They had made their plans, he just hoped that they would reach the walls today! This, however, was the only way that they could hopefully retake the city. Slaughtering the enemy. He fought on and on, abandoning thought for renewed action: the quicker they got on with it, the sooner they would succeed, please God!

"Hold!" A shout went up from the commanders as the men would have carried on down towards the jajozeli defence and the enemy launched an arrow-storm uphill, the lethal darts whistling though the air. Most soldiers managed to raise their shields in time, but across the field, hundreds of men from both armies died, or fell sorely injured.

The battle continued, speeding up at some points whilst a lull descended in other places, as the allies kept up their offensive with grim determination. They had estimations, of course, but they did not know how many jajozeli soldiers there were inside the city. The allies had decided to take as much of the ground before the new outer perimeter wall around the curve of the road and the river as they could, using only their initial vanguard, if at all possible. Holding the land outside the wall here to the north of Clirensar at least would mean that their engineers could get to work, destroying these defences.

Jerryn considered uneasily that he had been practising for this moment for years, he, the soldiers and the other nobles who had trained as he had. Now that he was fighting for his life, the lives of his friends and companions, he found that his reaction time sped up, even though the physical weight of his mail hampered his movements; he was fighting by instinct, it seemed. Men launched themselves at him, screaming obscenities, flourishing their weapons; men he must cut down before they killed him in return. It was foul. He had guessed it, of course – Sevanter had warned him. The dismemberment of a living man was brutal, blood spraying like fountains, and not every blow delivered was fatal. He left quite a few men injured, armless, bleeding heavily from wounds in their heads, necks or throats – praying that he would not loose strength or his courage! Inwardly, he hated it, because his power made him so much more sensitive to the emotions and the pain of those around him, friend and foe alike. It was worse, he thought, reading the pain the injured and dying were suffering, but he blocked it, his teeth gritted as he concentrated on his power and the momentum of battle, of working their way through the battlefield, through the cacophony. Fighting on horseback certainly provided them with an advantage, yet it was still risky. He saw riders and horses killed, not just footsoldiers. His closest compatriots all stayed mounted, at least, although their horses occasionally seemed determined to escape the melee! He, Pualyn, Tymain and the others just struggled to stay within view and shouting distance of each other.

"How are we doing?" Jerryn asked the High-King, as his small group finally caught up with the leaders, later that afternoon. His body was aching from the weight of the mail, the attack and defence required, the strain on so many muscles. Yet he still felt charged, although he could feel a deep tiredness beneath it. "Is everyone safe, sir?"

"Pretty much, Jerryn." Mhezal sighed. "But there are thousands of soldiers beyond those ramparts and probably thousands more inside the city itself."

"Ought we to burn Clirensar then?" He had considered the action with cold logic, trying to be dispassionate, but the mere thought of it filled him with horror. "Dear Arven, my head won't work properly!" It was as if the pause in fighting, in protecting his own and others' lives had slowed his responses. Tiredness was draining his concentration, now that the immediate threat had faded slightly.

"I know, I feel the same." Mhezal assured him. "We will have to keep that option in mind and pray that it won't be necessary." He turned quickly as a pocket of fighting swept suddenly closer across the muddy, bloody-stained ground, and they were far too busy again for conversation.

*

By nightfall, the jajozeli forces outside the northern ramparts had all been slaughtered and the exhausted allied combatants began retrieving their injured and dead, torches blazing as the light faded from the sky. Whilst the initial allied force had been fighting, other men from the allied camps had come down the sweeping road to dig out defences for a new ditch and rampart close to the edge of the trees, within clear sight of the enemy but at the top of that slope; there were sharpened stakes aplenty and the soldiers made short shrift of making a ditch and rampart, a good few miles long on either side of the road, to be manned by more troops. This was a line designed to block any advance to the north by the enemy below, extra security; a clear sign of their determination to succeed at all costs. As they finished off, muddy and tired, the remaining combatants, blood-stained and exhausted, marched or rode slowly back to the safety of the main camp trailing alongside the carts transporting their wounded and then the dead.

The soldiers washed if they had the energy, ate and rested; but the commanders and nobles talked long and hard as they were served with dinner, discussing their plans for the next day, along with what they thought about all that had occurred since the armies had collided.

"We didn't see any Generals in the battle." Jerryn voiced the fact that most of them had noticed, despite their necessary focus on staying alive. He was eating with relish: he knew now that he would never again suffer from being too scared to eat before battle. After so many hours of hard graft, he was starving.

"Yes, I noticed." The High-Prince said gravely. "I think they'll hold back as long as they can, the bastards!"

"Is that going to be a problem, Kerrenan?" King Marrand asked, clearly concerned. "Clirensar has excellent defences. Dear Arven, this will take moons!"

"Hopefully not, your Majesty." Commander Vedeigne assured him.

"If they get pinned down in the city, it'll be to our advantage: they'll have nowhere to run!" Pualyn declared fiercely.

"I like your spirit, your Grace." King Nemeth of Derravale said with a nod. "Be positive, that's definitely the thing."

"Thank you, your Majesty." Pualyn managed a genuine smile, for a moment.

"Amen to that." The High-King said, stretching. "Well, I'm for my bed, gentlemen, if we're all done, else I'll fall asleep right here!"

*

Over the next few days, the allied armies inched towards the city's outer defences; by the fourth day they recklessly took the defensive ramparts on the north bank of the Sare at considerable cost, but not losing anywhere near as many men as the jajozeli defenders. The surviving jajozeli fled back across the bridge or swam the river to safety on the southern bank, in the shadow of the city walls. Taking the ramparts was a huge boost to the thousands of allied soldiers as they marched down to this new front. Now, commanding that abandoned high ground, protected by the river, they could concentrate on the three city gates.

The only Generals they saw were directing their troops at a distance, which worried them all, especially the razine: their estimation seemed correct, that the enemy commanders would indeed hold back to the last.

None of the leaders had yet been seriously hurt or killed in the battles, but all of them bore injuries, ranging from the broken leg that had retired King Nemeth late on the ninth day, to the cuts, bruises, pulled muscles and so on that made so many more of them limp and ache as they rested as well as they could each evening, sometimes sharpened their weapons, talking.

As the allied forces had advanced, their engineers had been constructing siege engines and pontoons to enable an easier crossing of the Sare, using where available the materials that had formed the defences that they had taken, along with what seemed to be miles of planks and beams cut from the denuded forests. Some of the walking wounded were tasked with filling in the ditch and flattening the ramparts around the gates; their two camps behind them were more than adequate for the moment, and they didn't want to leave defences that a task force from the city could utilise easily. Now that the enemy were confined to Clirensar, hemmed in behind its ancient walls, they all breathed easier, but although many thousands of the jajozeli soldiers were dead and forming smoking pyres across the lower vale, to ensure that the health of the allied soldiers were not compromised, no-one felt any elation: the city was held against them.

The commanders sent out more patrols, carefully ranging through the countryside, a good few miles distant from the city walls, and their reports were pondered over with great scrutiny: it seemed that the enemy had denuded the whole area of the vale before withdrawing into Clirensar. Their soldiers were visible clearly on the ramparts they defended, but that seemed the limit of their sphere of influence, a wise strategy, everyone agreed. Allied soldiers now were sent to encircle the rest of the city: thousands upon thousands, with all the ancillary support required: equipment, food and tents and so on.

Jerryn and his companions all sat together, tired and resigned to the ache and burn of their abused muscles, the low-level headaches that beat behind their eyes. The reality of battle had shaken them all, but they were ready and willing to continue the next day; and the next; and the one after that, for simply as long as it would take, to eliminate the enemy and retake the city . . . But they were all sick of it!

"Are you all right?" Kerrenan and King Namayomn both came over with fresh jugs of the watered wine they now normally drank in the evenings. They had been there for twenty days by then and they were sick of it. "You look terrible, men."

"Just tired, Kerr, really." Pualyn admitted with a sigh. "Thank you." He held out his goblet for a serving of wine.

"And a bit disheartened, too." Jerryn added. "I know we're advancing quickly, all things considered, but it still seems far too slow! We can't afford to be stuck outside the city for long – we have to eliminate the jajozeli!" He shook his head.

"I know what you mean, Jerryn." Namayomn agreed, courteously refilling the other goblets in their hands. "But look, we control the countryside around the city again, we've killed at least eight thousand of the enemy, to less than half those losses on our side; and don't forget that we are gaining fresh troops and supplies regularly, whilst they are not! Our healers are exceptional, as well. Things could be so very much worse." His tone was hearty, but they could all tell that this was faked. No matter training and professionalism, it was a horrible business.

"Dear Arven, yes!" Sevanter exclaimed and shivered. They were scheduled to take a troop of guards the next morning, to try and see if they could view South Vale Farm and Callorton in safety; if they dared to venture somewhat closer to Clirensar's defences, despite their own troops that blocked any danger; and the thought of what they might find there was probably much worse than what they would actually find, after so many moons.

*

Dawn came all too swiftly as the spring advanced and everyone was up early for a hearty breakfast, before the massive siege engines would continue their assault on the city gates and walls, under the command of Commander Vedeigne. This, they assumed with some confidence, would continue to concentrate the enemy's attention sufficiently for King Marrand to lead a company of razine soldiers as support, as well as Jerryn, Pualyn, Sevanter and the Flame Guard around the Vale to the south. Their scouts reported that there were no enemy soldiers outside the city walls.

The group rode steadily, keeping at least a league from the bank of the Sare, making for a small crossing upstream well-known to Pualyn and Sevanter, keeping hidden behind trees and empty farm ranges where possible; they noticed that the bright spring green meadows and fields of the vale were frighteningly empty; even wildlife was largely missing, it seemed, likely disturbed by their presence, their violence. The farm animals which had been held south of the city during the winter, as reported by Captain Chasson, all seemed to have been eaten – there were none to be seen.

There was no sign of any of the enemy, except for the figures visible on the distant rampart and the city walls beyond; nothing amiss apart from the emptiness. Their own troops had long-since completed their circle to form an impregnable barrier to the west and south, right to the foot of the crag to the east; their soldiers were clear to see, their weapons shining. The small group carried on through countryside that was horribly familiar, yet full of hidden horror and danger; they all felt it, even the razine who did not have personal reasons for their intense emotions. They passed other little farms on the south side of the river, all empty, some ruined; the land was eerily quiet, despite their armies.

It took most of the morning to circle around to the lane that led to South Vale Farm, puddled from the rain that had fallen during the previous day, and overgrown; the hedges and verges were unkempt, some branches from bordering trees fallen and lying across their path. The fields beyond were ragged and completely bereft of the horses that had defined Sarant's stud, the well-woven stems of the hedges and wild plants on the verges gaining that new cover of a myriad greens, nature having no regard for their loss.

"This is a beautiful land." Kerrenan said quietly, fully aware of the collective distress of the group and most especially of Sevanter and Pualyn, who ignored the rest of them, riding ahead; they paused at the edge of the old orchard that had screened the range of buildings from the road.

"Oh, dear Arven no! This is worse than I ever imagined!" Sevanter groaned, staring at the remains of the farmhouse and barns which had been burned, leaving only blackened stone walls and a couple of roof beams hanging precariously, looking horribly like broken ribs. There were no signs of any bodies; the yard was empty. There were no chickens or other creatures in sight, other than a couple of large crows that leisurely flapped away from them.

"Sevanter, I'm so sorry. Salyn and Deanne, their children and the staff . . . oh, the bastards!" Pualyn fought back tears, looking at the ruins. "I'm so, so sorry -."

"They never stood a chance." The lieutenant said with an attempt at professional detachment, riding slowly forward as the rest of the group joined them. "Look how easily we moved through the countryside without being in sight of the city: it's a definite flaw, your Grace."

"This is tragic!" Marrand spat. "Dear Arven -." He broke off, dismounted and headed for the ruined doorway that had led into the pristine kitchen, wincing as he stepped on a couple of pieces of broken pottery, glancing at the remains of a bowl that he recognised. Everyone stared as he paused on the blackened doorstep, shaking his head slowly, before turning around and heading back towards them. "Nothing is left." He said regretfully to Pualyn. "I am sorry."

Jerryn spat curses, kicked his horse Vachane, which had been born here, and turned out of the yard, heading towards the little lane that led to the fields and the strip of woodland that separated South Vale Farm from Callorton; he knew these lands almost as well as the others, after all. He had spent many happy holidays here in Clirensar, here on the farm, especially when he was younger, when they had all raced about: children having fun fishing in the ponds, catching tadpoles, crickets, butterflies and grasshoppers, feeding the animals, when the world had been simple!

Fury and fear filled him: he had spent a great deal of his energy on the planning and execution of battle, trying to suppress the guilt he felt at all that had befallen the kingdom since he and Ethrayne had agreed to take the Flame of Arven, with no idea how anyone was going to survive. He, too, had known everyone who had lived on both estates, apart from the youngest children, he supposed with pain.

<Jerryn, stop!> Kerrenan shouted silently. *<Please take care -.>*

<I've spent most of my childhood here too!> He spat back, urging Vachane on at full speed. *<This is all our fault!>* He was trying to put his feelings into words, but very badly; he heard the High-Prince's projected curses following him.

<No, it bloody well isn't -.>

But Jerryn blocked the High-Prince's reassurances, racing onward. Across the fields and through the separating woodland, Jerryn slowed as he emerged into the equally overgrown fields beyond, the previously pristine lands of the self-contained Callorton estate where Sevanter and Lyria had grown up with their siblings, certainly in awe of the rich, privileged aristocratic family which owned the farm to the north and nearly all the rest of the vale besides, with their frequent royal guests . . . He stopped there by the edge of the trees, unwilling to continue. It wasn't his place to take over, for Sevanter and Pualyn were family; sickened, he realised that he could just see the blackened ruins of the buildings from here, emerging from the greening trees.

<*Dear Arven, no!*> He fought to keep control, though he longed to scream out his distress. There was sound from behind him, a curse as Kerrenan came out of the undergrowth, fighting to clear his cloak from ensnaring rose stems.

"Thousands on thousands are dead! How many more of our people will the jajozeli kill to try and capture me, Kerr? Will they sacrifice their entire army to see that happen? And what then? What might happen to-to the kingdom, to Iullyn if they imprison me, too?" He demanded angrily, his tone a harsh whisper. "If they hold Ethrayne and me, are we doomed?"

"We cannot answer that, Am'maiya, I am sorry." The High-Prince answered him quietly.

"Then surely we've not -." But Jerryn stopped there as the rest of the group burst through from the woodland, curbing his despairing words and began again, but silently. <*Then we* are *all doomed, Highness! We had better check that damned Book of Days for a prophecy detailing the end of everything and the rise of the Betrayer!*>

<*Forgive me Am'maiya!*> The High-Prince apologised humbly, bowing his head as the duke and lieutenant took the lead.

Pualyn would have spoken, but a clear boom of stone hitting stone broke through then; they realised that they had been hearing similar collisions for some time, but with less clarity: that CRASH! had echoed for miles across the vale and was followed by a notably audible cheer of support from the encircling soldiers.

"Excellent!" King Marrand said, smiling despite the clear worry on his face. "That's a strong hit, unless I'm mistaken, the siege is continuing well, gentlemen."

"Thank Arven!" Pualyn muttered, shuddered expressively and led them on to Callorton with Sevanter. "Let's find out what we can, before we head back, hey?" He muttered to his brother-in-law. "We ought to try and collate some news for Lyria."

"Yes." Was Sevanter's terse reply.

The farmyard was as weedy and empty as at South Vale Farm, all the old, well-built barns and house burned out. The chickens, geese and ducks had gone, as had all the other animals; probably for food, they surmised. One sight deeply disturbed them: the hefty farmhouse door had been deliberately propped up against the blackened porch wall and a body had been nailed to it moons before, leaving stained and ruined tatters of clothing and most of the bones piled haphazardly on the ground, where they had been gnawed and disturbed by vermin.

Sombre, his jaw clenched, Jerryn picked up a rusty shovel half hidden in emerging nettles, and strode on past them to clear grass, where he started to hack at the ground. Pualyn and Sevanter found tools to help him, all silent, all holding tight to their emotions. With three of them working, it did not take quite so long to dig a grave. Marrand, Kerrenan and Tymain gathered the remains up respectfully, wrapping them in the king's cloak, whilst the rest of the Flame Troop searched the area for more bodies, to no avail. They buried their countryman, or woman, pressed down the soil, laid stones on top, and said fervent prayers to him and the innocent dwellers of the two farms, before setting off back. The accompanying BOOM! of the rocks hitting the walls and the gates gradually growing louder.

* * *

CHAPTER 32

Buoyed by their High-King's acquiescence, if slightly disappointed at being unsuccessful at obtaining his whole-hearted approval, the five razine captains who had formulated their audacious proposal of attack, met together at the Pilgrim's Arms in a newly reconstructed Saremouth, some distance from the port's administration buildings. The presence of five massive razine ships at anchor in the deep water just off-shore made everyone, from Garrison Commander to lowly fisherman, feel much more secure and Lord Kierven and Commander Taess had been pleased to receive private visits from Captain Ashanner and Captain Phellos, briefly explaining the reason for their congregation.

In fact, the men, separately, had rubbed their hands together in glee at the thought of Cal'Badon's possible destruction and wished them Godspeed on their voyage. The attack on their city as part of the diversion for the quiet occupation of Clirensar had hit them hard, amongst many.

The Orbain Pearl and Mador Opal had been joined by the Jaece Pearl, Veddock Pearl and the Cerris Opal; the other ships of the fleet were elsewhere in the world's oceans and out of range; but the five captains between them had nearly two hundred and fifty razine crew, including themselves, to call upon, in addition to their human troops, all of them experienced, hardened marines.

Over a hearty, four-course meal in a large, private dining room at the inn, the captains made their plans. The two Opal ships would range ahead as scouts, to destroy all jajozeli ships that might interfere, then sail on to the south of the Badon Inlet by the last quarter of the moon of Rhellay. The five ships would attack at the dark of the moon, with deck based mangonels to throw fire effectively and the intention of wakening the fire of the earth that kept the region ice-free.

They knew well that they would be hard-pressed, but their combined power as razine was considerable and war-by-talent was a concept so far ignored by the razine since the initial war with Gregnor's followers, more than eight hundred years earlier. The humans amongst them would manage the firing of the mangonels and lead the hand-to-hand fighting.

"I just wish we could have brought more of our colleagues into the equation." Captain Amdor remarked. He was older than all the others there and he looked it, with a craggy, lined, ruddy face and white hair that tended to stick out; with his pale, blue eyes that protruded slightly, there was the look of eccentricity about him, but he was a sober master of the Cerris Opal and had been for nearly two centuries. "It isn't a small place like Newventure Bay, after all. I'm sure Cal'Badon is well defended."

"There are over four hundred and eighty of us, Amdor and even the youngest men in our crews are seasoned fighters." Captain Phellos asserted calmly. "And they're hardly going to expect an all-out attack by the reticent, timid Protectorate ships, are they?"

"Well, that's true, Phellos." Captain Eltham, master of the Jaece Pearl, agreed, nodded fervently. "But it's -." He fell silent at a knock on the stout door.

"Enter." Captain Ashanner called.

Lord Kierven and Captain Dhell stood in the doorway and the old fisherman from Rothern grinned and bowed low to Captain Phellos as both men stepped into the room and shut the door smartly.

"Evenin' Cap'ns." He offered in his usual drawl.

"Ah, excuse our interruption, good Captains." The lord of the city said rather nervously, sensing a brewing antagonism. "I've been thinking about what you told me, and I've discussed the matter quietly with my crews and the guard, and we would be greatly honoured to join you in your attack. But, completely separately, it seems that with this gentlemen's input, there's been quite a bit of discussion between your Protectorate crews and the locals since you came ashore." Then he grinned.

"Captain Dhell, what on Iullyn are you doing here? You've never come near Saremouth before." Phellos pointed out crisply. "Isn't this range rather out of your usual fishing grounds by a good few tens of leagues?"

"Hss, Ma'am!" Dhell said with a bow. "Heard you're gonna burn Cal'Badon so I had a word with people an' hitched a berth; d'ya want some help? And there're quite a few pissed-off folks who'd just love to give you a hand after all that's happened here in the south."

"Blood and sand!" Captain Skendon of the Veddock Pearl rose slowly to his feet, staring and then began to laugh. "Brilliant!" He exclaimed.

"I'm going to *murder* Lunde!" Phellos declared then, crisply. "Captain Dhell, did you get them *all* drunk, hmm, in Rothern?"

"Me, Cap'n? Never!" The old man replied, hand on heart, grinning broadly. "Knew you must be plannin' summat, though, when you went up to Tenum City. An' it's a fine sight, Cap'n: never before have we had five of your ships berthed anywhere in Tenarum at once." His eyes twinkled as he shook his head.

"How old are you, Dhell?" Phellos continued, but her glare was fading slightly into amusement. "You're too old by far for combat, surely -."

"I'm probably younger than you, Cap'n." He said with a shrug and Kierven laughed. "But we can't stand by, even if we only are good for't basics. Most of the lads I've spoken to here're strong and determined, on me 'eart." And he bowed again.

"He's right there." Lord Kierven added then. He was young, a man in his early thirties, but a seasoned merchant with a fleet of ships trading north and viewed the coming conflict with enthusiasm. "The news has spread through the harbour area anyway, without the captain's input and those who haven't gone inland to fight at Clirensar are those who know the sea the best. If they haven't dare venture near Cal'Badon before, they still know the ocean and they certainly know their weapons, Captains."

The five razine exchanged glances, all of them grinning with appreciation.

Captain Ashanner rose to his feet and bowed. "Then you had better join us, gentlemen." He came across the room, shook their hands heartily then went to the door and stuck his head around it. "More wine and extra goblets, please." He instructed the maid loitering in the corridor.

"At once, my Lord." She said with a curtsey.

"It will be very dangerous, my Lord Kierven." Captain Eltham warned him, later that evening. "This is war, not commerce: you and your crews and the volunteers might all die, as might the rest of us."

"I've dealt with pirates, Captain, I'm not a complete novice, you know." Kierven told him, grinning without rancour or offence as he perused the map on the table, partly covered by their goblets. "I volunteered for the fighting last autumn as soon as I heard the awful news, you know, but King Marrand wrote back that I was better off guarding Saremouth and continuing my shipping ventures. Very nice of Marrand and a nice profit, here and there, but now it's time to get involved: they've cost us dear, torching our wharves, killing Sarant and Riyala, takin' Clirensar like that. Burning Cal'Badon would be a bloody good start."

"Good for you, my Lord." Captain Phellos commended him with a grin.

"Thank you, Captain Phellos. May I say, your actions are quite legendary, and it's been an honour to finally meet you." Kierven said enthusiastically.

"Thank you, my Lord. Let's all get to our ships and prepare to begin our voyage, shall we?" She suggested, rather tired of the clear interest and flattery of so many much younger men, however politely and gallantly done. She did admit to herself, however, that the thirty-three-year old Lord of Saremouth was a most handsome fellow and a superlative captain and businessman aside.

*

Three days later, two large Tenarean merchant vessels were equipped and ready to sail south with their allies, supplied by Lord Kierven. With the sea in his heart, he was more often on the open ocean than present in his castle above the port. Having returned from Horann, a city on the east coast of Jaece, less than ten days earlier, he had regretfully limited his involvement to the pair of his own ships that were currently in port and himself as captain of one of them, although he admitted that the Sweet Rose and Crimson Rose were smaller than the razine craft by some fifty feet, bow to stern, although they were swift. He brought in another two thousand men in total.

Captain Dhell led a large group of local volunteers, fishermen and dockworkers who filled the cabins on the seven ships with extra bodies and a willingness to fight.

The captains had met on the wharf there after, most uncharacteristically, all attended the cathedral for early prayers led by the local priests, now exchanging a few last-moment prayers for good luck, re-iterating the care that they each should take, observed by a crowd of thousands, who clearly wished them well. They felt keenly the danger they faced and hoped that some input from the clergy might give them some much needed luck and protection.

"Well, let's get started, shall we?" Captain Ashanner said, gazing at the water, for it was nearly high tide. "Good luck and may Arven be with us all."

"Amen." They all answered seriously.

"We can only do our best, Captain. Thank you again for letting me and my men be a part of this." Kierven said earnestly with a bow. "We'll do our utmost, I promise you."

"Thank you, Kierven, let's go." Phellos said.

As the local fishing boats set about taking the razine captains to their separate commands about the estuary after an intense few games of dice for the privilege, one crew had won the honour of transporting Phellos to the Mador Opal; she smiled to herself, this was perhaps the craziest idea that any of them had ever had and, whether they succeeded or failed, they would certainly be famous as the lunatics who had taken on the enemy with only seven ships and less than seven and a half thousand men and razine!

*

Ten days onwards, after some bracing weather and, thankfully, no sign of enemy craft on the ocean, the seven ships were approaching the rocky point that protected the Badon Inlet, an innocuous name for a vast sea channel that led deep into the mountains that guarded the port so well.

They were sailing in a loose arrowhead formation, with Ashanner ahead and he viewed the land that was a mile or so distant across the choppy water with unease. The end of the northern spur of land was a sharp-edged, steep sided stack that was host to innumerable seabirds in this season, the dark grey rock covered with centuries worth of shit. A steep, wave-cut curve joined it to the northern extent of the mountains, bare rock for the most part and sheer to the cold, grey sea. The steep edged cliffs and crags averaged only a couple of hundred feet, but they were unassailable. It was a view he had seen before, many years ago now and it still filled him with a certain amount of dread.

It was stark and forbidding and the mouth of the channel that led inland from the ocean was a good few miles wide there, showing just as forbidding a range of cliffs to the south; it was a singularly unappealing inlet into which large, monochrome waves breaking with suicidal enthusiasm against cliffs and steep slopes of a similar shade, to both north and south. The only approach was by sea and the greatest danger was that the small invading fleet would meet enemy craft emerging from the city at its western end and so loose the element of surprise that they had prayed so greatly for. Once in the curving inlet, they didn't imagine that there would be many hiding places available to them.

"Well, here we go. Arven protect us all!" He muttered, turning the wheel so that the Pearl turned to starboard, glancing back over his shoulder to see the Cerris Opal closest, the other ships all strung out now, but they would change their positions once within the Inlet, for they had set their plan out clearly and they all knew where they must be. Ashanner just prayed that they would not encounter any enemy ships just yet!

A mile onward, sheltered somewhat from the harsh southern wind that had been such a challenge for some of their voyage, the ships set anchor within shouting distance, giving each other plenty of insults, of course and wishes of luck!

Kierven as Captain of the Sweet Rose, Captain Leo of the Crimson Rose and Captain Amdor of the Cerris Opal were tasked with holding the attention and neutralising the forts that would initially focus on their approach. At daybreak, all seven ships had run up the standards of the Jajozeli Empire, which would be displayed until, please Arven, they sailed away from this forbidding place. They knew that there was at least one fort protecting the length of the inlet and, logically, there would probably be more, considering the strategic importance of the city to the enemy; and if they all displayed the right flags, they at least should get within shouting distance! The razine would appear to be in charge, posing as Generals from Enlath and would silence any questioners imperiously from the defenders regarding their unfamiliar ships.

Such was their plan: simple and audacious. Once the forts were neutralised, the other four ships would shoot ahead under the cover of the old moon to attack Cal'Badon at the head of the inlet. They were all aware that their scheme relied on a considerable amount of pure luck and the superstitious sailors of both races and continents prayed diligently as they made their preparations, organised their weapons and supplies. The crews of the Pearl and Opal ships were all familiar with the devices of the Betrayer, but they felt horribly uncomfortable at displaying them, however necessary it was.

It was evening when the Cerris Opal, alone, showing the stark flags of the Empire and deliberately lacking some equipment that had been stowed away from its usual position on deck, slowly approached the dock of the cliff-based Cal'Dernal on the north-face of the inlet, the crew in plain black and Captain Amdor imposing in similar clothing, glaring at the local guards as they scurried to attach the ropes thrown across the gap, as the ship's sails were furled.

"Watch out!" He bellowed in jajozeli. "Capturing this vessel cost me a number of valued crew. Who's in charge here?"

"C-Captain Scarm, Lord General. He's been sent for -."

"Good." Amdor commented, scanning the compact fort ranged in levels above his head. There were two docks angling out into the deep-water channel, just long enough to form a small harbour of sorts: this was a guard post, nothing more, situated on the steeply climbing rock face; it was formidable, and, positioned on the curve of the cliff, it had a good view for miles both north-east and south-west along the inlet. A wall separated the dockside from the fort structure and access was only by one six-foot-wide gate that opened inwards to reveal a small, flat area and the bottom six or seven feet of a steep flight of stairs, obscured by a thin, tall man who stepped through and bowed politely to the 'General'.

"Good evening, my Lord General. Pirris! You've captured an 'Opal'!"

"Yes, the bastards damaged my ship six days ago, so I took theirs." Amdor stated grimly. "It's been a long trip, Captain; is there any chance of a drink and a meal? We can exchange news. The crew have some purloined Rothern red and they're willing to share it."

"But-but of course, my Lord General. Have you travelled this way before? Cal'Badon is at the head of the inlet, two days further you see – they have much better facilities -."

"Stars, no man! It's been moons since we left. We've got to stretch our legs and we're sick of bloody fish! Lead on, Captain. You can fill me in on recent news." Amdor continued, not giving the awed captain time to protest, dismissing his protests with commendable arrogance. He followed the thin man up the steps to the fort above. "Bring that barrel, we all deserve a drink after the last moons!" He ordered his crew, filing off the ship behind him.

"At once, Lord General." His first officer, Forran, shouted back.

It was always beneficial for local commanders, especially if human, to pay court to any passing Generals or ranking jajozeli-razine, if one wanted to retain one's rank, advance, or even to simply survive in the empire. Excellence was vital in everyone. The captain of the fort was most insistent, on hearing how the visiting 'General' had succeeded in capturing the Opal, to entertain him and his crew. His subordinates were clearly just as keen to get off the ship after a long voyage from Enlath and a lavish dinner was provided. Captain Amdor was easily able to discover the call-signs that worked between the three cliff-bound forts and the city that they protected: bonfires on the fire-level, three steep flights of steps above the roofs of the fort, which could be see easily from Cal'Passe at the opposite shore, most of a day's further journey inward; thereby the signal could be quickly advanced as required, to warn Cal'Badon.

By the middle of the night, in a chilling reproduction of the taking of Clirensar, every jajozeli in Cal'Dernal was dead; the hundred replaced with twenty Tenareans and First Officer Forran as the razine in charge. They stripped the fort of most of its food supplies and Captain Amdor sailed on towards the equally unprepared Cal'Passe at dawn.

*

Cal'Passe, under Captain Wesse; then finally Cal'Lilse, under Captain Yoclayn, fell with equal ease. Clearly, the jajozeli could not envisage the hated razine and their pet humans duping them in such an audacious manner; and the Generals who might have been able to sense the danger were, to their great relief, absent. That had been their real fear, of course: the presence of even one jajozeli-razine at one of the guard posts would almost certainly have scuppered their attempt to pass through, right at the outset.

They had found two points where they had been able to moor more or less out of sight for of course, they could not guarantee that any jajozeli ships would not venture along the inlet. One was a rocky bay, backed with vertiginous cliffs, situated behind a brush-covered headland, almost the first vegetation they had seen along the channel, although they had sailed a good fifty miles by then. The second site was similar, an area of deep water, into which a huge waterfall dropped like thunder, behind the screen of an ancient rock-fall. It was not perfect by any means, but to superficial glances, they might survive any other watchers.

Now, just outside of sight of Cal'Badon, the three Pearl ships and Captain Phellos's Mador Opal waved thanks and farewell to the Cerris Opal and the Rose ships and set off at first light, all showing the jajozeli flags. Most observers in the city ahead would probably assume that four blatantly razine ships which had clearly passed the guard forts without incident or problem, were controlled by their own people: an unprecedented coup! That was what they hoped, their prayers still fervent.

On the Mador Opal, Captain Phellos glanced up at the Betrayer's standard with evident distaste as they continued past the towering snow-covered, cliff-based mountains that had grown steadily in height the further inland the inlet had led. These largely pathless mountains had rendered the eastern regions of Zanezli inaccessible; it was a cold, unfriendly, unwelcoming land.

"Are you all right, Captain?" The elderly fisherman, Dhell, asked; he had noted her glowering glances at the standards, now and again and the striking woman was usually far too confident and able to let something so inconsequential bother her.

"Not really, Captain Dhell." She admitted, hunching her shoulders for a moment. "There are traitors in my family: my great-grandfather's brother on my mother's side betrayed the Protectorates and abandoned Arven when the Betrayer caused such destruction in our lands, all those centuries ago. It's awful: he helped kill so many innocent people, human and razine indiscriminately and his descendants will still be doing the same . . . I *hate* them!" There was a deadly intensity to her voice that he had not expected.

"Well, Captain Ma'am, you're not going to go around recklessly puttin' yourself in danger just because of a few bad'uns in the family. Hold back a little is my advice." He said calmly, grinning, to her evident astonishment. "Not spoken to my idiot brother and his stupid wife for thirty years, actually. Still, they're only bleedin' irritatin', not traitors, but y'know what I mean. Personal revenge is a bitter thing, y'know: got to think o' that girl, Lady Ethrayne and Clirensar an' all. Not risk y'self, Ma'am."

"Dhell!" She snapped his name, then sighed, for behind her she could hear her first officer, Lunde, laughing aloud. "Shut up!" She growled, turning to glare at him.

"Of course, Captain, at once." Lunde answered with a sweeping bow. But it took a lot of effort, it seemed, and he had a grin fixed to his face, his eyes shining, for most of the day.

*

The four ships slipped along the narrowing inlet, all too aware that the mountains now pressed down upon them; the towering cliffs on either side had only got higher and steeper, now merging into snow-topped peaks like knife edges. The effect was heightened because the channel was now only a mile or so wide and the light even at noon was minimal, mountains, cliffs and water all shadowed, except at the edge of the sky, where sunlight occasionally showed on the peaks. It was very quiet, only a few gulls called as they dived into the water for fish.

In the fast-fading afternoon light, those with good eyes could see, some distance ahead the deep but narrow river channel that flowed into the sea and beside it the steep-sided, deeply shadowed valley beyond where the outlines of walls and roofs could be discerned. There was clearly a whiff of sulphur in the air, plus smoke or steam above the rooftops that made the city seem ethereal, somehow.

The sky above was still blue, around the gusting clouds, but the looming peaks blocked the sunlight almost completely; it must be a very gloomy place, most of the year, almost perpetually shadowed, surrounded by its protecting ranges.

Clearly the approach of four 'captured' razine ships had raised a great deal of interest. The dockside was packed with men and jajozeli-razine, all cheering enthusiastically with their expectations, for why should they imagine anything other than the obvious?

"Thank you, thank you, thank you." Captain Ashanner said, nodding graciously, as the Orbain Pearl was helpfully tied up right in the centre of the wharf, by a couple of eager soldiers.

<*Are you ready?*> He sent on a tight focus to his cohorts of both races and an answering cheer went up, echoing around. <*Right, here we go -.*> "For Arven and the Am'maiya!" He yelled in Selithian at the top of his voice. "*Now!*"

Arrows rained down without warning from the Orbain Pearl and her sister ships, slaughtering the front ranks of the jajozeli who had gathered to greet them. The enemy could only stare, aghast, disbelieving, for one crucial moment as their fellow soldiers died around them and Ashanner and his fellow razine did what so very few of them had ever had the stomach to attempt before: they linked their talent under the Captain's guidance and blasted out the mind of every General and other jajozeli-razine civilian within a mile!

<*Yes!*> That was Phellos, exulting, her ship heading past the other three, heading to port, towards the southern side of the dock front as planned.

Everyone on the wharves that fronted the waterfront was motionless on the floor, stunned or dead. Those who had melded their power to murder felt sickened at the odd burst of pleasure that had accompanied their attack, running intensely through each of them. It was one of the effects which sometimes occurred when they were so emotionally involved in what they were doing and another reason why the razine rarely used their native power to physically attack their enemies. Conversely and revoltingly, it was rumoured that the pleasure-factor was specifically used during the intense training of the jajozeli-razine Generals.

"Don't dawdle, let's go!" Ashanner cried, shaking himself out of a momentary distraction at the horror he had inflicted. "You know what to do, let's get to it!"

Dutifully, his crew, the Tenarean contingent and the fighters from the other Pearls, leapt down onto the sturdy, tarred planks and set off towards the gate that gave admittance to the city, whilst he paused, concentrated hard, and proceded to make nice big holes in all the craft of all sizes berthed along the waterfront; with at least three ten-foot wide holes in every ship's hull, they sank immediately and would probably be almost impossible to refloat, especially quickly. Grinning, he jumped down onto the dock and drew his sword. The sounds of horns blasting, and shrill shouts further inland clearly told him that the alarm had been raised, but he was confident that he and his cohorts would prevail.

<*Take care, Phellos! See you at dawn.*> He sent, running on.

<*Watch your back, Ashanner. Arven go with you!*> Phellos replied, concentrating on minute adjustments as her ship closed on the dock, so its fenders only kissed the stones.

Lunde leapt out and fastened the ropes with quick hands, then waved his arm widely. "Come on men! Let's get going!" He shouted.

There were a few soldiers spilling out through a gate at their extreme left and south side of the wharves, but these were disposed of easily and the attackers broke into every building in turn in that area, checking them for occupants, then torching them with cold efficiency. The allies spread out around their Captain, Phellos's striking hair hidden in a kerchief, taking care to eliminate any jajozeli in their path, for her self-appointed task – and no one had been able to dissuade her from it – was to activate the volcanic substrata that kept the inlet from freezing in the bitter winters, which would otherwise have rendered it useless for more than half the year. Guarding the Mador Opal for her return, Captain Dhellos watched her vanish amid the nearly night-shrouded but starkly fire-lit buildings, gripped his sword tightly and continued to pray.

"C'mon lads, keep alert, we've got a job to do here: they're dependin' on us to keep the Opal safe for our escape." He barked roughly to the largely grey-haired residents of Saremouth who stood with him. "Dear Arven, it's goin' to be a long night."

*

The city was large, laid out in a clearly military-based grid pattern, giving the allies surprisingly easy access to the entire place. There were walls, but they were mediocre when compared to most defences, Clirensar's for example for, of course, Cal'Badon was completely protected by its position and its forts.

The murders of so many innocents at the enemy's hands, from

Newventure Bay to Arven's Palace at Car'Agasse in the far north of Iullyn and everywhere in between, gave the severely out-numbered Protectorate and Tenarean combatants the strength to maintain their impetus, the razine gritting their teeth and using their power to kill whole swathes of the enemy.

Reaching the imposing range of administration buildings, they found them well defended in the centre of the city, but the defenders were dismayed at the uncharacteristic ruthlessness of the allies, as the complex was set ablaze around them. This dismay turned into a sudden loss of confidence, or so it seemed, a heartening occurrence none of them would have expected from the supremely confident, lethal jajozeli of both races. Captain Ashanner led the attack, abandoning the use of talent for the satisfyingly physical effort and clash of weapons. It seemed that most of the city's inhabitants were fighting here, but all of them were systematically cut down; the invaders' focus and determination seemed to prove them unstoppable. The allies watched in great satisfaction as the standards of the Betrayer vanished in flame, cheered and carried on their advance, flushing out every defender as they went.

The massive city seemed, however, strangely empty; if the thousands of soldiers now occupying Clirensar had been based here, the swathe of empty buildings were explained: administration, cook houses, barracks all unoccupied, especially on the western side of the city, right up to the city walls, five miles inland, where an imposing gate gave access to the main road to Ban'Lerracon.

The allies fought on. It was easier, in part, than they had expected but war is never easy and none of them were complacent. By the middle of the night, it seemed that they were primarily engaged more in checking, clearing and burning. Captain Skendon of the Veddock Pearl was severely injured, and his place was enthusiastically taken by his first mate, Lieutenant Carron, whilst he was carried away back to his ship, protesting every inch of the way, despite his shattered femur that had been hurriedly splinted, a tourniquet halting the bleeding. Most of the city was burning now and, gradually, the rather depleted allies started making their way back towards the seafront. They had lost nearly a hundred combatants in the battle, most of them bore injuries of varying seriousness, but their losses were surprisingly few when compared with those of their enemies.

"Dear Arven, I hope Phellos is all right!" Ashanner remarked to Lieutenant Hachorn as they kept watch at the landward side of the wharves, trying to differentiate solid from the stark shadows cast by the many fires reflected strangely from the mountains and the clouds above. "It'll be morning all too soon and we'll have to leave as planned: we can't deviate from what we agreed. Too many lives are at risk."

"Aye, sir, you're right." Hachorn agreed, sounding tired but admiring. "We have to trust her and Lord Arven as well!"

*

There was no protective wall on the southern side of Cal'Badon where the crew of the Mador Opal were advancing. The blocky series of buildings ended abruptly with a plain pavement that ran off towards rougher ground to the south and west, an area over a mile wide and nearly a league from the inlet's lapping water to the solid base of the mountains, now intermittently visible in the guttering light of the fires that were spreading unchecked across the city behind them. Ahead of them, starkly clear in the darkness, were some small, brightly burning, forbidding-looking pools that seethed with a sulphurous power.

"Dear Arven, what an evil looking place!" Lunde muttered staring out at the strange sight. "Perfect for the local inhabitants: it stinks!"

"Yes, and it's ideal for what we want." Phellos sheathed her sword and rolled her shoulders to ease the ache she had developed. The group had had some intense fighting to pass through this portion of the city since they had landed but had made it through to their goal. "Spread out. I'll call you if I need your aid."

"Aye, Captain. Dear Arven, be careful, Phellos!" He added, concern in his voice.

"Go on with you, Lunde, you sound like Dhell." But she flashed her first mate a grin that belied her inner concerns and took a deep breath of the clearly sulphurous air. As the group of over two hundred headed out in a wedge-shape back into the cover of the remaining buildings to torch them, she closed her eyes and reached out and down with her talent, her power, intending to use it in a way that she had never even imaged before; yet the entire concept had seemed just *right* to her when they had all discussed it so intently, setting out their options and their approach. Instinct had led her to claim this task as her own and the razine usually followed their instincts.

Using her power, Phellos realised that the ground below her feet seemed to include a seething mass of hot water and semi-molten rock almost within physical reach, a vast force which seemed to be only barely contained and controlled by nature . . . Taking a second deep breath, feeling herself tingling in reaction to the sheer amount of talent that she was pulling together . . . Time slowed as Phellos reached out and down, moving steadily but confidently and it seemed that she was breathing in rhythm to the movements and fluctuations of the earth, the impossibly hot magma and gasses and super-heated water . . . The physical danger vanished, the actual fighting, the city; all her attention was fixed underground, as her power flexed, and she worked to control forces few had ever dared to touch.

Surrounding her at a distance and out of sight, her crew and the Tenarean volunteers ranged about, killing any remaining jajozeli they came across, keeping their now deeply entranced Captain safe, all too aware that the night was passing.

Gradually, expanding her reach, increasing her concentration, the moment of *rightness* came closer, closer . . . "In Arven's name, rise!" She shouted aloud, lifting her arms above her head, feeling her power thunder down into the depths of the earth.

Almost instantly, the ground below her feet bucked violently in almost a wave-like manner and then an explosion ripped through the ground to her left, knocked her flat to the ground; suddenly, two hundred yards away, pulsing, molten fire erupted, spilling out of the earth with a strangely thick, muddy consistency, with pressure behind it, spouting twenty or so feet into the air; the heat was phenomenal.

Phellos got heavily to her feet, utterly exhausted by her efforts, but elated. "There, that'll keep the bastards out of the area!" She murmured with satisfaction, quietly amazed at the success of her plan.

Then, without warning, there was a second explosion, not from the ground, followed by a flash of massive talent that did not bode well at all. Instinct told Phellos that their enemies were closing in.

* * *

CHAPTER 33

The weather warmed as the days passed, the ship heading north across the boundless ocean and Ethrayne cut down one of her worn tunics, removing the sleeves, finishing it neatly during the long evenings she was forced to spend with the Generals. She continued to spend as much of her free time as possible out of the way on deck, under a piece of sailcloth turned into a sunshade near the bow, when allowed.

Yet another day dawned and Ethrayne awoke, creeping out of the cabin as usual. Straightening the tunic that had been pulled on quickly, she glanced back down the dimly illuminated passage where she was forbidden to stray and ascended the ladder to the main level, heading for the galley where General Whillan glowered at her and served her breakfast from the clever, brick-built stove that provided safe cooking facilities in the cramped space; again, very much as normal. Ethrayne ate the porridge quickly, thinking that it had got a bit thinner over the last few days, then dutifully thanked him and left to climb onto the main deck, balancing the flat bread and cheese and mug of tea with well-practised ease.

She supposed that, considering that they had been sailing now for so long, even the fullest cargo holds would grow depleted with the creative cooking practised by the chefs and the hearty appetites of everyone board. It was proof of Whillan and Sepphar's skill that the steadily dwindling resources had hardly impacted on the quality of their meals.

Stepping out into the sunlight, the planks already warm under her bare feet, the girl's mood lightened immediately; even after more than a moon at sea, every unavoidable moment spent near the king, his presence and power and that of his lieutenants still shredded her nerves day and night, she could not grow accustomed to them at all. At least, here on deck, the pleasant warm breeze, the sunlight playing on the azure ocean, the endless vista of sea and the bowl of the sky somehow seemed to dissipate their all-encompassing dominance a little.

The sun was a huge golden orb less than a finger's breadth above the horizon, the sea a glittering shimmer of sapphire blue, the sky above that lambent, clear shade that would earn any dyer a fortune if it could be replicated in cloth. Stretching, Ethrayne looked about cautiously and saw Generals Garrtnor, Jallon and Benthan talking together at the wheel on the stern deck, so she made her way to the port rail halfway along, set her tea carefully on the deck and nibbled at the bread and cheese, staring at the deep-blue waters that were broken by the passing of the ship, the white wavelets a sharp contrast as the craft advanced. She gazed about, noting a few wide-winged birds which soared far above, or dived like arrows into the water to emerge in a moment, gulping fish down; absently she reached for her cooling tea, sighing softly. It was beautiful, yes, but alien somehow. Soon enough, Ackat, Thellor or one of the others would call her for the obligatory combat practice, but at least she could rest, until they were all up and breakfasted.

Turning towards the south, drinking the last of the tea, Ethrayne actually started for there, right on the edge of the horizon, loomed what at first sight seemed to be a far-distant mountainous vista; she blinked and shivered despite the warm, humid air and sunshine. The dark grey mass must be clouds, vast clouds, but the weather had been consistently lovely for at least eight days, the only clouds had been tiny, brilliant white and soon vanishing before the heat of noon.

"There's a storm coming, the wind's changing." General Tynsyn remarked from behind her and Ethrayne almost dropped the tin mug, for she had been so absorbed in the scenery that she was unaware of his approach.

"Those clouds are very dark, my Lord General." She answered politely.

"Certainly, and this is not the time of year for storms." He elaborated, grinning at her unease. "It could be interesting."

It did not sound like any kind of interesting that she had ever heard of and Ethrayne recalled those awful first few days aboard the ship, plunging through massive waves, the seas a strange shade of chilling grey-green and the sky a complex, rain-pelting variation of deep grey. But, viewed in the early sunlight of these tropical seas, this bank of cloud was somehow darker, the base shaded from the sunlight and, as the morning advanced, propelled by the strengthening wind, it towered almost unimaginably into the sky, higher and larger as if trying to cover the entire ocean and scrape the very stars. Ahead of it, the smooth water swiftly vanished and was replaced by actual waves that grew progressively larger.

Combat practice was forgotten that morning, which she considered to be worrying, for the routine of her mornings had been relentless, taking place almost despite the worst weather, until now. For the first time in days, Ethrayne felt suddenly chilly and, once Cavaln was up on deck with the others, she went back to their small cabin for a jerkin before emerging again almost at once. A colder wind gusted more forcefully at them, although the hot sun still beat down, climbing inexorably towards midday. The encroaching weather was strangely fascinating, although by now the clouds were covering over half the sky. Then, it started to rain, hard cold drops the size of crowns, or near such. The beautiful blue seas were transformed into a cold, steely grey-blue that looked at least as ominous as the huge clouds.

Ethrayne shivered, moving over to the mid-point of the deck, for the king stood on the stern deck surrounded by most of the experienced sailors and they talked, gesturing a great deal. Cavaln, Whillan and Sepphar were watching the discussion from by the entrance to the cabins and both the chefs and the woman looked serious; Ethrayne knew well that all three of them had cheerfully acknowledged how little they knew about the craft and art of sailing. To the girl's eyes, they all looked concerned and Ethrayne shivered and moved right up to the bucking bow, her unease growing; the wind seemed stronger, the rain harder, falling in stops and starts, then pounding down, the waves larger and larger and again, the weather caught and held her attention.

Around her, quickly and efficiently, the sailors got on with their assigned tasks: the sails furled tight away on the masts; the lines tightened; the water barrels on deck secured, as were the two boats and every knot and connection examined. It didn't stop raining.

"Get to your cabin, girl." General Herstyn ordered shortly and unexpectedly from behind and Ethrayne turned to see him stagger as the bow of the ship plunged into a steep, greenish-walled gully between foam-topped waves. He held a stout rope in one hand, which he proceeded to lash to the rail in the bow. "Don't dawdle, they've taken in the sails and even fitted the shutters. Get below, you fool, or you'll be overboard -."

A sudden flash of lightning temporarily blinded them, and it seemed to hit the mast, to be almost instantly followed by a deep roar of thunder that drowned out whatever he was saying. Both of them ducked automatically in reaction and then Herstyn grabbed her arm and hauled her back along the slick deck as a wave suddenly broke across it, the water icy cold against her feet, staggering at the increasingly erratic movement of the ship as they made for the door to the interior; it took a moment for the General to open it, both of them stepping quickly into the sudden darkness as he slammed the door closed and released Ethrayne and she blinked, now able to see clearly, for the lamp ahead was burning more brightly.

"Get to your cabin! Stay there!" Herstyn ordered, almost shouting, for the rapidly approaching storm seemed ridiculously louder from inside, accompanied by the creaking and protests of the ship itself.

Ethrayne obeyed him, glad of the ropes that were strung along the corridor and down the ladders, ropes which she had not had cause to use since she had grown used to the movement of the ship. Carefully descending, memory proved to be much more useful than her eyes at the wild patches of light and shadows cast by the swinging lamps. As she climbed down the ladder, she considered a sight from up on deck that she had only just got around to considering: the king, wrapped in a large dark cloak, had been stood at the wheel of the ship, surrounded by the most experienced Generals, holding their course, despite the howling wind and the rain and spray that had suddenly drenched them.

She shivered. *Tynsyn was right.* She acknowledged to herself, staggering down the second ladder; the pools of light from the lamps, moving widely, were even more useless on this lower level. *But his definition of* interesting *is bloody peculiar! Oh, dear Arven, help us!* But, she wondered, was it even appropriate to pray when she was surrounded by enemies, striving to keep control amid the storm?

The creaking of the ship was more noticeable, surrounded by the structure as she was, but the howl of the storm was far louder, and she slid across the planking more than stepped, unlatching the door to the little cabin and entering a far dimmer area than she had expected, for it could not even be noon, she guessed.

Dear Arven, might the ship sink? She considered then, uneasily. She had wished for her captors' deaths on many occasions, but to imagine her own death alongside them, no! That was peculiar, odd, worrying. She shivered at the impact of the thoughts as they suddenly hit home as hard as the waves on the hull , for even such a well-built ship might be overwhelmed by a bad storm.

Closing the door, fighting against the temporary angle of the ship that nearly threw her back out into the passage, Ethrayne shook her head, then made for the closed shutters, wanting one last glimpse of the outside for some strange reassurance perhaps, although she didn't really know why. But there was no view of storm-tossed waves or the cloud-covered sky, when she pulled one open, puzzling for a moment – for there was nothing to be seen except a pierced, close-fitting metal plate outside the fragile glass of the windows and, recalling what General Herstyn had said earlier, she supposed that these were the shutters he had mentioned. The light level now was non-existent, dark.

It seemed that the Generals had been busy, whilst she had been transfixed, watching the storm developing; but hanging over the stern of a bucking ship and somehow fixing metal sheets over the wide banks of windows seemed quite as stupid as balancing atop the masts as they frequently did!

Ethrayne shrugged as she fastened the inner shutter, taking one staggered step to reach her narrow bunk, climbing onto it and bracing herself as best she could against the wall, ignoring the crash of the waves, her wet clothes, pulling one of her blankets up and around herself for warmth and comfort; it was growing increasingly chilly, she realised . . . It was lonely, sat there on her own in the dark, but although she wondered where the Generals were, she was glad to be by herself: they would only have mocked her fear, she knew that for the truth. And she was desperately afraid; she thought the weather had been awful when the ship had first left Cal'Itase, but it was nothing, nothing at all, when compared to this! She sat there, hanging on tight, praying to Arven, trying to ignore the increasingly loud protests of the ship itself against the battering it was taking, and trying to ignore her own increasing hunger and thirst, for it had been nearly noon when she had been called below and now it felt like a very long time had passed since breakfast . . . But there was no respite and the storm seemed relentless, except to worsen.

*

The cabin door opened without warning, slamming open back into the passage and a small ball of light entered the cabin, revealing a tall figure behind it, carefully closing the door again. Ethrayne sat up, her heart pounding with a sudden unexplained fear. It had been long since she had decided that it was safer by far to lie down on her bunk rather than struggle to remain sitting up, although the movement of the ship was so violent now that it seemed that she was going to be thrown right out of the bed with every relentless mad plunge it made, ascending or descending waves which seemed almost vertical.

"Pirris!" Ackat's voice said loudly in disgust and he staggered, then swore graphically and unexpectedly so that, despite her rising fear and discomfort, the girl managed a small burst of laughter that sounded more than a little hysterical. "Still here, are you, brat? Enjoying the weather?" He asked, almost sliding further into the cabin and grabbing hold of the door frame and the end of her bunk. "Bloody storm!"

"What's happening?" She asked and she, as Ackat, was shouting to make herself heard. "How long has the storm been raging? Is it nearly over?"

"We'll ride out the storm." Ackat answered in a bellow, but he did not add any details. "His Majesty wishes you secure against injury." The ship lurched off to port, then starboard, steeply upwards and he staggered again. "I'd stay laid down if I were you. I've got rope here to stop you falling out." The General braced himself, then lashed a length of thin rope between narrow hooks that Ethrayne had noted set both into the plank wall and the outer side of the bunk frame; she had wondered what their purpose was and now she knew, as the rope made a sort of zig-zag webbing above her from upper chest to knees, something to keep her more secure, she supposed; tight, but not tight enough to imprison her: she could easily remove it.

"You can remove it yourself, but I'd leave it in place, girl: a fall in this could easily break bones if you tumble out and we'll rather too busy to check on you for a while." He yelled.

"It's been ages since I came back inside, and you've not exactly been overly concerned with my wellbeing!" She retorted quickly.

Ackat flashed a brief, mocking grin, then passed her some other items. "Here's water and some dried fruit." He ignored her statement, otherwise. It explained the two bags, one small one, made of canvas, one large and leather, were laid on her midriff. She caught hold of them as the ship continued to buck, shooting down a steep slope, then instantly up another. He grinned again; the small globe of pale light was the only constant, it seemed: staying put despite all else and he could obviously see the fear that she battled with all her strength to contain and control. "I'll lock you in, girl: there's no point putting you at further risk -."

"What? No, don't you dare -." She protested, holding tight to the items, held back by the ropes that now served to constrain her. But Ackat had wheeled out of the cabin, taking his light with him and the door had been shut again in a moment, the sound of the bolt being slid across clear despite the encompassing noise. "I hate you!" She yelled recklessly, fighting against a sudden rush of panicked tears.

*

An age passed, she thought. It was unbelievably worse than being locked in the bottom of the ship or the dungeon had been, feeling the ship shuddering with every massive wave that struck it, again and again and again, hearing the roaring gale outside that only served to worsen, sounding like a ravening beast rather than a storm. Time passed horribly slowly in the darkness of the small cabin, yet it had been a very long time since Ackat's appearance. Exhausted and terrified, Ethrayne lay in her bunk, every muscle tensed, holding tight to the lashed rope that had, despite her earlier misgivings, probably saved her from being physically thrown onto the floor on quite a few occasions.

Intermittently, greatly daring, she had endeavoured to eat a little dried fruit and sip a little water, but simple overriding fear had dampened her appetite. She was certain that the ship would be smashed to kindling!

The sheer, unstoppable force of nature that had been unleashed even surpassed the power of the Betrayer, in her eyes. It felt as though the storm that had swallowed them would never let them go, never spit them out: it would hold them forever before it covered the whole of Iullyn, its unstoppable waves and winds flattening the continents. The Betrayer, who had imprisoned his God and stolen a goodly portion of his power, would now never prevail . . .

Then, unexpectedly, strangely, Ethrayne could see him, the king, in her mind; he still stood at the wheel, drenched to the bone, his cloak long-since gone, fighting the storm with his own physical strength, but its might was overwhelming. It was mad, her eyes were closed tight, but she *could* see him in her mind, although the deck was shrouded in soaking darkness, except when jagged forks of lightning erupted in momentary fractured patterns across the sky. She knew, somehow, that Gregnor had been stood there, lashed to the wheel, battling for control ever since she had descended to the little cabin, aided as far as possible by his Generals; Jallon, Benthan, Unwynn, Garrtnor and Eduren were doing all they could. She could sense his bone-deep chill and exhaustion as clearly as if it were her own, but she didn't understand why. She could also sense his implacable will: his determination that they would beat the storm. He was fighting the storm as if it were a physical being, using his power as much as brute strength. Waves were almost swamping the deck as they struck the structure, again and again.

The rest of the group, the other Generals, were all huddled in the main cabin above, all braced with ropes even as she and she could sense their fear clearly as well, but she knew that the king was not afraid . . . Although the world was surely at an end!

The ocean seemed to be boiling: the waves, in her strange vision, were unbelievably massive. Ethrayne squeezed her eyes shut even tighter and tried to banish the strange double image of her captors, for she was certainly not concerned for *them*! But she prayed constantly, speaking aloud even though she couldn't hear her own voice, using the words to somehow, very slightly, calm herself. "Dear Arven, please just let it end . . . Don't care if I die! Just end it. Kill them! Oh, please!"

The sky was black. The sea was somehow black and grey, delineated by the lightning which lit up the waves like mountains, the shape of the massive ship, tossed about like a tiny toy, momentary blinks onto a scene of complete horror. Ethrayne saw Jallon fighting to stay upright as a wave crashed right over the stern deck and heard it thunder down above her, trying to drive them under . . . Benthan slid a good ten feet before halting himself, coughing and spluttering, luckily grabbing the end of a line when he was desperately close to the rail and the endless furious black water beyond.

Still clear in her mind's eye, she saw and then sensed every General raising their individual inborn talent, their power, and passing it eagerly to their master . . . Grimacing horribly with the effort, he added their talent to his own, and it was vast! Ethrayne had not gained any real controls over the power that she had been gifted with so long ago in Tenum City: she had not had the daring to pursue the learning begun with Bahlien and Lurco, had been starkly warned not to, in fact. Therefore, she had no protection, no way to buffer her mind against their immense strength, which was why Cavaln and Thellor's lovemaking had so traumatised her: the lack of knowledge and the ability to block her mind from them and their inimical power. Now, in the absolute hell of the storm, Ethrayne was concentrating so much on her fear at the sheer enormity of the weather, it served to make her more vulnerable than ever. The power that the jajozeli-razine passed so freely, to be controlled by the king, also flowed through *her* and it built up inside her: unstoppable, painful in the extreme and utterly unnatural! . . . Ethrayne screamed, unable to stop it or dispel it. And it sparked her own talent, the power of the Flame of Arven, deep within her . . .

<NO!> Ethrayne screamed loudly inside her head, trying to stop it, to fight it, anything at all! Yet she was helpless, alone in the tumultuous darkness. *<Stop it! Get out of my head!>*

<I need your strength.> Gregnor's mental voice was clear and menacing inside her mind, despite the deafening sounds of the storm that drowned out even her own scream of agony.

<No! I'd rather drown right now!>

<Don't be ridiculous, give me your power!>

Clutching her hands tight to her head, Ethrayne screamed again, for the forces inside her were unbearable: she felt as if she would explode. Not even knowing what she was doing, working at some deep, instinctive level, she tried to wrap up her power tight within her, whilst simultaneously striving to force *out* the touch of his mind and strength.

<Go 'way! It hurts!> She protested again in panic, sobbing desperately. *<You're hurting me!>*

But her protests and feeble attempts to stop the Betrayer were ignored. Ethrayne was helpless as Gregnor simply reached into her and took her power . . . The strength that he controlled then: hers, his own and that from his willing servants, was possibly greater than the sun itself . . . It broke over and around the girl, a massive avalanche and wave of power as it was used against the natural force of the impossible storm . . . All her senses were overloaded by the enormity of it . . . Screaming, unconsciousness took her.

* * *

CHAPTER 34

A loud bang woke her and Ethrayne opened bleary eyes to brilliant sunlight pouring in from behind her head. She tried to sit up, but struggled against ropes that held her down, craning around to stare out through the windows at the bright blue sky.

"Oh, dear Arven!" She croaked through a very dry mouth, her fear rising, confused. Then the unexpected sight of a figure sliding into view, hanging incongruously by ropes from above, jolted her memory: he was outlined by the clear sky, temporarily obscuring the sunlight streaming in. Ethryane then recalled the extended horror of the storm that had battered them so relentlessly. Frankly, it was a miracle that they had survived.

Slightly calmer, remembering more, she pulled herself up and set about unfastening the rope that had held her in place, now aware of a throbbing, thudding ache that filled her head to bursting. She knotted the length tidily, then set her feet down on boards that felt peculiar simply because they were so still, and she stretched mightily, easing muscles which had been tensed for far too long.

Turning to the window, Ethrayne wondered if Cavaln had opened the inner shutters earlier. She could see Dahne, Ollyn and Shaille suspended from various ropes, working to remove the surprisingly thin metal sheets that had undoubtedly saved the wide bank of windows from the massive pounding fury of the waves, and thus the ship from certain destruction. The sheets seemed to be about seven feet long by four feet wide and the Generals lifted them easily, exchanging banter that she could clearly hear, their light tones and insults finally convincing her that they were safe: the storm had passed.

"Thank you Lord Arven, I think." She murmured, pulling off her crumpled jerkin quickly, for the air was hot and humid. She found tepid water waiting for her in the wash room, so she washed, dressed, then opened the windows, tidied her bed, picked up the rope, water sack and the bag of dried fruit. Ethrayne lifted the latch on the door almost fearfully, but it opened, to her relief.

The passages were as dim as always, lit by the ever-burning lanterns, but there was a smell of damp even here and the planks seemed a little wet to her bare feet, although she wasn't sure if they were: it had been a horrible period of horrible events; the storm-tossed seawater could easily have burst through the doors or hatches, after all. She shivered, remembering the deafening sound of waves crashing repeatedly onto the deck two levels above, wondering just how close they really had come to sinking.

Ethrayne left the bags and rope in the empty galley on the level above, helping herself to cooling porridge and a bit of cheese, gulping down a mug of fresh water. This meant that *someone* at least had had the opportunity to do some form of cooking already, although it was still early. She ate the porridge quickly, then took the cheese, more dried fruit and the refilled mug up to the main deck, exactly as she had on the morning of the storm.

"You're up." Garrtnor remarked easily from above her, only his head visible where he leaned over the rear rail of the stern deck, pulling one of the ropes that held a shutter up towards the horizontal with Thellor at his side. "Good morning, girl."

The air was warm, smelling of wet wood and water but with undercurrents of rottenness as if it blew across overripe vegetation, soft, mild. Ethrayne shivered, nodded a greeting to the Generals and quickly moved away from the area, heading towards the starboard rail.

The planks here certainly were still wet, although the surface under her feet was already warming up as the sun rose higher. Part of her noted that things here on deck seemed different, somehow: more Generals and the sailors were gathered near the main mast, busy at some tasks, so perhaps some damage had been caused; then she saw that both boats were absent and the framework that had held the port skiff and some of the railing alongside were missing, the ends of the woodwork splintered, scrape-marks visible even at a distance. That visible proof of the power of the storm on such well-built structures caused her to shiver again.

As always, the presence and native power of the Generals reacted on her mind and body and, considering how drained and wrung out she felt, it somehow seemed to make her aching head worse, but that fact and her breakfast were almost forgotten as she stared out at the brilliantly green island visible a few hundred yards away across a sweep of pale turquoise water, strangely edged by a long, sweeping curve of pale rock only just below the level of the sea, an arc made plainer by the striking difference in the colour of the water around it. The island was almost completely covered in thick forest, as far as she could tell. Gazing out, then down, Ethrayne could see that the ship was moored fifty yards or so from the rock structure, in smooth, clear, midnight blue water out of which the strange formation emerged like a rugged, platform-studded cliff. Across the mirror-smooth pale lagoon, the lumpy-hilled island was bordered by pearl-white beaches that reflected the sunlight like a mirror.

It was as if the storm had never occurred, apart from the strident sound of wood being sawn and the earnest conversations that accompanied it, over by the main mast and then over on the stern deck where the shutters were neatly stacked.

Ethrayne shivered, feeling someone approaching and she turned to see Ackat closing on her. Glancing at his face before she quickly turned back to the view of the island, she thought that he looked deeply tired.

"Don't forget your breakfast, you look pale." He advised and glanced over at all the industry by the mast. "We sustained some damage in the storm, so we might be here for a while. The island isn't large enough for you to get lost on, so his majesty said that you can go ashore if you wish; and look, the longboat's coming back." He pointed across her, ignoring her instinctive duck away, then carried on his way towards the others.

Ashore? That concept was certainly pleasant: the chance to escape their stifling presence for a while and Ethrayne finally finished eating, watching the craft being rowed smoothly across the lagoon, its shadow on the bottom disturbing native inhabitants, great and small: many other shadows darted away in defence, which was interesting. There was a notch in the rock bordering the underwater rock formation, somehow looking almost like a crack in the stone, through which the deeper water met the shallow, and it was through this that the boat manoeuvred, rising slightly in the swell, Allun and Cavaln on the oars, rowing strongly. There were baskets of produce by their feet containing roundish shaped things, bunches of leaves and so on, as if they had been foraging for food.

Cavaln called out and Ackat returned to the rail as the boat was made fast to the ship, then the baskets were attached to lines and hauled up quickly, whilst the two Generals easily climbed the net that hung down and over the rail, stretching as they straightened their backs after the unaccustomed exercise.

Looking at the three of them, unobserved for a moment as they discussed the foodstuffs, Ethrayne knew that she had been correct with her initial thought: they also looked tired, their faces etched with weariness. Again, she wondered how long the storm had pounded them; how long she had been unconscious; just how long ago the Emperor had used her power to support his own . . . But she knew that she was also scared to discover the truth. Still out of sorts, her head aching despite the fresh air and sunshine, she sighed and cautiously approached them.

"May I go ashore, Lord General?" She asked as Allun laboriously picked up two baskets, handing one to Sepphar as he came over to assist them.

"Don't see why not, you're no bloody use here. Just keep out of our way, brat!" He answered ungraciously. He had never bothered with her at all, so his unrelenting rudeness was better in her eyes than the false politeness and snide insults she endured from most of the others. "Get yourself some water, something to eat from the galley and you'll need your boots. Be quick!"

"Yes -." And she turned back eagerly to the stern; the chance to escape the confines of the ship for the first time in well over a moon, since they had left Cal'Itase was far too good to miss. She had lost count of the days now. "Thank you." She added politely, already nearly at the entrance to the lower levels. Hurrying, she dashed down to fetch her boots then halted at the galley, now adorned with the neatly stacked baskets, where she hefted the water skin that she had left earlier; it held at least a pint, she guessed, so that would serve, along with the dried fruit to which she added a bit of cheese and a few of the double-baked hard biscuits that formed a great part of their lunches. Hurrying back up to the deck, she found that Sepphar had been joined by Khaen, Masson and Tynsyn, dropping empty baskets into the boat below.

Ethrayne hung back to pull on her boots, trying to find a way to attach the bag and water skin around her so that she could descend the netting for she hadn't yet had to negotiate it -.

"Get down here, brat, or swim!" Masson shouted from below and so she clambered over the rail and began to climb down, her burdens an uneven weight on her left-hand side, without any more concerns.

*

Stepping out of the boat into the bubbling edge of the sea lapping on the gleaming white beach, Ethrayne felt her feet sink slightly into the wet sand and followed the quickly moving Generals towards the lush greenery which marked the edge of the forest beyond. The gently sloping beach here was nearly fifty yards deep and high water probably only occasionally reached the tree line, protected as the island was by the reef and lagoon that encircled it. *Reef,* a word she had never heard before, delivered by General Khaen. The air was very humid, smelling of water, rotting vegetation and salt and she noted a stream purling down into the sand where it meandered and vanished; reeds and tall grasses were visible at the edge of the trees and it seemed that the Generals were following the stream into the shade ahead, for clear footprints in the sand marked their route. They were discussing food, drink and fixing the ship, but Ethrayne didn't pay much attention, concentrating on walking on land that didn't move, a great peculiarity; and on widening the distance between the three jajozeli-razine and herself.

The vast variety of the woodland ahead was spectacular, even at first glance, but it was much more humid under the trees and after all that time locked in her cabin, the girl longed for a period of sunshine, free of worries and woes. Birds called, both raucous and musical and she caught a glimpse of bright plumage through the trees and other creatures scampered away, out of sight, though thick undergrowth.

"Heavens!" She murmured, looking around and realising that she had not any idea what any species here was; nothing was familiar at all.

Slowly, Ethrayne smiled for she was finally alone: the Generals had all forged on ahead into the trees and were now out of sight, although she could hear them, their voices muffled. It felt simply wonderful, even if only for a short while, to be alone. She had not been ordered to follow them, to assist them; Ackat had said that she could not get lost – but she could certainly try to, she decided. First, she turned about and left the steamy, oppressive heat and stink of rotting greenery for the sunlit beach.

The azure sky was clear, with only a few tiny wisps of cloud far to the north; the treacherous sapphire ocean was as smooth as a millpond, with hardly a ripple to move the mass of the ship anchored by the reef edge. In contrast, the sand was a brilliant white, shining in the sunlight almost with the beauty of gemstones. Ethrayne stopped and sat down on the shifting stuff to pull off her boots, for her feet were hot and the warm grains felt strangely soft and wonderful when she stood up, boots in her left hand and the bags on her right shoulder. She orientated herself and set off along the beach in a southern direction, only determined to get out of sight of the ship, for a while at least.

There was some evidence of storm damage here: a few freshly uprooted trees; some peculiar, large green fruits cast widely along the strand; the tide line clear along the edge of the undergrowth, displaying debris from the deep: pale rock, seaweed, dead fish and even bleached driftwood were cast up in random piles. Ethrayne walked, gazing about her, glancing back every so often to check how far she had advanced from the ship, smiling, humming, her heart lightening even though her headache still lingered.

Finally, hot and thirsty, the girl stopped and sat on a fallen tree trunk as if on a horse, rubbing her bare feet through the warm, gritty sand, eating and drinking with relish, for even such ordinary rations seemed a feast. She saw a pretty spiral shell lying half-buried by her left foot and picked it up, admiring its iridescent interior and red- and yellow-striped exterior, no larger than her thumbnail. That find took her down to the waterline, the sea warm on her toes, where she gave herself up to some serious beachcombing. As well as many more pretty shells, some broken, some inhabited by funny little crabs, Ethrayne found more worked wood, some silvery, curved along the edges and covered with odd, dried shells; some more recent, less rounded by the waves; there was also a large, encrusted nail; hanks of old, rotting rope, also with shells attached; the business-end of a battered shovel and even, lodged next to odd purple and pink tentacled blobs in a shallow, rocky pool, a gold coin which was almost as large as half her palm. She put some of the prettier items and the coin into one of her boots.

Suddenly, Ethrayne wished she could show Jerryn this beautiful place, so different to anywhere in Tenarum . . . It made her feel his loss greatly. She paused to take another drink of the warm, stale water and realised that the Lightning was out of sight, since the line of the beach had turned towards the west. Sighing, acknowledging the inevitable, for the sun was now sinking slowly towards the horizon, she turned around and set off back the way she had come, trying to walk in her own footprints when she could see them, paddling in the edge of the lapping waves, realising that her mood was darkening a little: the welcome interlude was nearly over, she had had a short period of respite -.

Ethrayne was jolted abruptly out of all levels of happiness in an instant, when she clambered for a second time over a large tree trunk that lay across the beach. Almost immediately, most unpleasantly, the sense of her captor's power returned with a vengeance, causing her almost forgotten headache to increase drastically in intensity. She stopped, leaning on the gnarled trunk and looked up with dread: the king was striding towards her along the beach! He was still a good distance away, but no-one could bare her nerves like he: he was completely unmistakeable.

"Oh, dear Arven no!" She whispered to herself, fighting an almost overpowering urge to flee. Instead, with obviously faked nonchalance, she stepped up out of the wavelets, gulped, and walked up onto the hot, dry sand. Her legs were shaking terribly, so she was almost glad to sink to her knees in polite acknowledgement of his presence, for she felt that she would collapse anyway; and, strangely, the king as he approached was surrounded by a hazy, rainbow-shaded halo which caused her eyes to water and smart even more than the brilliant sunlight reflecting off the sea. The ache in her head became suddenly much more acute. She hated herself for it, but she didn't dare to even attempt to ignore his power, his authority, especially after what he had done so easily during the storm.

"I wondered just where you'd got to. Stop cringing, child!" His tone went from neutral to sharp in a breath, making her jump. He snorted at that. "Show a little backbone! Up on your feet, quickly now."

"Y-your Majesty." Ethrayne murmured, getting up, swaying a little as one foot slipped in the sand, then stifling a groan as the rainbow halo went somehow jagged, assaulting her eyes and her head with ultra-thin knife blades.

"What's wrong? You look terrible, child." He asked, closing the distance between them as she sagged, taking hold of her chin, studying her closely.

Despite the jagged halo and her pounding head, Ethrayne could see that the king also looked very tired: his face was lined, there were dark circles under his eyes and they seemed to lack the gleam and fire of power that usually marked his gaze. For the first time, she could see some of his great age.

"I, I-I can see rainbow lights around you, M-Majesty, there are strange shapes, my-my head hurts." She admitted in a quiet tone, longing to retreat from his painful touch, trembling.

"Yes, I can imagine that it does. You want to know what happened." Gregnor acknowledged as he released her and grinned, turning, striding off along the beach towards the fallen tree that she had clambered over only a short time before. "Come along." He commanded, sitting down on the trunk and pointed to the sand, nodding as Ethrayne slowly advanced and sat down, deliberately out of reach, squinting to try and control the horrible vision of her eyes.

"The truth, Ethrayne, is that that bloody storm nearly sank us: you may have noticed that a longboat was ripped away, and considerable damage was done to the main mast; there's a whole list of things that need fixing because of it! We were tossed about like a cork for nearly three days and, early yesterday morning, you will remember that I took some of your power."

Ethrayne shuddered visibly at the memory and went cold despite the sunshine and the heat around her. "I . . . I could see you, fighting at the wheel in the darkness . . . they all gave you their power. Bu-but you hurt me!" Her tone was sharp, recalling that vision.

"If not for your strength, girl, then the storm would have destroyed the ship around us." Gregnor said calmly. "It was your input that saved us, however unwilling you were -."

"I would have sooner drowned!" The girl spat back recklessly, his gratitude raising her anger. "You ripped that power from me! I had no defence, Sire -."

"For one with no training, child, you were putting up an admirable fight." He told her, and that admission stunned her – if it was genuine, for surely he lied? But why would he? Confusion filled her.

"You hurt me, your Majesty, my head is still pounding -."

"Stop whining!" His words, so cold, cut short her list of sullen grievances and Ethrayne shrank backwards again. "Your power saved us, but if you actually saw what it was like up on deck, you should understand why I lacked the time to leave the wheel to come and explain our need to you. As it is, you and your talent belong to me, Ethrayne."

"I belong to nobody!" Ethrayne spat back instinctively, but the king laughed aloud with evident amusement at her defiance.

"Child, you are a delight. Why do you think I sent Lord Ackat to watch you, then to capture your home with my army, expending many thousands of lives, simply to get you into my hands, so soon after you and the prince received the Flame of Arven?" Gregnor paused, waiting politely, but he seemed satisfied with the slight shrug of the shoulders which was her response. "Logically, sensibly, as I imagine that fool Bahlien will have assumed, I would make no move to take you away: a pair of untrained adolescents would be far too immature and ignorant to be of any use. You would not understand even the tiniest part of the events unfolding around you." His tone was cool. "And that is all true, yet I wanted you, and Jerryn also, if the opportunity had arisen. Because *I* will train you. *I* will reveal to you the wonders of your God-given power, not those idealistic razine fools! One day soon, child, you will belong to me: mind, body, soul and power!"

Her gaze fixed on the sand pushed upwards by the toes of his highly polished black boots, Ethrayne shook her head fervently, ignoring her throbbing headache. "I won't, M-Majesty! Not ever!" She declared, but her mouth was dry, the words slow to emerge, almost sticking on her tongue.

"*Ever* is a very long time, Ethrayne, and I wouldn't lay any bets on the alternative outcome: my servants, my Generals and I can be most persuasive. Now come, you'll get sunburn if you stay out in the sun too long. You can bring your new-found treasures, too."

Gregnor rose and the girl got slowly to her feet, but deliberately dropped her boots so that her shells, stones and the coin spilled out onto the sand. Instantly, the atmosphere around her changed. Despite the tropical heat, Ethraye could feel the king's displeasure like the Lerracon glacier. All trace of amusement had vanished utterly. His gaze was locked on hers, his eyes blacker than night, but he said nothing: his expression alone promised dire punishments if she dared to disobey him for another moment -.

"By Car'Agasse, Ethrayne, you are reckless for one so young, with so much to lose!" He said very quietly, smiling almost approvingly, although his gaze was still dangerous. "You may brace yourself, but you know the price of disobedience -."

Stood uncertainly, slouching, before him, unable to look away, Ethrayne could only gasp as that throbbing headache became sharp needles of utter agony shooting through every single part of her mind and body. Her vision blurred with tears; she fell helplessly to the sand as her limbs failed, fighting suddenly for every labouring breath, writhing at the pain filling her . . . It seemed that an age at least passed before the king's power ebbed away, before she could sob, groan . . . Another age before the pain eased with a horrible, lingering slowness . . .

"One day, little Wielder of the Flame, you will learn the sense of obedience and your life here amongst us will be much more bearable." Gregnor said calmly. "You should know that I am merciless, and I always get what I want, eventually.

"Now get up, pick up your finds and come along."

"Y, yes your M-Majesty." Ethrayne finally managed to whisper, tears stinging at her eyes, struggling to make her body obey her; it felt as though she had fallen down the hundred-odd stairs from her tower prison in Ban'Lerracon, every part of her felt bruised and agonising. It took all her strength, but she got to her knees, fumbled in the sand for the small handful of items which had caught her interest, returning them, sand covered, back into her boots and retrieved the water and food bags before she slowly and shakily got to her feet. Gradually, the pain in her body eased, but the intense headache remained, now thumping hard behind her eyes.

At that point, terrified, she remembered sharply what Archpriest Bahlien had related about the night when he had escaped from Car'Agasse with his life and the Flame: their God frozen in unbreakable ice, the halls full of the dead bodies of men, women and children, running with their blood, all murdered by the Betrayer! And *he* was the Betrayer, this stern, cruel razine man before her! He had no mercy.

Unmoved and patient with her slow progress, the emperor of the jajozeli-razine watched her struggle to her feet, malice in his eyes. Then, he turned and set off back up the beach, leaving the girl to follow as best she could, every single part of her body aching in reaction to the pain that he had inflicted upon her. Strangely, he continued to talk with her as if nothing untoward had happened.

"We'll be here for another day at least, probably two, which should be enough time to rest and recuperate, fix the ship and garner some fresh supplies." He said. "And I meant what I said, girl: if not for your power, the ship would have sunk and us along with it. As it is, we've been blown far off course, which isn't very surprising when you remember the strength of that storm."

Ethrayne shuddered, recalling their helplessness in the teeth of it and was struck by a thought that seemed integral to her own situation. With great daring, and most politely, she asked fearfully. "Ex-excuse me, your Majesty . . . but you possess a great part of Lord Arven's might . . . Surely, surely you cannot . . . die?"

Gregnor laughed heartily at that. "Die? I don't know, Ethrayne. I haven't met anyone strong enough to even threaten my health for centuries, girl. If the ship had disintegrated, perhaps I would have floated atop the waves like a seabird whilst my faithful lieutenants sank gradually to the bottom of the ocean. And maybe you are rather more impervious to death than you might have believed: you and your prince share the rest of your God's strength, after all. I imagine you never thought of that, did you?"

"I -." Ethrayne stopped dead, stunned. But, of course, she hadn't. The very idea of it was chilling. "But, but I'm only human." She protested weakly.

He laughed again, shaking his head at her obtuseness, probably. "You and your prince have not been '*only human*' since the pair of you accepted the Flame of Arven, girl. You will learn to control yourself and your power soon enough; it should not be too painful, if you actually do as you are told!"

Ethrayne did not reply to that. There was nothing she could say that would not be construed as argumentative or insulting. Her head pounding, she trudged along the beach, tired, aching, sticky with sea-salt and gritty from head to toes with sand. She would have stopped to drink from her water skin, but the king kept up a brisk pace that sorely tested her strength, making for the obvious outline of the longboat, now distantly visible against the flat vista of the light turquoise lagoon and the deep blue sea, the huge ship oddly tiny beyond. He kept on walking.

"Excellent, it looks as though they are preparing a meal." Gregnor remarked after a while, indicating the thin line of pale smoke visible in the afternoon sunshine ahead and to their left, grey against the sky. He grinned back at her. "And you are sunburned, girl, you should have worn a hat."

"Y-yes, your Majesty." She mumbled as they approached the stream, turning finally from the brilliant late afternoon sunshine into the deep shade that had earlier repelled her. The shelter of the forest was suddenly very welcome, a huge relief after the relentless glare of the sun that had pounded her since her arrival on the island, although she had not realised it until now.

Suddenly, without warning, she was staggering and from more than the after-effects of the king's punishment -.

"Careful." His hands caught her, this time preventing her from hitting the ground and dimly Ethrayne felt herself being lifted up and carried through the thick trees, as her mind drifted almost into unconsciousness, although she could feel the discomfort of his touch, his proximity; her eyes were closed, her body unresponsive, but she was still able to hear voices ahead, then around her, her head fuzzy as if stuffed thick with wool.

"Your Majesty! I'll take her from you. Please, do sit down." A voice exclaimed, perhaps Ackat, perhaps not, and someone else took hold of her.

"Thank you, but honestly, I am not as exhausted as all that." The king assured them with an easy laugh. "She's light enough, Tynsyn."

"Yet after all that you have worked with during the past four days, you must be weary, Sire." The General continued, evidently concerned.

“What has the brat been up to this time, Sire?” That was Cavaln, her voice testy.

“I suspect sunstroke amongst other things.” Gregnor said, moving away and Ethrayne felt herself being lowered to the ground, onto a blanket, her head lolling beyond her ability to control it. “Totally untrained as she is, she felt the effects of our united power most uniquely . . . Is that wine, Thellor? Excellent, thank you.”

Cold cloths smarted for a moment as they were pressed to her burning face; an arm under her shoulders lifted her head and cool fruit juice was slowly dribbled into her mouth; swallowing was the only reflex she could command, drinking enough to finally assuage a need she had not realised that she had. Helpless, gradually Ethrayne fell asleep, as the jajozeli-razine chatted in a group around her.

* * *

CHAPTER 35

Ethrayne woke languorously to dawn's early light, shining horizontally through the vegetation. There was a great deal of birdsong, none of it familiar. She felt, all things considered, surprisingly alert and rested; that horrible headache had completely vanished overnight, although the skin on her face, neck, arms and upper chest felt hot, tight and very sore. Lying there on a reasonably soft surface, almost too hot under her covering, she could smell wood-smoke, rotting vegetation and an almost overwhelming sharp scent of herbs or some unfamiliar plants around; she opened her eyes wide to a peculiar roof of shimmering leaves, an oval of clear, deep blue sky delineating a glade surrounded by the forest canopy.

Her full memory returned then: of getting sunburnt, there on the beach; of angering the king so much that he had punished her; and fainting!

<*Oh, you idiot!*> She scolded herself, slowly sitting up, her skin stinging acutely, feeling oddly tight. <*Have you no sense at all? Sunburn!*>

She had been covered with a blanket, lying on more, set on top of a base of cut vegetation that smelled sharply green and herbal, at a distance from a cheerfully burning fire on a flat piece of ground where more of the cut vegetation was strewn on a grass-like plant that grew ankle high in the glade; this was surrounded by thick undergrowth which had clearly been hacked back in many places. The stream that she had seen at the beach purled along to her left, forming a little pool in the sandy soil, next to which cooking pots and crockery had been neatly stacked. Other piles of blankets and various bags were laid here and there. It looked like a very well-appointed campsite.

"Awake, are you?" General Whillan commented, coming in to view from through two bushes to her right, a load of green and red oval things in his arms and she jumped. "Pirris, you certainly did catch the sun!" He commented.

"I can tell." Ethrayne answered, grimacing, rising slowly; but apart from that clear discomfort, she felt fine: there was no pain or dizziness in her head, messing with her eyes.

"Cavaln left your bags over there." Whillan pointed to a small pile by a shrub with long dark leaves and small yellow flowers. "You ought to wash, but I'd wear your boots: there are sharp thorns, and some of the insects here bite and sting. If you go upstream a hundred yards or so, there's a larger pool." He pointed to her right, past a tall tree covered in what looked like a very sharp, spiked bark, its branches somehow all growing out from its very top, covered in long palmate leaves. "It's private; everyone is off gathering food or working on the ship: you won't be disturbed. "Go and get washed and changed, you can eat when you get back."

"Yes, my Lord General." She replied meekly. It was a good suggestion: she could feel the salt-water residue on her skin and there seemed to be sand stuck everywhere, itching and painful on her burnt skin. Ethrayne found that her small collection of shells and things had been set neatly on a stone, and she had to shake quite a lot of sand out of her boots before pulling them on; she located her bags, with soap and a towel laid on top, then approached the narrow space where the woodland reclaimed the land, but found that there was a bare line by the stream that looked like an animal track, set straight through a longer grass that, catching her skin, seemed rather sharp edged. The slope increased slightly, the stream bubbling along musically and she passed through a deep shade, with dappling evident ahead, the singing of the birds still loud.

The pool was sheltered by undergrowth, some like peculiar, overly thick, eight-foot high reeds, well protected from sight and the glade was much larger than the one by the camp, nicely open to the sky. There were a few birds there that flew off, calling loudly, and a surprising number of bright butterflies in attendance, dancing up from wet earth to bright flowers in a haphazard, drunken manner, then back again.

Ethrayne waded out into the pool fully dressed, shivering for a moment, before ducking down into the waist-deep water to strip off, sliding through it back to the bank to retrieve the soap. She scrubbed herself and her hair twice all over, moving carefully over the sunburn, then washed her clothes, leaving them draped on a bush in the sunlight which had begun to shine down as the sun rose in the sky; drying herself, she changed into just about her last set of clean clothes, a loose shirt and leggings. She determined to wash all her other clothes after eating, if she could.

Returning to camp, she was most of the way through a hearty breakfast and enjoying it when General Cavaln appeared, a large pair of leather saddlebags on one shoulder, a jar in her left hand.

"Ah, the sunburnt brat." The woman greeted her mockingly. "Up and breakfasting, yet still with no sense at all under the tropical sun! Finish your meal and I'll treat the burns." She indicated the jar, then set it down. "Of course, one good turn deserves another: you can do my washing."

"Very well, my Lady General." Ethrayne acquiesced, spooning up the fish and vegetables that Whillan had served her, as Cavaln made herself a cup of tea before helping herself to the fish dish. "You're not using this stream for drinking water, are you, Lord General?" She asked Whillan in concern.

"No, we're collecting drinking water from a spring that emerges from a fissure over there." He pointed in the opposite direction, smiling slightly. "You can wash away in peace, with no soap in your supper, I assure you."

The soft, pale salve from the jar almost miraculously eased the discomfort of her smarting skin, although it did smell rather pungently of herbs, when spread about. Cavaln suggested she try to keep the treated areas out of water for it to work effectively.

The girl accepted her washing without complaint and carried both sets of bags back up to the now fully sunlit pool. Having fashioned a hat from a couple of large leaves, a rough clothes line from a thin but strong creeper which was wound about one tree (she pulled it down and fastened it to another a good twenty feet away) Ethrayne set about scrubbing clothes with as much care as she could, given the lack of hot water. She relished the work, to her surprise, for she was alone, with time to think, but with a task: scrubbing, soaping, rinsing, wringing over and over, her leggings rolled up, kneeling in the soft, damp ground by the pool, just glad to be busy. It took most of the rest of the morning, but she did finally get every garment washed. Her hands were wrinkled and smarting, her back aching a little, but she didn't mind.

The chore left her mind free and she had a great deal to consider. Somehow, the knowledge she had gained was equally exhilarating and terrifying, she acknowledged towards the end of her work. Ethrayne realised that the king had only related the truth: they had survived the storm only because he had so ruthlessly ripped away her power and she shuddered, growing cold despite the heat that surrounded her like a massive blanket. She simply could not comprehend just how, physically and mentally, he had fought and beaten the storm's destruction. His strength and power were terrifying.

Everything else that Gregnor had told her frightened her deeply, as she supposed he had intended. To finally learn just *why* she had been brought out of Tenarum was chilling in the extreme. Any training by the jajozeli-razine would surely be just as awful as combat practice; and if *he* was involved -! She shuddered.

Oh, dear Arven, why did you Choose me? She asked silently, wringing out the final pieces of washing. *He, he wants to* own *me! How on Iullyn can I possibly fight him when he, he can hurt me like that? Oh, it would be better if I had drowned!* She fought against a surge of panic as she shook out the last items of Cavaln's clothing, hanging them neatly on the third creeper that she had turned into a washing line. "You should have Chosen someone else!" She muttered aloud, her tone dull.

"Stop wallowing in misery, girl! Be useful, come and help me with dinner." General Whillan's voice came unexpectedly from the left and she physically jumped, his approach had been silent. "You've got quite a laundry going, haven't you?" He grinned at the lines of dripping clothes. "You'll notice we men are not so concerned about such matters. Come on, they'll all be hungry from their exertions. Bring the bags and soap."

Not having the spirit to argue this time, Ethrayne picked up the bags left by the pool, shaking off some very odd-looking ants and followed him back down the slope. The campsite was even tidier than when she had left earlier, apart from by the fireplace, where vegetables, fruit and four large silver-finned fish were piled on huge leaves. She was directed to cutting up the vegetables and fish, as the chef shaped six large loaves, setting them before a hand-built oven to rise; Whillan had lit a bright fire with bark and twigs and was now feeding it carefully.

"There, that's the bread nearly ready to bake, let's get the rest of the meal started." He said with satisfaction but looked askance at how badly she had cleaned the fish. "I thought Thellor was joking, you know; you've obviously never worked in a kitchen, girl. Clearly you'd be better in a laundry or as a dressmaker."

"Ha, ha, ha." She growled at that, washing her hands free of gleaming fish scales in the stream behind the fire pit. "No, I'm certainly not a cook." Then, unable to stop the question – for she had wondered it for ages now but hadn't dared ask before – Ethrayne asked. "But isn't this rather an odd job for a General, sir? Cooking?"

Whillan laughed aloud at that. "I've enjoyed cooking since childhood and it was my hobby, when I wasn't doing my real job: logistics. But because of my expertise, I've become his majesty's official chef, especially when travelling. Most cooks would balk at trying to create fine meals on a deserted island or building a bread oven from scratch." He waved towards the oven, where the fire was starting to burn merrily and spoke matter-of-factly rather than boastfully. "Of course, I drop back into logistics when required, usually when planning for war or the stationing of troops around the Empire."

Ethrayne frowned. This General, at least, alone amongst them all, did not seem to be quite as monstrous as the others and he wasn't too offensive, either; but she remembered what the dream-Arven had said on her journey to Ban'Lerracon: it was fixed in her mind and after the king had talked of '*owning her*', she knew that she would never, ever, trust any of them.

"Well, your efforts are not irrecoverable, I suppose." Whillan continued critically. "You'd better fetch plenty of water: take the buckets through there and walk ahead, you won't miss the spring. You can't wreck that, at least."

"All right, my Lord." She replied tartly but was glad of a reason to get out of his way, although hauling water was bound to be heavy. She hefted the buckets and wove her way through a grove of shrubs covered in long pale leaves shaped like spear heads, following a thin trail that brought her to a spring welling up out of a bright, mossy hollow edged with various flowers, forming an almost oval pool before it wandered away through the thick vegetation and out of sight. Ethrayne lingered there for some time, before setting off back laden with the water, which she did her utmost not to spill.

To her intense dismay, the jajozeli-razine were all present in the camp when she returned; the king and all the Generals were sat about, sipping at watered wine and talking as they waited for dinner; at least, she realised with some relief, the sailors were not, with their intense stares; perhaps they were eating on the ship. Ethrayne gulped, longing to just drop the buckets and run and hide somewhere, quite sick of the impulse really, but unable to halt its appearance; she wove between them and set the water down close to the fire as Whillan indicated, then edged over to her blankets, fortunately away from the others, sinking down and hoping that they would continue to ignore her; also, she was hungry again, waiting as patiently as she could, smelling the bread, the meal, cooking. Nervously she fingered the small pile of shells, stones and the coin which King Gregnor had insisted that she bring back the previous afternoon, but without really seeing them.

"Ah, dinner!" Jallon said eagerly, and she looked up. He had bruises on his face and arms that she had not noticed the day before; and Benthan, who had also been on the stern deck, struggling mightily during the storm, had a long cut down his left cheek, as well as more bruises. She supposed that she had been too wound up in her own discomfort to notice their injuries.

The jajozeli-razine crowded about the fire, jostling in a friendly fashion after their master had been served; Ethrayne did not get up until they were all sat down, serving herself the deliciously scented stew and the warm, fresh bread, moving quickly back to 'her' space. It wasn't *very* often that one of them had knocked a plate out of her hands, but she had been the butt of their cruel humour too many times, in her opinion.

They talked, clearly at ease after the hard work of the day. Some talked about the ship and her damage; about how far they guessed they had been blown off-course; about the food and the excellent, surprisingly rich supplies they had found on the island. Ethrayne relaxed very slightly; hopefully the evening might continue without any humiliating incidents.

"I want everything back on-board ship by noon tomorrow." The king was saying in his conversation with his servants.

"We will be ready, your Majesty." Ackat assured him. "We're in the process of re-filling the water barrels. The remedial work to be completed is now almost all cosmetic finishing off, rather than anything operational."

"I've amassed a good amount of produce: fruit, tubers, seafood and so on. It would be a pity to waste the bounty this island has provided us." Sepphar, the second cook, said then, which explained the scratches on his hands and arms, Ethrayne assumed.

"We will add the island to our charts, Sepphar. If we sail north, we'll get a second reference point from the stars." Jallon stated. "It will be a useful addition to our voyages in the future, that's for sure."

"Certainly." Gregnor rose to his feet. "Thank you Whillan, that was delicious. Let's carry on clearing up before nightfall." He led the way out of the camp and nearly everyone followed him.

Ethrayne was already resigned to being forced to do the washing up, so that was not a surprise, but at least Cavaln went to fetch their now dry washing, before covering her sunburned skin with more of the salve.

"I think General Whillan will sooner cut off his own hands before he ever lets you near his knives and produce again, girl." The woman remarked with a laugh.

"Good." Ethrayne replied. "Thank you." She added politely. The king's cold evaluation of her and Jerryn's future still dominated her thoughts. These people meant her nothing but ill . . . She was forced to subservience, so frightened of him . . . and she was so lonely.

*

Tasked only with helping pack the equipment that had been brought off the ship, and the surprising amount of fresh produce that had been gathered on and around the island and piled about the glade, Ethrayne had no time to worry the next day; she spent most of the morning carrying bags and bundles down to the beach. Checking the site that they had occupied for anything mislaid, a suggestion from Masson which she was grateful for, since it meant that she had a little more time to herself, she found an exquisite flint arrowhead about the size of her little finger, which she absent-mindedly added to the little bag that she had fashioned for her beach treasures. Other than that, nothing had been left behind apart from the empty fire pit and the bread oven which Whillan had built so carefully.

The sun was almost directly overhead when she finally climbed the netting onto the Lightning, noting that the broken section of railing had been replaced along with the other works, and set foot on the baking hot deck, feeling the gentle movement of the ship almost thankfully; she had not realised that she had felt uncomfortable back on land, so stationary underfoot, until she was back on the ocean.

Shaille was directly behind her, so Ethrayne moved across the broad deck to the opposite rail, moving almost up into the bow some distance up from where some of the other Generals were gathered, gazing downward into the deep blue ocean and, curiously, she did likewise, wondering what they were looking at.

"Oh, dear Arven!" Shock hit her like a physical blow as she stared down at some human bodies floating in the water, pallid against the sapphire shade; four, no five people, dressed in what looked like the ragged remains of Tenarean-style clothes. They were clearly dead; what was worse, far worse, to her mind, was the sight of a group of massive, silver- and blue-striped stream-lined fish that had risen out of the depths to bite hungrily at some of the corpses, their teeth triangular in huge mouths, and instantly effective at dismemberment. "But, but where have they come from?" She demanded in horror, then bit back a cry as a body was knocked closer to the ship by the muscular tail of one razor-toothed monster; below, she clearly saw the face of a woman she had known for most of her life: Rosalla, one of her mother's maids, who had been an expert with her needle. "Rosalla! Oh, dear Arven no! But, but how were she, they here?"

General Allun laughed coldly as she gripped the rail and sobbed. "The prisoners are in the forward hold, brat; where else would they be?" He stated. "Some were killed in the fury of the storm and have been disposed of -."

"Disposed of?" Ethrayne almost shouted the words as she turned on him. "B-but I would have sensed them! Why did I not sense that they were on board? Some died, you say, but who has survived?" She demanded with an imperiousness none of them had witnessed before. "Is anyone injured -?"

"Silence, girl!" Garrtnor cut through her furious questions. "You had no need to know about the contents of that hold, so their presence was blocked from you -."

"*That hold's contents?*" She spat the words, utter shock dispelling the last vestiges of necessary caution that usually ruled all her interactions with the jajozeli-razine. "These are *people*, General! People! An-and I had no idea! You've had prisoners crammed in some space below our very feet, in some dark, airless cabin? Like animals? Oh, dear Arven! You, you evil monsters!" Ethrayne took a deep breath, so intent on voicing her distress and anger that she did not even realise that, most uncharacteristically, the Generals were drawing away from her, almost as though she was as dangerous as the sea creatures feasting on the bodies in the sea below. She could not see the golden glow emanating from her body, lit from within by her power, clearly visible despite the brilliance of the tropical sun; the Flame of Arven, fed and released by her rage and upset. "Take me to them! Now!" She demanded furiously, behaving as she had never done before, perhaps subconsciously mimicking her captor's demeanour. "You can't treat people like this -."

"Silence!"

The one voice that could have cut through her near hysteria bellowed out, a sound like thunder. Ethrayne froze in dread. Gregnor followed that shout with a hard punch that, matched by his vast power, simultaneously knocked the girl partway across the deck, to be brought to a halt by the base of the wooden housing for the landing boat, and suppressed her rapidly rising strength as a dampened blanket would smother a fire.

"I will not permit such disrespect!" As he had two days earlier, on the beach, he slapped her badly focussed mind with his power and her unregulated talent faded back down, smothered out of existence at the pain that flashed through her.

Ethrayne could not move, her muscles frozen for one endless moment, the rising distress and hysteria shocked out of her by his sudden, unanticipated violence. Her face, her head and her back were all agonisingly painful, quite apart from the assault on her nerves. Blood ran freely from her nose, down into her throat as well as down her face. She gurgled, involuntarily coughed as it felt as though she could not breathe, almost screaming at the agony; she tried to retreat yet was unable to shrink away as the king reached down to pull her onto her side. Her agonising coughing halted finally, before she spat an inordinate amount of blood onto the deck at his booted feet. Then, helplessly, she vomited more blood -.

"Have some care, brat!"

The girl groaned, covered her bloodied, painful face as well as she could with shaking hands and sobbed almost uncontrollably, as her blood flowed steadily, forming a small, dark pool between her and Gregnor.

"Sorry, I'm sorry, please, please don't hurt the prisoners -." She managed to mumble, her words almost unintelligible, her voice thick with blood. "Dear Arven!"

Gregnor knelt beside her, ignoring the blood, and forced her hands away from her face with a firm but not painful grip. Ethrayne could do nothing: her body and head hurt far too much for her to try to move. Quaking with fear, she could only close her eyes as Gregnor stared intently at her blood-stained, damaged face. He turned back to the Generals with a frown.

"Shit!" He spat with feeling, moving one hand to touch her back, again ignoring her utter fear and almost animal-like howl of discomfort, running his fingers downward. "Double shit! Cavaln, Harton, I've broken her nose and strained her bloody back! I'll hold her -."

"Wha'?" Ethrayne knew what this meant and reacted in horror, waving her hands frantically but futilely. She had never felt as much pain as this, not even from her crushed left side and leg, after Ackat had lifted her out from under her father's dead stallion; she knew how broken noses were fixed. But the king and General Harton turned her rather gently over onto her back, all things considered. "No – *no* -."

The three of them paid her absolutely no attention, her blood flecking their faces and clothes as Cavaln hauled up the bottom of Ethrayne's shirt to mop away some of the mess, so that she could see the extent of the damage caused by Gregnor's blow. Harton held one arm firmly, the king the other. Ethrayne made a strange, strangled sort of shriek as the woman took hold of her throbbing nose. She gurgled, helpless. More blood spurted for a moment as there was a second audible crack! That sound made not a few of the circling Generals wince. The girl slumped in shocked agony, breathing irregularly, shivering uncontrollably, as both healers carefully turned her back over onto her side and the king quickly got up out of their way.

"Pirris!" He said with deceptive brevity. "Every time we get the brat clean and obedient, she gets covered in blood!" He glanced down at the quivering, sobbing girl as Cavaln attempted to clean up a bit more blood from her face.

"Sire -." Garrtnor began in a tentative tone.

"Wait!" He gestured slightly and the finely upholstered divan from his sitting room appeared some feet away, plus a pile of soft, brightly covered cushions. "Get the girl on there, carefully!" He warned. "Clean her up, get her changed, tend those injuries."

"At once, your Majesty." Harton assured him quickly.

"You -." Gregnor glared indiscriminately at the rest of the group, yanking his blood-stained boots off with evident disgust. "Can get the deck scrubbed clean and ensure that the slaves are secure. I simply cannot believe that none of you thought to simply slap the girl out of her shock!" His tone was scathing at the least.

"I, well, it all happened so swiftly, your Majesty." Thellor answered meekly.

The king snorted derisively. "You are my trusted servants. You have received the highest, most specialised training and none of you have balked at any of the tasks you have undertaken on my orders before. Yet here you stand, a group of experienced Generals, seasoned over many decades service, too nervous of a single girl's hysterical lack of control to even *smack* her? She is usually nearly as wary of you as she is of me. After the last few days, she would have quietened down swiftly enough. She is a mere child, not a lioness!" He raked them all with a scathing, contemptuous glare that matched his tone and strode, in his socks, towards the stern deck. "Get out of my fucking sight!"

"Your Majesty." They replied as one, bowed deeply, and cleared out of their master's way extremely quickly.

*

Ethrayne came to sometime later, when she was carefully lifted from the hard, hot deck and laid on a softer surface nearby, moved out of the bright afternoon sunshine into a blue-tinged shade, or so it seemed, with her eyes closed. The movement jarred her back terribly and her whole face was agony, her head pounding -.

"Ow!" She breathed.

"Hush." General Harton's voice growled above her head. She heard water dripping. "It's entirely your fault, brat!" She flinched, painfully, as a warm, wet cloth gently touched her face without warning. "Hold still."

<*Tisn't, it's your fault.*> She spat back in return, her mental tone as bruised as the rest of her. <*Hateful . . .*>

He chuckled as he carefully dabbed at her face with far more care than Ethrayne would ever have imagined. Then, that done, her attention was caught, as her shirt, boots and leggings were removed quickly, although she protested frantically -.

<*Don't -*> An indistinct, futile remonstration, really, as all sorts of fears struck her.

"Stop fretting, girl." Cavaln's voice sounded calm, distant. "Harton is a healer. You are safe enough."

Her alarm was only growing, yet oddly formless: she was in too much pain, too distressed, to react properly.

The woman washed her body, the water cooling against her hot skin, as she lay helplessly propped up against Harton, as he held another cloth to her nose, which was still leaking blood. Tears ran from aching eyes which were nearly swollen shut, and she had some trouble focussing when she forced them open; Ethrayne could not bear to look down at herself, her naked body, for to do so would only confirm one of her worst fears, her utter helplessness amongst them. Looking past the healers, she noted that, strangely, a small, pale tent now surrounded the three of them, blocking the sunlight, the cloth billowing in the sea breeze.

But that was nothing. Despite her fear, however, she could only concentrate on the throbbing agony which filled her; the disgusting taste of blood in her mouth; the harsh, laboured sound of her breathing; the fact that any movement on her part was impossible . . . She cried out again when they turned her another time, gently, onto her side on the bed, which triggered more nausea, as her body purged itself of the last of the blood which she had swallowed. Ethrayne hardly noticed the two hands moving up and down the length of her back, the woman's palms growing surprisingly hot as they touched her, an odd sense of *tingling* around the area that hurt so much, where she had collided with the boat's housing.

There was just misery, pain, and the awful knowledge that her captors' had managed to conceal a group of prisoners right beneath her feet on the ship . . . Ethrayne fought the cold logic that asked just *how* she could have known of their presence when most of the ship's inner spaces were prohibited to her, and the king had also used power to keep her ignorant of their existence? Recalling the horrific afternoon when he had ordered Fionn's death, after he had mutilated and slaughtered her attacker mere feet from her, she felt revoltingly nauseous again and despair filled her. She should have known!

Cavaln finished whatever she was doing to her back and then both healers helped her into clean clothes, straightening whatever garment it was, pulling it down smoothly and decently as Ethrayne was eased onto her back, propped up slightly with cushions. The salve to ease her sunburn was applied; a cool, wet cloth was laid over her smarting eyes; a drink of fresh fruit juice was held to her lips, but swallowing was not easy, although she was thirsty; a further cloth was placed in her hands, so she could wipe at her still-dripping, agonising nose herself; a blanket covered her.

"Rest, if you can." Cavaln suggested finally, sounding tired. "There's water here, if you need to drink more." She guided her right hand down to a metal cup on the deck below, easily within reach.

<*Thank you.*> Ethrayne managed, so wrung out by her ordeal that she just longed to be left alone. She heard their footsteps receding; the sounds of scrubbing had stopped . . . Misery took her, dimly interrupted by the sounds of the ship moving, so perhaps their interrupted journey had resumed, although she had been too occupied to notice . . . She lay there on the bed, half concealed in the little tent, listening to the sails billowing, the ship moving through the waves, indistinct conversations . . . but she was too frightened of the pain that she had experienced to even shift her position, frozen in place, unable to relax a single muscle . . . Slowly, after an age, the sunlight faded into night through the cloth, and she still lay there tense, her face throbbing agonisingly . . . *Wish we'd all drowned!* She spat uselessly. *Oh, Rosalla! Mamma, Papa . . . I'm so frightened! So alone!* She could recall with perfect clarity what the king had said on the beach, his icy explanation for capturing her; her life was no longer hers to control, it seemed. She was helpless, utterly helpless! She and Jerryn were fated to destroy everything and everyone they held dear!

There was no merciful fainting that night.

*

It was evening by the time that the king had finally got a grip on his temper, the glow of the vanished sun bright on the western horizon and across the endless ocean. He summoned the Generals to the stern deck, where he stood tall at the wheel, steering north, the sky darkening from the east, stars winking into visibility; the small canvas tent that held the injured girl fading from sight in the middle of the deck, although her presence was clear to him, her fretful, frightened restlessness.

Warily, the group of highly competent Generals gathered around him, but none of them stood too close, even so.

"We should have a clear run from here." He stated levelly. "I know it has been rather ridiculously manic for the past few days since that storm abated but, honestly, I cannot believe that you all permitted yourselves to be outdone by our prisoner: she's barely an adult amongst her own people, men, she doesn't even understand how to control herself yet!"

"Erm, that might be the problem, your Majesty: her lack of control." Thellor answered after a short silence. Their master was evidently waiting for *someone* to respond sensibly.

"How so? Are you not Generals? Do you not possess considerable power of your own?" His tone was sharp, his gaze blazing.

"Well, your Majesty, that's true. I slapped her hard, that day we left Cal'Itase, but she was simply a frightened brat then. Ackat cut off all her hair, teaching her a lesson on their way south." The large jajozeli-razine paused and shrugged; physically, Thellor was the largest of the Generals on board and although the king topped him by a good few inches, he was still the bulkiest. Nothing much worried him in life.

"But we felt her fighting you, during the storm, Sire." Ackat admitted, flexing fingers that still slightly ached from his participation in the scrubbing of the blood-stained deck. "Even *we* can tell that she has a massive potential: the power inside her is vast and we know she fought well, fought you strongly, even though she knows nothing at all . . . It wasn't that we did not *want* to stop her hysterics quickly, your Majesty, well, we -."

"That lack of control she has could destroy us, your Majesty." Garrtnor finished simply with a shrug. "She was furious, losing far too much control in her hysteria; we could all feel it and, I'm afraid to admit it, Sire: her talent frightens me!"

"Her fear of what you told her on the island fills her mind and that probably contributed to her fury as well, your Majesty." Whillan said quietly. "Her fear, ignorance and shock certainly compounded into something far stronger than we ever would have expected: she doesn't understand it all and that terrifies her. Her distrust of us has been constant, yer her terror of you and the purpose you revealed is vast; she must learn control."

"You *must* start teaching her, Sire." Tynsyn stated gravely, inclining his head almost apologetically at the bluntness of his words. "Perhaps it's her proximity to your own formidable presence that has sparked her talent to new heights, but this voyage does seem to have done so: she was nowhere near as volatile in Ban'Lerracon."

Gregnor considered their hesitant words, immensely glad that he always sought intelligence as well as native ability in his primary servants; the intensity of their training took the youngsters they began as much further than the civilian jajozeli-razine population could even imagine.

"Very well, gentlemen and lady." He inclined his head to Cavaln. "Your recommendation and concerns are noted and, I must admit, they are most relevant. I only wish I had not damaged the girl again!" He sighed. "Very well, I will begin by training her to control herself. It should prove interesting and she will certainly detest every moment of it: she hates being within a hundred feet of me! How is she, Harton?"

"She is most discomforted, your Majesty, but cleaner at least." The male healer replied and grimaced. "Cavaln has partly eased the bruising to her back and gave her a little pelande in fruit juice, so she should not try to do anything at all tonight; it will inhibit action, quite apart from her injuries. Overall, she will probably heal quickly."

"And how do you feel, Cavaln? That sort of healing is the rarest, the most tiring. Thank you for your work."

"Thank you, Sire, but I'll be fine after a good night's sleep." Cavaln replied and chuckled aloud. "Harton is right: the girl will recover well, once those huge black eyes and the bruising subside, anyway." She stated with a lot more authority than she usually showed, as the most junior General and she smiled as the king raised one eyebrow in query. "Whillan is correct: she is in deep shock, Sire and she needs to rest completely for at least tomorrow: her mind is in turmoil, quite apart from those physical injuries."

"Very well General Cavaln, thank you. I am very glad I trusted my instincts to involve you in this business, you are most insightful, concerning the girl."

"I am honoured, your Majesty." The young woman bowed low.

"Well, if that is all sorted, gentlemen, lady, you can all seek your beds. I will keep helm and keep a watch on our challenging little prisoner until the middle of the night."

* * *

CHAPTER 36

Exhausted, her head aching fit to crack, Ethrayne watched the tent around her slowly become visible as the sky began to lighten. Finally, after a night's fitful rest, she was lucid enough to wonder where she lay; the tent was not large, so that she could have touched the canvas on both sides without moving more than her hands, and she was aware that this was not the little cabin below decks, that was for sure . . . Thinking back to the events of the previous afternoon with some difficulty, around her pain, the fury and the resulting panic which had controlled her, she realised that she must be on deck, for the flap of sails above her, now, was unmistakeable; then, vaguely she remembered someone giving her drinks of water during the long night when she had been distressed, helpless, rearranging the comfortable pillows behind her aching back . . . but . . . Oh, dear Arven, everything hurt so much!

More tears ran down her face, stinging her swollen eyes as she tried to pull herself upright, but she fought the pain of her head and face even as she noticed the slightly lessened discomfort of her back and ribs – she recalled vaguely they had felt as if they had shattered when the king had struck her. After a great deal of effort, she sat up, slowly setting her legs over the side of the divan, only then realising that her well-worn clothes from the day before had been replaced with her nightgown. She remembered her helplessness aginst them -.

The effort of getting up had made her head spin, this time, rather than pound with pain, but Ethrayne did not dare to move further. After what she recalled of the previous afternoon, she wasn't that brave, or stupid; her head, back and ribs might not hurt as much as they had, but her face certainly did; all of it: her skin abnormally swollen and tight, her bones feeling as though they had been smashed. Nor could she open her eyes properly, which had formed part of the irrational night-fears which had assailed her, that she was losing her sight, too. Miserable, frozen in that position because she was now scared of doing herself further damage, her back twingeing, Ethrayne did manage to reach the water cup on the deck and emptied it; although swallowing hurt, she needed the liquid far more. Stuck there, she spat silent, graphic swearwords and hoped that one of the hated Generals might come to check on her, now that the sun was rising.

She could not get Rosalla's dead face out of her mind . . . the fish, seeming to fight over her body . . . wondered how many other prisoners were locked up somewhere in the depths of the ship – imagining a small space like the one she had been shoved into, after Thellor had thumped her . . . The realisation still shocked her, that she had not known of their presence . . .

"Pirris! If your handsome young prince could see you now, girl, he'd run away screaming!" Cavaln remarked heartily, pulling open the pavilion's canvas flap and admitting brilliant sunlight that caused the girl to quickly shield her eyes, even as she choked a brief, painful sort of laugh that grated all the way up from her stomach, for the statement was amusing, in the dark mood she still felt. "You really do look terrible. Let's get you on your feet, shall we?"

Some time had passed, for the sun was well above the horizon now, but Ethrayne still felt as bad as she had before dawn. Trying to keep as straight as possible, she shuffled forward slightly from her position, then the General finally assisted her, hauling her upwards by her upper arm.

"Ow!" It was more noise than word, but she was glad when her legs did hold her, although she swayed a little, clutching at the nightgown which covered her, her head spinning for a moment, then settling, although all the rest of her discomfort remained.

"Let's get you to the cabin." Cavaln said calmly. "Come along and don't worry, you should be fine, I worked on your back and ribs yesterday, the pain should ease."

Ethrayne glanced at her briefly from her unfocussed, swollen eyes, stooping, then dared to take one step then a second as Cavaln moved back to hold open the flap, so that she could emerge into the new day, stepping on the hot planks, using her left hand to keep her eyes shaded. She moved slowly, the General leaving her to make her own way towards the stern and the girl advanced, her gaze fixed on the entrance to the cabins, determinedly ignoring all the others out on deck. It seemed to take a lifetime, but she reached the oddly stifling gloom of the corridor, shuffling along; her ribs surely ached as she descended the first ladder, carefully lifting the skirt of the nightgown out of the way as she stepped down, holding tight to the rungs, but not so much as she clambered down the second, into the deeper darkness, Cavaln just above her.

"You've done well." The woman said, as she entered the sunlit little cabin, one hand shaking as she took hold of the edge of the bunk for support. "I'll check you over, strip."

"Wha -?" Speaking was a mistake, for the pain of her face was increased. She jumped as Cavaln slammed the door shut.

"For the -." Sounding exasperated, Cavaln took hold of the fabric of the garment at her shoulders and shook Ethrayne slightly. "I'm a healer, brat. Undress, or are you suicidal enough to argue?" Her gaze was forbidding. "No?"

Emotions swirled within her, complex, confusing, choking; Ethrayne shivered, not daring to respond and meekly removed the nightgown, glad that her eyesight was hampered, hanging her head.

"Right, stay still for a moment." Cavaln said with her usual professional detachment, ignoring the girl's automatic flinching as her hands touched her front, then directed her to turn around to stroke her aching back, before telling her to sit down on the bunk, moving away then back with a bowl of water. "The bruising of your back and torso will fade soon enough, but as for your face -." She pursed her lips and sighed a little. "That will take time. Now hold still: this *will* hurt a little." This time she grinned at her patient, squeezing out a cloth over the water bowl. "Believe me, I know: my great uncle broke my nose during practise once, I looked as horrific as you do . . ." She carefully dabbed, ignoring her victim's hissed protests, her flinching movements. "Mmm, looks like your cheekbone is damaged too: you've got lumps the size of apples appearing all over, girl."

Ethrayne flinched again; for it hurt almost as much as when the king had struck her, her nose especially felt abnormally swollen. Cavaln's ministrations hurt a great deal and there seemed to be something astringent in the water that smarted in all her injuries besides. <*Ouch!*> She uttered silently, describing every part of her misery, pain and humiliation, sat there naked as cooling water ran down her body, fighting against more tears.

"Stop whining, it's your own fault!" The woman said cheerfully, scanning her face, wiping the excess water from her throat; both the cloth and the water in the bowl were reddened now. "There, you'll do. Now, get dressed: the formal gown is still in your bag. You will take breakfast with his Majesty -."

<*No!*> That was a cry of absolute fear and Ethrayne hid her swollen face behind her hands, shuddering.

"Hurry now: he will be waiting." And with a cool smile, visible through her slightly separated fingers, the General departed.

Into Ethrayne's frightened mind came her latest memory of the king: her brief glimpse the afternoon before of his furious face, his flashing, fiery dark eyes as he had struck her with what had seemed like all his strength, matched with the power that had suppressed her rising hysterical power and crazed ranting. Now her fear of him had increased to gut-wrenching proportions, yet she knew that refusal was not an option, no matter how she longed to hide uselessly in the cupboard under her bunk.

Dear Arven, help me! She prayed desperately, shuddering again . . . But- but *he* was waiting, probably impatiently.

That knowledge finally gave her the impetus to move, reaching for the bag that she had not noticed lying beside her on her pillow, containing the various underclothes and the fine silk gown which went over them, terribly creased but clean and soft at least. Fumbling, she quickly pulled each layer on, the under gown with its tapes and then the bright outer gown, knotting the sash tightly before she ran her shaking fingers through her unruly hair, not even caring how it looked. Moving very carefully, she threw the slightly blood-stained water out of the window, set the bowl neatly in the little wash room and stowed her bag back in the cupboard before, barefoot, she opened the cabin door.

"Good." General Thellor stood in the passage, leaning on the back on the ladder, clearly waiting for her to emerge and he smiled slightly at her jump of dismayed surprise. "Don't dawdle, brat: you're expected."

He gestured expansively for her to precede him, but she froze: her fear suddenly choking her as her blood had -. “Move it!” He bellowed, and she scurried past him at once, pushing past a rather indignant Eduren and Sepphar without even noticing them: up the ladder, around and up the next, to advance a few halting steps and stop dead before the king’s sitting room door.

<*Enter.*> Gregnor’s voice was clear in her head and Ethrayne could sense amusement. Her fear was almost a horrible physical thing within her, but she forced herself to move, one hesitant step forward, still praying uselessly for deliverance, or death, her hand shaking just as much as her legs as she lifted the latch, pushing the door open to flood the passage with light, stepping through, her gaze fixed desperately on the carpet. Closing the door, turning back to face the broad windows, she started to bend, to kneel -.

“Get up before you fall over, girl. Come and sit down.” He ordered, and she froze, shivering, stuck mid movement as her muscles spasmed uncontrollably.

“Your Majesty -.” Was what she meant to say with desperate politeness, but the pain of her face caused the words to sound almost unintelligible as she slowly straightened, hesitantly raising her head so that she could see where she must advance to. The king was sitting on one side of the table in front of the window, an empty chair to her right, opposite him. He wore plain black and indicated to that seat, smiling broadly, looking well satisfied. Ethrayne felt sick; did the state of her face amuse him?

As if he had heard her thought, and of course he could do so, her host chuckled. “Ethrayne, you look terrible, sit down, have some tea.” He said lightly.

The girl risked a moment’s glance into his face, met his dark, hypnotic gaze and quickly locked her gaze on the white tablecloth as she stumbled forward on her shaking legs to take her seat, perched awkwardly on the very edge of the chair. As she moved, the king poured a pale, steaming liquid into two gold cups, setting one before her.

“Thank you.” But, again, her voice was mangled, hoarse and pain shot through her face.

“Why do you not just reply in your mind, girl?” Gregnor suggested, as if to an imbecile. “There’s no point croaking in such an ugly fashion, now, is there? I have invited you here for breakfast but, looking at you, I really do not know if you will be able to eat. Perhaps the resourceful General Whillan can rustle up something suitable.” He chuckled; Ethrayne could sense his satisfaction.

<*Thank-thank you, your Majesty, but I-I’m not hungry.*> She lied, suddenly aware that it would be virtually impossible to tell falsehoods to any other talented being; most would be able to read the lie and thus the truth clearly.

The king shook his head slowly, as if regretfully. She could see it, even though her eyes were fixed on the table. “You threw up everything you had eaten yesterday up on deck and practically all over my boots, Ethrayne. You *will* eat for I will not permit you to neglect your health. No!" He raised one finger slightly when she shifted, intending to protest and she shrank back. "Drink your tea."

Ethrayne took hold of the warm cup in both hands and it rattled audibly against her teeth as she sipped, swallowed and sipped again. There was something pleasant in the hot liquid, but she couldn't define it, although it was soothing as it went down.

"Lime blossom." He said lightly. "You won't be able to taste it, but it's gentle on the palate and stomach." He glanced away, and the outer door swung wide to admit both Whillan and Sepphar, bearing laden trays.

"Breakfast, Sire." Whillan said and they laid two covered fine gold dishes before their master, a basket of rolls in the middle of the table and a covered bowl before Ethrayne, along with gleaming cutlery, a water jug and cups of beautifully chased silver.

"Excellent, chefs and is that broth? It should suit her well, thank you." The king said, and they bowed and departed.

Ethrayne sat there, still clutching desperately at her mug, as Gregnor lifted the lids on his platter to reveal sausage, delicately fried fish and steamed vegetables.

"Eat, child." He ordered, breaking open a roll to fill it with fish.

Setting down the mug, Ethrayne lifted the cover, looking down at a bowl of creamy-looking soup, smooth and steaming. Despite her proximity to the king and, despite her terrible, all-encompassing fear, her stomach growled prosaically. She set down the lid, picked up a spoon and tried it; the spoon felt sharp, painful against her bruised lips as she swallowed, but the soup tasted just as bland as the tea, although it went down pleasantly. She could not tell what it contained, but she suspected it was fish and she ate with as much decorum as she could, despite the need that she had not noticed until now . . . But her captor, opposite, was far too great a presence to be ignored; most of the way through the broth, she dared to glance up at him through her lashes to find him gazing right at her, his expression unreadable, and her remaining hunger died abruptly. She set the spoon down and picked up the half-empty mug of tea, simply to seem polite as he finished the last bites of his breakfast, then dabbed at his mouth with a pristine napkin.

"Your nose is bleeding a little, here." He handed the cloth across the table and Ethrayne took it, tentatively pressed, winced and shivered at the sight of even more blood, bright crimson spots on the white fabric. She had seen far too much blood in the past moons -. Rosalla, Foinn and Sally loomed again in her memory and she shivered. Somewhere inside, she felt anger at the fate of so many innocent people, but it vanished like mist in sunlight as the Betrayer's overwhelming aura filled her mind anew.

<Thank you, you Majesty.> She ventured in a subdued tone, carefully folding the napkin to hide the stain and laying it beside the bowl.

"Keep it." Gregnor waved his hand again. "Well, child. I was going to have my Generals' train you, but it appears that your lack of basic control can scare even such experienced combatants as they, else I would not have had to intervene, yesterday: your insubordination would have been dealt with appropriately." His tone was neutral, he at least was not shouting at her, but his matter-of-factness was chilling.

<*Your Majesty – I -.*>

"Apologising now is ridiculous, child." He stated. "You did not know that there are hostages on board. We hid them from you simply because I knew you would overreact and, seeing those bodies without warning, you very predictably lost control, because you are young, stupid and ignorant of the power that you hold. Your nose is bleeding again."

Ethrayne raised the cloth, pressed carefully, then clutched it between both hands, twisting it tightly into a short rope.

"You must learn to control yourself: your tongue, your emotions and your mind. There is no alternative to obedience, child. You *will* learn. You will obey my commands. How you proceed is quite up to you, of course, but I cannot really recommend the way you have chosen so far, Ethrayne, so I strongly urge that you reconsider your position over the next few days. If you want to continue trying to fight me, you will suffer much worse discomfort and privation than you feel now, I promise you; and we do have prisoners from your home on board, remember." He grinned broadly at the horror he could read in her mind and see in her eyes, clear despite her injuries. "Why are you looking at me like that, Ethrayne? I am not the one with a broken nose, huge black eyes and a strained back, am I? You knew exactly what you were taking on a year ago, my dear; and if you did not, then blame that meddling fool, Bahlien!"

<*How-how could he possibly have warned us that you are . . . are so cruel?*> Ethrayne had quickly amended her thought, but – *you are evil* – hung there as clear as the sun between them and she ducked her head, shrinking into her seat fearfully. <*That wa-was very rude, Sire. I-I am terribly sorry.*>

Hesitantly, she shoved the chair backwards, knelt, her heart thumping, fully expecting to suffer his rage . . . Yet, silence filled the cabin for far too long before, unexpectedly, Gregnor chuckled with apparent good humour.

"You are reckless, my Lady. I will forgive your lapse, this time, but I meant what I said, child: you *will* obey me, so work on your manners and curb your tongue and your hostility."

<*I-I will try my best, your Majesty.*> She quavered.

<*You bloody well will! If you offend me, child, then you will suffer, so keep that in mind*!> He replied silently, his voice almost a bellow within her head. <*You will rest today and tomorrow, but the following day you will return here after breakfast with the stones, shells and coin you collected on the island. Get out of my sight!*>

Ethrayne slowly bowed her head, then got up from her knees. She was not stupid enough to ignore his warning. Then she simply fled, tears pricking at her smarting eyes, but she did manage to close the outer door quietly. The main deck was only a few steps away, and she emerged into the brilliant sunshine with only a moment of relief, for the light stung her eyes far more than she had anticipated, so she halted, shielding them, but even blinking hurt terribly now.

Seeing some of the Generals busy outside, she fled back into the dim passage and carefully descended the ladders, managing to reach her cabin without meeting anyone else, although she could hear dim footsteps and conversations. Politely, she stopped to knock on the door, checking that Cavaln was absent and slipped inside when there was no reply, shutting the door and wishing that she could lock it, lock them all out! She got up on her bunk and arranged the blanket and pillow next to the window, carefully leaning back, shivering uncontrollably again; she tried to cover her face in her hands, but it hurt far too much to touch . . .

Oh, dear Arven, I truly wish that that storm had destroyed the ship! She wailed in silent misery, her tears stinging painfully as they ran down her swollen face. *I wish I was dead! Kill me! Find someone else, better, stronger, to, to fight!* And she sobbed, although the paroxysms were agonising. *I can't disobey him! I daren't disobey him!*

Finally, after what he had said on the beach a few days before, the Emperor of the Jajozeli-Razine, the Betrayer, had delivered his ultimatum and she did not have any way out, no way at all.

Oh Lord Arven, Jerryn . . . Bahlien, Lurco for-forgive me! She hoped against all common-sense that, somehow, they might hear her half across the world. *I-I can't fight him! They-they kill people for-for fun, here! You wouldn't recognise me! He . . . he is cruel . . . oh, I wish I was dead!* Ethrayne shuddered, recalling far too many shocking and pitiless occurrences since she had been captured.

Death certainly not being an option, of course, she spent as much time as possible for the rest of that day and the next, alone. Hunger and thirst forced her from the little cabin, to ascend to the main cabin, to eat Whillan's nutritious broth and to endure the Generals' usual taunts and she could not, dared not, answer back. Warned by the king, in no condition to endure any form of punishment and completely terrified by his confident account of her future in his hands, Ethrayne hunched down, all too aware of her weakness, her helplessness; she ignored them, but it was very hard to achieve, especially as she remembered that the king had told her that they had all been scared by her loss of self-control! But she would have ignored jibes at court in Tenum by rude minions or equals . . . She would not have demeaned herself by replying . . . Perhaps it was because she knew exactly what the consequences would be, why talking and eating were so difficult. But it was not easy.

The night that followed her breakfast with King Gregnor was somehow much worse than the one before, for she was fully conscious and in too much discomfort to rest. Breathing through her mouth, the sounds harsh and loud, her face throbbing almost in time with her heartbeat, she tried to lie still and not disturb Cavaln in the other bunk. She spent those horrible, long hours trying to think of some way, any way at all, in which she might be able to escape from this bottomless chasm that she was trapped within. But there was no escape that she could imagine. Three women had died here already, as well as the others she could not identify; many more prisoners were threatened! Despair filled her.

Ethrayne greeted that second morning out from the island with gloomy resignation; she still had not slept a wink and she could feel her exhaustion like a physical presence within her. Her eyes were now swollen practically shut, she still couldn't breathe through her nose, but at least her nose had stopped leaking blood, although it felt as though it was now at least twice as large as her fist. She crept out of the cabin at first light, or just after, served herself porridge which was much harder to eat than soup had been, but filled her stomach wonderfully, then moved to the bow of the ship, staring despairingly across the endless ocean, until she heard Cavaln's voice, whereupon she fled back to the small cabin, the heat only assuaged slightly by throwing the windows open wide . . . The day passed at an agonising slow pace but, inevitably, evening came around and she was finally summoned to the main cabin for dinner.

King Gregnor did not acknowledge her presence in the main cabin, but he watched her almost all the time, or so she believed, trembling terribly as she sat eating the soup that had been prepared for her, along with, greatly daring, some little bits of softened flat bread, which only really needed swallowing, soaked in the soup. Tears stung at her eyes, partly due to her injuries as well as her unhappiness, and she strove to keep her emotions contained, her gaze fixed on the table top, her free hand clenched in her lap. The jajozeli-razine talked idly around her, tall and threatening, but she could only focus on *him* and, naturally, her own dilemma.

"Ethrayne."

The girl jumped in her seat and some of the Generals laughed a little. "You-your Majesty?"

"You really ought to rest tonight, I am aware that you have not slept." Gregnor informed her in a light tone. "General Cavaln has prepared you a draught." He lifted a plain tin cup and handed it to Ackat, so it passed between Generals at the table until it was set before her, the liquid within it a pale, opaque orange.

"May-may I enquire whether it is poison, your Majesty?" Ethrayne asked in her rough, gravelly voice, suddenly full of fatalistic daring.

He laughed aloud at that. "No, it's only a sleeping draught, child. Drink it now, go to your bed and you will sleep. I will see you after breakfast, as arranged and don't forget your items from the island." Ethrayne flashed a moment's glance at the king, then at the cup, doubt filling her, but she slowly picked it up. "Drink it, Ethrayne." He commanded. With a shiver, she downed the stuff in three swallows. It tasted sharp, sweet, yet also oddly herby;

she licked her lips to remove any traces, set the cup down and hazarded a second look at Gregnor at the far end of the table; his gaze was sharp, measuring her yet again.

"Go to your cabin, the drug works quite quickly. Good night, child."

"Your Majesty, my Lords, Lady -." With a careful half bow as she rose, Ethrayne stepped around the bench and chairs and left them, closing the door with relief. Feeling slightly light-headed, she descended the ladder and entered the small cabin below, immensely relieved to be excused another long evening in their presence. She quickly made her few preparations for bed as her light-headedness increased; lying down, pulling the blanket over her body just because its weight was comforting, she tumbled almost instantaneously into sleep.

*

She woke gradually to a day already fully light, for dawn had long-since passed, one of few that she had missed during nearly every day of the voyage. Ethrayne sat up and stretched, aware then that her body did not hurt as much, and her mind was blessedly clear of that numb exhaustion, although her face, of course, felt just as bad. Stretching for a second time just because it felt good, she threw off the blanket and stood up, nearly stepping in a bucket of warm water that had been set by the foot of her bunk. Obviously, someone thought that she should wash again, which amused her, she had always been fastidious regarding cleanliness.

The usual business of rising, washing herself and what clothes she could, plus dressing in shirt and leggings took a little time, then she picked up the pouch that she had made to contain her beach treasures on the island, which had been stuffed in her bag; she fastened a thong about it to make a handle to loop around her wrist, then she tidied her bed, folding her blanket and nightdress neatly, all too aware that she was delaying leaving the cabin. She wondered why the king had told her to bring those things; it made no sense to her, but she supposed there was a reason for it, he might even explain it . . . As she finger-combed her hair, she shuddered with a touch of ice that belied the hot air entering through the open window.

Although the sun was not very high above the horizon to their right, it felt later. Breakfast had been cooked and Sepphar glared at her as usual, as she served herself porridge, spreading fruit conserve on one of the rounds of flat breads which were still slightly warm. She ate the porridge as quickly as she could, lodged out in the doorway to keep out of the chef's way, thankful that her jaw was at least starting to allow her to chew a little, not that that was necessary with porridge, of course; then she took a mug of tea and the bread up to the main deck, eating, drinking and staring out at the sunlit water as usual, enjoying her seeming solitude as some of the Generals and crew got on with tasks elsewhere on board.

<*Come, Ethrayne, it is time for your instruction to begin.*>

She nearly dropped her mug as Gregnor's voice sounded in her head and shivered again. <*I-I will just return my cup to the galley, Sire, if I may?*> She ventured in a shaky whisper and sensed his consent. Tossing the last bit of bread over the rail for the fish or seabirds, Ethrayne hurried below, exchanging the single mug for a broad tray containing the gleaming gold teapot with its black, shining handle and cups at Sepphar's command, leaning heavily against the side wall for balance as she ascended the ladder. Pausing, taking a deep, audible breath, she tapped nervously on the door and heard the king's call.

Again, he was already sat at the table, this time gazing out at the wake of the ship, waving her curtly to sit down.

"You can pour, put your bag of shells on the table." He said.

"Yes, your Majesty." She whispered, but still stood there uncertainly in the middle of the cabin, the tray shaking in her hands.

He glanced around and grinned, showing his large white teeth to good effect. "Sit, girl. Have you *ever* just done what you were told to? Once in your life?"

"Err . . . probably not, y-your Majesty." Ethrayne admitted truthfully, setting the tray down, taking her seat and pouring a darker shade of hot liquid into the mugs. Only then did she take the cloth bag from her wrist, place it by the teapot, then politely set one mug before him.

"Before we begin, I have something for you." Gregnor held out his right hand which had been empty a moment before, but now it held what was unmistakeably a large, ornately decorated silver-framed mirror. "Take it, child and look." He held it up, so the mirror was facing her, his eyes shining with malice, his smile just as twisted as she stared at him in brief horror. "Go on."

Nothing could have prepared her for the reality of her injuries. The acute pain of his blow, the blood and discomfort following had been somehow separate, or so it seemed. Ethrayne stared, aghast, at a short-haired, utter stranger with a revolting, misshapen face who was staring back at her. She set the mirror down as quickly as she dared, fighting against tears and some nausea.

Almost all her face was bruised, from her jaw to her brow; her eyes were swollen, blackened and still as nearly closed; her nose really did seem to be the size of her fist and her left cheek and jaw line were also lumpy and misshapen. Overall, she was completely unrecognisable, and she wore an indelible mask painted brilliantly in black, purple, red, green and yellow . . . <*No-no wonder everything hurts so awfully, S-Sire.*>

"Ha, good!" He laughed aloud at her silently whispered words, for a breath or two. "That is your warning, girl: of what will happen each time you might think of defying me or neglecting your lessons. You have a great deal to learn, and I imagine that some of it will not be easy to master, but if I am certain that you are striving to succeed, you will not be censured for slowness.

"You will learn to control yourself, your mind and the power which resides within you. In a few days you will also resume your combat training, so at least you will not be able to complain of boredom." He grinned again at the dismay and fear that she felt, that she was emanating. “So, to begin; you should not need to write anything down at this stage. By the way, I recall that you were learning to read and write jajozeli before we left Zanezli?”

“Yes, your Majesty. I was having difficulty with-with tenses.” She whispered.

“Hmm. Well, language studies can resume when we reach Ban’Ganleth. As you may already know, child, we razine hold an innate force that most humans lack: power, talent, strength; it could even be called magic, I suppose. It lies within us and we control it and utilise it using our minds. You know who created us first and then humans, experimenting, it would seem.” His tone was steady but seemed disapproving. “Some razine have a great deal of power and some do not; most humans don’t have a jot of it, yet a very few of you do, and perhaps you and the prince were actually naturally born with a measure of talent, even I do not know.” Gregnor shrugged slightly. “Personally, I suspect that you were. There is a sort of logic there: even imprisoned as he is, frozen, Arven might well be able to somehow influence the focus of his prophecy and it would make the addition of a portion of his own power slightly less of a shock to your human minds and bodies if you already possessed some.

“You stopped short of describing that moment of transition to me, when the Casket opened for you, and we will certainly discuss it in the future, Ethrayne, but for now you need to start with the absolute basics: learning how to use and control your mental muscles. To which end, you will find that these will be most useful.” He reached across the table to pat the small pouch.

Large within her mind was the name: Ban’Ganleth, the words echoing now in translation – Fortress of the Master. It was not reassuring.

“Excuse me, your Majesty, but, but may I ask a-a question?” Ethrayne ventured after a moment, asking despite her intense fear, lifting her cup in both hands and taking a sip of the cooling liquid, it was still flavourless.

“You may.”

“Th-thank you . . . I, we wondered how you could possibly have known to prepare for Jerryn and myself growing up? The prophecy is ancient. Archpriest Bahlien said that Lord Arven ignored the book after it was written . . .” Her voice faded out and she kept her gaze fixed fearfully on the cup in her hands. Hopelessly, she expected that her bone-deep terror of the Betrayer would never lessen.

“That day, on the Solstice, I absorbed some of his power, his strength and it’s the easiest way to describe it, I suppose; it has been wrapped around my soul for a very long time, after all. Actually, that’s a very good question . . .” Gregnor considered in silence for a time, his face calm and Ethrayne sipped at her tea in growing dread. “I have never seen the book, but I learned of its existence and, somewhat, of its contents through the powers that I control, when I had mastered them. I knew almost immediately when you and the boy were born. Oh yes, I was expecting your births and I knew then, over seventeen years ago, that you would be the ones to take the Flame, the ones chosen." He smiled widely at the amazement Ethrayne revealed. "I have been rather impatient during the greater part of the last two decades, waiting for you to reach adulthood. I will use this knowledge of his prophecies to my own end – which is why you are here!"

Ethrayne's astonishment gave way to, well, she sensed a roiling mixture of raw fear, awe and an undercurrent of anger that she knew that she must conceal from the king at all costs at his cold, unfeeling explanation.

"Now empty out those things you collected on the beach."

The objects made a very small, sand-specked pile on the tabletop: seven shells; four little stones; the gold coin, plus the delicate, tiny flint arrowhead.

Gregnor picked up the gold coin and the arrowhead, seeming to weigh them in his hand and gazing at them intently, then selecting each stone and shell in turn for equal appraisal. "An interesting collection; the arrowhead is nearly as old as Iullyn itself, I've no idea how it ended up on a tiny island in the middle of the ocean; the coin now belongs to me, it's nearly four hundred years old, I see; you have rose quartz, granite; amethyst and an actual chip of sapphire. I want you to pick up one of these things and look at it. This is where you study will begin, Ethrayne, with these objects."

Ethrayne looked at him, the frown obvious in her mind if not on her heavily bruised face, then fixed her gaze back on the tabletop. "I-I'm afraid I-I do not understand, Sire." She whispered fearfully.

He rolled his eyes and even sighed slightly. "Listen, child and look and use your mind. Here." He dropped the small arrowhead into her palm. "Look at it, child: study the marks created by the man who made it all those millennia ago, the shape of it, the very rock it was chipped from. Open your mind and look through that too. Go on -."

She shrank back in her seat, shaking visibly. "Y -you are scaring me." She quavered, alarmed by his intense tone and expression. "I-I will try, your Majesty -."

"Just look at it, girl." Gregnor interrupted, but as if he was deliberately curbing his impatience. "Ignore my presence for now and look."

Ignoring the world-sized, mind-scrambling presence of the emperor of the jajozeli-razine was profoundly difficult, when he filled her mind and her being so completely but, by fixing her gaze on the small, flaked, intricately shaped fragment of pale greyish stone, Ethrayne did study it with her eyes. After quite a while of *this is really, really, stupid!* ringing in her head, that opinion also faded, and she actually did begin to see some of the details of the small thing; it was as if the tiny curves that shaped the blade of the arrowhead became a little more visible somehow . . . fascinated despite her fears, she stared and stared -.

"Oh, it's gone!" Ethrayne had blinked for a moment longer, perhaps the ship had moved differently, or something else entirely. Now, the arrowhead was just a small, grey, delicately shaped piece of flint. But Ethrayne felt exhausted, as if she had been sparring for half a morning with the Generals, and not sat at ease staring at a fragment of rock.

"Hmm, that's a start, excellent, child." Gregnor said almost approvingly from across the room. At some point he had moved from his seat at the table to the divan on the other side of the cabin without her noticing, silently watching her all the time. And, amazingly, she realised that she *had* forgotten his overriding presence confusing and frightening her. "Take the things with you. I suggest that you go, eat something and rest up on deck for a while. I will see you again in the morning."

"Y-yes, your Majesty." She faltered, all her fear returning with its full strength as she crammed the shells and so on into the rough pouch then rose quickly to her feet, shaking . . . but she had to pause, for her head span wildly and her eyes showed strange jagged shapes for a moment until, as it abated, and her vision returned to normal; she backed away, knelt and then almost ran from his sitting room.

How very strange. She thought to herself a while later, sat out of the way on the main deck by the remaining housing for the landing craft, leaning on the boat in the shade with food and water close to hand. *It feels like only a short time yet it's well after noon now, so was I sat there just looking at my arrowhead for most of the morning? But-but nothing happened!*

Yet, deep inside, she knew that her assessment was not strictly correct: now somewhere within her, she could sense a tiny flicker, a *movement*, almost a *presence* that she had not felt since her capture. She felt strange, too: she almost had a headache, but it wasn't that exactly; her skin felt tender, as if she had brushed against nettles, but it was fading quickly, and her eyesight was now somehow a bit clearer, as if her time of intense concentration had caused a degree of change within her, or so she tried to describe it.

Bahlien had said that her acceptance of the Flame would alter her, but after so many moons of fear and inertia, she supposed, the process of learning, forcefully, how to use this talent would have other effects . . . After all, over an entire year had passed since then! That was frightening: a year or more since her betrothal to Jerryn and their acceptance of the Flame! . . . But she could only wish that the king, the Betrayer himself, was not teaching her! That she was in Tenum City or Clirensar; that the horrors of the jajozeli-razine had never descended upon them all, to cause so much horror and destruction!

The Betrayer's assertion of his purpose had shocked her to the core: that she, and Jerryn as well, would be used by him to destroy their God! She just could not accept it – it was so contrary to what the prophecy had said, the verse identifying herself and Jerryn – yet Ethrayne could not even start to puzzle out how she, alone, might ever be able to counter the king's demands.

* * *

CHAPTER 37

"Beware, they're attacking!" Savalle yelled in selithian, just before he died with a sword-thrust through his spine. The shout went up, now repeated from all quarters; although unwanted and unexpected, the new thrust by the enemy had been perceived and the warning was now spreading out from the central square of the city, even as the jajozeli-razine advanced.

Master Cheltor had instigated opening the portal upon receiving the faint, rather garbled warning from Cal'Badon as the razine had attacked his colleagues with their minds. Such was his speciality, what he had been trained to: sensitive to a level far beyond most jajozeli-razine, he was the Lord Defender of Zanezli as well as Weapons Master. Creating and guiding a gateway across the continent was not easy, but his focus on the alert was absolute and the Generals and civilian jajozeli-razine present in Ban'Lerracon had all complied with his command and hurried to give him their strength. Even so, the night was passing before the gateway was stable enough to permit the armed force to advance through it, to walk in a heartbeat or two into Devacknon Square, appearing amid flaring garish lights through a portal from Ban'Lerracon. Cheltor had been the first of the fifty Generals through and had taken grim delight in slaying the young razine sailor giving the rather shrill warning.

Humans, especially from selith, usually considered the razine to be immortal, impervious to blade or illness, but the reality was quite different: they could be killed, but not easily, by either humans or razine; although their innate power and generally faster instincts gave them a good level of additional protection. Master Cheltor was one of the best combatants in his emperor's service, which was why he was not called *General*; hence his almost constant presence in the combat halls, training his subordinates and peers.

"Spread out, get to the docks, destroy their ships!" He bellowed to the largest number of Generals. "The rest of you follow!" He led them southward through the largely ruined city, drawn by the sense of power and the explosions that were so clear in that direction, fire reflecting brightly from the bare sides of the mountains above. The ground moved slightly beneath his feet, as if some huge animal was starting to wake from sleep, and a shiver of unease ran through him.

Forewarned, the allied attackers halted their retreat to the docks, to turn and face the enemy who were swiftly engaging them. Ashanner urged the humans amongst them to return to their ships, to get ready to sail, but most of them, both Protectorate and Tenarean, disobeyed him. Armed jajozeli-razine closed on them with grim intent, fresh to the fight and the allies were far from fresh and no longer had the element of surprise on their side; all of them, no matter how strong or talented, were weary to some extent.

Captain Eltham blasted out the buildings which were still standing further up the street where he and his crew stood, as the jajozeli-razine closed on them, but the destruction to the Generals was minimal; the group of about five, he was sure there were others close nearby, were yelling at the tops of their lungs, in a mixture of anger and defiance as they ran forward. "Get the bastards!" He shouted, using the words and the volume to diminish his own rising fear and stood fast, his sword held low, his gaze shifting quickly from form to form. Lifting his blade, shouting "For Lord Arven!" He sliced through the ribcage of the General just to his right, feeling the enemy die; he blessed the presence of his crew who blocked the others attacking as he wrenched his blade free of the bone that had temporarily trapped it.

The fighting was intense for some critical moments and although they did kill the Generals, it was certainly not without loss: Lowel and Tanag died, protecting an injured Syme, the youngest man in the crew, now bleeding from gashes in his abdomen. Eltham and his first officer, Vesstelyn, hoisted the man up off the ground and bore him carefully back towards the dock as others of their company engaged the remaining Generals, single-mindedly determined to eliminate them and largely succeeding. From all around, it seemed, the fighting had renewed with a vengeance.

The wide area before the burning warehouses was full of combatants. The group of fourteen edged around the space as best they could, attacking the enemy where necessary, now focussing far more on saving their precious ships, the only means of their escape: without them they were worse than dead! But it would be better to destroy the vessels themselves than have them taken as spoils of war by their sworn enemies.

Ashanner and Lieutenant Carron were back to back, fighting three looming jajozeli-razine, their weapons clashing and ringing; then, they had one opponent less; the third one was down, blood pouring from his chest; then the second was cut apart.

"Save the ships!" Eltham bellowed, turning to assist Vesstelyn who had supported the unconscious Syme during the short battle. "Go men, go!"

"Aye, Captain!"

But the fighting continued; both sides desperate to win through to the ships, as many of the Tenareans died, paying with their lives in their determination to do their duty to their allies. There was no quarter given, for there was too much history, too much hatred on both sides. There were few amongst the injured who would not soon die from their wounds, unless treated quickly.

Ashanner and the rest of the surviving force of Tenarean and Protectorate volunteers finally met the defenders of their ships, having cut down the enemy, but at huge cost: the dock ran with blood, was littered with bodies; they now counted less than half the men they had landed with, including six walking – or carried – wounded.

"We've got to get out of here!" Ashanner yelled. "There are more Generals nearby; we've got to warn Kierven and Amdor, or we're all worse than dead!"

"But what about Phellos?" Carron from the Veddock Pearl demanded, ducking at a loud explosion somewhere to the south. Lurid fire lit the sky. "We can't leave her -!"

"Calm, you fool!" Lieutenant Hachorn interjected. "Phellos and her men would not thank us for putting everyone else at further risk. That volcano is rising: this whole bloody valley's going to vanish by dawn; dear Arven, she's amazing!"

They studied the remaining parts of the city that they could see, through the smoke, fire and darkness as their remaining men and razine quickly boarded the ships, having quickly set a wall of fire to isolate the dock as far as they could from encroaching Generals. The Mador Opal, however, was invisible, still out of sight; although the sky above the mountains far above was starting to lighten slightly, just a hint of grey visible, the inlet was not only as dark as ever, but a stinking murk was spreading fog, or cloud, or smoke, there was no real way to tell, but the sulphurous fumes gave them warning of what would come, catching in their throats.

"No." Ashanner overrode their objections, although he sympathised with their argument: he had to work hard to suppress his own feelings, and it hurt. "We have to get out, now! We cannot leave the kingdoms defenceless whilst we have life and sails. We all swore on our God's name on what we have to do now! Phellos knows the risks as well as the rest of us and we'll pray to Arven constantly that the Mador Opal and her crew are already on their way to the ocean. Let's go, men!"

But they were the last ship to leave the burning dock and Ashanner kept his gaze on the southern area of the dock as Hachorn brought the Orbain Pearl about, slipping out into the safety of the inlet, beyond reach of land-based enemies, heading away from the danger of the shaking expanse of Cal'Badon, watching the fires they had set spread outwards, meeting other, hotter, fires, as they sailed away towards the dawn.

*

Captain Phellos watched the tall, thin figure emerge from the perimeter of the surrounding buildings with no change of expression; here was the bastard who had made the portal from Ban'Lerracon and she would be thrice damned if he survived their meeting!

"Most creative, woman, I admire your style." Cheltor said calmly as a spurt of brilliant orange fire headed towards the sky, painting them all garishly before the light vanished again.

"You will address me as 'Captain', General." She answered, her heart in her boots for a tense moment, although she would sooner have jumped into the awakening volcano than admitted that fear to anyone.

"Ah, the infamous Captain Phellos, most marvellous. I am Master Cheltor, Lord Defender of Zanezli in his majesty's absence." His cold eyes shone in an unnervingly feral way in the intermittent light cast by the spewing birth of the volcano and his long sword also reflected the firelight and the magma.

"Really?" Phellos's tone was cool. "Then I will have to do my best to deprive the Betrayer of your existence!" Without warning, she attacked -.

"Ha! Good, Captain!" The habit of appraisal and comment in his day-to-day role was not to be lightly cast aside. Cheltor took a side step and attacked in turn, both blades shining intermittently with red and orange flares. There was no more chance or attempt at conversation, only the ring and scrape of swords colliding.

The jajozeli-razine was every bit as competent as Phellos had expected; he was a skilled swordsman and frighteningly fast. She honestly suspected that her own skill might not be quite up to his professional level yet was counting on his use of so much power, the sheer physical and mental effort in creating the portal gateway that she had sensed, to slow him down a little. She tried to ignore the fact that she had been spending her own strength freely on awakening the volcano which was now bucking the ground violently beneath her feet.

Fighting for her life, as her opponent fought for his, she could only pray that her crew and the rest of the volunteers had made it back to the ships and to freedom and long life! Whatever else happened this day, Cal'Badon would soon vanish in unquenchable fire, never again to send ships out to terrorise and destroy the innocent on land and sea. Phellos willingly gave herself to that fire, to the furtherance of Arven's Prophecy and the two young Am'maiya . . . But she would do her utmost to kill Cheltor first.

In the area around the open expanse where Phellos and Cheltor battled, other equally intense fights took place, although nearly all of them were resolved, either one way or the other, a great deal more quickly. Tiring, her arms burning, her legs feeling a little shaky, her lungs starting to labour, Phellos set her jaw, all too aware that her enemy was grinning broadly; although he was clearly also tiring, his stamina and skill were truly as great as his title of Master warranted, no matter his age. It felt as though they had been duelling for an age, but much less time had passed -.

A sudden new stripe of bright pain flared across her ribs, added to the ones on her left arm and her right thigh: long cuts from her enemy's sword, that hopefully were not deep or wide. Phellos had inflicted similar damage on Cheltor: fortune had been with her! Garnering her strength, dancing away although her legs were trembling even more, she thrust again, using her weight behind it to knock his long, lethal blade aside. And was amazed when her sword sliced an arc from his brow, through his left eye and down his cheek, blood pouring suddenly from his face -.

"Bitch!" Cheltor lunged forward, knocking her weapon from her hand by the sheer strength of his body. He dropped his own sword and Phellos screamed in shock as a long knife was rammed home through her right shoulder, followed by a swipe from his leg that knocked her feet from the ground. "Take that, *Captain*!" He spat, pulled his dagger from her body, then used the hilt to hit the woman hard over the head with it, twice and she stopped struggling, rendered insensible.

As if her incapacitation had been a signal of some kind, the increasing rumbling of the volcanic forces below his feet became a great blast of fire and sound, deafeningly loud, as Cheltor staggered, staring from his one remaining eye at a fountain of liquid fire that was shooting at least a hundred feet into the air barely a hundred yards away, if that. Concern showed on his lined, blood-covered face for a moment then, ignoring his own injuries, he bent down to retrieve his weapons, taking time to wipe the blades clean with a cloth before sheathing them. He picked up the unconscious woman with a grunt of effort and hoisted her, just, over his right shoulder, wincing slightly as he slowly straightened, then set off at a tired trudge towards the waterside some distance away. Clearly, the only possibility of escaping this conflagration would be by ship: he could not have raised a portal if his life depended on it. Which it did, he reflected with a moment's grim smile.

The dock area was also growing foggy with the smoke from the fires set by the damned attackers, but he noted an increasing stink of sulphur amid the other fumes, hot and metallic, all of which caught sharply in his throat, nose and lungs as Master Cheltor advanced, limping, blood running, cooling, down his face and his front, Phellos' body seriously hampering the speed with which he could advance; there seemed to be no one around who could assist him: he could see only smoke and darker fumes eddying about.

The range of wharves off to his left were burning furiously by the time he caught sight of the large ship standing almost ethereally at the edge of the dock to his right, its masts and rails almost hidden in the murk. Wincing, he drew his sword again, for he did not yet know whether the craft was held by friend or foe: he had heard nothing for ages; after all his cohorts could all be dead, and the Protectorate bastards would just cut him down -.

"Master!" A dark figure emerged from out of the shadows on the deck as he advanced, and he recognised General Shuim by his large, muscular outline as much as his voice. "You-you're injured, sir -."

"Later, Shuim." Cheltor turned his head as another, even larger explosion rocked the ground, even affecting the water, tossing the large ship slightly, painting everything with fiery scarlet light from the ground to the peaks of the mountains behind. "You hold the ship?"

"Aye Master, but it was close." The jajozeli-razine was heading down the gangplank and quickly took the unconscious woman from his superior. "There are seven of us and five prisoners: two razine, three humans and -." He flinched and ducked as another spout of liquid fire flared up somewhere towards the centre of the city. "Blood and shit!"

"Let's leave, yes?" Cheltor suggested drily, already unfastening the thick ropes from fore and aft that held the ships secure. "Before we're roasted?"

Shuim had negotiated the gangplank easily, but the older jajozeli-razine climbed the slope slowly, grimacing slightly, feeling his age as he had not ever done before. The General set the woman down on deck, hauled up the ramp with enviable ease, then stamped loudly on the planking. "Hoy! On deck you lot! Move, Generals!" He yelled. "It's time to leave, gentlemen!" Behind him, Cheltor was slowly pulling in the rope at the rear of the huge craft, then limped determinedly to the bow to do the same.

"Pirris!" General Tegene came outside from the dark hole that was the doorway into the ship below the raised stern deck. "Now that's impressive!"

"Shut up, Tegene. We've got to get this ship out of range or we're all dead." Master Cheltor growled, the rope heavy in his arms. "I may have beaten all of you regularly at combat for years, but I know absolutely nothing about sailing ships."

"I know something. Robonnare, Alach and Pasqua know more than I, Master." General Tegene stated, shaking his head at the on-going and unstoppable destruction of Cal'Badon. "The prisoners are secure; oh, another one." He glanced down at the still unconscious woman.

"The previous captain." Cheltor explained briefly as the others burst out onto the deck and the slightly shorter and stockier Pasqua climbed to the stern deck and started bellowing orders which the others quickly obeyed. "Thank the emperor for some brains." He muttered, wincing as he dropped the rope then sank down onto the deck not far from where Phellos lay. He would be no use yet on board the ship, and he could start quelling the bleeding from the woman's slash down his face; his shirt, he had noticed, was wet with blood.

Slowly, under General Pasqua's direction, the ship was shoved away from the wharf and the hot wind from the conflagration and growing volcanic activity filled the sails dropped by the Generals who were balancing from the yardarm of the main mast.

"Pirris! You should see the city from here!" Alach shouted down in dismayed awe, staring out over Cal'Badon as it turned from city to volcano. "There are three craters now and a fourth is spewing up lava near the city gates! Oh hell!" He exclaimed as, frighteningly quickly, burning rocks suddenly began flying with deadly intent, some reaching impressive heights and distances from the volcano; by some miracle, all of them missed the ship entirely although quite a few landed, hissing and exploding, into the sea, which seemed to boil as they hit! The city was vanishing, it seemed and soon all the dead, Protectorate, Tenarean and Jajozeli, would be immolated together.

By dawn, the Mador Pearl was nearly two leagues down the inlet and the Generals had relaxed enough from the initial threat to finally deal with the injuries of Master Cheltor and the semi-conscious Captain Phellos, both of whom were borne to the main cabin under the stern deck where General Shuim took charge. General Tegene suggested that he try and find something to make breakfast with, or even just a drink, but he was clearly dismayed by the size of the tiny galley below. Pasqua was in command, and the other Generals were also on deck, keeping a close eye on the spouting liquid fire and the flying lava that were now reaching maybe a good few thousand feet into the sky and growing; the sound of lava evaporating the sea water at the end of the inlet was also loud, and gritty steam, fumes and smoke were billowing out beyond their position, shrouding the steep-sized fjord in murk nearly as impenetrable as the night had been. Even the sea was covered with dust and grit.

"Well, Master, I'm afraid I can't save your eye." Shuim admitted regretfully, having cleaned the five-inch gash that Phellos had given his superior.

"I thought not." Cheltor said coolly. "Just stitch me up, then see to the woman. I'll think we'll need the good Captain Phellos."

"Oh?" The General enquired.

"Later, Shuim. I need to speak to Tequan there in Ban'Lerracon." The master told him shortly.

*

Further down the inlet, the Pearls headed as swiftly as they could in relay towards Cal'Lilse, waving a Tenarean flag desperately from the bow: the pre-arranged warning for the expected quick departure, just in case the Tenarean ships hadn't got their earlier warning of waving lit torches, to get them moving from where they had been moored; but there were the ships ahead of them, thank Arven!

The day seemed to have crept along for them as they had sailed all too slowly away from their enemy's burning stronghold, blessing the hot wind that aided their advance. Although their lookouts had stared out until their eyes ached, searching the inlet around and behind them since first light, they had not seen any sign at of the Mador Opal, a fact which concerned all the survivors. But even in the pre-dawn darkness when they had all fled to their ships, it had been clear that Captain Phellos had begun something awe-inspiring and unstoppable: the city was burning, collapsing . . . They all prayed for her, her crew and the Tenareans who had volunteered to accompany them whilst she had awakened the beast of the volcanic forces beneath. Now, in the cloudy, smoky, indistinct light of day, the topography of the inlet seemed to funnel the sounds of the explosions quite spectacularly and the burning lava, now miles behind, was still visible as a distant fiery glow.

Lord Kierven's Sweet Rose soon joined them, leaving nothing behind in the strategic fort but oil-fuelled fires in every building. The nobleman's heart had sunk, seeing the lack of the Mador Opal instantly as a very bad omen, but he praised his crew warmly as they sailed eastward into the indistinct day.

"This entire venture depended far too greatly on pure luck along with aid from Lord Arven." He remarked heavily to his first officer. "T'would have been a miracle indeed if everyone had come out of it alive and whole, may Arven bless their souls."

"Amen."

*

Advancing cautiously under as much cover as the eruption could gift them, concealed amid the dust clouds, steam and smoke that were being blown from the land down the inlet, General Pasqua hung back, keeping close to the dark northern slope to gain more concealment. His watchman, General Robonnare, uncomfortably ensconced in the crow's nest atop the main mast, his nose and mouth covered with a damp cloth, could see the very tip of one of the Pearl ship's masts far ahead as she headed into clearer air sailing into the east, and so becoming more visible.

<Wait, the shores straighten ahead, there's a view for leagues.> Robonnare told his new captain. *<Are you really going to follow them, Pasqua? They outnumber us considerably.>* There was a measure of doubt in his mental tone.

<Don't be stupid, fool. We're waiting for Master Cheltor's input. I just want to get out of this potential death-trap alive, with our prisoners.> Pasqua replied shortly. "Drop the anchor!" He yelled to Tegene. "Keep watch ahead and on the volcano behind us, too." He ordered and headed for the main cabin.

Master Cheltor sat to one side, his sword belt naturally still around his hips, bandages wrapped around his left thigh, both upper arms and across his face, hiding his left eye completely. Shuim was leaning over a second figure, the captured captain who sat on a stool, naked from the waist up as the General finished wrapping a thick bandage around her right shoulder, breast and upper arm. There was a second bandage about her ribs, below her breasts, but the lesser cuts on her arms and thigh, almost mirroring the ones that she had inflicted on Cheltor, were just dabbed at as Shuim finished his work. Her red hair was tousled, her face pallid; she had lost quite a lot of blood from the knife wound, for her torso was streaked with it and it had soaked into her leggings. Despite her discomfort and disquiet, however, she was resolutely maintaining a stoic silence regarding her injuries.

"We have stopped, Master Cheltor. The enemy were briefly in view, heading for the ocean." He reported respectfully.

"Dear Arven, what sort of terminology is *that?*" Phellos commented in a tone of low contempt. "Who put you in charge, idiot?"

Pasqua stared at her for a moment. "Master Cheltor did, actually, woman, since I know the most about ships of all of us."

"There, done." Shuim stated.

"Then I will pray to Arven for a storm to quickly sink us!" The woman said levelly as, slowly and carefully, with only one workable arm, she pulled the ripped and blood-stained shirt Shuim had removed earlier back over her head.

"Shut up, Phellos." Cheltor ordered but in a mild tone. "You might have destroyed Cal'Badon rather effectively, but you, along with some of your crew and your ship, now belong to the Emperor of the Jajozeli Empire. Gornen, take her to the hold, and restrain her well." The last was a bellow. His lungs certainly had not been affected by his injuries.

Another General quickly came through the door and grinned. "As you command, Master Cheltor." He said respectfully. "On your feet, bitch!"

"My name, General, is Captain Phellos." She retorted but could not halt a visible wince of discomfort that she quickly suppressed, as the jajozeli-razine deliberately took hold of her right upper arm and pulled her upright.

"Pleased to make your acquaintance, *Captain.* I'm sure, however, that you are going to deeply regret ever meeting us!" He laughed coldly as he marched her out of what had been her cabin, a large, scar-faced General who had suffered few injuries during the battle.

"That I do not doubt." She sighed quietly.

The lower passage was unlit, until Gornen made a small sphere of light that bobbed along near the beams of the low ceiling; they both had to duck a little to advance. The forward hold, it seemed, had been hurriedly rearranged when the jajozeli-razine had wrested control of the vessel. The boxes, bundles and food supplies were now piled rather messily in the passage, whilst Phellos found herself joining a clearly dispirited group of frightened, injured men and razine locked where her main cargo had been.

"Captain!" Lunde cried sharply in dismay as Phellos found herself bound tightly at wrists, ankles and knees by the General in the doorway, then knocked to the floor with no regard for her injuries.

"Oh, damn it, Captain!" Old Dhell muttered succinctly as the hold door was slammed shut and locked firmly, leaving them in complete darkness. "I hoped you got to one of the other ships, Ma'am!"

"Damn the bastards indeed, good Captain Dhell." Phellos answered with a sigh, trying to ease the discomfort of her bandaged shoulder. "Who else has been captured, Lunde?"

"Rynn, Captain." Rynn piped up from over to the left, one of the newest members of her crew; the young razine had joined at Lerat nearly a year earlier.

"Zeron, Captain." One of the middle-aged men of her crew stated levelly. "I was here with Dhell when they used their talent to neutralise us, the bastards."

"Fereyne, Captain, Ma'am." Another voice stated in selithian, one of Lord Kierven's men. "I'm sorry we failed you, Ma'am -."

"We have not failed, gentlemen. I released the volcano and its might from beneath Cal'Badon, and our companions are well ahead sailing towards the open ocean, apparently; that's why the ship is presently at anchor." Phellos related with some satisfaction. "We might wish that we had died after that bloody General Cheltor raised a damned portal; he's a weapons master of note, it seems, but I nearly killed him and we've dealt the bastards a huge blow: the city is turning into a vast pit of molten rock, it seems, so it will be completely unusable for decades at least; there's nothing else of use in this inlet, if the men leaving have destroyed the forts as they intended, so we've hopefully limited or even stopped their depredations on this side of the continent." She hissed as she jarred her shoulder.

"Captain, are you badly hurt?" Dhell asked in concern a moment before Lunde could speak; the old fellow was most solicitous, and she managed a grim, toothy smile in the darkness.

"Well, Cheltor and I were exchanging blows for quite a while and both of us were injured. How about you lot?" Was all she admitted.

"Nothing worth mentioning, Captain." Lunde said with stout bravado, but Phellos knew that he was lying. With her power, although still exhausted from raising the magma and from her injuries, she could tell that he had suffered concussion as well as a long gash to his back; Dhell was nursing a mass of cuts and bruises where he had been literally thrown to the dock from the deck of the ship; Rynn had been patched up with bandages around his abdomen, although fortunately the knife had missed anything vital; Zeron had similar wounds to his back and shoulders, whilst Fereyne had both a broken shoulder and a broken nose.

"That's good, I suppose, it could be worse for all of us. Let's rest." She suggested with mock cheerfulness. "At least we can stretch out in here."

"Aye, Captain." Dhellos agreed promptly. "It's larger than my fishing boat, isn't it?"

"Well, yes, I suppose it is." And she had to suppress a half-despairing burst emotion at his ready answer. She had hoped that everyone else had got away, for so she had prayed, during her desperate battle with Cheltor; but neither had they escaped through death.

Phellos winced again, her injured shoulder agonizing. The General had cleaned it and bandaged it, a courtesy she had not really expected, but with the bonds confining her wrists and the ones on her legs, she could not get into a comfortable position on the bare planks of the hold and she supposed that her cohorts were having similar problems. The fact that their enemies had taken the time to tend them was rather worrying, to her mind: it did not bode well for them and she was quietly concerned at their captors' purpose. They all knew what the jajozeli-razine were capable of and she breathed deeply, resolving to hold off fear at all costs for it would only weaken her.

Time passed slowly in the darkness, as they felt the swell of the sea beneath them, hearing the occasional boom reverberating from the mountains around them, as the ground heaved at the head of the inlet. Huddled on the planks, hungry, thirsty, restrained by their bonds, the prisoners could only lie there helplessly, wondering in silent trepidation what was happening and what the future would hold for them, in the merciless hands of their enemies. No one came. It felt as though a lifetime had passed before they finally heard the anchor being raised and the Mador Pearl slowly set off.

* * *

CHAPTER 38

The campaign to re-take Clirensar continued apace. Duke Pualyn had stated bleakly, his face pale but resolute, in their first meeting after their return from the heart-breaking remains of Callorton and South Vale Farm, that the only safe way to enter the city that he could think of was to use the siege engines which had been designed and constructed as part of their strategy as their main weapon, or else lose thousands upon thousands of men storming gates that likely concealed who knew what defensive structures. The commanders, both noble and military, argued this for a day, but in the end they all agreed with Pualyn's bleak assessment.

The engineers and mathematicians were then in charge for a period, poring over plans and calculations, improving and improvising the frameworks to throw even larger rocks, or bundles of spears or something else; fire was suggested, fuelled by bitumen or pine resin, but each adaptation was worked through quite slowly, the calculations checked, so as not to endanger those working the machines. The soldiers fretted at the delays incurred, but it was impossible to advance otherwise; it was painful to see the city, so loved by many, so vital to the region's and the kingdom's economy, being steadily destroyed, but no one could think of any alternative.

Once the engines had been adapted, the rest of the army simply had to defend them. The enemy commander sent out sorties at the start of the siege, but these halted after the latest horrific assault, during which at least five thousand jajozeli had died, more of a bloodbath than a battle, to the attackers' minds. The beautiful and carefully managed coppiced woodlands that edged the Sare valley were in real danger of disappearing entirely, so much wood was required to burn the bodies that littered the ground, threatening all their health.

"D'you think that that bastard in charge is discouraged in any way, at losing so many soldiers?" Jerryn asked Pualyn, after the latest mounds of the enemy dead had been systematically consumed by fire; the stink had sickened them all, whichever way the wind had blown. They were both on horseback, on a hilltop a good half a mile from the city walls, looking out over the hard, heavy, dangerous work going on at various points around the city, surrounded by the Flame Guard as always.

"I bloody hope so." The young duke responded coldly. "He deserves it, certainly." He still harboured a single-minded determination to slaughter General Tequan himself, no matter what else happened or what obstacles were in his path, and nothing anyone could say would persuade him to pursue a slightly less risky agenda. "It's going to cost a fortune or maybe two to rebuild the city, perhaps more and I bet they've stolen the contents of the treasury and everything else of value they've found!"

"Yes, I agree, Pualyn." Jerryn agreed with a heavy sigh. "But even if it takes the rest of our lives and most of the money in Tenarum, we will restore

Clirensar. You know, I thought this part of the siege might take much longer; that's what all the professionals say, isn't it, in those hugely heavy books purchased from the universities in the Protectorates, that we studied when we were younger? It's been six days since our people started throwing rocks and there are already some bloody big cracks in the city walls."

"But cracks aren't going to let us in, it still will take time, Jerryn, don't get your hopes up." Pualyn said and managed one of his now rare smiles. "You'll see, we'll rebuild the city walls twice as thick next time, and then nothing will dent them. Don't forget that we've been refining the designs every few days, judging by what's happening. I think your father was rather surprised to discover he had such a flair for engineering."

"Yes, all those figures and angles make my head spin, frankly." Jerryn commented.

"Liar, I've seen you sat there poring over the plans." The duke countered and stretched in his saddle. "I tell you, I'll be glad when this is over, provided we survive the next few days, Arven willing."

"Amen to that." Jerryn said earnestly. "But it's all this hanging about I hate: it's somehow worse than the initial battles were: we were too worried to consider just how terrible it would get; and Arven only know what we'll find when we do finally get inside the city? I sure as hell didn't think about the end of the process." He shuddered.

"Are you sure you were thinking at all, Highness?"

"Probably more than you were, Clirensar." The prince laughed slightly and Pualyn, after a short pause, did also. "Come on, let's find some lunch: I'm starving."

"We could mark the day using your stomach, lad."

"Oh, shut up, Pualyn; then Lennarn can try to rob more pennies from us at Stepping Stones or dice."

"It was a bad day when that man learned to gamble, for the rest of us, anyway. Why can't you use your magic to turn the dice in our favour, hey?" Pualyn complained and the valet grinned broadly, winking at the guards.

"Sod off." Jerryn stated with familiar affection, but the banter set him thinking. His conversations, his jokes, were all a mask – he could not get his fears out of his mind, or his regret that he was unable to use his power as Captains Phellos and Ashanner had asserted, in their venture to destroy Cal'Badon. Both Mhezal and Kerrenan had assured him that his ability was improving, but he knew that he was only advancing slowly in his mastery of what he had naively considered he would command easily, after more than a year! He resolved to ask the razine more about the power which he could quite often sense deep within himself, but it was peculiar to consider using it *properly*, as he used his hands, for example, rather than mostly exercising his mind as he strove to protect himself from everyone else's fear and anger. With the days slowly passing, spring now advancing, he could feel the Flame inside, late in the night when he was drifting towards sleep, something simultaneously both alien and part of him. It was frightening to acknowledge that he bore a third of his God's strength inside him . . . he and Ethrayne had been so innocent, so ignorant.

Dear Arven, please protect her from our enemies! He repeated the heart-felt prayer again; the words were almost always in some part of his mind: he was determined to utter the prayer at least five times a day, even if their God was imprisoned helplessly in ice and sick of hearing the words.

*

"So, we should be able to advance on the city tomorrow?" King Marrand asked eagerly, as the commanders came together for the evening meal that night. "The other gates are neutralised? You're sure of that?"

"Yes, unless the jajozeli can fly, your Majesty." Commander Vedeigne grinned; they were rather pleased with the massive pits dug before the south- and west-facing gates of Clirensar and the huge ramparts made from the soil and rocks from those holes. It had been risky, but the soldiers digging had been protected by 'roofs' constructed from shields fastened together and a second layer of wet cowhides; in this way, no matter what the defenders had thrown down from the walls, it had mostly been deflected without causing much injury. Those two gates could now be held securely by only a few hundred allied soldiers each, unless the enemy were particularly tricky and illogical. The western pit had filled with river water, whilst the southern pit was too deep and wide for any ladder to cross without a number being lashed together; they hoped so, for it had been an enormous undertaking for the already worn soldiers and their superiors, since Jerryn had suggested that they all help in the work. Isolating those gates at least meant that their forces were safer from large-scale sorties, leaving only the north, river gate, accessible for the enemy locked inside Clirensar.

The rocks lobbed into the city had certainly caused a great deal of damage, but despite their excellent engineers, it was a broad form of attack, lacking any real finesse and they could not really depend on the massive mangonels to pulverise the entire length of the walls. Yet again, their plans had been refined.

The mood in the plain command pavilion was still serious, if rather more positive that it had been a moon before battle had commenced. Although, of course, awful events might occur again the future to put them at a serious disadvantage, the allies had acquitted themselves well as a group thus far. They were no longer novices. Even the newest volunteer walked with assurance now, yet most of them still detested the job that they were undertaking, even if their enemies were doing their utmost to slaughter them in return.

Any sensible defender, of course, would concentrate his soldiers around the gate that the attackers would throw themselves against. But they were not sure whether General Tequan was sensible, or logical. Well over fifteen thousand jajozeli lives had been thrown away so far in the conflict. It seemed that Tequan's master, the Betrayer, counted those lives not at all, unlike the allied kings and commanders who, conversely, fretted probably too much over the lives spent in trying to liberate Clirensar.

"There's something foul waiting for us inside those gates, I'm sure." Jerryn was convinced of it and most of the others agreed with him, especially after that brief discussion with General Tequan so many days before. "I just wish we could prepare for it, whatever it might be!" The city must have had its full complement of citizens, of course, when the jajozeli had occupied it, as would the castle on the crag above. After the brutal deaths of Shan, the duke, duchess and their entourage, Jerryn could not imagine what might be the fate of the people held hostage by such pitiless enemies.

"But we are prepared, Jerryn." The High-King tried to reassure him. "When we finally get through those gates, past the walls, we will all progress most carefully, expecting pit-falls and traps with every step; the enemy have had plenty of time to construct all manner of things to hurt our advance. But we will neutralise them. We will advance and retake the castle."

The prince nodded agreement, but his mood had darkened. *<And it's because of me!>* He added silently, his worry evident. "*Dear Arven, I feel like such a coward -.>*

<Am'maiya, you are no coward. And this is for all of us – we all *must stand against the Betrayer. You cannot assume any guilt for the betrayer's evil! There are risks enough without you and Pualyn being right in the vanguard.>* Mhezal countered firmly. *<We are leading, and there will be fighting enough for everyone, I'm sure.>*

<That's what's worrying me most, your Majesty.> Jerryn admitted quietly. *<There's no alternative: we must destroy the jajozeli, but so many families will lose their fathers, sons and brothers . . . I keep praying that we are worth their loss!>*

<You are gaining wisdom, Jerryn and, like you, I and the others can only pray that our cause is worthy enough.> The razine said.

*

Some strange-minded individuals, whilst appreciating the sheer hard work of the infantry and the technical advances of the siege engines, took a rather different approach to the task of freeing Clirensar from the jajozeli. Instead of looking at the walls and gates of the city, they studied the great limestone cliff that formed its eastern side and, indeed, the actual edge of the castle above. This extended from the bank of the river, forming a natural barrier at the east of the wharves at the foot of the city walls to the north, and stretched south, a pale precipice jutting out of the green grass and rubble that formed its foot, a good two hundred feet tall if it was an inch, topped by the rear of the castle.

"We could climb that crag, you know." Captain Robard stated one evening to the High-Prince, when he had delivered his usual report on food supplies and sanitation.

"What crag?" Kerrenan had asked; it had been a long day and he was unusually tired, having been up since before dawn, supervising the additions to their water supplies.

"That crag, Highness." Robard pointed in the direction of the city, although they were in the prince's tent. "The one the citadel's stood on."

"It's sheer rock, how on Iullyn could anyone climb it?" He asked, shaking his head. "And, more importantly, *why* would anyone climb it?"

Robard grinned and shrugged. "We like climbing cliffs, me, Lieutenant Harrisen, some others. We even go out into the Edge Lands beyond Lerat to the north and scale those crags, bottom to top; you wouldn't believe how exhilarating it is!" He paused and grinned broadly, a tall razine with greying hair and soft grey-blue eyes in a square–jawed face. "We do it because it's exciting, but we've been thinking and planning a little; if anyone *could* get up that cliff when the occupiers were all concentrating on the front of the castle and the gates for instance, it might be possible to get over the walls above and attack the bastards from the rear. They certainly wouldn't be expecting it, would they?"

Kerrenan looked at him for a long moment. "You haven't been drinking, have you, Robard?" He asked in a level tone. "That's the most bloody ridiculous idea I've heard yet! We don't have time for stupidity, Captain."

"Actually, it's not ridiculous, your Highness, not if you think about it properly." Robard protested, but in a mild, reasonable tone that exuded confidence. "You have never climbed rock faces for the challenge and amusement and I bet none of the jajozeli have either. They won't be considering the remote possibility that anyone would even attempt to ascend that cliff to attack them, it looks far too smooth to climb, at first glance." He grinned again, a mischievous expression that made him look almost like an errant schoolboy. "But it isn't, you know."

"It isn't what, Robard?" The High-Prince asked, in a slightly weary tone. "Stop smiling like you've stolen an entire cask of wine and got away with it. Dear Arven, explain! I'm tired, man."

"Harrisen and I went to look, yesterday, when we were off duty: just marching about the perimeter, and we climbed a good thirty feet up from the base in a short time: it's full of useful little cracks and ledges, as far as we can tell; and those of us who know what to do could climb it rather easily, bearing ropes and weapons, and we could haul up less confident men and kit by those ropes, then go and attack the enemy in the most secure part of their stronghold. No one from the citadel above could possibly have seen us there at the base for a moment, there're overhangs and bushes near the summit, undergrowth at the bottom. If we had a hundred men or so – and there are ten of us amongst our army who like scaling rock faces – then we'd have ten each to guide up the face, say; and then we could possibly make a real difference, couldn't we?"

Kerrenan stared at him. "You know, this year seems to be the year of the absolutely ridiculous suggestion. First it was Ashanner and Phellos' idea to attack Cal'Badon and now this! I ask you! Robard, this is madness! For a start, you have no idea whether you'd even be able to get over the walls above the edge of the cliff."

"True, but Duke Pualyn would probably know, wouldn't he? We could ask him: he grew up there, he knows the castle intimately." Robard suggested instantly, unconcerned at the High-Prince's negativity. "Of course, there're bound to be guards around even on the back walls, but it doesn't look as if any extra breastwork has been added to them, as far as we can tell. And we could always descend quietly again if we can't get over, fasten the ropes to a safe point and climb down, before we hauled anyone up."

"You're very confident in your abilities, Robard." Kerr noted. "But, dear Arven, what about losing your grip and falling? That ground below the cliff is covered in rubble; we had a look in the area, in case of any caves or passages leading into the rock and it's a mess of rubble. You'd be dead and very broken if you fell, dear Arven!" He shuddered. "And you'd have to climb at night, so there'd be no visibility. No, it's too dangerous, Captain."

"But your Highness, for the risk to a few of us – only ten men initially – we might be able to significantly assist the final assault on the castle, when that moment comes." Robard continued in his persuasive fashion. "You really wouldn't miss those few from the main conflict who have the knowledge to climb the rock, which might help save thousands, or hundreds, at least, when the gates are stormed. I'm confident we could initialise it, you know; and we could put together a plan, highlight the sort of equipment we would need, which is only very good, long ropes and maybe some iron hooks. Please, your Highness, could I put a proposal together and maybe ask Duke Pualyn about the layout of the castle? We will not attempt it, if the commanders veto the plan, of course, but for a bit of effort on my part, please?" He paused. "It's only a waste of mine and Harrisen's time, after all, in addition to our official roles."

Kerrenan looked at the razine, a level-headed man who was considerably older and more sensible than he was himself, generally. He must be confident, he acknowledged to himself and felt a strange mix of emotions inside: a surge of excitement that such an audacious scheme might possibly succeed, plus doubt that it was at all possible.

"All right, Robard, you can ask Duke Pualyn if he might agree to assist your hare-brained plan and come up with a proposal to set before the commanders, but I don't really think that they'll support it." He conceded. "And you've got two days."

"Thank you, your Highness and honestly, you won't regret this; I'll get on with it immediately." And Captain Robard dashed off like a man a good few centuries younger.

*

Reports finally came upstream Saremouth from Lord Kierven and Captain Ashanner, giving details of the success of the destruction of Cal'Badon, the loss of Captain Phellos and so many others. It was bitter-sweet, that so many brave individuals had been lost, and amazing to hear even a little detail regarding the volcanoes that had emerged from the very earth to wipe out the city.

The arranged discussion for the climbers' proposal took place two evenings later, during the dinner-meeting that extended beyond the usual reports from the scouts, supply logisticians and regular patrols that took place earlier. Unlike Ashanner and Phellos' intentions for attacking Cal'Badon, Captain Robard did indeed create a most detailed presentation, including drawings of the projected route up the nearly eighty-yard wide cliff-face, the sorts of knots that he would suggest to hold the soldiers secure on the rope, one of which he brought in to show its strength, and a report on what he intended to do, if and when he managed to scale the castle walls at the top of the precipice. He spoke confidently and was clearly at ease, even when describing a process that was alien to nearly all his audience.

"His Grace has provided Harrisen and me with a great deal of information on the layout of the castle." Robard bowed politely to Pualyn, who was sitting beside Prince Jerryn with a non-plussed expression on his face, as if he were struggling to decide whether to laugh or be amazed at the plan. "Clearly, the enemy didn't think of scaling the cliff; they hardly needed to, if they managed to sneak a few Generals or soldiers through the main gates: and the lack of awareness of the population around Clirensar after their take-over certainly points to some such subterfuge." He sighed. "It was clearly an audacious scheme, for who, logically, could have anticipated it? Perhaps, this idea of ours is equally as audacious, as mad as the High-Prince declared. As to whether they have not even considered the precipice as a possible risk, we cannot assume anything. They are Generals, after all. But we will hopefully be able to clamber over the wall at a critical moment and startle them enough that a hundred and ten allies will make a considerable difference to the outcome." He straightened, produced a final sheaf of parchments showing a detailed plan of the layout of the walls and buildings that abutted the cliff top and grinned widely from face to face, his eyes twinkling.

"I know that most of you think we're crazy, I can read your thoughts and faces, but, well, it's something that might actually work, at a minimal risk to the entire allied forces. I'll leave you to discuss the matter, your Majesties, my lords and gentlemen, but if you come up with any questions, please just ask Harrisen or myself, we will be happy to answer them. We've done our best to cover most sensible propositions, but we acknowledge that we might not have thought of everything." He bowed low and strode from the pavilion, leaving silence in his wake.

"He's mad!" Duke Agamn of Amorry commented after a moment, but he reached for one of the sketches of the cliff front which Robard had prepared, frowning down at it. "I've never heard anything so completely ludicrous!"

"Oh, I don't know, Agamn." His king, Namayomn, countered, shifting his shoulders. "He's certainly identified a route that no one's considered before."

“Because no one’s stupid enough to climb up precipitous rock faces, your Majesty.” Commander Vedeigne muttered. “Dear Arven, can you imagine it?” He shuddered.

“I take it that you don’t want to volunteer, Commander?” Jerryn asked with a smile.

“Dear Arven, no, your Highness!” Vedeigne exclaimed vehemently. “Men like them might like such a challenge, but the sheer thought of hanging off a cliff with all that air beneath my feet fills me with horror.” Then he smiled happily. “But I’ll say this: I never would have expected a suggestion such as this, not ever, so I might be willing to wager that the enemy haven’t. I’ve watched your faces and all of you were clearly as stunned as I was at the captain’s proposal. Might it work? You know, it’s a possibility, your Majesties, my Lords.”

“It’s audacious, but it’ll delay our advance, surely.” Tarlan, the Crown Prince of Derravale objected. “We have been delayed enough by the adaptations to the siege engines and surely speed is of the essence, gentlemen?”

“Yes, but once we begin our final assault, we have no idea how long it will take; it won’t be over in a couple of days, that’s for certain.” Marrand countered seriously. “Our advance will be slow, and I can’t see that the alternative plans of this small group would hinder the main business of taking the north gate in any way.”

“What do you think of Robard’s idea, Pualyn?” Jerryn asked, aware that his friend had been very quiet on the matter, although he must have known of it, to draw plans of his castle home. “I bet it’s something you’ve never considered.”

“Dear Arven, no! But, from our point of view, Robard’s right: surprise will be on their side and I must admit that there are be parts of the ramparts over the cliff where enterprising men possibly could gain access to the castle, unless the enemy have done some amazingly invisible stonework, which I doubt.” He shrugged. “It might well work, and it would surely be to our advantage if even a hundred men could assault the castle from the rear, if the rest of us were holding their attention. It might swing the advantage in our favour – and we need all the luck we can get.”

“Amen to that.” Jerryn sighed, wondering if they might possibly take the castle, considering the trouble which had assailed Ashanner and his fellow captains – leaving the Mador Opal to burn, most likely, with their audacious plan which had succeeded with the loss of Captain Phellos and many other brave men. His sense of foreboding was only increasing, day on day. He could dimly sense the jarring power of the Generals holed up in the city and the discomfort of it, his concern for the safety of his father and his friends across the kingdoms, did not help. He could only keep his shields high and do his best, although he knew that the jajozeli-razine would be waiting for him to enter the city.

In the end, swayed by the duke’s support, the commanders agreed to assist Captain Robard, Lieutenant Harrisen and the others get to the point where the could assail the rear of the castle once the army were advancing through the city below.

On hearing of this, the next morning the rock climbers started finalising their requests for equipment such as ropes, hooks and so on with complete enthusiasm, and put out the word for volunteers to join their ascent of the cliff face. A surprising number, to the commanders' amazement, did so. Apparently, scrambling up vertical rock faces was more popular than anyone had imagined.

* * *

CHAPTER 39

Again, Jerryn didn't sleep, the night before the next phase of their attack was due to begin and, in the end, he got up and dressed and alternately paced the tent restlessly or stood still, fighting an anger he knew to be futile. All in all, he decided, on towards dawn, he absolutely hated war, but, until such a primitive tool was no longer required in the world, he supposed it was best to master it.

And, the truth boiled within him, wasn't that what he and Ethrayne were supposed to do: to end the need for war by freeing Arven and destroying the Betrayer? He shivered, there in the darkness, realising again just how deeply he was missing his betrothed, how much he feared for her safety; yet, surely, he was the one in the most danger now, facing injury or capture every day. Thank Arven, Ethrayne was safe in their enemy's hands; uneasily, Jerryn remembered how he had protested at Archpriest Bahlien's description in the autumn. How naive he had been! And now they were about to advance and spend far too many lives, to try and break through the gates into the city! Jerryn knew that he was dreading it. And the enemy were always watching from their vantage points within Clirensar, so they were fully aware that the allies were planning another attack. Quietly, he spat curses, dreading the day.

Dawn arrived all too quickly. Their plans, equipment and men were all prepared, along with replacement siege engines in case of breakages along with metal-work and wooden beams, in addition to the huge mounds of fresh supplies brought in from Foston. So many nights had been spent poring over their plans after each day's fighting: the building and arrangements organised, that it was almost a let-down for *the day* to finally arrive: an anti-climax of a vast proportion.

The eve of their assault, of course, had been largely sleepless for many, ordinary soldiers as well as Jerryn and the other commanders. So much was resting on their hard work and efforts now on in. It was heartening, however, to be moving to this point and not just circling the city, not able to begin to retake it!

The first light of that day was initially marked by the cessation of the actions of the machines lobbing rocks rhythmically into Clirensar, as the allied forces gathered on the now dusty, mud-churned field on the outer curve of the River Sare, watching the High-Prince who was commanding the mixed group which, protected by the innovative interlocking-shield roof that they had devised, was driving an enormous iron-tipped tree trunk towards the massive gates that gave admittance to the city; the ram was resting on a specially low slung wheeled cart that took the oak tree's great weight, it's massive, thick wheels moving ponderously but inexorably across the dusty ground. The sound of the ram colliding with the ancient timbers of the gate was deep and seemed to travel right through the ground as well as through the air.

BOOM! Again. And again. And again. Rhythmically, almost like a huge drum. It seemed that the damaged walls on either side of the gates shivered slightly with every blow. BOOM!

The defenders poured molten lead down onto the crew pushing the battering ram but, with their locked shield roof, the injuries sustained from the red-hot metal were, luckily, negligible. The allied soldiers amassed out of bowshot of the walls watched and jeered, cheers and shouts echoed up and down the valley as the assault continued.

The sun had moved perhaps only three finger breadths or so above the horizon when the first few initial splits finally showed in the thick gates which had already taken so much battering from the siege engines. Finally, to the attackers' relief, the wood was starting to weaken, and the cracks quickly lengthened and widened as the men kept ramming the tree trunk against it.

Another huge roar set any remaining wildlife in the area into instant flight when the great gates burst open with a crash which could be felt as well as heard across the Vale, followed by another deafening BOOM! A twenty-foot wide part of the wall to the left crumbled into a mess of rubble without warning, raising a huge cloud of dust and debris. It was nearly noon by then. As arranged, as drilled into them, the ramming crew quickly hauled the battering ram backwards out of the gateway and shifted to the left of the road to permit the fiercely yelling vanguard through, five thousand volunteers comprising men and razine from every army, under the High-King. Behind them, hundreds of archers waited in lines, bows and arrows held loose in their hands, ready and poised to fire.

There was a moment where everyone at the front of the army seemed to stop in their advance – staring for a moment, freezing, astonished – for a fifty-foot high wall had been built right across the main street, maybe a hundred feet inside the gates. It was a solid-looking barrier upon which a company of the enemy soldiers were confidently stood, shaking their weapons, jeering.

"Well, that's unexpected." Mhezal commented drily, before raising his sword to point it straight at the wall. "Burst!" He shouted in mendor. A flash of power ran, raising goose-bumps and shivers through the minds of everyone within five miles before, to the allies' amazement and the enemy's dismay, the stones of the wall began to topple as if there was no mortar fixing them; no solid ground supporting them; as if a river had washed its base away, or an earthquake had shaken its solidity to wreckage. The jajozeli on the parapet ran for their lives as the wall collapsed, leaving a heaped mass of rubble in the thirty-foot wide street, nearly as high as the buildings to either side, dotted here and there with the bodies of those who had not been able to retreat in time. "Attack!" Mhezal yelled then, rousing his troops from their momentary abstraction.

"Good God!" Jerryn remarked to Kerrenan, from their vantage point out of arrowshot of the walls; the High-Prince had retreated there, his men having moved the ram further out of the way of the armies. "How? I mean, Lord, that was *power*!"

"Father doesn't often display it, but he has talent beyond most razine." Kerrenan said with a grin. "He's been itching for something physical to do for days, though it will tire him considerably. Quite soon you'll be able to do things like that just as easily, Jerryn."

"Yes, if you give me another few years to study, maybe." The young man grimaced.

"You've been improving in your focus, Jerryn, you're far too hard on yourself." The High-Prince answered. "Yes!" He exclaimed, as a jajozeli flag was replaced with Arven's.

His enthusiasm was contagious and Jerryn found himself grinning broadly. "Well, we've been planning for this for moons, it's good to take the next step!" He agreed, then sighed a little. "Though we'll have to rebuild the entire city -." Then he ducked, along with everyone else in the vicinity, at a loud explosion that sent a cloud of dark smoke into the sky from within the city. "Dear Arven, I'd rather be there than here!" He fretted.

Slowly and carefully, the troops advanced through the ruined gates and over the remains of the wall, protected to a certain extent by the arrow storm of their archers, sweeping their combatants off the walls and rooftops. Some soldiers began trying to clear the rubble of the inner wall out of the way, handing it back out beyond the city gates as the others strode forward, all grateful for the presence of the razine amongst them: able to give warning or an odd, mental sort of shielding against arrows and missiles from the rooftops above.

The next two thousand men to enter Clirensar simply concentrated on getting to the rooftops themselves, with bows, arrows and hooked lines; the buildings lining the main road were swiftly broken into and the upper levels quickly attained, where they began to range outward to secure the area around the gate for the purposes of both advance and, if necessary, retreat. Keeping hold of the ground that they had taken was certainly a priority. No one wanted to do this monumental task a second time.

To their dismay, it quickly became apparent that the enemy commanders had altered the layout of the city during their occupation. It appeared that the detailed maps they held might well be useless: buildings had been torn down, other walls and different routes constructed, around the fixed points of the cathedral and the castle above. Reports were gathered and passed back along the companies: '*don't rely on the maps, go carefully; and make plans if possible as you go*'. Their advance, it seemed, would be far slower than anyone wanted, but that would surely be preferable to rushing into a situation where they might lose men unnecessarily.

"It looks like a labyrinth in there." Mhezal reported wearily late that evening, having returned to the command pavilion after hours of slow, careful progress. He was as tired, as aching and as dirty as anyone he had led that day, battle taking no notice of rank or position. "It's a complete muddle! I'm sorry, Pualyn, but it is." He continued after taking a drink of wine. "Buildings are pulled down or ruined, roads are blocked, and new roads are lined with removable barriers at some points I think. They've really worked hard at making the city impenetrable since they took control, and it will slow us down considerably, just trying to work out if a construction is solid or designed to collapse on us! Let alone neutralising any traps they've made! And we've not had a sniff of a jajozeli General all day, not a one!"

He had passed on command to Colonel Varle of Derravale for the securing of their occupied portion of the city overnight; about five thousand men were now ranged throughout an area a couple of hundred yards on a side, where they lit lines of bonfires to assist the guarding, to prevent the enemy from sneaking up in the darkness.

"The Generals are holed up in the castle?" Pualyn asked heavily, then answered his own question. "Well, of course they are, it's the strongest defensive structure in the city. They'll want us to work for every step to the top of the crag. And they've trashed the city!" From what he had seen from the periphery, the state of his home had completely shocked him: he had not expected to find such a drastic alteration since the moons of occupation, even though, logically, he knew he should have done. The wholesale destruction had reawakened his depression.

"Truly, your Grace. Well, there's no help for it: we've got to keep advancing, even if it is a step at a time, at a snail's pace." King Marrand said, trying to return some positivity to the meeting. "We control all the hinterland, don't forget Pualyn: there is nowhere for the enemy to go, they cannot escape, and we know all the sally-points and secret exits."

"That's what's worrying me, Marrand." King Namayomn of Amorry growled. "They'll be trying to kill as many of us as they possibly can; wholesale destruction indeed."

"And trying to get their hands on me, of course." Jerryn interjected then. "If they took me hostage, Arven forbid, they'll be able to walk right out unscathed -."

"Over my dead body!" Kerrenan retorted vehemently. "It'll never happen!"

<*Then there is no chance or uncertainty in battle, highness?*> Jerryn asked rather acidly, so that no one else could hear. <*No matter how well protected I am, we can't guarantee a bloody thing and you know it!*>

"Well, at least Robard and Harrisen are positive – they're amassing all sorts of equipment for their part of the assault and training volunteers." Mhezal said, finally, ignoring that negativity.

*

Thousands of jajozeli died, in fierce and single-minded defence of their positions, over the next four days as the allies slowly and painfully advanced, carefully removing the traps, demolishing defences and making their own. By the fifth evening, they held the northern half of the city entirely; by the afternoon of the ninth day, they held Clirensar, up to the castle walls which loomed ominously above them in a way that none of them had ever before considered: the castle was a truly formidable structure. It was depressing to stare up and up at the Betrayer's standards flying from the towers in wind-swept defiance.

In addition, they had found no sign of any survivors from the jajozeli occupation of the city, although, shockingly, they had found bodies in various states of decomposition and heaps of bones as well, strewn all over; both in the streets and in many buildings as well. It was frightening to discover that after all their moons of worry, the citizens of Clirensar had been apparently massacred: men, women and children alike. There were old bodies, rotting in gibbets; nooses hanging from the bell tower of the cathedral and other high points – evidence that some poor souls had died recently, in agony. Children as well as adults. It was chilling to see the myth of the jajozeli fabled cruelty proved as fact.

Nerves were very taut as the commanders rested that ninth night in the range of servant's and ancillary buildings at the edge of the cathedral complex. They had thought to use the cathedral itself as a new headquarters, but the old edifice, with its ancient buttresses and high windows seemed to have been deliberately targeted by the servants of the Betrayer. Many - not only priests and priestesses, had been assaulted here, before they had been slaughtered. There was a palpable air of desecration about the place to Jerryn's senses that went far beyond the piles of filth and corpses and the wanton destruction which had occurred there. . Even walking into the previously hallowed space made him almost physically sick; he had had to stop, breathing deeply to control it, whilst his guards and companions had begun to search the building.

"I can't stay in here: they've deliberately destroyed Arven's sanctuary!" He muttered to Tymain, looking around a heart of horror rather than what had been a peaceful, hallowed hall. He did not start to feel better until he had walked up and down the perimeter courtyard for a while. Most men wondered what had affected him, but the razine amongst them could feel what he had experienced, and it was oddly reassuring to see that Mhezal, Kerrenan and the others were just as pale and sickened as he had been.

A group of the walking wounded had already volunteered to start cleaning up the cathedral and its associated buildings, as others were removing the bodies and the debris from the streets, continuing the movement of masses of food, equipment and all the associated ephemera of war that was required for the movement of the commanders and thousands of allied soldiers who guarded the hard-won perimeter of the city, and continued to search the rubble, possible tunnels, existing buildings, cellars and even the sewers to flush out every last trace of ambush and threat from the enemy. Some additional traps and groups of well-armed, determined enemy soldiers had been found in their midst, but not as many as they feared: the talent of the razine was central to the location of the danger-points, along with the intimate knowledge of Pualyn and other denizens of Clirensar, in securing their own safety. But still, the razine returned to search for a second or even a third time, just in case!

On searching the cathedral area in the centre of the city, the advance guard had found the large pilgrims' hall the best remaining space to house the command: its sheer size and associated kitchen, sleeping rooms, offices and dormitories were ideal for the group; and, after a finger-tip search of every nook and cranny and a necessary scrub, it looked much more comfortable than even the best-appointed tents and pavilions; most of them agreed that they felt more secure with solid walls and slate roofs surrounding them, guarded by thousands of their own troops.

"Dear Arven, I'm sick of this place!" Pualyn muttered, shrugging his shoulders expressively that first night when they had moved their equipment into the city, safely encamped in the visitors' dining hall that adjoined the ruined cloistered garden which had previously been such a delight. He, like all of them, was leaner, stronger from the physical work of battle and in fact it was strange that they had all managed to wash and change properly, discarding their chain mail with relief. A large group of soldiers had worked hard at a meal, after cleaning out the kitchen, serving a better meal than they had enjoyed recently, though many of them did not notice. Tymain was now passing along the pulled-together tables where the commanders sat, bearing a jug of watered wine, followed by Lennarn with a second, filling goblets and mugs. "It keeps jarring me: things have been altered so much, the entire city just feels so wrong!" He shuddered with feeling. Many houses had been pulled down, streets rearranged, barriers erected – yet, far worse, were the bodies left seemingly at random, some killed quite recently – their cadavers not yet reduced to bones.

"Yes, I agree." King Marrand said. "It's certainly quite deliberate, of course: to wound us all. The atrocities here likely match those suffered across Mendor after the Betrayer brought war upon that continent, having imprisoned Arven. I'm sorry, Pualyn."

"Well, we know for certain who's to blame, your Majesty: that bastard in charge up in the castle and his master!" Pualyn jerked one thumb in the general direction of the citadel looming above the cathedral's rooftops. "So many folks must have died -." His voice cracked slightly, but every man spoke up and nodded their agreement, admitting to their own distress: the cathedral's central hall had been stacked high with human remains; there had been even more clear evidence of the atrocities committed against the priesthood and the general citizens, in many places. The knowledge sickened them, wounded them, yet it also tempered the nerve of every soldier of all ranks, increasing their determination to succeed.

"Thousands and thousands, men, women and children." Jerryn nearly whispered the words and shivered. "They are cruel, bred to serve their master, the Betrayer, without question. Emotion, morality and common feeling are leached out of them in childhood, it seems. He has created a realm of monsters, trying to make them in his image, mirrors of his own depravity." With a sigh, he looked around the tables, and shrugged. "We owe it to our dead to destroy the jajozeli!"

"Amen!" Pualyn grated and they all raised their cups in a toast. "Destruction to our enemies!" Everyone repeated his words.

*

The main gate to the castle faced south-west, halfway along that range of the roughly diamond shape of the complex within its walls. It was atop a gravel-strewn steep slope up which the road zig-zagged in the open.

Any approach, of course, would be a nightmare, beneath the well-armed defenders that filled the high walls directly above, brandishing their weapons, yelling loudly even as the sky to the east started to lighten. Now, from the safety of the far edge of the large rubble-strewn square that bordered the steep way and hopefully out of reach of arrows or other missiles, the advance forces could see the Generals who had so far proved absent from every single confrontation from the war of attrition that had, finally, brought the allies to the final push. There were about fifteen of them, their power clear, all dressed in black and grey, stood as two groups above the gates that would give admittance to the citadel, surrounded by a good few thousand ordinary troops.

"At least there are more of us left than there are of them!" The High-Prince commented, his tone dark. "Bastards! That's a truly well-constructed outer wall!" He continued in a lighter manner and nodded.

"Thank you." Pualyn offered a quick grin, although his face was pale under his tanned skin. "It's pretty much perfect from the inside; that's how my ancestors designed it, at least, although we never knew who we were meant to be guarding against . . . wolves, maybe, or bears from the mountains to the south, the odd bandit over the centuries . . . oh, shit!" That was almost a moan.

"Yes, I agree, our old castles and forts are all built most robustly, but before the Betrayer we had no enemies. Hessarth and other capital cities are the same – we rebuilt Lerat, of course. Perhaps some influence from Arven suggested defensive construction, I don't know." Mhezal suggested then, frowning. "I might pursue that with Archpriestess Gailla at some point in the future."

"Philosophy, your Majesty?" Crown Prince Tarlan enquired coolly.

"When we have time for such." The High-King answered steadily, his gaze level as he shifted in his saddle.

In the end, ignoring the fact that it took a great deal more time and effort to achieve, the combined armies set about using some of the tons of building stone and roof slates to turn that hundred yards or so of lethal approach into a virtual tunnel on its uphill slope. They constructed large barriers from beams and doors throughout the city, that could be lifted into place, to protect the builders, a mish-mash of metal and wooden structures held together with rough metal frameworks that acted as shields, proof against most of the almost continual barrage of missiles from the castle walls that were mitigated, as far as they could do so, by the razine 'blocking' their soldiers – in effect, using their power to divert the arrows, fireballs, rocks and so forth relatively harmlessly. Even with determination and goodwill and extremely hard work, they managed less than ten feet a day.

Jerryn assisted in this shielding after the first day, under the High-King's tutelage and found the process exhausting. Even though the razine used their strength as a group and thereby increased their overall effectiveness enormously, as a novice the prince discovered that even the concentration required to focus properly left him as tired by noon as if he had been fighting all day.

"You're actually doing very well, Jerryn, but this is a hard task, one that many do not try to master until they are rather capable at other roles." He was reassured by Mhezal's opinion, when he complained at his own weakness. "We're all assisting for a set period, more or less; don't try to strive all day, man! And look: hardly anyone has been injured."

"It's like trying to hold an anvil above one's head for a day." Jerryn wiped sweat from his face. "Am I really helping, or are you humouring me, your Majesty?"

Mhezal shook his head and Kerrenan laughed aloud. "You'll be much stronger than most of us when you reach maturity, Jerryn, but you're starting very well; as father said, don't try to do too much at a time, though." The High-Prince suggested.

"All right." He conceded and frowned. "Have you heard from Captain Robard lately? Are they organised?"

"Dear Arven, yes!" The High-King breathed a chuckle; reassuringly, even he was finding the block of the enemy missiles difficult today, as it seemed that a whole wall had been dismantled to enable the stones to be thrown down from the castle walls with deadly intent. "He and Harrisen have their equipment in place at the base and are just itching to begin, when we give them the word."

"I hope they're patient men: this is going to take forever!" Jerryn grumbled with a sigh, looking up the slope at the defenders atop the wall; again, a couple of Generals were visible now, clearly keeping an eye on them. "D'you know, I'm surprised they haven't emerged to attack us, though; they have the advantage of the crag and any sortie wouldn't be a final commitment: a well-armed company could destroy the wall our men are building quite simply, and we wouldn't find it an easy matter to stop them."

"Yes." Kerrenan agreed, also glaring up at the gates. "When we get closer, I expect they will, but we've still got a good distance to go." He sighed and shook his head. "Dear Arven, I'll be so glad when we've taken the castle!"

*

Captain Garane of the Flame Guard was one of the men killed late in the evening, three days later, when the jajozeli did launch a surprise assault that cost both sides a good few thousand men; the fighting raged down the steep road for most of the night, garishly and unevenly lit by torchlight. All the commanders were involved there before the castle; there was no chance to ensure that Prince Jerryn or Duke Pualyn or any of the kings were not in the vanguard.

When the gates initially opened, on that warm spring evening, Marrand and Mhezal looked at each other. "Shall we send them?" The King of Tenarum asked doubtfully and the High-King grinned and rubbed his hands together as he had, by mind-speech, given the command to the waiting rock-scrambling group who had been loitering at the eastern edge of the wharf, ready and waiting. This might not be the final assault, but it was the first time the gates had been opened since the allies had stormed into the city. They certainly didn't want to be pushed back: too many had died to get to this pivotal point.

"Robard and his group are on their way, Marrand. They're taking double the number of men we initially assessed." The High-King said. "Let's take the castle if we possibly can!"

*

The ten razine, in the quickly fading light that was obscuring the eastern face of the cliff as the sun vanished behind the distant western hills, ascended the cliff with a speed that, to the other men and razine waiting at the foot, was nothing short of spiderlike. Each had long coils of rope with hooks slung around their bodies and their weapons were fastened to their backs; climbing in mail was hard, but none of them cared to proceed without it.

Robard was the first to make the point where the natural rock met the cut stone of the eastern defensive structure of the citadel, finding his way up the cliff by touch and instinct alone, it seemed. There was even a sort of ledge, almost three feet wide in parts, where he could sit, uncoil the rope and hook it into a crevice where the metal stuck and ground quietly. *<Rope descending!>* He silently warned the razine below. *<Start climbing when you're ready.>*

<Aye.> A reply came from Cull on the ground, backed by an evident enthusiasm that made the captain smile.

Lieutenant Harrisen was next to reach a point further along the ledge and both estimated that they had ascended as quickly as they had hoped: the sky beyond the light-blocking crag was still showing a vague orange light that was steadily fading, even though it was now pitch-black on the rock face. *<I'll take charge here, Robard. You'd better see if we can get over the wall.>* He said drily, puffing slightly as he checked his own rope for security. *<Rope descending.>* He also called down. *<It'd be a complete bitch if we're stymied by the wall itself!>*

<Have faith, Harrisen! Trust in Arven.> Robard said breezily. *<See you soon.>* And he got up, heading to the north, his left hand caressing the base of the wall, the sound of his footsteps on the rock only a faint crunching that was swallowed by the overriding sound of the wind at this height, gusting along the crag, making the flags on the poles far above crack every so often.

After some yards, the shelf widened and began to climb; his night-vision showed him only a higher section of natural rock, as far as he could tell and the stonework to his left abutted up to it, fitting securely, but his fingers could feel a slim crack or gap between the wall and the natural limestone, as if perfect abutment had been impossible for the masons who had laboured so long on this impressive construction. The crack was only a few inches wide and seemed, when he ran his hands upwards as far as he could reach, to vary in width. Also, he could feel the bottom level of the building stone, which heartened him even more.

<*Excellent! We should be able to climb up here: there are finger holds aplenty.*> He sent with a satisfied air. <*Thank Arven! Send the men to the right but tell them to lean to the left: it's a narrow ledge at first.*>

<*Yes, we have six up so far.*> Harrisen replied. <*And two more nearly up. Take care.*>

For some unknown reason, climbing, heights and narrow pathways had never worried Robard, not even in the dark – which was a first; vertigo was unknown, he never felt dizzy or unsure of his footing. He reached up with his right hand and found a gap that three fingers fitted easily into, his left clasped the top edge of one of the stones that made up the wall and raised his left foot so that his toes rested on another edge. In this way, he hoped to ascend the final thirty or so feet and, thanking their God all the way, he did so, peeking over the parapet rather like a small boy warily checking that a landowner was out of the way before dashing in to an orchard to steal fruit.

<*I'm up!*> He sent cheerily.

<*That's bloody wonderful! Get out of the way, let's secure the wall: they're starting to climb behind you.*> Was the answer from Cull, close at hand, as Robard edged over the wall and down onto the walkway, which seemed empty. Judging by the faint sounds of shouting and banging that he could now hear, the battle for the gate was occupying everyone's attention, which was better than they had hoped, truth be known. It was now full dark, but there were a few torches around on the perimeter wall that showed it was otherwise empty; it seemed that the sentries had been called to join the general melee, which was even better! Robard crouched down, unfastened his weapons from his back and continued to thank Arven, even as the first of the Tenarean climbers slipped down from the parapet, his mail grating slightly on the stone. The entire group wore dark clothing, to hopefully blend in with the enemy.

"Shit!" The man whispered, his voice quivering, hunkering down to Robard's left and reaching for his own secured weapons. "Oh, shit, Captain!" It was a simple statement of mingled terror and elation that made the razine crack a broad grin.

"Get yourself straight, then secure the far side, Dann; you've done well, thank you." He stated approvingly, buckling his sword belt, straightening his weapons.

Behind him, a second, then a third; regularly, the 'crazy' volunteers reached what would probably turn out to be the most precarious of rest points, until the two hundred and ten were ranged out across the back edge of the citadel, all pretty sure of their position in relation to the yells, clangs and screams coming from the area across the buildings, where a great deal more light was shining, some from torches, others from fires, or so it looked.

"Let's advance: a hundred-and-five each to left and right, as we arranged. Move carefully, I think it's about the middle of the night by the moon, may Arven protect us all!" He hissed.

"Amen!" They whispered as one, and the group set off, so far, so incredibly, somehow invisible to the enemy.

*

After so many days of relative tedium and inactivity, it was a relief to abandon thinking, talking and straining his mental muscles for simple action. Jerryn battled with the rest of the Flame Guard, Pualyn and Kerrenan, working step by step up the road they were striving so hard to command, towards the castle that was so familiar, yet so chilling: home to Pualyn and Ethrayne, yet a nest of monsters. His arms and shoulders ached terribly as he hacked, thrust and fought and killed, his feet slipping in the gore that covered the cobbles, the mail increasingly an uncomfortable weight, even though it saved his life on numerous occasions. His companions, his friends, were close beside him. They all pushed relentlessly but so, so slowly up the road; whilst the enemy strove desperately to push them back down again.

"For the glory of Arven!" He shouted, knocking another jajozeli soldier aside with the side of his sword; stunned, injured or dead, he did not know, in the darkness. It was heartening to hear the words taken up by his compatriots around him, despite the horrible screams and shouts and the deafening clash of battle, of weapons ringing, or of making final and horrible contact with living bodies.

"For Arven!" Echoed from thousands of throats, as distinctive as bells, from the walls above and the ruined city below.

Eventually, when the half moon was sinking towards the west into cloud and lower, thicker cloud was covering most of the sky to the east, promising rain before dawn, the first twenty or so fighters attained the flat space before the massive gates, pressing the jajozeli who had worked so hard to destroy them back against the ancient wooden structures where they had no escape, cut down as more and more allied soldiers reached the level ground. Cries of. "Arven!" Continued to be shouted out. The jajozeli were shouting other things, unintelligible. Jerryn and his group followed on, advancing eagerly.

Then, amazingly, sounds of fierce fighting and yells could be heard from *within* the castle, behind the gate that blocked them. "Arven! For Arven and the Am'maiya!" Rang out, amid shouts of dismay; it seemed that the intrepid rock climbers had succeeded beyond all expectation or even belief. Their fight was not swiftly concluded, even so: it ranged on and on, until, with a loud boom! and a harsh creaking, the gates opened slightly inwards, revealing only a crack, a thin view of badly lit bodies struggling, fighting beyond.

"Get in here!" Captain Robard yelled from the archway above the gate, waving one arm enthusiastically, then ducking a spear that sailed past to his left. "For Arven and the Am'maiya!" He cried, then vanished.

Jerryn swore rather graphically, from where he stood, only about fifty feet now from the level area. "I don't suppose I really thought -!" He muttered and swore again.

"Same here, Jerryn." Kerrenan uttered different curses in admiration. "Crazy buggers!"

"Bloody brilliant!" Pualyn breathed, then swore himself. "Damn it! I'm going to have to rebuild the rear wall of the entire structure, if we survive!"

Jerryn had to quickly suppress a completely irreverent burst of laughter that threatened to take over. "Come on, let's get in there!" He yelled, brandishing his bloodstained sword. "They're vastly outnumbered now! Who's with me?" The men around then shouted agreement.

<Jerryn, you're meant to stay back from the van, away from the Generals.> Kerrenan said silently, his tone respectful. *<They're very tricky bastards -.>*

<Yes, but, by Arven, Kerr, what would you do, if you were me? And it's not as if we're outnumbered, is it? We must have killed most of the jajozeli by now -.>

<But it's the Generals we're worried about!> The High-Prince continued.

<Dear Arven, yes! We have the Generals to eliminate. But I can't stay further back, I can't!> Jerryn shrugged. *<And it's not as if it's just us men alone: you're here, all the Protectorate razine. I'm going in.>*

<I have a bad feeling about this!> Kerrenan's tone was worried. *<You will stay by me, Am'maiya, at all costs. I know what you asked your friends to swear to, but* I'll *do my best to keep you safe. I promised your father and mine also.>*

<Very well your Highness, thank you, but what will be, will be!> Jerryn's gaze was straight and unafraid, despite the horrors they knew would await them beyond the gates; the last stand of the jajozeli-razine. *<I'll keep close and alert, I promise.>* And he strode forwards with the mass of soldiers, men and razine shoulder to shoulder. He briefly wondered where his father and the High-King and the other commanders were, sure that he wouldn't have been able to bull his way through what he knew would be their stern, unwavering instructions to remain further back in safety; they were nowhere in sight, although he guessed they were not far away. Everyone wanted to take part in what would be, hopefully, the final all-in fighting action.

The soldiers at the front, already on the level, were using brute strength to open the gates wider and awful deep grating sounds accompanied the slow movement of the huge leaves, inching inwards until, with a great crash, the left-hand-side flew backwards, all resistance suddenly gone. The allies dashed through, finding broken beams and stunned jajozeli who had been trying to hold the gates; the remaining dark-clad rock-climbers were fighting manfully for their lives against a mass of the enemy.

"For Arven!" The shout went up again, and the jajozeli were outnumbered: hundreds of men and razine seemed to be advancing into the first courtyard of the castle, and Robard's remaining men cheered loudly, the sound deafening as it echoed off the surrounding walls and buildings.

"Help us hold the walls!" Lieutenant Harrisen yelled from above their heads, waving one arm urgently. He, Robard and some others were being sorely pressed by a larger group. Instantly, at least a hundred of the allies were racing for the steps which led up at various points and the fighting above on the battlements was soon as fierce as in the courtyard.

Quickly, the jajozeli were being pushed backwards through the archway that led on to the castle as more and more soldiers flooded through the outer gate, Jerryn, Kerrenan, Pualyn and the Flame Guard amongst them. Flickering torchlight lit up the moving bodies more than the daylight that was now growing, though it was weakened by the rainclouds that indeed had blown over and now had started to drizzle, which at least cooled them at first.

Amazed, Jerryn stopped for a moment, looking from point to point, shocked at the savagery that seemed to have descended upon the combatants; desperate pitched battles were taking place everywhere he looked, somehow more terrible than anything that had happened before, simply because this was Ethrayne and Pualyn's home, their castle! A fierce excitement filled him anew, negating his bone-deep weariness at fighting half the night. After so much heartache, sheer bloody hard work and worry over the last moon and a half of action, it was exhilarating to finally reach the castle's outer court!

He took a breath and ran to the rescue of one Derravane soldier being menaced by two burly jajozeli soldiers and cut one down, then continued with his small group as close as they could keep, despite the jostling bodies and pockets of fighting, heading under the arch and into the huge main courtyard that fronted the central keep.

Heavy fighting occupied them all within moments for the jajozeli were as reckless as anyone could be, faced with almost certain death. The ranks of the allies could only determinedly hold their ground and survive, cutting down the soldiers of the Betrayer as quickly, as competently, as they could. Determined to succeed, to take the castle back. They were all so busy, so focussed on staying alive, that neither Jerryn nor Kerrenan realised at first that they were soon separated, although Sevanter, Karne and Lennarn managed to just stay within sight. Pualyn, Tymain and the Flame Guard had also been diverted. There were only a few of their own men with him, the prince saw with a sinking heart, as he finally had a chance to pause, to look around.

Then, in a heartbeat, the atmosphere in the courtyard utterly changed. Jerryn shivered as power assaulted his senses: fury and hatred hit him so hard, it was almost physically painful. He had to pause and shake his head to try and dispel it, as a burst of fear filled him. *Shit! Perhaps I should have obeyed them, after all . . . But it's too late now!* He thought to himself, trying to mask that fear with bravado.

"Generals!" Kerrenan's bellow sounded harshly even above the fury of battle. "Beware!" <*Jerryn, to me!*> He sent.

Oh damn! Jerryn abruptly remembered just how frightening the aura of the blonde General had been on that day over a year ago above Tenum City; then, how scared he had been, seeing the bearded General who commanded this force that had held Clirensar and his cohorts, speaking to Pualyn and his father before the city. Now, power assailed him from far more than one enemy jajozeli-razine.

Swiftly, he turned about, but he couldn't even see Kerr, for far too many groups of fighters separated them. His fear was mixing with a tinge of despair: General Tequan was after him, he had wilfully ignored that one cold fact. This whole campaign, involving the destruction of Ethrayne and Pualyn's family and Sevanter and Lyria's; occupying the city and murdering both its innocent population and thousands upon thousands of soldiers had been instigated by the enemy simply to facilitate *his* capture as well as Ethrayne's! He began to spit swear-words under his breath. <*Where* are *you?*> He asked the High-Prince, turning, setting out towards the gate, bolstering his courage, stepping over bodies and rubble with the other men in the group following.

<*Yes, this way, back towards the gate-.*> Kerr replied in an urgent tone. <*Don't stop. Run!*>

<*Ha!*> That was a silent shout of triumph, yet although it drowned out some of Kerr's response, it was not from very close by, but from just within the courtyard to Jerryn's left, he thought. <*There you are, boy!*>

"We'll guard you, Highness." Sevanter declared determinedly and Karne and Lennarn nodded. The other soldiers were fully occupied in their own fights of their survival. "Go."

There was still a good chance of retreating, then! He thought with relief and set about forcing his way, so slowly, back towards the promised safety of the archway to the outer courtyard, a step at a time -.

Amid the struggling figures, the piles of bodies that threatened to trip them all, the melee of humans, razine and jajozeli, Jerryn stared back towards the castle, his attention caught by the clear and strong menace exuded by one tall being, the commander, Tequan, who moved confidently and surprisingly easily through the battle. Gulping, turning back to face the danger, Jerryn could only pray that he would be strong enough to hold his own in a duel, despite his deep tiredness, facing one such as this, a man over half a foot taller than he, fresh, hugely strong both physically and mentally. He knew that the razine were mortal: he had seen enough of his compatriots killed, after all, but could he kill the General?

"Bastard!" Rang out then, as loud as Kerrenan's warning shout had been and Jerryn glanced to his right, to where Pualyn stood some distance way, somehow also alone, his surcoat shining in the light which was growing around them. Standing tall, grim faced, the young duke then followed that assessment up with an entire litany on the commander's antecedents and unsavoury habits, delivered most eloquently, as befitted a man of his rank and education.

"Ah, good morning your Grace. Welcome home."

The fear that the simple sound of Tequan's voice evoked in the prince was ridiculous, he thought, even though the commander was now concentrating on Pualyn and not himself.

"I am so pleased to meet you again." He waved his right hand, indicating the castle and city at large, smiling. There was a clear element of mockery in his words as he closed on Pualyn; everyone else still alive was melting quickly out of the way.

Pualyn snarled as he attacked, his sword ringing as it knocked the General's blade aside. Tequan laughed, moving swiftly for such a bulky man, swinging his broadsword as if was weightless; his left handedness probably often proved a great advantage, but the duke simply transferred his blade to his left hand likewise: being ambidextrous had never proved such a godsend!

Jerryn continued to try and retreat away from the duel, but the surrounding, ongoing fights impeded him, as it did the razine and his friends; they were all struggling through knee-deep mud, it seemed, for all the progress any of them were making, trying to keep from being spitted on some enemy soldier's sword as they advanced. Not everyone was battling for their lives, however; not a few were stood, transfixed, as Pualyn and Tequan fought, and these spectators also blocked their movement, their retreat. Jerryn kept glancing around, praying for Pualyn's survival, but Tequan was taller and bulkier and his big frame, wild hair and beard were a bluff: he was fast and light on his feet, his thrusts and movements uniformly smooth, graceful . . . Pualyn was leaner and he was strong, a superb swordsman; his skill with weapons was legendary amongst those who had trained with him since childhood in Clirensar and Tenum City, as well as since this war had begun.

It seemed that the two were very evenly matched, although Pualyn, like the rest of them, had been fighting for most of the night. Their faces set with concentration, the duel continued, their weapons ringing, scraping, sparking as they collided again and again and again . . . Then, in a moment it seemed that the General misjudged slightly: putting just a tiny amount more weight behind his thrust, perhaps. In the blink of an eye Pualyn bent athletically around the long blade and his Black Fell-forged sword ran unstoppably into the General's chest, as close to his heart as possible. Tequan's expression instantly became one of utter shock. Blood ran from his mouth as his young opponent yanked out his blade with a grunt, changed his grip, tossing it into his right hand with a flourish and beheaded him with one swift stroke.

"For my parents, Lyria's family and everyone else you murdered." He said evenly and smiled, relaxing with a breath as the General's body collapsed.

A huge cheer of approval went up from every throat of every allied soldier there.

"Very well done, your Grace!" Jerryn shouted across, raising his own sword in salute, relief flooding him. It was strange: yet again, feeling a razine, even a jajozeli-razine die so close at hand was jarringly intense, revolting, to one with the abilities he was gaining, involving power which he could not block out. But he also was damned pleased that the enemy commander was dead.

"Thank you, Highness -." Pualyn looked back, grinning, as he finished the honorific then the smile vanished from his face, replaced by shock. "Jerryn! Beware, look out -!"

Sevanter shouted out then and Jerryn span around, to see Lyria's brother being beaten backwards by a group of jajozeli.

"Jerryn, go!" Karne shouted his tone urgent, just to his left, followed by a harsh scream and the prince saw his friend and servant die at that moment, a long, sharp blade impacting horribly in his head. Jerryn staggered as he fell, just missing being knocked over by Karne's body. Then, awfully, Lennarn cried out agonisingly, just out of sight beyond the soldiers who had killed Karne -.

Oh, hell, no! Jerryn thought with bitter regret. Then, even as he drew breath, straightening, something struck him hard in the middle of his back and he did collapse; only a sense of self-preservation, the fear of being helpless on the ground, gave him the impetus to twist as he fell, locking his hand on his sword hilt. It hurt incredibly: the blow, the weight of the mail, but Jerryn gritted his teeth, struck back as best he could, his left fist colliding solidly with someone's neck, for whoever had knocked him down was also unbalanced.

Calling upon all his strength, Jerryn got back to his feet and thrust with his blade at the scar-faced General there, slashing him right across the face. The jajozeli-razine screamed as much as Karne had, a shocking red line erupting with blood across both cheeks and his nose, pale bone revealed. Yet, despite this, the General still tried to fight back! Jerryn blocked his unsteady thrust, feeling sickened: he could sense his opponent's pain, but he dared not leave a conscious, dangerous enemy alive. He attacked, gritting his teeth, hating the sensation as his sword sliced into the General's chest, crunching through the mail and bone beyond, nearly getting stuck, as he yanked it back. The bastard was dead, anyway!

<Ah ha!> A voice said clearly in his head, a shout of exultation.

"Oh, shit!" Jerryn muttered to that, turning to his left with his fear choking him, to see at least five or six Generals closing on him, only a few feet away. "Shit, shit, shit!"

<Jerryn!> That was the High-Prince again, but their contact was shattered as, without any warning and completely out of nowhere, there was an intense pressure in his head, a pain which seemed somehow far greater than he could absorb. Jerryn felt it like a sword-thrust right through his mind and it was agonising! The High-King had used his power as a physical force to destroy the wall that had blocked the road at the entrance to the city, but this, this was an amalgamation of the power of all the remaining Generals, unified,

combined and used as a weapon against the allies. He gritted his teeth against it, determined not to cry out at the discomfort and, dear Arven, it was terrible! It weakened his body, ruined his coordination; then part of him realised that the pressure, the pain and immobilising strangeness was not just affecting him. On the edge of his vision, for he dared not shift his focus, he could see both men and razine collapsing, some more than others; many were screaming in agony, whilst others reeled, stunned, on their feet.

As a weapon it was brilliant, he acknowledged, even if part of him was aware that it could not be sustained for long: that much he had learned over the moons from the razine. It was terrible, it was unstoppable, occurring without warning with such a devastating effect.

No, you bastards! He uttered the silent protest, striving to do all that Bahlien, Kerrenan and Mhezal had taught him. But somehow the sensation only worsened, and his own power was somewhere lower than his boot soles, along with his spirit: he could do nothing to counter it although he tried, determinedly straightening, aware that only a moment or two had passed although it felt like a lot longer. Jerryn noticed all of that in the blink of an eye as he tried to make his mind and body work, knowing that he must, or be captured. *Damn them all to hell!* He spat silently, all too aware of their threat, their strength, their collective power surrounding him, as if trying to weaken his resolve if it was at all possible -.

Obviously, the enemy knew who he was: they could sense the slight power within him, quite apart from identifying him from his surcoat. Jerryn took a breath as the small group launched themselves at him, moving silently. He raised his sword and prayed yet again.

Dimly he could hear people shouting, but he could only concentrate on these three jajozeli-razine now, attacking him and it was clear that one of them was the physical focus of the terrible blast of power. Beyond them, he saw that the other Generals were stood shoulder to shoulder, their backs to him, making a barrier between him and any assistance. There were no allied soldiers left standing in this part of the courtyard.

Fighting for his freedom, Jerryn thanked his instructors for the six or seven years that they had pushed him, always pushed him, and worn him out. He had faced three enemies at a time before, in the many battles he had been part of since this campaign had begun, but never three like these! Fighting, battling them as best he could given the obstacles on the ground and his own weakness due to their powerful assault, he noticed odd things at random, thrown into his head: the oldest looking of the three had thick, wavy black hair and a bleak, grim light in his hazel eyes; the one who appeared youngest had light brown hair and an open, handsome face; the third, who might be somewhere in between, had darker brown hair and an old scar set diagonally across the left-hand-side of his face from broken nose to jaw. But none of them looked 'evil'; any one of them could be razine rather than their deadly enemies: the feel of their power making a separation that was profound and absolute, created by the Betrayer. It was only that and their intent, their focus on their master's agenda, which set them apart.

<*That cut must have hurt.*> Part of his mind decided, all weariness forgotten in the simple necessity of protecting himself. And he noted, out of nowhere, that all three jajozeli-razine were not much more than a few inches taller than he.

Spinning, focussing tight with his mind as he had been taught, Jerryn caught scar-face right across the throat with the edge of his sword and felt relief flood through him for a moment as that General fell back, bleeding profusely and certainly neutralised: Jerryn could feel his pain for an instant before he managed to block it, thankful that he had eliminated at least one of them! *Thank Arven!*

But there were still two more of them, and although they were only intent on capturing him and thereby constrained somewhat, the Generals were both swift and capable fighters.

He was aware, at the edge of his notice, that his companions were desperately trying to assist him, but other Generals and jajozeli soldiers were blocking them fiercely; dimly he could identify Pualyn, Tymain and Kerrenan shouting, striving but failing to break through the living barrier, no matter how many they managed to cut down.

I bloody-well walked right into this, this is simply all my fault! Jerryn castigated himself using every curse word he had ever heard, the rhythm of the words in his head matching his movements as he attacked and attacked, trying to force the two Generals away into the line of jajozeli blocking them from his friends, trying to disable or kill them -.

A far more physical agony affected Jerryn a moment later and, still, only a short time had actually passed since the terrible pain had begun to affect them all: he was punched hard in the face, a blow that set his ears ringing, just before his lower right arm was struck with the physical weight of the black-haired General through the flat side of his sword. He cried out, dropping his own weapon from a hand rendered useless; he felt bones grinding as he tried to hold onto the hilt and failed, hearing the sword ring as it hit the cobbles.

"Ha – I've got you! You're ours, you bastard!" The black-haired General held out his hand and Jerryn felt even more pain rendering him weak at that moment: he couldn't even *think* straight! He wanted to fight, and he struck out with his left fist, but his coordination had gone, due to the power assailing him, it was only a glancing touch against the man. The jajozeli-razine, only inches away now, quickly cut through Jerryn's sword belt as, at the same moment, the brown-haired, younger General punched him hard in the face for a second time when he in turn managed to deliver a better-aimed blow to black-hair's cheek; his dagger had gone with his belt, out of reach.

Dear Arven, his right arm hurt so much! Jerryn grimaced; he had bitten his tongue at the blows he had received, and he could taste blood, his ears ringing. His cheek and head were aching fit to crack, the jajozeli-razines' power still flaring through him, weakening him just enough that the two bastards could take over. One General quickly locked his hand tight in his hair as the other jajozeli-razine laid a long, slim blade at his throat with a flourish, the steel cold and lethal against his windpipe. Jerryn still struggled, however, although the grip on his hair hurt; then it was followed by a hard, accurate knee in the groin that rendered him utterly weak and breathless, despite his mail. At that point, the man with black hair took his left arm in a painful, locked hold that severely threatened those joints and bones. The pair quickly shoved him into movement, heading at a half-run back towards the castle, even as the debilitating pain in his head but not his balls very slowly began to fade.

"Don't even think about it, bastard, or I'll break every bone in your hand and keep going!" The black-haired General threatened intently, his breath hot on Jerryn's cheek as he tried to pull away, to kick out as they forced him onwards -.

<Jerryn! Where – what -?> Kerrenan's voice bellowed fearfully in his head, sounding somehow weakened. *<Shit! Jerryn!>*

<Don't put anyone in danger, Kerr. Secure the castle. Ow!> Jerryn broke off his silent instructions as the older General tightened his grip and he felt his left elbow and shoulder joints grate horribly. His right arm was useless, agonising. Despite this, he still struggled again for a moment, tried to break free, but to no avail.

"Jerryn!" That was Pualyn's voice, not too far away, clear above the clash of weapons that was beginning again as the allies started to recover from the power that had knocked them flat. He sounded anguished. Jerryn hoped he and the rest of his friends were still unhurt, but that blast of power still affected him -.

"You can always proceed from here with no friends left alive, boy. Silence!" The older, black-haired General threatened in his ear, keeping up the relentless pressure and marching him as fast as they could advance towards the dark entrance to the stores and kitchen quarters, the plain range of buildings leading off to the right of the main castle with its fine elevated entrance, which was now behind him.

One on his right, one on his left and Jerryn could feel only discomfort from their proximity, along with the intense pain throbbing through his right arm, hanging useless, flopping painfully at his side and jarred with every step, banged by the brown-haired General who still held tight to his hair, moving close enough that their mail shirts scraped harshly against his, the physical discomfort replacing the slowly fading mental pain that had so weakened him at that critical moment. Jerryn could only obey, startled, somewhat cowed by the sheer physical pain of it and overwhelmed by the cold triumph he could sense within his captors even as he tried unsuccessfully to think of a way to fight back, to escape. Slowly, the ache of his groin eased as well. Behind him, he could hear the allied forces gaining their feet, their senses, as they recovered and continued the battle, fighting desperately to reach him as he was hauled into a dim corridor. A heavy door slammed shut behind them and was locked by brown-hair, cutting off the tumult outside in the courtyard.

Quickly, there in the passage, the Generals hauled off Jerryn's mail shirt and padded undershirt with absolutely no care for his broken arm, dumping them on the floor, then searched him thoroughly from head to foot, even checking his boots for concealed weapons. The air was cold, his shirt felt clammy against his sweaty skin and Jerryn shivered at that and the discomfort of their touch. They found his gold chain at once, the one that had belonged to his mother, with the large silvery pearl attached and, since they had been fighting, Ethrayne's betrothal ring fastened with it. This was quickly removed, the black-haired General stuffing it into a pocket in his uniform. Jerryn hissed, fighting back both nausea and fury for neither would be of any use at all: he could feel the bones grinding in his right arm even more now, delivering stabbing pains through his flesh.

After only a few moments delay, his captors hurried him on, still with the knife at his throat, that fist locked on his left arm, a burning torch held in black-hair's free hand, marching him swiftly and confidently into a different corridor, down a flight of dusty steps, along and down. He could hear voices somewhere nearby, echoing strangely; people moving, their weapons' clinking. Were the enemy planning another ambush here? Behind, Jerryn finally heard one distant blow on the outer door, but the Generals took him around a corner, through a series of empty storerooms, firmly closing and locking the doors behind them, even removing the keys. A landing there actually led up a further flight of steps and, now, other than their breathing, the sound of their boots scuffing slightly on the stone floor, silence surrounded them.

"Halt!" A different, taller, blonde-haired General stepped out of a doorway ahead and Jerryn jumped in uneasy surprise at his appearance. They had descended three levels by then and were a few hundred yards from the main courtyard, or so Jerryn guessed. His legs were shaking, only partly because he had been up for over a day, fighting for half the night without a pause; his broken arm was throbbing agonisingly in time to his heartbeat, his privates and the contusions on his face ached likewise and the discomfort was spreading. He felt weak, useless.

"I'm glad you're here, Sarlock." The brown-haired General admitted. "I've only basic healing skills and his arm's smashed."

"I can tell. The boy looks beat." The new General commented. "That's why the Commander ordered me to wait here for you, Jaike: basic training is all very well in most situations, but a healer's skill is required here. Nice work, by the way, neutralising him. Let's go." And he strode off ahead of the three of them, imposing in his black and grey.

The Generals' route through the lower reaches of the castle was one of great familiarity, Jerryn realised through the discomfort that was increasing in both his arms, for the iron grip on his left arm never lessened. The enemy had had moons to gain a great knowledge of the citadel, after all, probably as good as Pualyn's and far better than his own. They forced him on unerringly, without a pause, the fresh torch slowly burning down.

Jerryn wondered if they meant to go to ground somewhere down here, beneath the complex, perhaps somewhere secure; yet their route was always downwards, now traversing ancient passages and narrow, steep stairways he didn't think he had ever seen before despite those years of childhood exploration, noting the increase of dust and cobwebs: this area had not been used for years upon years. Yet that would be dangerous, he amended after a moment: they would be found, eventually, surely. So, was there really a way out down through the crag to the open air, he wondered? But Robard and Kerr and many other experienced razine had discounted the existence of any escape route or cave system within the cliff and the steep hill behind which supported the castle.

General Sarlock turned abruptly and ducked through a narrow doorway and Jerryn was shoved after him, finding himself in a small, dusty room containing only three sets of leather bags. "So, tell me what's been happening?"

It was a slightly disingenuous question, Jerryn thought, for surely any razine of either type would be aware of the mental assault which had struck the allied soldiers and the jajozeli-razine commander's death. He was starting to recover more from the pain of that mental assault now, but his body felt just as weak as ever and the power of the enemy was sharp, alien and uncomfortable in his head and body, almost as painful in a way as his injuries.

"That bitch's brother killed Tequan!" The older, black-haired man retorted suddenly, grabbing Jerryn's injured arm so that he could not halt a cry of pain.

"Careful, Oxttyn! So, Tequan is dead, but we have the boy! That was why we came here, after all, you especially, if you care to remember! The Am'maiya needs to be able to use his arm again, we daren't leave him in this state, our master would not be happy! Anyway, the commander knew the risk, that's why he took their attention just now, we all did; any of us could also be dead. He took their focus and it killed him. He died honourably. I bet the rest of them are dead as well, by now! Anyway, he'd already lost his command: you heard the communications from Master Cheltor. And *this* is what we came for!" The other said, his tone stern, commanding, although Jerryn decided that he was younger than the one called Oxttyn. "Give me a moment. Leave the boy alone, by the emperor, if you value your own health!"

"General Sarlock." Oxttyn conceded and Jerryn tried to finally start to catch his breath as the brown-haired one (Jaike, he had called him, he remembered), turned to the bags, rummaging and pulling out things seemingly at random.

"Don't fight, boy, or you'll regret it." The new General snapped angrily at Jerryn as he moved slightly, and he gulped as the newcomer grabbed hold of his privates, still aching from that earlier blow, and twisted tightly so that he gasped, his body automatically trying to fold up protectively. Dear Arven, it hurt! The General kept up the pressure for a moment, glaring threateningly, before he released him. "Understand?"

Jerryn nodded once.

"I asked a question, boy. You had better answer!" That warning was delivered with a fist in the stomach that forced most of the air from his lungs.

"Yes, I understand." Jerryn forced the words out, his voice rough. Violence was a bloody successful way to ensure control!

Oxttyn used his dagger to cut away his right sleeve as Sarlock ran his fingers lightly up and down Jerryn's arm, making him flinch.

"At least his bone ends are mostly aligned for now. I'll do what I can, but we'd better get out quickly, then I'll set it properly later." Sarlock muttered, yanking hard on his wrist. "Pass me the splints and the bandages, Jaike."

"General Sarlock." Jaike already had the items in his hands.

"You've got no chance of escaping!" Jerryn said defiantly, biting his lips hard, wincing, limiting himself to a groan at the fresh pain inflicted on his arm. He knew they were just empty words with no substance, no truth to them.

"That's what you think, boy?" Oxttyn slapped Jerryn hard across the face, even as the other man started lashing lengths of wood around his forearm with quickly ripped strips of his shirt sleeve, following that with a bandage across the area where one bone had protruded, the wound bleeding and already bruising. His arm hurt horribly but somehow he gave no more reaction of it to his abductors. Jerryn swallowed, there was more blood in his mouth now and he hesitantly raised his left hand to wipe his lips.

"Careful, Oxttyn!" Jaike spat with a glare. "Pirris!"

Oxttyn grunted, glaring at the prisoner. "Soldiers have already lit fires in many places beneath the castle on our route to this point, boy. The bitch's brother and your friends will be rather too busy trying to save this heap of rubble in case it falls down around their ears, before they can even think about starting the search for you!"

"Dear Arven, you bastards! You've destroyed the entire castle?" Jerryn hurled with reckless anger but broke off, wincing again as Sarlock tightened the last strip of material on his arm, secure just below his elbow.

"You'd better be quiet, boy, if you know what's good for you!" He ordered, arranging a sling neatly around Jerryn's arm, fastening it securely behind his neck, before he produced a dark cloth that he wrapped twice around their prisoner's face, pulling it tight, a most effective gag that caught his lips painfully against his teeth, knotted roughly at the back of his head.

<*Don't!*> Jerryn protested, struggling, although he knew it was pointless.

"Silence!" Oxttyn glared and raised his fist meaningfully again before the prisoner's face. "Tie him, Jaike."

Gagged, with a length of rope in a loop around his neck and now able to smell a faint hint of acrid smoke that had already bypassed the many locked doors and steps that separated him from the surface and his friends and family, Jerryn was helpless as the three Generals marched him on quickly, weapons in their hands, the packs they had prepared over their shoulders, carrying fresh torches as they continued into the deep darkness beneath Clirensar.

<*Jerryn!*> That was an agonised call from the High-King somewhere above.

<*Sire!*> He answered swiftly, but a sudden heavy blow to the back of his head stunned him, fire and pain blossoming and he fell, insensible, to the floor.

"That'll shut the boy up, let's go." Oxttyn growled, sheathing his dagger, handing the torch to Jaike and then bending to haul Jerryn up, laying him over his shoulder.

* * *

CHAPTER 40

Jerryn awoke groggily. A place at the back of his skull hurt sharply, the rest of his head just pounded; his right arm throbbed in sympathy with his head; whilst his body ached and his mouth, behind the painful gag, was bone dry and tasted revolting, his tongue swollen. Instantly, clearly, he had remembered all that had happened, which explained most of the pain he felt. He was laid on cold stone, no wonder his back ached. He opened his eyes to stare upward at a strange, irregular roof in what, he realised, blinking in a dim wash of light, seemed to be a natural cave. Shifting his position slightly only confirmed that his ankles and knees were bound tightly, his left arm raised above his head, his wrist fastened to something behind him.

Where am I? Is this still today? He wondered uneasily and coughed hard, painfully, behind the gag that kept the sound contained. Despite his question, however, part of him knew that it was still the same day, but he wasn't sure how. Somewhere out of sight he heard movement, and a shadow moved as General Oxttyn came into view, even taller and more imposing from the floor he realised, moving from the right.

"Good, you're back with us." He stated, glaring. "I suggest you do as you are told, boy: you are the means to bring my family and myself back into favour, after that episode with the brat! Behave, else I'll kick you firmly into obedience!"

As he raised his right leg and lowered his huge boot almost into Jerryn's shocked face, the prince believed him, even as he struggled to understand what the General meant . . . favour? His family? Was the 'brat' Ethrayne? What on Iullyn had happened?

"Understand?"

<*Ye-yes, sir.*> He replied, the only way to communicate through the gag.

"Not sir, boy. My Lord General." Oxttyn snapped and that large boot slammed hard into his side and another pain was added to the rest. "*Understand?*"

<*Y-yes, my Lord General.*> Jerryn's mental tone was very meek, cowed by the General's instant use of violence, but already he was trying to think of a way, anyway at all, for him to escape. Ethrayne, of course, had attempted it and so would he, if he could do so!

"Just keep that in mind." The General said, leaning down to unfasten the rope that confined his left wrist so tightly, then pulling him into a sitting position before looping the rope back around his throat. "I strongly suggest you cooperate. You'll walk when I order you to; you'll stop when I tell you to, and you will not try to communicate with the bastard razine or make a sound, boy, else prisoners will die!" He undid the ropes at the prisoner's ankles and knees and hauled Jerryn to his feet. "You're thirsty and you'll get water later, if you behave. You can piss over there."

The cave had seemed to have a roof nearly as tall as the cathedral, from the ground, but the uneven roof was barely high enough for the General to stand upright in, a smooth-walled empty oval with a floor that sloped down towards the light which highlighted the odd shapes of an outcrop. After he had relieved himself, Oxttyn's grip on the rope around his neck tightened as he shoved him forward, and Jerryn stumbled on numb feet into what was a completely smooth passage in the limestone, descending to the left. Downhill, the light was a bit brighter after the darkness and a short distance on, Jerryn could see that it was real daylight leaking around a jumble of undergrowth-covered rubble that rested partly on the rock, but mainly on dark, damp, smelly earth.

General Sarlock was stood by the opening, seemingly alert, his hand on his sword hilt, his gaze forbidding but Jerryn paid him little attention for he stared, amazed and appalled: there, kneeling bound on the wet ground to the General's right and guarded by ten hard-faced jajozeli were three prisoners dressed in filthy rags, also bound and gagged. They gazed up at him with despair in their eyes.

"You no doubt recognise these slaves, prince?" Oxttyn demanded and Jerryn nodded quickly, even though he wasn't sure that he did. "I will introduce them: Benner, captain of the household guard; Poppy, maid to the old duchess and Hella, sister-in-law of the new duchess. All kept here carefully by Commander Tequan and waiting just for you. If you misbehave, boy, then these three will suffer agonisingly." He paused as Jerryn choked behind the gag, quickly suppressing all sorts of protests. "Now get down on your knees and don't move!"

Hostages! Hostages against his compliance! Jerryn's thirst faded as simple dread took over along with nausea, for how could he possibly try to escape his fate when these poor, terrified souls would be tortured and killed? What could he do, but obey? He sank down onto the wet ground, jarring his right arm of course, the rope still tight on his neck, now in the hands of one of the soldiers, trying to suppress any reaction, taking a closer look at the prisoners.

Poppy, a middle-aged woman with greying hair, muffled a sob behind her tied hands, tears trickling down her dirty, bruised face. Jerryn thought he recognised her, one of Duchess Riyala's maids, but there had been many ladies. Hella, he did remember: a pretty girl in her twenties with soft brown hair and smiling eyes, who had been wedded to Dettar, Lyria's oldest brother, a mother, although he could not recall her childrens' names; she also looked thin, terrified and badly used, with cuts and bruises on her face, her hair matted and dirty; as was Benner, a previously solid officer who was now only a shade of his former self, his face thin, his dark eyes bloodshot and scared. Jerryn felt even sicker, just trying to imagine the sheer brutality they must have witnessed and been subjected to since the jajozeli-razine had taken the city, so many moons before.

Gradually, the light faded away ahead of them, beyond the overgrown rock-fall that almost completely hid the entrance to the cave system. On his knees, feeling the water slowly seeping into his clothes, aching all over, Jerryn wondered what his friends were doing, how his father and Pualyn were managing and just how the Generals intended to get them out of the base of this crag when he knew that the allies would be targeting it for attention. Quietly, desperately, he reached out within his mind as he had been taught, only to meet a strange barrier that had been clearly constructed by his captors: it somehow felt *jajozeli* to him, anyway, and touching it only increased his inner discomfort.

From where he stood in the narrow gap at the side of fern-covered rocks, Sarlock glanced back at him and grinned in a self-satisfied sort of way.

<Don't try that again, boy, or you and the others will suffer!> He warned silently.

Slowly the darkness blanketed them. Jerryn's thirst now burned at him, along with the other discomforts and humiliations he felt, but he supposed the General could sense his thought, so he did not demean himself by complaining. His fellow prisoners probably felt even worse than he did -.

A low hoot, rather like the call of a little owl, sounded from outside and Jerryn's heart thudded in his chest. Sarlock stuck his head out outside and repeated the noise, the sound echoing slightly in the cave and Oxttyn chuckled quietly as he and the soldiers quickly got to their feet, their weapons and mail jingling quietly. Jerryn was dragged up and shoved past the cowering hostages until General Sarlock took hold of the hair on his head, then Oxttyn came up and grabbed his left arm before they both set out into the darkness, escorting him. Clearly, they didn't want him to try anything stupid, but Jerryn didn't think he dared, not when the other prisoners were at risk! He could just about hear the others stumbling along behind as he was pushed on and, without being able to see anything at all in the darkness, he was tripping over stones and tussocks and lord knew what, although the enemy moved like cats.

High above, the rainclouds which had poured water on the fighting armies had dispersed, and stars gleamed, remote and beautiful in the distant heavens, leaving the thick undergrowth in velvet blackness. Jerryn blinked to try and clear his vision, quickly glancing around; soon he became aware that behind him, the night was blocked by a looming, deeper darkness that must be a hill, one of many on this side of the city, he recalled; also, by briefly craning his neck and glancing backwards, far above and at a distance, he could just about see the great mass of the crag upon which Clirensar was constructed. Distant torchlight was visible high above on the walls that the rock climbers had ascended, seeming almost as tiny as the stars. His heart sank even further. Somehow, the jajozeli-razine had managed to find a passage from the crag that led out beneath it and into the countryside beyond; no wonder the razine hadn't found any caves at the foot of the cliff! Now they were downstream of the wharves and pretty-much out of reach of any rescue! His heart quailed and despair filled him.

At least. The thought came to him unexpectedly, a little boost to his sinking spirits. *At least they had to carry me all that way: if he hadn't knocked me senseless, I could have walked. I hope they all ache abominably!*

The Generals must have been communicating silently for secrecy's sake, for the only noises he heard were natural: an owl, off in the distance; a fox barked, somewhat closer; the rustling of leaves in the wind, which would certainly cover their movements and, somewhere not far ahead, the gurgling sound of the river Sare. Jerryn tried to make his eyes see more, despite the darkness, but he could only just make out the hillock and the crag behind; ahead was invisible, although it appeared that where he was now stumbling along, marching under duress through thick vegetation on very soft ground, seemed to be a good foot or two below the land to either side. He wondered if they were perhaps in a stream gulley and found his supposition confirmed when Oxttyn and Sarlock directed him straight into a smelly, soggy muck that sucked at his boots, getting wetter the further he stepped, slurping, but it was much quieter than the natural sound of the river racing past ahead. They waded through about six feet of knee- to thigh-high water and mud, until the rippling, black but slightly sparkling Sare was right before them. Jerryn thought fearfully that he was going to sink forever into the cloying, stinking mud which was trying to claim his water-filled boots: with one arm useless, a rope on his neck, he was helpless -.

<*Here.*> A voice whispered in his head and Jerryn shuddered at the touch of the General's power. Something long and flat had glided almost silently up from the right and a rope was tossed out for the Generals to grasp, whilst a hand, Jaike's, grabbed his shoulder and hauled him from the mud, into much colder water that splashed quietly against him. The General yanked him over the gunwale into the bottom of a boat with only a few muffled bumps and Jerryn's silent curses as he banged his broken arm repeatedly, dragged further to the right and out of the way, crouching down on his knees, his head resting down on them as ordered. He could hear the others climbing aboard, one woman whimpering slightly, despite her gag and he knew that Sarlock was right behind him, gripping the rope on his neck anew, pulling it tight. He spat silent curses as the boat rocked slightly against their weight to the side, before they spread out a little, he was shoved down flatter, his broken arm pinned beneath him and it hurt! The only good point was that the river water and the stinking mud could drain out of his boots, but that just made the rest of his clothes wetter. He heard an oar being employed, to push them away from the muddy bank, turn the boat about . . . then they were out in the current and being carried away from Clirensar.

*

Shivering in his wet clothes, his arm aching desperately, parched and exhausted, Jerryn did not dare to move until he felt hands removing the gag from his mouth, then one of the soldiers helped him to sit down and handed him a water skin; it was certainly not a General. The assistance was rough, admittedly, but to sit was better by far than being laid achingly on his front. The feel of water in his arid mouth was simple bliss. He swallowed, coughed as quietly as he could, drank until the water skin was removed – and the gag was refastened just as tightly.

"You'll get more later, perhaps." General Jaike said quietly from where he sat at the tiller, to his right. "Remember, boy: silence or the slaves will suffer."

He shuddered, huddled there, the rope a firm reminder of his position, now tight in Oxttyn's fist. He tried to get his bearings even as he wished that he could ease his cramped muscles. As far as he could tell in the shrouding night, the boat floated in the middle of the river which was at least a good hundred feet wide close to the city, widening as it flowed towards the sea; he guessed that they must be passing the ruined farms east of the city; fields and woodland; land that they had all surveyed since their arrival. Straining to look back upstream, Jerryn realised that he could no longer see the torch-topped crag that held Clirensar; he had no idea how fast the boat was moving, as he looked about, seeing nothing but various levels of darkness. Oxttyn tightened his grip in warning. He wondered, shivering at the cold wind on his still-wet skin, how his father would react to the news that his captors had escaped so easily! *Damn them all to hell!* He spat miserably, the malice evident in the Generals' auras choking him as much as the rope about his neck.

Helpless, exhausted, he watched clouds hide the stars above, only able to guess at the passing countryside for an age until, eventually, his eyes gritty from over a day without sleep (could he discount unconsciousness, he wondered?), the first faint light touched the horizon ahead to the east, a mere slight wash of grey. The soldiers passed around the water skin to the prisoners again, before a large, brown canvas tarpaulin was unfolded from the bow of the boat.

The prisoners were all forced to lie flat in the bottom of the boat, severely restrained in Jerryn's case, and the cover was stretched out over the greater part of the craft, hiding the contents from view, as if protecting a cargo from the weather. It was a design which had been in use on the Sare and the other main rivers of Tenarum for two centuries at least; he assumed that the craft must look innocent enough, guided by the cloaked Generals, ten labourers spread out near the bow, their weapons and mail all concealed, going with the steady flow of the river.

Stifled somewhat by the dark canvas only just above his head, aching in mind and body, Jerryn eventually drifted into an uncertain sleep where he was menaced by massive, hulking figures, to wake slightly more clear-headed, to what turned out to be a slowly darkening sky. Somehow, despite thirst and a terrible hunger, he had slept half the day away.

"The sleeping beauty awakens." Oxttyn grated, his tone conveying mostly menace. "How's your arm, boy?"

<It-it is painful, my-my Lord General.> Just in time he remembered the title: this was not the time to antagonise his captors, when he was so helpless in the bottom of the boat. To his intense embarrassment his stomach gurgled, and his bladder was screaming for relief. *<P-please, sir -.>*

Their silent, mocking, laughter was the only answer and Jerryn was unable to block the sharp, malicious amusement that the jajozeli-razine let him sense; probably they had done something else, made some barrier, to stop him using his slight power in any way, for the all controls and blocks that he had been taught by the razine appeared useless.

Misery filled him for a while, until a memory surfaced from the previous day, from just before everything had fallen apart around him: the delight on Pualyn's face as he had decapitated that bastard Tequan, exacting some well-deserved retribution! The death of the commander of the occupying force did much to buoy his flagging spirits -.

"I suggest you dwell on some other event, boy, else I'll start my own retribution on your hide!" Oxttyn said, kicking him roughly at the top of his left thigh as he helped Jaike start to roll back the tarpaulin. The soldiers were folding it carefully down from the front, letting the fresh night air in now that there was no chance of being seen.

<I don't understand, sir. Ouch! My-my Lord General.> Jerryn immediately amended at a second kick, fearing for his ribs.

"Your little bitch cost me my son!" The General hurled the words viciously, yanking Jerryn to a sitting position by his hair.

<Y-your son, my Lord?> He quavered. *<Do you mean Ethrayne?>*

"Whom else?" He kicked Jerryn again, then cracked him hard almost exactly where he had been knocked out the previous day and, the lump still very tender, his headache returned with a vengeance.

"Oxttyn, the fault was Inajo's!" Sarlock interjected then firmly, laying one hand on Oxttyn's shoulder as he raised his huge fist, towering over his prisoner. "His mistake alone, not the girl's. And most certainly not his majesty's. You will leave the prisoner alone!"

General Oxttyn gazed with furious eyes at the taller man, kicked the prisoner hard again, then a third time, making his ribs ache; his burning eyes held Jerryn's gaze in the fading light and he was unable to control his bladder when faced with the threat there: this General hated him beyond sense. Intense embarrassment filled him, as well as relief, but Jerryn was all too aware of his complete helplessness! The Generals facing each other right above him seemed frozen. He assumed they were wrestled mentally for authority, control. Finally, snarling, Oxttyn strode to the bow.

"Watch your mind and your tongue around General Oxttyn, boy." Jaike warned him in a low voice, moving over to unfasten the rope that had constrained his neck since his capture. "He bears a grudge and *you* are its focus as the brat is far out of his reach!" He then removed the gag from around Jerryn's head.

<But-but Ethrayne -.> Jerryn stuttered mentally, for his lips were swollen and painful from the gag, his mouth revoltingly dry.

"The pair of you are a focus of some kind, it seems, beyond sensible expectation." The younger General shrugged, then reached for a water skin and a second bag being offered by one of the soldiers, pulling out a strip of dried meat. "Eat and drink quickly: the cover will be replaced soon for security."

Confused, miserable, frightened and ashamed, almost every emotion existing boiled within him, but they were all negated as Jerryn finally could assuage his burning thirst, before attacking the tough, salty strip that would certainly keep him well occupied as chewing practice. He wasn't fooled into thinking that this one small piece of food would fill him, but it had been nearly two days, he guessed from a quick breakfast well before dawn on what had turned out to be their final assault on the citadel, since he had eaten a thing. Yet at least that awful sensation of desperate hunger receded a little, as he chewed and swallowed.

The other prisoners were further towards the bow, cringing away from General Oxttyn and the guards who were ranged close, but he could sense that both Sarlock and Jaike were close and watching him intently and the proximity, the sense of their power thrilling Jerryn's nerves.

"I should have stayed at the back of the assault!" He muttered unhappily to himself, thinking back to his reckless stupidity, overruling Kerr and Pualyn before the gates.

General Sarlock snorted. "It would have made no difference, boy: you were always our one goal once the brat had been captured. We would have taken you within a few days, no matter what you or your elders devised, or where you were guarded!"

"You'll never get through Saremouth, my, my Lord General. There are ships and the razine: they will block -." Jerryn stated defiantly, surprised to realise that he was reassured by Sarlock's arrogant response.

This time, Jaike chuckled coldly and answered. "Oh, we'll get through Saremouth, boy! It might cost the locals a few more lives, a little more damage, but we'll reach the sea safely." His tone was confident. He proceeded to tie Jerryn securely, replaced the gag and the canvas was pulled back out and secured to cover the boat. By then it was full night. Later, a hard rain fell, drumming loud on the tarpaulin. Some, of course, found its way into the bottom of the craft, soaking the prisoners with cold water. But at least they were covered.

Jerryn lay still, his broken arm hurting even more than it had when his weight had been on it the previous night, trying to get enough mental control together to properly *concentrate*, to try and raise even a tiny part of the power that he had been learning how to use . . . But he was worrying about Oxttyn's intense hatred, his mention of Ethrayne. Dear Arven, what had occurred? He wondered. Also, he was fretting about the safety of the other prisoners: the threat to torture or kill them if he rebelled. He knew that he was not cold-hearted enough to condemn anyone to pain and death, no matter what! He tried to clear his mind, again and again, but failed. Meditation was nigh-on impossible . . . The aura of the Generals, also, was sharp, cold and uncomfortable, almost painful in his head . . . The night passed, the boat moved down the river, rocking choppily now and again as they crossed confluences with the many other streams that met and joined the larger river . . . He achieved precisely nothing at all as he tried to concentrate – except, once, late in the night, a very brief touch: someone else's sense of relief -. Then the barrier, the block that the Generals had created around him slammed down hard and he was left with only an even more intense headache. All his worries returned, and despair plunged him into the depths . . . It kept on raining.

Eventually the night gave way and the canvas took on shape and colour above him as the boat continued downstream. Jerryn wondered if he was imagining it, but it seemed that he could sense a heightened alertness in the Generals, although he could see little except a bit of the frame of the boat and the canvas above him; all three were ranged behind him and he could only really see parts of their legs if he craned his head painfully over. He supposed they must be closing on Saremouth, or the populous area upstream of it . . . but there his imagination failed, he was just worrying that more people would die. General Jaike's assurance of their advance only unnerved him further.

They floated on, accompanied by continuing rain, which only cleared sometime in the afternoon, the air oddly chilly. There was certainly a heightened tenseness in the air, Jerryn had not been mistaken, but the Generals did nothing different to any other travellers, he thought. They would be leaning at the stern. He heard them calling hallo! to the masters of passing craft heading upstream, or perhaps people on the riverbanks. He heard noises other than polite greetings: the moos of cows, the raucous sounds of ducks and so on and, clearly, the sounds of birds in flight overhead: geese or ducks, he guessed, hidden above the canvas, now and again. It was an ordinary day in the eastern vale of the Sare, the farms, villages and little towns that were dotted about, completely unaware of the danger slipping past, the threat of three Generals and their soldiers who were prepared to wreak havoc in their total determination to take him from Tenarum. Awful images filled his mind: the destruction of Callorton and South Vale Farm and in Clirensar itself and Jerryn prayed fervently that the craft would be allowed to continue unchallenged, the innocent locals completely unaware of the dreadful violence passing so close to hand . . . His hunger and thirst had returned, almost as burning as the previous day.

It was growing dark yet again when something finally changed and Oxttyn steered the boat towards the left-hand bank. There were no lights visible, no hamlets close to the river around them. The soldiers removed the tarpaulin; the stars were just starting to appear through a rustling net of tree tops, they were moored by a stand of tall trees on the edge of the river, the woodland and undergrowth completely unable to block a chilling breeze that made the prisoners all shiver now that they were uncovered. They were released from their bonds, allowed up and provided with water and more dried meat, then allowed to climb onto the bank, accompanied by the guards, to relieve themselves and stretch their aching legs briefly.

"We are close to Saremouth." General Oxttyn informed Jerryn when the two soldiers marched him straight back to the boat. He could hear more muffled crying from Poppy and Hella and he could sense their wretched fear; it made him feel quite sick again. "We will continue later tonight."

"They will know you are on your way, my Lord General." The prince dared to diffidently point out, wondering why Oxttyn would bother to tell him such information. "They will search every single boat coming down the river, I'm sure -."

"Shut up." The General ordered, but not in a fierce, angry way; his opinion did not count for shit, Jerryn supposed. They laughed at him.

The night passed slowly as the half-moon crept across the sky, dodging clouds with dubious success. It was chillier tonight, Jerryn and the prisoners feeling it acutely through their damp, inadequate clothing. The moon was sinking towards the distant hills in the west when the prince was trussed up again, but this time he was not gagged, although he was fastened up tightly alongside Poppy, Hella and Benner, all four of them forced onto their knees in the stern; Jerryn was right beside Oxttyn with Sarlock at his back at the tiller, General Jaike in the prow and the soldiers close beside them with their weapons loose. The tarpaulin was tidily packed away, and they resumed their journey, long oars set out, ready for use.

Arven protect the people of Saremouth, everyone! Jerryn prayed. Knelt there, wedged uncomfortably against General Oxttyn's muscular legs, he found the onset of dawn both faster and slower than normal, relishing the opportunity to remain upright, having been confined on his back for two days solid. The ropes that tightly bound him, the shivering of the others increased his fear as, gradually, the woodland and farmland they swept past were replaced by cottage gardens, then the dusty, messy outskirts of a large settlement. Boats, barges and larger craft in various states of repair were docked at various rickety wharves that stuck out over the edges of the river, the muddy foreshore now visible. The sun had only just risen ahead of them when the boat moved out into the wider estuary.

"There." General Jaike pointed quickly to left and right then straight ahead. "As reported, Oxttyn: the Orbain Pearl, Veddock Pearl, Cerris Opal, Jaece Pearl, local ships and -." He laughed aloud. "There's the Mador Opal."

"Tricky." Oxttyn glanced from side to side, clearly assessing the situation. "So, the survivors from the sacking of Cal'Badon have returned to honour. Man the oars!"

The ten soldiers moved to the middle of the boat, working the eight oars between them, perching on the narrow boards fitted for the rowers who usually manoeuvred such craft when adjustment was required. Sarlock took the tiller and Jaike stayed in the bow, poised, alert.

"Oh, damn it all! Captain Ashanner!" Jerryn gasped, suddenly recognising the man at the wheel of the gigantic ship on their left that approached swiftly, which seemed intent on sinking them. Suddenly, he recalled the report that the attackers of Cal'Badon had used power to subdue the jajozeli, probably exactly as they had all be struck so hard in Clirensar! It was devastatingly effective.

"Keep back, bastard, or the prince will be sorely damaged, and these others will die!" Oxttyn roared, laying a knife at Hella's cheek; the woman screamed shrilly on cue, as if it had been rehearsed for a dramatic play.

"You're surrounded, General!" Ashanner shouted back, his face set. "Phellos has blocked you most effectively. Surrender! Release your prisoners! You won't get a hundred yards!"

"Not a hope, bastard!" Jaike shouted back from the bow, grinning broadly. "Keep your ships well away. Saremouth can burn again for all we care!"

Dear Arven! Jerryn prayed, gulping in fear as the Orbain Pearl swept past far too close, so that the shallow craft rocked nastily in its wake the murky water suddenly looked very dangerous, lapping hungrily at the gunwale. The ship was so very big! *Do I want to drown? Should they just sink us -?*

<Jerryn!> That silent shout was unmistakeably the High-King's and the prince stared up at the stern of the Pearl, turning in the current, to see Mhezal beside Ashanner, his gaze intent. But, he wondered in confusion, how on Iullyn had the High-King managed to reach Saremouth before them? Horses could gallop, but had to be changed, whilst the boat had glided along on probably the straightest, quickest route.

He came for me! The thought came to him suddenly, a horrible feeling of guilt only worsening his fear: too many people had died already!

<NOW!> Sarlock gave a mental bellow that probably even the humans could hear, as the Sweet Rose and the Crimson Rose closed in from the right. Then, a moment later, there was a loud CRASH! A BOOM! The sound was echoing from the Veddock Pearl, the ship furthest away and closest to the ocean. Practically everyone in the vicinity turned to stare first at that razine ship and then, open mouthed, at the swinging arm of the mangonel on board the Mador Opal, before it was hauled back again, creaking; as the crew of the Veddock Pearl raced desperately to put out fires, another burning missile flew overhead to land with awful effect on the roof of one of the warehouses on the northern bank of the river.

"No!" Ashanner cried in heartfelt anguish. "Phellos!" His voice was clear across the water.

"Oh, damn it!" Jerryn whispered in shocked disbelief. "The bastards! You took Captain Phellos's ship!"

The High-King, audibly, started swearing sulphurously, as did some of the other people on board the ships that had been about to block and board Oxttyn's river boat. The Generals laughed and jeered, well pleased at their deception.

"We hold your dear friend's ship; she and the other survivors are also our prisoners, bastard razine!" Oxttyn used the insult indiscriminately, relishing the telling, his voice carrying across the water. "Now, Master Cheltor can keep raining fire upon you; we can mutilate a few civilians –." Poppy wailed this time, again almost as requested. "Or you can retreat, drop anchor and live to see another day!"

<*Jerryn -?*> Mhezal's contact was broken and Jerryn winced as pain struck his mind hard from the power the Generals were expending.

<*The prince belongs to his majesty, idiot leader of soft-minded idiots! Do not interfere or he will suffer much worse than a broken arm and some bruises!*> Jaike warned, as those on the Mador Opal prepared the mangonel again and, in a moment, a second burning mass thumped down amid the crew still working to contain the liquid fire that had previously fallen on the Veddock Pearl.

<*Very well, General.*> The High-King acquiesced heavily, with obvious reluctance. <*Am'maiya, I'm so sorry -.*>

<*Get out of our way!*> Oxttyn spat. <*You have moments, bastards, or the prisoners will start suffering!*>

Their voices echoed painfully in Jerryn's head. The aftermath of the sudden attack was almost as though a massive wet blanket of despair had fallen in a moment over the estuary and the city around it, as the small boat he was cowering on bobbed along over the increasingly large waves, propelled by the current and the sweating soldiers at the oars, heading out to where the Mador Opal menaced the allied ships, now displaying clearly the Saremouth-made standard of the Jajozeli Empire, cracking sharply in the wind that was rising from behind him, from the land. The other craft were swiftly moving to berths out of the main river, men hauling desperately on ropes, all except the Veddock Pearl, still trying to smother the lethal fire. He could hear muffled, urgent commands there.

His knees and his mind numb, Jerryn watched the huge ship they were closing on, noting its dark-stained timbers, the thick netting that hung down the outside of the hull amidships, the height of the masts; he noted that it hardly seemed to move on the rocking waves that threw the little river boat all over, drenching him and the others with cold spray . . . The sun was shining, shaded somewhat by the half-furled sails; the sky was clear, midsummer was close approaching, after all, the air warm. It was a good day for a voyage, perhaps, but not the one he was about to undertake so unwillingly . . .

<*Oh, dear Arven, please, take care.*> He sent silently, but he did not know whether his plea escaped the jajozeli barrier. <*Protect yourselves, look after my father, I'm sorry!*>

The motion of the little boat increased awfully, for the water was choppier in that area, the swell riding in from the ocean meeting the current of the river and the wind in an unexpected, unpleasant manner; but the soldiers rowed relentlessly, Jaike issued directions. The boat was alongside the ship all too quickly. Two soldiers hung relentlessly on to the bottom of the net, striving to hold the boat relatively still, whilst Oxttyn untied Jerryn from the other prisoners, hauling him up. They were all hindered by the waves now breaking over the gunwale as they were shifted by both the river current and the waves, almost crashing fatally into the hull of the Mador Opal. Jerryn flinched and staggered as, from the chest down, he was drenched by an even larger wave which broke over the side, running around them, leaving inches of water in the bottom of the boat. It was freezing! The other prisoners gasped and screamed a little, whilst the enemy did not to react.

Quickly the rope was secured twice around his waist and under his arms, then tossed up to the ship; it was caught by a General up there and pulled tighter as Jerryn stumbled and the boat bucked.

"Climb." Oxttyn ordered.

"Oh." Jerryn glanced down at his right arm, took a breath and shuffled forward through the water now mostly covering his boots; a step, a second; then he was before the net, the huge ship moving crazily at a completely different tempo to the tiny boat on the sea. Praying silently, he stepped across a suddenly horribly wide gulf of glinting water, grabbed with his left hand, pulled his left foot onto the net at a higher point; but his right boot, sodden, nearly slipped . . . he hung there, frozen, completely unable to move from his position with only one hand as the ship moved wildly.

"Move!" Oxttyn shouted. "Climb, you cowardly, useless coward!"

That stung, along with the long string of swearwords. Jerryn gritted his teeth, tried to brace his feet and slid his left hand a little way up the net before the rope tightened under his arms and it was hauled up . . . scarily, he found himself hanging at a distance from the ship, holding on as tight to the netting as he could with his left hand, as the ship moved, dipped – and he hit the hull hard when the waves shoved the ship the other way. Dear Arven, that was unnerving! The people on deck continued to drag him up the side of the ship, his right arm banging on every bloody knot of the net, it seemed as he suppressed his reaction to the pain, did his best to climb. But then he was at the level of the gunwale, trying to brace himself and not fall over onto the deck. Hands grabbed him as the ship pitched, nearly throwing him back to the sea, which would have been preferable; but they pulled him over onto the deck. Just below, he could hear the women's cries as they were forced up the net in his wake, Jaike and the soldiers cursing them.

"That wasn't so bad after all, was it?" Sarlock and Oxttyn had climbed up behind him, their bags over their shoulders and they laughed aloud, at the success of the mission perhaps. They were dripping with water just as much as he.

Jerryn shivered and turned slightly to stare up the estuary, noting that the decks of the razine and Tenarean ships were now full of people, staring back.

"So, you survived, General Oxttyn. Excellent news." A new voice remarked. “It’s good to see that you have assisted so well in finalising his Majesty’s plans.”

“For the honour of my family, Master Cheltor.” Oxttyn replied, standing to attention. “The Am’maiya is ours.”

“Finally, we can set sail for Enlath. Well, let’s get you out of that rope.” The length that had hauled Jerryn up the ship’s side was quickly unknotted. He was free of bonds, but a large hand closed hard on his right shoulder. “Move, boy.” Jerryn flinched: it was the sort of voice he recognised from all his years of weapons training and the lined, lean, cold-gazed figure before him, even as sorely injured as he was with a startlingly bright red healing scar amid the fading bruising so prominent across his face, certainly confirmed his supposition.

The deck seemed enormous, the vertiginous masts with the sails cracking in the wind, a wave causing him to stagger, the movement alien, unknown. He had heard the anchor being hauled up and glanced again towards Saremouth as he was marched towards a dark doorway beneath the stern deck, startled to realise that they were already heading out to sea: the towers of the castle were more distant, the ships a little smaller. They had passed the Veddock Pearl and he was relieved to see that the fires had been extinguished.

He was leaving the other three prisoners, whom he realised that he had not even dared speak to yet; they were shoved roughly towards the bow where a hatch was open. He heard commands from above him, speech from the sailors; part of him realised that they were all jajozeli-razine. Then, he was in a dim passage and his view vanished.

“Let’s sort your arm out, boy and you can rest. Sarlock, with me.” The tall, imposing General said, steering him firmly towards what seemed to be a dark doorway under the stern deck. “Welcome to what was the Mador Opal. We call it Phellos’s Folly now.”

* * *

CHAPTER 41

"This way!" Pualyn yelled, turning as others hammered desperately at the locked door that blocked them, racing his way along the building to a door fifty yards to the right; he and those following him had to leap over bodies laid all over the cobbles to reach that side entrance to the guard room, seriously slowing them, but they ran through rooms and corridors that were partly filled with rubbish, heading left, trying to catch up with the Generals who had abducted the prince.

The young duke's knowledge of the citadel was complete, right down to the oldest cellars, but the jajozeli-razine had a head-start on them: doors had been locked, slowing them down again and they occasionally faced determined groups of enemy soldiers whose sole, desperate, purpose seemed to kill them or die, delaying them! Pualyn picked up one lighted torch from a bracket, others copied him, as they headed for a staircase.

"Where the hell are they going?" Tymain demanded, after they had descended two flights of dusty steps into complete darkness. "Are there any secret passages here, Pualyn?"

"Not that I know of in this part of the castle, and none into the bedrock." Pualyn slowed, breathing heavily. "Of course, there *might* be . . . oh, shit! There might be. Come on!"

"We certainly explored enough when we were children, Pualyn, but I suppose we might have missed places." Sevanter said, doing his best to keep up with his brother-in-law, for he had sustained a long slash to a leg and others to his shoulders and head, during that horrible period when Jerryn had been isolated by the Generals. His face was set, as he limped along with them, ignoring the blood-loss and the discomfort, heartily offended that he and the others had been rendered so ineffective.

"Stop! Wait!" The High-King said, raising one hand in warning after some time. "I smell smoke, Pualyn, let's not rush ahead: clearly the bastards have carefully set traps for us."

"They'll not escape!" Pualyn asserted stoutly, even though he knew that he was only hoping for success. "Carefully, then, your Majesty." He led them on, fifty men and razine, through a series of barrel-vaulted cellars into another corridor, and the smell and the slight pall of smoke only increased. Ahead, they could now hear fire crackling, then a heightened roar, a little like a wild animal, as something flammable caught hold -.

"Back! Get back!" Kerrenan shouted, as there was a deep rumble, a crash and thick clouds of dust and rubble were added to the thickening smoke. "Oh, damn it all! We can't do anything but extinguish these bastard fires, else the castle will be down around our ears!"

"But Jerryn's down there! We've got to rescue Jerryn!" Pualyn's tone was anguished.

"We'll do our damnedest, Pualyn, but not until we've secured your home." Mhezal said heavily. "Where's the closest well?"

The duke stared at him, his fear and distress clear to all of them. "Shit! I've got to do exactly what Marrand had to do to me, in effect: tell him we've lost his son?" He asked rather plaintively. "Oh, damn -." He started to swear rather eloquently.

There was another crash and they started to retreat as quickly as they could, looking nervously along the corridor towards the site of the fire.

"Water, Pualyn, we need water!" Tymain stated urgently. "And buckets man, lots of bloody buckets! Come on!"

Pualyn shuddered. "Water! Buckets! Come on!" He took the stairs two and three at a time, but he was slowing as he climbed. Finally he was thinking again, his mind clear of that awful flood of furious panic. "We'll get organised, start others searching the citadel methodically when the fires are out. Dear Arven, we're losing so much of the day. That bastard really planned this minutely, didn't he? Wish I could kill him again!"

"They split us up very effectively, didn't they?" Kerrenan agreed heavily, keeping level with him. "We had fourteen Generals to eliminate in the courtyard to get here. Yet you killed their leader and that's fifteen more Generals out of the way for good!" He grinned in a very satisfied way. "And you fought Tequan with great skill, congratulations, your Grace."

"Thank you, your Highness." Pualyn managed a grimace in return. "Fifteen?" He shivered at that confirmation. "Shit!"

Behind them, Sevanter and Tymain barked rough laughs, before they and the others began to cough; the smoke was thickening.

Returning to the main courtyard, they found that a state of organised chaos had descended as the other kings and commanders, under Marrand, started the movement of bodies, the collection of equipment. He turned, his hand on his sword hilt, as Pualyn and the others reappeared. He looked tired, his face lined and there were blood stains on his mail.

"Your Majesty. Generals captured Jerryn . . . We chased them, but there are fires burning in the cellars. Dear Arven, I'm sorry, Sire but we cannot advance until the lower levels are safe, the fires out." Pualyn explained quickly, rubbing at his smoke-reddened eyes.

"I heard it from Robard and Vedeigne, Pualyn. Oh, clever, clever bastards! They planned every step, didn't they?" Marrand shook his head, obviously suppressing his emotions as much as the rest of them. "Hey, you're one of the duke's men -." He called to a weary captain who had just laid a bushel of arrows on a barrel nearby. "Look lively, man: buckets, water; his Grace here will direct you! Let's get this citadel secure!" He barked. Another man determined to try and suppress his fear and sorrow in more hard work.

"At once, your Majesty."

"Lieutenant Sevanter, for Arven's sake, go and get those wounds bound before you lose too much blood." The king glared at the man, sagging where he stood. "Don't argue, we've lost too many good men today. I won't lose anyone else. Go on. You, Private Calle, help him."

"Yes, your Majesty." Sevanter bowed deeply, wincing at the injuries he had been trying to ignore.

*

Pualyn and Tymain coordinated the smothering of the fires, of which they found five in various places towards the east of the citadel, some less successful than the one which had collapsed the ceiling during their initial attempt to find Jerryn, fuelled by broken furniture and lamp oil. They also had a company of jajozeli soldiers to eliminate, the men who had lit the fires. Not even Pualyn dared to try and find a route around the lower cellars yet, to risk more dangerous collapses; whole rooms had vanished into blackened rubble. There was no route that they had yet found which led around that risky area and they supposed that the damned Generals had probably reached their escape point out of the castle by now. It was late afternoon by the time that they emerged from the cellars to find that King Marrand, King Namayomn and Crown Prince Tarlan had set up a healer's station in the servants dining hall, whilst the walking wounded from previous battles set about beginning the task of clearing the mounds of rubbish that so many moons of occupation had created and, most importantly, the cooks set about preparing a meal in the vast kitchens.

The High-King had left the firefighting to others and found a quiet room above the guard's quarters where, supported by Kerrenan, he concentrated his innate talent on trying to find Jerryn. There was a barrier, however, set most securely around him: the prince was effectively hidden until, suddenly, one call got a quick response before he felt a sudden, intense pain, then nothing.

"Damn them! They've knocked him out, Kerrenan, somewhere near that cliff to the east. I thought there'd be a sally point into the city below, you know, but perhaps there's a crack or passage downwards; its limestone, after all! Let's tell Pualyn: we need to get the wharves and river patrolled quickly. Bastards!"

"I agee, Father, but what can we do?"

"We live in interesting times, Kerr." His father stated sadly. "Let's start looking for Jerryn: if there *is* a way down, it'll be some time before they reach level ground."

"I'm so sorry, Father. I tried to stay close to the Am'maiya, but there were so many enemy soldiers around we were split apart, overwhelmed."

"We know. We saw. Marrand understands. I imagine the commander planned it that way: separate the prince from as many people as possible, especially we razine . . . You did your best, Kerrenan, don't flog yourself with guilt." Mhezal sighed.

The High-Prince only grunted an answer to that.

It took time to assemble a group of razine for Mhezal's plan to hopefully trap the enemy; the soldiers were scattered about the castle and city on various missions, from trying to find alternate routes through the fire-damaged lower levels; to conducting a room-by-room search for any jajozeli; to carting out the dead and bringing in more of their vast array of supplies; to tending the injured. So many thousands of soldiers, intent on so many vital tasks.

"Dear Arven, I'm exhausted." Pualyn muttered, sinking down on a filthy tabletop in one of the household offices, his face despondent. "And look at the state of this place! I bet there's no one left. I pray there's no one left alive, with all we've found so far!" He shivered.

"Look at the price we've paid, Pualyn: Jerryn was correct, wasn't he?" Tymain pointed out diffidently. "The jajozeli were focussed on him as soon as we entered Clirensar."

"Aye, by Arven, it seems like it. The Generals had moons to search for any possible way they could get into the rock beneath our feet and moons to chisel their way through, if necessary! Oh, damn, I need a drink!" He got slowly to his feet. "Let's find the others, we've going to have to set some engineers to shoring up those damaged areas -."

"We'll sort that later, Pualyn." The High-King had stuck his head around the door. "I've set the appropriate standards on the flagpoles, sent messengers to Foston. I thought it might reassure everyone watching from outside. Marrand has some Pellerton red to hand."

"What are we going to do about Jerryn's capture, your Majesty?" Tymain asked, rubbing at his face vigorously.

"Kerr and some others are outside, checking the wharves and the cliff face. They'll patrol the river too; others are on alert in the city, around our perimeter, in case the caves open there. But -." He sighed deeply. "Let's face it, we've no idea where any passage might emerge, how long they'll wait, or how well prepared they are."

"Oh, they were well prepared, your Majesty." Pualyn agreed. "I suppose we ought to start trying to make this place habitable." They nodded sadly in agreement.

"The main structure seems intact, Pualyn; the rest is mainly rubbish and deliberate defacing of the castle. We should be able to clean up and sort it out quickly enough, I'm sure." Tymain tried to make light of the broken windows, walls, furniture and so forth so clear to all of them.

*

The High-Prince's group of razine started their patrol at the wharves set below the crag which formed the eastern wall of the city and the castle far above it. As a precaution, they moored every boat and barge remaining on the river together under armed guard, but they suspected that the Generals already had their escape-route completely set up and ready for their egress at night; logically, that's what they would all have done.

Fighting a dark despair that was usually completely alien to his nature, Kerrenan did his utmost to locate any cave systems running down through the limestone but did not find much that was any use. The openings they investigated were all too small for fully grown adults to squeeze through, and although there *were* passages inside, not even their combined power could find any exit points.

"Back to eyes and ears, then, let's go." Kerr said with a sigh. "Right, half of us will mount up, the rest on foot; we will split up – a hundred and fifty on this bank, a hundred to the north. We'll track slowly up and down until nightfall, and fresh eyes and ears can take over then; those bastards will be out here somewhere!"

But even so, riding or walking up and down the river banks; investigating streams, hollows and dark spaces along the way for five miles inland and two leagues or downstream, and with a boat rowing up and down in addition, they found nothing. Darkness fell; other men and razine relieved them. Noises could be heard, naturally: animals moving about; calls of various types; owls hunting; an odd thump! once or twice. But although they were all diligent, alert and determined to succeed, they found absolutely nothing.

Then, shortly after first light, the now obvious escape point was discovered; although the extremely muddy pool that had filled the stream bed in that hollow had been studied, no one, of course, had thought to wade up it and try and push through the apparently impenetrable vegetation at the base of the uneven, gorse-covered hill, a good half mile or so from the actual crag.

By dawn, an exhausted Kerrenan admitted defeat. He had refused to rest and had walked up and down on the south side of the river bank all night, searching with his power for Jerryn's familiar presence – he prayed he would prove easy to find, but, naturally, he had been completely blocked by the jajozeli-razine; the High-Prince had been sure that the enemy would break out of concealment overnight, hidden in the darkness.

Receiving the news of the discovery of the footprints with a fatalistic calm, Kerr stared at the marks of passage in the margins of the pool that had been fed by the stream, then struggled through the muck up past his knees to the very bottom of the slope, disappearing through the undergrowth and his muffled yet echoing stream of curses told them all they needed to know: the Generals, of course, were quite capable of concealing such a place and, obviously, they had. The High-Prince emerged still swearing, glaring, foul mud covering most of his clothes, to wade straight into the river.

"A couple of you take supplies, ropes and plenty of torches and follow the cave up and back. Have we got parchment and charcoal?" He asked, climbing soaking wet but a little cleaner, out of the water, his boots spouting water. "At least Duke Pualyn will have one escape route for the future." His tone was cold.

"You really ought to rest, sir." A captain offered diffidently, holding out the reins of his horse.

"When I've reported to our leaders, Cannort. Thank you."

*

There were copious amounts of both hot water and breakfast up at the castle and Kerrenan was shown to a suite with a bath as soon as he had reported to Commander Vedeigne what they had discovered, too late. It was immensely galling that the enemy had snuck through in such a manner, but even Kerr knew that they had done all they could to locate Jerryn in the circumstances. He bathed, ate a little, then fell asleep on a clean, comfortable bed despite the sense of guilt that filled him; it was stupid, he knew, to apportion himself responsible for the failure, when everything that could have been done had been done. The enemy had simply outsmarted them.

It was early afternoon when he woke, dressed in clean clothes that hardly contained any heavy metal work, put dry boots on his feet and found his way through the castle to the High Hall, which looked and smelled freshly scrubbed. The commanders were clustered around a large, badly battered table, poring over maps.

"Kerr, did you get some rest? Are you hungry?" Pualyn asked, looking up at his approach. "Please, fetch the High-Prince a meal." A soldier hurried off.

"Thank you." Kerrenan stretched. "I must have slept, I don't remember." He broke off then, holding in the automatic apology.

"Your people have found a whole labyrinth of passages and caves rising up and around from that hidden entrance in that hill, Kerr." Lieutenant Sevanter said admiringly. "Another group are still moving upwards inside the cliff, and the whole area seems riddled with caves. They're making plans as they advance and have found where the cellars become the caves, but the fire-damaged sections will prevent their egress that way."

"There was a narrow crack, that apparently was full of rubble and hidden behind more, forming the connection, right in the corner of a tiny room full of ancient boxes; none of us had any idea of its existence." Pualyn marvelled, shaking his head. "Apparently it had been made larger, to accommodate people."

"Well, what have you decided whilst I slept?" The High-Prince asked, as the soldier returned with a tray holding bread, soup, sausages and cheese, a second bearing wine and beer for the group at large. "Thank you."

"I will take a handful of people to Saremouth: warn the city and the ships, so we'll hopefully be able to intercept the Generals at the estuary, or maybe upstream." His father stated gravely. "With the Pearls and local ships, we'll be able to block them easily -."

"I'll join you -." Kerr began, but broke off when Mhezal shook his head.

"No, you stay here and help the coordination, Kerrenan: there might well still be traps or enemies within these old walls." He ordered and Kerr nodded acquiescence.

"I want to be there." King Marrand stated then, his tone calm, but with the air of a man expecting argument.

"Your Majesty!" Commander Vedeigne protested. "I, excuse me, but you *can't* -."

"I bloody well will! I'll keep out of the way. But I've got to be there." Marrand replied.

"Very well, Marrand, I don't see why not; you are ruler here, after all and you won't be in danger. But you have not asked me how I propose to reach the port before our enemies when they have the advantage of at least half a day on us." Mhezal pointed out, smiling.

"Well, *I* was wondering I must admit it, even if Marrand isn't. So how can such an impossibility be achieved, your Majesty?" King Namayomn enquired dutifully with his eyes wide, his voice expressing breathless wonder.

The High-King laughed. Namayomn was quite willing to ask questions and viewed the world with great enthusiasm, for a man in his early thirties. He was well capable of command, but also acknowledged that others sometimes knew a great deal more than he, and that knowledge never upset him, unlike some others in the command structure. "We will use our power to make a portal, a gateway, straight to Saremouth. You can call it magic, I suppose; we don't very often make these portals for it's very tiring and it can be quite uncomfortable. That was what Ashanner meant in his report on their attack on Cal'Badon: the enemy Generals were able to fight back at the end of the night, because they created a portal from Ban'Lerracon which carried them across those intervening mountains.

"Right, gentlemen, let's get armed up again. We will reconvene here shortly. I want six volunteers." He glanced at the razine around the hall, who nodded.

"Very well, thank you, Mhezal." Marrand turned and hurried out, Orthen right behind him; the High-King and six tall, stern-faced razine followed.

"Magic?" Lord Gorman asked of the hall at large. "Dear Arven, whatever next?"

Kerrenan smiled, but he was obviously preoccupied as he ate quickly. "It looks spectacular, but as my father said, it's very tiring. I've made a portal twice in emergencies and it put me flat on my back both times, a bit like wearing two lots of mail and fighting all day or trying to climb a mountain. Worse than we all felt yesterday, definitely." He tried to describe the sensation then shrugged. "It's bloody useful, but I don't like it."

"Will your ships still be at Saremouth?" Duke Agamn asked.

"Yes, your Grace, they're resting and re-stocking their supplies, getting goods for trade. And I know Captain Ashanner is still praying that the Mador Opal under Captain Phellos makes it back to safety at some point; he is most distressed that there has been no sighting since they left Cal'Badon. It was her talent that raised the volcano, after all."

"It is most certainly magic!" Lieutenant Sevanter affirmed politely. "And Lady Ethrayne and Prince Jerryn will one day be so talented?" He wore his bandages as if embarrassed at his weakness but was moving a little more easily than he had the previous afternoon.

"One day soon they will, yes." Kerrenan agreed with a sigh. "And much more besides. They'll eclipse my father and me for sure."

The men considered his confident words. Tymain smiled: it seemed that some of the nobles still had difficulty with the concept, even after a year, judging by their expressions. He had been keeping a personal note on who had trouble with the very existence of the Am'maiya, just because it seemed prudent – though they would probably never require such protection from a man such as he, when they could command so much of the Flame of Arven . . . He prayed that Jerryn was all right, that Lady Ethrayne was as safe as possible, yet again.

The two kings and the razine soldiers returned in a group, all fully armed, mail and weapons jingling musically, helms on their heads, both kings wearing rather damaged surcoats.

"We'd better move the table, gentlemen, if you please." Kerrenan suggested, winking at Pualyn, now clearly looking forward to the spectacle, if he could not be part of the force heading to Saremouth. "That's it, over by the far wall; Lord, what's this made of, your Grace? Iron?"

"Simple oak, your Highness." Pualyn protested.

"Humph!" He said, as they set the table back down by the wall.

"Thank you, Kerrenan. Please, everyone please stand back, I don't want to injure anyone by accident with this." Mhezal said, standing alone in the centre of the hall, raising his palms facing outwards at shoulder height. Everyone stared avidly; the men of the kingdoms hardly dared to blink as the High-King straightened, took a deep breath, and exhaled. The six razine were ranged around him in pairs and adopted identical poses, two to his left, two to his right and two facing him. Marrand stayed where he was, surprise on his face; he shivered, as did Tymain and some of the others, as power flared in the great hall, invisible but tangible . . . Then light flared like pale lightning from their hands, all focussing on a single point some ten feet before Mhezal, the white-ish light somehow spinning itself into a sphere about five feet above the ground . . . The power in the hall increased until even the most unimaginative could sense it: their teeth on edge, their skin itching, the hair on their heads and bodies even standing on end; some men shivered at its touch . . . There was a *crack*! A far brighter flash and the ball of light vanished, leaving an oval opening that, viewed from behind the High-King's position before it, showed a four-foot wide and eight-foot high view of bright green, with a few clustered buildings visible to the right, trees to the left, the grey-blue sea shining beyond.

"Dear Arven!" Nearly everyone there repeated Tymain's words.

"Your Majesty?" Mhezal gestured politely. "Will you join me?"

"My word yes, thank you your Majesty. I'll take care." Marrand grinned wickedly at the others despite his worry and stepped forward at Mhezal's side.

"Just walk, Marrand and don't be concerned, for it will feel odd." The

High-King advised.

And together they advanced, stepping from the old tiles of the High Hall onto lush green grass, the six razine close behind them. Marrand shuddered as there was a strange lurch, a stink of an odd metallic nature; he felt almost dizzy for a moment as he stepped across so many tens of leagues in a moment. The rest of the commanders watched, amazed, as the small group stepped out into clear sunshine - then vanished from their sight as the gateway suddenly ceased to be with a burst of harsh noise, another flare of light and that harsh stink.

*

"Bloody hell!" King Marrand shook his head, staring around him, seeing the sea, the estuary, city, ships exactly as they should be amid the flatter countryside of the coast. "Oh, dear Arven!" He shuddered again as if at an icy draught in an aftermath to the travelling. It had been momentary, he supposed, but it had felt horrible.

"I know, the sensation is quite unpleasant; come along, please. I've told Ashanner to warn Lord Kierven, or I don't know what he might think at what they will have seen." Mhezal smiled and they all set off towards the pale line of the road that wound towards the city gates, a quarter of a mile away. "You've got to admit, however, that it's arriving in a manner that certainly gains everyone's attention."

Marrand grimaced. "Is this actually going to do any good? Can we rescue Jerryn, d'you think?"

The tall razine sighed deeply. "Honestly? I can only pray, Marrand, like you. This has obviously been planned meticulously by the enemy, so it all depends on what their intentions are; how they will bypass Saremouth; whether they're perhaps expecting one of their ships to pick them up; who they've been in contact with on their side. I'm praying, Marrand, that we can block the Generals' route and regain your son."

"Oh, please Arven we can!" The King of Tenarum breathed.

The city gates opened, people emerging to meet them, a mixture of men and razine, some clearly injured. Getting closer, Marrand recognised Captain Ashanner and Lord Kierven, the enthusiastic sea-trading Lord of Saremouth.

"Your Majesties, welcome to Saremouth!" Kierven said, bowing low, his eyes wide; the razine had obviously told him who was approaching. "My word! How may we assist you?" He bowed again and gestured politely. "I can tell from your faces and from what Ashanner related earlier that there is trouble somewhere. Please, come up to the castle."

Served a restorative goblet of wine, the group sat in silence in Kierven's meeting hall, digesting the news delivered. Nothing else needed saying, for now, which Marrand was grateful for; anger, guilt and fear raced around inside him, despair following close upon those emotions, threatening his equilibrium. All his concerns for the kingdom that had been focussed on poor, lost Ethrayne were increased infinitely, it seemed . . . Part of him wanted to scream and curse Arven soundly, although that wasn't fair; Jerryn had known of the danger, had warned them all that he was the enemy's target, and his son had not shirked from his duty. No, it was the Betrayer . . . He felt cold for a moment and took a large gulp of wine, trying not to let his fears show.

"Oh, damn it all!" Kierven said eventually. "So, the Generals are on their way downstream? Well, of course they are." He answered his own question. "It's quick and easy to travel on the river at this time of year, there are so many craft. If they set off last night well, three or four days at most, likely three to reach us – the river is clear, there are no barriers." He frowned, thinking. "I suggest that we wait a little, keep watch upstream and then blockade the estuary."

Marrand had to smile at his boyish enthusiasm and uttered more silent prayers for Ethrayne, Jerryn, the kingdoms and all the thousands who had died in the capture and freeing of Clirensar.

That evening, at a hurriedly arranged yet sumptuous dinner, the destroyers of Cal'Badon and the liberators of Clirensar exchanged basic details of their separate, audacious campaigns. It was very strange, almost disrespectful in fact, to reduce the intense planning, their hard days of fighting and their slow advances to such short narratives and Marrand supposed the men and razine who had willingly and courageously sailed into the heart of enemy territory so boldly, felt the same as he. Amazingly, despite all their reservations, the attack on the southern port had succeeded, although at a terrible loss and not simply because the brave, resourceful Captain Phellos had not returned from awakening the fire of the very earth! He added another prayer for her and her cohorts, for good measure.

"You must be weary, your Majesty." Lord Kierven said, noting his king's introspection amid the conversations. "You have had a busy couple of moons, and the night passes. It is wonderful news that you actually ousted the enemy and retook the castle yesterday! That is a great success, despite your terrible loss, I know. We will meet for breakfast. Let me show you your suite, Sire." He rose to his feet.

"Thank you, Kierven, I apologise for my silence, it's just -." He shrugged, as they left the hall.

"I know, Sire; we all felt the same when the Mador Opal failed to rejoin us once Captain Phellos had raised the volcano: fury and misery filled us -." The younger man grimaced. "And that was nearly twenty days ago now. You will be so frightened. I wish there was more that we could do and, well, we can pray and plan as best we can. Please, let me guide you, your Majesty." He turned towards the sweeping staircase, but Marrand saw the shadow in his eyes and realised that the Lord of Saremouth had taken the death of the brave, beautiful, strikingly unique woman badly, however he tried to deny it to himself. He himself had been stunned by the fire, the presence of Captain Phellos on those few occasions they had met before the captains had left to set off on their dangerous mission.

*

The next day passed in a flurry of preparation on board the four razine Pearls and Kierven's two ships, in addition to many other small boats and craft in the vicinity, once the news got out regarding the impending intended escape by the hated jajozeli with Prince Jerryn their prisoner. Experienced men were sent upstream to watch for suspicious-looking craft sailing downstream, and the rebuilt wharves and dockside were emptied just in case; although this was only the second day, the city was made ready for action.

Of course, the only boats arriving coming downstream were well known, guided by local folk. All craft were accounted for. By nightfall, despite their knowledge, the tension was still great enough to be cut with a knife.

"I bet they'll try and come through at dawn." One of the local fishermen nervously suggested. "Everyone's busy at dawn, 'round here, Majesty. If there's a ship out there -." He shook his head and sucked his teeth.

"I think you are correct, Captain Vicaro." High-King Mhezal agreed, to the man's open-mouthed amazement and he smiled. "Instinct, Captain, instinct." He tapped his nose. "But however it specifically works, we all depend on it."

"Oh, bloody hell!" Marrand clenched his hands into fists. "Hell – hell – hell!"

That night passed, sleepless, as the men and razine moved to their respective crafts. Mhezal joined Captain Ashanner on the Orbain Pearl, whilst Marrand and three of the razine soldiers remained with Lord Kierven on the Sweet Rose with strict orders to keep out of the way. Commands that neither man intended to obey.

They all waited impatiently, the stars moving all too slowly, wheeling along to the west at a snail's pace until, beyond belief, there was finally a faint hint of greyness that showed the eastern horizon, banishing night and, unlooked for, as everyone stared east in relief at the arrival of a new day, that was surely the Mador Opal, heading towards port! As it came, a figure on the stern deck, details hidden by the increasing light behind, waved most enthusiastically. The crews on the waiting ships all waved back as the ship came on and the sun rose bright behind it -.

"There!" Lord Kierven pointed upstream to a long, low river boat coming down right in the middle of the stream. "There they are, look!" His tone was fierce. "Let's go!" He ordered.

Marrand watched, his heart in his mouth, as the Orbain Pearl swept towards the small craft, where ten soldiers rowed; there was a General in the bow; people were huddled together at the stern – one of them his son, knelt there at the feet of two more Generals -.

Captain Ashanner shouted, from the northern bank opposite, but the words he called were not clear across the water, for the wind was rising towards them from inland. The General replied contemptuously, his tone evident even if the words were not. Marrand clutched at the rail tightly as it seemed that Ashanner's ship would crush the little boat into the depths of the river. Then, oddly, he felt power -. The mental bellow of the command thrilling through them -.

Every single person turned in shock to the Veddock Pearl, then swivelled to stare at the suddenly swinging arm of the mangonel at the bow of the Mador Opal that was cranked back. The crew and Captain Skendon were instantly, desperately, trying to quench the fire that had been dropped upon them. As the rest of them watched, aghast, another missile flew out of the contraption to hit the tiles of one of the long storage buildings on the north bank of the Sare.

"Oh, dear Arven no! Please no!" Lord Kierven whispered, sounding sick, his face grey. "The bastards!"

"No! Phellos!" Captain Ashanner's shout of loss and shock echoed from bank to bank.

The Generals on the little boat jeered, shouting coldly and precisely in selithian, threatening them and their prisoners. But Marrand was not really listening to the insults and demands, his brain had frozen in denial and disbelief. They heard screams, women's screams, from the boat: as he had dreaded, his son was obviously not the only prisoner. The enemy's escape was assured, if they held the Opal, he realised then.

Suddenly, more fire rained down onto the Veddock Pearl and, instinctively, everyone watching on every ship and on land flinched in horror.

<*Jerryn!*> Mhezal's shout, however, broke through Marrand's inertia, for when had he ever been able to hear razine mind-speak?

<*The prince belongs to his majesty, idiot leader of soft-minded idiots! Do not interfere, or he will suffer much worse than a broken arm and some bruises!*> The General shouted confidently in all their heads.

"Oh, damn them all!" Marrand muttered in horror as the High-King reluctantly agreed to the terms, as more threats were delivered, as he saw his injured son roughly shaken by his captors.

What else could they do? The captains obediently turned their ships, moving smoothly back to the docks and they were forced to watch the little boat, looking smaller and smaller as it moved into the wider channel, slowly approach the Mador Pearl, watch Jerryn, they supposed, be hauled up onto the ship by rope, the others following quickly.

Marrand stared, tears in his eyes, as the Mador Opal raised her anchor almost before everyone was over the rail, the mangonel poised again to rain destruction upon them. She set her sails, the standard of the Betrayer shining, clear, the whole time, turned elegantly and headed into the newly risen sun. Despair filled him. He had watched the enemy abduct his only son and heir, take him away for some evil purpose! He wondered if anyone from Phellos's ship had also be captured . . . It was very hard, he found, not to curse Arven now.

* * *

CHAPTER 42

Everyone there at Saremouth, whether on board ship or on the docks, who was not directly involved in extinguishing the last flames that had so threatened them, watched the Mador Opal vanish into the newly risen sun on a beautiful early summer's day that now was as cold as the depths of the southern winter.

Standing there on the deck of the Sweet Rose, Marrand had had one last glimpse of Jerryn's face; small, hardly clear at such a distance, as the boat had rowed quickly past; he had thought his son looked drawn, pale, frightened; that was certainly how he would have felt, in his place. In his mind, he could see the little boy of five that Jerryn had been, just one random image out of countless memories: lying on the hearthrug in Sarant's private sitting room, it had been a winter visit, with an equally small Ethrayne, an older, bigger Pualyn and a number of wriggling puppies, giggling, whilst Riyala and his sorely missed wife, Tanallyse, laughed as they tried to restore order and get them to bed . . . But what had happened to the world? How had so much been destroyed in a single year? First Ethrayne and now Jerryn stolen away -.

Dear Arven, please protect them! He prayed desperately.

Aboard the Orbain Pearl, the High-King remembered his first meeting with an already ancient Bahlien, on his accession to the throne, when the then acting Archpriest had told him of the prophecy in the Book of Days. Surely his memory was wrong, surely it was not over three hundred years ago? He had been concerned: two young humans were surely not going to be strong enough to contain so much God-given power! How could they possibly face the sheer might and the ruthlessness of the Betrayer? But Bahlien had convinced him that they had no real say in the matter: their roles would mainly be ones of support when the young couple accepted their destiny . . . And now, barely a year after they had taken the Flame, he and all his people had failed! They had effectively helped condemn these courageous youngsters, who were barely even adults, to a terrible fate!

Captain Ashanner mourned the loss of Captain Phellos: brave, beautiful, independent and brilliant who had excelled, taking on their exclusive male world, ensuring the defence of the Protectorates and the Selithian Kingdoms, winning the respect of everyone she met and, besides, raising profits with her cargoes . . . Knowing the cruelty of the jajozeli-razine, especially since it was she who had single-handedly raised the volcano, he prayed fervently that Phellos was already dead and followed that up with a prayer for the prince and those other poor souls.

"Bastards!" He spat, coming back to himself. "Those bloody clever bastards! Sire, if we had only known -."

"How could you though?" Mhezal asked impatiently, watching the ships around them tie up at the docks, wishing to get off the ship, go and find a large wine skin perhaps. "If they could knock everyone in the castle area sideways with power, razine and human both; poised to grab Jerryn and hide their exit point from Kerr and everyone else who had been looking . . . The bloody bastards didn't have to do anything at all to make us believe that the amazingly resourceful Captain Phellos was coming to our rescue. Dear Arven, protect them!" He sighed deeply. "Let's go. We've got to face Marrand. I suppose we ought to return to Clirensar."

"Berthing promptly, your Majesty. Dear Arven, I only wish -."

"Aye, don't we all?" Mhezal sighed heavily.

It only took a short while and they were back on the southern dock, all of them very self-controlled, their faces pinched and rather pale: it had been a traumatic morning.

"Have you told Kerr that Jerryn is beyond our help?" Marrand asked bluntly. "We should get back. Pualyn will need our assistance."

"Yes, of course, Marrand." Mhezal agreed. "I'm - ."

"We all regret it and apologising for things we could not have anticipated gets us precisely nowhere." Marrand waved one hand dismissively but the razine were not fooled: it was all an act, and who could blame him? He hurt so much inside, it felt as if he had been stabbed! Those in power sometimes required the strongest armour around their feelings.

In the end, it was nearly noon when the High-King was ready to raise the portal, for Lord Kierven and the other ships' captains, led by Ashanner, insisted on accompanying them, all weighed down with wineskins and some delicacies from the lord's cellars.

When the razine-raised portal appeared, shimmering strangely, in the muddy field north of Clirensar, there was a great flurry of activity about the city as the temporarily fixed gates were opened wide and the young duke met them at the bridge over the Sare, alone but for the High-Prince.

"We are pleased that you are back safe, your Majesties, gentlemen. Please, come on up to the castle. It's still pretty basic, but we've been cleaning up, just to keep occupied." Pualyn said with a low bow. "Dear Arven, I'm so sorry your rescue failed."

"As are we." Marrand said and gestured. "Let me introduce you all as we go, gentlemen, Lord Kierven of Saremouth you may know."

"I thought you looked familiar, my Lord, it must be years." Pualyn greeted the older man politely.

"Four at least, your Grace." Kierven was equally as formal.

"And Captain Ashanner of the Orbain Pearl; Captain Eltham of the Jaece Pearl; Captain Skendon of the Veddock Pearl; Captain Amdor of the Cerris Opal." Marrand continued.

"Captains, my Lord and so you led the attack upon Cal'Badon; we salute you." Kerrenan said rather unhappily as they set off up the road, the gates being closed behind them, the soldiers of all armies saluting them. "Your loss, as ours, is terrible."

"Aye, terrible indeed." Captain Ashanner's tone was sad. "It's nice to see you again, your Grace."

"And you, Captain." Pualyn tried to smile but failed. "May I ask why you are all bearing wineskins and bundles?"

"It's my idea actually, your Grace: to celebrate our successes and to drown our woes together." Kierven replied with a poor attempt at humour.

There was a certain amount of drinking later in the High Hall, but an awful lot more talking went on as the participants in both groups did their best to describe all that they had been through since their last meeting. Jerryn, Phellos and the others lost were mentioned sadly and with great respect. At dinner, however, Marrand got to his feet and urged that they stop regretting and worrying and start planning: their goal, of course, was to liaise with the Archpriests and to work towards rescuing the Am'maiya. His short, impassioned speech ended with a heart-felt prayer to Arven that raised a rousing cheer.

*

Pualyn had had his own suite cleaned out for King Marrand, and they had worked hard to clean more for the other kings and commanders. His parent's suite had been badly damaged by the occupiers and was not going to be usable until the problems had been rectified; he himself had claimed his sister's rooms although, strangely, many items including her four posted bed, clothes, curtains, carpets and even her sewing box had simply vanished; whereas everything else apart from the shredded remains of her wedding dress seemed to be untouched. He, Orthen, Tymain and Sevanter had carried in furniture from elsewhere in the castle the previous afternoon; it had certainly kept them busy.

Alone, finally, the young duke had finally acknowledged his deep fear for his sister, the evil she might be facing brought home with stark reality seeing the destruction of so much, never mind the even more obvious 'object lessons' left for them to find: the bodies of emaciated family retainers who must have died only a few days before in revolting circumstances to be still recognisable! Pualyn prayed that Ethrayne was safe, unaffected by such evil as they had seen here. He had considered destroying the whole structure, discovering yet another well full of corpses, but logic won: the city's strategic importance was undeniable, it would simply be folly to try and rebuild the castle elsewhere, or even atop the existing base, the costs prohibitive!

Seeing the deliberate vandalism that ranged from tower to cellar; now acknowledging the single-minded ruthlessness of enemies who had held his home chiefly to get the best possible opportunity to take Jerryn into captivity, no matter how many lives were lost; it was chilling, along with the realisation that practically the entire jajozeli force had been wiped out. Tens of thousands of them had been killed, other than the few who had escaped with the prince, on top of the probable tens of thousands more allies who had died for Jerryn and to secure the kingdom! It affected him deeply.

Pualyn prayed that Ethrayne and Jerryn, along with anyone else in the enemy's hands, were as safe as possible. That night, he finally slept properly for the first time in moons, it seemed, although Ethrayne, Jerryn and his parents walked through his dreams with Lyria. Killing the leader of the jajozeli had laid some of his worries to rest, the one who had slaughtered his parents and so many others; he was still pleased that he had managed to despatch him in straight combat although he knew full well that it had been luck, as well as his own skill, that achieved that end: General Tequan had been a damned fine swordsman, it had been a bloody close thing.

*

Morning came, blustery and sunny, and, after a hearty breakfast, Pualyn led his friends and the surviving members of the Flame Guard from the High Hall, hoping to finish their search of the castle, cataloguing damage and so. None of the tasks allotted either to officers or the common soldiers were pleasant, but all were necessary. Groups of engineers were still down in the cellars of the castle, carefully clearing the collapses caused by the fires that had so facilitated the Generals' escape with Jerryn, starting to rebuild supporting structures where required.

The kings and commanders were discussing the great sea voyage that would be undertaken by the Mador Opal to reach Enlath: four moons at least, the ships' captains asserted to the horror of most of the group, with likely few opportunities to take on fresh water or supplies.

Ashanner wondered uneasily whether the jajozeli had raided towns along the coast before sailing into Saremouth; he was not sure how much supplies the Opal had had in storage. He offered to return to port and so sail out and check on the safety of the settlements to the south.

It was mid-morning, when a soldier came to inform them most politely that visitors had arrived. Duchess Lyria, her maid Greta and Archpriest Bahlien, with a troop of soldiers.

"Here?" Marrand spluttered, looking around the rather worse-for-wear hall at the other men. "Dear Arven, it's hardly suitable -. Look at your home."

"Then you require ladies to undertake the cleaning, your Majesty. We might do a rather better job than soldiers." The young duchess stated, sweeping in regally, despite her plain travelling clothes and her pale face, her hand on the old Archpriest's arm.

"Your Graces -." The High-King greeted them with a sweeping bow, as the group rose to their feet.

"It's entirely my fault, your Majesties." Lyria stated with a smile. "As soon as Pualyn's letter arrived, saying you were close to taking the city, I started organising: there are thirty women with us who have volunteered to help with the cleaning up. You've made quite a good start, for men." She conceded, glancing into the corners at the mess that still lingered.

Kerrenan started to laugh at that and quite a few of them joined in as Lyria, Bahlien and Greta were quickly shown to seats and wine poured.

"Lyria has the soul of a garrison commander." Bahlien admitted with a huge sigh and a wide smile. "As soon as I passed on your message that you had taken the outer city, Mhezal, our young duchess flatly insisted that we set off with our accompanying ladies from Tenum. She would not take no for an answer: she had everything planned."

"Tymain, will you go and bring our duke and Lieutenant Sevanter, please? They're somewhere in the castle." Marrand asked and the young man bowed and hurried away. "You have heard that Jerryn has been abducted, my dear?" He asked tensely.

The blonde woman nodded gravely. "His Grace told me at once, your Majesty." She admitted.

"I myself felt that explosion of power quite clearly, Marrand, even four days north of Foston. It was shocking." Bahlien said sadly. "I have brought the Book of Days with me, but I myself have not been able to find anything useful at all within its hallowed pages. Please, if any of you want to read through it, do feel free." That explained the heavy-looking, bulky bag that had been slung across his body and now rested close by on the table. "We feel such guilt, Lurco and I."

"We all feel guilty, your Grace." The High-Prince admitted.

"I realise that you have suffered terrible losses, quite apart from his Highness's capture, but I am so glad that you are safe, that you have freed Clirensar. I have little experience, of course, except that simply terrifying afternoon when Ethrayne was taken away, amid so much bloodshed." Lyria faltered and took a deep breath to settle herself. "The graves and burnsites around the city will be prominent in the landscape for centuries." She shivered. "The whole world has changed, hasn't it?"

"Yes indeed, dear Lyria." Marrand agreed wearily.

Small talk occupied them nicely for a while until. "Lyria!" Rang from two throats simultaneously; Pualyn and Sevanter had both stopped in the doorway, staring in shock and some disbelief, then the soldier grinned and waved her husband forward. Tymain entered behind them bearing a new wine skin which he quietly laid on the table beside King Marrand.

"Oh, Pualyn!" Lyria pushed back her chair, leapt to her feet and met Pualyn halfway across the hall, laughing and crying all at once, thanking Arven for keeping so many of them safe. She squealed as Pualyn lifted her up and span around, kissing her soundly.

"But, hang it all! Lyria, how are you here? The city is a complete wreck -."

Grinning, Lyria explained again. "I bullied the archpriests and everyone else until they relented. I've brought thirty hard-working ladies to assist in getting this place and the city back to normal." She answered as he set her back down. "We won't get in your way, Pualyn, I promise."

"Dear Arven!" The duke blustered for a moment, shaking his head.

"Oh, *please* let me help, Pualyn! It's been dreadful, waiting day after day for those sparse messages that came back to the palace. This is our home!

There can't be any jajozeli left alive in the complex, surely? I've just got to help as well, after everything. I owe so much to you and your family!" There were tears in her eyes, but she managed a weak smile.

"Well, no, Lyria, dearest . . . heavens, you've brought a troop of women with you?" Unexpectedly, Pualyn chuckled; it was quite ridiculous, but she, Bahlien and Greta were nodding agreement, and they seemed very pleased with themselves. "Who am I to stand in your way, your Grace? But it's going to be a bad job in parts, you know."

"Yes, we know." Her tone was sober.

"We took a day at Elyssa and Banley's inn at Foston to get organised, let Greta tell her parents how she is; we arrived at the last fort last night and we left the group there at the edge of the vale. I bullied the soldiers with us to get some of the tents and kitchens organised." Bahlien admitted. "They can be here in a short time."

"Then we'll start in the morning." Pualyn agreed. "And you have just completely ruined *my* surprise announcement, dearest." He complained rather plaintively, pushing his hair back from his forehead.

"Oh, what might that be?" Lyria asked archly, grinning at her brother who was shaking his head.

"I found the keys that Steward Pentar and Reeve Thomur would have held, and the treasury does not seem to have been touched at all, your Majesty: it was securely locked -." Pualyn paused at the cries of surprise around the hall -. "And I found this letter on top of one of the caskets that held some of the family's assets -."

"Your grandmother's pearls?" Lyria asked, her quivering hands at her mouth. "Oh, your lady mother loved those, Pualyn. Are they still safe?"

"Aye and the rest with them." His tone was cool, but his voice shook as he continued. "Everything . . . The letter, here." He unfolded a rather blotchy palimpsest of great antiquity and cleared his throat.

> "'Greeting Duke Pualyn.
>
> 'Thank you for the use of your home. We have taken all we wanted: the Am'maiya, not your gold, yet your steel was most welcome.
>
> 'Your wealth is intact, and you will likely need it all in the years ahead, preparing for the inevitable occasion when your sister and the prince, broken by our Master to his service, return to assist him in destroying your civilisation! Prepare to lose, servants of a defeated, defective god.'"

He paused and took a breath. "I'm glad I killed the bastard so convincingly!"

"Do they learn their offensiveness at school, d'you think?" Sevanter asked Tymain.

Pualyn grinned. "So, it seems that we're actually not quite as poor as we feared, my lady, your Majesty." He bowed first to his wife and then to Marrand.

"Good, because hard-working cleaning ladies won't just work for free, my lord Pualyn." The duchess replied primly before anyone else could speak.

*

Three days had passed and the small but effective group of women, aided and abetted by ladies from Foston, were moving steadily through the castle.

Archpriest Bahlien had set the great Book of Days in the centre of the scrubbed and now highly polished table in the High Hall, and a few of the kings, officers and lords had glanced through it, although no one had yet sought to read it properly. Maybe it was its legendary reputation that deterred them, perhaps something else entirely, but although they had all sworn their oaths to Arven, had fought hard and shed blood for their God, perhaps the *reality* of the myths that governed their lives was too immediate for even the razine amongst them.

Tymain popped in to the hall on his way to a delayed breakfast, to report that the engineers had stabilised the greatest part of the collapse that had prevented their initial pursuit of Jerryn's abductors; the cellars and the greater structure were no longer in immediate danger of falling in.

"That's good news." Pualyn agreed, looking up from the parchment that he had been scribbling on, stretching his right hand which ached slightly. "In fact, it's bloody good news. You know, I thought we'd lose something huge like half the castle. Have you eaten yet, Tymain?" He had risen early, along with Lyria who was leading the clean-up in person, whilst he was checking inventories and accounts.

"No, not yet, but -." Tymain paused, suddenly feeling an urge to look at the Book of Days, although the vast size of the tome awed him; he had never been much of a reader and books were expensive. "Go on ahead, Pualyn, I just want to -." And he sat down at the table, pulled the Book closer and opened it.

Pualyn watched him for a moment. Tymain was frowning down, his forefinger moving under a line of writing, his mouth silently saying the words that he read there. But it was rude to stand there staring, so he turned and left the hall, shutting the door quietly. Tymain never heard him leave.

"Have you seen Tymain?" Duke Agamn asked, when he entered the dining hall, quickly serving himself steak and eggs. "We were going to continue gathering scrap iron together this morning."

"He's just picked up the Book of Days, Agamn, he may be some time, judging by the look on his face." Pualyn answered lightly. "He told me that that huge section of ceiling and buttresses in the cellars is stable, then – he just sat down by the book and opened it. He hasn't even eaten."

“Then we had better not disturb him, Pualyn.” Bahlien said with a lenient smile. “I wondered who the book would attract, of all of you.”

“How strange.” Lyria frowned, considering, smoothing her plain linen gown that had become a uniform of a kind for the diligent cleaning women of the kingdom. “Are you saying that the Book of Days is a-a lodestone, Bahlien?”

His smile broadened at her hesitant description. “Yes, for the right people, my dear; don’t ask me how because I have no idea, but I suspect that young Tymain will not be our only reader. He may discover a passage or a meaning that we past students of its pages have completely overlooked; that was how I found the prophecy regarding Jerryn and Ethrayne in the first place.”

“That’s very peculiar.” The High-King commented. “But would it not be so much easier if important information was just there in plain sight on the page, Bahlien?”

“Well, yes, but the Book of Days was not written by men or razine but by Arven himself and that just seems to be the way it has always worked, I’m afraid.” The old razine explained with a smile and a shrug.

“Obviously the mind of our God is definitely not like our own, but surely that is what makes him our God, because he is so different?” King Marrand suggested, sounding puzzled. “I mean, we must be rather mundane in comparison, even the notable of us.”

“It might be one reason, yes.” Bahlien agreed, getting to his feet. “I will take some food and drink for the young man to break his fast when he remembers his needs.” He bowed his head politely to the table at general, picked up a jug and a serving plate holding bread, cheese and cold cuts and left the hall.

“He is a very singular person, isn’t he?” Pualyn asked politely.

“Oh, yes indeed.” Kerrenan agreed with a smile. “Archpriestess Gailla learned everything she knows from him; he’s quite unique.”

“I agree.” His father added, then chuckled, as if at some memory.

*

Sustained by the occasional bite of food or gulp of drink placed close at hand, which he never tasted or even really noticed, Tymain read steadily through the book, feeling its words somehow sinking deeply into his heart or soul; nearly all of it made absolutely no sense at all, but there were points where the words were clear. ‘And behold, my loyal servants. In the time following the promise . . .’ was the first, the passage describing Jerryn and Ethrayne, ending ‘In the hands of the Betrayer always lies despair.’ It made him weep a little, silently, even as he read on.

Then, a long time later, another section jumped out at him:

“‘Despair will wring our hearts,
Yet out of trial and tribulation,
Out of slavery, even,
Will emerge such Strength,

Such Fury as may even break
The bonds of Imprisonment.
From the loss of Self
Will emerge Power enough
To shake beloved Iullyn.
The Sister of the Iron Duke,
The Son of the Eastern Realm ~
Despite The Betrayer's despicable
Evil, such Evil as
Good people cannot envisage ~
In time they will break
The bonds that then Imprison them.
They will be free to rest in the Arms
Of the One Betrayed.'"

He read aloud, the archaic script as clear to his eyes as if it were printed letter by letter for a child at school and shivered deeply, suddenly realising that he sat in candle-lit darkness, that he was desperate to relieve his bladder and then that the Archpriest sat opposite at the great table, charcoal stick in hand, having clearly just written down what he had read aloud.

"Your Grace, I -."

"You have done us all a great service, young man." Bahlien said seriously with a soft, rather sad smile. "You have found the next passage of the prophecy, although it's not the most hopeful for now, is it? How do you feel?"

"I well, gosh, have I been reading *all day*?" Tymain got up, stretching his muscles with a sigh. "Me? But, excuse me, your Grace -." He made a dash for the narrow doorway that led to a privy beyond a plain waiting room and emerged a short time later, frowning a little, his mind clearer, *remembering*. "Am I really the first to find that prophecy?" He asked plaintively and the old razine nodded. "Dear Arven, no! We can't tell the king or Duke Pualyn of-of '*such evil as good people cannot envisage*'!" His tone was anguished.

"We will hope to highlight '*they will break the bonds that then imprison them*', young man." Bahlien answered gravely. "The whole message must be imparted, Tymain, or the results might possibly alter. Iullyn, all of us, might end up burning in eternal fire -." He paused as the young soldier shuddered. "I don't think anyone has gone to bed, you know; they're all waiting in the dining hall. Come and tell them the next Prophecy, Corporal Tymain."

* * *

CHAPTER 43

Jerryn was pushed through a second door just inside the passage, which opened into a bright room that clearly showed Phellos's personality, although the prince only dimly realised that. The tall, scarred General was at his shoulder, Sarlock just behind and two more jajozeli-razine stood waiting – and his inner discomfort and fear increased.

"Sit." He was pushed to a stool near the wide bank of windows, where General Sarlock removed the grubby sling and started to unfasten the knots holding the splints in place on his arm. "The Prince of Tenarum, welcome." The tall, commanding, injured General was speaking, his remaining eye shining bright as he stared at Jerryn.

"Sir." He finally managed to speak, around a grimace as the splints came away and the throbbing of his arm worsened. It was only at that point that Jerryn realised that he could understand the jajozeli language and, amazingly, had been speaking it too. He groaned, at first disbelieving his own ears and mind, then understanding the continuation of what Mhezal and Kerrenan had been describing, regarding his power: it had happened with the Protectorate language, mendor, without any outside interference and obviously had again, when faced with the new tongue spat at him by these unfriendly enemies. But, dear Arven! He still found it hard to believe, that his power had affected the change quite naturally.

"You will address me as Master Cheltor, boy." The tall General stated crisply. "My colleagues you will address as Lord General, do you understand me?" And he glared coldly. "You will mind your manners, else you and your fellow prisoners will suffer the consequences; ask the survivors brought from Cal'Badon, when you meet them: Phellos will encourage your obedience, I'm sure."

"Oh, indeed she will!" One unknown General now spoke with malicious amusement and laughed.

General Sarlock was checking the alignment of Jerryn's broken bones. "Don't move, boy." He ordered and yanked at his arm much harder than he had in the castle cellars. Jerryn bit back a cry of discomfort, trying to ignore the bloody wound caused by the protruding bone and the horrible mass of swelling and darkened bruising that covered his swollen arm. "There, that should do it, but he'll have to rest it for it to heal properly, Master. We must be mindful of the injury, as well." The healer reported, cleaning the area, before roughly rubbing a salve on the wound and bruising.

"Indeed, General Sarlock. When your arm is mended, boy, I will undertake your training myself to bring you back up to strength. It will be interesting to compare your skill to your betrothed. You *are* betrothed to the brat, aren't you? Ha! I thought that would get your attention." Master Cheltor barked a laugh as Jerryn sat up straighter. "Yes, I instructed the girl for some moons during the winter, and I must say that she also showed a deplorable lack of sense. I really do recommend obedience: we have a long voyage ahead of us."

"Yes, Master Cheltor." Jerryn muttered, wincing as the General started wrapping clean bandages around the splints that were placed back along his forearm. "Can I, may I ask, Master? General Oxttyn, he a-attacked me, on the river . . . he mentioned his son, Lady-Lady Ethrayne and retribution. But . . . she wasn't hurt, was she?"

"Were you injured?" The General asked promptly.

"I, well, I don't think so, not too seriously, Master, he-he kicked me." Jerryn admitted uneasily.

"He did kick him a few times." Sarlock admitted, finishing off the bandaging and refitting the sling. "I reminded him to restrain himself, however. The prisoner isn't more than bruised, I'm sure. I can't sense any other serious injuries, Master."

"General Oxttyn would do well to remember that afternoon completely." Master Cheltor snapped. "His son presumed – well, let me say that Inajo disobeyed all directives and his majesty took his life in payment. The brat was shaken, but unhurt. Our colleague was sent to Clirensar in the depths of winter to begin restoring his family's honour or freeze to death!"

Jerryn choked at that terse explanation but stopped himself from demanding more details.

"General Oxttyn will restrain himself. And you, boy, will be most respectful, for not only your own well-being depends upon it: if you want your fellow prisoners to eat regularly. If you want them to remain relatively healthy, I strongly suggest meekness on your part!"

"Y-yes, Master Cheltor."

"Excellent. Shuim, take him down; the prisoners are allowed food and water." Cheltor ordered.

"Aye, Master." Shuim pulled Jerryn up by his hair, then punched him hard in the stomach, twice, so that the young man half-folded in on himself, stifling a groan, trying to hide his dismay at this new humiliation from beings who could sense his every discomfort. "Move, boy!" He ordered, releasing Jerryn who attempted to stand vertical but with little success. "Soft!" Shuim commented in derision to Master Cheltor.

"He'll soon harden up adequately, we'll see to that." Master Cheltor answered with a cold laugh.

With a full water skin over his shoulder and what looked and smelled like a pail of gruel in his left hand, Jerryn uncomfortably and reluctantly followed the General back out onto the deck, staring with wide eyes at the vast expanse of green-blue waves that now surrounded the ship; the coast of Tenarum and the large estuary of Saremouth were already tiny in the distance, a good few leagues away, hazy and indistinct. He prayed that the Protectorate ships would not try to pursue them, prayed that no one else would die because of he and Ethrayne! He staggered slightly as the ship was lifted by a large wave, completely unused to the movement; he shivered at the wind that cut through his tattered shirt and concentrated on following a straight route along the deck towards the bow where a hatch was open. There were other Generals around, all staring at him, but he kept his gaze fixed on General Shuim. If he didn't look at them, perhaps they wouldn't hurt him. He hoped not, anyway.

Descending the nearly vertical ladders with the bucket in his left hand and his right arm strapped up was not easy, but Jerryn found it less of a challenge than he had climbing the netting up onto the ship: down was easier than up and there was just enough width there for him to use the bucket itself on the rungs as a balance; the prospect of a meal after these appalling days of enforced starvation was too good to throw away, especially when he suspected the other prisoners would be equally as hungry. A short, lightless passage followed, to a thick wooden door that the General opened with a key and a thick bolt. The prince was pushed into a foul-smelling dark space and the door was slammed shut and locked on his heels.

"Is that Prince Jerryn?" A female voice asked from the darkness to his right, sounding weak and tired.

"Captain Phellos?" Jerryn answered as heartily as he could manage, all courage and hope leaching out of him. "Yes, it's me, I've got food and water here -."

"Thank Arven!" That was a Clirensar-accented male voice to the left.

"I agree, Benner. Who's closest? Zeron, help his Highness sit down; you're injured, aren't you, Highness?" Phellos easily took charge. "*Please* don't drop the food!" She urged.

"I wont, Captain . . . I've got a broken right arm, some cuts and bruises, but otherwise I'm pretty much all right, so far." He replied politely, shocked at the hunger he could sense in the other prisoners, worse than his own. Someone touched his legs and Jerryn almost jumped; the bucket was found, removed from his hand and set down on the planks, before the unknown hands supported him, so that he could sit without falling in the darkness. "Thank you, but please, Captain Phellos, call me Jerryn." He carefully took the water skin's looped handle from over his shoulder. "Here's water, too." And, after a few gropes, it was taken from his hands by someone on his other side. "By your eagerness, I suspect that our worthy captors are a little lax regarding mealtimes?" He made it a light-hearted comment and one male voice ahead of him snorted in agreement.

<Indeed, but later, young man.> Phellos replied silently. "Right, where are Poppy and Hella? Beside me, of course. Let's get you two and Benner fed, along with Jerryn. Pass that pail, gentlemen, thank you."

The stuff in the bucket was barely warm, had looked pale and mushy out in the sunlight and tasted of meal or lentils of some kind, slightly seasoned with onion, proving very bland, but at least it was filling. Jerryn ate his quite soggy handful as slowly as he could, relishing the resulting fullness if not the consistency or flavour of the food, then drank, but Phellos silently warned him not to drink his fill: there was not enough water for them to do so.

"So, what happened at the port, Jerryn?" Phellos asked after a while, when everyone had finished eating. "Benner here wasn't too sure; please can you tell us?"

"We are far out from Saremouth now, the coast is receding, and I doubt the Pearls or Kierven's ships will sail after us." Jerryn remarked, wincing, for his stomach muscles were still aching from Shuim's blows. "Not with the threats General Oxttyn made, or the attack on the razine ship in port." Slowly, carefully, he briefly described what he had seen, and the crewmen muttered amongst themselves, sighing deeply at the danger so narrowly averted. "I thought we would be drowned at one point, when Captain Ashanner crossed our route, I'm sorry about my terminology, Captain, but, unfortunately, we weren't. Sorry, Benner, Hella, Poppy." He commented with a sigh. "It's been a frightening few days since I was captured, four days ago. But these people must have been prisoners for moons. I can say that the allies have re-taken Clirensar. Duke Pualyn killed General Tequan in single combat and-and here we are . . . Sorry." He shrugged in the darkness, fighting a sudden fear.

"Glad to hear Tequan was despatched. Who brought you here?" Lieutenant Lunde asked after introducing himself.

"General Oxttyn, General Sarlock, General Jaike, and ten soldiers. Oxttyn hates me . . . he hates Ethie, I mean Ethrayne, much more; something happened in Ban'Lerracon. I expect the remaining Generals in Clirensar are all very dead by now. How many are you? Were you all captured at Cal'Badon?"

"Forgive our rudeness, Highness -."

"Jerryn, Phellos." He reminded her with an attempt at a chuckle. "And you've obviously had a bad time of it."

"It's not been fun, Jerryn." Phellos also tried some false humour. "We have me, Lunde and Rynn who are razine, plus Captain Dhell, a very brave fisherman from Rothern, Zeron and Fereyne who were also members of our crew."

"I'm honoured to meet you all. Poppy was one of Duchess Riyala's maid's, whilst Hella is the sister-in-law of the new Duke and Duchess -." The woman sobbed at that. "Captain Benner was a household guard. Damn it, I'm sorry, Benner." Jerryn admitted.

"That's a'right, sir I'm just a man-at-arms." That gruff voice said, confirming his identity. "Young Pualyn killed General Tequan?" He demanded fiercely. "Thank Arven, the bastard's dead!"

"Yes, decapitated him. Glad to impart some good news." Jerryn replied. "But it's terrible, Phellos that you were captured, despite your victory."

"Rousing a volcano is a strange sort of victory, Jerryn but yes, we were successful. Cal'Badon was turning into quite an impressive fire pit when these ignorant Generals got the Opal away from the dock." She stated. "I injured

Cheltor, as you will have seen, but he disarmed me before I could finish him: stabbed me in the shoulder!"

"The scar looks very impressive around his face, there's still bruising, so I imagine you came very close to success there too, Captain." Jerryn noted, having participated in and seen enough hand-to-hand combat over the last few moons to have a relevant opinion. He sighed. "And then Oxttyn wouldn't have been able to use the river as an escape route . . . oh, damn it all!" He took a deep, rather shaky breath to calm himself. "It's Oxttyn I'm scared of most, though I haven't met the rest yet, have I?" He briefly explained the matter, as far as Master Cheltor had confirmed it, and shivered. "He hates me because his son was killed by his own master?" He shuddered at the thought of what might have happened.

"They ain't very sane, Highness." One of the Protectorate sailors confirmed then. "They moored up twice on the way to Saremouth, north of Newventure Bay we suppose. Pretending to be the Opal, I expect, for who'd expect the enemy after all? They slaughtered both villages, killed everyone, fired the buildings and boats, loaded up all the animals, food and water . . . O'course, it's moons to sail to Enlath from this side of Selith -."

"Enlath? That's half around Iullyn, isn't it?" Jerryn asked, his courage failing. "It took Pualyn a moon and a half to reach Lerat!"

<Calm, Jerryn, please.> Phellos's silent voice was as weary and as wounded as her ordinary one; clearly, she and the others had suffered considerably since their capture. *<We'll be imprisoned here for moons and our captors are complicated, with nasty habits, not just that one who bullied you. I expect most of us here are alive simply to provide entertainment and to keep you obedient. I'm deeply sorry, Jerryn -.>*

"Oh, damn it all!" He muttered.

*

Time passed with a terrible slowness there in the complete darkness of what, Phellos explained during that long day, was a space some twenty-five feet long and fifteen feet wide, one of four cargo holds at the bottom of the ship. There was nothing there but themselves and a single bucket that, of course, was completely inadequate for its purpose.

The mere concept of incarceration in such conditions was appalling, but Jerryn gritted his teeth and did his best to control his horror, for surely everyone else felt just the same and they were all in this together.

Such insanitary arrangements were unpleasant, yet the darkness was far worse and Jerryn found its effects more challenging even than the terrible thirst and hunger which soon became second nature to him, meals for the prisoners being delivered rather infrequently. He had been lately practising how to make light globes in his lessons with Kerrenan, had been doing well; but here, now, such capabilities were beyond him and he realised that Phellos and the other razine were similarly constrained.

The ten of them were huddled close together, for a little warmth and comfort, and the darkness felt a little less oppressive when you could touch the person next to you, hand to hand. Jerryn could not imagine what Hella, Poppy and Benner had suffered during their imprisonment in what had become their prison for moons on end; nor what Phellos or her men had been subjected to since their capture at Cal'Badon. All were suspiciously quiet on such details, but after his nightmare journey from Clirensar with the Generals, he was beginning to realise that perhaps the legends of the jajozelis' evil were under-exaggerated, that anything was possible of such monsters.

They were sat in darkness, with only the movement of the ship around them, sometimes manageable, sometimes plunging through what seemed to be mountainous seas; unlike the three prisoners from Clirensar, Jerryn didn't feel even remotely seasick, for which he thanked Arven profusely; occasionally they could hear footsteps above or beside them as the Generals walked along the passage on some task, or they caught muffled, indistinct voices in conversation. It was impossible to calculate the time of day beyond their prison.

It must have been a day at least, Jerryn guessed imprecisely, before he felt calm enough to try to sleep, his fear uppermost – in addition to the painful throbbing of his arm, and the desperate hunger that soon returned to haunt him; it was as if the tasteless handful of mush had never been consumed. He spent a long period huddled up in silence, simply trying to absorb the grim reality of their situation; then conducted a silent conversation with Phellos, who reluctantly acknowledged her weakness, trying to survive on meagre rations with her injured shoulder, but who was nevertheless positive in a way that Jerryn admired wholeheartedly, even if he could not emulate her confidence.

<*I am sure that your betrothed is being guarded most carefully, Jerryn.*> She stated, realising how frightened he had been by Oxttyn and Cheltor's brief descriptions of the events that had led to the death of Oxttyn's son. <*Ensuring the safety of the Am'maiya would be paramount: their king would hardly permit any risk to your lady.*>

<*That isn't very reassuring, Phellos! If that was what Oxttyn's son attempted . . . oh, dear Arven -!*>

<*Jerryn, we're in quite enough bother here, please don't go making yourself more trouble!*> She urged him sympathetically. <*It happened moons ago, whatever it was. I am certain that your betrothed is safe . . . Perhaps not happy, but safe. The Betrayer* would *ensure that.*>

Jerryn reached up with his left hand to scratch at one cheek, then the other; he was starting to really hate his stinking state, the growing whiskers that were making his face itch – missing the annoying necessity of shaving. <*Yes, I know you are correct, Phellos. Dear Arven! This is, it's just-.*> Words failed him there, but images span in his head that expressed what he felt, and he felt the captain's silent, mental agreement. <*And here we are, waiting on our captors. I bet they make me clean out this space, dear Arven, I* hope *they make me clean out this hold at some point! If I'm well-behaved and polite and subservient, we all get to eat, too, I hope.>*

<And what do the rest of us do, lad, hey?> Lunde asked, breaking into the conversation with false brevity.

<You? You know already, Lunde: you ensure my obedience, my manners, my meekness, of course.> He replied with a shudder. *<And, by Arven, they'll bloody get them, I promise!>*

<They'll probably hurt us anyway, Jerryn: don't forget, their interests are often perverse. You at least should be inviolate, like your young lady, but the rest of us -.> Phellos shrugged both physically and mentally at that.

<But, Captain -.> Jerryn stopped and took a breath. *<Oh, dear Arven I hope not!>* But his prayerful words were not delivered confidently, after his journey to the coast. *<May I ask you? I have no power at all now, beyond mindspeech . . . It's as if our absorbing of the Flame never happened last spring, Captain . . . I'm scared.>* He admitted after a great deal of worrying consideration – the apparently complete lack of that power which had been a circling force within his body for over a year now, alarmed him. The power of the Generals, or something, had knocked his strength and ability away.

<Aye, injury, lack of food and drink, pain and our enemies domination frequently reduce their prisoners' power, Jerryn – its how they stop people like us fighting back. I raised the fire of Iullyn to destroy Cal'Badon, and now I can't even make a light globe . . . We couldn't sink the ship if we tried for the entire voyage, let alone knock one of the bastards out . . . I'm sorry, Am'maiya.> The woman answered unhappily. *<If you can, you should try to meditate, however, since you are what you are . . . At some point, you will regain the power of the Flame, I'm sure.>*

<Oh, shit!> Jerryn shuddered at her explanation, which confirmed his own supposition and only increased his feeling of utter helplessness. *<I will try, Captain . . . I promise.>*

*

Days passed with a creeping slowness even snails could not have equalled; they had received five further meals, spaced widely apart, before a General came with soldiers bearing buckets and Jerryn's earlier prediction was proved accurate: he was ordered to clean the hold. Even with a short-handled shovel, a scrubbing brush and sea water, it was a hard job to complete, one handed; the other prisoners were marched away up onto the deck, whilst he scraped, scrubbed and did his best, determined that their well-being and perhaps even lives hung on how well he worked. At least, after a lot of sweaty effort on Jerryn's part, the stink was dispelled a little, the mess was eliminated; the planks were wet, but clean. He leaned back, stretching his back, wincing -.

"Not bad, boy." An unknown voice remarked sarcastically from the doorway behind him. "I bet you've never scrubbed anything before in your life!"

"My Lord General." Uncertainly, Jerryn turned to gaze up at an auburn-haired individual with hazel eyes, as tall and as muscular as the rest, with a cruel smile on his lips. His left hand trembled from the work and he did not dare to get to his feet yet, for menace exuded from the stranger, stinging him.

"Lord General Robonnare to you, boy. Get up, bring the equipment."

"Lord General Robonnare." He acknowledged quickly.

Jerryn bundled the buckets and brush and shovel all together; they were heavy in his left hand as he stepped as quickly as he could into the dim passageway. He was all too aware how foul he smelled as he clambered up the ladders and out onto the main deck, into gusts of chilly rain blown on a sharp wind, the sky and the vast ocean both grey and menacing. The other prisoners were all huddled by the bow on their knees and the prince finally saw their faces, pale, drawn, the men's visages bearded as he was, cuts and bruises clear; and, most prominent, their shadowed eyes uniformly held only fear and despair.

The buckets were taken from him and two of the jajozeli soldiers brought over fresh buckets of seawater that were simply poured over the group of them; it was breathtakingly cold, stinging awfully in their eyes and their many cuts, leaving them shivering, yet a little cleaner overall.

General Robonnare grabbed Jerryn, dripping wet, the salt water stinging in the gash in his broken arm and dragged him to the first mast, where he was lashed tight with rope around his body; sheer fear made him struggle, but a few hard blows to his face and torso ensured obedience, blood running from his nose.

"Please!" He begged. "Please d-don't -."

"Silence, boy, else it'll be worse for the others." He hissed, kneeing Jerryn hard in the groin.

Laughing, two of the Generals grabbed Poppy from the midst of the group. She screamed shrilly, but they ignored that.

Jerryn stared, appalled, but did not dare to breathe a single word of protest as she was raped, for General Oxttyn stood right beside him now, grinning, as if daring him to fight or shout out. Helpless, he could sense the satisfaction and lust in their captors, such awareness only making the attack even worse, for he could not block it.

It was a prolonged assault: every General apart from Master Cheltor took part in it. Sickened, Jerryn watched because he must, realising that there were much worse things in existence than the (so simple in comparison) horror and violence of battle and he was probably going to witness every single one of them! Poppy fainted, in the end, her screams long-since choked down to heaving sobs, an ordinary woman of middle years thrown into a nightmare come to life. Jerryn prayed desperately to Arven, although it didn't really help, but it did keep him focussed on keeping silent.

Eventually, the Generals dumped her to one side, Jerryn was released and the group were locked up again in what was now the safe darkness of the hold, with food and water, besides. They comforted Poppy; ate and drank, yet none of them talked much, shocked and shattered by the unnecessary violence that had descended. Jerryn considered, then, how death could, seriously perhaps, be preferable to life.

*

The ship continued into the wide ocean; days passed, but day and night were indistinguishable, marked only by the unannounced arrival of those buckets of mushy food at odd intervals. Every so often, Jerryn had to clean the hold, then usually, but not always, endure the torture of one or more of his fellows, there on the main deck. This horror was seldom avoided except in the roughest weather and they all learned far more than any of them had ever imagined they might, concerning the violence and indignities meted out, seemingly at random. Rape was common for any of the group, as were floggings, beatings and worse.

Despite the darkness and the terrible privations they were subject to, as well as the terrible food, their injuries gradually healed, until new ones were delivered.

Only Jerryn was exempt from the wholesale violence, forced to watch every agonising session from the main mast, trussed up securely before, if blood had been spilled, he was required to scrub the deck clean; and if he was a little slow or missed a speck, he himself was then beaten, or whipped, the Generals always careful to avoid his right arm. After one punishment session when Zeron had been eventually knocked unconscious, his blood coating the dark planks that the prince had had to scrub clean, Jerryn had descended back to the hold with the usual meal and stale water, distributing it as usual, but he himself could not eat: he felt weak and utterly sick and terrified, huddled up in despair, fighting silent tears.

Is this my fault? He asked himself silently, his misery blocking even Phellos's attempts to reassure him. *Dear Arven, how can any of us survive this? I wish I was dead! We've got – m-moons to travel!* That knowledge was somehow even worse.

Later, when his self-loathing and utter depths of misery had lifted a little, Phellos and Lunde edged across and both embraced him, one on either side, just offering support, comfort . . . But any attempt at hope or comfort was useless, here, although he appreciated their presence.

The strangest thing that occurred, he dared not reveal even to his friends: one night, when everyone was sleeping as well as they could, Jerryn clearly sensed Ethrayne's mind close to hand even though he could somehow tell that she was really half the world away; so clear was her presence that he sat up as quickly as he could, feeling her touch, as familiar as ever -. <*Jerryn!*> She said in a tone of relief. <*Oh, Jerryn -!*" Then the contact vanished, before he could respond, yet he treasured that brief contact more than gold, holding it close in his heart and mind to lift his spirits.

Days followed days. Gradually, Jerryn noticed that his right arm was pretty-much usable again, although it felt weak, which was shocking: had they really been incarcerated here for a moon or so? He told his fellows that his broken bones had mended, although Fereyne's shoulder, broken at Cal'Badon, was slower to heal, and their dismay and surprise was as great as his own.

The Generals had kept an eye on the passage of time, it seemed and Jerryn found himself up on deck, alone, a few days later in the late morning, when General Sarlock declared him fit, removing the bandages and splints. Then, to his dismay, Master Cheltor claimed him for a practice session although he had done little for over a moon but scrub floors at odd intervals, and this unarmed practice against such a strong, implacable opponent was merciless and humiliating. The other Generals watched on, jeering and hurling insults at Jerryn, who was flat on the deck, dazed, for most of the bout as he strove to get his muscles to work as they used to, Cheltor barking commands that he tried his utmost to obey, to avoid yet another hard blow.

Finally, as the sun sank towards the west, he was released to the hold with a bucket of food and, surprisingly, slightly better spirits than he had felt since arriving on board. Proper physical exercise, even though he had been so shockingly slow, was far preferable to seeing others attacked and beaten for his 'education' and their captors' enjoyment.

Although he was still having to clean the hold, Jerryn found that the violence against his fellows became less common. He was on deck most days from then on, facing one or another of the Generals, sometimes two or three in combat, always shouted at, naturally, by Cheltor who certainly proved to be the Master he claimed. With extra exercise came actual daily meals, only one, but much better than before. The random violence against the others continued, however and nothing Jerryn could do, he imagined, would halt it entirely.

Then, late one evening, long after Jerryn had returned sweaty and exhausted to the hold, the ship came to a stop, the sound of the anchor dropping loud in the space: they had docked, probably in the Bertaan Archipelago, Phellos suggested, hundreds and hundreds of leagues across the Faell Ocean. Amazingly, hot water and soap was provided to the prisoners for washing themselves and the hold, along with clean clothing for all of them. Lastly, *real* food was provided: meat, bread, vegetables and cheese, for a couple of days at least.

To their shock however, Hella was dragged away during this period, screaming in desperate fear. They did not see her again, never discovered what had happened to her.

*

All too soon, the ship set sail again and the collection of islands set so randomly in the middle of the ocean were passed by, although it took many days to sail beyond them. Then, most unwelcome, the combat and torture sessions resumed and the violence against the prisoners worsened, also. Dhell was beaten to death on one beautiful, sunny day. Jerryn had cried out, purely in shock and horror, which led to the extensive rape of Phellos and General Oxttyn informed him coldly, with a sneering smile, that this was happening simply because the prince had protested, so he had better bloody learn to keep silent until spoken to! Again, everyone but Cheltor abused her. It seemed that the Master had different perversions to the others, although he certainly enjoyed watching the spectacles when they occurred.

That sunny day led to Jerryn himself feeling the Generals' almost uncontrolled violence at first hand, for an intense fury filled him at the indignities meted out to his friends, their complete helplessness and he finally told their captors exactly what he thought of them, their ancestors and their habits, whereupon they released him from his bonds at the mast and proceeded to beat him, painfully and eventually, into unconsciousness.

Jerryn awoke to darkness, feeling nothing but agony through his body. A tiny part of his power, actually working, told him that it was the morning after the violence had stunned them all. He could feel a hand on his left arm, Phellos's, and reached up with his right hand to pat hers.

"You're awake, finally." Phellos said with evident relief. "Dear Arven, Jerryn, you shouldn't have -."

"Oh, fuck that! And fuck the jajozeli-razine! Bastards!" Jerryn replied, groaning as he strove to sit up. Dear Arven, everything hurt! "I just couldn't take it anymore, I'm so, so sorry, how do you feel, Phellos?"

"Pretty much as bad as you, lad." She answered with the grim humour that they attempted after each nasty episode, which caused the prince to curse again. "I'm only sorry that Cheltor got me, us. I prayed then that those flying burning rocks would sink the ship: then we would have all died in the fire descending on the city!" Phellos hissed, pulling her strained muscles painfully. "None of us would be here then." And she sighed.

"No, I'd be slogging, probably still barefoot, through those mountains to Ban'Lerracon instead. You know, Captain, when I thought of a sea voyage, I must confess I imagined something a little more luxurious than this, d'you know what I mean? Something less stressful, too, without all the scrubbing involved. This is most disappointing." Jerryn murmured, repeating a litany of curses in his head.

The red-haired woman choked a laugh that was almost half a sob and they embraced, simply to feel a sympathetic body close, acknowledging their weakness and their need. The others joined in, all feeling particularly low.

"Am'maiya, your lady is most fortunate to be betrothed to such a fine young man. You must keep strong, Jerryn." Phellos said with fierce intensity.

"I'll try, Captain, Ma'am but, oh shit! I don't want to meet their master if his servants are this evil!" He declared. "Can we sink the bloody boat from here, d'you think? We're somewhere near the bottom, aren't we? I'd rather drown! I know my power is non-existant now, but surely we could damage the planks somehow, or something?"

"It's a ship, lad, and you mean the hull." Lunde corrected him automatically. "They're jajozeli-razine, though; they'd know instantly if we tried to sabotage the hull or anything else, Jerryn, but it's still a good idea."

"Damn it. It floats on water, so if I say it's a boat it is a boat, Lieutenant." Jerryn replied with an exaggerated sigh. "I'd throw myself over the side, but I bet they'd pick me up, the bastards! Oh, dear Arven. Ow!"

Moving suddenly caused most of his body to protest most strongly. "I – only – shit! Poor Dhell . . . oh, I'm sorry -." And, finally, Jerryn wept, his inner armour severely cracked if not quite broken into shards.

As expected, food and water were a long time coming after the prince's transgression, but the combat sessions continued relentlessly, along with occasional periods when Jerryn was separated from the rest and forced to learn to write jajozeli, which occurred after the physical exercise. The letters were strange, the grammar stranger, but he determinedly did his best to take in their sparse explanations, sat in the main cabin with Jaike or Gornen glaring at him, scribbling peculiar shapes on parchment. He did not dare to ask questions now: he just obeyed their commands, especially since the beatings and torture also continued, at intervals.

More affected by all the horrors which had occurred around him than he had first realised, Jerryn quietly tried starvation as a weapon, refusing three meals in a row; he did not discuss the matter with any of his fellows, determined to find a way out, the only way out he could think of. His death, he felt, would stop the violence against the others; it would ruin the Betrayer's intentions; it was all he could think of, to escape this hell! Yet when he did not eat the fourth delivery of the usually tasteless food served, although his insides hurt from hunger, especially after each day's relentless physical exercise, the Generals hauled him up on deck in a cold, driving rain, trussed him up there to the main mast as normal and simply force-fed him.

There were too many of them. Nothing he could do would stop them, their hands tight around his throat and jaw, someone holding his head still by a hank of hair and they suppressed his gag reflex as well. To ram the point home completely, they also used their power to strike at his mind with pain when he continued to try and struggle, however uselessly. He never found out how they had known that he was not eating, but they did. It was painful and humiliating. Master Cheltor promised dire and revolting consequences against the other prisoners if he dared such a stupid move again.

Lunde and Fereyne, separately, both managed to provoke the Generals enough to escape into the finality of death during their last sessions as victims whilst Poppy, who had always been the quietest and most frightened of the group, just willed herself to die in utter despair, refusing all food and water; the Generals only laughed at that, forcing Jerryn, Rynn and Zeron to throw her corpse from the ship.

Gradually, day by day, his life in Tenarum faded out of his mind. Ethrayne . . . reclaiming Clirensar . . . receiving the Flame of Arven, even; all the points of his life before his capture receded as fear and horror took precedence. It seemed, now, that this nightmare voyage would never end. The Mador Opal would circle Iullyn for eternity and they, the prisoners, would just exist. Suffering.

* * *

48667649R00305

Printed in Poland
by Amazon Fulfillment
Poland Sp. z o.o., Wrocław